UNFETTERED III

UNFETTERED III

New Tales by Masters of Fantasy

EDITED BY
Shawn Speakman

GRIM OAK PRESS
SEATTLE

Dust jacket artwork by Todd Lockwood
Interior chapter illustrations by Kaitlund Zupanic
Book design and composition by Rachelle Longé McGhee

Signed, Limited Edition ISBN 978-1-944145-33-0
Trade Hardcover Edition ISBN 978-1944145-23-1
Emerald City Comic Con Exclusive Edition ISBN 978-1-944145-34-7
eBook ISBN 978-1944145-26-2

First Edition, March 2019
2 4 6 8 9 7 5 3 1

Grim Oak Press
Battle Ground, WA 98604
www.grimoakpress.com

For my father, Richard Louis Speakman

Who taught lessons that will last a lifetime

"I think you have a moral responsibility, when you've been given far more than you need, to do wise things with it and give intelligently."

—J. K. Rowling

"A scar is never the same as good flesh, but it stops the bleeding."

—Robin Hobb

CONTENTS

FOREWORD
by Jacqueline Carey

Shawn Speakman didn't have to do this twice; and he certainly didn't have to do it a third time! And yet here it is, *Unfettered III*, with another fantastic lineup.

The original *Unfettered* anthology was conceived as a way to help Shawn retire medical debt after being treated for Hodgkin's lymphoma in 2011. The proceeds from subsequent volumes go toward cancer research and assisting other writers, creatives, and their supporters with medical debts.

Perhaps you're looking at this stellar array of authors who have contributed short stories or novellas and asking yourself, "Huh, why would so many heavy hitters in the field just donate their work?" The answer is twofold, and the first part is that Shawn's simply a heck of a nice guy. Many of us (and I count myself as a member of the *Unfettered* crew, having a story in the first volume) have worked with him for years in a variety of capacities, and we know him to be a tremendously generous supporter of his fellow writers.

The second reason is that each and every one of us knows we could find ourselves in the same predicament. Writing fiction for a living means existing with a great deal of uncertainty—and a lot of responsibility. It's not a job that comes with benefits. It's not a job that comes with health care. It's not a career in which you can reliably predict your income from year to year. A book might take off . . . or it might tank. Who knows?

At least with the passage of the Affordable Care Act, it's easier for authors and self-employed people of every ilk to procure health insurance. But as of this writing, the ACA remains under attack by politicians who don't have to worry about their own health care—and the plans that actually are "affordable" carry staggeringly high deductibles. There are very, very few of us in the field who can be confident that we aren't one devastating diagnosis away from severe financial peril—and among those few who are, you can be damn well sure that we have friends and colleagues who are at risk.

So we do what we can. We write stories. We do our best to infuse the world with the wonder of magic and the beauty of science. With the help of people like Shawn, we use the tools at our disposal to lift up and support our community of science fiction and fantasy writers, and the broader community of humankind.

Enjoy, and know you're doing good in the world!

Jacqueline Carey
Author
October 2018

INTRODUCTION
The Power of Three

I had no idea what the future would hold when I planned *Unfettered* in 2011.

In truth, how could I? The present took precedence over that future. I spent every day recovering from two surgeries and six months of chemotherapy—necessary evils to combat the greater evil of cancer. Knowing I must, I fought to create *Unfettered* from nothing. I gave little thought to a future in publishing, of writing, or even what the next day could bring.

Now, seven years later, I look back fondly at that time, remembering how my author friends rallied to my banner. They did so again with *Unfettered II,* to raise money for others in similar dire straits. Now the publication of *Unfettered III* continues that mission. These authors contribute works of the fantastic because they believe in the power of our geek community making a difference. In short, they believe in *you,* the reader. It warms my heart to no end.

But as I sit here writing this introduction, I am reminded that the true power of these anthologies resides within their pages—great stories written by authors at the top of their game. And *Unfettered III* has both, no doubt. I never thought one day I'd publish a Shannara tale. Or a Dune entry. Or any part of the Wheel of Time, let alone a novella-sized Perrin story. Or powerful new contributions featuring gorgeously wrought prose from writers like Seanan McGuire, Callie Bates, and Naomi Novik. Or grimdark by Anna Smith Spark, Anna Stephens, and Mark Lawrence. The list goes on and on. I am humbled by *Unfettered III*. I think you are in for one helluva read!

That is not all though. *Unfettered III* is why I keep publishing and hope to do so for many years to come. I can see that future now. These anthologies are a testament to great storytelling but more than that. It shows the character and strength of our reading community—and our humanity. We rise to help others when they are down; we fight for those in need when our needs have been met.

And magic is within the words and hearts of us all.

Shawn Speakman
Editor and Publisher
December 2018

UNFETTERED III

Callie Bates

THIS STORY HAS BEEN RATTLING AROUND IN MY HEAD FOR ABOUT A decade—if I'm honest, ever since I first saw *Pirates of the Caribbean: At World's End*. While that may seem an unlikely beginning for this particular short story, Davy Jones's heart box got me thinking. Why would anyone really want to part with their heart? What would it feel like; what would it mean for them? And what could possibly make them change their mind?

A personal note: this story features a character battling leukemia. As a cancer survivor myself, I've long sought an opportunity to portray a fraction of the emotional and physical intensity of this experience in fiction. More than anything, I've wanted to show how complex cancer can be; how it doesn't necessarily rob us of life but instead can make each moment all the more vital. We don't just survive cancer. Cancer can show us how to better appreciate the depth and power of our own hearts.

Callie Bates

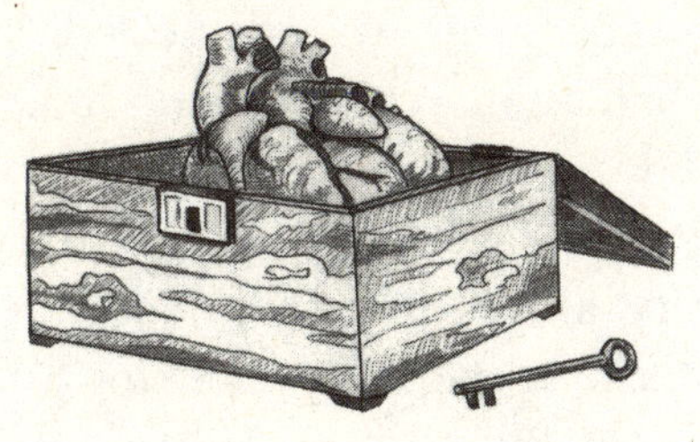

THE HEART BOX

Callie Bates

1. Before

What he had before the accident:

Barbecues
God
Vacations
Children (their faces a blur of memory and
perpetual motion)
A shared bottle of wine
A spouse (the lavender smell of her hair)
Laughter
Swing sets
Parents (who seized the grandchildren in their arms
without seeming to notice anyone else)
His heart

2. *After*

His heart ached, though his wounds healed. It ached when he woke, it ached when he bicycled to work, it ached on his lunch break, and it ached most of all when he came home. He sold the house and boxed up all his belongings, donated dresses and dolls and toys to charity, and moved to an apartment as blank as a chalkboard, its sterile windows overlooking a parking lot and a blackened, sickly river. But his heart still ached, and even the cardiologist said she could do nothing for him.

"But it *aches*," he said.

"There isn't anything wrong with your heart." She offered him a mother's smile. "Maybe you need a meditation class. Yoga. Self-love. Do you have a faith?"

On the wall above her computer station hung a portrait of a woman in a red dress, her head haloed in a golden nimbus, her gaze as gentle as it was fierce. The sight of it gutted him, for reasons he couldn't explain.

"Faith?" he said. "How could I have that?"

He had hoped for a prescription. A procedure. Something. Anything. But he walked empty-handed out of the clinic's beige corridors.

There were other ways, though. Other methods. He had a friend. Most people have a friend like Larry, when they need one, though if he'd thought about it he might have wondered whether Larry was really a friend to anyone.

Even Larry thought the idea a bit extreme. "That's gonna kill you, dude. Heroin would be safer."

"It won't kill me." He couldn't stand to think about heroin, or alcohol, or the myriad ways of coping that were not love or faith or lotus position. He did not want any of those answers. It was simple: he wanted to feel nothing.

In the end, Larry sold him the box, but he didn't take Larry's offer of help or even the antibiotics.

"You're going to be dead," Larry said—but, well, wasn't that the point?

He went back to the colorless apartment. First he called his boss and explained that he needed a week off—mental health time. He tried not to hear the relief in her voice when she said he must take as long as he needed, that he should just call when he was ready to come back.

He hung up the phone, locked the doors, and opened the windows. Summer had died into autumn, and its warm golden light transformed the barren room. Birds sang in the scraps of trees along the turgid river far, far below him. He closed his eyes. His dad had been a birdwatcher—not a very good one, but he knew his way around a pair of binoculars. The birds were some kind of warbler, he thought. Their song wrapped shining filaments of sound around his heart.

If he did it, he knew the birdsong would mean nothing to him.

He went into the kitchen and got out a knife, the sharpest one he had. Before he could think much more about it, he stripped off his shirt, mopped a cotton ball with some antiseptic, and began to cut. It took a long time and when, at last, the heart came out, he realized he hadn't given much thought to sewing the wound back up. But when he patted the skin back into place and wrapped it with cotton gauze, it began to scab over.

The heart was smaller than he'd imagined it would be, and more scarlet. It thumped in his hands.

He put it into the cherrywood box he'd gotten from Larry and fixed it with a padlock. Already the gentle numbness had begun to settle in, a soft static that filled the gaps where his heart had so recently beat. He took the box and nestled it in the back of the closet in his bedroom, where it disappeared behind white shirts and gray suit coats. Then he laid down on his bed and fell asleep.

3. *After*

Sometimes in the night, he heard it beating, the twinned rhythmic pulse echoing from the box, playing to his defenseless ears. He turned over in bed, trying to shut out the incessant sound of it, but still it beat.

4. After

He stopped aging. New floors clambered up from the top of the building; a fresh swimming pool was installed; the river vanished behind a concrete wall. Babies wailed and grew to screaming toddlers, who became shouting children, who transformed into sullen teenagers who finally went off to college, and the hair stayed the same dark color on his head. The lines of his mouth did not shift; the crease between his eyebrows did not deepen.

"Someone's going to notice," Larry said, his own stomach now grown soft, the fringe of his hair whitened. "Maybe you should think about moving." He glanced around the spartan walls of the apartment. "It wouldn't take much."

He did not agree. At work they had ceased to notice him: another figure in a gray suit producing black numbers on white paper. He could have been anyone. The people in his apartment building had long since stopped trying to talk to him in the hallway or invite him over for dinner; they had forgotten the story that once worried them so, the story of a man driving home from vacation at the beach with his sunburned, sandy family, his parents crowded into the middle of the van singing along to Joni Mitchell, his wife with her feet on the dashboard turning her toes in time to "Both Sides Now," the kids barricaded in the far back behind sand shovels and buckets and inflated beach balls and books. They burst open upon impact, the beach balls. Somehow, in all that rushing noise, he heard them break.

"I'll stay here," he told Larry in the voice that was his now, the one with no color and little sound.

5. After

The carpets in the hallways grew faded, and the parents who opened their doors to returning college students began to fade out with them, evaporating to the suburbs, and new people moved in—young buttoned-up would-be professionals who reeked with the eager odor of hope. But as soon as they got promotions, they moved on; they did not want to be in the aging building beside the concrete-bordered river, with the carpet that smelled of time.

Still, in the night, he heard the heart beating in its box, like a clock stuck on one hour, or a bomb waiting to detonate.

Only one emotion seemed to remain for him: the longing for the heart to go silent.

6. *After*

"Come in," his boss said, "and close the door, Tim–Tom?" She glanced surreptitiously at the file on her tablet, but the letters blurred. *Maybe it wasn't Tom or Tim at all,* she thought, *maybe it was another three-letter name like Eli or Ian.* Maybe she was getting a migraine. It must be from all the stress.

He stood patient, waiting. She was his seventh supervisor in more than fifty years; this, the first time he had ever been called into the shiny monochrome office. He had long since forgotten that office summons used to elicit a tight sensation in the gut, and the faint dampening of the hands, and the humming worry, *what about the kids* and *will it be all right*; a worry that faded into reassurance when his supervisor revealed that he had in fact been called in for a raise. A reward: something he had not even dreamed of in decades.

"Sort of funny," the boss said, making a noise that did not sound funny, "you and I are some of the only people left. I'm sure you've been feeling the clock tick down. We all have."

He thought of the heart box, but obviously she didn't mean that–she didn't know it existed. He said nothing.

She sighed. "All good things must come to an end, Ted–Terry. Friday will be the last day our doors are open, so my time has come too. You've been a good employee these last fifty-three–" *fifty-three?* she thought–"years, and now it's bon voyage."

Or maybe she should say happy retirement? She didn't know. He didn't look old enough to retire, or to have worked fifty-odd years. But then she had a migraine aura coming on and couldn't focus on his face.

He walked out, staring into the offices he passed. Desks sat vacant; shelves gaped like maws. In reception, something electronic buzzed and buzzed into empty space.

It wasn't necessary to pack his things, since he no longer had the kind of personal possessions that populate an office space—family photos, certificates, artwork. He shredded some papers because it seemed like he should, and deleted all the files on his computer. He left his stapler, White-Out, and calculator, and took his pens.

As he walked home, he became aware that something was missing. He put his hand over his chest and realized it was a sense of regret.

7. *After*

A new family moved in next door. Their cardboard boxes and bicycles blocked the entrance to his apartment, and one of the boxes had broken open, spilling stuffed teddy bears holding hearts between their paws and fuzzy pillows and a pair of unicorn slippers with shiny gold fabric horns and cunning black eyes.

"Sorry, sorry!" the young mother exclaimed, rushing over to thrust everything haphazardly back into the box. Red color blossomed in her cheeks and sweat shone on her forehead. Her thick curly hair had wrenched itself free from her ponytail. She waved the unicorn slippers at him. "Nice style, huh?"

"Mom, those are mine!" A girl shouldered through the door—about eleven years old, in a black T-shirt and running shorts, a ribbon tied jauntily around her head. No hair grew from her scalp. She was bald—entirely bald.

She seized the slippers and dashed back inside.

The mother cleared her throat, and he realized that his gaze had not moved from the place where the girl had been. The woman didn't look upset, however; mostly tired. "She has leukemia. That's why she's bald."

"Oh," he said. Now, he thought, would be the time to feel something, if he could.

She studied him. Her eyes were black and held a hard obsidian glimmer, as if she knew what it was like to build a wall around her heart and guard its entrance fiercely. With decision, she stuck her hand out. "I'm Malorie—Mal. My girl's name is Clara."

He shook her hand as much from reflex as anything else.

"I'd invite you to dinner, but . . ." Her gesture encompassed the disaster in the hallway.

"I'll help you."

He didn't know where the words came from, but he had a memory of a white slate house, boxes overflowing a van, dropping a bassinet from the top staircase landing and breaking the cheap wood in half. His pregnant wife, flushed with effort, falling against him, laughing.

He carried in the teddy bears and boxes of books, a wad of carpets, several shaky lamps, a desk. The movers, being either hard-hearted or poorly paid, had left most of the furniture in a pile next to Mal's old snub-nosed sedan. Together he and Mal wrestled two mattresses up the stairs, since they wouldn't fit in the elevator. Next came a dining room table and an assortment of mismatched chairs, each painted a different shocking hue. Set up in the living room, it all made an impossible jumble, nothing like the silence and order of his place next door.

Mal collapsed on a sagging blue futon and said, "Oh my god, I need a beer."

He looked over his shoulder. Clara watched him furtively across the mess of boxes. She pointed at a red and white cooler set on the kitchen floor, then vanished into her bedroom.

He fetched Mal a beer and got himself one too. They both lay back on the couch and stared up at the ceiling, a cracked and dirty white.

"Thanks for helping," she said. "As you can tell, I don't have a man around to haul heavy things anymore."

"Where's Clara's father?" he wondered.

"Divorced forever ago. Good riddance." She sat up, wiped her forehead, sipped her beer. "With her medical bills, we couldn't afford the rent on our old place."

He recognized, again, that this was another moment when he should feel something. Say something. *I'm sorry*, perhaps. But he didn't.

"Thanks again," Mal said, standing up now. "But if you don't mind, I'm going to start organizing this mess."

8. *After*

Clara was following him down the alley, her shadow jumping out behind his, past dumpsters and parked cars. When he glanced back, she hid with a quick breathless sound.

Mal had asked him to look after the girl in the afternoons before she got home from work (the second of her three jobs), since at the moment he had nothing but time on his hands. He had interviewed for six positions, but so far no one had offered him a job . They seemed to look right through him. *This is good work*, they said, handing back his file, their eyes already searching for the next person.

He couldn't just live on in the apartment, though as he hadn't taken a vacation since the last one forty years ago, he had saved up a good amount of money. Still, eventually he would run out of funds for rent and groceries, and Clara alone seemed likely to pauperize him with ice cream cones. (He couldn't seem to say no.) He needed help. He required an answer for why he was fading into almost-invisibility, for why he kept living on with no end and no purpose, and there was, as far as he knew, only one person who could explain.

He turned the corner. The house squeezed in between two other buildings with a disgruntled air, its roofline askew, as if the proximity of its neighbors had caused it to buckle. An enormous hand-painted yellow sign occupied the entire right front window: PSYCHIC.

Underneath, in more conventional font, it read: FOR SALE.

He ran up the steps. Rapped on the door. Peered through the windows to the empty, dusty floorboards inside.

"Who are you looking for?" Clara asked, behind him.

"Larry." Except Larry had not used his knowledge to prolong his own life. Forty years ago, he had been in his thirties; when he last saw him, a decade ago, Larry's flesh had grown soft, his hair white. Now, approaching eighty, he was gone. Retired, nursing home, dead, it did not matter. He had no way to find him. No way to end this.

"Don't you have a phone number?" Clara piped up.

He did, but it had been disconnected. This morning, after the last fruitless interview, he had thought that was one of Larry's quirks. Now he saw otherwise.

Clara edged up beside him, read the sign. "*You* know a psychic?"

He glanced at her, baffled.

"You always wear business suits," she explained. "Business people don't go to psychics."

"There's a lot you don't know." He had already left the porch, striding back the way they had come. If he couldn't find Larry . . . but then Larry might not be able to fix the problem in any case. Larry might say this was the inevitable outcome of what he had done to himself.

Clara trotted to keep up with him. Today she wore a bright yellow scarf wrapped around her bald head.

"You don't feel sorry for me, do you?" she asked as they approached the alley.

He blinked. The question came far from his thoughts. "Why would I?"

"Because I have leukemia. *DEATH!*" she sang it out in sudden, dramatic tones that echoed up and down the soot-stained walls. He glanced at her, and she grinned.

"Do you feel sorry for yourself?" he asked. The world of feelings seemed an impossibly foreign country.

"No. Well, sometimes." She chewed at her bottom lip. "But there are people out there with no home and no families. People getting *torn* from their families. All I've got is, like, maybe dying."

"Aren't you afraid?"

Afraid of the chill: the emptiness. Of saying a name and having it be only a word in the mouth.

"I'm more scared I won't get to live all the life I want to." She glanced at him. "I'm a *little* scared, though. You are too."

"No," he began, thinking of that formlessness; that absolute, ringing silence; that ultimate erasure.

Clara touched his elbow. The warm brush of her fingers startled him. No one had put a hand on him in a very long time. "It's okay," she whispered. "Actually, it really scares me a lot. I pretend it doesn't because it makes me feel better."

He swallowed.

"My mom says everyone who's died is with us all the time." She lifted one shoulder. "We can feel them if we pay attention, like a red thread wrapped around our hearts."

9. *After*

He took the heart box from the closet, past the same jackets and shirts that had hung there long ago, and set it on the marble surface of the kitchen island. Every part of the apartment lay quiet and still, gray and unchanging as it had been when he first moved in. Next door, Mal had painted the living room mustard yellow and the kitchen fire engine red. (At midnight, when she finished the third job. The thumping had woken him up.)

The box sat on the counter, its cherrywood turned dark over the years, its once-crisp edges softened. It occupied the marble with the authority of an icon: something raw and powerful from a more potent age. It beat and beat and beat.

A rattle at the door: Clara breezed in. She'd stolen his backup key and now let herself into his apartment whenever she liked, trailing books and ice cream, the scent of fresh grass and school textbooks.

"What's that?" she asked, pointing at the heart box with the core of the apple she was eating.

"Nothing," he said. "Just memories."

Yet he left it there.

10. *After*

His phone rang, rang into the night, and when he answered Mal sobbed something incoherent into the line. All he understood was one word. *Hospital.*

He threw on his clothes, and he ran—down the streets, across the freeway overpass. The nighttime city smelled of gasoline and pavement and gathered hopes and marsh grass and the dreams of all the people he passed. The lights on the wide, wide road poured on and on into the darkness like fireflies, or souls.

He ran, the breath flashing hard in his lungs. But no heart pounded in its cage. He had no heart to tighten as he skidded over the curb and through the gleaming glass doors, past the reception, down the white linoleum hallway to a blank wooden door where Mal stood talking to a man in a pale green coat. Then she saw him, and she was too strong for relief to overwhelm her face, but she reached out and closed her warm hand around his palm, twining her fingers through his, so hard the pressure dug into his bones.

He had no heart, so how could he feel this: the crawling, grappling desperation, the words that wouldn't come, the question too immense to be asked.

"She got up when I came home at midnight," Mal said. "Came into the kitchen and collapsed—"

The doctor shook his head. "She needs to take her medications regularly. She keeps skipping. If she would just—"

He interrupted, driven by a need so profound it struck him like a pressure between his shoulders. "Is she—"

"She's on fluids now," the doctor said.

"She's in deep trouble," Mal said, "with *me.* She can't scare the hell out of me like this."

"I'm sure she's given both of you quite a scare," the doctor said. "Though if she kept a more regular schedule . . ."

"I know," Mal said, and terribly, her voice cracked. "I'm doing the best I can."

Her fingers tightened on his, and he held back, held her up. He wanted to say, *I will help.* To declare, *I will be there for her.*

"Well," the doctor said, "we'll talk to Clara when she's awake. Best to let her rest."

Mal nodded, and the doctor left, and he stood there feeling the blood race through his veins even though it had no destination—even though, when they entered the room, Clara was safe, tucked on her side in the hospital bed, the purple bow knocked off her forehead. They sat on the beige chairs by the window and watched her eyelids flutter through a dream, and Mal put her fingers over her mouth and whispered, "Ed, I thought that was it. I thought . . ."

He looked at her, at the tears winking unshed in her eyes, at the fierce curve of her lips and the bold tumble of her hair. Mal put a wall around her deepest feelings because she felt *everything*. And somehow, she was big enough to hold it all.

"Clara's so strong," she was whispering. "And she pretends none of this fazes her, but I know that's not true. I tell her she's been given this, and it might feel like a curse, but it's her chance to feel it all. The grief and the fear and the pain—yes, all of it. It's what it is to be alive."

He looked at Mal, at their still-joined hands. "She's strong, and so are you."

"I know. But sometimes I get so tired of being a rock. I get tired of being strong, and so does she."

"I want . . ." he began, and stopped because the words tasted like stars in his mouth: strange and bright and foreign, something that should not belong to him. He had not wanted anything in a long time—except that he had wanted nothing.

"What do you want?" she said. "Ed?"

He looked into her black eyes. "How do you know my name?"

"You told it to me the day we met," she said, starting to laugh, "you lunatic. Imagine going all these months thinking of you as that guy next door!" She was laughing so hard now that she snorted, and pressed her face against his arm, and then she sighed and remained there, snuggled in. When he looked down at her next, she had fallen asleep.

11. Now

He has returned from the hospital with a tired Clara and a steely-eyed Mal (who drove the snub-nosed sedan). He has closed himself in his pristine apartment, where an ice cream stain darkens the carpet by the door. He approaches the counter where the organ that once dwelt in his chest beats and beats and beats, only now he realizes it's not just the rhythm of something lost, it's a summons, a plea, it's the way home.

He wants:

Color
The pounding in his chest when he runs
Hope
Gray hairs
Fear
Presence
Strength (for Mal and Clara, when they can't be strong themselves)
Clara (to be there for her last chemo, for every night and day when she needs him)
Mal (to hold her up, when she needs to be held; to let go, when she needs to be released)
The past, the present, and the future
To feel (everything)

He puts his hands to the wood, and opens the box.

Lev Grossman

PROBABLY THE HARDEST SINGLE REVISION I'VE EVER HAD TO MAKE WAS cutting this section from *The Magician's Land*, the third book in the Magicians trilogy. I was almost done with it when one morning I woke up and realized that the opening was moving too slowly. So I had a stiff drink, wrote a new first chapter, added a subplot, and then ripped out about thirty thousand words, including this bit.

I love it, but it didn't fit in the story anymore. So I'm overjoyed to finally see it in print.

The passage is a fragment, but it doesn't require much context. Plum is a senior at Brakebills, an exclusive college for magic in upstate New York. She is a tough, upbeat person, but born under an ill star—a curse that she knows will catch up with her once she graduates and leaves the safe haven of college. Plum is haunted by two people: a charmingly arrogant rival named Wharton, and a mysterious phantasmal being with whom she had a close brush earlier in the book.

Plum studies with Professor Coldwater, who as a younger man was the protagonist of *The Magicians*. She's working on a piece of advanced magic that she hopes will win her the senior prize. But like so many things in life—for example, novels—it won't work out exactly the way she planned.

Lev Grossman

EVERYBODY SAID IT WOULD HURT

Lev Grossman

Plum didn't see the ghost again after that night. For a week whenever she passed a mirror she was afraid to look for fear that she'd see that glowing blue face looking back at her instead of her own. But she never did. All she ever saw was Plum.

She was relieved and, after a while, also just a tiny bit disappointed too. In a perverse and vaguely suicidal way, Plum missed the ghost. She wondered whose ghost she was, and how she died, and why she was still here. Probably she wasn't here for the fun of it. Probably she wasn't a nostalgic alumna haunting Brakebills out of school spirit. Probably she needed something; all else being equal, Plum would have liked her to get it and go wherever retired ghosts go. Just so long as that thing wasn't, you know, to kill Plum.

Frankly before this she hadn't even thought ghosts were real. So taken all in all the whole thing had been quite an eye-opener.

Plum was just a few months away from graduation, and she could already feel the impending forcible expansion of their horizons outward in all directions. Academic work was starting to feel like one of those childish things it was time to set aside, as the verse sayeth—but unfortunately where that was concerned there was something that she couldn't set aside, which was her senior thesis project. She had an eye on the senior prize, which came with an attractive, outstandingly cushy yearlong fellowship at St. Margaret's, the magical university in Edinburgh. Plum wanted that fellowship. It was Professor Coldwater's class that gave her the chance.

Professor Coldwater never mentioned their little adventure with the ghost again, which was fine with Plum, because she didn't think there was much more to say there. Yup, sure, there had been a bonding moment in the senior common room, but she wasn't going to make a big buddy-movie out of it. Still, she'd been curious about him after that. He knew magic that she did not; in fact he knew magic that she hadn't even known she didn't know. She wanted it. So she took his class on mending, which wasn't hard, though it was harder than she expected, and she kept an eye on him.

She didn't see much, or not at first at anyway. Just every once in a while you'd get a peek at something slightly nonstandard. You never knew what would bring it out—a chance remark, a question, some weird secondary magical effect nobody expected. Then his eyes would go blank and he'd turn and run at the blackboard like it was a window he was going to throw himself out of and go nuts on it with the chalk. Plum followed as best she could, though he knew some weird notations that didn't even look terrestrial to her.

The day with the bottle had been like that. Plum had solved the set problem a bit differently than you were supposed to—rather than attack the bottle and the water separately, she'd taken a flyer on exporting the entropy of the whole bottle-and-water system into the surrounding atmosphere, thereby restoring it to order, more or less. She'd finished up with a few touch-ups from an elective on glassworking she'd taken in second year. It made sense in her head. But then somehow the bottle had gone all TARDIS on her.

Speaking of keen: Professor Coldwater had practically almost smiled when he saw it. He seemed to think it was important. He seemed to think she should pursue it. And so, while her classmates slacked and slumped their way through their last semester at Brakebills, she seemed to be pursuing it as a thesis project.

Plum finished out her audit of Mending and signed on for a senior independent study with Professor Coldwater. This had the nice effect of getting her assigned a private workshop: a pleasant, clean-swept, cubical room on the top floor of the lab building, with a shelf for her books, a cabinet for her stuff, an indestructible table for her to blow stuff up on, and two tall eight-paned windows through which the winter sun streamed and had its long wavelengths stripped out (not magically, that's just physics), resulting in a cozy greenhouse effect.

Her first move was to scrap the bottle, and the water, and start over with something a little more substantial: a glass cube a yard on a side, fused at the seams, with one side left open. Her hope was that the magic wouldn't care too much about the difference, because the presentation would be a bit more dramatic for the benefit of the Prize Committee, who were known to be partial to a bit of theater. Also you could learn a lot more about what's going on with a container that you could actually stick your head into. She lucked out: the effect still held.

At first she'd figured that this was fundamentally illusion magic, a trick of perspective. But now that she could actually get a look at this thing, and the more ways she figured to measure it, the less likely that seemed. The box really did seem to be physically bigger inside. And that raised all sorts of other, weirder questions. Like, where was the extra glass coming from, of which this larger box was formed? Where did the extra space come from for that glass to exist in? Basically what the hell?

Fortunately, senior projects were blessedly pragmatic exercises, and the examiners didn't really care that much why something worked, on a theoretical level, as long as it consistently, repeatedly did. So she went after the experimental side of things for a while. She broke down the original spells she'd cast in Mending class into their component effects, swapped them round, enhanced some, dropped others, more or less at random, just to see what would ensue. What ensued was the melting, discoloration, evaporation and explosion of a whole dynasty of glass cubes, the expense of which she had to justify to the projects committee, who were at pains to point out that glass cubes didn't grow on trees, or at least not in this plane of existence anyway.

If Plum were a betting girl, she would have bet that she would take the prize. She was, to be totally un-modest about it, a pretty sharp magician, and she'd lucked into a really not insignificantly useful magical effect, which she could exploit in a very tangible, awardable way. Her only real liability was political: Coldwater hadn't done her a ton of favors in that respect by more or less adopting her as a protégé. He didn't seem that popular with the faculty, except with Professor Bax, who seemed nice enough, though he had a tiny bit of a boob-looking problem where Plum was concerned. But the only reason Bax wasn't low man on the Brakebills academic totem pole was that Professor Coldwater now occupied that position.

Even then Plum would have had it pretty well sewn up if it hadn't been for of all people Wharton—he of the pencils and the wine. Wharton had been assigned a private workshop too, right next to Plum's, and she could not help but notice the steady stream of senior faculty going into and out of it making interested, encouraging sounds and nodding to each other. Wharton would never have been so careless as to hook up with a politically compromised faculty member like Coldwater; his advisor was Beauclerc, a middle-aged psychic specialist of Quebecois extraction with clear and unembarrassed designs on Dean Fogg's job. He was almost obnoxiously Deanish-looking: I mean seriously, who actually goes to a barber and says, *I would like a Van Dyke beard please*? What is the path in life that leads you to that decision? And a prizewinning protégé like Wharton was exactly the kind of accessory a Dean-in-waiting like Beauclerc coveted.

Wharton was just one of those bastards on whom the gods smiled. Sometimes Plum suspected him of magically exporting his own entropy, pushing it out of his system, so that he lived inside a personal bubble of perfect order and good fortune. Moreover she suspected him, almost certainly unfairly, of exporting his entropy onto her, thereby doubling the chaos in her own personal bubble.

None of this mattered really. Plum knew as well as anybody, and better than most, that the senior prize was just another piece of academic hoop-jumping, exactly the kind that Plum felt she was currently outgrowing. It was just that Plum really wanted that fellowship.

Plum was not a sulker or a brooder. She knew this about herself. But occasionally, once in a blue moon, she was fully capable of something like panic, and whenever the subject of graduation came up she could feel panic drawing near. Panic had her scent, and it was stalking her on its huge paws, with their prickly claws and their soft, smothering pads. Plum was not a grind, but she operated very, very well within the confines of an academic setting. Outside—it was embarrassing to admit it, but the world outside of Brakebills made her nervous. She liked to know the rules of the game, and she had not fully parsed the rule-set of the outside world yet. There just didn't seem to be any structure to it. It was all entropy: chaos left to run riot.

Brakebills had seemed to her like a safe place. She'd felt sure that Fillory couldn't find her here. She'd been wrong about that, but at least it had taken a few years. She needed another bolt-hole to hide in. She needed to put Fillory off the scent, buy some time. She wanted to slow down time, throw a wrench in the works, so the seasons wouldn't turn quite so fast. The mills of the gods, they ground slow, but not slow enough for Plum's taste.

In that light the St. Margaret's fellowship had taken on a holy golden glow. A fork was coming up in her future, and the St. Margaret's fork held so many good things: windy streets and skeevy Scottish bars and weird Highland magical lore and skinny pale boys with good hair and compelling accents, and above all another year behind a fat thick defensive cordon against which bad things could batter themselves senseless, because they were not getting in. Not by the hair. Chinny chin chin.

This is what she wanted from magic. Magic had taken from

her, and lo, it would give to her as well. It would set the world right. It would make her safe.

And then maybe, once she was safe, she could even think about fighting back.

But whenever she imagined the St. Margaret's fellowship, the annoyingly handsome figure of Wharton (was that his first name or his last name? She didn't even know) always pushed his way into the picture and took over the role of protagonist. Instead of her, Plum, with her stupid box-that-was-slightly-larger-inside. Once when she peeked, collegially of course, into Wharton's workshop, she saw him manipulating hundreds of steel balls which wove in the air around him in complex patterns, doing God knew what but looking hella impressive.

Wharton knew a thing or two about theater too. Somehow his magic always seemed so much more magical than hers.

Professor Coldwater stopped by every few days to check on her. He would peer into her latest box, knock on the sides with his knuckles, sometimes stick his head or other extremities inside. After a month she'd made some respectable if not spectacular progress.

"It's getting bigger," Plum said. "It's about half again as big by volume. So that's something."

"That it is," Coldwater said. His voice sounded weird with his head in the box. He took it out. "Did you try sticking a couple of intensifier clauses onto that entropy spell?"

"Being as we're trying to intensify the spell, yes, I put some intensifier clauses into the entropy spell."

That was, like, the first thing she tried.

"How many—?"

"All of them."

"Did you—"

"I put in the Flemish one that I'm not supposed to know about."

"Right." He fingered his chin and looked at the box. "What about some dampers?"

"Damping and intensifying at the same time."

"Right."

"That is a pointless thing. Why would I do that."

It irked her the way he walked in and felt free to just dick around with this thing she'd been slaving over night and day.

"I don't know."

"So why do it?" Hands on hips.

"Because then we'll know."

She felt some bitter satisfaction when it emerged that damping and intensifying the spell at the same time did, predictably, eff-all. But then it turned out that the very act of damping and then stripping out the dampers had some kind of intensifying effect—wax on, wax off—which made no sense whatsoever, but hey, magic, it's a journey of discovery. Assist to Professor Coldwater.

But she wanted to add, just for the record, that there was something weird about Coldwater's emotional investment in this project. She was going to give him the benefit of the doubt that he didn't have an inappropriate crush on her. If that was the secret, she was going to be really disappointed. And kind of skeeved.

Meanwhile, in non-magic-box-related news, Plum was going to graduate in about six weeks. The Fifth Years were already reverting to a state of nature. Everybody who'd been holding their breath for the past five years started letting it out. Even socially anxious, usually authority-respecting students began conducting risky experiments with sass. Professors went on with the show, but the students just looked at them like, can you not see the volcanic explosion of sun and green leaves that is occurring right outside the window? Our little world is ending, it's crashing into the rogue planet Summer, and you want us to pay attention to dimorphic thought-vectors or whatever?

Plum proposed a complex regime, instantly universally accepted, whereby parties would be thrown by specific groups in specific venues, chosen semi-randomly via a complex matrix, and an elaborate system of awards, knighthoods, etc. should be awarded to those who showed outstanding bravery and fortitude in attending same. Even as she proposed it the idea struck her as kind of lame and fratty, but it immediately went viral anyway.

But Plum did not herself earn her knighthood. She had always been a social butterfly, but in those last six weeks she did her best to cocoon herself and turn back into a social caterpillar. Most nights she spent in her top-floor workshop, or in the library deciphering old tomes and rifling through the boxed papers of medieval magicians with really bad handwriting. Almost as indecipherable were the technical articles she called up from the one reputable scholarly journal of magical studies, the *Analecta Magi*, the house style of which seemed to be more about making you feel like an idiot than about conveying information. As far as Plum was concerned, however complicated your idea was, if you couldn't explain it in a paragraph of clear simple language, you were trying to get away with something.

Though her own idea was getting complicated to the point where she was on the point of flunking her own test. She spent a lot of time just sitting staring at the glass box, which stared back at her looking like a huge cubical cyclopean eyeball. Things had progressed to the point where she could actually get bodily into the box, and sometimes she'd do that and just sit in there cross-legged. She'd put so many spells on the damn thing, she could no longer even remember what they were, and she was scared to start erasing them again for fear of knocking off one she really needed.

It was no good doing a reveal magic on the thing. It just looked like a nasty multicolored snarl. Maybe it would be enough, as it was, to get her the prize.

One afternoon Coldwater found her like that, sitting in the box like a toad in its hole. She couldn't even look at him. He stroked his chin.

"I can't tell you what to do," he began.

"And yet."

"And yet I'm telling you what to do. Wipe it all out."

"What?" She didn't look at him. Plum had reached the point in the process where she thought that no force on earth or in heaven could induce her to lift her head from where it lay buried in her hands.

"Scrub it out. Scrub it clean and start over. You've got too many conflicting spells to get a clear magical effect. You've got a fix here where you've fixed the fix, which then broke another spell, so you had to fix that. There's too much interference."

". . ."

"What was that?"

Plum lifted her head out of her hands.

"I said, I do not have one of those. Fixes where I've fixed the fix, et cetera."

"You do. Do you want me to show you where?"

Plum shook her head.

"Think about it," he said. "You still have two weeks. You can make it."

That night Plum thought about it, there in her workshop, till about two in the morning. She couldn't go on, and she couldn't go back. When she opened her eyes the blue girl was watching her.

It could have been a trick of the light, except that it wasn't. The ghost wasn't there in the room, she was in the reflected light on the windowpane—hardly more than a stray highlight, blue sky in the middle of the night, smeared and distorted. She neither moved nor spoke. It was like watching a fish from the safety of the dock.

Plum and the girl watched each other for a long minute. The ghost's eyes were all-blue, solid blue, the same as the rest of her, which made her look blind. But Plum didn't think she was blind.

"What do you want?" Plum said.

The girl's blue eyebrows knitted. Her expression was hard to read. Wrong question? She didn't know? She knew but she wasn't happy about it? No way of knowing.

"Who are you here for?" Plum said. "It's not me, is it? So who?"

The ghost swam deeper into the reflections on the glass and was lost.

Plum watched the window where the ghost had been for a while. The wind rattled the pane. Then Plum walked over to the glass cube and destroyed two months of work. She wiped it clean of magic. She broke her staff and drowned her book. Then she walked back to the House, through the trenches of drifted snow and the bitter early-morning cold, and went to bed. She would start over fresh in a few hours.

The next day she skipped her classes and started over, building up the lattice of spells around the cube all over again, carefully and methodically this time, no false starts, documenting everything properly. Over the next two weeks the interior of the cube gradually expanded again. It opened itself up, bloomed inwardly, became a tiny model world. Worlds within worlds.

The day before the Prize Committee review Professor Coldwater breezed into her workshop.

"How's it going?"

Being as how he had now seen her in states of extreme tiredness and dishevelment and emotional decrepitude, a certain informality had crept into their conversations.

Plum brought him up to speed on the latest technical developments, which at this point were pretty minor: tiny tweaks and hinks and yoiks, mostly far to the right of the decimal point. He'd been right, she'd gotten more space this time, by a couple of feet. It was a question now of wringing the last couple of inches out of this thing.

"It looks good, Plum," he said. "It's great work. I hope you're proud of it."

"I'm proud of it. I'm still not sure I'm going to win."

"It's good enough to win. I have no idea if it will, but it could. That's all you can do."

"So I'm done?"

Coldwater didn't answer right away.

"What?" she said.

"All I can think of is that you might try tweaking the Circumstances a little. Get a little more power out of them."

"The Circumstances."

She'd established the Circumstances two months ago. She'd worked that stuff out before she cast the first spell.

"Not the big stuff. The tertiaries, the stuff about the caster's motivation, that kind of thing. I don't think you've allowed completely for how you feel about this project."

"I don't know what you mean."

Plum folded her arms. She felt suddenly defensive.

"I just meant, you're going to have to be honest with yourself about how badly you want that fellowship. Or at any rate, you're going to have to be honest with the magic. You can't lie to the magic."

He left. She frowned at where he'd been standing. That's it, she thought ungratefully. Go post some mini-letters or whatever.

She unwove a couple of the big spells, the bulwark enchantments, and thought some more, and then, as the afternoon wore on into early evening, she rewove them. By the time he came back, bringing her a cold supper of lamb and brussels sprouts from the dining hall, the room was a foot bigger on all sides. She was a proud person, but not so proud that she couldn't thank him. In a funny way he was a little bit of a father figure to her, she realized. A father-in-art.

"Mind if I go in?"

"Knock yourself out."

He stooped and began awkwardly insinuating his lanky frame into the box.

"It helps if you go in backward," she said.

She sat down heavily on the old industrial-looking office chair that came with the workshop and creaked its springy back as far back as it went. All of a sudden she was exhausted. It was late afternoon, and the thickening golden sunlight was full of dancey motes, and she thought about all the sunlight she'd missed out on this spring, and all the motes, how instead her whole spring had gone into this box that would probably be tagged and put in a basement somewhere afterward if it even won the prize at all.

Professor Coldwater was still in the box. You could see into it; she'd thought at first she might see a tiny scaled-down Coldwater walking around in it, but actually what she saw was a segment of full-sized Coldwater, thigh-to-chest, as if the opening of the box were a window into a much larger cabin.

She wondered what he was up to.

"Coming in," she called. Then she crawled in and stood up too.

It was like being in a giant ice cube. Or really it was like nothing so much as being in a big glass box. She'd expected Coldwater to be taking careful measurements and kicking the tires and generally doing a big technical inspect.

Instead he was just standing there grinning like an absolute loon and looking at his fancy silver pocket watch, which was ticking away loudly and happily.

The Prize Committee viewing took place in a small auditorium; graduation was the next day after that. A small audience had gathered to watch, as it usually did: well-wishers, ill-wishers, humorous commentators, wet First Years who were actually interested in the academic part of it. They were joined by the seven sweaty-palmed students who had actually done the senior projects, sitting in the front row. There was some good-natured mutual sizing-up, but Plum and Wharton were the only two seriously tipped as prizewinners.

Still, everybody had his or her moment on the modest wooden stage. Rosie Ray-Mermin, still in braces, with a coin that alternated heads and tails, heads and tails, every time. Ilya Fan, with a flame that burned bubblingly in a tank of clear water (which, you know, technically, sodium and lithium and cesium and something else burn in water, non-magically, though granted they don't burn as prettily). Aryanna Palomides displayed a mouse, peeking out of her cupped hands, which—she swore on a stack of necronomicons—turned into a rat with the full moon. Kate Schlossberg demonstrated a seed that grew into a sunflower and then withered and died and dried, all in the space of a half-hour. Plum liked that one and kind of wished she'd done it, even though the actual magic was brazenly derivative. She would have given it a twist. Something like, it's a different flower every time.

Then Plum's box was brought out and placed on the stage. The committee—six in all, including two outside examiners, one of them a woman in a hijab—stood and walked in slow circles around it, and then, one by one, rather creakily, stooped and entered, as if they were visiting royalty reluctantly accepting the hospitality of an Inuit. Plum hadn't counted on them wanting to go in, but they seemed to feel obligated. It took ages. Edinburgh was a tiny dot receding into the distance.

Think, Plum. We need a *coup de theatre* here. Those withered fucks were ruining it, with their genteel fucking skepticism.

The last examiner, a corpulent man with a flamboyant waistcoat, was inside and knocking the walls dubiously with a cane. Plum walked over to the box, confidently, as if she'd planned it all along, and picked it up with the examiner inside. She turned it upside down. The auditorium went silent. It was no heavier than it was when it was empty—the extra mass was somewhere else, as she'd thought it would be—and the gravity inside kept its own independent orientation, as she was fairly sure it would. The fat guy peered out at his colleagues, upside down but in no way inconvenienced. He hadn't felt a thing.

Applause. Plum curtsied and turned the box right-way up, then went back to her seat in the audience flushed with triumph. That's how we do it.

Last of all, it was Wharton's turn. Plum would have been reluctant to follow an act like the one she'd just put on, but on he came, wearing the charmingly self-deprecating smile of somebody who had never been pricked by the tiniest shard of self-doubt. He wheeled a squeaky cart on which sat a bin of shiny steel balls, each about a centimeter in diameter; it looked as though he'd made markings on them, though it was hard to be sure from the audience. The examiners smiled expectantly.

Wharton closed his eyes and began muttering under his breath, like someone saying grace. Then he opened his eyes and took a steel ball, whispered something to it confidentially, and tossed it into the air, where it commenced a complicated orbit.

He kept whispering and tossing, and the orbits got more and more complexly interwoven the more balls got up there. There were exactly 101; for some reason it was important that the number be prime. When he was done the balls formed a loose sphere about 10 feet on a side, constantly in motion, never touching—you would have heard the *click*. It was like watching a busy aquarium full of tireless little silver fish. It was hypnotic.

It was also a relief. That was it? *That* was what she was so worried about? Oh my stars and garters. She'd thought the balls were going to create some complex electro-magnetic lightning effect, or form the face of some extra-dimensional being that would talk to them, or at least melt and merge into a giant molten bowling ball. It was just a kinetic spell! There was no mystery. It was just a big, elaborate, very labor-intensive kinetic spell. There wasn't so much as a syllable of new magic in it.

She was home free. She was running downhill. Plum would have laughed out loud, except it would have been unseemly. Instead she just sat back in her chair, pulled up her knees and hugged them, and waited for what she knew would come.

Everybody said it would hurt, and itch, but usually when people say that about something you get all ready and then you're almost disappointed at how little it actually does hurt and itch. But this son of a bitch really did hurt. And itch too.

She's ditched her parents to go change after the graduation ceremony, but now she stopped, arrested by the sight. Plum studied it in the mirror: Brakebills mirrors would show you your back, if you asked them nicely. The tattoo really was beautiful. She'd never thought of it as her kind of thing at all, but now that she had it she loved it. It had become her kind of thing, or maybe she had become its. Everybody's was slightly different; Plum's was black with just a few of the letters and symbols in red and orange, a lot of runes and Greek letters and less easily identifiable symbols, arranged in overlapping wheels, and a big Greek cross off-center within the star.

There was a demon in there, somewhere. She tried to feel it, curled up and dreaming, or maybe pacing the floor of its cell and ranting. But she felt nothing.

Except the pain. She welcomed it. Also the pain in her skull, and the dryness in her mouth and nausea in her stomach. Bring it on, world. Come on, stomp all over me, you fucker, prove to me that I was right about you all along. You think I can't take it? You already took your best shot. Plum was still a little drunk.

Goddammit, she thought, and she sighed. Kate fucking Schlossberg. You never see it coming. She would never look a sunflower in the eye again in her life.

Well, graduation had been a suitably final blowout, anyway. She'd done some self-medicating. She may have medicated a few other people too along the way, it was hard to recall a lot of specifics. She definitely knew she made out with Wharton, after all that. Christ. She would submit all the goings-on to a personal ethical self-review at some point, and the appropriate parties would be duly chastened. But not yet. All in good time.

Someone knocked on her door. Plum froze and pretended not to be home. After a minute whoever it was went away.

The pain of the tattoo was already turning less like the tiny bites of a million fire ants and more like a dull ache. Like she'd been beaten with a sack of oranges. They'd put some kind of icy ointment on it after the procedure, to accelerate the healing. The whole thing had been a trippy, horror-movie sequence. The descent, the candles, the deep peace of the underground chamber, but also the fear of being buried alive, outside the defensive cordon.

One kid wouldn't do it, sat down outside the circle of candles just watching them and swigging whiskey till he threw up and passed out. They had a near worst-case scenario when one of the cacodemons got loose in the middle of it. Fogg, who was maybe getting a bit too old to perform the operation, and definitely a bit too drunk, lost his grip with the tongs when it was halfway into Chelsea's back. The damned (literally) thing pushed off with a clawed foot, taking skin with it, and took off running, keeping low, skittering through people's legs and bowling over the brazier so that hot coals spilled everywhere. Guys bellowed, girls screamed. Plum, to her lasting pride, had been one of three or four Fifth Years who hadn't completely lost their shit and instead hammered the thing with kinetic spells till it was pinned and wriggling flat against a wall.

At which point Fogg strolled over and tonged it up off the ground like it was no big deal.

"Right," he said. "I guess this one's free-range!"

But you could see he was rattled.

Chelsea, nursing a nasty scrape, was so freaked out that she didn't want it anymore; plus, candidly, she thought it might be a little shopworn now. So Plum adopted it, and Fogg put it in her back instead. It seemed like a scrapper.

She felt too bad to go back to bed, but she didn't want to hide in her room. She didn't want to be anywhere or see anyone. She resolved to find a private spot in the Maze. Bylaws being what they were, she wasn't allowed to wear her Brakebills uniform anymore, so she got into street clothes instead. They felt strange, comfortable but cool and alien—it made her think of changing back into regular clothes after a long day spent at the beach.

Her head wasn't so much painful now as just missing, like she'd erased it, and not well—it had smeared and smudged, the paper ripped. She could see from here graduates picnicking with their families on the Sea. Her parents would be out there too. She should be with them. She would find them soon.

But not quite yet. She set off into the Maze. It would be good to sit by a cool fountain for a while. She realized she was crying.

She had no plans, not one. She'd pretended to herself that she was afraid of Wharton, that the fellowship was a longshot, but deep down she'd been *so sure* they would give her the prize. Without quite admitting to herself that she was doing it, she'd let all the rest of it slide.

Where would she go? She suppressed a soft wail. Oh, she would manage. She had friends from the years above, good enough friends that she could go crash with them. She could go to Portland or Vancouver. There was a clutch of ex-Illusionists three years older than her who'd set up an invisible floating island in the Caribbean. She had a standing invitation. There was so much to do out there, so many problems you could use magic to solve, so much magic to learn, so many weird and interesting places to go.

But not for her, she thought. Not for Plum. Plum was marked

out. A painted bird. She didn't belong out there. The universities were the safest places, the most carefully hidden and heavily fortified. There must be a graduate program somewhere that could take her this late.

Plum sat on the rim of the fountain; the black water looked brackish and unrefreshing; it seemed to be giving off heat rather than absorb it. A topiary gazelle was near-frozen in the act of leaping across a gap in the hedge, nearly closing it off. Plum didn't know when she had ever felt so alone. She would pull herself together soon—ten minutes at most. But first she was going to let herself fall apart.

She didn't even look around when she heard somebody thrashing their way past the rogue gazelle into her private cell of misery.

"Plum." It was Professor Coldwater.

Oh God. She hadn't spoken to him since the debacle of the Prize Committee. She'd hoped to get out of here without talking to him again at all. Plum didn't need to be told that you can't win'em all, that she'd tried her best, to keep her chin up, she'd go far. She knew those things. If one could win them all, then she would have. She'd rather hoped Coldwater knew her well enough to understand that it was not necessary to impart that information to her. She'd given him more credit than that.

But it was obvious that she'd been crying, and guys only knew one way to react to that. Well, there were worse fates. As she well knew.

Plum didn't get up.

"Too bad about the prize," he said.

"Too bad," she agreed.

Maybe if she facilitated, they could get this over with faster.

"The sunflower really wasn't that impressive," he said. "It wouldn't have been my call."

"It was warmed over, dressed-up, boiler-plate magic!" she snapped. She'd thought she could help herself, but it turned out she couldn't.

Professor Coldwater—Quentin, she supposed she should call him now that she'd graduated—put one foot up on the rim of the fountain and looked up at the statue, which was of the nymph Daphne caught midway through her transformation into a laurel tree. He was still dressed in his academic robes from the ceremony.

"Listen. Plum. What are you doing this summer?"

She shrugged.

"Damned if I know. Why?"

"Because I've got a project I'm working on, and I could use an assistant. How would you like a job?"

Mark Lawrence

This is a tale from the Red Queen's War trilogy, books which sit in the same world and time as the Broken Empire trilogy. This story focuses on Snorri and Tuttugu, both (eventually) staunch companions of Jalan Kendeth, from whose point of view the Red Queen's War trilogy (starting with *Prince of Fools*) unfolds. The emotional core of those books comes from Snorri's backstory, and I have often wanted to explore it further. So I have.

The story dates to Snorri and Tuttugu's youth, before Tuttugu earned his nickname by eating twenty chickens in one sitting. On the face of it, it's an adventure with trolls. The main focus, however, as in many of my stories, is really character development. In this case how fatherhood begins to work its changes on young Snorri to deliver the man we meet in the books.

Mark Lawrence

A THOUSAND YEARS

Mark Lawrence

Trolls are seven kinds of bad news. A troll will rip off a man's head and suck out the eyes as easy as a child picks and plucks a flower. The thing with its foot on Snorri's chest was not a troll. It was something much worse.

Three days earlier, the priest Ingolf Magnorson had arrived at Eight Quays with the setting sun at his back and a challenge before him. His faering, rowed by two blind old men and hung about with the skulls of lesser wolves, bumped against the mooring post.

"Jarl Torsteff has charged me with finding warriors worthy of a place at the high table in Valhalla. Odin has blessed this venture with blood and with fire. Glory awaits the men who bring our jarl the heart of the Iron Troll." Ingolf offered this challenge to the crowd gathered at the long quay. The priest wore a vast stinking bear hide and had one eye covered with a leather patch, though Snorri had heard that there was nothing wrong with the eye beneath. On Ingolf's right shoulder perched an elderly raven. It seldom left, judging by the white trails of bird shit that reached down front and back. The priests from Einhaur often kept ravens in tribute to Huginn and Muninn, who sat on the shoulders of Odin One-Eye.

Olaf snorted, coming to stand at Snorri's elbow. "Has he forgotten to bring Muninn?" He stood on tiptoes to see, lacking Snorri's great height, fat where his friend was thick with muscle. "Forgotten Muninn. Get it? Muninn is named for memory!"

"I got it," Snorri muttered from the side of his mouth. "Do you have any funny ones?"

Olaf scowled. "All my jokes are funny. Some just require more beer to appreciate than others."

"Perhaps," said Snorri, "he only thought to bring Huginn?" He paused. "Huginn is named for thought, so he *thought* to bring—"

"You stick to killing people with an axe. I'll do the jokes."

"The Iron Troll!" Ingolf raised his voice as new arrivals made it down the steep slopes from the village. "Jarl Torsteff has offered a bag of gold and a place in his mead hall to the man who kills it."

Olaf snorted again. "Stories are as close as I want to get to a troll. And even then I need a bellyful of ale first." He kept his voice low as the men closest to the water asked their questions. "They say this one wears armour! Imagine that! The damn things are murder on legs in just their skins."

Some of the older men were already turning away, returning to their boats or the terraced land where they coaxed a living from what dirt could be found between the stones. Others, who had more recently returned from raiding with Jarl Torsteff, began to boast, telling troll tales, though none save Ulf Greyheart had ever fought one.

The crowd built to around forty, the bulk of the men and women of Eight Quays with a fringe of snot-nosed children. Most of the youngsters were blond, though a scattering had dark hair too, some as black as Snorri's own. Even little Karl was there, Snorri's boy, two summers to Snorri's sixteen, his hair white as new snow. His mother's had been the same, too white, as if it weren't something real but stolen from a dream. Mhaeri had died the day she first saw her child. Maybe the gods had decided there was only room for one of them in the world.

"Here, you!" Snorri's mother appeared in her apron to scoop the infant away.

Snorri's eyes prickled, as they always did when he thought of Mhaeri, and a dull, unfocused anger filled him, trembling in his limbs.

"How big is this troll?" a man shouted.

A woman yelled something Snorri didn't catch but that set the fishwives around her cackling lewdly.

The Eight Quays crowd had the air of an audience seeking entertainment rather than of Vikings itching to take up axe and sword in the name of their jarl. Einhaur lay far away, and a jarl was not a king. Not quite a king even in his own hall, and this far up the Uulisk, his authority was more of an appeal to old loyalties. He did not order men to join his raids. Rather he tempted them with talk of gold and glory. Such temptation had led Snorri's own father onto one of the jarl's longboats and seen him sail into southern seas on a voyage from which he had yet to return after more than a year. Rumour had it that new longboats would come soon, calling for more warriors. Snorri had already decided to go.

From the rickety quay before his boat, priest Ingolf was describing the Iron Troll's predations among the villages on the north shore of the fjord. Snorri gazed out across the dark waters of the Uulisk. Four miles wide and unknowably deep. But, however deep it might lie, in a hard winter the ice would spread from shore to shore, joining hands in the middle. Some winters it was thick enough for the whole village to march out onto it for the Yulefest and stamp for the return of the sun. Thick enough for trolls to cross. Even an armoured one of unusual size.

"We should go," Snorri said.

"Ha!" Olaf punched his arm. "Maybe you *can* do the jokes too."

"We are all the Uuliskind, after all," said Snorri. "North shore or south should make no difference."

"Comedy is about timing," Olaf said. "You have to know when to stop."

"We should be ready to bleed for our brothers," Snorri said.

"Oh gods, you're serious." Olaf sighed.

"Ingolf says we have a duty." Snorri repeated what the priest had said a moment before.

"You have a duty to raise your son," Olaf said. "That's the hard path. Not rushing off every time the jarl calls for axes."

"You're too young to be an old woman, Olaf." Snorri slapped his smaller companion's shoulder. Harder than he had intended. Hard enough to stagger his friend and put him on his knee. Instead of helping Olaf up, Snorri raised his head and called out. "I will go!"

Courage is most often a collective property. It needs to be sparked. Like an avalanche in the high passes it will lie hidden, disguised as everyday life, and then with one small action, everything can be set in motion.

Snorri's lone voice gathered others, and soon the slope was ringing to lusty cries demanding vengeance for the fallen, demanding retribution, demanding blood.

Later, when they climbed the slope back to their homes, Olaf was furious with Snorri.

"You'd rather die than raise that boy? Is that it? The mighty Snorri afraid of his own son?"

"You shut your mouth, Olaf Arnsson," Snorri growled.

But Olaf, red-faced and panting from the climb, was having none of it. "Something good went out of you the day Mhaeri died."

"You talk like an old woman." Snorri veered away across the bare rock, leaving the path. It was true though. Something good had gone out of everything when the last breath left Mhaeri and her body lay abandoned by her spirit, the baby howling beside her.

"Snorri!" Olaf called after him but chose not to follow across the slickness of rain-wet stone.

Snorri hunched his shoulders and went on toward his parents' home. Karl would be in bed by now, deep in his dreams. When Karl had been a baby, Snorri would watch him sleeping. Sometimes he would reach out with a big, calloused hand, large enough to wrap about his son. The hand would stop, tremble, and withdraw as though the boy were a burning coal, too fierce to be endured.

Snorri had given his heart once. Too young. Too freely. And she had died, taken by a foe there was no fighting. His whole life Snorri had met every challenge, taken on boys twice his size, hunted with his father in the depths of winter, entered into battle with a howl of joy that frightened his friends almost as much as his enemies. Fear had been a stranger to him. But now . . . now, after the hurt that Mhaeri had done him just by dying, things were different. He had come to know fear. The fear of losing what he loved. And the defense had been a simple one. He had armoured his heart and set his child in his mother's care.

It had seemed on the night of the priest's arrival that all in Eight Quays were prepared in the very next moment to leap into their boats and row to the north shore. But when the cold morning rolled in from the east and the sun's eye stained the fogbanks on the fjord with crimson, there were only five who gathered at the long quay.

Snorri had slept poorly, brooding on Olaf's words. The truth of them grated on him. He should stay and raise Karl. That's what Mhaeri would have wanted. Though she had been just fourteen when the baby came, and perhaps if bringing him into the world hadn't killed her, she would have been as poor a mother as he was a father. They had both been too young. She always would be too young now. Locked in his memory. And he was still too young.

His mother hadn't argued with his decision to hunt the troll. "Like your father you are." Then she'd nodded toward Karl in his crib, just the white blond of his hair visible above the red wool blanket. "Him, he'll probably grow to be the same. All of you a hundred times more ready to stand with your axe to protect your babies than to clean the shit and puke off them. You think the harsh realities of life are tooth and claw, spear and sword. When the real fight is right here, tearing a living from the ground, raising a child to know how to live in this world." She had shaken her head and given it up. Words don't change hearts.

Snorri nodded to the men as they arrived. None of them so large as him—he'd taken after his father in that, standing halfway between six and seven feet, and with a natural inclination to muscle—but these were men who had been tested time and again.

Audun ver Boldorfson came first, five years older than Snorri, a big man with a blond beard and a reckless smile. They had been rivals in the past, but now he came with his round shield, iron bossed, and a broadsword taken from the Red Vikings of Hardanger.

Erik Red Beard stumbled down the slopes, grumbling and perhaps still drunk. A narrow man bulked out by a black wool coat, good with bow and knife. He had two girls not much younger than Snorri. The eldest of them, Freya, had caught Snorri's eye, though he had taken no steps toward her.

Some of the tension went out of Snorri when Ulf Greyheart came striding along the shoreline, his mail shirt sounding like soft metal rain as he raised his arm in greeting. Over his shoulder he bore a six-foot poleaxe, blade on one side, hammer on the other. Ulf practiced the lesson that he had once been taught in scars: Never get close to a troll.

The men were loading their gear into Ulf's boat when the fifth member of the hunting party came down from the huts.

"Go home, boy," Erik grunted. "This is man's work."

Olaf stopped in his tracks, looking half relieved, half angry. It was easy to understand why Erik Red Beard would call him a boy. At sixteen, Olaf had clouds of red fluff on each cheek where Erik had a luxuriant beard. He was short. Fat, despite the long hunger of winter. Worse, he was no warrior. More times than Snorri could count, he had seen his friend back down from a fight, deflect hostility with humour, run if need be, and if all else failed, just lie there and take his beating.

Snorri hefted his father's axe, Hel. The double-bladed head was a wicked piece of steel from the old days, the weapon passed down their line for generations. His father had left it in his care when he sailed last, claiming a völva had advised him to do it for luck. But Snorri knew that if Snagga had truly consulted a witch, then the völva must have told him there would be no returning from the voyage. He wouldn't part with Hel just for luck. Snorri's mother had told him, after the first year passed with Snagga gone, that his father had known his wyrd. He had known the path the gods had set before him, and handed over the axe knowing that this would be his last chance to leave the chain unbroken.

"Why did he go then?" Snorri had asked.

"When the Norns reveal a person's wyrd it is a gift. To try to turn from it would be to offer insult, and no good would ever come of that."

Snorri looked up from the memory reflected in the blade of his axe to see Olaf still standing there at the start of the quay, defiant, yet scared. Olaf was always scared. It was in him like his bones were. Part of who he was.

"My friend, I need you to watch out for Karl if I don't come back." It was the least hurtful refusal Snorri could manage. Even so, he saw the hurt in Olaf's face.

"Undoreth, we." Olaf began the clan-song, taking his hatchet from his belt.

"Don't do it," Ulf rumbled, untying the boat's prow from the quay post. "This isn't for you, lad."

Olaf scowled, his face reddening, and continued. "Battle-born. Raise hammer, raise axe, at our war-shout gods tremble." He took a breath. "I'm of age, same as Snorri."

Ulf shook his head. "But you are not the same though."

Even so, he beckoned Olaf aboard. When a man of the Undoreth formally invited himself to battle, none could deny him. "Get in and try not to be in the way. You'll be wanting one of my spears." He nodded to a bundle wrapped in oiled skins. "Your little chopper's only good for kindling. You don't want to get close to a troll. The other side of a fjord is ideal. Arrow range maybe, but you won't get to loose many shafts. If you find one at the end of your spear or poleaxe, you'll get one chance, if you're lucky."

Olaf sat down in the stern, pale all of a sudden. Snorri frowned, sighed, then nodded his appreciation, all in the space of one breath. He bent his back to the oar, dipping, pulling, launching them toward the distant shore in a series of smooth surges.

None of them spoke. Nervous chatter was unbecoming in a Viking. Snorri watched Olaf and, behind him, the huts of Eight Quays receding into the distance, the goats becoming dots of red scattered on the slopes.

As he rowed, and thought about Olaf's foolishness in joining them, it gradually began to seem no more or less foolish than any of them being there in that small boat. Around the winter fires, "going on a troll hunt" meant doing something suicidally foolish. Arne Deadeye was going on a troll hunt goading Erland Eskilson like that. Bera Aslaugdottir was going on a troll hunt returning to her drunken wife-beater of a husband. And surely the Iron Troll would see little difference between Olaf and Snorri. All of them in that boat were as children to a troll.

Olaf's crossing the fjord was, Snorri thought, the greatest feat of bravery of any there with him. Olaf lived with fear, and yet he had overcome it for the sake of friendship. He had nothing to run from, and still he chose to come.

Snorri wasn't sure what the others were running from, but he knew that the great warrior he hoped to become was running from responsibility, running from a tiny boy and telling himself the child would be better with his grandmother than with his father. He was running from that, and pushed by the restless need for challenge that had driven him all his life. It made him feel less of the man he wanted to be to call it a need for violence. But sometimes on a rare windless day, he would see himself in the cold surface of the fjord and recognize that he had no place among the herd, however much it saddened him to know it.

The Eight Quays hunting party put in at the hamlet of Rolf's Rock. All the villages on the north shore were smaller than on the south. Rolf's Rock made Eight Quays look like a southern town. Snorri could easily see why they needed help. Those who came to greet the hunters from their boat were old, beaten thin by the years. The young escaped this shore any way they could, but these were the roots of Viking strength. The harshness of an upbringing at the edge of survival set aside a young man's fear. It made him see an axe as opportunity. He would return with foreign riches or die and feast in Valhalla. Either choice was better than scrabbling to squeeze a crop from thin soil in the brief gaps between bitter winters.

"Has the troll been seen here?" Ulf took command, addressing a tall old man wrapped in wolfskins, standing straight despite the burden of his years.

The man shook his head. "Where that one goes, little remains standing." He indicated a woman watching from farther up the slope, a grey-haired crone, bent like a wind-shaped tree. "Myrgiol survived Uttgar. Nothing remains of that place."

"Uttgar. The cottages beneath the Ram's Head Rock?" Ulf asked. "Magyar Uteson's place?"

"The same."

Snorri had heard of Magyar Uteson, though not of Uttgar. Magyar's silverwork was much sought after. Even Jarl Torsteff was said to have goblets worked by the old man and his apprentices. Any other smith of such skill would have set up shop in Einhaur, but Magyar was said to find his muse only in the place he'd been born.

Ulf led the way up the slope to talk to the woman, the others trailing behind with the locals following. Olaf puffed along beside Snorri, struggling to keep pace with his friend's longer stride.

"Old Mother." Ulf stood before Myrgiol and inclined his head, respectful of her years. "We have come from Eight Quays to kill this troll of yours. First, though, we have to find it. Tell us what you remember of the night it came to Uttgar."

"It came by day." She watched Ulf with eyes that were the same startling green and blue as the crater lake Snorri had once climbed for two days to see.

Ulf shook his greying mane. "Trolls hunt by night."

"He came by day," the old woman said. "Roaring something across the slopes. It was almost words. We saw him from the step-fields. Magyar came out from his workshop. His three lads got their spears, Old Arne had his great axe, though the fool could hardly lift it at his age, and Young Arne had the sword that was all Jarl Torsteff gave him back of his brother. The rest of us hid in our huts."

"What did he look like?" Snorri asked.

Myrgiol stared as if noticing him for the first time, even though he was the biggest man there, and likely the biggest she had seen in a long life. "You're very young," she said.

"Old enough to have a son in the world and to have taken other men's sons from it." Snorri tried to soften the words with a smile. "It would help me to grow older if you would tell us more about the beast."

Myrgiol sucked at the remaining stumps of her teeth, brow furrowed with the pain of remembering. "My boy, Thorson, sailed south three times before the Red Vikings took him." She spat on the rocks to clear the name of the Red Vikings from her mouth. "He told me about those southern knights, so thick in their iron that an arrow can't find an inch of skin to kiss. Like lobsters he said they were. This troll looked like the picture Thorson's words put in my head."

Audun snorted behind Snorri. "Where would a troll find knight's armour?"

"And what sort of man would it have been made for to fit a troll?" Erik asked.

Ulf shook his head. "Trolls are cunning. Clever at killing. But they've no use for weapons, not even a club. I thought maybe one of them had wrapped a dead man's chain mail around its shoulders as a trophy. This though . . ." He shook his head again. "I've seen southern armour, down in the port of Den Hagen. Metalwork like that takes tools to put on a man. Those noblemen who sit in their steel, on horses bigger than any you've seen . . . they can't get into or out of that armour by themselves. They need a trained servant to lock them into it."

The men gathered at the edge of the hamlet to depart for Uttgar.

"You should stay here, Olaf. Guard the boat." Red Erik pointed to Ulf's boat, hefting his pack as he did so. "You've crossed the

Uulisk with us. That will be something to tell your mother."

"Enough," growled Snorri. "He said he's coming."

Erik, old enough to be their father, looked from Snorri to Olaf. "What can he do apart from eat?"

"He's funny," Snorri said. "Before this is over we'll probably need a laugh or two."

"Nothing funny about a fat boy being ripped open by a troll." But Red Erik shrugged and walked away, clutching his bow.

"Funny?" Olaf hissed at Snorri's side. "Is that the best you can say for me? How about the fact I'm cleverer than the rest of you put together?"

It was Snorri's turn to shrug. "If you were clever you wouldn't be here."

They left for Uttgar in the early afternoon and hoped to reach it by nightfall. The troll had struck settlements to the west, some closer to Rolf's Rock than Uttgar in the east, but Myrgiol's report was the most recent. The Iron Troll had killed Magyar Uteson no more than three days ago.

Before Ulf led them from the sorry cluster of huts, Olaf had asked Myrgiol one last question. "All the others are dead. How did you survive?"

"I heard the troll kill the men who stood against it. It came against them roaring an unearthly cry, over and over. It was still roaring as it tore down all our huts. When I saw the sky and felt the pieces of my home fall around me, I closed my eyes, lay still, and prayed to Lady Freya to take me to the holy mountain."

"And then what happened?" Snorri had asked, after one of those long silences that old people sometimes stumble into.

"Nothing." Myrgiol turned her curious gem-like eyes on him. "I opened my eyes again and sat up, and the monster had gone off shouting into the mountains. So I came here."

The ruins of Uttgar lay in darkness by the time the hunters came there. They made their own camp in the lee of a steep ridge of granite running down into the fjord. The summer had yet to make its brief appearance and crowd the air with mosquitos, a fact Snorri was glad of. He had heard that mosquitos could be found the world over, but that everywhere had exactly the same number. In Viking lands, however, there were only a handful of days warm enough for the bloodsuckers to endure, and so on those days, the folk of the north got their entire year's allocation in one fog-like monthlong swarm.

They kept a cold camp and set a watch. Snorri took the last hours, first sitting beneath the stars watching his breath plume and listening to the darkness for any sound of approach. Then, as whispers of dawn chased the lesser lights from the sky, he stood and paced to and fro along the ridge. He tried to make sense of the grey confusion of shapes where Uttgar stood. Slowly, the shadows ebbed, a tide withdrawing into the black depths of the fjord, and the ruins lay for all to see, their riddle unraveled by the sun's eye.

"Odin's teeth!" Olaf came to join him.

"You've never in your life sworn by Odin, let alone his teeth," said Snorri.

Olaf sniffed. "Just trying it out for size, now that I'm a warrior. Besides, I've never in my life seen a log-walled hall that's been knocked down like it was a child's toy."

Snorri nodded. The sight had taken him aback too. He had seen the aftermath of raids on villages, the dead lying where they fell, curled around the wounds that killed them. But always it had been fire that did the greatest damage. Once flames sank their teeth into timber, the only end was ashes and black ruin.

Audun, Erik, and Ulf joined them. Together the five men explored the splintered remains of Uttgar. The sod-roofed huts must have been much like those in Eight Quays, little more than green hummocks from a distance, grass growing thick enough for goats to jump up where the roof came nearest to the ground and spend the day grazing above the occupants' heads.

"Hey!" Audun stood, lifting something bright in his fist.

The others came to see. Audun opened his hand. A bar of silver gleamed across his dirty palm. "From Magyar's workshop, I guess." He frowned. "Don't trolls care for treasure?"

Ulf took the bar and echoed the younger man's frown. "They covet gold, gems, whatever shines or sparkles. This they would take."

"There's another." Erik moved quickly to claim it from the dirt.

"Don't they like to eat too?" Olaf looked slightly queasy.

"Of course," Audun snapped. As a child he had beaten Olaf often through the years. It stopped the day Snorri felled him with a log, though he was twelve and Audun seventeen.

"Why didn't it eat him, then?" Olaf used his foot to lift a slab of sod from the fallen roof to reveal a man's pale face, the side of his head a wet mess of red and white and grey. "Or that pig?" He nodded to the creature that had come nosing round the tumbled wall of another hut.

"It won't be hard to track." Snorri moved more of the scattered sod aside to reveal what he had first thought to be a posthole.

"Is that . . . a footprint?" Olaf asked, bending for a clearer view.

The imprint was far larger than any man's foot, unnaturally straight-edged, and deep as a wheel rut from a laden cart.

"What do we do?" Audun asked, sounding more boy than man.

"We take the silver and whatever food we can carry," Ulf said. "And then we do what we came to do. We hunt."

By noon they crested the ridge and eyed the descent into the next valley. On the heights Snorri stood amid the lingering snow and turned to look down on the Uulisk, its grey waters beaten flat beneath the sun, glimmering here and there where the east wind could tease out a ripple. The troll's footprints were black against the white, the icy crusts of snow squeezed back into water by its weight. Where there was no snow and only rock they followed by the marks its feet left on the stone.

"I've never been farther north than this," Snorri said.

"I've never crossed the fjord before," Olaf gasped, coming last to the ridge and leaning, hands on knees, to catch his breath.

Snorri kept his eyes on the view, all the vast reaches to which the Malvik jarls laid claim seemed spread before him. "You should not have come."

Olaf straightened at that. "We're friends, aren't we?"

"We are."

"Well then," Olaf said, and sat heavily on a boulder, reaching for his waterskin. "Besides, I owe you. For keeping me safe all these years."

Farther along the ridge Audun snorted but said nothing.

"I stood in front of a few bullies for you, Olaf. I can't be saving you from the Iron Troll." From what he'd seen, Snorri doubted he could save himself.

"We'll see who saves who." Olaf gulped from his skin.

"Ha!" Erik slapped Olaf's shoulder, causing him to choke. "You were right, Snorri. He is funny!"

The trail led north and east. Far ahead the Bitter Ice waited, but Snorri could not imagine that the troll roamed such great distances. Its lair would likely lie no farther than another day's travel.

"I wonder what it was shouting," Olaf said.

"Shouting?" Snorri frowned.

"Yes, the old woman said it was shouting. Not roaring."

Ulf came up behind them, shaking his head. "You focus on where its mouth is, not what noise is coming out of it. We're hunting an animal. Armour or no. A brutal animal."

As the day wore on, Snorri sensed a change in Ulf. The warrior was a serious man not given to wasting his words, but somehow he seemed to grow more quiet and more grim-faced with each passing mile.

"Trouble?" Snorri asked later when they paused where two ice-gouged valleys came together.

"The troll is taking us to Dragsil."

Snorri blinked. "Dragsil is a real place?" In the long winter many tales were told, and not all were true. If a story began "North of the Uulisk," then you knew to take it with a pinch of salt. Apart from along the fjord's shore, nobody lived north of the Uulisk. The land between the Uulisk and the Bitter Ice lay in great folds of frozen rock. No crops could be grown there. Even the hardiest goats starved.

Ulf nodded. "My father saw it with his own eyes." He sighed, tugged at his beard, black but streaked with iron grey, and carried on toward the northern valley.

The others followed, unspeaking. The tales told that Dragsil was a place of the Builders. The chambers carved into the mountainside had survived the Day of a Thousand Suns, though the people inside had not. It was said that the tunnels were still, so many centuries later, haunted by the ghosts of those who had died there. The priests of Odin warned against all such places. There were, they said, no doors to Valhalla to be found within.

The setting sun showed them the peak that the troll seemed bound for, painting its sides a cold red.

"Who has a tale of Dragsil?" Audun asked at camp after they had eaten. The boldness of the request was undercut by the hint of fear in his voice.

Ulf and Erik grunted and shook their heads.

"I remember one," said Snorri. "Only the bones of it though, not the full telling. It seems to me that Dragsil is mentioned in many winter tales, but almost always as a place that the hero avoids. Or somewhere a cruel jarl threatens to send someone."

"So . . . 'going on a troll hunt' and 'a visit to Dragsil' are pretty much the same thing," Olaf said. "Just another way to say 'a very bad idea.' And we are going to Dragsil on a troll hunt."

"Scared, Olaf?" Audun taunted from his furs.

"Always," Olaf agreed. "But I would rather be scared in Dragsil than most other places. I spoke to Groa about Dragsil."

Audun barked a disbelieving laugh, but it was true. When the old witch had come to Eight Quays two summers previously, few had dared the interior of the hide tent she had pitched up on the step-fields. The priesthood and the völvas had scant regard for each other, and many men would cite the priests' counsel as their reason for avoiding old Groa and her ill-smelling tent, but the true reason was fear. An older kind of fear.

Of all the boys and young men of Eight Quays, only Olaf had bowed his head and entered, calling out his greeting ahead of him. Snorri had thought Olaf would be the last to consider it, but later had to concede that his friend had a different sort of courage.

A bravery bound closer to curiosity than to pride, more suited to withstanding the unknown than the danger of a blade.

Olaf had never told Snorri what the völva had said to him among her bones and talismans, but he told them all some of it now.

"Groa asked me how I knew Odin existed. How I knew he lived and breathed. I had to think about that, because völvas don't ask idle questions. I said to her that I knew because I had been told so. Because he is in a thousand stories. Because his name is written in stone.

"She told me that there is a difference between a life that is, a life that was, the story of a life, and the story of a life that never was, but that these differences are hard to pin down. Like the aurora they shift, and overlap, and change.

"She told me that the Builders made machines of many kinds, and that some of those machines were made just to watch the Builders and to store the stories of their lives, and to give them new lives inside those stories. Groa said the ghosts of the Builders are not true spirits but the memories of those who died, their stories, stored in the machines that watched them all their lives. She told me that there are many such stories, untold numbers, down in the deep and hidden worlds of their machines."

Olaf fell silent, and Audun snorted again, but Snorri knew that his friend had shared something of worth. Before they slept, Snorri went on to tell the bits of the winter tale he remembered, but he only had fragments. Sigurd of Hardanger, a hero of the old sagas, had set his mind on braving Dragsil's halls and taking the treasures that surely must have been left there by the kings before the suns. The warrior had come with axe and sword, blessed by the gods and their priests. He had wandered empty hall after empty hall, and eventually had slept before quitting the place in disgust.

Sigurd returned to the Uulisk to find it settled on both shores by a people who knew neither his name nor the names of the jarls to the south and west. He walked on through a changed world where towns sat on what had been barren shore and where even the völvas had no memory of him. He had been erased from his own life.

"Or," suggested Olaf, sleepily, from the dark mound of his bundle, "he just slept for an awful lot longer than he thought he did."

They came to Dragsil early on the next day. Snorri laboured up the slope behind Ulf, who seemed immune to fatigue. The others were strung out behind them, Olaf far below. It had been Snorri's idea to outpace him. That way there would be at least one survivor to tell their tale. And he wanted it to be Olaf.

Ulf and Snorri sat on an outcrop watching the others toil up the mountainside. The windows and doorways of Dragsil gaped a few hundred yards above them, dark and empty. Stretching south and east, the land heaved and rolled like a sea caught in a high wind and suddenly frozen in place. Some rock faces caught the sunlight, others lay in shadow, and in all that vastness there was nothing, not man nor tree, to give the eye scale.

"That," Snorri said, indicating the panorama of stone and sun, "is how I know that the gods live."

Ulf grunted an assent. He didn't speak again until Erik arrived with Audun hard on his heels, red-faced and gasping, having struggled to close the gap between them.

"If this were a troll we would have smelled it by now." Ulf stood, leaning on his poleaxe and staring up at the empty windows cut into the rock. "Trolls stink. But this one has walked two days without scat or sign."

"At least it should be easy to find." Snorri was ready for the fight now. The Builders' ruins were the end of this journey. He would meet whatever challenge they held and he would win or he would lose, but it would be done.

"Odin watch us." Ulf raised his weapon to the cold skies. "Thor watch us." It wasn't a plea for aid. It was a demand for witnesses. "Undoreth we."

Snorri, Erik, and Audun joined in, voices loud. "Battle-born. Raise hammer, raise axe, at our war-shout gods tremble."

Without further talk, the four men began the last climb, while hundreds of yards farther down a slope of broken stone that was closer to vertical than to horizontal, Olaf Arnsson scrambled upward with grim determination, spit flecking his lips, too little breath to spare for cursing.

Ulf had brought torches and a single precious lantern fueled by whale oil. He had anticipated that their quarry might run to ground. A troll is best avoided, but if a man's wyrd sets one in his path, then better to meet it in the open beneath a noonday sun. So seeking one out in its lair was a new kind of foolishness.

The empty halls of Dragsil were far more extensive than Snorri had ever dreamed possible. Even the dwarves of legend had never carved such spaces into the roots of the mountains.

The four men passed a hundred chambers and saw nothing but stone and dust and rust. The place felt old and lonely and empty. Snorri's skin didn't prickle beneath the gaze of hidden watchers. The corridors didn't echo with the sorrow of a vanished people. It was just deserted.

All that changed as they advanced along a seemingly endless tunnel that ran straight as a die into the mountain. Its ceiling was arched, and low, so that Snorri had to dip his head just an inch. He wondered how the troll had squeezed its bulk this way, but the floor bore not just the scratches of its iron shoes but a host of such scratches, as if the troll had made this journey a thousand times before.

In that long corridor, Snorri felt himself walking back through the years, with decades and centuries falling behind him. The air grew warmer and tainted with alien scents, some remembering the blacksmith's forge but others that bore no comparison and grated on his lungs.

They stepped at last from the corridor into a wide, round chamber with a domed roof too high above them for lantern or torch to drive away the shadow.

Perhaps thirty large alcoves gave onto the main chamber, their tall arched openings equally spaced around the room. Pieces of what looked like plate armour scattered the floor, though Snorri had never seen such metalwork before and relied on descriptions he'd heard from others, who had likely never seen it either. Some of the pieces looked to have been made for giants. Huge articulated metal limbs lay here and there, some disgorging a confusion of what looked like steel snakes, powdery residue, dark stains.

Ulf led the way in, holding his poleaxe almost vertical, with the heavy blade higher than his head. He moved slowly toward the center of the chamber. Erik followed, stepping around the detritus, turning like a dancer, an arrow strung to his bow straining for release. Snorri and Audun brought up the rear, Snorri clutching his axe two-handed, Audun with a shield on one arm and a torch in that hand, in the other a broadsword.

As they neared the center and began to see into all the recesses, it became apparent that the lantern hanging from Ulf's wrist and the torch in Audun's left hand were not the only lights in the chamber. At the back of three of the alcoves were glowing patches, the light unearthly and offering no illumination. Some patches were round as eyes, glowing with the greens and violets of the aurora. Others held the hot orange of the forge coals or the dull red of cooling iron.

"This is a place of spirits," Audun hissed above the crackle of his torch.

"Perhaps," Ulf replied in a conversational tone. "But that's less dangerous than a troll nest, so be thankful." He began to advance on the alcove with the most lights.

As they drew closer, Snorri could see that the red glow was leaking from either side of some large, dark object that blocked the source. Closer still and their own lights began to show them what stood before them.

"What in the name of Hel is that?" Audun gasped.

Snorri craned his neck. The thing was a giant, ten yards tall, so armoured that no inch of flesh showed. The head lay hidden in a great helm perforated with small holes through which a light like that of a banked fire could be seen.

"This is not our prey," Ulf whispered and began to back away.

Snorri reversed without argument. There were no objections

to be offered. Firstly, the creature could crush them like a man crushes ants beneath his heel. Secondly, the tracks they followed could not have been made by the giant before them. And finally, it could not have left the chamber by the corridor. It was too large to fit more than an arm down that passage.

Snorri took another step back, gaze still fixed on the steel visor pinpricked with the light of a dying fire. Jarl Torsteff's longboats had come down the Uulisk each seating forty rowers. The giant before him looked capable of hoisting such a vessel above its head.

The howl that came from behind them was so loud, so startling, and so alien that it nearly unmanned Snorri. He found himself on the edge of dropping the axe that his father and grandfather had carried into many battles. He found himself poised to run, a stranger to himself. The anger that filled him was at his own cowardice, but it served to turn him round.

"MMMmmmmmRRRRRYYYY!" The blast of sound came again, like nothing that a human mouth could make, or any animal that Snorri had heard.

The Iron Troll was far smaller than the giant they had been backing away from but far larger than Snorri. Just as reported, the armour on it allowed no flesh to show. Red Erik's first arrow shattered into splinters against the troll's face, or rather what must be the visor of a helm fashioned to look like a face, though more like the head of a beetle than of any troll Snorri had imagined.

"MMMMMmmmmmrrrRRRRRYYYY!" The sound blasted through a mouth that lay behind a rectangular slot protected by thick metal mesh. A shard of metal, a piece of a sword perhaps, jutted from the side of the slot, bedded in the mesh. Snorri took comfort in seeing that something had once at least partially penetrated the troll's armour.

"Undoreth we!" Ulf's poleaxe swung down in an arc that saw the blade impact where neck and shoulder joined.

The troll's ironclad hand closed on the poleaxe shaft and jerked the weapon away with such sudden force that Ulf was thrown across the chamber, the first ten feet without touching the ground.

Snorri's paralysis left him and he leapt to the attack, swinging his axe into the creature's side. Audun followed, bellowing, sword raised high. Another of Erik's arrows caromed from the creature's armour.

Snorri struck again, a solid blow. It was as if he'd hit a boulder. Audun landed a swing with every ounce of the strength in his thick-muscled arm, and the transmitted shock of the impact shook his sword from numbed fingers. A moment later the troll knocked him aside with a backhanded slap that shared much in common with a sledgehammer blow to the face.

"mmmmMMMRRRYYYY!" The deafening howl echoed through the chamber.

Snorri replied with his own roar and swung at the monster's face, but somehow found himself on his back, his vision swimming, though still good enough for him to see the great metal foot descending toward him.

"Undoreth!" A figure that had to be Ulf returning to the fray hurled itself at the troll.

The iron foot pinned Snorri to the ground despite his best effort to roll clear. As the weight mounted on his chest, causing his ribs to creak and driving the air from his lungs, Snorri saw Ulf swing toward the troll's face with his hatchet.

Only it couldn't be Ulf. Too wide for one thing. And Ulf would never get that close to a troll. It was his rule number one. Snorri blinked away tears, or blood, and saw Olaf, arm extended high above his head, strike the shard of metal that was trapped in the troll's mouthguard. Snorri groaned, and not just from the pain of the rapidly growing pressure that would very soon crush his chest. Olaf had had a good plan. If he could hammer that shard deeper through the hole it had already made in the troll's armour, it would skewer the monster's head. But instead his swing struck the side of the metal fragment and knocked it out, sending it flying into the dark.

"Maylee!" the troll screamed, its voice almost human now.

One of Erik's arrows struck the black globe of its right eye and ricocheted away. Snorri rolled his head back, dying, unable to breathe, his vison going dark. As soon as the troll shifted its weight from its other leg, he would be a red mess of broken bones and pulped organs. The troll glanced down at him and moved to do just that.

"Maylee!" came Olaf's shout.

In that moment the troll froze, its vast body seizing up mid-action to become as still as any statue ever carved in Odin's name.

For several heartbeats none of them moved. Snorri's pulse pounded in his ears. His flattened lungs laboured in vain to draw breath.

"Maylee? Chitholg lagga namastay?" The voice that came from the troll still buzzed and broke and wavered in loudness, but now it sounded almost like a woman's voice, a woman's voice mixed with fear and hope.

"I don't understand you." Olaf ran to Snorri's side and tried without success to lift the iron foot from his chest. "You're killing my friend."

"Icanthen, Maylee? Dottirsname gefahren?" The pressure eased, then lifted entirely. It seemed to Snorri, as he drew his first breath in far too long, that the troll had changed its way of speaking and was using a language he almost recognized.

"I don't speak the empire tongue," Olaf called as he tried to drag Snorri clear.

The troll said nothing for a moment, though it did lower its foot as Snorri finally managed to roll out from under it.

"Norsenmen, is it that youarre?" the troll asked.

"Yes! Norsemen," Olaf called.

Snorri tried to sit. His breath wheezed in and hissed out, as delicious as life and agonizing at the same time.

"Why did you say my daughter's name?" the troll asked, the woman's voice growing clearer with each new thing she said. "And why"—a light began to flow from the troll's huge iron hands—"am I within a mechanical?"

And there before them, as if she had spilled from the troll's grasp, stood a woman made of white light, as if her image were somehow seen among the shifting of a hundred hanging cloths, each disturbed by a sea breeze. She stood as tall as Olaf, statuesque, long haired, clad in strange garments not meant for the chill of a northern spring. She turned dark eyes on Snorri as he struggled to his feet.

"Your daughter is Maylee?" Olaf asked, peering at her with his head bowed, for surely she was from Asgard.

"This is the Drevja base in northern Norway." The woman looked around. Where her gaze fell, lights flickered in the walls. Some stuttered into life, others failed and died away, but within moments the place was better illuminated than any jarl's hall. Ulf and Audun lay motionless where they had landed. Erik had backed to the far wall, but his bow hung forgotten from limp fingers. "A maintenance hub for hydroelectric stations."

Snorri had been impressed by the goddess's swift mastery of their language, but now she seemed to be relapsing into a foreign tongue.

The woman waved a hand at the giant they had backed away from earlier. The glow behind its visor intensified, and with a loud grinding noise, it took one step forward to stand at the entrance to its alcove.

"Why did you say Maylee's name?" She looked grave, sorrowful.

"You were shouting it." Snorri snarled the words past his pain. "*That,* was roaring it." He gestured past her toward the motionless troll with his axe.

The woman's eyes widened and she turned toward the troll. "How strange. I haven't been out of the deep nets for . . ." She frowned. "Well . . . a thousand years. There are so many other worlds, it's easy to forget that this one even exists. But a thousand years! I hadn't thought it anything like so long." She looked back to Olaf and Snorri. "Well, it explains your appearance at least. But not here . . . why are you here?" She narrowed her eyes, seeming suddenly alarmed. "Your kind should not be here. There is infrastructure that needs protecting. We can't have you burrowing, damaging the network, breaking memory banks." Behind her both the troll and the giant flexed and began to lift their great hands.

"We tracked that!" Snorri indicated the looming troll. "It was raiding our villages. Killing and looting—"

"Not looting," Olaf interrupted. "And did it kill any who didn't first attack it?"

"We saw the dead, and Myrgiol—"

"We saw people crushed in the ruins of their homes," Olaf said. "But were they dead because the troll attacked them or . . ."

Snorri considered what the troll could do if it wanted to kill someone. Their body would be scattered in small pieces or little more than a wide red stain. "Or it was searching for something!"

"Or someone," said Olaf.

"The troll . . ." Snorri frowned, trying to think past his pain. "It was looking for Maylee. Calling for her, but its voice was broken."

"Where is your daughter?" Olaf asked softly.

"Dead." A shudder ran through the light that made the woman. A ripple of darkness. "She died a child, back on the first and last day of our war. Too young to be rendered in the system." She looked down at herself. "Like this." And then, as if she had been studying something behind her eyes and had only now seen the truth, her face changed, her mouth losing its hard lines and going slack. "Oh." The word fell from her lips. She took a moment to gather herself. "It seems this unit and others have been acting on undirected overspill commands." She noticed their confusion. "My dreams," she explained. "These machines have been acting on my dreaming, if you like. I have . . . strong . . . dreams."

"This . . . troll," Olaf said, "has been searching for your daughter because you still dream of her?"

The woman looked away as if seeing something else. "This unit and eleven others scattered across the world. Most are too broken to comply, but twelve were able." A sadness took possession of her face. "I will seal the data leak. There will be no more searches." She looked to where Ulf and Audun lay. "I am sorry for your friends. Did they have children?"

Snorri shook his head. "Not Audun. Ulf has two grown daughters living in Einhaur." He had thought himself finished, but his tongue had more to add. "I have a son, two years old."

The woman's face flickered between the sadness that held her and a second face, alarmed, eyes held by some distant scene.

"I must go. Other matters demand my attention. And you must leave. It would be unwise to linger here." She paused and focused on Snorri. "Watch over your son. Keep him safe. No parent should outlive their child—it is a hurt that endures. And if that hell should ever fall upon you, then pray with all your heart that you are not given a thousand years to suffer the memory of that loss."

And with that she was gone.

In five loud strides the Iron Troll retreated to an empty alcove, and as it pressed its back to the wall, all the lights went out. Only the flickers of flame still lapping the stone where Ulf's lantern had been smashed, and the fire from Audun's fallen torch, remained to illuminate the chamber.

Ulf gave a groan and rolled over. A glance told Snorri that Audun would never rise again.

"Quick." Olaf hurried to Ulf's side. "Let's get out of here."

And so it was that Erik and Snorri followed Olaf back out into the brightness of the day, helping Ulf Greyheart between them.

They sat on the lower slopes, taking bread and water, glad to be alive, speaking of what they had seen and of Audun's fall. It was, they decided, a warrior's death, and he would be welcomed into Valhalla as a man who had faced both giants and trolls.

Ulf sat with his head bandaged and counted through the silver they had taken from Magyar's workshop. A bar for each man.

"You earned this, Olaf Arnsson." Ulf handed the largest bar to the boy. "My apologies for doubting you. Forgive the foolishness of an old man. Any who are raised on the cold shores of the Uulisk are worthy of respect."

Olaf stowed away his silver and lay back next to Snorri. "Will you take the ship with the jarl then? When his sails come east for men?"

Snorri shook his head. "A man shouldn't run from what he fears. Even if it's into battle. You know what scares me, Olaf. You always did. But you waited and let me understand it for myself." He would have said more but his mouth wouldn't shape the words, not without quavering. Pride is a strange thing, and Snorri had fought enough battles that day, and so he kept the words inside. He would let pride command his tongue, but not his actions.

He would return to Eight Quays and lift up that little child he had made with Mhaeri, and he would give the boy his heart just as he had given it to Mhaeri, and he would defend that boy with arm and axe from all that he could. But if a foe came that he could not defeat. A fever in the night. The grey wasting. A cruel trick of Loki's choosing. Then yes, his heart would break again, and yes, he feared that more than the claws of any troll. But he would face it, and if he lived a thousand years, he would live them with that pain. Because his friend had shown him that the true challenge that stands before a man is often right before his eyes, and runs deeper than any axe can cut.

Delilah S. Dawson

THE TALES OF PELL WAS BORN IN A BARBECUE RESTAURANT IN THE Dallas airport when my dear friend Kevin Hearne pitched me a series of stories based on lovingly flipping fantasy tropes. Despite the fact that its existence is completely ridiculous and highly improbable, *Kill the Farm Boy* is now out from Del Rey Books, with *No Country for Old Gnomes* and *The Princess Beard* to follow. This is our first short story in that realm—my attempt to question why quests must always be blessed by the Elders, and why "Elders" needs to be capitalized, and why very old people offer children very old candy that is covered in very old cat hair when obviously nobody wants to eat that. Maybe those questions don't have answers, but I've tried, by dinkum. For more Pell fun, including finding out who you would be in that mystical land, visit TalesofPell.com.

Delilah S. Dawson

AMONG A THRONG OF BILIOUS OCTOGENARIANS

A Story from the Tales of Pell

Delilah S. Dawson

(with Kevin Hearne's blessing)

> "Young folks never appreciate the utility of a healthy, functioning sphincter until it fails them. Go on, caper and cavort, eat that spicy food while you can! Just know that from diapers you emerged, and to diapers you will return."
>
> —Jussi Rompers, in *Gastroenterological Daredevils I Have Kilt*

It befell in the days before people kept track of such things that a foine young lad met a pixie, and the pixie did anoint him, and the young lad said, "Oh, gross! Is that mucus?"

"It's *magic,* you ungrateful snoot," the pixie said, discreetly wiping her wand on her sock. "In case you hadn't noticed, you've been anointed. You're going to be a great king one day. Or possibly just a passable king, or maybe even a terrible one. The greatness bit is up to you, but I'd suggest aiming for passable or better, as beheading is messy and, frankly, a lot more fun for the crowd. But I've done my bit, so now get on with it."

"Get on with what?" asked the foine young lad, whose name was Barthur. He was a smallish and gangly and pasty human with the sort of hands and feet everyone assured him he would probably grow into.

The pixie shrugged and rubbed her nose. "Get on with your destiny."

"But I'm to be a squire!"

"A squirrel?"

"A squire!"

"So aim higher. Be a king. Find yourself a quest."

"A quest?"

With a sigh, the pixie put her hands on her hips and considered the boy. "Yes. That's how you make things happen. You go do something important, and people say, *My, that foine young ladde has a sort of god-like halo, or perhaps it's just the sun, but we should most definitely give him a crown and start painting his face on pennants and things and make him king, and maybe he'll make our hideous life in the sodden mire ever so slightly more tolerable.* That's simply how it's done. Rescue a princess, slay a fire-breathing dragon, find a glowing thing. Heck, go after the Holy Quail; at least quails don't breathe fire! All I can tell you is that nothing fateful ever happens to squirrels who sit around polishing other people's lances all day."

And with that, she flew off in a serpentine pattern that suggested she'd already hit the bottomless mimosa bar at the local halfling brunch spot.

Now if there was one thing Barthur knew, besides the fact that his tunic was indeed befouled by pixie mucus, it was that one simply did not set out on a quest without first gaining the permission and blessing of the Elders. These sage old souls were considered wise beyond belief, their joint knowledge encompassing all of history, geography, culture, art, magic, and a sort of general knowledge referred to as Potpourri. And so Barthur dabbed uselessly at his tunic and wiped the layers of stable grime off his face and went to knock on the grand oaken door of the St. Jocomo the Squat Elder Home and Hostel.

Knock, knock, knock, he knocked, and then once more, sharply, for emphasis, so they would know he was a Lad of Certainty.

Knock!

Barthur's hands were shaking, and it seemed like all his blood had pooled in his feet, leaving his head more stupid than usual, and he couldn't believe that a little pixie mucus had emboldened him so. To approach the Elders for a blessing—that was the stuff of heroes! And he was just a squirrel—er, squire! But he was here and committed to his path, and someone inside was shouting "Not it!" and footsteps were slowly pattering toward the door, and if he turned to run away and got caught, it would be very awkward indeed.

"Heh?" someone shouted through the thick, carved oak.

"I am Barthur, son of Buther, here to seek audience with the Elders," Barthur said, pitching his voice low.

"Heh?"

A little louder and squeakier this time, he said, "I am Barthur, son of Buther, here to seek audience with the—"

"Heh?"

"I AM BARTHUR, SON OF—"

"Is someone there?"

"CAN I COME IN, PLEASE?"

Seven locks slowly clicked on the other side of the door, accompanied by the sounds of grunting and the licking of dry lips. The door opened just wide enough to show a safety chain and a rheumy eye set in warm brown skin under an awning of quavering white eyebrow.

"You delivering food?" the man barked in a fug of chowder breath.

"No, sir, I—"

"Flowers, maybe? Candygram? Birthday card? Perhaps a fruit bouquet with the pineapple cut into little stars and dipped into not quite enough chocolate?"

"No, but—"

"Are you Ermenegilda's granddaughter? Because if so, we need to talk about your dress."

"My tunic?"

The old man cleared his throat and whispered, "It's a bit mucusy, kid, and that's coming from a blind guy. Unbecoming too. Kids these days. With their raised hems and whispering."

Barthur firmed up his chin and forced his noodley spine straight. He spoke loud and sure, making an uncomfortable amount of eye contact. "Sir, I'm here to speak with the Elders. I am Barthur, son of Buther, and I have been anointed this day and sent on a holy quest—"

"Oh, is that it? Come on in." The chain slid, the door opened, and a bright light blinded Barthur as the old man shouted, "Hey, listen up! This kid has a holey vest. Needs patching. Who's got the sewing basket?"

Barthur found himself in a room simply dripping in candles and thick with the odor of mothballs and soup and portent. Five low, squashy chairs formed a semicircle facing the door, and on those cushy chairs he saw five donut-shaped cushions of fine gnomeric handiwork, and on each donut-shaped cushion sat an aged person with a long, fine beard of white or gray. These enigmatic folk were pruneish about the face, their eyes black buttons sunken amid taffy-like wrinkles. One dark-skinned old man had an ear horn, and an old woman with toast-brown skin and apple-red cheeks was knitting a solemn-looking sweater. The other two Elders, if Elders they were, looked vaguely like his Aunt Sandy and were staring off into space as they puffed on pipes. He couldn't tell if they were male or female, much less if they were awake. The man who'd opened the door was rummaging in an old basket, muttering about mouse dookies.

"The Elders," Barthur whispered to himself.

"Heh?" the old man who'd opened the door asked again, holding out a very dull needle in a vaguely threatening manner.

Barthur gave his best bow, staying just far enough away so he couldn't get poked with the needle, should the old man decide he was a threat. "O GREAT ELDERS, I SAID IT'S AN HONOR TO MEET YOU."

"It's not beet soup, it's chowder," the knitting Elder said. "And there's not enough to share."

"No, I'm not here for soup, it's just that—"

"Well? Take the needle and fix your dang tunic. You look ridiculous," the first Elder said, handing Barthur the needle and returning to his chair. Barthur noted that the old man in question was wearing a short flowered robe over a long plaid robe and wore plush slippers featuring yellow duck faces, but he had to assume that this was considered less ridiculous and more eccentric when one was attuned to the higher spheres. Barthur held the needle carefully between thumb and forefinger and stood, breathing in the rich, thick air of the ancients and coughing a little at the pipe smoke as he regarded the grand personages before him.

Every child in the village had heard tales of the Elders. Wise, learned, powerful, gifted, they were the rulers in spirit of the people, a guiding star in the increasing confusion of a society that all agreed was constantly falling apart at the seams. Long ago, in their ancestral lands, long before the Giant War, back when they'd been merely the Middle-Aged, the Elders had ruled with absolute power and magnificent benevolence. They'd led their people here, directing the building of this very town and drafting the Writ of Getting Along and Not Being Arses that still governed the land. Barthur realized he was holding his breath and released it silently so that he might continue to listen for any wisdom they might impart instead of passing out.

"That's not my niece Ermenegilda. It's some strange boy. A hooligan. And he's not fixing his vest," the knitting Elder said, and Barthur was now sure she was a woman, even though her beard was as long and gray as those of the men. "He's quiet, though. Might be an idiot. Someone offer him a butterscotch."

The old man who'd given him the needle now held out a crystal dish of candy that looked like lint-covered gallstones. When Barthur didn't immediately take one, the old man shook the dish at him aggressively. "Eh?" he said. "All children enjoy candy. Keeps 'em quiet."

"I'm not here for candy, good sir," Barthur said, trying to get things on the right track and avoid ingesting anything that resembled pancreatic excreta. "I come to you, the Elders, in hopes that you will grant me a quest and bless my holy . . . uh. Quest. A pixie hath anointed me, and—"

"That explains the mucus."

"Yes, so I'm anointed, and—"

"Are you a Chosen One?"

That made Barthur stop and blink. "*A* Chosen One? Do you mean *the* Chosen One? The pixie didn't use those exact words, but I do assure you that I've been anointed. I'm to be a king someday, the pixie said. I mean, uh, *yon pixie hath decreed.*" Barthur felt that distinct loosening in the bowels one gets when one realizes one is royally botching up something important. This audience wasn't going at all as he'd planned.

"Hmph. Kings. So you're a future politician, eh? That's your chosen career path? Back in my day, children worked in the mines, and *we liked it.*"

"Well, the ones who didn't like it died in the mines," the woman interjected.

"That's not a mime! It's just some mendacious young rando come to rob us!" shouted the Elder with the ear horn.

"No! No, I'm not . . . robbing anyone. And I'm not a mime. Or a squirrel, to be clear. I just wish for your blessing and a quest. Honestly, either would do at this point; I'm not picky."

Barthur knelt, head down, which forced him to look at a stain on the tattered old rug that appeared to be cat barf.

"Look, sonny," one of the Elders said—the Aunt Sandy–esque one in the middle, judging by his excitedly swinging feet. "You seem to think we're the folks who go around spouting writs and giving out halos, but we ain't. Those folks were from a different lodge. The Elders—well, we're more like a loosely knit cabal. Every town or city has 'em. Or maybe you're thinking of the Welders, which is a totally different group, or the Box Elders, which are trees. But we don't truck with blessings and quests here at St. Jocomo's. We do weaving and fiber arts. I think the Elders in Okesvaa were into flower tiaras for a while, which is probably closer to a crown? Or was that macramé? Point is, we're not the folks you're looking for."

"But surely you can see the glow of the anointed around me?" Barthur said, standing up and waving his arms a bit.

"Can't see much, sonny. Eyes are going fast. But we don't do magic, either. Lost our last witch four years ago, and she was only good for talking to cats, which was about as useful as a bucket with a hole in the bottom since the cats just ignored her and borfed where they liked anyway."

"Rest in peace, Malefibeth," one of the Elders said, pouring out a chunk of soup from his cup directly onto the floor.

But Barthur wasn't done. "At least tell me what it means to be anointed? To have the Aura of Fate wreathed around me? Am I destined for greatness, or is death still, like, a really big risk?"

The knitter spoke this time, although her needles didn't stop clacking. "Tell me this, tell me that?" she mimicked. "You tell me how many stitches of worsted alpaca to cast on to start a proper cap, and I'll tell you everything I know about pixie mucus," she barked. "Which, in both cases, is not a dang thing! Can't a body mind its own business anymore? Not all folks are handy with quest-giving, you know. It's rude to make assumptions."

Barthur deflated. "Look. Things are bad in the world today. Taxes are high, the earl is all but useless, we haven't figured out how to have a king yet. My parents can barely make ends meet, and the price of chickens is down, and when that pixie anointed me, I suddenly had this feeling, deep in my—"

"Bowels?"

"No! In my chest. It entered me like a ball of white-hot light—"

"Yes, yes. In the bowels. I know that feeling. Too much fiber!"

"No! No! It felt as if God had entered me—"

"Gross!"

"Argh!" Barthur stood, furious, his hands in fists. "Please let me finish!"

"Rude," the knitter grumbled. "Young people are always interrupting."

Barthur gritted his teeth. "Look. You might not be *the* Elders, but you're still elders. You're old. You're wise. You have arcane knowledge. You've witnessed generations of triumphs and failures. You must know something about staying alive successfully. I just want a quest. Some direction. Tell me what to do. What to seek. Who to save." He raised an arm as if hefting a mighty sword, looking into the cobwebbed rafters as if a shaft of sunlight fell from heaven upon him through the thatch. "Tell me how to elevate my people from the muck and bring about an enlightened era, as is my anointed destiny!"

As if in response, a thatch-tortoise fell through the ceiling and onto the floor, moaning a little as it scuttled away under a table. The closest Elder grabbed a stick and slowly chased it with murder in his eyes, thwacking its shell, and Barthur deflated a bit more.

"Just . . . help," he whispered.

"Help you? Pfft. Look at us," one of the Elders muttered. "We're old and stale like last week's donuts. We're doing the only thing we can do, which is tell you that we can't do anything."

"But you can at least give me your blessing," Barthur said.

"He just wants dressing?" shouted the Elder holding the ear horn.

"Who's undressing?" barked another one. "Stop that right now. Bodies are shameful!"

Louder, Barthur repeated, "Your *blessing.* I wish to undertake a quest to . . . to . . ."

He looked down, frustrated. Irritated by the heavy press of mothballs and soup and cough drops and smoke. Annoyed by the fact that the Elders weren't what he wanted them to be, what he'd been told they were, what the legends promised. Angry that life was so greedy with direction and surety, seeming to apply it only in hindsight to those who had failed.

Being anointed wasn't enough, apparently, to set one on a path.

But then he saw something. A shape. The crusty, hairy, gooey thing sticking to the carpet. Round, with little fluffy bits. It looked a bit like . . . like a . . .

Good heavens. Could it be?

And then he knew! He knew his quest!

Barthur rose, and in the voice of a future king, he spake, "I will find the Holy Quail!"

For just a moment, the room went silent, and all the Elders looked at Barthur, their jaws dropped and their eyes mostly open.

"What did you say?"

"I said my quest is to find the Holy Quail! The pixie mentioned it, but now I know for sure! The quest is in my heart! All I need is your blessing. Or even . . . just . . ." Barthur scratched his head. "Not quite permission. Maybe you could just say that it was a decent enough thing for a foine young lad to do?"

"Do what? Graffiti and lollygagging?"

"No, my quest to find the quail."

"Definitely mind the pail," an Elder muttered. "Don't kick it. We pee in there sometimes."

Barthur shook his fists at the heavens, or at least at the thatch.

"I WILL FIND THE HOLY QUAIL!"

"Doesn't exist," the middle Elder said, shaking his head. "Legends and folly."

"But didn't the Elders hatch it from a golden egg? That's what the legend says."

The middle Elder groaned. "We keep trying to tell you, kid—there's elders with a lowercase *e* and Elders with a capital *E* and then again there's ELDERS in all capital letters with little flourishes. That's the one you're looking for, and it's the one we definitely ain't. We're just a local branch of a social club. These Elders you're all so anxious to find—the ones who bred fancy glowing quails and gave out blessings? They're gone. Dead. Dust. Left nothing behind but debts, soup recipes, and a mangy old bag of quail feathers. That's kind of the key thing about being an elder in general—you're always one step away from the grave."

He gave a firm nod and picked up a mug of thick soup, which he began to mostly spill down his beard with a shaky spoon, although Barthur was glad to see some of the bigger bits made it into the man's mouth, and that he might be able to squeeze some drippings out of his beard later.

"Fine," Barthur snapped. "Fine. If not your blessing, if not your guidance, then could you at least give me directions toward the famed Laddy of the Lake? Perhaps he could—"

The oldest, baldest Elder threw up his hands in a puff of dust and possibly dander. "See? There you go. Laddy Whosits. You young folks think all old people know each other. Well, I never heard of him. Now if you want to be a true foine ladde, just go back home and do what your parents tell you. We need strong young backs to run the economy and produce the soup, and old folks can't stay safe if all the youngsters go running off willy-nilly with these . . ." He squinted at Barthur, who felt quite small under that withering glance, for all that the old man had the muscle strength of a boneless goose. "Quests," the old man finally finished, but it looked like he had meant to say something much worse and had held back only because he was running out of soup and would probably ask Barthur to fetch more shortly.

"Staying home and doing nothing never fixed the wrongs in the world," Barthur barked back. "I'm part of the next generation. It's my duty to make the world a better place!"

"Balderdash," the knitting Elder muttered. "Nothing can do that."

"You're wrong. With all due respect, which isn't much, you're wrong." Barthur stepped forward, and his form was wreathed in a golden light that smelled a bit like spring flowers and honey, and his squeaky, cracky voice took on the timbre of nobility and power. "I will make the world a better place. I have been anointed, and it is my destiny, and I pledge my body, mind, and heart to this quest. I will find the Holy Quail, and tenderly keep her, and collect her Eggs of Wisdom and Truth, and—"

The old man with the ear horn poked a finger into his hairy ear. "Did somebody just shout down my earhole about eggs?" he screeched. "I don't like eggs in my earhole! They hatch!"

"The point is," Barthur shouted, clearly beyond maintaining any sort of patience, "I'm going, and I would like your blessing. Will you give it? Honestly, just a simple head nod will do at this point in time."

One of the Elders who had not yet contributed stood on

wobbly legs and raised his bushy white brows so that he could look each member of his party in the eyes. And then he turned to Barthur, catching him in a steely glare. Under his scrutiny, Barthur stood up straighter and puffed out his chest, wishing to be everything a hero should be.

"No," the Elder finally said. "Can't go sending young people on foolish journeys. Wouldn't be any young people left to do paperwork and sweep the floors. Stay here, do what your father tells you, and pay taxes like everybody else. That's how stability happens."

"But what about the evil plot of the Dark Lord Fitzherbert?" Barthur challenged. "Staying home won't stop that, and I hear he wishes to outlaw soup."

The Elder waved a hand. "Dark Lords have always been terrible, but they've never changed the taste of soup. We survived by not angering anyone with a wand. Silly little quests won't make anything safer. A bunch of kids with hope in their hearts never changed the world, and that's the sorry truth." He blinked at Barthur and frowned. "Kids these days. Being weird. Just be normal. Weirdos never get anywhere, you know."

Barthur turned a shade of red his mother had warned him about, one that would've been quite pretty on a flower but made him look like he might be having a medical incident.

"Weirdos *can* change the world," he growled.

"Weirdos can change my diapers when they can't get a job," the old man shot back.

The warm glow of destiny had been replaced with the burning glow of rage. "I think we're done here," Barthur said, turning away without bothering to acknowledge the Elders. The standing one collapsed back onto his pillow with a slippery squeak fart, and they all took up their pipes and knitting and soup again as if nothing had happened.

"But I'm still going," Barthur muttered under his breath. "I will find the Quail."

"What?" the Elder with the ear horn shouted. "You found the mail?"

Barthur stopped in the open door and turned back. "Oh,

nothing," he said with saccharine sweetness. "Thank you for your time, o wise and truthful Elders."

"Remember, kid: meek and silent is the way to get along each happy day!" the knitting Elder shouted. "Rhyming songs are always true!"

Barthur let himself out, muttering, "I wish everyone knew the real truth about the Elders."

And then a strange thing happened.

Barthur heard the soft, sloppy pop of magic, and the pixie mucus on his tunic peeled itself off the fabric in a blob, rose up into the air like a particularly nasty soap bubble, and floated right through the closed door. Barthur waited a moment, curious, and heard an even louder pop on the other side, in the room where the Elders sat.

"Oh, gross!" one of the Elders cried. "It's all over me. Somebody call a nurse!"

"The nurse left because I kept grabbing her betonkus!" another Elder cried. "We got blackballed from the agency!"

Another Elder shouted, "We couldn't pay 'em anyway! We're out of money! I stole it all to support my cat hoarding habit! That's why I was always in charge of the petty cash drawer! You knobs never suspected a thing!"

Another one yelled, "I'm not really deaf! I just hate listening to you people."

"If you think that's honest, wait until you hear what I did with that vase you painted for my birthday! I use it to pee in at night!"

"I peed in it before I gave it to you because you said you didn't like my hat!"

Barthur smiled to himself as he listened to the Elders shouting their truths at the top of their feeble lungs.

So that's what pixie magic could do.

Perhaps his anointing was real after all.

"Oh, excuse me," someone said, and Barthur looked up to find a boy about his age, but with black hair and golden skin and a shoddier tunic decorated with a very familiar greenish gooey splotch. "Is this where I might find the Elders?"

Barthur gave the kid a tired smile. "Let me guess. You got anointed?"

The boy's mouth fell open in surprise. "Yes! How did you know? It was by a pixie! Who found me toiling in the barn and chose me for greatness and bade me go on a—"

"A holy quest."

"Yeah, but everyone thinks I said vest."

"Lot of that going around."

The kid stared at the door, then stared at Barthur. "You going in next?" he asked. "Maybe delivering something that'll butter them up?"

Barthur shook his head. "Nah. I'm just going on my own dang quest. I don't need anyone's permission or blessing to do good in the world. I don't need the Elders. Turns out they're actually rubbish."

"Cor, what a bad boy," the kid said with a tone of awe. "Say, I'm Dancelot. What's your name?"

"Barthur."

"Nice to meet you, Barthur."

They shook hands in a manly sort of way, and Barthur looked Dancelot up and down. He could see the Aura of Greatness there, under the mucus stains.

"Tell me, good Dancelot," Barthur said, "how do you feel about quail?"

Brian Herbert & Kevin J. Anderson

When writing major novels in the Dune universe, we have also had ideas for smaller portraits or vignettes. One of the ideas that came back again and again was an exploration of the Sardaukar, the ruthless and greatly feared military division that served the Imperial House. In the novel *Dune,* the Sardaukar are key players in the overthrow of Duke Leto and the downfall of House Atreides. They brutally attack the city of Arrakeen and hide their treacherous involvement by wearing Harkonnen uniforms.

This seemed to run counter to a military code that was so deeply based in honor and loyalty. How could the Sardaukar, with their tradition of honor and dedication to the Imperium, possibly serve the loathsome Baron Harkonnen? How could they agree to support such an unprovoked sneak attack? We wanted to delve into the background of one of those characters, how he became a Sardaukar in the first place, and what he believed.

This story takes place during the Battle of Arrakeen, one of the crux points in the novel *Dune.* House Atreides is famous for their own code of honor, which collides with Sardaukar honor in this story. In Frank Herbert's great novel, a Sardaukar Colonel Bashar appears in one brief scene, confronting the Baron and notifying him that the Emperor has ordered a clean death for Duke Leto, without torture.

We believe "Blood of the Sardaukar" stands on its own as a compelling story, but it also enriches the classic scene in *Dune.*

Brian Herbert & Kevin J. Anderson

BLOOD OF THE SARDAUKAR

A Tale of Dune

Brian Herbert & Kevin J. Anderson

The fires of battle had already begun in the city of Arrakeen, shattering a quiet and secure night.

He had a name, but his identity was the uniform and the brotherhood of the Sardaukar, the undefeated elite troops of Emperor Shaddam IV, though now the uniform was false, with loyalties obscured. And Colonel Bashar Jopati Kolona wasn't so sure of his core identity—not on this night, not on this mission. But he had his orders, and he was a Sardaukar.

Arrakeen was the largest city on the desert planet of Arrakis, the seat of House Atreides, newly installed planetary governors in charge of vital spice production for the Imperium. It was also a trap.

Jopati rode inside one of many heavily armored dropships that emerged from an enormous Guild Heighliner in orbit, part of the clandestine Harkonnen attack force augmented by the Imperial military.

On their way down, he saw the aerial bombardment of Arrakeen's slums and warehouses, sparking the first waves of chaos and disrupting Atreides defenses. Low, weathered buildings exploded into dust and flames. When the troop carrier landed hard among the fresh rubble, side doors opened to disgorge the uniformed troops. The colonel bashar led his men, disembarking in a fluid, coordinated motion.

Racing into the streets, the disguised Sardaukar carried projectile weapons and explosive launchers because the Harkonnens liked to kill mass numbers of people from a distance, but Jopati and his troops also carried bladed weapons because they preferred more intimate combat.

He ran ahead through the streets, raising his black-gloved hand. "Eliminate any resistance, but don't get distracted. Our objective is the Residency, and Duke Leto Atreides will mount a significant defense."

One of the gray-uniformed men beside him snorted. He was not even breathing heavily as they dodged around a broken-down groundcar. "Waste of time."

"Just another day," said a second man, shifting his projectile rifle to aim into the shadows of a narrow alley, where Jopati saw only huddled figures. No threat.

He said in a stern voice, "Confidence is good, but don't underestimate this Atreides Duke." He smelled the chemical smoke whirling up from the bomb blasts. The air was so brittle and dry here, each breath felt as if it held scouring shards of sand.

Arrakis was a hellish place. Offworlders who worked here by choice could command ridiculously high wages, while other inhabitants were stuck here because they had no place else to go or no way off planet. Jopati had no patience for their whining complaints. This desert world could not compare to the blasted wasteland of Salusa Secundus, the Imperial prison planet the Sardaukar claimed as their home.

Ahead, the great blocky building of the Arrakeen Residency looked more like an illuminated, huddled fortress than the palatial home of a wealthy planetary governor. The walls were thick and square, and the grim architecture reflected decades of Harkonnen rule on Arrakis. Baron Harkonnen and his predecessors were not known for their appreciation of beauty nor their patronage of the arts.

The well-lit Residency stood not far from the Shield Wall, the towering cliffs that protected the city from the dangers of the open desert. The perimeter lights flickered, and more beacons went on as alarms sounded. Atreides guards were already trying to shore up their defenses after the first explosions from the dropships.

The colonel bashar knew his foes could not stand against this well-coordinated sneak attack. The Landsraad might howl and dispute the treacherous actions of the Baron, but Jopati knew full well the accepted treacheries of Imperial politics. He had lived through it himself. The Emperor's role in this overthrow would be covered up, and any hint of Sardaukar participation would be erased. The Landsraad members who objected too strenuously to the treatment of their beloved Duke Atreides would be paid off or, if necessary, assassinated.

Given the sheer number of deadly troops rushing through the city, the outcome of the assault was certain—two legions of Sardaukar descending on the desert planet—one full legion of ten brigades sweeping through Arrakeen itself, and the second legion dispersed to Carthag and other cities around the desert world. They would swiftly remove any Atreides resistance and install Harkonnen-friendly administrators and military peacekeepers.

As his men approached the Residency, launching explosives to disrupt any organized defense, Jopati resented being forced to wear these Harkonnen uniforms, but to his trained eye he could see the difference in how his troops moved, because their service to the Imperium made them better than any other soldier, better than any other human. They were the elite, feared Sardaukar, ferociously loyal to the Padishah Emperor, as bonded to the Imperial throne as a Suk doctor with unbreakable Imperial conditioning. No false uniform could hide that fact from any astute observer.

The lieutenant next to him touched the comm in his ear and grinned. "The house shields are down, Colonel Bashar. Our traitor did his work."

"Acknowledged. We can move right in." Jopati placed his hand on his kindjal, his fighting knife. He was itching to confront the Atreides guards. "Kill anyone necessary, but we have special orders regarding the Duke."

"The Baron will want him himself," said the lieutenant.

"He will, and he's likely to have him," Jopati answered. "But the Emperor gave me explicit orders that Duke Leto is to die cleanly and without torture. I'm to see to it personally. With the enmity these Great Houses feel for one another, the Baron may have . . . difficulty obeying those instructions."

Baron Vladimir Harkonnen was loathsome, not just because of his gross obesity but his carnal, pedophilic appetites, his vicious personality, his utter lack of honor. Thinking of the Baron made Jopati feel dirty in his Harkonnen uniform. He did not care about the politics of Arrakis, or the monopoly on spice production, or the disgusting nature of the Baron himself.

As they ran toward the Residency's main gates, he saw a line of Atreides guards rallying for the fight. Jopati's Sardaukar let out a great roar of challenge and swarmed ahead as explosions continued throughout the city.

At one time, the Atreides Duke was the only person he hated more than the Baron. Now he wasn't so sure.

Almost two decades ago, Jopati Kolona had been on the other side of the same situation. When he was only fourteen, his noble family, House Kolona, were the victims of Landsraad betrayal, a power play by Duke Paulus Atreides—Leto's father—to increase the prominence and profits of House Atreides.

Jopati was the son of Count and Countess Kolona, hereditary rulers of the planet Borhees. He was one of eight sons, five older and two younger. House Kolona had been a member of the Landsraad, faithful if unremarkable citizens of the Imperium for more than a millennium. Borhees was a small planet with a tolerable climate, wealthy enough to be desirable but not enough to be powerful.

In his early teens, Jopati had already known the map of his future, how he would one day become a regional administrator for his Great House, a man who needed to understand bureaucracy and leadership, but who never expected to face many challenges.

That all changed when Count Kolona argued with Duke Paulus Atreides during a Landsraad council session. It was after Imperial laws were changed—conveniently and coincidentally, it seemed—to place House Kolona at a disadvantage, and Paulus pounced on the opportunity for himself. At the council session, Jopati's father filed an appeal and waited for the slow judiciary to grind its way toward a decision.

No one had expected the outright attack from House Atreides.

The warships and nighttime raid had been a complete surprise, and the Kolona house shields had not been activated. Jopati's mother and oldest brother were killed before they even knew what was happening, having gone out to stargaze on an open tower. A stray explosion struck the rooftop, killing the Countess and the heir. Unprepared for a fight, the Count rallied the rest of his family and whisked them into the hills with little more than the clothes on their backs. All the while the household guards battled the Atreides invaders, giving the Count and his surviving sons time to escape.

Jopati's father had looked sick, angry, and determined. "We will fight one day," he assured the boys as they fled through back passageways. "But it will be a long struggle, and we are not yet ready for battle."

Before that, Jopati had only known peace. Any conflicts were political, such as arguments on the floor of the Landsraad Hall or local Borhees disputes among fur farmers and spider weavers. Before the Atreides Aggression, as his father called it, the greatest emergencies the teenage boy had seen were an unseasonable ice storm that caused widespread damage, and floods that wiped out river villages. In his youth, Jopati had never fought in actual combat, though he had been trained in fencing and hand-to-hand shield fighting—more like a court dance than a clash for survival. Naïve and oblivious, Jopati had been too young to see the real threat posed by Duke Atreides, until the infamous sneak attack.

After that, when the Count led them to his hiding place in

the hills, Jopati was astonished to see just how prepared his father actually was. Years before the attack, he had constructed hidden redoubts in sheltered areas and supplied them with weapons and food. Jopati's older brothers knew about the redoubts before he did and had drilled for the unlikely eventuality of an attack, but the teenager had been considered too immature for that information.

Now, after years of harsh training and vigorous military service ingrained in his bones, Colonel Bashar Jopati was deeply disappointed at his father for not establishing more palace defenses and not preparing for a frontal attack. The Sardaukar officer found it ironic that the Atreides themselves were now facing a similar nighttime surprise attack. . . .

For many months the survivors of House Kolona hid in the hills and launched regular guerilla attacks to drive out the Atreides forces that had planted their green-and-black banner on Borhees. Duke Paulus administered the world in the name of Emperor Elrood IX, but he rarely set foot on his new holding. Through intermediaries, Count Kolona continued to file complaints in the Landsraad, and the resistance managed to gain some support, more out of sympathy and vengeance for the murdered Countess and their eldest son than out of any wishful thinking for the golden days of House Kolona. Under occupation, the people of Borhees noticed very little change in their daily lives.

Jopati himself went out on a few guerrilla raids against the Atreides oppressors, which seemed like adventures to him. Inside the protected redoubt, his father continued to spit poison and hatred toward the treacherous Duke Paulus.

After months of hit-and-run harassment, the Duke—or was it the Emperor?—reached a breaking point. The hiding places in the hills were discovered through a spy or a traitor. Military troops swarmed into the hidden redoubt, ruthless fighters wearing the familiar but hated Atreides uniforms. They blasted the sealed entrances and ferreted out the weapons stashes, lookout posts, and satellite command centers. The Kolona guerilla fighters had no chance.

The men in Atreides uniforms were the most efficient and

brutal soldiers Jopati had ever seen up to that time in his life. They showed no mercy. With a sweep of his sword, one man beheaded the Count before he could even activate his shield belt. Jopati's four older brothers were also killed before his eyes. Jopati himself had a knife in each hand and fought to protect his two younger brothers, Telso and Kem, each of whom had a small sword. They expected to die.

The colonel bashar who had killed the Count faced the boys, raised his sword, and laughed. "You show fine mettle, lads. Are you young enough to be trained into something better and strong enough to survive? Or will you foolishly throw your lives away on fruitless revenge?"

Jopati had been so terrified he didn't know how to answer. When he hesitated, the colonel bashar swept his sword sideways, and Jopati held his ground, knowing he was about to die. But the officer controlled his stroke and merely smashed the two knives out of Jopati's hands, leaving him with sore wrists, numb fingers, and nothing else to fight for.

Only later did Jopati learn that the military force consisted of Sardaukar wearing Atreides uniforms so that Duke Paulus would receive the credit, or the blame, for wiping out House Kolona.

The colonel bashar, a steel-hard man named Horthan, took Jopati, Telso, and Kem to the Imperial prison planet, where they were sentenced to be erased, the last members of a rebellious house of the Landsraad. He dumped them inside the oppressive prison complex, but gave them one last chance to survive before torture and execution. Tragically, his youngest brother Kem, only eight years old, died within the first month. Jopati had not seen Kem for days until his bloody and battered body was tossed in front of their cell one night, a tender, barely-alive toy that—to Jopati's rage and disgust—had been passed around among the prisoners.

Jopati and his scrappy twelve-year-old brother Telso did manage to fight off the advances of the prisoners. He was physically strong, athletic in his movements, and quite good with his extended fingers, gouging at the eyes of anyone who tried to come for him or his only remaining brother.

After the two young men passed that first test, Colonel Bashar Horthan took them out of the labyrinthine prison complex. The boys thought they were being rescued when, in fact, their lives would become far worse.

Salusa Secundus, a blistered and windy world that had been devastated in an atomic holocaust by a renegade House millennia earlier, was considered one of the worst planets in the Imperium, a place of fitting punishment for those foolish enough to commit crimes against the Emperor. The prison itself was only part of Salusa's purpose, though. The deadly environment was a testing and training ground to produce the fiercest, most ruthless fighters in the known universe: the Imperial Sardaukar.

Initiation into this elite brotherhood was not so much training as a delayed, agonizing execution, considering how few recruits lived. Early in the horrendous ordeal, the colonel bashar addressed the determined or frightened candidates on a training field in a bleak wasteland. "Long ago, during the reign of Prince Raphael Corrino, the noble House Sardaukar was convicted of plotting against the throne. They were sentenced to Salusa Secundus, where they were expected to die." He swept his gaze across the shivering trainees. "But the ones who lived became the toughest fighters ever.

"Prince Raphael offered them a chance to redeem themselves, when he recruited the surviving lost souls for a desperate military operation, and they saved his rule. Since that time, the greatest fighters serving the Emperor have called themselves *Sardaukar*—not just descendants of that noble House Sardaukar but any prisoners who proved themselves worthy, the survivors of Salusa Secundus." Horthan's stare was like a weapon. "Are you worthy of being Sardaukar?" He looked at all the candidates who stood before him under the harsh sun. "Are you survivors?"

Jopati and the others cheered and made their vows, but later most of them were killed during training, though not the Kolona boys. Horthan took the pair, the last of their Great House, and taught them to fight and survive. He gave them the tools they needed while doing his best to kill them.

In one of their tests, Jopati and Telso were turned loose naked out in a glassy hot canyon; they had to find shelter from fiery windstorms and fight off packs of bloodthirsty predators with nothing but rocks. Surviving that, he and his brother were rewarded with knives, then turned loose to fight the beasts again, more of them this time. Telso survived such ordeals for two years, growing strong and hard, but he died from the bite of a poisonous reptile during group maneuvers—not yet a man by his years, but he died like a man.

Jopati was the only remaining member of House Kolona, unrecognizable from the fresh-faced young man who had hidden in the hills with the Count. All because of the hated Duke Atreides.

Soon even the Kolona family name became buried under scars, blisters, and armor when Colonel Bashar Horthan promoted him to the rank of lieutenant among the Sardaukar, an accomplishment that had more meaning than Jopati's entire family tree.

The Sardaukar had become his family. . . .

The tall date palms burned in front of the Arrakeen Residency like macabre, smoky candles. On this parched and desolate planet, trees should not have existed at all, but Duke Leto must have had some purpose in keeping the trees where all the people could see them. Flaunting his wealth and water perhaps? Or offering a symbol of hope?

Whatever his thinking, the Duke's plans and dreams would die with him this night. With the house shields sabotaged from within, the Residency was vulnerable to outside attack. The colonel bashar led his forces against a line of hardened Atreides soldiers. The kindjal was Jopati's preferred weapon, a long knife slightly curved, carefully weighted. It was a personal blade, requiring more finesse than a long sword that allowed an attacker to strike from arm's length.

In his false Harkonnen uniform, Jopati faced an Atreides captain, a deeply tanned man with three ornate metal pins on his chest, apparently awards for service or commendations for valor. The captain's uniform cap was askew from when he and his men had rushed out of the troop barracks to form this frantic defense.

Seeing how easily the renowned Atreides fighters had been surprised, the colonel bashar realized a weakness he had not previously considered. Atreides honor was legendary and Duke Leto's adherence to that core principle had made him a hero among the Landsraad. Leto was revered, celebrated, and even *liked* among the other noble houses, enough to intimidate and annoy Emperor Shaddam IV. But that unwavering devotion to honor also created a blind spot for the Atreides. Despite all their suspicions and precautions, they had not given enough credence to the possibility that one of their own could betray them so completely.

They had a traitor in their midst, very close to the Duke.

With his shield belt surrounding him in a comforting hum, Jopati threw himself upon the Atreides captain, his kindjal raised while his opponent defended himself with a longer sword. Their body shields sparked as they crashed into each other. The shimmering Holtzman barrier slowed or deflected any rapid thrust, forcing their desperate battle to become more of a slow dance of thrust blades carefully deflected, points dodging, slashing, stabbing.

"Harkonnen scum!" the captain snarled.

Jopati responded with a hard smile. "You don't even know who you're fighting." He found it insulting to be considered a member of that vile house, but that was part of the plan. Even though Jopati knew he would kill this man, he could not reveal the deception. The Sardaukar had their own code of honor.

The Atreides captain managed to slice his arm with the sword tip, surprising Jopati. He had looked forward to fighting some of the legendary protectors of House Atreides, the troubadour warrior Gurney Halleck, the Swordmaster Duncan Idaho, even the old Mentat, the Master of Assassins Thufir Hawat, but this guard captain was his opponent now. Warm blood trickled down the gray sleeve of his Harkonnen uniform, and he was angry with himself. A Sardaukar should never have been wounded by a mere unnamed captain.

Seeing the splash of blood, tasting just a hint of victory, the Atreides man surged forward. "For the Duke!"

Jopati brought up his kindjal to deflect the blade of his enthusiastic opponent. The body shield blocked what would have been a death blow, and Jopati countered with a much more calculated strike, gliding the kindjal tip through the other man's shield, thrusting into his body slowly, steadily, pushing the tip between the captain's ribs, cutting deeper, all the way into the left side of his chest.

"For the Duke," Jopati whispered as the man died, falling at his feet.

Around him the other disguised Sardaukar dispatched their opponents, leaving dead Atreides soldiers strewn across the Residency grounds. The first ranks of attackers had already broken inside and were swarming through the corridors. By now, Jopati assumed that Duke Leto had been subdued and captured, his concubine and son possibly killed. The Baron would be unable to control his twisted desire for vengeance, but Jopati had his own orders from the Emperor himself, and had to intervene.

He respected the loyalty of the Atreides troops. Few other noble families could command such devotion—Baron Harkonnen certainly didn't! Jopati saw the reason for it himself, and even understood it. He knew from firsthand experience that Duke Leto was no ordinary political leader.

It was not easy to turn against this nobleman.

Jopati thought back years ago, to a time when he'd held a lower rank. . . .

On Salusa Secundus, a violent and strictly regimented existence, Jopati Kolona had received a new uniform to go with his fresh commission as a lieutenant. Then, after further years of grooming, he received an assignment more challenging than the most dangerous survival exercises he had faced.

He was sent to Kaitain to become one of the Emperor's elite guard in the Imperial Palace itself.

Though raised as a noble son on Borhees, the new lieutenant now found that he was a stranger to civilization. With their machinations and schemes, the nobles were just as predatory as the poisonous Salusan reptiles, but in a different way. Jopati wore a formal uniform, ate well, and slept in comfortable quarters, but never let his sharp edge of wariness and violence grow dull. His life, loyalty, strength, and skills were sworn in service of the Padishah Emperor, a man who had previously been only a symbol, a name that Colonel Bashar Horthan invoked while shaping the recruits.

Emperor Shaddam IV had ascended to the throne after the death of his father, Elrood IX. Now in his later middle years, Shaddam had reddish hair held in place with delicately scented pomade, an aquiline nose, sharp intense eyes, and thin lips that never smiled. The Emperor loved to surround himself with uniformed Sardaukar and reveled in well-choreographed military parades in the great plaza. Shaddam enjoyed standing at one of his tower windows to watch the precision spectacle from a safe distance without risking interaction with his own subjects.

Jopati had no friends among the Sardaukar, since he had learned not to allow any personal weaknesses. He served as ordered, and because his days in the palace did not involve a constant struggle to survive, he had time—too much time—to remember his murdered family, the destruction of his noble House through the schemes of Duke Paulus Atreides . . . how the guerilla fighters had hidden themselves in the hills, only to be overrun by Sardaukar wearing false Atreides uniforms. He did not understand how Duke Paulus could have been aligned with old Emperor Elrood's wishes.

Though Jopati did not resent what he had become—a far superior human being and an incomparable fighter—his anger toward the Atreides had festered inside him, so much that he did not grieve when he learned that Duke Paulus had been killed in a bullfight, gored to death by a maddened Salusan bull. Yet he felt cheated that he'd not had the opportunity to do it himself. . . .

Years later, hardened into Imperial service and having successfully performed several risky missions to increase Shaddam's power, Jopati had been on duty in the cavernous palace throne room, standing at attention, when he was shocked and disoriented by a supplicant who presented himself before the Golden Lion throne.

Duke Leto Atreides himself.

He was a dark-haired man with gray eyes and hawk features, not dissimilar to Shaddam's appearance. He exuded confidence, having comfortably settled into his role after the death of Duke Paulus. Wearing a civilian suit with the Atreides crest on the jacket, he strode into the throne room in an erect soldierly posture, crossing the expanse of polished stone tiles accompanied by a young man, his bodyguard and Swordmaster, introduced as Duncan Idaho. Jopati's fellow Sardaukar guards immediately gauged the potential threat posed by the Swordmaster, but Jopati riveted his attention on Leto.

This was the heir to the House that had overthrown his family, that had killed the Count and Countess Kolona and all of Jopati's brothers. This was Duke Leto Atreides, who ruled the planet Borhees as an auxiliary holding, taking the profits for his own coffers on Caladan. Jopati did not doubt that Duke Leto was just as treacherous as his father had been.

Leto paid no attention whatsoever to the Sardaukar guards as he walked up to the throne carved out of a block of Hagal crystal. His bow before Shaddam was polite and respectful but not obsequious. "Cousin, it is good to see you again," Leto said. "It has been awhile since I had personal business on Kaitain."

Jopati narrowed his eyes and felt emotions roil up, hard memories of death and vengeance. He was a loyal Sardaukar, but he was also the last surviving son of the fallen House Kolona.

Shaddam lifted his hands in an impatient gesture, even though Leto was already rising from his bow. "I'm always happy to see you, cousin." Jopati recognized no warmth or welcome in the Emperor's voice. "It is a good sign that you don't come here often, because that means your rule is smooth and without problems. I wish I could say the same of more Landsraad nobles."

Leto smiled. "Perhaps it is because I'm content with my Caladan fief and not desperate to increase the power and influence of House Atreides."

"I wish I could say the same of more Landsraad nobles," Shaddam repeated, then coolly raised his eyebrows. "House Atreides has more holdings than just Caladan, though. You administer the planet Borhees as well. I receive my tithes from you for both worlds, at least according to my treasurer."

Coiled with rage, Jopati did not dare make a move now, could not draw his weapon and attack Leto Atreides before the court, though as a member of the Imperial Sardaukar he had the ability to move throughout the palace. He had allies who would follow his commands without question. He could find a way to abduct Leto, interrogate him, and kill him. Would that be sufficient to balance the scales for House Kolona? Duke Paulus was already dead, but the sudden death of Leto might settle the debt.

The Duke's expression grew more serious. At his side, Duncan Idaho stood stoic and alert. The Swordmaster seemed completely content, utterly loyal. Although Idaho was not to be underestimated, Jopati felt certain he could defeat him. Regardless of whether they were evenly matched, Jopati had the added leverage of vengeance and surprise. The Swordmaster didn't know the dark stain on Atreides history.

"Yes, Borhees is a secondary holding of House Atreides," Leto said. "Previously, the planet was administered quite capably by House Kolona, but my father assumed control of the planetary operations." His voice hardened. "In a manner that has always puzzled me, and now I am very disturbed by it."

Jopati tensed but made no move, showed no reaction. The Emperor raised his eyebrows, showing only mild interest.

"I've already presented a petition to the Landsraad," Leto continued. "It is highly unorthodox but perfectly legal, so I see no reason why it will not be approved. I came here as a courtesy to inform you."

Shaddam frowned, obviously more tense. "What is it you find so important?"

"I have come to believe that our administration of Borhees is not legitimate. It always seemed peculiar that my father would have made such an atypical move on such an unusual target. House

Atreides did not previously seek expansion beyond Caladan. Then why Borhees? My father only spoke of the matter rarely, and if I ever asked him about it, he seemed genuinely distressed. Once, he told me it was a stain that could not be washed away."

Jopati felt cold inside. His arms were straight at his sides, his hands clenched quietly and unnoticed into fists. The thought of Leto Atreides even speaking his family name seemed like a sacrilege, but the nobleman's words gave Jopati pause. He watched the Emperor's reaction, how he sat on his throne, puzzled and intrigued.

"What nonsense is this? Borhees was granted to House Atreides by right of conquest when your father responded to a ruling. Evidence showed that House Kolona was prepared to go renegade after being accused of embezzling from the Imperial treasury." Shaddam looked down at his fingers as if considering a manicure after the discussion was over. "But that was many years ago. Is Borhees not a profitable holding? Are the people troublesome and causing unrest?"

"No, Sire, neither of those."

Shaddam pursed his lips, seeming to grow impatient. Jopati listened in stony silence, wanting to scream out thousands of questions.

Leto said, "In studying my father's records to instruct my young son Paul in leadership, I came upon some troubling documents. I suspect that the entire operation was not, in fact, instigated by Duke Paulus, and that he merely provided political cover for Emperor Elrood." He paused to let the revelation sink in. "Many of the Kolona holdings were absorbed into the Imperial treasury, though Elrood's name was kept entirely out of it. House Atreides received a substantial payoff for facilitating Elrood's plans and for my father's silence." His hard gaze was locked upon Shaddam, who sat motionless upon the throne. Leto lowered his voice, speaking in the tone of a friend to his cousin, "I know you had no great love for your father, Sire, and although you had no knowledge of this illegal scheme to crush a member of the Landsraad, it cannot be a complete surprise."

Jopati felt a knot in his stomach. What was this Atreides Duke doing?

"I came here to Kaitain to rectify the situation," Leto said.

Duncan Idaho glanced at his Duke, and the look on his face was one of complete satisfaction, almost bliss.

Shaddam's expression darkened. "Rectify? How?"

Aloof, Leto ran his left hand through his long dark hair. "I have already petitioned the Landsraad Council, releasing details of this unconscionable plot. Any noble House could have been the victim of such a world-grabbing scheme, and they are relieved that your father's ire didn't fall upon them." He straightened. "Although all known members of House Kolona are dead, the Count and Countess and their sons, there are still extended family members who can claim to be legitimate heirs. I offer to return Borhees into their care."

Shaddam half rose from the crystalline throne. "Why would you do that? It paints a shadow across my reign!"

"Not yours, Sire—your father's, and he is long gone. I know that you, dear cousin, would wish to do the moral thing, the *just* thing. The Landsraad members applauded my decision, and I believe they are voting now. We can expect the results soon."

Duncan Idaho's firm lips began to quirk in a small smile. Jopati couldn't believe what he was hearing.

Into Shaddam's stunned silence, Leto continued, "My father hammered into me the idea that honor is the most important thing in any man's heart and mind. I don't know why he was forced to accept the blame and the credit for what he did to House Kolona, but I intend to provide a righteous example for my own son. This is the honorable thing to do. If the Atreides cannot follow the course of honor, then my House is like a Guild ship without a Navigator."

The Emperor could do nothing to stop Leto's plan, because it was already in motion, already publicly announced. If he interfered with the Landsraad vote, Shaddam would look corrupt as well as complicit in what Elrood had done. A masterstroke, Jopati thought, and it would greatly increase Leto's standing among the Landsraad. They would love him for what he had done.

Failing to find a counterargument, the Emperor abruptly dismissed Leto, who bowed again and withdrew with his faithful Swordmaster.

Unable to believe or process the startling information he had just heard, Jopati Kolona watched the two Atreides men depart. He felt off-balance, and wondered about the true motivations of Emperor Elrood IX. Previously he had blamed Paulus Atreides for the entire affair, but what if the late Atreides Duke was merely camouflage, coerced into cooperating?

And Leto . . . the young Duke might have kept his silence. In stepping forward, he had everything to lose and nothing to gain.

Except honor.

Jopati decided he might have to reconsider. Perhaps he liked this Duke after all.

That had been years ago.

Now, following orders, the colonel bashar dispatched his troops throughout the Residency of Duke Leto. The fighting continued, and many of his men—Sardaukar!—had been killed in hand-to-hand combat. How could that be possible?

The Atreides were indeed fierce and determined opponents, valiant foes. Thufir Hawat ran the household troops with an iron fist, and against any normal attack by mere Harkonnen troops, they would likely have been victorious. But not against Sardaukar.

By now the Baron Harkonnen's own ship had landed nearby, which he used as his base of operations on Arrakis. As soon as Colonel Bashar Kolona locked down the Residency, he would report to the Baron and insist that he follow the Emperor's orders about the manner of Leto's death. Jopati had conflicting reports about whether Duke Leto had already been captured or killed in the fighting.

In the courtyard of the Residency, soldiers dragged bodies in Atreides uniforms into lines on the brick pavement, while the fighting continued around the perimeter. Jopati had personally killed twelve during the assault.

Fires burned through the night. Military aircraft cruised across the skies through a maze of smoke columns. Booming rumbles echoed from the fringe of the city where heavy artillery, archaic weaponry deployed by the Harkonnens, pummeled hide-out cliffs in the Shield Wall. No one expected such retrograde technology in this day and age, and they were not prepared for it. The Atreides troops who had fallen back to the shelter of the cliffs were being pounded. The dull, booming sounds were like the persistent drumbeat of a funeral procession.

The uniformed troops ransacking the Residency and destroying anything that bore the Atreides hawk crest were real Harkonnen soldiers. Jopati didn't care about them. His Sardaukar troops followed their orders exquisitely, and so did he. He felt unsettled, since the events of this evening reminded him so much of the downfall of House Kolona. The turnabout seemed appropriate and poignant, the perfect way to balance the scales of justice . . . if such scales still needed to be balanced. But Duke Leto Atreides had already settled that score without being coerced, because it was the right and moral thing to do.

Jopati was a Sardaukar officer, but he had no name that anyone remembered or noted. It was not possible for him to rise up, reveal himself and claim the Kolona holdings on Borhees. That possibility had long ago been erased, but he did not yearn for it. He was content with knowing that his relatives had their rightful holdings back. He was a Sardaukar now, so nothing else mattered. He followed the orders of the Padishah Emperor, but he had his own code of honor, a personal matter guiding his actions.

At the far side of the Residency, in the open landing field with guard towers and a small hangar, shouts erupted along with the clang of metal. He saw a furious fight, a lone man in an Atreides uniform against three true Harkonnen troops and two disguised Sardaukar—and the man was holding his own! Jopati jogged forward, saw his other Sardaukar watching the combat with detached interest. They stood with weapons that ranged from heavy launchers to small hand knives. They did not doubt this one man would be defeated, but they marveled at his bravery and fighting finesse. His skill was honed even sharper through desperation.

Jopati recognized the lone Atreides fighter: Swordmaster Duncan Idaho, the man who adhered to the Duke's code of ethics. In precisely controlled strokes, he dipped his blade through the body shield of the nearest Harkonnen fighter and gutted him, then withdrew. With a kindjal in his other hand, he stabbed a Sardaukar in the kidney, a mortal wound. The Sardaukar stumbled, unable to believe the death blow he had just received.

Jopati froze, and the other Sardaukar cried out at the fall of their companion.

In efficient fashion, Idaho dispatched the two remaining Harkonnen soldiers and drove back the second Sardaukar, then bolted for the Harkonnen ornithopter on the landing field. Its running lights were still on, its engines powered up.

Along with Jopati, the rest of the Sardaukar in the vicinity lurched into action, no longer just watching the duel. Idaho was a blur of speed, leaving his victims behind. He dove into the cockpit, and without even closing the plaz door, he revved the skimmer engine and set the articulated wings into a blurring flutter of motion.

One Sardaukar reached the ornithopter before Jopati, just as the craft lifted off the ground. The man grabbed for the struts and clung by his fingertips for a few seconds as the 'thopter rose, then dropped back to the ground from the height of a few meters. More Sardaukar rushed across the landing field, but Idaho had control of the aircraft now. He pulled higher, circling away as he increased speed.

Jopati snatched a large-caliber launcher from one of his fellow soldiers. "Give me that." He wouldn't be fighting the Atreides Swordmaster hand-to-hand, as he had hoped, but he could still shoot down the aircraft with a projectile. Even the fastest 'thopter couldn't outrun an explosive shell. He shouldered the weapon, activated the power pack, and looked through the targeting hairs.

After this night, nothing would remain of House Atreides, no more than was left of House Kolona once the Sardaukar swept in and eradicated the guerillas in the hills.

Idaho zigzagged in the air, flying evasive maneuvers, but Jopati knew he could take down the craft. He had his orders. Idaho was only the Atreides Swordmaster, but a high-ranking target nevertheless.

It was not Jopati's decision whether this treacherous attack on the Atreides was just or not. Even if Leto had redeemed himself by restoring the Kolona holdings years ago, too many other events had been set in motion, and Jopati could do nothing for the Duke.

He tracked with the launcher, centering the ornithopter in the targeting crosshairs. The shell was ready, the target in his sights.

He had his orders.

He pressed the ignition stud and launched the projectile, which whistled through the atmosphere in the direction of the fleeing 'thopter.

Colonel Bashar Jopati Kolona knew what Emperor Shaddam expected of him in this night's operation, but the details of the execution were somewhat vague. Jopati was the Sardaukar commander.

And he intentionally missed.

The explosive shell screamed along its trajectory and detonated just shy of Duncan Idaho's craft. Jopati's troops stared after him as the ornithopter sped away, darting among flowering explosions in the sky. The aircraft's running lights went dark as Idaho disappeared into the curling smoke.

Jopati handed the launcher back to the uniformed man who stared at him in silent disbelief. Both the Atreides and Sardaukar had codes of honor.

Gesturing toward his men in Harkonnen uniforms, the colonel bashar marched them into the Residency for one last encounter with Duke Leto Atreides.

Terry Brooks

THE HISTORY IS THUS: THE ONCE-DRUID BRONA, SEDUCED BY HIS PURSUIT of dark magic, was forever transformed into the Warlock Lord—whose evil would be the downfall of the Four Lands and the death of the Races. Against him, the Elven King Jerle Shannara wielded the fabled sword that bore his surname and triumphed. Or so it was believed. But though the Dark Lord was driven out . . . he was not destroyed.

The Druid Allanon knows only too well the prophecy passed down to him by his late master: that eventually the Warlock Lord will return. Now, after hundreds of years, that day seems imminent. And the time is at hand for the Sword of Shannara to once more be brought forth from its sanctuary to serve its ancient purpose. All that remains is for a blood descendent of the Elven house of Shannara to carry the blade into battle.

With ever more portents of doom on the horizon, Allanon must seek out the last remaining Shannara heir, who alone will bear the burden of defending the Four Lands' destiny. But with agents of darkness closing in from behind, unexpected enemies lying in wait ahead, and treachery encroaching on every side, there can be no certainty of success. Nor any assurance that this desperate quest will not be the Druid's last.

"Allanon's Quest" is the prequel short story to *The Sword of Shannara.*

Terry Brooks

ALLANON'S QUEST

Terry Brooks

The storm clouds scudded across the night sky in roiling clumps that blotted out the half-moon and stars and enveloped the land beneath in heavy shadow. The woods surrounding the village of Archer Trace, fifty miles north and east of the city of Arborlon, stirred uneasily. The trees swayed, and their leaves shivered with a metallic rustling as wind tore at the branches in sharp gusts and rain pattered heavily against the leaves. A drop in the temperature had already announced the storm's arrival, the air damp, chilly, and raw. Intricate patterns of lightning flashed, and bursts of thunder rumbled from across the eastern edge of the Sarandanon.

Allanon pulled his black robes tighter and his hood closer as he entered the Elven village, passing the first of the outlying buildings and making his way along the empty pathways. Candlelight burned in the windows of a few cottages and huts, flickering behind glass panes or through open shutters, and this small light was sufficient to guide him on his way. But most of the buildings were entirely dark. The residents had either gone to bed in anticipation of an early rising or down to the taverns that provided the main source of entertainment for the village.

Had anyone been looking through windows or shutters, or had he been careless enough not to disguise his coming, he might have been observed. But Allanon was not the careless sort, and he had used his Druid skills to change his appearance sufficiently that he seemed little more than another of the night's shadows. To anyone looking, he simply wasn't there. It was a Druid trick—one he had perfected during his early years, when he was just learning his craft. Bremen, who had taught it to him, was already gone by then, so he had mastered it on his own, expanding on his existing skills.

But while Archer Trace was the sort of miserable place where inhabitants and visitors alike made it a point to watch one another closely, there was little vigilance on this night. The foul weather did not invite the monitoring of those abroad, and the pleasures of the taverns provided a more attractive lure. So Allanon passed into the village relatively unseen, traveling along its single roadway to a cluster of ragged buildings that were illuminated by torches wedged down in iron brackets beneath their weather shields, fighting bravely to stay lit against the onslaught of wind and rain.

Slowing, he looked for the sign that would identify his destination and quickly found it: THE DRUNKEN FOOL. Big, bold letters—no doubt a reference to its patrons. But if it could provide him with the information he needed, what did the nature of the business or its patrons matter to him? He had come all the way from Arborlon on this slim hope of success because time and opportunity were growing short. And rumor alone was enough to send him on what others might have dismissed as a fool's errand. Lives were being snuffed out, and all that mattered might soon be gone—something that would prove disastrous to the Four Lands. If even one of those he sought could be saved, he had to do whatever it took to make that happen. There was more at stake here than his discomfort and risk.

He cast aside the magic that let him remain unseen as he pushed his way through the tavern's heavy door and into the smoky interior, then looked about. The room was crowded—more so than he would have expected, given the size and condition of the village. Most of the tavern's denizens were Elves; no surprise there—this was their homeland. But it appeared as if everyone who lived in Archer Trace or might even have been passing through had gathered. A few heads turned to look at him, but most turned quickly away. A man seven feet tall and possessed of rough features and a dark scowl did not draw many extended looks. He ignored the few looks he received and waited for the barkeep to acknowledge him. When the man gave him a nod of recognition, the Druid turned his attention to a small table in the back of the room and the two men who occupied it. A moment later, both men rose, having suddenly decided that it was time to leave although neither could have said why.

He gave it a moment, then crossed to the table the men had vacated and sat down.

After a few minutes, the barkeep wandered over.

"Long trip?" He was a large, heavyset man with big features and a dour look. For an Elf, he looked downright sullen. "I know everyone in the village," he added. "You've come from somewhere else."

Allanon nodded. "A cold tankard of ale would ease my weariness."

The barkeep nodded and wandered off, and Allanon looked around at the room's patrons, his gaze moving from face to face, making sure that nothing seemed out of place and no one appeared to be a threat. By the time he had finished, the barkeep had returned.

"Anything else?" He set the tankard of ale down and waited. "Something to eat, maybe?"

The Druid shook his head. "Do you know where I can find a man called Derrivanian?"

"Might. What's your business?" "My business is my own."

"Maybe so, but I don't like sending trouble to other people's doorsteps. Trouble finds them quick enough without my help."

"I intend no trouble." Allanon brushed the rain from his shoulders and sat back. "He is an old friend. I knew him when he served as record keeper for the Elessedils."

"Oh, you know of that? So maybe you are a friend. But where's the proof? What's to say you aren't here to collect a bill or cause some other sort of mischief?"

Allanon gave him a look. "Derrivanian is an old man with an old wife and an old dog, and he hasn't got much of anything to give and no history of ever having done anyone harm. Why don't you just tell me where he lives?"

The barkeep shook his head. "I need something more than your word before I tell you anything. I don't much like the look of you—all in black, dark-faced, and grim. You're a big man used to getting his way. Well, I'm a big man, too, and I'm not afraid of you."

Allanon went very still. "It isn't me you should fear, barkeep." He locked eyes with the man. "Ask yourself this. Are you sure enough of yourself that you would risk a meeting with some who might not ask any questions but simply tear the information from you? Would you risk a meeting with those they call Skull Bearers?"

The barkeep paled. "Do not speak that name in here!"

"What name should I speak, then? I gave you Derrivanian. Should I give you another? The Warlock Lord's name, perhaps? Or is there another you would prefer me to speak?"

The barkeep backed away. "I want you out of here! Take your business elsewhere and seek your answers from another."

Allanon shook his head. "I have no time for asking others. I have chosen to ask you, and I will have my answers now. Look at me. Where will l find Eldra Derrivanian?"

The barkeep tried to back away, but suddenly his strength failed, and he found himself rooted in place. His face tightened with his efforts to free himself, and it was clear he saw something new in the Druid's eyes that made him realize what he was up against.

"Answer me," Allanon ordered.

"Take the road west out of the village." The barkeep was speaking in a different voice, one dredged up from the dark places you hide when you are very afraid. "Go about five hundred yards. Look for a fence and a wooden gate inset with the carved image of a rooster. He can be found there."

Allanon nodded. "My thanks. Now forget you ever saw me. Forget this conversation. Forget everything but your purpose in coming to my table with my tankard of ale." He paused. "What was it you wanted to ask me again?"

The barkeep's eyes, which had lost focus, suddenly seemed clear again. "Something to eat, maybe?"

When the barkeep had left the table, Allanon took a few minutes to finish the tankard of ale, relishing the cold liquid flowing down his throat and the fire it brought to his belly. He stopped examining the patrons and the room and delved deep into his own thoughts, musing on the Druid abilities he had developed since leaving Bremen to his fate at the Hadeshorn all those years ago. Sometimes, it seemed like a dream to him. He could still see the old man walking out onto the glistening black rock of the Valley of Shale to the edge of the lake's waters and into the arms of the Shade of Galaphile, then being carried beyond into the mists. He could still remember standing alone afterward and wondering how he could manage what he had been charged with doing.

He was only fifteen when Bremen had left him. Only a boy. But he had been strong, both physically and mentally, and he had only grown stronger with time. And he had used that strength in ways that now made his name a household legend.

He had restored Paranor to the world of men, using the Black Elfstone entrusted to him by Bremen, and made the Druid's Keep his permanent residence. He had brought a fresh contingent of Elven Hunters—supplied at first by Jerle Shannara, then by those Elven Kings who had succeeded him—to act as protectors of the Druid's Keep and the Sword of Shannara, which had been set within a block of Tre-Stone and placed in a vault, there to await the day when Bremen had promised it would be needed again.

Then he had slept the Druid Sleep, deep and dark with magic that let time and aging pass him by.

But now the day that Bremen had promised had arrived—the day for which Allanon had been preparing himself all his life. A life that, because of his extensive use of the Druid Sleep, spanned almost five hundred years.

So fifteen years of age was a very long time ago, and that boy he had been was very far removed from who he had become.

He lifted his eyes from the tankard and looked out across those years to the many, many people he had left behind. He was in the prime of his life, while all those he had known as a boy and a young man were gone. It was a strange feeling to realize that so much had passed him by. It was a hard way to live your life, but he was the last Druid—the only Druid—and he wondered where he would find another to succeed him. He had looked, but no one seemed right for the weight of what he would have to ask of them. Who would willingly accept that burden? Worse, only someone who fully understood what it meant to shoulder such a load, and what responsibilities came with it, would be the right choice.

But that was another problem for another time, and this night was meant for other work.

He pushed back from the table and rose. The tavern seemed busier than ever, the bar crowded with laughing, shouting, jostling people. All the tables were occupied. He was barely on his feet before a pair of young men hurried over to claim his space, pausing only long enough to make certain he did not object. He nodded to them and walked away—ignoring the barkeep, who ignored him in turn—then moved back through the door and out into the night.

Wrapped in his cloak, he trudged up the muddy roadway, head bent but ears and eyes alert for sound and movement. The rain was a slow, steady downpour that had already soaked the ground and was now being channeled into low places to pool and settle. He kept to the drier parts of the sodden path as best he could, moving westward toward his destination, thinking about what he hoped to accomplish. So much depended on what Eldra Derrivanian remembered or what he had written down, or even what he might be able to divine. It had come to this: a sort of crazy guessing game as to who might still be out there that the winged servants of the Warlock Lord hadn't already found. Someone who hadn't already been revealed by traitors and sycophants eager to preserve the lives they were assured of losing. Someone who hadn't already been turned or killed.

Someone who might still have courage enough to do what was needed to save the Races.

But this was Eldra Derrivanian, and he might not care about saving anyone.

Two weeks earlier, Allanon had thought his search a lost cause. He had known of the Warlock Lord's imminent return for months. All the signs were there for anyone who could read them. Winged fliers had been spotted in the North—Skull Bearers patrolling the night skies over the Knife Edge Mountains, bathing in the waters of the River Lethe to armor their skin by day. Bodies of travelers had been discovered in the surrounding regions, ripped to shreds and partially devoured. People and animals alike had gone missing, never to be seen again. Fire bloomed in the once-dead volcanoes that riddled the Charnal Mountains, and deep rumblings shook the earth at regular intervals.

The prophecy that Bremen had passed on to him all those years ago was coming to pass. Brona, the once-Druid who had fallen victim to his own pursuit of the dark magic and evolved as a consequence into the Warlock Lord, had not been destroyed as most believed. The Elven King Jerle Shannara had not successfully wielded the sword forged especially for this purpose, and though the Warlock Lord had been defeated and driven from his mortal body and the Four Lands, still he was only diminished, not dead. One day, Bremen told the boy, the Dark Lord would return. To that end, the Sword of Shannara must be kept safe and made ready for an heir to the Elven house of Shannara. When the time came, whether during Allanon's lifetime or the lifetimes of his Druid successors, a Shannara heir must take up the Sword and stand against the Warlock Lord once again.

It was easy enough simply to acknowledge this truth and set it aside for another day, which is what Allanon had done. He had made certain the Sword of Shannara was kept safe at Paranor and gone on with his life. Years had passed, with no indications of the expected return. Other matters had occupied his thoughts and his time. Eventually, hundreds of years later, the prospect of the Warlock Lord's return was all but forgotten.

Even so, he recognized it when it happened, and he understood what was needed to keep the people of the Four Lands safe. But he had acted too slowly. He had failed to anticipate the nature of the approach the Warlock Lord would employ to make certain the Sword was not used against him a second time. The Sword itself was anathema to both the Dark Lord and the Skull Bearers; they could barely stand to be in its presence, let alone touch it for even an instant. So lacking the means to take it for himself, Brona chose instead to eliminate all those who might one day use it against him. He decided to wipe out Jerle Shannara's line.

Systematically, he killed all those who were scions of the Elven house. Since Jerle Shannara's direct descendants had all died of natural causes within three generations of his own death, the Warlock Lord needed only to search out those distant relations who carried even a trace of his Elven blood. Allanon did not realize at first what was happening. And by the time he did and began his own search, he found himself arriving too late to save any of the ones he sought. By then he was in steady communication with the young Elven King Eventine Elessedil, and the two of them were working together to glean any references or scraps of information about Shannara descendants from the Elven genealogy records and histories that might help in their search.

It was Eventine's last message that had brought Allanon to Arborlon two weeks earlier and set him on his current hunt.

"You've had no luck finding an heir?" the young King had asked him after they had settled down in one of the private reception rooms. Eventine had only recently ascended to the Elven throne following the death of his father. Already, Allanon believed the Elf's potential was enormous. His charisma, his strength of character, his concern for his people, and his ability to act quickly and judge fairly suggested he was a king in more than just name.

"No luck at all," he answered. "Every single source has yielded only the dead. We are running out of time."

"And out of names. I have exhausted my sources here. Are the Druid Histories and your personal records of no further help?"

Allanon was an historian of some note and a meticulous keeper of records. He had made a concerted effort to write down the names of Shannara heirs over the years, recording deaths, births, and marriages. But even he had not been able to follow every thread in the line, and so the possibility existed that a man or woman possessing Shannara blood could still be found.

"I am out of ideas. I have nowhere else to look."

"I thought as much. But there is one other possibility we have overlooked."

Allanon had been surprised. He had thought their search had ended with the deaths of the entire Waylandring family in Emberen a week earlier. He had thought there was no one left. "Who have we missed?"

"Not a descendant of Jerle Shannara, but a man who might know of one that we do not. His name is Eldra Derrivanian. He was the keeper of the genealogical records for the members of the royal families and the Elven High Council for many years. He was there even before my father. His knowledge was phenomenal, even for a keeper of records. He could trace almost any branch of their lineage from memory. He kept his own set of records in addition to ours, and he took those records with him when he was dismissed from service just before my father died."

"Dismissed? I sense a problem."

"You are not mistaken. Derrivanian left under very unfortunate circumstances. His son was killed while serving in the Elven Home Guard. The killer was never found, and the reason for his death remained a mystery. The circumstances surrounding the event were suspicious, and Derrivanian could not let the matter drop. He demanded that my father do more. But my father was old and dying by that time, and failed in his efforts. Derrivanian was so distraught he began to ignore his work. In some cases, he deliberately sabotaged it—in small ways at first, and later in much more extensive ones. When my father found out what he was doing, he dismissed him. Derrivanian appealed to the High Council for help but was rebuffed. In the end, he left Arborlon in disgrace."

"So he has no reason to want to help us."

"You will have to discover that for yourself."

"You know where he is now?"

"He was seen in the village of Archer Trace only a week ago, discovered by a member of my Elven Guard during our searches for the descendants of Jerle Shannara. Finding him was a complete accident. He is living there with his wife. Both are quite elderly. If he still hates the Elessedils as much as he did in the time of my father and remains resentful of his dismissal, it may be difficult to persuade him to help. But he might have his private records with him, or some memory of a member of the Shannara family that could lead us to an heir."

"And you believe that if he understands the magnitude of the danger to the Elven people—to his people—he might be persuaded to put aside his anger?"

Eventine had shrugged. "You are the best one to find this out, Allanon. You are, in all likelihood, the only one who can persuade him."

So here he was, off on another fool's errand, searching out an Elf who had no love for the Elessedils and a lasting bitterness toward his own people for their failure to support him in his complaints against the Elven throne. But it was the best chance left to him. Better yet, he might, for once, be one step ahead of his enemy. Derrivanian was not a member of the Shannara family, and so the Warlock Lord and his minions had no reason to seek him out. This time, Allanon believed, he might find the object of his search alive. This time, he might have a chance to discover information that was unknown to the Warlock Lord.

And if so, maybe all was not yet lost.

He was almost completely beyond the limits of Archer Trace when he passed the fence with the rooster carved into its gate. He paused to study the house it warded. Lights burned in the interior—enough to indicate that someone inside was still awake.

He watched the windows for movement but saw none. He cast a net of seeking magic to spy out hidden dangers and found none of those, either.

Satisfied, he opened the gate, went up the path to the heavy wooden door, and knocked.

Immediately, he heard movement within. "Who's there?" a man called out.

"A stranger to you," Allanon answered. "But I bring news from Arborlon that you will want to hear."

There was a long pause. "There is nothing I wish to hear from Arborlon and its Elves. Go away."

Allanon sighed, his dark face implacable. "The barkeep at The Drunken Fool seemed to think it was important enough to send me this way. Why not hear me out?"

Another pause. Then the locks released, the door swung open, and weak candlelight spilled out into the rain.

The man who stood there was bent with more than just the weight of years and the infirmities of age. Reflected in his eyes were anger and frustration, which spoke of injustices suffered and endured. Bitterness was there, and an expectation of further damage, waiting just around the corner and still out of sight but there nevertheless. There was weariness and a deep sense of resignation.

There was something else, too, but it took a moment for Allanon to sort it out from the rest of the burden this man bore.

There was fear.

"What do you want?" Eldra Derrivanian snapped at him. Then he paused. "Wait. I know you. You're the Druid Allanon."

"We've never met."

"No, but you were at the King's court and before the High Council often enough. I know you, even if you paid no attention to me. Now get out of here."

Allanon moved his foot swiftly to block the door. "First, you will hear me out. Once you've done that, I'll go my way. But not before."

Derrivanian stared at him balefully, then turned his back. "Do what you like. It means nothing to me."

Allanon entered the room and closed the door behind him.

He glanced around quickly. The room was small, sparsely furnished, and unkempt, and smelled unpleasant. Dishes were piled in a washbasin, and clothes were strewn about. He felt right away that something was wrong, but other than the obvious, he couldn't decide what.

"Where is Collice?" he asked.

Derrivanian's wife. The old man hesitated, then nodded toward a door at the back of the room. "Asleep. Sick. She tires easily these days. She goes to bed early. What is it that you want with me?"

Allanon moved over to the tiny kitchen table and sat, waiting. After a moment, Derrivanian sat down across from him. "I require your help," the Druid said, leaning forward, elbows propped on the table, chin resting atop his folded hands, eyes fixed on the old man. "And I hope you will agree to give it after you've heard what I have to say."

"My help to do what?"

"To think back in time and try to remember something for me. To use your exceptional mind to call up something that perhaps no one else can. And if that fails, to peruse your private records to jolt that memory."

The old man rubbed at his face. He was unshaven, and his cheeks and forehead were deeply lined. His ears drooped with age, and his slanted brows were shaggy and gray. His salt-and-pepper hair was wild and stiff as he ran his fingers through it. "Whom do you seek?"

"Anyone who is an heir to the Elven house of Shannara."

The other was silent for a long moment. "The Warlock Lord has returned, hasn't he? The rumors are true."

Allanon nodded. "He has returned, and he has brought his Skull Bearers with him. He is hunting down and killing all of the Shannara kin so that the Sword cannot be used against him again."

"How many are dead so far? Wait. Don't tell me. All of them, right? All that you can find, in any case. If you need my help, it must be as a last resort. How did you even find me?"

"An Elven Hunter searching for news of an heir saw you."

Derrivanian shook his head. "I was hidden here for three years. No one knew. I found some small measure of peace. And now this." He sighed. "I don't have any love for the Elessedils. I don't even have much love for the Elves, no matter if they're my own people. None of them did anything for me when I needed their help. They let my son's death go unpunished. They let his murderer go free. They tossed it all aside like it didn't much matter."

Allanon held his gaze. "This involves more than just Arborlon and the Elessedils. The survival of an entire world is at stake. I need you to put your anger aside."

"Do you? Too bad. Why should I bother? Why should I care about the world or anything else?"

"Because you don't want it on your conscience if everything goes wrong, and you could have done something to prevent it. Come, Derrivanian. You're been a good and faithful steward for too many years to throw it all aside when it could mean so much to so many if you could help. Stand up for those who can't stand up for themselves."

The old man rose and walked away, stopping to look out a window—perhaps contemplating what he saw, perhaps only gathering his thoughts. He was silent for a long time. Allanon let him be. Too many words of persuasion would have the wrong impact on this man. It would be better to let him come to the right decision on his own.

"You seem a strong man, Allanon," he said finally. "Is that so? Are you as strong as they say?"

Allanon kept quiet, waiting.

"Because I'm not a strong man. I am a weakling and a coward. I've lost a son, and I don't—" He stopped suddenly, shaking his head. "You don't know what you will do until you are faced with a situation that tests you. You think you know, but you don't."

Still, the Druid waited. But he couldn't help wondering as he did so what it was the man was trying to say.

Eldra Derrivanian turned back to him. "There is one last possibility, one last man who may have been overlooked by the Dark Lord. He is a distant relative, born to the son of a son of a cousin once removed from the direct line. His bloodline is true, though. He would have enough of the Shannara in him to serve your purpose. His name is Weir. Shall I tell you where he can be found?"

Allanon nodded slowly. "Tell me everything."

Allanon departed the cottage shortly afterward, pulling his hood over his head and his cloak tightly about his shoulders, hunching down against the onslaught of rain. He had what he needed to find the man Derrivanian had named, including the location of the place where he could be found. Weir lived on a farm well outside any town or village, north of Emberen, close to the southwestern edge of the Kierlak Desert in country that was just barely Elven and in no way friendly. It was a day's journey in good weather and more in bad. It was better traveled by horse than afoot, and so the Druid went back into Emberen to find a room in which to spend the night before seeking a mount for the morrow's journey.

He was still troubled by his visit to Eldra Derrivanian. Something about it didn't feel right. The man himself, the words he spoke, his actions—none of it. He realized suddenly that there had been a mattress in one corner of the front room, shoved off in a corner. Why was Derrivanian sleeping there when his wife slept in the back room? Or was the bedding for someone else? His wife's sickness could account for the state of the cottage, but there was a furtiveness to him that was troubling.

On the other hand, this was a man whose life had been a shambles for many years, a man who had exiled himself from his people and his previous life and gone into the outback of Elven civilization. He had lost his son and his position and the respect of his King. He had become an object of scorn and pity and outright suspicion. Everything he had built his life around was gone. Perhaps it wasn't so strange that there seemed to be no substance to him.

Allanon spent the night at a rooming house set apart from the taverns, and in the morning he procured a horse and set out. He rode north at a steady pace, through the forests, following a series of trails and paths toward the Streleheim. At midday, he passed onto the plains. The terrain changed abruptly, trees giving way to empty space and shade to heat. The rains had moved on, but the earth was left sodden and muddy, and the sun turned the standing pools to steam.

He let his horse meander across the uneven ground so that it could find decent footing, his thoughts straying to the task ahead. He was already thinking about what he would say to this man Weir to persuade him to take up the Sword in defense of his people. Over the past few weeks, he had composed dozens of arguments and hundreds of reasons for all those he had thought he would encounter in his long, fruitless search. In the end, he had needed none of them because there had been no one alive to persuade. If the same was true this time as well, he wasn't certain where he would go next. Back to Derrivanian, perhaps. He wasn't entirely satisfied that he had been given the truth.

But the hard fact remained that he still hadn't found the man or woman he needed, and the time left to do so was growing short. If Weir refused him, what would he do then? There was nothing to say the man wouldn't say no. Most would decline any sort of involvement in this business, no matter its importance and urgency. The danger was enormous, the risks terrifying. Jerle Shannara had been unable to kill the Warlock Lord, and he had been a king and a warrior. How could anyone expect an ordinary man to do better?

And, yet, that was what would be required. That was what would need to happen to end what had begun all those centuries ago.

He should have planned better, he chided himself. He should have known this time would come sooner rather than later, and he should have found the ones he needed and prepared them. He should have kept better records and spent more time sizing up the heirs who remained. He should have protected them all from what had happened.

He should have done so much more.

The day wore on, and the sun moved westward across the sky toward the horizon. As he neared his destination—a place called

Rabbit Ridge—a man herding sheep passed into view. Allanon rode over and hailed him.

"Well met," he told the man.

The man just stared at him, saying nothing. Allanon could read what was on his mind. He wanted nothing to do with this huge, black-cloaked rider with the grim countenance and imposing presence.

"I'm looking for a man named Weir. He lives on Rabbit Ridge. Do you know of him?"

The herder spit. He pointed left, made a warding sign, then turned away abruptly and hurried on, clucking to his sheep to move them along faster. Allanon watched him go, but he did not wonder at the man's reaction. In his place, he would have done the same.

He rode on, watching the shadows cast by his horse and himself lengthen in front of him, noting the twilight's approach. Not much farther, he thought. Then he would have his chance to persuade a man with no desire to place himself in harm's way that this was exactly what he must do. He wondered if he would find in this man the strength of character and courage and decency to invoke the magic of the Sword. He wondered how the man would react when he heard what the Druid had to say. He had rehearsed the moment so often without ever having come this close to experiencing it. He had prepared himself repeatedly, and all for nothing.

Would it be for nothing again?

He found Rabbit Ridge, a thickly wooded and rough piece of ground, and rode his horse up its slopes. Poor land for farming, he saw, mostly scrub and sparse stands of timber and rocky ground. Sheep might do well here. Was that what the man farmed? He hadn't asked Derrivanian. It hadn't seemed important then and probably wasn't now. Still . . . He was going to ask a farmer to come with him to stand against a monster. It was insane.

He reached the apex of the ridge and urged his horse along its length toward a broad stretch of grasslands that ran like a ragged carpet to the door of a house and barn. There were sheep in a fenced pasture, milling about, moving first in one direction, then in another, looking stupid and lost. He felt a sudden kinship. His eyes shifted to the buildings. There was smoke coming from a chimney attached to the house but no sign of occupants. The barn was big and empty-looking; the hinged doors facing him stood open to the darkness within.

The last of the daylight was fading as he walked his mount to the porch that fronted the house and climbed down.

"Hello the house!" he called out. "Anyone?"

No answer. He didn't care one bit for what that suggested. Draping the reins of his mount over the porch railing, he climbed the steps to the door and knocked.

Still no answer.

"Hello! Anyone?" he repeated.

He walked the length of the porch to peer through the windows. The house looked inhabited. It was well kept, with furniture intact, dishes set on a table, and ashes banked against a stack of wood burning in the hearth. It looked as if the owner had just momentarily stepped away.

Not that there was much of anywhere to step away to.

Except the barn.

Allanon left the horse where it was and walked toward the open doors, keeping a careful eye out for trouble. He had survived enough attempted ambushes and traps to be mindful, and he was not about to fall victim now. He glanced around the farmyard, but other than the sheep in the pasture, there didn't seem to be anyone or anything about. Even so, he fully expected to find Weir in the barn since he wasn't in the house and didn't appear to be anywhere else close at hand.

But when he got there, the building was empty. He walked far enough into the shadows for his eyes to adjust. The stalls were empty, the floor bare, and the interior of the barn silent. He glanced up at the hayloft, but there didn't seem to be a ladder at hand that would allow him to climb up.

He decided to make a more complete search of the level he was on. He walked into every stall, examined every corner, poked through the hay mound, and looked inside the tack room. There was a toolshed attached to the barn, but the door that led into it was outside. So he exited the barn and walked around to where he could have a look. The shed was filled with hand tools, a workbench, and scrap metal. Nothing there, either.

He closed the door to the toolroom and walked back around to the front of the barn, glancing up momentarily to where the hayloft opened out on the yard.

"Up here!" a voice called suddenly from behind.

There was a man standing on the porch, waving. Allanon stared. Where had he been before? "Are you Weir?"

"I am," the other said. "Come closer, where we can talk."

Allanon started back toward the house. He was no more than ten feet from the man when he noticed the nervous shifting of his horse in the dusty yard, the stamping of hooves, and the sudden shaking of his head.

A warning . . .

Too late. The man on the porch moved first, one arm whipping up sharply, a throwing knife streaking toward the Druid and burying itself in his chest. Allanon tried to react but was a fraction of a second too slow. He staggered back, stricken.

Immediately, a whole raft of armed men emerged, pouring out of the house, out of the barn, seemingly out of the ground, howling and brandishing weapons of every stripe. Allanon threw up a protective shield of magic, throwing back as many of his attackers as he could. He dropped to one knee to make himself a smaller target, then yanked out the knife as he tried to gather his strength. To remain where he was would mean his death. Once they sensed the extent of his weakness, they would be on him.

A handful broke through, but he was back on his feet to meet them and flung them away as if they were straw men. He moved quickly, rushing his attackers. They stumbled back from him, none of them eager to stand his ground against this angry giant. But one in their midst, a big man like himself, was shoved forward by the rest, perhaps to champion their failed efforts, perhaps out of desperation only. All dark fury and cold intent, Allanon was reaching for him when he caught sight of archers rushing forward and drawing back their bowstrings. The Druid barely had time to act. Snatching the tunic of the man in front of him, the Druid whipped him about and used him as a shield. A cluster of arrows struck the man, who jerked and went limp. Allanon threw him down in disgust and brought up his protective magic once again.

Those of his attackers still able to do so came at him, some throwing knives, some firing arrows, some using slings, all trying to bring him down. But he was warded by his magic and not so easily reached. His attackers were thrown back again. Even those remaining at what seemed a safe distance found that the Druid magic could reach them easily, and they were tossed aside as well. Bones snapped, and lives were extinguished. Twice more the attackers came at him, and twice more they failed to reach him.

Finally, their numbers reduced by more than half, they turned and fled into the fields and the surrounding countryside, the desire to fight gone out of them.

Allanon clung to one of the uprights supporting the porch roof, watching them flee. Derrivanian's help had been worth nothing. He would have to go back and start over. Once he healed, of course. Once he felt strong enough to do so.

Dizziness washed through him, and a glance down at his robes reinforced his suspicion that he was losing blood rapidly. He pressed gently against the knife wound, trying to staunch the bleeding, using a thin skein of healing magic to help close the ragged opening.

He was engaged in that effort when the Skull Bearer appeared.

He didn't see it at first, but he heard the slow beating of its wings. Then it was swinging around from behind the farmhouse, making no effort to disguise its coming, settling in slow, insolent fashion onto the corpse-strewn yard in front of the porch. Black-scaled from head to foot, and long-limbed in a way that made its crooked arms and legs seem all out of proportion, it was warded by the cape of its huge wings. Eyes, bright and expectant, glittered from beneath a heavy brow that shadowed its rough-hewn face.

"Druid," it hissed at him.

"You arranged all this," Allanon replied, making it a statement of fact.

"I did."

"Why go to such trouble?"

The other's breathing was deep and rough, as if its lungs could not manage to draw in enough air. "Because the Master wishes it. Because it pleases me. Do you know what you have done this day? You have put an end to your last chance at preventing our return."

Allanon stared, uncertain what the creature was saying.

"The man lying at your feet, the one you used to shield yourself? He is Weir, and he is the last of the Shannara. The last hope you had. We would have killed him ourselves, but you saved us the trouble."

Allanon felt despair fill him—what had he been manipulated into doing?—but his expression never changed. "Is this your hope, creature? I think a man who sold his services to the Warlock Lord was never the Shannara we needed, and killing him is of no importance." But doubt still nagged at him. What if the man had been an innocent, trapped, like himself, by the Warlock Lord's forces? What if his last hope truly was gone?

The great wings drew close about the dark body. "Think what you wish. It matters not the least to me. But your end draws near, Allanon. Like the man lying at your feet, you are the last of your kind. Time will not save you."

"Do you intend to finish what your assassins started?" Allanon asked the Skull Bearer. "Because your power lessens in daylight, does it not?"

The other hissed at him. "Why bother to kill you? I have come to bear witness to your misery. You hide it well, but your despair is revealed nevertheless. You hoped this man would save your people, but now that cannot happen. Worse still is the way it was accomplished. You were betrayed, Druid. The one who sent you gave you over to me. Think on that. Then do with him what you will."

The Skull Bearer spread its wings and began to lift away, circling upward into the sky.

"My brothers and I will return for you soon, Allanon!" it called back to him. "Watch for us!"

Then the creature was gone, and the Druid was alone.

Allanon chose not to spend the night in the farmhouse even though his knife wound was serious enough that it would be wiser to stay where he was. But with dead men all around him and the prospect of the Skull Bearer changing its mind and making a return trip—perhaps with others for company—the Druid decided it was better to put a little distance between himself and the day's events. Using his magic to strengthen himself as best he could and setting course for friendlier ground, he mounted his horse and rode south into the forests of the Elven Westland and found refuge with friends in a small outpost miles from anything.

There he allowed his wounds to be treated by the wife's practiced hands and took to bed, where he slept undisturbed for thirty hours. Then he rose to wash himself and eat and drink for the first time in two days, and went back to bed.

It took four days of rest, traditional healing skills, and Druid magic before he was fit enough to travel again. At the end of that time, as dawn broke and the day began, he reclaimed his horse, bid his friends farewell, and set out for Archer Trace.

His plans for Derrivanian were still unformed. He understood his options, and he knew that, when the time came, he would have to choose among them. But his thoughts were dark and tinged with anger, and he did not want to get too close to them until he understood for certain what had happened. It was too easy to conclude that he already understood everything. But he had believed that once before, when going in search of Weir, and it had almost been the death of him. This time he would be more circumspect and less resolute about what he thought he knew.

He rode through the day at a steady pace, but he made frequent stops to rest and took time to eat and drink and replenish the magic that healed his wounds. He breathed in the spring air, feeling warmth in its breezes, the first hint of summer's approach.

It was a time of rebirth in the world, the yearly beginnings of new life and fresh possibility. He wanted to feel just a little of that, wanted to hold it in his heart and draw from its strength.

Twilight approached as he came to the edge of Archer Trace and turned down the roadway that would lead to the cottage of Eldra Derrivanian. He no longer bothered to consider what he was going to do, even though it was not yet decided. He would know when he faced the man. His instincts and his intellect would show him the way. He was a Druid, after all, and a Druid always knew.

He reined in his horse at the gate bearing the rooster carving, left it tied to the fence, and walked to the door of the cottage. Derrivanian opened the door before Allanon reached it.

"You're alive," the old man said, and in the tone of his voice, Allanon detected an unexpected note of relief.

They stood on the porch staring at each other. "Why did you give me up to them like that?" Allanon asked finally.

Derrivanian shook his head. "I wasn't offered a choice. Come in. I will tell you everything."

They entered Derrivanian's home, which looked exactly the same as it had when the Druid had visited the last time—counters and dusty furniture cluttered with pieces of clothing and unwashed dishes, mattress and bedding shoved into one corner, and the bedroom door closed.

The old man beckoned the Druid to the kitchen table, asked if his guest would like a glass of ale and, on receiving a negative answer, turned his back to pour one for himself. He studied the glass a moment, then returned to the table. Once again, the two men sat across from each other in the mix of fading daylight and approaching night.

"I did not want you to be killed," Derrivanian said.

"That's very reassuring." Allanon kept his voice steady even though he was seething. "But if you didn't want me killed, why did you put me in that situation? You aren't pretending you didn't know what they would do, are you?"

The old man shook his head. "No, I knew exactly what they intended. The Skull Bearer told me when it came to find me several weeks ago. I don't know how it found me, but it did. It explained very carefully what I was to do and why I should do it. It told me that if I failed, Collice would die. If I did as I was told, she would be allowed to live. That was the choice I was given."

He rubbed at his eyes, and his knuckles came away wet. "It was plain enough. I was to let myself be seen by one of Eventine Elessedil's Elven Hunters. They come through here regularly, guarding against the Warlock Lord and his minions. Once I was identified, it was virtually assured that word would get back to the King. Because of my knowledge of Elven genealogy and your need to find a Shannara heir, you would be sent to speak with me. For something as important as this, no one else would do. When you came, I was to tell you of Weir. The Skull Bearers knew of him already, having tracked him down on their own. But he was an evil man and in no way likely to take up the Sword and become a champion for the Elves. He had already announced to the Skull Bearers that he wished to be an ally of the Dark Lord. What he didn't realize was that it had already been decided he would be used in another way."

"As a lure to attract me." Allanon saw it now.

"Yes. But not for the reason you think. Not to kill you. The Warlock Lord had something more insidious in mind. Since Weir was the last of the Shannara, what Brona wanted was for his death to come at your hands. He wanted revenge against the Druids for the terrible harm Bremen had caused him all those years ago when he forged the Sword and placed it in the hands of Jerle Shannara."

Allanon's expression hardened, but still the knowledge served as a balm to his heart. He might have destroyed the world's last hope, but he had not killed an innocent man. "But if you knew it was a trap, why didn't you warn me? I could have helped you protect Collice."

Derrivanian was already shaking his head once again. "You couldn't have helped. No one could. And warning you wasn't possible. If I had told you anything other than what I did, Collice would be dead. The Skull Bearer was in the back room with her when you were out here talking with me."

Derrivanian's face was haggard, and his eyes were filled with despair. "Don't you see? I had to choose between you and Collice. I had already lost everything else that mattered in my life. I was not about to lose her, as well."

He leaned forward, the fingers of his hands knotted together. "The Skull Bearer cautioned against saying anything that would warn you. If Weir did not die by your hand, if anything happened to change that outcome, if you learned it was a trap—even by accident—it promised it would return for Collice."

"But you believed I might survive anyway?"

The old man could hardly bear to look at the Druid. "I hoped as much. Judge me as you wish. I deserve it. It was a roll of the dice with lives at stake. I knew the risks. I simply took the choice that seemed best at the time. I wagered your life against Collice's."

Allanon looked away. "You should know that the Skull Bearer still lives. I was too weakened from the struggle to destroy it."

Derrivanian shrugged. "It doesn't matter. It will gain nothing by killing me now. It's too late. I tricked it."

The Druid's eyes locked on him. "How did you do that?"

The old man had a strange look on his face. "It was surprisingly easy. I knew that no matter what happened, it would return for me eventually. It never intended to keep its word. Once I had done what it wanted and tricked you into going after Weir, it would have no further use for me. It would wait for a time, then it would come back to finish me."

He paused. "If I were in its place, I would do the same. But it waited too long. It made a mistake. It should have started by making very certain that Weir was indeed the last of the Shannara instead of wasting time playing games with you."

Allanon stared. "What are you saying?"

"When I told you that Weir was the last of the Shannara kin, I lied. There is another. Weir was not the last."

"Another heir? Are you lying this time, too?"

The old man shook his head. "It was necessary to tell you that Weir was the last. The Skull Bearer was listening. I was betraying you, but I was also using the betrayal to reinforce what the Skull

Bearer wrongly believed. If you lived, I told myself, I would give the name to you. If you died, there was probably no hope for any of us. In any case, I would not allow my knowledge to fall into the wrong hands."

Allanon could hardly believe what he was hearing. "So you're sure? There really is another? Weir was not the last?"

Derrivanian shifted his gaze, first to the door, then to the windows, as if to reassure himself that no one else was listening. "There was a boy who was orphaned as a child, a boy whose father was an Elf and whose mother came west from the Borderlands."

He paused. "The boy approaches manhood now, but he is not yet fully grown. His parents were good people, intelligent and responsible, the right sorts. It may be so with this boy."

"His name?"

"Aren Shea."

Allanon shook his head in rebuke, his dark face intense. "I recognize the name. But a fever took him while he was still very small, shortly after his parents died. That was years ago."

"Yes. Tragic. He was the last of his line. The burial service was poorly attended since there were no longer any living relatives among the Elves. He was buried and forgotten. Even by you, it seems. Though you can visit his gravesite in Arborlon, if you wish."

The Druid paused. "Are you saying he didn't die?"

"Exactly—though I arranged for the circumstances surrounding his death to look as convincing as possible."

"Because you knew. Even then. You knew he would be hunted."

"His parents were killed under mysterious circumstances. Just before this happened, his mother brought the child to Collice and asked her to take him. She sensed the danger, I think. The women were close friends, and the boy's mother knew my wife could be trusted. She asked Collice to keep him until she was certain the danger was past, then she would take him back. But if anything happened to the parents, we were to fake the boy's death, then convey him to her brother's home in the Borderlands and tell no one what we had done. We were to hide the truth from everyone so that her son might have a chance to live."

"So you did as she asked? And the Warlock Lord and his Skull Bearers have not discovered the truth?"

"They have no reason to suspect the boy still lives. No one in the whole of the Westland knows the truth."

"You are certain of this?"

"As certain as I can be. You will have to determine if I am right or not for yourself. The boy's name is different now. He is called Shea Ohmsford. He was given his uncle's surname. He resides in the village of Shady Vale in the forests south of the Border Cities."

Derrivanian gave a weak smile and a shrug. "I have done what I promised myself I would do if you returned. It is the only thing I can offer as recompense for my behavior. I hope you can understand." Then he gestured toward the door. "You should go now. Find the boy. Save him."

Allanon rose. "You should take you own advice, then. Leave here immediately. Take your wife to Arborlon and ask the King for protection."

The old man shook his head. "I sent her away to stay with friends the moment the Skull Bearer left to follow you. I asked them to hide her until they heard from me. I don't know where she is."

"Then join her. Do so before the Skull Bearer comes for you."

The other man smiled, but there was no warmth. "No, it's too late for that. It was always too late." He took the glass of ale he had brought for himself and drained it. His eyes fixed on Allanon. "Do you really think we would be safe from the Warlock Lord and his Skull Bearers in Arborlon? Do you think we would be safe anywhere?"

"Eventine Elessedil is not his father. He harbors no bitterness toward you. He is dedicated and compassionate. He will do his best to protect you."

"I am the only one who can do what is necessary to protect Collice, and I have done it." He gestured toward the glass. "You see this? A permanent sleeping potion. The kind you hear about all the time. I am putting myself beyond the Warlock Lord's reach. I know myself. I am weak, and if pressure were brought to bear,

I would give up everything I know. But if I can't talk, I can't tell."

Allanon stared. "You took poison?"

"I have betrayed you once. I would do so again. I would betray everyone. But I could not bear to let such a thing happen." He shrugged. "I have lived my life doing the best I could. I would like to think I died in the same way." He was already slurring his words. "Maybe, if you have the time, you could tell Collice . . ."

Then his eyes fixed, his head fell back, and he was gone.

Allanon rose, lifted him out of the chair, and laid him on the mattress in the corner. He placed a blanket over the body. It was the best he could do in the time he had. He couldn't stay longer. He would tell someone about Derrivanian on the way through town.

He stood for a moment, looking down at the body. The old man had ended things on his own terms. He was probably right about his wife. Once he was dead, the Skull Bearers would not bother hunting her. There was no longer a reason.

He went outside into the twilight, wondering if Eldra and Collice Derrivanian would have found sanctuary in Arborlon as he had advised, or if they were both better off now.

He was uncertain, but the choice had not been his to make.

Minutes later, he was riding east toward the Borderlands and the hamlet of Shady Vale.

David Anthony Durham

After my Acacia epic fantasy trilogy, I turned back toward historical fiction, wanting to write something along the lines of *Pride of Carthage*, my novel about Hannibal's war with Rome. I had another enemy of Rome that I was keen to write about: Spartacus.

Alas, this writing thing is a funky beast. When I wrote *Pride of Carthage*, I'd only written literary historical fiction. When I began *The Risen* (the Spartacus novel), I'd written three epic fantasies and a bunch of science fiction stories for George R. R. Martin's Wild Cards series. In the process, I'd mutated. I was weird and geeky in a way I hadn't been before. This manifested in a desire to write *The Risen* as a horror/fantasy novel. My publisher wanted the straight historical novel that I'd signed up for. Ultimately, I delivered that. But the monsters didn't sleep.

When I had the opportunity to contribute to another of Shawn's wonderful anthologies, I knew that I wanted to write a sample of the dark places my mind went with an alternative version of ancient Rome. That's what I'm offering here.

David Anthony Durham

KNEELING BEFORE JUPITER

David Anthony Durham

It was to be the best day of my young life.

The first fifteenth of March since I had turned sixteen. The day on which I officially—before the eyes of all of Rome—became a man. And not just any man, but one of the nobilitas who truly ruled Rome. I had slept the previous night in a white woolen tunic. I strived to keep it immaculately clean. I ate my evening snack with my head jutting far out before my body, and I drank water uncolored by wine. I didn't pull Thana, the chamber slave that had my ardor then, into bed with me. I didn't even give in to the desire to bring myself to climax. Such sacrifices, but worth it. I had made it through the night unstained.

In the early hours of the morning, family and friends, senators and merchants gathered to honor me. As they milled about, slaves washed and dressed me in a purple fringed tunic, a garment of youth and one that I would wear for only a few moments more. When my father called my name, I entered the crowded room. I strolled in, as composed as I could manage, to applause and shouts of my name. My mother's eyes fixed on me with admiration. And my younger brothers? Their eyes shone with envy, which to me was just perfect.

I carried to the altar the golden ball that had been mine since childhood. I pushed it away, a thing belonging to a boy, something I was to have no need for anymore. I stepped up onto the dais where my father waited for me. Marcus Licinius Crassus, the richest man in Rome, greeted me stern-faced. He was always stern-faced, his head as solid as a boulder, his features carved of stone. He motioned for me to disrobe. I shrugged my tunic from my shoulders and took the white toga from my father's fingers. I stood awkwardly as various hands draped and tugged the garment into place.

The journey to the Forum was a mad festivity. At first, I made sure to keep my eyes from rising to the bright, cloud-studded spring sky. A few days previous my father had an augur read the skies for me. The motion of the birds in flight, the man ruled, were most favorable. Hoping to keep it that way, I made sure not to see any signs that might revise my fortunes. I didn't want an errant pigeon to put my future in jeopardy.

I forgot my trepidation soon enough. The streets thronged with revelers. I walked at the vanguard of my own procession. Strangers shouted my name and sang my praise. Some tossed flower petals to soften the way before me. Behind us, a throng of the impoverished followed, bellowing the loudest of all. I knew they were hoping for a meal at my father's expense, but no matter. The moment buoyed, pushed me forward.

In the Forum, they spoke my name. It rang out in the center of Rome, just as the names of famous men had before me. Despite the tumult, I could hear the tribunes inscribing my name on the tabularium, where it would be forever. Already, I was part of the history of the nation.

From there all of us new men traveled in a boisterous pack to the Temple of Juventas. We bowed before the goddess of youth and offered her a coin for her grace in seeing us from boys to men. Nor did the banquet back at our city estate disappoint. I had worried that my father's thrift would make for a Spartan affair.

Marcus Crassus had simple tastes and cultivated the same in us, much to my dismay. This time, however, the food and drink was all I could have hoped for. The slaves anticipated every desire.

Cassius Longinus, one of the serving consuls, stopped in to raise a glass to me. He declared me the foremost of the new men in terms of potential. "I have high expectations of you," he said. "You will have a fine military career ahead of you. And then . . . the Senate and high honors. I see it all quite clearly."

Outwardly, I accepted this with the stern humility appropriate for a Roman. Inside was a different matter. Inside, I hid layers of fears. How was I to ever live up to what was expected of me? I had trained as hard as any of my peers, but none of them had achieved the physical prowess, the stamina and speed and bravery common to nobiles. I had marveled at displays during various games. I had seen men—even old men to my eyes—lift weights above their heads that I could not even budge, or leap over walls taller than several men's height. I had watched Actorius Naso best Gaius Pompey's fastest stallion. A man outpacing a stallion! And he was not the only one who could do it. At the games celebrating the end of the campaign season, I had watched nobiles officers move at incredible speed when dueling captured Bithynian prisoners. They struck blows that lopped off limbs and set heads spinning in the air. The foreigners didn't stand a chance against them. It had been incredible to behold, skills seemingly the sole province of nobiles.

My uncle had once told me how, on campaign in Spain against a Carpetani rebellion, he sensed an ambush that his scouts had missed. The Carpetani were well-hidden, in a perfect spot to shoot down on them as they passed through a narrow defile. If he hadn't spotted them, many lives would have been lost. "It was a cold morning," Uncle Lucius said. "I could see the heat their concealed bodies gave off." He tapped a finger to his temple. "That is the benefit of nobiles eyes. You'll have them as well when you're a man."

Such feats had left me burning with envy, yearning for the day I would receive the training to make me a comparable warrior. I was plagued by the fear I would not be up to it. How was I ever to reach their standard? Why were my eyes like any other eyes, no better suited to spotting an ambush than the lowliest beggar on the streets? I feared my vision wasn't even very good. The world blurred in the distance, and I couldn't make out objects that others could. I took some comfort in the fact that my peers all seemed equally mediocre compared to their elders. But it was a thin comfort, a sheet instead of a blanket against the cold.

When I went to my rooms to change from my wine-stained toga into a fresher garment in preparation for one last meeting with my father, a welcome distraction presented herself. The slave girl, Thana, had been arranging my pillows and sprinkling the sheets with scented oil when I stepped in. Seeing me, she bowed her head and moved to flee. I almost let her, but as she turned, the fabric of her tunic flared. I caught sight of one of her bare breasts. What a breast it was. I had strived for views of them from her first days in the household, nearly a year now. More recently, I had attended to them with much more familiarity.

Emboldened both by my new status and by the wine sloshing in my belly, I grabbed her and slipped my hands inside her tunic. "Not now!" she exclaimed. "There are too many guests."

The fact that she attempted to refuse me was a sign that we had grown too familiar. I didn't mind, though. I'd never in my life wanted a girl as much as I wanted her, all her softness and curves, the pleasures she'd been giving me the last weeks. The things we did together in the dark stunned me to think about in the morning. With her, I truly was a master. That was something I rarely felt in my father's shadow. I knew my father wouldn't care for my fondness for her, if he knew of it. But that mattered less now. I was a man, wasn't I?

There was a sharp rapping at the door. A slave called my name, saying my father awaited.

"Can it wait a moment?" I snapped, trying to stop Thana from pulling away.

"Master, your father himself sent me to fetch you."

That wasn't good. Thana got to her feet. I grabbed her before she could leave and, pulling her against me, whispered the things she should be ready to do for me when I returned.

Walking down the corridor behind my father's upright, prim slave, I hoped it would be a brief meeting, and then I'd return to Thana and complete the evening in the manner I most preferred. When the servant turned out into the courtyard instead of taking the stairs to my father's rambling offices, I called, "Where are you taking me?"

"Master, your father awaits you in the temple."

The temple was a small structure built in the round, a personal tribute to the goddess Juno. My mother, Tertulla, had convinced my father to dedicate it, arguing that the goddess's blessing would be a boon to the family's prosperity. It sat somewhat lower down on the grounds, on the far side of the gardens, past our private bathing pools and near the southern entrance gate. A back entrance, as it were. The spring night had gone chilly. The sky above—which I looked up into without fear of seeing omens, for such things weren't augured in the night heavens—had blown free of clouds and twinkled coldly, as if each star was a gem of ice. Trudging down the stairs behind the slave, I had half a mind to chastise him for not having suggested I wear an outer tunic. The walk was short, however, and brisk, enough so that I stood a moment outside the small structure, catching my breath.

The slave, having delivered me, took his leave and withdrew.

When I pushed the door open and entered, I found that my father was not alone. In the warm, dim candlelight, a dozen or so senators mingled about the room. They all wore the togas of their status, all of them my father's age or older, grey-haired or soon to be so. The murmur of their conversation vanished as I stepped into the room. The men turned to study me, their faces funereally grave. Not one of them held a wine cup, and no slaves were to be seen. A room full of nobiles. No servants to attend them? That was passing strange. It was such a marked change from the euphoria of the day that my pulse quickened.

Most confounding of all was the presence of a woman. She wore a woolen palla, pinned with little adornment at the shoulder. The garment hung bulky enough for an old maid to hide herself beneath. And like one of those, a veil draped her head. If there was any doubt as to her office, it was dispelled by the red and white ribbons woven around her shoulders. A Vestal Virgin. Her face was lovely, round and ripe with youth. I could see nothing of her figure, hidden as it was by the voluminous folds of her palla, but from the slim contours of her arms I imagined that the folds of her gown hid a figure that should not be hidden.

"Publius, my son," Crassus said, "come stand before us."

I did so. The men and the lone woman arrayed themselves around me.

My father continued, "You might have expected to meet with me alone." He bowed his head, acknowledging, it seemed, that secrets had been kept, ones that were now about to be revealed. "We have among us ten senators, representing various tribes." He named them in turn, illustrious names from prominent nobiles families. "We have a representative of the Flamines, the order of priests that keep Rome in the favor of the gods. They are here as witnesses."

I asked, "Witnesses to what, Father?"

Crassus cocked one of his prominent eyebrows. He held me in his gaze long enough to convey his displeasure at being interrupted. "They are to witness your entry into the nobilitas. There is one last stage in your transition to manhood. In the house of each new nobilis this same ceremony is taking place this night. Listen carefully to me, son, for this—now—matters more than all of it."

"He must swear secrecy," the priest said, "before you say anything more."

Several others murmured agreement.

I restrained the urge to roll my eyes. I assumed my friends Sextus and Volero would be going through the same tiresome ordeal. I looked forward to joking with them on the morrow.

"Swear to keep what passes here secret," my father said. "For all the days of your life, you may only speak of this to other men of the nobilitas, and to the Vestals, should you have occasion. Swear now, on our ancestors' spirits."

I did so.

"You know of how Numa Pomplilius created the college of the

Vestals long ago, during the time of the kings," my father said. "You know that the Vestals worship the goddess Vesta. You know that they keep alive the flame of the sacred hearth. You know that they have many duties, and that their service is at the heart of Rome's good fortunes. You know that they are vowed to chastity, and that no man can claim to have taken blood from the womb of a Vestal."

The virgin accepted the praise as her due, with startling composure for one so young.

"There are some things you do not know about the Vestals. Indeed, about what it means to be a Roman nobilis at all. There is a reason Rome has become a great power, a reason our village beside a river crossing came to be a great city, with a glorious past and a future too bright to behold. Our gifts have been given to us directly from Jupiter. It is through him that we triumph against all that face us. Hannibal came at us with the rage of Ba'al to aid him, and yet we defeated him. So it's been with all the others. Only once have we been truly defeated, by the Gauls that sacked our city and defiled our treasures. But that is a discussion for another time." The man's eyes flicked to the other senators, making him look momentarily ill at ease. "Yes, that's for another time. Tell me, Publius, have you heard of the feats of Roman senators in battle?"

"Of course, Father. Every boy wants to achieve such victories himself."

"You have seen the speed and strength of our nobiles warriors? How no regular soldier—no matter how gifted—can stand against one of our own? How even gladiators of the arena are no match for a Roman nobilis?"

"Yes, Father."

"I've told you it was Roman discipline and techniques that account for this. That's true, but there is another reason for it. We are blessed with the blood of Jupiter." A platitude, I would have thought, except that he looked deadly serious and full of import. "The ancients don't tell us when we received this gift or exactly how. They say only that it is our duty to honor it, and to never forget it came from Jupiter himself. Numa Pomplilius, in his wisdom, saw that the gift was too powerful a thing to go unchecked.

He established the rules by which it's passed, and initiated the college of Vestals to keep it pure. Since that time, only Vestals have made new men. Have you heard and understood everything I've said so far?" Crassus asked.

"Yes, Father," I answered.

I spoke too eagerly. I realized as much when my father frowned. No face could match Marcus Crassus's for skill at expressing disapproval. "I see that my words are just words to you. And here I'd told these men that you esteemed your father above all other men and would listen with reverence."

"We told you he would listen with only half a mind," one of the senators said.

"It is that way for all of us," another man added. "Just have him take the blood."

My father bowed his head and beckoned the priestess forward with his fingers. She came, moving with the chaste reverence Vestals always displayed. Her face was as pretty as I'd thought. Soft-edged, large brown eyes and a bloom of lips that I couldn't help admire, but her gaze was candid in a way I wouldn't have expected. She looked at me like a man would. Like someone that could take my measure and judge me.

She asked, "Are you worthy of my blood?"

For a moment, I thought she was offering me her virginity. But there was nothing like that sort of submission in her eyes. "I hope that I am, priestess."

She made a fist and twisted her right wrist around, showing it to me. Her other hand came up between us. Her two smaller fingers were curled; the two longer ones straight. A cap ring tipped the end of one. It narrowed to a sharp, barbed point. She placed the tip of the barb on her wrist and sliced it across her flesh. For a moment, nothing happened. And then a line of crimson appeared. It beaded at the center of the slash and began to flow. The priestess held the bloody wrist out. "Drink."

I drew back a step, horrified at how fast the blood pulsed from the wound and splashed to the floor.

My father whispered sharply, "Do as she says."

I started to protest, but the priestess snapped out her undamaged hand and grabbed me by the neck. I felt the point of the finger ring press against my skin. I tried to twist away, but the grip of the girl's arm was like iron. "Drink." She slammed her bleeding wrist against my lips.

For a few moments, writhing in the priestess's grip, I was terrified by her strength. Blood found its way into my mouth. It coated my teeth. It poured past them onto my tongue. I gagged, choking on the warm, metallic liquid. My lungs burned and my head began to swim. The world fogged around me as I moved toward unconsciousness. Before I fell into it, my throat opened. I began to drink. Blood. It was liquid, but swallowing it was like gasping for air after being under water, luxurious and complex like no wine had ever been. I hung, limp in the priestess's grip, drinking it in and breathing through my nose. I had never sucked at life so fervently. Breathing and drinking. Drinking and breathing. I could barely tell the two actions apart.

I lost sensibility. When I regained myself, I had crumpled to my knees. At some point the priestess and the others had departed. My father had me disrobe. He draped clean garments over me, a simple night tunic. He had me wash my face and hands in a basin of water, and made me rinse the blood from my mouth. He pushed my body through these motions, a closer intimacy than we had ever shared.

"You did not comport yourself well, Publius. What matters is that it's done. You've got the blood in you. You won't feel the change immediately, but it will come soon. The first yearning comes fast."

I almost asked what yearning he meant. But didn't I already know? Hadn't that been what I'd just felt and given in to? "No," I said. "I won't drink like that again."

"When the hunger is upon you, you will feed it. Come."

I trudged behind him, sullen, feeling more like a boy than I had before becoming a man. I was repelled by myself, but at the same time the salt taste that lingered in my mouth made me yearn for more. My belly, full of a virgin's blood, felt strangely like the contented center of my being. How much had I drunk? And what of the priestess? I felt so full of her blood that I couldn't imagine she had any left inside her. My front teeth ached, no doubt from the violence the priestess did me. How was it possible that she was so strong? My father had said that others were going through the same thing, but I couldn't believe that. Whatever had happened was a humiliation all my own. I was sure I would never talk about it with my friends or anybody else. Perhaps I could tell Thana. She was just a slave, after all. Her judgement of me didn't matter. Having formed the thought, I quickened my pace to catch up with my father.

Stepping into my room and coming around from the screen of my father's broad shoulders, I at first didn't understand what I saw. A naked girl hung from a chain in the center of my room. The chain had been run through a hook in the ceiling. It pulled her arms taut above her head. Her toes just barely touched the floor.

Thana. I rushed to her, trying to lift her up to take the strain off her wrists, whispering her name to wake her. I cradled her head in my hands. Unconscious, her features had all the form of beauty but seemed strangely lifeless, unanimated.

My father walked up beside me. "You should know by now that nothing that happens in my house escapes my notice. I know you like this girl. There is reason to, as I know well." He pinched her chin and turned her face to the light. He made a sound low in his throat. The touch of his finger on her chin and that sound told me everything I needed to know. Instantly, I hated him. I pushed him away. He allowed it. "You've become too attached to her. That ends today, on the very day you become a nobilis. Three days hence, after you've done with her and recovered, I will take you to the temple of Jupiter Optimus Maximus, and you will make offerings to the god. Believe me, Son, you will worship him like you never have before."

I shouted for the slaves to help me.

"They will not come," Crassus said. "Publius, leave this girl to hang. When your hunger tells you what to do, obey it. She will feel nothing. She's in the hold of a potion that will keep her until you are ready for her. You may rage, but I'm being more generous than I need to be. My father did not offer me my first in such a civilized manner." He turned to leave.

"But . . ." I stammered. "But what am I supposed to do with her? I won't do it, but what?"

Marcus Crassus did something very unusual for him. The edges of his lips rose. The creases of his face deepened. He smiled, his teeth looking particularly fearsome in the lamplight. He said, "When the yearning comes, you'll know what to do."

As soon as I was alone, I got Thana free. I set a chair upon a chest. Standing on it, I could lift the chain enough to free it from the hook. She collapsed on the floor. I picked her up and carried her, chain dragging on the stones, to my bed. I laid her out and pulled a woolen blanket over her. I went to find a key to unlock the wrist cuffs. I got only as far as the door. It had been blocked from the outside. I banged on it, shoved it, kicked it, but it did no good.

Back in bed with Thana, I lay next to her. I watched her sleeping face and stroked the light strands of her hair. I apologized for her treatment and promised that on the morrow we would leave for one of the country estates. My father couldn't stop me now that I was a man. We would live unwatched and do as we wished and all of this would be forgotten. I would finish my education and begin to make a name for myself. If my father wouldn't support me, I would build my own fortune. Marcus Crassus had done it. Why not Publius Crassus? Perhaps I would buy her—it would only take the right price—and free her someday. My mind was a tumult of schemes and plans. If I became a rebel—an outcast even—I wouldn't have to live up to the impossible standard. In that, Thana might free me.

I loved her all the more in the light of it. I adored the shape of her lips and flare of her nostrils. Her skin pulsed with life. It glowed like coals in a low fire, giving off heat without flame. I closed my eyes and touched the tip of my tongue to her naked shoulder. I would know her from any other woman simply from the touch of my tongue. Opening my eyes, I noticed the pulsing of the artery running up her neck. For the first time since I'd arrived in the room, lust stirred low in my abdomen. I climbed from the bed and sat down in a chair a little distance away. I would not force myself upon her, not when she was asleep from some potion. I sat watching, the fingers of one hand feeling my front teeth. They throbbed dully. Strangely, I could feel the touch of my fingers on the enamel.

A little later I was back in the bed again. I tugged the blanket down and studied the curves of her breasts. She mumbled and moved her head from one side to the other. I could hear her heartbeat. I could see the tremor of it in her soft flesh. I leaned down and pressed my ear against her chest. The heat of her brought my excitement back. That and the sensation that with each beat of her heart I could sense blood surging through her entire body, sliding down arteries, warm and full of life. I could feel the way it filled her. I understood the mechanics of her body like never before. I understood all of her, because I understood the beauty of the blood that gave her life. I had to be closer to it.

That was why I lifted the blanket and slipped on top of her. She wouldn't mind, I thought. I loved her, and she loved me too. She would wake and kiss me, and I would tell her of the things I'd decided. I wanted to be with her, that was all. I was sure she would want that as well. When this mad night is over, I thought, everything will be set right.

It wasn't.

That was why, a few days after that night, I sat in the gardens waiting for Gaius Julius Caesar to arrive. My father had tried several times to speak to me. I'd railed against him every time. What happened was his fault, and I hated him for it, all the more for the smug manner in which he named my emotions as absurd, unmanly, and not suited for a nobilis. "You must get over this, and soon," Marcus Crassus had said that morning, before leaving to survey an estate he'd just purchased near Casilinum.

I sat stiff, the sun of midmorning turning my skin hot. Though I was some distance from the nearest slaves, I could sense them.

The man that pruned the bushes down in the terrace below annoyed me, just by being there and by the fact that I knew he was there, though I couldn't see him. It was as if I had a sense of perception that I'd not had before. Not sight, because I didn't have to set eyes on them to know where they were. Not smell, for it wasn't through my nose at all. Not sound either. Somehow, I sensed their movements through the heat of their bodies, and through the blood that gave them life.

A voice beside my ear startled me. "I think you'll find," it said, "that only another nobilis will ever manage to sneak up on you from now on."

It was Julius, crouching just behind the bench I sat on. He grinned, an expression that on him always made him look like he'd just completed a sexual conquest and was pleased with himself. He mussed my hair. "How goes it with Little Monkey? I understand you've come into your blood and are a man now."

"Don't call me that anymore," I said.

"Little Monkey? I've always called you . . ." Julius craned his head back and studied me. "All right. You're a boy no more. Shall I call you by your full name from now on?"

"Publius will do."

He pulled a face of exaggerated concern. "Publius, why do you look so glum?"

Normally, his humor was infectious. Not today, though. There was too much on my mind. I needed to unburden myself. I couldn't do that with my father, much to the man's annoyance. With Julius it was different. Though a protégé of my father's, he'd long been like an older brother to me. With him, it was possible to say the truth.

"Something is wrong with me," I said. "I did something horrible to Thana."

"I presume that's the name of your slave girl."

"The way I took her . . . I didn't intend to. It just happened. I wouldn't have . . ."

"Of course you wouldn't have, Publius. You're a kind lad. Too much so, I think."

"Kind? Julius, I forced myself on her. She wasn't even awake at first, but I—"

Julius knocked on my knee with the knuckles of one hand. "She was a slave. Awake or sleeping doesn't really matter. Some girls are rather more engaging when asleep, actually."

"Stop making light of it!" I slid away, turned on the stone, and faced him. "They made me drink a priestess's blood. She gripped me and made me do it."

"Vestals are surprisingly strong, aren't they? Sometimes I think we've got it all wrong. We should give our women the blood and send them off to war like Amazons. Then we men could play at sport, eat and drink, and bugger slave girls. Or boys, for that matter."

I pressed on. "But afterward, with Thana. She awoke to my touch and was scared, at first, confused. I wanted her badly, like I've never wanted anything or anyone. She gave in and joined me, and when I was about to have my pleasure I . . ."

I knew the word that came next, but it seemed so feral and animal that I didn't want to admit it. As I thrust inside her, working toward climax, I became more and more aware that my motions matched the rhythm of her pulse. I saw it in the artery of her neck, right there beneath my panting mouth. I kissed it, ran my lips over it, touched it with my tongue and felt the surge of blood and the glorious warmth of it. The two of us were completely in unison, even the beating of our hearts. I ran my tongue across my teeth and found them different than before. Still sore and sensitive, but also reshaped. There were two small, sharp protrusions that hadn't been there before. They were hidden behind the screen of my other teeth. Noticing them for the first time, I knew what they were for. And, knowing, my orgasm began.

"I bit into her neck," I said.

"Of course you did." Julius crossed his hands on his lap as if he heard such confessions regularly enough that it bored him.

"I mean really bit her, like an animal!" I said. "I sucked at her neck. These teeth . . ." I tried to show them, but they weren't easy to see. I knew because I'd tried to find them in a hand mirror and had failed. "I don't understand it. I hate now to think of what I did. She thrashed and screamed out, but I didn't care. So long as I drank her blood my pleasure went on. It was like nothing else ever had or ever would matter more than that feeling."

"There is no pleasure to match it," Julius said. "It rose with each swallow, didn't it? And dipped with each pause. But it went on so long it seemed it would never stop. It was so complete that you were lost to anything but thirst and pleasure. It lasted so long that when it finally subsided, you were too overcome to regret the flagging of ecstasy. Have I got it right?"

Miserable, I nodded that he did.

"Then have heart, Publius." Julius gripped me by the shoulder and spoke for the first time without any humor edging his words. "You experienced the same thing we all do on the night we become nobiles. There is nothing wrong with you. The blood of Jupiter is within you. It needs to be replenished. If you think fondly of this slave girl, then remember her fondly because she was your first."

"My first? I'll never do that to another—"

"Ah, but you will. Listen, you seem to be very slow in realizing that a great mystery has been solved. All your life, you've marveled at the things nobiles were capable of. Now, you are one. The blood of Jupiter has made you what we nobiles all are: the masters of the earth. You may have thought your father just talking hyperbole, but he wasn't. Tell me, do you see things differently than you did before? Colors are brighter. Images sharper. Sometimes, when you are close to someone, it seems like you can see the blood flowing beneath their skin. Am I right?"

I didn't answer, though each thing was true.

"You can sense living beings around you even when you can't see them. You will find that you are faster than you ever were before. Stronger too. Next time you train you'll be a greater warrior than any seasoned foot soldier. When I was a boy, I used to catch ill for no reason at all. A walk too long in the cold. A night spent away from my own home. I was weak. The most miserable years of my life were the ones just before I reached maturity. I despaired forwarding my family name. We're patricians, but hardly distinguished ones. How was I—sickly and with a feeble constitution—going to build our fortunes?" He smiled. "I see you may have had some of the same thoughts. Neither of us need to have feared."

"Why did my father not prepare me? Why didn't he ask me if I even wanted this?"

"That is the way it's done. If you were told ahead of time, you might not believe. You might talk out of turn and reveal it to others. That's something you must never do. You see now why you've been sworn to secrecy? If word of this spread to the populace . . . Or to foreign powers . . . All of us—Vestals and citizens—would be in grave danger, no matter our individual powers. We keep our secret to preserve our lives and our status. Once a boy becomes one of us, he shares the covenant. It's done. There is no going back. That, Publius, is the Roman way. And believe me, you will find your life much improved. Crassus wanted me to say as much to you."

"For you to say the things he can't be bothered to?"

"Do you have to curdle every kindness?" I had a response to that, but Julius spoke over me. "Here is what you should know. You are still mortal, but you have powers beyond other men. You'll grow into them. Enjoy it, but don't grow too cocky. You have the blood of a god in your veins, but that does not make you a god. You may lose your head. You may take an arrow to the heart. Things like that will kill you just the same as any man. You may lose limbs and can die from such a thing like any man. But unlike any man, you can heal from grievous injuries. If you take blood from others, you recover quickly. You'll be the match for any normal man, but that doesn't mean you don't have to fear them. You still have the appetites you always had. Food and drink sustain you, but only blood strengthens you."

I stood and paced. Two maid slaves passed on the terrace above and entered the house. I could sense them in the room adjacent. It was faint, but even the stone didn't stop me from knowing where they were. It was, I acknowledged, an incredible thing. I didn't know yet if it was a gift I was willing to kill for. "Who are all these others that I'm supposed to drink from?"

Julius looked at me, amused. "Why Publius, have you understood nothing about how things work? Rome conquers. We enslave. So long as we have slaves, we have all the blood we need. Our slaves feed us. What more complete way to serve a master?"

"Will it always be as it was? The way it was with Thana?"

"Taking the blood doesn't need to be a sexual act, though that's an enjoyable way to do it. Just don't run through all your father's female slaves. He wouldn't appreciate that. The only thing you must know, Publius, is that when you feed, you must always feed completely. Drain them until they die. That's part of the covenant. We can't have slaves as living evidence against us. It's enough that there are dead bodies to dispose of. Messes to clean up."

"No one would believe them if they spoke of it," I muttered.

"Are you done complaining, or do you have more?" When I didn't answer, Julius continued. "Here is what we're going to do. We'll talk as long as you like. I'll help you to understand your gifts, to appreciate them. When you're ready, you and I will walk to the temple of Jupiter and make the offerings your father has left for you. You'll thank the god as you should, and then you'll get busy with the starting of your career."

I didn't refuse. I did say, "I won't forget her, you know. I won't forget what I did to her."

Julius nodded. "No, I don't suspect you will."

Later that afternoon, Julius escorted me to the temple. We climbed the Capitolium under a gloriously bright sky. From that high vantage, I took in views of Rome that sparkled with a clarity that continued to amaze me. How much I hadn't seen before! Such cramped, jostling grandeur, buildings and temples piled on top of each other. I could have stood for hours taking in the details of the architecture, the stains in the stonework, the cracks in structures that I'd never have been able to see before. I felt I could gaze right into windows and view the lives inside. Along the Tiber, I could pick out men in their boats, and I could make out individual leaves in the boughs of distant trees.

Julius pulled me on, mumbling that I shouldn't stare so hard just yet. I might see an omen I'd rather not.

The Temple was still being rebuilt from the fire that had destroyed it nearly ten years before. Quintus Lutatius Catulus had yet to dedicate it, and it was not open to the public. For us newly risen nobiles, though, on the occasion of our indoctrination into the covenant, exceptions were made. We entered as did others, through the massive pillars that framed the entrance. We paid homage to Juno Regina on one side, and to Minerva on the other. But it was at Jupiter Optimus Maximus's feet that we gathered to make our offerings of thanks and eternal fealty.

My eyes found my friends. Sextus just down the row of young men, and then, on the opposite side of the great statue, Volero. They both looked shaken, anxious to talk. Had they killed a slave as well? Had all of them committed the same bizarre crime? I looked to other faces, still wanting to see kinship with them, some sort of absolution for my crimes, even if only because others shared in it. But there were too many things written on their features. Some of them, I thought, held themselves with a smug superiority they hadn't demonstrated just the day before. Perhaps they hadn't all gone through the same ordeal.

Either that, I realized, or . . . they had enjoyed it. Despite my horror and grief, hadn't I to admit that I had enjoyed it like nothing I'd ever experienced in my life? Didn't I know already that when the yearning took hold of me again, I'd have no choice but to feed it? Couldn't I tell that for the first time in my life my body moved with a grace and perfection I'd thought forever out of my reach? Wasn't it already true that I would take none of it back, not even to live that life of poverty with Thana? To all these and more, the answer was yes.

With my peers, I bowed at the god's feet and gave thanks for what he had made me into.

Seanan McGuire

IN THE SUMMER OF 2017—SUMMER FOR ME, IN THE PACIFIC NORTHWEST, winter for Oceania—I traveled to Australia and New Zealand as a guest of their respective national science fiction conventions. Being a zoology-oriented person, I spent a great deal of my trip poking into the local flora and fauna, talking to naturalists, and studying the history of humanity's influence on the two nations. I also had the opportunity to go into the Tasmanian brush to see the site of the last verified thylacine sighting.

The thylacine, or Tasmanian tiger, is very important to me, because it represents so much about mankind's interactions with the natural world. This was a completely unique, completely innocent animal, wiped out by human intervention . . . or so we currently believe. I devoutly hope that the thylacine is still out there somewhere, hiding, waiting for a chance to come home. This story is the manifestation of my hope . . . although through a rather dystopian, science fictional lens.

Seanan McGuire

STRIPES IN THE SUNSET

Seanan McGuire

Crimson—the crown jewel of the otherwise unremarkable Lakeland Zoo, which had never quite been able to forge a distinct identity for itself—went into labor just before midnight on Tuesday, December 19. Zookeepers and veterinarians rushed to the side of the six-year-old Siberian tiger, while members of the zoo's social media team stood by with cameras and computers, ready to share the entire process with their eager audience. After the blood had been sponged away, of course. The public couldn't get enough of Crimson, but they didn't like to be reminded that she was a predator. The one time a video had been posted showing her in pursuit of a rabbit that had managed to tunnel into her enclosure, well . . .

It had been a miracle that any of them had still been employed when the dust settled. No one was going to risk a reprise.

"You're doing so good, sweetheart, you're doing *so well,*" cooed the lead veterinarian, a twenty-year veteran of the zoo and its sometimes-labyrinthine internal politics. She knelt by the tiger's side, occasionally stroking her flank with one gloved hand, making soothing noises in between words of fawning praise.

The rest of the veterinary staff, who were either more intelligent or possessed of a more finely honed sense of self-preservation, depending on who you asked, kept a safer distance. It was best for the tiger if she could deliver naturally, without excessive use of drugs or restraints. It was best for the staff if their faces were still attached to their skulls by the time the cubs came. It was a delicate balancing act, made more difficult by the fact that Dr. Fisher seemed incapable of treating her larger, more dangerous patients as anything other than her beloved friends.

Crimson lifted her head, eyes rolling wildly, and snorted. The rest of the care team took a step back. Dr. Fisher gave her flank another stroke.

"Good girl, who's a *good* girl, yes, you're doing *so well*, my girl. So very, very well." Her tone changed only slightly. It was enough to make it clear to the observers that she was no longer speaking entirely to the tiger. "What's her blood pressure? Someone give me an update, so I know whether we're moving toward an intervention."

"This is your reminder, as requested by the legal staff, that once you use the word 'intervention,' it might be time to move away from the massive apex predator," said one of the vet techs. "Her blood pressure is good, everything seems to be within normal ranges for her age and size. She's going to have a baby."

"She's going to have more than one, if the ultrasound can be believed," said Dr. Fisher, giving Crimson's flank another stroke before lifting the tiger's heavy hind leg and checking on her progress. A slow smile spread across the woman's face. "In fact, I believe she's going to have a baby right now."

The first of Crimson's cubs came into the world with a refreshing lack of trouble, sliding straight into Dr. Fisher's waiting hands. She passed the baby on to the vet technician who would weigh and clean it, and returned her attention to the perplexed tiger, who was starting to sniff around for her missing baby.

"It's all right, sweetheart, you're doing fine, just fine," she said, in a soothing tone. "Come on, good girl, let's get that second baby out, okay? I know you can do it."

Apparently, so did Crimson.

The three cubs, all born in quick succession, were weighed, cleaned, and photographed before they were returned to their mother, who had already done the work of cleaning herself and started to growl lowly at the attending humans. Dr. Fisher set the last of the cubs down by its mother and rose to move away. Then she froze, a perplexed frown on her face, seemingly heedless of the increasingly agitated predator in front of her.

"Dr. Fisher?" said one of the vet techs anxiously. "You need to move. She's not sedated."

"Something's wrong," said Dr. Fisher.

Hands grasped her shoulders and yanked her away right before Crimson's warning swat passed through the space where Dr. Fisher's thighs had been. The tiger, eager to get back to her babies, did not pursue. Uncharacteristically, Dr. Fisher didn't complain about being moved. She was still staring at the babies.

"Something's *wrong*," she repeated.

"They're healthy, they're feeding, nothing's wrong," said one of the other techs. "Three babies, two male, one female. We should all be very proud of our girl."

"Three brand-new Siberian tigers," said a member of the social media team, virtually glowing with the thought of what this would be worth in terms of attendance numbers.

"No," said Dr. Fisher, still staring at the cubs. "That's not what we have. That's not what we have at all."

By morning, reports had come in from zoos around the globe. A mated pair of thick-billed parrots in a zoo in Texas had hatched a nest of five eggs, two of which looked remarkably like their parents, and three of which, even mostly featherless and underdeveloped as hatchling birds always were, already showed distinct morphological differences. A mink had given birth to four pups, three of which were nearly twice the expected size, and which had already nearly exhausted their poor mother with their nursing demands.

A little eagle had laid an egg substantially too large for her system and had died shortly after, leaving her single potential child to be incubated by zoo staff.

Dr. Fisher, who had sat up all night with pictures of the cubs and her research library on big cats of the world, was already waiting outside the zoo director's office when he arrived for work. He looked at her wearily, bracing for her latest diatribe about feeding regiments or enrichment activities for the animals.

"Can this wait until after the press conference to formally announce the cubs?" he asked.

"It's about the cubs," she replied.

He sobered instantly. "Come inside," he said.

Only after they were seated—him on the safely authoritarian side of his desk, with its weight to protect him from the outside world, her on the outside, the supplicant's side, where she would remember her place—did he lean forward, resting his weight on his elbows, and ask, "What's the problem? Is something wrong with one of the babies?"

"No," she said, and waited for him to relax before she said, "there's something wrong with two of the babies. Only one of them is a Siberian tiger. We can't present them to the public. Not yet. We need to run more tests, we need to sequence their DNA, we need to—"

"You need to calm down." The zoo director slumped back in his seat. "They came out of a Siberian tiger. We have it on video. Their father, also a Siberian tiger, donated the sperm that was used to conceive them. We have that whole process on video, God knows why, sometimes I feel like I'm running a very niche pornography studio when these animals get involved. They're Siberian tigers."

"Except that they aren't," said Dr. Fisher.

"Karen. Please."

"As I said, I need to run more tests before I can be sure, but I think we're looking at a pair of Caspian tigers. They're extinct, Paul. They've been extinct for decades. Don't you think we should know exactly why our purebred Siberian tiger is giving birth to cubs that belong to a subspecies that died out years ago?"

"You're seeing things," said the director. There was a sudden hard note in his voice. "You need a break. Go home. I'll make sure your rounds are covered for the day."

"I'm telling you what I saw."

"And I'm telling you that we do not have inexplicable extinct baby tigers. We have two cubs with slightly unusual markings and a clear genetic history. You need to sleep. Go home. I'll see you tomorrow. Or not, if you need more time to recover."

The threat in his words was impossible to dismiss. Dr. Fisher stared at him for a long moment before she stood, straightening her jacket, and said, "When you realize that I'm right, I'll expect an apology."

She left the office without another word. The director watched her go, sighed, and turned to his computer. There was much to do before the cubs could be shared with the world.

In a zoo in Boston, a red hartebeest gave birth to two foals, one of which resembled its mother, the other of which was a pale sandy color that hadn't been seen in a hundred years.

In a zoo in Vancouver, a lioness retreated to her den, where she delivered three cubs, snarling at any zookeeper who tried to get close enough to examine them. It would be three weeks before she allowed them to be seen, and observers commented on how two of them, while healthy, were surprisingly small, with dark brown—almost black—hair rimming their ears. The boy cub had matching smudges below his jawline, indicating that his mane, when it grew in, would be surprisingly dark.

Births were not unusual for the zoos of the world. So many of them were involved in conservation activities that it was only reasonable that they should be regularly breeding, expanding their stock in terms of genetic diversity and strength. Secondary to the conservation concerns was the fact that baby animals were always good for attendance, and "you can't look at zebras with the lights off." The more healthy, viable births a zoo had to announce, the better off they would be.

Even so, it would seem strange, later, how long it took for anyone to realize what was happening, or to question *why*. In a community populated by naturalists and animal-lovers, even the slightest deviation from the norm should have attracted immediate attention. And it did, it did. It was just that it attracted the attention of the probable and plausible, which said that it was not outside the realm of possibility for cubs to be born and chicks to be hatched with unusual coloration or morphology; that recessive genes existed.

The breaking point, when it was reached, was reached in a wildlife rehabilitation center in Tacoma, Washington.

Eliza looked at the wide-eyed, worried faces of the teens in front of her, and hated her job, just a little. "I'm sorry," she said. "We can't accept pigeons. They can't be released back into the wild, and treating them only to euthanize them when we run out of space isn't fair. I can't help you."

"But we're not sure it *is* a pigeon," insisted one of the teens, pushing the box toward her. "Please, can you just take a look? It has a broken wing, it's not going to get loose."

Eliza sighed. "If I look at it and say that yes, it's a pigeon, will you go?"

"We will," said the other teen. "Promise."

"All right."

Eliza opened the box.

The bird inside was a juvenile, but old enough that its adult coloration had mostly come in. It was crammed into a corner of the box, narrow head up and watching warily, one wing dangling limply at its side. Her breath caught.

It looked like a pigeon. It *was* a pigeon, just not a band-tailed pigeon, not a common city bird, feral descendant of someone's abandoned, beloved pets. The feathers on its breast were a rosy pink, a color so characteristic, so impossible that she would have known it from a single feather. But a feather could have been a hoax, a lie, a pointless prank. This was a living, breathing bird.

"Yes," she said in a dazed tone. "You were right to bring him here."

"Him? You can tell it's a him?" asked one of the teens.

"Oh, yes," said Eliza. "We can help him. Thank you. Please fill out this form," she pushed a clipboard toward the teens, "and indicate *exactly* where you found him." She closed the box. She had to close the box. If she didn't stop looking at the impossibility that it contained, she was going to start crying, and then she would never be able to finish doing what needed to be done.

Half an hour later, with the teens gone and the door securely locked, she picked up the phone and called the chief veterinary officer.

"You're not going to believe this," she said. "I barely believe this, and I'm looking right at it. But you need to get down here. Two kids just brought me a live passenger pigeon."

The pigeon, unaware of his own importance, huddled in the corner of the box, beak pressed to his breast, and waited for the hurting to stop.

A hastily assembled expedition to the underpass where the teens had found the pigeon uncovered six more, both males and females, all in perfect health, all absolutely, unquestionably passenger pigeons. It didn't matter that none of the people gathering them up had seen a live example of the breed. They had books, and they had reference films, and they knew a passenger pigeon when they saw one.

Press conferences were called. Announcements were made. A relic population of passenger pigeons: a chance for a dead species to return. A miracle. They called it a miracle, over and over again, as behind the cameras, ornithologists from around the world gathered to search through the eggshells and the nests looking for some sign of where these birds had come from. Where there were a few, the reasoning ran, there might be more.

All they found were common city pigeons. Their seven passenger pigeons were all of an age. It was a mystery; no question.

Mysteries yearn to be solved.

Dr. Fisher squinted at her inbox. Every evening brought another spate of email from zoos around the world reporting on the inconsistencies within their breeding programs. Animals—healthy, normal, genetically sound animals—were giving birth to offspring they couldn't possibly have given birth to. Genetics didn't work that way. All nature was not an incubator for everything else.

But the evidence was there, as undeniable as a Caspian tiger . . . or a passenger pigeon.

The evening's mail brought with it the news of two dodos hatched by an ostrich, and what several people suspected was a moa hatched by an emu. "If it is a moa, we can expect a lawsuit from the government of New Zealand demanding it be delivered to them," wrote the keeper in question. "What do we do? The native people of New Zealand own the genetic code of the moa, but this is a unique specimen, and legally, it's probably an emu."

"Deal with it when it happens," Dr. Fisher typed. "Has anyone else got a Caspian tiger?"

Futures were discussed. Plans were made. The odds were good that none of them would account for anything, but plans were comforting things to have.

It was unlikely, based on the discovery of the passenger pigeons, that these miraculous, impossible births were confined to the zoos of the world. Ironically, it was extinction and poaching that were buying them the time to plan for anything at all. In a world where there were almost no tigers, how many odd-looking cubs would be spotted in the wild? If someone saw a cub, they were probably looking through the crosshairs of a rifle.

The Caspian tigers in Dr. Fisher's zoo should never have existed. Now that they did, they were very likely to once again be the last in the world. If they died, they would carry their species with them into extinction for a second time, and it seemed unreasonable to ask the world for another miracle resurrection. This was the only second chance the human race was going to get.

They had to do it properly.

"I don't understand," said the young woman, her hands folded in her lap, a miserable expression on her face. "If everything is working the way it's supposed to, why can't we conceive?"

Dr. Marlowe had been helping patients achieve their dreams for nearly twenty years. She had kept abreast of developments in all forms of fertility treatment, from the hormonal to the surgical, and if she didn't know how something worked, it was unlikely to have been legalized for use on humans. She was touted on all the message boards and in all the private forums as being the woman with the answers.

Looking at this couple, who had come to her like so many before them, hoping for a miracle, she had never felt further from the answers in her life.

"Well," she said. "Sometimes it can take a while for everything to fall into synch."

She spoke the platitudes like they were somehow new, like they had never been spoken before, while inwardly, she was raging and confused. Nothing was working. They followed the steps as they always had, combined the genetic material as they had always done, and . . .

Nothing. There hadn't been a single pregnancy out of her office in months. She worried for the couples who still came to her, still looking for their miracle. More, she worried for her staff and her own reputation. This couldn't be the way it ended. This couldn't.

The announcement that two confirmed Caspian tigers were being raised in an American zoo was neatly buried under the announcement that no human babies had been born for a full month anywhere in the United States. The additional announcements about impossible animals were similarly buried. Only a few countries continued to report normal birthrates, and there was reason to believe, based on information coming from those regions, that the reports were lies.

In a small town in Oregon, a domestic cat nursed her litter of kittens and sea minks, purring all the while, unaware that the world was changing.

"The animals and the fertility rates are connected; they have to be." The man who spoke was old enough that his three children were grown, and several of them had already had children of their own. The current situation was largely academic to him. It was frightening people. Frightened people were unpredictable. He wanted that to stop. As to the rest . . .

There were too damn many babies around these days as it was. Maybe a little break was exactly what the doctor had ordered.

"But how is this happening?" The man behind the desk had not risen to the position of leader of the free world by refusing to listen to his constituents, if only so he could be sure of what needed to be hidden from their innocent ears. "Surely someone has some idea."

"It's happening on a global level, as near as we can tell," said one of the few women in the room. She was smart, she was savvy, and she was twice as skilled as any of the men around her at feeling out which way the wind was blowing. She had to be. It was the only way for someone like her to break into the boys' club that they still represented. "Scientists around the world are looking for a cause. If there's something for them to find, they'll have it soon."

"There has to be something for them to find," snapped the President. "Things like this don't simply *happen*."

The woman, who had watched as her daughter's cat gave birth to a litter of sweet-faced flying foxes the size of kittens, said nothing.

When faced with the impossible, historically, humanity has risen to the challenge: has reached out to find the place where improbable and actual collide, chart it, and in the charting, make it so.

Not this time.

Around the world, scientists wrested supposedly extinct animals away from their caretakers and vivisected them, looking for the answer to a question that no one was entirely sure how to phrase. Why were things that had long since been written off as dead and gone returning, and why in such an impossible, improbable manner? What was determining their birth rate? Why had humans stopped getting pregnant? Were all these things the same question, or were they a chain of questions, barely connected, tangled in the same string of illogic and confusion?

The zookeepers began hiding their charges, spiriting them out of what should have been their safe havens and tucking them away in garages and attacks, rented storage lockers and the back rooms of certain trustworthy animal rescues. Arrests were made. Still there were no answers; still there were no causes.

Time passed. Time always does.

The Caspian tigers, heralds of this bright new world, paced in their enclosure, eyes on Dr. Fisher. They knew the veterinarian well enough not to be disturbed by her presence, but they didn't trust her, any more than they trusted any human. They were wild things, for all that they had been raised by human hands. They had always been intended to be wild things.

Dr. Fisher stopped, looking at them. The tigers looked back.

"You're going to die in here," she said. "You're never going to be free. You're never going to hunt, or kill, or fade into the shadows. Humans have long memories, and they blame you more than you can possibly understand. Not for anything you did. For existing, and for being the bellwether of a change that they can't turn aside. They ask themselves what they did, how this could possibly have happened, why, why, why. They never ask the reason that it took so long. But Nature would have her due, wouldn't she? We broke too many of her toys. We had to be removed."

If anything, the process—inexplicable and impossible as it was—had been as kind as it could have been. No human babies, no, but no babies of other species born to human parents. No resurgence of the Neanderthal in a neonatal ward, no proof of their replacement.

She had her suspicions about the gorillas, and what some of them might carry in their bellies, waiting to be born.

She hoped that this time, the coming custodians would be kinder.

"The world may not have loved us, but oh, how we loved you," she murmured to the tigers, watching them move, all elegance and potential behind the clear plastic wall. "We loved you to death, and now you're back to return the favor."

The tigers said nothing.

The kangaroo scratched her ear with one vast hindfoot, relieving the itch. Her joey was a few feet away, snuffling at the ground. She barked to call the young one back. It was large, yes, but not large enough to leave her yet. That would come soon. She could feel the next joey stirring, ready to take the pouch for its own.

Her child was strange, stripes across its back, body too low, head too long, but she groomed it all the same before it scrambled back into her pouch, and she was content. This was as the world should be.

All around her, kangaroo mothers tended thylacine children, their stripes shining in the sunset, and nature moved on.

Marc Turner

As the title "All That Glitters" suggests, my short story takes a sideways look at the risks connected with the pursuit of wealth, and, by extension, the value of more important things in life—a theme particularly relevant considering the origins of the *Unfettered* anthology. The tale also delivers a generous serving of revenge, with a side order of humour. Oh, and dragons, of course, because you can never have too many of those. Although they aren't quite the same creatures of marvel for those unfortunate souls who are about to find themselves staring into the beasts' golden eyes . . .

Marc Turner

ALL THAT GLITTERS

Marc Turner

From her hiding place behind a rocky ridge, Castella looked down on the dragon's carcass in the shallows. Breakers tugged at the creature, dragging it shoreward before releasing it to settle back again. The moonlight flickering off its copper armour made it seem as if the beast were aflame.

Beside it, a dozen shadowy figures worked to extract the dragon's precious blood from its veins. It was dangerous work, Castella knew. If the liquid splashed your skin, it would burn like acid; she had a small scar below her left eye to prove it. It was grueling work, too, prising apart the overlapping scales and hacking at the flesh with boarding pikes. But if there was one type of work Castella didn't object to, it was work done by others to her imminent profit.

Considering the perils involved, the workers on the beach were going about their labour with imprudent haste. Doubtless this was due to the trumpeting of more dragons to the south, for the blood of the dead beast would draw others of its kind like sharks. And there was no shortage of dragons abroad in the Rubyholt Isles at present. With Dragon Day less than a week away, the creatures were being lured to the Dragon Gate in readiness for the Hunt.

Castella had been dodging the wretched beasts all week. Just yesterday she and Araline had seen a silver dragon maul a Raptor brigatina off Summer Point. But the creatures hadn't been having it all their own way, as the carcass in the bay proved. The scales across the dragon's neck were crumpled like a cheap suit of armour. And since no earthly weapon was able to damage the plates, the creature must have fallen foul of the beast that dwelled in the Dragon's Boneyard, then limped to this place to die. The sound of its death cries had clearly drawn the people on the beach just as they had Castella.

She looked over at Araline. Her companion was studying a piece of driftwood. With a series of languid movements, she turned it in her hands as if she were trying to work out which way was up. Everything the woman did seemed elegant, but maybe that was because she was standing next to Castella when she did it.

Castella caught her eye and nodded toward the workers. "They're Squall clan," she whispered.

"How do you know?"

"The man with the headscarf and the ponytail—that's their krel, Malavon Tempest."

Araline stiffened. "*The* Malavon Tempest. The man who keelhauls crewmen just for staring at him the wrong way?" Her look turned suspicious. "The man *you* used to sail with until a year back."

"No, a totally different Malavon Tempest," Castella muttered.

And he *had* been a different man when she first met him a year ago. Flushed with the honour of being promoted to krel, he had had a spirit and a fire to him that had drawn Castella like a feathermoth. The feeling had been mutual too. In fact, he might even have fallen enough for Castella that she could tell him she wasn't really a sandclaw hunter and dragon rider in her spare time. The relationship hadn't lasted, of course; nothing good ever did.

Araline regarded her impassively. As ever, Castella had no idea what her friend was thinking. For seven months they'd been working together, yet all Castella had learned about the other woman in that time was that she liked keeping secrets. They had met in

Skarl on midsummer's eve. Trying to rob the same waterfront warehouse, they had blundered into the same drugs deal and been forced to flee on the same leaking skiff. In retrospect, that debacle had set the tone for their working relationship to follow.

"We'd better tell Dresk about Tempest," Araline said at last. By rights the dragon's carcass belonged to the warlord of the clans, because the island upon which the corpse had washed up—the Cross—was in Spear territory.

"What's the point?" Castella replied. "By the time we get to Bezzle, Tempest will be long gone. Then it'll be our word against his that he was ever here. I've got a better idea." She gestured to the top of the beach and a cluster of pearlshell flasks containing siphoned-off dragon blood. "I'm going to steal one of those."

Araline stared at her. "You're mad."

"Relax, it gets worse. You're going to help me."

"I am?"

"Here's what we'll do. I'll creep down and hide behind that dune there"—Castella pointed to it—"then you'll stir up the sea around the dragon's head to make it seem as if the creature is still alive." Araline was a water-mage, so manipulating the waves would be easy for her. "While the Squalls are changing their breeches, I sneak in, grab one of the flasks, and sneak out again."

Araline pretended to consider. "Let me get this straight. Your plan is to trick the Squalls into thinking a dragon they've been drawing blood from for the last quarter-bell isn't dead, then walk across twenty paces of open sand without anyone spotting you."

"More or less."

"Sounds like less to me."

Castella grimaced. "Have some faith," she said. "When have my plans ever gone wrong before?"

The mage resumed fiddling with her piece of driftwood. "Well, there was the time when we tried to take back our boat from those Raptors, and they were woken by that cough."

"Your cough."

"Then there was that business with the sunpearl divers in the Outer Rim—"

Castella raised a hand to cut her off. For all Araline's reservations, Castella knew her friend would go through with the plan because the money they stood to make should set them up for years. Besides, Castella's scheme *would* work. Judging by the way the Squalls' heads came up at every sound, they were already twitchy about the prospect of a gate-crashing dragon. When Araline stirred the waters about the copper beast's head, the mere possibility of the creature still being alive would capture the clansmen's fullest attention.

With luck, Castella could tiptoe in without the Squalls even knowing she was there.

And so it proved.

Two hundred heartbeats later Castella was back at the rocky ridge, clutching her prize. That had been too easy. After grabbing the flask, she had crept away so slowly she'd felt *sure* someone would notice her. But the beach behind her remained silent. No cries of outrage, no demands for her to stop.

There had to be a catch, though. Life loved knocking Castella down just to see how quickly she bounced back up again.

That was when she noticed that Araline was not alone. A step behind and to one side of the mage was a man holding the largest crossbow Castella had ever seen. Even in the darkness, Castella could make out the zigzag burn of a lightning bolt on his neck—the symbol Tempest now branded onto his followers as if they were cattle. Castella didn't recognize the man from her time on Malavon's crew, and she seemed equally a stranger to him. A handspan shorter than Araline, he sported a self-inflicted haircut and a smile with more gaps in it than teeth.

When Castella caught Araline's eye, the mage had the decency to look sheepish about being caught.

"That's close enough," Gap-Tooth said, pointing his crossbow at Araline. "One false move and I put a bolt in your friend's back."

The size of that crossbow, his quarrel would probably punch straight through Araline and hit Castella as well. She raised her hands. "Take it easy," she said in a low voice.

Gap-Tooth glanced at the flask she was carrying. "Put that down," he said.

Castella looked around. The ridge hid her from the Squalls on the beach, and the continued silence suggested Gap-Tooth hadn't yet alerted his companions. That got her thinking. "You don't have to turn us in," she told him.

He snorted.

"If you take this flask to Tempest, what do you think he'll do? Throw you a party and let you keep half the blood as thanks?" Castella shook her head. "The only thing Tempest is generous with is the lashes from his whip. Most likely he'll blame you for letting me steal the flask in the first place."

From Gap-Tooth's expression it was clear he knew this was true. Along with his wariness, Castella saw a greed and a calculation she could play on.

"If you give him the flask," she went on, "no one wins except Tempest. Whereas if you take it for yourself, he probably won't even miss you when you're gone. We won't stop you."

Araline surprised her by speaking. "The Nine Hells we won't!"

Castella blinked.

Araline tried to turn to face Gap-Tooth, but a jab from the Squall's crossbow kept her looking forward. "If you steal the blood," she said, "how do you plan on getting off this island without a boat?"

"I'll take yours," he replied.

"And what about the sea dragons? How will you avoid them?" Araline paused to let her words sink in. "I'm a water-mage. You need my help."

Castella took up the baton. "Plus even if you could get to Bezzle," she said to him, "what would you do then? Do you know someone you can trust to broker a sale? Someone who won't rat you out to Tempest as soon as he sees the zigzag mark on your neck?"

The Squall said nothing. A shout from the direction of the beach made him startle. But the cry was more of pain than alarm, so likely all it signalled was that some poor sod had splashed themselves with dragon blood.

"Don't get greedy," Castella continued. "The blood in here"—she nodded to the flask—"is worth maybe a hundred thousand sovereigns. Split three ways, do you know how much that'll make you?"

Gap-Tooth's eyes widened in alarm. Evidently no one had warned him there'd be maths in this conversation.

"Over thirty thousand sovereigns," Castella said. "Easy money if we work together."

"And how do I know you won't shoot me in the back first chance you get?"

"Because you're the one holding the crossbow, that's why."

Gap-Tooth sucked his lip as he thought. His gaze flitted all around. Far behind him, the cross-shaped rock formation that gave this island its name was a deeper dark in the gloom.

Castella tensed. If Gap-Tooth's answer was no, she would rush him. A crossbow like his would be harder to maneuver than a galley in a storm. Maybe she could reach him before he brought it to bear, or maybe she would dive to one side when he aimed at her. Then Araline could gut him before he could shoot. The mage's knives were never far from her hands.

"You've got a deal," the Squall said at last, and Castella released a breath she hadn't realized she'd been holding.

"Good," she said. "Now point that damned crossbow somewhere else."

"Hah! Not likely."

"Fair enough. But we get to keep the dragon blood."

"No way. Pass it here."

Castella suppressed a smile. She had laid a trap for Gap-Tooth and he had obligingly walked straight into it. "If you insist," she said, then tossed the flask to him underarm.

Pearlshell was sturdy enough that it would survive a fall on rock. But instinctively Gap-Tooth flung out his right hand to catch the flask.

Just as Castella had been hoping he would. Because if he was using one hand to hold the flask, he couldn't also be gripping the crossbow with it. Supported by only by his left hand now, the weapon dipped, such was its weight. The bolt pointed at the ground.

Araline spun around, silver glinting in her hand.

Castella didn't see her friend land the killing blow, but suddenly Gap-Tooth dropped both the flask and his crossbow. He clutched his throat, blood bubbling between his fingers. As he sank to his knees, Castella saw in his eyes that familiar look of disbelief as he confronted the truth of his mortality. Then he slumped on one side, twitching like a grounded fish.

Castella held herself still, senses straining for any sign that the Squalls on the beach had heard. The only sounds, though, were the restless murmur of waves, the scratch of tools on dragon scales, a man's voice—Tempest's?—ordering the workers to make haste. Around Gap-Tooth, a red pool was spreading. Castella shivered. Strange how a flask of dragon blood was near priceless, yet the cost of a human life was so cheap.

Araline stooped to clean her knife on the Squall's tunic. Her gaze strayed to the dead man's crossbow, and for an uncomfortable moment Castella pictured her friend lifting the weapon and turning it on her. Araline was Castella's best friend, but a hundred thousand sovereigns would test even the strongest bond.

"That was close," Araline said.

"Too close."

A pause. "You'd really have given that guy the blood to release me?" Araline asked.

"Of course."

"Why?"

The question left Castella feeling strangely self-conscious. "Why not? Not everything is about money."

"We're thieves. What else would it be about?"

"You make it sound as if you wouldn't have done the same for me."

Araline chuckled, her gaze sliding again to the crossbow. She extended a hand to the weapon, but there was a playful edge to her smile that suggested she wasn't serious about taking it. Maybe.

At that instant the crossbow bucked on the ground, discharging the bolt in its slot. There was a twang so loud it set the air humming, a flash of black. The quarrel pinged off a rock. Stone chippings fell in a patter. From the beach came enquiring shouts, faint over the roaring in Castella's ears.

Araline was the first to react. "Let's get out of here!" she said, snatching up the flask.

The arrow loosed from Tempest's ship, the *Destiny,* traced a grey arc through the night before landing in the sea beside Castella's boat. Another followed it, then another, the first falling short, the second whistling overhead.

Castella and Araline had led a charmed life for the past quarter-bell, jinking through a maze of waterways between islets while dodging a steady rain of missiles. After Gap-Tooth's crossbow had gone off, they had sprinted for their boat, hoping to slip away before Tempest realized what was happening. But even as Castella was casting off, she'd seen the topmasts of the *Destiny* appear above the treeline on the northern shore. Now the ship was slowly reeling her in like she was a saberfin caught on a line. It was just a matter of time before it overhauled her.

Araline had summoned up a wave of water-magic beneath their boat, but the wave beneath the *Destiny* was larger. Clearly outrunning the Squalls wasn't an option. So what now? Hide? Castella and Araline would need to break line of sight first, and what were the chances of that? Double back, perhaps? If they sailed past the *Destiny,* by the time the bulkier craft turned they would be halfway to freedom. But that would mean running the gauntlet of the *Destiny*'s archers, and at such close range the women would be easier to hit than miss.

Even as the thought came to Castella, a missile thudded into the transom behind her with an impact she felt through her buttocks.

In the darkness ahead, she spotted a sandbar connecting two islets, moonlit water beyond. She pointed it out to Araline.

"Go over!" she shouted above the hiss of spray. "Over!"

Araline nodded.

The boat picked up speed, and Castella gripped the rail. As the sandbar approached, the wave of water-magic beneath the boat reared higher. It carried the craft halfway across the bank before breaking and receding. There was a scrape of sand and stone against the hull, and for a heartbeat Castella thought they would be marooned. Then the boat's momentum took them skidding and scratching the last of the way and into the sea beyond.

Araline summoned up another wave, and the boat sped off across the silver ripple of the bay.

Alas, the maneuver bought them only a moment's breathing space. Due to the size of the *Destiny*'s keel, the Squalls couldn't use the same route without running aground. But most of the islets in these parts were barely a stone's throw across, meaning Tempest could simply steer around the nearest one before continuing the chase.

Castella's boat rounded a promontory. To either side were forested shorelines, in front, the corpse of the copper dragon beached on the Cross. Castella grimaced. *Great.* Somehow she and Araline had managed to steer their boat in a circle. All that time, and all those arrows dodged, to get precisely nowhere. In a way, that summed up Castella's life to this point.

Another arrow thumped into the boat, and she crouched low. From the *Destiny* came calls for them to surrender. This was the end of the road, Castella realized. There was nowhere left to run. Her only chance at survival lay in dumping the flask of dragon blood in the bay and hoping she and Araline could slip away while Tempest looked for it. And he *would* look for it, she knew. Because while Castella had left four other flasks on the beach, their riches would never satisfy the Squall krel. He was the sort of man who would toss a sovereign into a wishing well to win his heart's desire, then climb down afterward to retrieve the coin.

"Head for the dragon," Castella told Araline.

The mage changed course as instructed.

An arrow whined past, close enough for Castella to feel the wind of its flight against her cheek. No more putting this off. She stood to face the *Destiny* and held the flask up high to catch the crew's attention.

"You want this?" she shouted. "Go get it!"

Then she hurled the flask as far as she could over the port rail. It plopped into the bay and disappeared beneath the waves before bobbing back to the surface.

Immediately the *Destiny* turned in that direction.

"Now go!" Castella said to Araline. "Give it everything you've got!"

"And here I'd been taking it easy up to now," Araline grumbled. Still she managed an extra burst of pace that set the wind rushing in Castella's ears. Spray thrown up by the boat's passage was cool against her face.

Ahead, the dragon's carcass moved closer. It looked like a pile of copper coins in the shallows, and Castella thought of the fortune she had just thrown away. The Corinians in particular valued dragon blood as a poison, and as a means of summoning dragons at their whim. *A fool and her money are quickly parted*, Castella's mother would say, but Castella had never understood that adage. After all, if a fool were such a fool in truth, how had they come by their money in the first place?

She looked back at the *Destiny.* The ship weaved across the bay, seeking the flask. Castella thought you could see Tempest in what had once been her favourite spot on deck—at the starboard cathead. "Do you see it?" he was yelling to his companions, but evidently the response was not to his liking for heartbeats later there was a squeal and a splash as a crewman was pushed overboard for a closer look.

In front, the bronze dragon's carcass rose from the sea in a wall of glistening scales. Tracing the line of its spine was a ridge of triangular plates, hooked and tapering to points. "Stop us here," Castella told Araline.

"Are you kidding? Tempest could find the flask at any time!"

"I just want a moment."

Araline huffed her reluctance, but the wave beneath their boat subsided. As the fizz of water faded, Castella could hear more clearly the voices of the Squalls and the trumpeting of a distant dragon. The boat sat down on the swell.

On the *Destiny,* torches had been brought to the rails to

illuminate the sea. Two barges filled with sailors were lowered to the water to help in the search. They were looking in the wrong place, though. Castella had thrown the flask ten ship-lengths from the Squalls' position, and the wave of water-magic beneath the *Destiny* was washing the thing farther away with each heartbeat.

"Why are you grinning?" Araline asked her.

Castella hadn't realized she was until now. It was time to come clean to her friend. "Because even if Tempest finds the flask," she said, "he'll be in for a disappointment."

"How's that?"

"Before I threw the flask away, I emptied the dragon blood into the sea."

Araline slowly matched Castella's grin. "Nice," she said. Then her expression turned thoughtful. "But . . . if you poured the blood away, won't it draw more dragons to this place?"

"Dragons like that one over there, you mean?" Castella said, pointing to the beast now approaching from the west.

Covered in silver scales, it slipped silently from behind the cover of an islet. Above the waterline only the top of its head was visible, and the horns protruding from its brow cut through the waves like sharks' fins. So absorbed was the *Destiny*'s crew in looking for the flask, it took them a while to spot the creature. Panicked cries rang out, then shouts to flee. But the dragon had already closed half the distance to its target. The sea about it bulged.

Tempest didn't stay to rescue the men in his two barges. A wave of water-magic formed beneath the *Destiny*, and Castella scowled. If the dragon targeted the barges first, if would give the krel time to escape.

But the beast did not go for the barges first. Instead it flashed toward the *Destiny*, passing between the smaller craft and setting them rocking. The silver flicker of its body seemed to fill the bay. With the glimmers on the water, it was hard to tell where the dragon ended and the reflections of moonlight began. From the *Destiny* came calls to speed up, pleas to the Sender for help.

The dragon lowered its head and rammed the ship beam-on. There was a splintering crack, a chorus of screams. The *Destiny* tipped drunkenly to starboard, the wave beneath it dissolving to foam.

Castella gave a contented sigh and settled on the boat's oar-bench. And to think just heartbeats ago she'd been the one facing death. There was nothing like the feeling of avoiding an appointment with the Lord of the Dead, especially when you sent a man like Tempest in your place.

Araline hesitated before sitting beside her. "Are we just going to watch?" she asked.

"Of course not," Castella replied. "I thought we'd break out the juripa spirits, make a proper celebration of it." Never mind the money from the dragon blood, she could have made a fortune by selling tickets to watch this.

The dragon slammed its tail onto the *Destiny*'s main deck. Splinters flew. The ship tilted once more, and a dozen sailors were hurled into the sea. They started thrashing through the waves toward the nearest islet.

"Odd time to go swimming," Castella said.

Araline nodded. "Do you think they know there's a dragon in the water?"

"The signs are all there."

Castella felt an unwelcome prickle from her conscience at the thought of all the sailors that would die this day. But they had chosen their side when they picked Tempest for a captain. Indeed, she was more saddened by the fate of the *Destiny* itself. She had been there nine months ago when Tempest seized the ship from a gang of Mellikian privateers, even led her own boarding party against the enemy quarterdeck. Strange how she missed those days. For a brief period, every dawn had marked the start of a new adventure, and Tempest had been a man to share it with.

Aboard the *Destiny*, three brave souls grabbed boarding pikes and charged the dragon. Their weapons deflected off the creature's armoured plates with a tortured screech of metal. The beast seemed not to notice. It brought its tail whipping down again. It tangled in the rigging, and the *Destiny* slewed round. Castella examined the newly revealed port side where the dragon had rammed it.

"You know what the sad part about this is?" she said.

"I'm struggling to see one myself."

"If Tempest dies, he'll never know that I tricked him by pouring the blood away."

Araline considered this. "That is a shame," she said finally. Then, "What is it about you and Tempest, anyway? I know you've got history, but it seems harsh to want him dead just because he left you."

Castella shot her a look. Did her friend think her so petty that she would desire a man's death out of spite alone? "He didn't leave me. *I* left *him*."

"What? Why?"

Castella looked away. In the bay, the dragon glittered like frost. "Because one of the crewmen he so famously keelhauled was a friend of mine."

He'd done it for no other reason than that he'd found Castella and Ven together one day, laughing and drinking. Mistaking it for something it wasn't, Tempest had flown into a rage. Castella could still remember the moment Ven was pulled from the sea following his keelhauling, half drowned and cut to slices by the barnacles on the hull. He'd been little more than a boy. Castella had been forced to watch as he was nailed to the main mast and left to bleed out. He'd cried and begged for his life. Through it all, Tempest had laughed—he and everyone else in his godforsaken crew.

Castella had tried telling Tempest the truth, but he hadn't believed her and he had cared even less. *I can't risk losing you*, he'd said. As if Castella had been his to lose. Later, he had locked her in his cabin together with the rest of his trophies. Every day he would come to inspect his prizes, until one night Castella had escaped by picking the cabin's lock and diving overboard.

Pushing the memories aside, Castella watched the dragon smash the *Destiny*'s mizzenmast with one sweep of a taloned foot. She wondered if Tempest now regretted his decision to search for the flask of blood. She had told him once that greed would be the death of him, and so it was about to prove. Even if Castella had had to give fate a nudge in that respect.

Araline regarded her shrewdly. "You planned this all along, didn't you? You never expected to get away with the dragon blood. You *wanted* Tempest to chase you so you could lure the dragon to him on open water."

Castella did not try to deny it. She felt bad about not telling Araline her plan beforehand, yet there was time to make it up to the mage. The flask of blood might be lost, but there should still be blood in the dragon's carcass. And if there wasn't, the rest of the creature's body remained valuable. Dragon meat was said to be a delicacy in the same way that everything that tasted ghastly was. Then there were the beast's scales to consider. Hacking them free was a task beyond Castella, but if she told Dresk about the carcass, he would send a few capable butchers to do the job. And reward her for the information too. Or reward Araline, more accurately.

The silver dragon crunched through the *Destiny*'s main yard, and the spar came crashing down. Most of the Squalls had already jumped overboard, but Castella could make out Tempest still on deck, struggling under the weight of a small chest. Even now he was trying to save his treasures. Castella forced a smile. Her plan had worked. How could she ever have doubted herself? There were enough people already to do the doubting for her.

Just then, Araline's gaze fixed on something in the distance. "Hey," she said. "You see that island over there? The one with the hill?"

"What about it?"

"That stone at the top—that looks a bit like the Cross, doesn't it?"

It did, Castella decided. Same height, same jagged protrusions on either side. In fact, the more she studied it . . .

"It *is* the Cross!" Araline said.

Castella frowned, wondering why that mattered. Before, she'd assumed she and her friend had sailed in a circle, but who cared if they'd landed on another island instead of the Cross? Easy mistake to make when you were fleeing for your life in the darkness. Plus it would be simple to retrace their steps to the island later.

Something niggled her, though, and it took her a heartbeat to chase the worry down.

She felt her guts twist.

Because if the Cross was over there, the body of the dead dragon would be there too. Which meant the carcass couldn't also be *behind* her now.

Her thoughts were interrupted by a slithering sound at her back, a low growl, then the splash and drip of something rising from the water. A wave cuffed the boat and carried it away from shore. But not far enough to Castella's mind. She could feel the chill of the dragon's breath against her neck, sense the weight of its regard.

She exchanged a look with Araline. Her friend was glaring at her like this was all Castella's fault, and this once she might even be right.

"Shit," Araline whispered.

That about summed it up, but this was hardly the time to get philosophical.

Castella's response was hushed but urgent. "Go, go, go!"

John Gwynne

This story is set in the Banished Lands, taking place some forty years before the events that occur in my series the Faithful and the Fallen. The protagonist in this short story is a young woman named Rhin, daughter to a dying king. She is intelligent and ambitious, and craves the praise of her father.

If you have read the Faithful and the Fallen, you will remember Rhin at a different stage in her life. She's a character who seems to have stood out to many of my readers. I thought it would be fun to write about an earlier, formative moment for her, a moment where she takes the first steps along a path that will lead her to greatness and fame, or perhaps the right word is *infamy*.

I'm honoured to be asked to contribute a story to *Unfettered III*. I love the ethos and heart behind the genesis of these anthologies, a coming together of creative people determined to help and support one another. It's a rare and precious thing in this world of cutthroat ambition.

Whether you are returning to the Banished Lands, or this is your first step into those dark, mist-shrouded lands, I hope that you enjoy this story.

Welcome to the Banished Lands . . .

John Gwynne

THE HEIR APPARENT

John Gwynne

Rhin contemplated the wooden board before her, the lattice-carved pattern upon it dotted with bone figures. They were polished and smooth from use. She pursed her lips, absently brushing a stray strand of her jet-black hair behind an ear as she leaned forward and placed a finger and thumb upon one of the figures. Then, deliberately, she raised her eyes to look at her opponent.

Gair. A giant of the Benothi Clan.

He was sat upon a stool on the far side of the board, a mass of meat and bone towering head and shoulders over Rhin like a granite cliff, small black eyes shadowed by his darkly brooding brows. A tattoo of vine and thorn curled around one wrist, spiralling up his muscle-slabbed arm. One hand tugged thoughtfully at his long, drooping moustache, black as the iron chains that bound his wrists and ankles.

Rhin moved her Brandub piece, a scrape of wood across bone.

"Do bhogadh," she said to the giant.

He sat there, his eyes shifting around the board, though the rest of him stayed still as stone, as if carved from the rock wall he was chained to.

"Your move," Rhin repeated to him, in Common Tongue this time, starting to doubt her Giantish.

"I know what you said, child," Gair rumbled, voice grating like grinding rocks.

I did say it true, then. And if I'd said it wrong, it would have been Gair's fault, not mine, for he is the one teaching me.

"Then you should make your move," Rhin said. *"Agus níl aon leanbh agam,"* she pronounced slowly, the words still strange to her, feeling like she had porridge in her mouth.

And I am no child.

"You *are* a child—" Gair rumbled, "you are like a spring flower, fresh-opened to the sun."

I am a woman grown, twenty-two summers I have drawn breath, learning all that this world has to offer.

"And what does that make you, then?" Rhin asked the giant.

He looked up from the Brandub board, intelligent eyes meeting hers.

"An oak," he said, "weathered and bowed by the unkind years." He reached out, moving his Chieftan a space from the safety of the board's centre towards the warrior Rhin had just moved.

Rhin arched an eyebrow.

"Moving towards danger," she said.

"What use is running," Gair replied.

"Your kin ran from here."

Gair raised his fists, a mass of hard-boned knuckles, and jangled the chains about them. Rhin heard the shifting of feet behind her, her shieldman moving closer, the rasp of a sword half-drawn.

Rhin raised a hand.

"Easy, Fallon," she breathed, knowing that her shieldman would take Gair's head off if he deemed the giant looked at her the wrong way, but knowing just as assuredly that he would obey her every word unthinkingly.

Her lips twitched in a satisfied smile as she heard Fallon's blade slip back into its scabbard, the whisper of his feet as he moved back into his normal stance.

"I did not run," Gair said, looking at the chains about his

wrists. His knuckles and the backs of his hands were notched and latticed with scars, evidence of how he had been put to the question when first taken prisoner after the Battle of Dun Vaner.

"Aye, and look where that got you," Rhin said, staring pointedly from his scars to the stone walls around them, the gaol that was Gair's home. Had been his home for five years.

The giant shrugged.

"Most of your kin ran, though. Fled, once they saw which way the battle was going."

Gair was silent a few moments, contemplating the board again.

"Ruad did not run," Gair's voice cracked the growing silence.

"No. But that is because he could not. My father slew your King." Rhin moved another warrior-figure, blocking Gair's Chieftan. He had five figures, one the Chieftan and four shieldmen. They began each game at the centre of the Brandub board, the goal of the game for the Chieftan to reach one of the edges. But first he had to find a way past Rhin's eight warriors that were arrayed around the board's rim.

"Ruad was not our King," Gair said as he moved one of his shieldmen to stand between his Chieftan and Rhin's warrior.

Rhin blinked and took her eyes from the board to stare at Gair. This was news to her. Enormous news, so great that she was not sure she believed the giant. Five years Gair had languished in this cell deep within the roots of Dun Vaner, the fortress of Rhin's father, Cambros the Bull, King of Cambren. He had taken this fortress from the Benothi giants, invaded their realm with his warband of heroes, and carved a bloody road to Dun Vaner. It was on the slopes before this very fortress that the last battle had been fought, ending when Cambros had fought and slain Ruad, King of the Benothi. Or so all had believed Ruad to be.

"You lie," Rhin said, arching one eyebrow.

Gair made a rumbling sound, much like the growl of a bear.

"I do not lie," he said. Raised his eyes to meet her. "I may hold on to the truth, let it seep out like the water that leaks between rocks into my cell, but I do not lie."

Rhin drew in a deep breath, trying to keep the excitement

she felt fluttering in her belly from showing in her voice.

"If not your King, who was Ruad?" Rhin said, masking the eagerness she felt for this new knowledge.

Knowledge is power, her father had told her many times. *Most battles are won here.* He had put a finger to his temple. *Long before a single blade is drawn. Knowledge is power, as is the wisdom and cunning to use it. Your brothers Ard and Cadlas are mighty warriors, skilled in battle, but you, my precious Rhin, you are the thinker.*

Rhin's heart swelled at the memory of her father's praise. She pushed it away, focusing on the giant in front of her, a swell of excitement rippling through her veins at the hint of what he had just said.

New knowledge. New power.

She had been visiting Gair in his gaol for many years, at first drawn by her inquisitive nature, just wanting to see and talk with a living, breathing giant. Most of the ones she had seen had lain dead upon battlefields. But somewhere along the way she had come to enjoy Gair's company. She believed him when he said he did not lie; she saw no falsity in him, a truth in him that was rare to see. At least, in her experience as daughter of Cambros, princess and heir to the throne of Cambren, most who spoke to her did not speak so plainly, and all had their own agenda. Gair was not like that, or so she judged, and she felt herself a good judge of people, had always found it easy to see to their hearts, their dreams and desires writ plain in their unsaid words. But that did not mean that Gair told her everything.

What other truths do you hold secret in that head of yours?

"I have been a friend to you. Treated you with kindness." Rhin looked at the Brandub board between them, a gift from her to Gair.

"Aye. You gave a great gift, but you also received one in return."

They had bargained truths before.

Rhin had quickly suspected that Gair was a deep vein of knowledge, one that she wanted to tap and mine. With kindness and companionship she had coaxed many secrets from Gair. The greatest one had been in return for this Brandub board. Gair had lived in Dun Vaner for many years before the coming of her father, and so he knew more about it than anyone else. He had told Rhin of hidden passages that threaded through the fortress, a secret tapestry that Rhin had used to great advantage, sitting and listening to her father's council meetings, to her brothers' hopes and dreams when they visited Dun Vaner.

And in those passages she had found something. Her hand drifted to a pocket inside her sable-trimmed cloak.

Not yet.

Gair's eyes shifted to Fallon behind Rhin's shoulder.

"You can speak plainly to me," Rhin said. "Fallon is my man, loyal unto death. He will speak nothing of what you say here. Will you, Fallon?"

"Not a word, my lady," Fallon said behind her.

Gair shrugged, a rippling of muscle. "Ruad was my Chieftan," he said. "The Lord of Dun Vaner, and the lands for many leagues around this fortress."

"But not King of the Benothi giants?"

"No."

"Who is your King, then?" Rhin asked, almost holding her breath with anticipation, desperate to have this knowledge, this token of power that she could take and gift to her father, once more proving her worth.

"Not King. Queen," Gair said.

Queen. Rhin felt her breath hitch in her chest. *A Queen, as I will be one day.*

"And this Queen's name?"

Gair lifted one of his carved bone shieldmen from the board and swept one of Rhin's figures from the table, opening a route to the board's edge, a glimpse of victory.

"Nemain," the giant breathed.

"Nemain," Rhin whispered. Frowned. "Not . . ."

"Aye. Nemain, once-wife of Skald, the First-King," Gair growled.

Rhin laughed. "You play with me. That was over a thousand years ago. I know you giants are long-lived, but . . ."

"Closer to two thousand years," Gair said.

"Do not treat me as a fool," Rhin snapped, a hint of iron creeping into her voice. "You may think me a fresh-faced spring flower, but I am no one's fool."

"I do not think you are," Gair said.

He is telling the truth, or what he thinks to be the truth, Rhin thought as she studied Gair's face, his eyes. *Nemain, Queen and wife to Skald, the first giant King. Two thousand years . . .*

She felt a thrill in her chest at that thought, her father's face filling her mind, once so strong, but now lined and stooped with age. *Could I save him? Help him live a thousand years? Two thousand? And for me. Old age, weakness, frailty, and wrinkles. Ugh. I do not want that to happen to me. To stay young and strong forever, now that would be something wonderful. Two thousand years . . .*

"How?" she said.

"I can see this is something you would like to know more of," Gair said, the hint of a smile twitching his long moustache.

Bollocks, Rhin thought, scowling in her mind. *I must learn to hide my emotions.*

"I feel that I am giving without receiving," Gair continued.

"You are in no position to bargain with me," Rhin said, looking at his chains.

"Not bargaining. Exchanging. A trade. We all want . . ."

"And what is it that you want?" Rhin asked, too quickly she knew, revealing her eagerness.

"To see the sky again."

Rhin let the silence grow, moved a warrior on the Brandub board, flanking Gair's Chieftan.

"I could do that for you," she said. "If . . ."

"Ask your questions," Gair rumbled, failing to hide the hint of longing in his voice.

Rhin made sure the glow of satisfaction she felt in her chest did not touch her face.

"How is Nemain still alive?"

"She drank from the Starstone Cup," Gair said.

"A faery tale," Rhin said dismissively with a wave of her hand.

"No. The Starstone was no faery tale. Why else did the Giants sunder into Clans? It was the Starstone, forged into treasures, that set us at each other's throats."

Rhin had heard these tales before, of the Starstone that fell from the heavens, of the Seven Treasures forged from them, of the following wars. One of the treasures had been a cup, fabled to have given health and long life to all those that drank from it. She had never thought of them as real before. Not until now.

Nemain, two thousand years . . .

"Where is this Starstone Cup?" Rhin asked.

"Ah, for that, I would need more than to just see the sky."

This is the real Brandub game, played with flesh and blood.

Rhin regarded the giant, delight coursing through her at the thrill of the game made real.

He wants his freedom.

And now I make my move.

"I remember my friends," Rhin said, holding Gair's gaze, the Brandub board forgotten. "If I were Queen and you were to tell me where I could find this Starstone Cup, help me make it mine, I would set you free."

She saw it in his eyes, a brief moment of hope, quickly masked, and she knew that she had him.

"*If*." Gair rumbled. "So much imagined and so little realised within that small word."

Ha, he still seeks to play this game, as if he can change the inevitable.

"*When* I am Queen," Rhin said.

"*If* you are Queen, *if* these chains are gone, with the sky above me and grass beneath my boots," Gair said, "*then* I will tell you where the Starstone Cup is to be found."

Rhin blew out a long breath. "You have a deal," she said.

Gair smiled, lines in his face deep as old leather. Another flare of the emotion that was his weakness. Hope.

"When," he agreed.

Rhin thought on that, felt a swell of pleasure at her victory, but at the same time a sadness. *That would mean that Father would be dead, that I had not saved him.* The thought of that settled into her, sinking deep, emotions swirling. *But I would be his legacy, would rule this realm for two thousand years. More.* The thought was intoxicating, and she imagined the day when her father named her heir apparent, the future ruler of Cambren when he was gone.

That is the key. The day my life will change.

She smiled. Then remembered what she had originally intended to talk with Gair about today.

"Until then, there is something else," Rhin said, reaching within her cloak. "I found something," she lowered her voice to a whisper, not that anyone was listening; Fallon always made sure of that. "Inside the tunnels."

"What?" Gair said, a flare of interest in his eyes.

"This," Rhin said, pulling a rolled sheaf of parchments from her cloak, tied with rotting linen. She untied it, carefully unrolling the parchment and angling it for Gair to see. It was covered with thick-scrawled runes. "I can read some of it," Rhin said, "after the Giantish you have taught me, but I cannot read it all."

Most of it.

Gair must have been reading from the parchment, for his lips were moving. He hissed, tugged at his moustache.

"What is it?" Rhin asked him.

Gair was silent.

"Remember, I am the one who will set you free," Rhin reminded him.

He looked up at her, then back at the parchments.

"A part-copy of an ancient book," Gair said. "Telling of our history, the Sundering, our Clans, and . . ."

"Yes?" Rhin prompted.

"The Earth Power," Gair breathed.

The Earth Power. I knew there was more to these parchments than cold history. What a day this is turning out to be.

The Earth Power was another faery tale, Rhin had thought. From the old sagas where some had learned how to control the elements: wind, water, fire, and earth. And sometimes even people, with the help of some blood and hair . . .

"Teach me," she said, almost a snarl.

Rhin strode along the corridor, Fallon's ever-present footsteps echoing behind her. She tutted at warriors who crowded the corridor, slowing her way. Many wore cloaks of red, men and women from Narvon, her brother Cadlas's realm, and others wore grey, marking their allegiance to Rhin's brother Ard of Ardan.

My beloved brothers and their retinues, gathered here like carrion-birds swooping above a battlefield, waiting to feast on the dead.

Because my father is dying.

Rhin turned and marched up a stairwell, moving swiftly up the large, giant-built steps. Her father, Cambros, King of Cambren, had sent for her, and something in the trembling in her blood told her that this meeting was important.

He is going to announce to my brothers that I am his heir.

Excitement gave her feet wings, and before she knew it she was marching along the corridor that led to her father's chambers.

A warrior stood at the doorway, tall and wide, thick with muscle and no visible neck that Rhin could see. His eyes fixed on Rhin.

"Dow," Rhin acknowledged her father's first-sword, greatest warrior in the realm of Cambren. With a grunt and a nod of his head, he opened the door for her but stepped in front of Fallon. Rhin waved a hand at her shieldman, leaving her red-haired warrior in the corridor with the mountain that was Dow.

I will tell Father of my news, of Gair's revelations.

She felt a taste of the satisfaction she knew his pride would give her, discovering she had extracted such secrets from a prisoner who had spent five years in Cambros's gaol, and one who had long ago been put to the question, yet still kept his secrets.

"Who is it?" a voice said from deep within the chamber.

The room was shrouded in darkness, a half-light from dying embers glowing in a firepit that only made the shadows feel darker and deeper. Rhin marched to shuttered windows and cast them open, a shaft of pale spring sunshine piercing the shadows. A cold breeze coiled into the room, stirring the ash in the firepit and causing the embers to flare.

"There you are," Rhin said, approaching her father.

He was sat in a high-backed chair, sunken into it. His face was pale, skin tight and pallid against the arch of his bones, a sheen of sweat covering him.

"Ah, it's you," said Cambros the Bull.

He did not look much like a bull now, or a King. Rhin felt the breath in her lungs hitch at the sight of her father. She had hardly seen him the last two moons, spending so much of her time with Gair since she had shown the giant her secret parchment. She had learned much.

But at what cost?

She had long known that her father was dying, had the wasting disease, but he had gone on for so long with no obvious change that it had almost felt like it was a lie. As if it were something that other people just said, a habit.

But now he sat before Rhin as if his body had been ravaged by some vast, cruel pestilence, his skin loose, hanging on his frame like a shrivelled old cloak. Where once his shoulders and chest were dense with muscle, now he looked like some desiccated half-corpse. His hair hung lank in sweat-soaked clumps across his face.

Worry and guilt swept through Rhin in equal measure, all thoughts of her discoveries with Gair falling away as she stared at Cambros.

"Oh, Father," Rhin said as she sank to her knees before him, clasping one of his hands between hers.

"Ah, my Rhin," Cambros breathed, phlegm rattling in his throat. He reached his other hand out and stroked her cheek, brushed a tear away.

"Death comes for us all, no escaping it," he said, mouth twisting in what Rhin realised was an attempt at a smile. "No point hiding from it. Now stand, I've wanted to see you, thought you would have come sooner."

"I've . . ."

Been busy. The words caught in her throat, none of her discoveries with Gair feeling important now. Just wasted time.

"I'm sorry," she said, rising, trying to brush hair from her father's face. Some of it came away in a clump and she stared at it in revulsion.

I should have moved quicker, pushed Gair for his information about the Starstone Cup. Maybe I could have saved him.

"There is something I have to tell you," Cambros said, his words turning to a wracking cough. He curled over, spraying blood-flecked spittle. He wiped his chin with the back of his hand.

Rhin stroked his hair, a hiss escaping her lips as more hair came away.

"Shave it off," Cambros muttered.

"What?" Rhin said.

"Shave it off. I will stand before you and your brothers on the morrow. I would not have them see me like this."

"Yes, Father," Rhin said, moving to find a bowl and fresh water.

She dabbed his face with a wet cloth, washing the blood and phlegm away.

"Use my knife," Cambros said, a hand reaching to his belt.

"I have my own, Father," Rhin said, drawing a blade from her belt.

"Is it sharp enough?" Cambros wheezed.

"Oh, aye," Rhin said, knowing it was razor-keen. She sharpened it each day.

Slowly, methodically, she cut away clumps of her father's hair, dropping it to pool about her feet. Once she'd sheared it close to his head, she washed the blade and began scraping the stubble from his scalp.

"I summoned you for a reason," Cambros said to her as she worked.

"Uh," Rhin grunted, focusing on her handiwork.

"I am dying, as you can well see," Cambros said. "It will not be long now." Rhin began to say something, but he silenced her with a grunt and a flick of his hand. "I will announce the heir to my throne on the morrow," Cambros said, "to you and your brothers."

Rhin's methodical scraping paused, a flutter of excitement in her belly rearing for a fleeting moment over the nausea she felt at finding her father in this condition. With an act of will, she resumed shaving her father's head.

"I will name Cadlas my heir," Cambros said.

A hitched breath as Rhin froze, a trickle of blood running down her father's scalp where her hands had twitched and she'd cut him.

"Cadlas," Rhin said, hearing her own voice as if through someone else's ears.

I was to be your heir. How can you name Cadlas, the sweaty oaf?

"Aye, your brother," Cambros said.

"You have always told me that I would be your heir. That Cambren would be mine to rule," Rhin said.

Cambros remained silent.

"Why?" Rhin whispered.

Cambros took a rattling, indrawn breath.

"He is my firstborn, oldest and most battle-hardened. And he is used to ruling, has done well with his fledgling kingdom of Narvon."

"Narvon," Rhin sneered. "He did not even name his kingdom after himself, but instead called it after his sow of a wife. How can you respect or trust such a fool?"

"He has done well, Narvon is thriving, and that *sow* of his is with child," Cambros said, a spark of his old self in his voice, though he trailed off, bent over coughing. Blood was on the back of his hand when he finished. He twisted in his chair to look up at Rhin. "Cadlas will have an heir, whereas you will not even consider a husband."

"They are all idiots," Rhin said, thinking of the many suitors that had called upon her.

"To secure a Kingdom, to establish a dynasty, you must have heirs. I thought I had taught you, prepared you, Rhin, but you stumble at the first stone. When you rule, you do not wed for love or passion. You wed for power, for the continuation of your name."

I do not need a husband, Rhin thought, *some foul-breathed, sweaty-handed half-wit who would expect me to bear him children and sit meekly by while he runs my kingdom his way.*

No. I will rule, my way.

"It should be me," Rhin said. A silence, only broken by the crackling embers on the fire. "I will take a husband, if that is what is required of me," she added, trying to keep the sullenness from her voice.

"It is . . . too late," Cambros said. "I do not have long left, I can feel death's cold breath on my neck."

"Father, please—"

"No," Cambros snapped. "You have failed at the first. . . . It cannot be you now. There is not enough time, and I must be sure of my Kingdom's fate. Cadlas will rule."

Rhin felt a cold anger filling her belly, coiling through her veins. She looked down at her father, a sad, pitiful figure where not so long ago he had been so strong and powerful. Her knife hovered over his head, Cambros's hair and blood on the blade from where she'd nicked his scalp. Options ran through her mind, the consequences snaking out in different directions like the threads on a spider's web.

Her knuckles tightened on the hilt of her knife.

"I am sorry, my precious Rhin," Cambros wheezed. "It is for the greater good of Cambren."

A long, sucked-in breath, Rhin's hand and blade trembling, and then she turned and walked away, her knife still clutched in her hand, not even bothering to clean the blade.

Rhin entered her father's chamber, her shieldman Fallon at her back. It was much changed from the day before. Bright spring sunshine filled the room, and there were a number of people milling around Cambros; her two brothers, Cadlas and Ard, both with a small retinue around them. Narva, Cadlas's wife, stood with Rhin's brother, her belly swollen with child. Narva smiled warmly at Rhin as she entered the chamber, nodding a greeting.

Rhin looked away from Narva, resisting the urge to curl her lip. She saw that her father was still sat in his chair, though he, too, looked different from the day before. He had been washed and was dressed in clean, fine clothing, wearing a green wool tunic braided at neck and sleeves, a bull embroidered upon one side of his chest, a broken branch upon the other, reminder of how he had slain Ruad, King of the Giants, to win his kingdom.

Though now I know that Ruad was no king, just the Lord of this fortress and the lands round about.

But no one else need know that. Knowledge is power, and I will hoard it like gold.

Rhin's brothers Cadlas and Ard saw her enter, Cadlas waving an arm in the air.

"Finally," Cadlas said. "Now we can continue. Rhin is here, Father," he said, reaching down to squeeze Cambros's arm.

"Ah, good," Cambros said. He smiled weakly at Rhin, who returned a smile with as much warmth as she could muster.

"You know why I have summoned you here," Cambros said. "I am dying, will soon make my walk across the Bridge of Swords, and so I must know that Cambren, my legacy, is left in safe hands. We fought hard to earn these lands, and I would know that our family will rule them long after I am gone."

"We conquered the west together, Father," Cadlas said, "and now we rule the west together. United we cannot be defeated. Besides, there is no one left to challenge us. Cambren will be in safe hands."

Does he already know? Has father already told him?

"No matter who you choose to sit on Cambren's throne when . . ." Cadlas's words stuttered, and Rhin was surprised to see what resembled genuine emotion twist his features and choke his voice.

"When I am gone," Cambros said the difficult words for his son. "Go on."

"Whether you choose Ard, Rhin, or myself, know that Cambren will be safe."

He does not know, then, or he is a better liar than I give him credit for.

Cambros patted his son's hand.

"So, I will say this now, before the plague that ravages my body addles my mind," Cambros said. "I will choose one of you, my children, to rule in Cambren when I am gone. You are all worthy, but the one I have chosen I deem best equipped for the task."

A cough rattled in Cambros's throat, but it passed and the dying King sat straighter. He looked at his three children, holding each one in turn in his gaze. "There will be no challenging my decision, either while I still draw breath, or after. My word on this is binding, and you will swear an oath before me and these other witnesses to honour it."

Cadlas and Ard nodded.

"I swear it," Cadlas said.

"And I too," Ard said.

They all looked at Rhin.

"My daughter," Cambros said, his eyes, still bright with intelligence, bore into her.

"I swear it, Father," she said.

"Huh, good," Cambros grunted and nodded to himself.

"Then know this, my kin; the one I would choose to rule in my place . . ." He paused, ran a hand across his shaven scalp and picked at the scab that marked where Rhin's grip had wavered as she'd been shaving her father's head.

Rhin's hand slipped inside her cloak, her fingers finding what she was looking for, cold clay, something wiry wound within it.

"Fola m'athair, gruaig as a chuid feoil, fonn mo ordú," she whispered.

Blood of my father, hair from his flesh, heed my command.

Her fist closed tighter around the clay effigy, the hair and blood of her father that she'd taken from her knife blade bound within it.

"Is é Rhin mo oidhre, suífidh ar mo ríchathaoir," she breathed, quieter than a sigh.

Rhin shall be my heir, shall sit upon my throne.

Cambros's lips twisted and he blinked, a shocked expression flitting across his face, quickly gone. His jaw worked, no sound coming from his throat.

Rhin muttered under her breath, her brother Ard's eyes narrowing as he looked from Cambros to Rhin.

"Rhin shall be my heir, shall sit upon my throne," Cambros said, the words escaping his mouth in a flurry.

Gasps around the room, Cadlas frowning, the broad smile upon Narva's face withering.

"Thank you, Father," Rhin said, stepping forward. "I am honoured by your faith in me." She stood before Cambros, who stared up at her. Again, his jaw worked, but no words came from his mouth.

She bent down to him and kissed his cheek.

"Cease your struggling, Father, it is for the greater good," she whispered in his ear. She felt the muscles in Cambros's throat working but knew that nothing could now come from his mouth that contradicted her will.

"My father, Cambros the Bull, has spoken," Rhin said as she straightened and faced her brothers. Cadlas was distracted by Narva hissing in his ear, but Ard was staring at her, frowning.

"We swore an oath to abide by his word. His will," Rhin said, meeting her brothers' eyes, daring either of them to oppose her. She knew Fallon was close behind her, could almost sense the trembling in his muscles as the possibility of violence reared in his blood.

"Are your oaths worth anything?" she challenged her brothers.

Cadlas looked away first, gave a sharp nod.

Ard remained silent.

"Brother," Rhin prompted him.

"I gave my oath," Ard eventually said, "I will keep it."

"Good," Rhin said and turned her back on her brothers, marching from the room. Fallon's footsteps followed her. In the corridor outside, another three hard-eyed men waited, mail-clad with swords at their hips, men she trusted, ready in case Cadlas and Ard had made different choices.

I hope for the best, and prepare for the worst, Rhin thought, allowing herself a smile as she strode down the corridor, Fallon and the others falling in behind her.

She led them deeper into the fortress, through wide, high-arched corridors, deeper into the rock-hewn belly of Dun Vaner, down spiralled stairs until water dripped from cracks in the wall and smoke from guttering torches was thick in the air.

Eventually Rhin stopped before a wide, iron-banded door.

"Keys," Rhin said. Fallon paused a moment, looking into Rhin's eyes.

"Are you sure, my Queen?" he said.

My Queen. I like the sound of that.

"It is the only way," she said to her shieldman. "Do it."

Fallon unlocked the door before her, swinging it open.

Gair the giant sat in the gaol before her, shackled to the wall by wrist and ankle.

Rhin strode in, her cloak swirling around her like mist, and stood before the giant.

"Are you my friend?" Rhin said to Gair.

He stared at her a long, timeless moment.

"Aye, Rhin fresh-flower. I am your friend." A half-smile cracked the lines of his face.

Rhin gave an almost imperceptible nod and then she walked to the far side of the room and reached her hand into a small alcove, fumbled a moment, then felt the mechanism and pulled on it. With a hiss and a puff of dust, the outline of a door appeared. She pushed it, revealing a dark tunnel.

"What are you doing?" Gair said, eyes wide.

"I made you a promise," Rhin said.

"When you are Queen," Gair breathed.

"Just so," Rhin replied, unable to keep the smile from her face. She gestured to Fallon, who unlocked the giant's shackles from the wall. Her other guards filled the chamber, tense and alert, hands on the hilts of their swords.

With a scrape of iron on stone, Gair stood on unsteady legs and stepped away from the wall he had been shackled to for five long years. His ankles and wrists were still bound, but this small step towards freedom was like an elixir to Gair. He stood straighter, his shoulders seeming wider, muscles flexing.

One of Rhin's guards tied a length of rope to the chain hanging between the iron collars that bound Gair's wrists and gave it a tug to check it was secure.

"Are you ready?" Rhin asked him.

"For what?" the giant breathed, unbelieving.

"To see the sky again," Rhin answered.

Gair's lips trembled.

"Aye," he rumbled.

"Torch," Rhin snapped, and Fallon took a lit torch from a wall sconce, the shieldman leading the way into the tunnel. Rhin followed, her guards wrapping around Gair and leading him by the rope, and then they were all marching through the encroaching darkness. The torch-light flickered before and behind, revealing rough-hewn walls slick with water, sounds both muted and echoing.

Fallon led them unerringly through a labyrinth of tunnels, wide-carved stairs winding downward, deep into the heart of the mountain slope that Dun Vaner was built upon, and then slowly they began to rise. Fallon had explored these tunnels with Rhin and knew where she wished to go.

The tunnel came to an abrupt end, a wall of stone before them. Rhin stepped past Fallon and found the hidden alcove, releasing the mechanism, and with a hiss of dust the outline of a door stood before them. Rhin pushed and daylight flooded the tunnel, making her blink.

She stepped out into a sheltered glade, wind-blasted hawthorns about them. Through the leafless branches Rhin glimpsed Dun Vaner's dark walls and tower, a sheer-blue sky beyond.

Rhin glanced back to see the bulk of Gair following, looming head and shoulders over the three warriors guarding him. His eyes watered as he stepped out into the daylight, but regardless of the discomfort, he looked up at the sky, a smile splitting his face. He stood still, closed his eyes a long moment, a cold breeze from the mountains stirring his black hair.

"Ach, but that is better than silver," he rumbled, opening his eyes to look about the glade.

"Where is it?" Rhin said.

Gair stared at her.

"The Starstone Cup. Our deal. Your freedom for the cup."

Fallon dangled the keys to Gair's shackles.

"The Starstone Cup," Gair echoed.

"Yes. Tell me where it is, and you shall be moved to a room with a window. If I find it where you say it is, then you shall have your freedom."

"For friends, that does not sound very trusting," Gair said.

"I am a friend, but not a fool," Rhin sighed.

Gair grabbed at the rope attached to his shackles, heaving the warrior holding it towards him. He seized the man's head in his two huge fists and gave a savage twist, a crack as the warrior's neck snapped, and Gair dropped the twitching corpse to the ground.

"Fool enough to bring me out here," Gair said, reaching down to draw the dead man's sword. It looked little more than a long knife in his hand.

The rasp of iron on leather as Fallon and the other two warriors drew their blades and threw themselves at the giant.

Gair shuffled to the side, his ankles still bound together, but somehow he kept his balance and swung and chopped as he moved, deflecting one blade and cutting into the shoulder of another warrior, ring-mail and blood spraying, the warrior staggering and falling.

Gair lunged for Rhin.

She had stood frozen, unbelieving for long moments, but now she stumbled away, the flat of Gair's sword grazing her head, sending her crashing to the ground, Gair lumbering towards her, towering over her.

Then Fallon was behind Gair, a slash and the giant screamed, fell to one knee, dropping his sword, the other warrior still standing, lunging at the giant, blade swinging high and down. Gair caught the blade in the chain between his wrists, launched himself forward, crashing into the warrior, and the two of them were rolling away from Fallon, coming to a stop with Gair's chains wrapped around the warrior's throat, his eyes bulging, face purple as Gair twisted his grip and iron links crushed the warrior's windpipe.

Then Fallon was on him, his sword stabbing and slashing, but Gair was using the body of the man in his grip as a shield, slowly clambering back to his feet.

Rhin dragged herself to her knees, felt blood running from the cut on her head into one of her eyes. She shook her head, staggered to her feet.

Gair was back on his feet, sparks flying as he fended off Fallon's blows with the iron chain hanging between his wrists. Then Fallon stumbled, his foot snaring on a tree root, and Gair was lashing out, fist crunching into Fallon's face, blood and teeth flying, Fallon crashing to the ground. Gair cast the dead warrior away and stood over Fallon, breathing heavily.

"HOLD," Rhin screamed, taking a staggering step towards them both.

Gair glanced at her, a grin twitching his mouth.

"You command me no longer," the giant said, lifting a boot to stamp on Fallon's head. But then he froze, one boot in the air, trembling as if pressing against some unseen force as it hovered over Fallon.

"Do I not?" Rhin said, her hand coming out from her cloak, clutching a clay figure, black hairs embedded within. She held it up before her for Gair to see.

"No!" the giant gasped.

"Step away," Rhin snarled.

Gair trembled, still trying to bring his boot down on Fallon, who lay dazed at his feet, but no matter how hard he tried, the giant could not finish his act. With a bellow of rage, Gair staggered away from Fallon, stood with his chest heaving, blood leaking from a dozen small wounds.

Rhin glared at the giant, feeling a cold hatred swell in her belly. She had thought, hoped, that Gair was her friend. Five years spent visiting with him, building what she thought was a friendship. She could have commanded him to tell her all he knew, used the figure back in the gaol, but she had wanted to know—part of her hoping, longing, for a genuine friend. Someone she could trust to stand at her side. Part of her had believed that Gair truly considered her his friend.

He was right, I was a fool.

No longer.

"I had hoped for an ally in you," Rhin said. "A new age, where giant and humankind worked together."

Gair just glowered at Rhin. His fingers twitched as he started to reach for her, his efforts frustrated by Rhin's clay effigy.

"That sword," Rhin said casually, "pick it up."

Gair bent and took a sword from the ground, one of the fallen warriors.

"You have slain two of my men, maybe three," Rhin said, glancing at the warrior on the ground with a bloody rent in his shoulder. "Almost killed Fallon, my shieldman."

She took a long, shuddering breath to control her anger.

"You would have made a good friend and a better guardian." She shook her head. "And now you have thrown it all away."

Gair's lips moved but Rhin waved her hand.

"Silence. Do not bother with your lies," she said. Gair's mouth snapped shut. "All I want from you is the location of the Starstone Cup. Where is it?"

"Lost," Gair said.

Rhin felt a wave of rage.

I want that cup. Must have it.

"Lost where?"

"No one knows," Gair said. "It disappeared in the retreat to the North."

"It is true, then, that you giants had it. That it grants long life."

"Aye, that was all true," Gair rumbled.

"You must know where it is, where it was lost."

Gair shrugged. "I do not."

Rhin sighed.

"Then you are no more use to me. Thank you for the lesson," she said.

Gair's eyes asked the question that his lips were forbidden to speak.

What lesson.

"I shall not be so quick to trust to friendship again. Now, take that sword and cut your throat."

The giant's eyes flared, the sword in his grip rising, muscles in his arms shaking, trembling as he fought to keep the sharp iron from his throat, but it moved ever closer, until the tip touched his flesh. A trickle of blood ran down his neck.

"Please," Gair breathed.

Rhin lifted the clay figure.

"Do it," she snarled.

Gair's muscles spasmed involuntarily and the sword sank into his neck, a pinprick at first, then deeper, Gair struggling, fighting with all of his will. Sweat dripped from his nose. And then with a shriek he rammed the blade home, deep into his neck, then ripped it free, blood jetting. Gair swayed and crashed to his knees, staring at Rhin, then slowly toppled onto his back, eyes glazing.

Rhin stood over Gair's body and watched as life fluttered and left him, a widening pool of blood spreading around him as it soaked into the ground.

"I told you I would set you free."

Deborah A. Wolf

"DANCING ON THE EDGE" IS A STORY THAT IS NEAR AND DEAR TO MY dark little heart. It details a very small but important slice of backstory for Yaela, whose presence is felt but not fully explored in my epic fantasy series The Dragon's Legacy.

Yaela's relegation to a background character is a deliberate choice on my part, and on hers as well. Born to royalty, raised in splendor and love for the first few years of her life, she finds herself outcast in a world that fears and misunderstands her magic, her appearance, her gender, and everything else about her.

This loathing of "other" is a common theme in my stories. Humans are driven by antipathy to act monstrously toward those we see as not like ourselves, and in doing so, we all too often create the very monsters we fear.

Yaela, like many of the more interesting characters I write and love, has done some truly terrible things in her life. It would be easy, if a reader were to sit down and peruse a list of these irredeemable acts, to condemn her as a villain and root for her demise.

And yet—as so many humans in literature and in the real world—Yaela is driven primarily not by fear, or bitterness, or an understandable thirst for vengeance, but by love. This love makes her relatable,

and admirable,
and very, *very*
dangerous.

Deborah A. Wolf

DANCING ON THE EDGE

A Story of the Illindriverse

Deborah A. Wolf

Akari Sun Dragon turned his murderous gaze from us, and the land sighed a great red-dust sigh of relief. I sighed as well, wishing that I might hope for such respite; the world had survived the killing heat and would thrive during the soft hours of dark, but I had no such assurance. For a girl such as I, dancing on the Edge of the Seared Lands, death burns down from the sky during the day and crawls up from the earth at night.

They would be here soon, men of the Edge come to pick at us girls like carrion-birds picking at a corpse. There was no hope for me. But my sister, my Haviva, might yet survive. So I woke her, sleepy-bones, before the others roused. I stole water to clean her face, her hands, her feet. I worked the last drops of sweet oil into her scalp and combed her magnificent hair till it sprang up all about her face, a great soft shadow. I smoothed oil across her lids to make her eyes shine, and a smudge of dust beneath to hide the dark hollows of weariness, illness, and endless aching hunger.

Haviva was hugely pregnant, but she was beautiful. Perhaps

it would be enough. For myself, I dragged the comb through my shorter curls and shook the worst of the dirt from my rags. There was no hiding my eyes, was there? Or the stink.

There was nothing good to speak of, so we were silent.

The rest of Hadl's nag of wives woke and began their own pathetic ablutions. Ahda, I know, would have liked to scold me for using the last of our hair-oil, but I stared at her with my eyes of Pelang and she did not dare. None could blame a sister for looking out for herself in times like these.

Ahda: yes, that was her name. Someone should remember that. It is likely all that is left of her. Ahda, and Nnadira and Kamya, and then of course Haviva and me. We wives were five where once we had been a nag of twelve, and we were being driven closer to the edge of the Edge every night. Our idiot husband had gotten himself injured and was no longer able to keep a place for us in this world. The best any of the others could hope for was to be sold to some other idiot, and survive another day.

The best I might hope for, I with my cursed eyes and wicked tongue, was a quick and merciful death in a land where death is neither.

Our husband, Hadl, roused himself eventually, with a great moan, and the rest of the wives fluttered to his aid. I kept Haviva back with a hand on her shoulder, and pressed my last treasure to her lips: a prickly red sabra pear, dusty and wrinkled but still good. Let it nourish *her,* not him. I was done providing for a stinking lump of meat not fit to protect a territory.

Her eyes widened and she squeezed my hand, but bit the fruit in half and made me share. The flesh of the pear stung my mouth, sweet and tart. I kissed my sister on either cheek. We shared life; likely enough we would soon share death, as well.

"Leave off, you stupid *buta.*" Hadl's voice cracked like an old leather whip and he flapped his hands. The nag of wives scattered like roaches, startled by the sound of his voice. We had been long in silence, lest some other mahl find us and make an end to us; that he broke it now with a curse sent a shiver down my spine. "Leave off! Is there water? Give it to me. Is there food? No? What good are you, then? Stupid *buta*." He hauled himself to his feet, and the stink of rot preceded him. "You will bring me food before morning, if any of you are left, or so help me I will kill you all myself."

The others quailed, more out of habit than anything. I ignored his whining and his threats, and prepared to help my sister make the climb to the land above. The distance from our dirt floor to the surface was too short by far—the farther out on the Edge a mahl lives, the shallower the cracks run, and these cracks in the parched earth are all that shelter life in the Seared Lands from the harsh sun. Still, it was a hard climb for Haviva with her gravid belly. Let the other wives cater to Hadl; he was an empty man full of empty threats, stinking carrion that did not know when to shut up and be meat.

The same had been said of me, more than once. And yet here I was, breathing the cool night air, and where were those who had mocked me? Smoking bones under the sun, every one of them.

It was time to be seen; it was time to be sold.

It was time to dance.

The rest of the nag wiggled their hips at these low men, they flicked their eyes and jiggled their tits and made come-hither motions with their hands. Even Haviva swayed through the rituals of seduction, false as a man's heart, plodding around in slow and clumsy circles, belly big as a moon. But not I; I, who had been a student of the great Ruaz, who had learned to dance the color red before I was four years old and whose *kahi'o e' anna* had once made a king weep, kept my feet still and my heart still and glared at them all. It would be a cold day indeed before such as *I* danced for such as *them*.

I did not dance for them, and so they did not see me, these men from the Edge with an appetite for girl-flesh. They saw the others, though.

Nnadira was bought away first, and then Kamya. Ahda was last; she was attractive, but there was that spark of intelligence in her eye that no man wants to see. The girls' lives were sold cheaply enough, and their new men slid past me and my sister with their lazy eyes.

"And what of these two? You are ignoring my best stock!" Hadl grabbed a handful of my sister's hair and shook her head at them in rebuke. "Look at this face! These ripe mamouleh!"

"Look at that belly!" The other man mocked, and his companion snorted laughter. "You think I want to wait for your whelp to come, just so I can kill it? If I want a woman with a ruined body, I will ruin it myself."

"Keep the child then, or sell it," Hadl whined. "Sell her as a breeder. Look at her skin, so fine and dark." He stroked her arm. "Look, she has all her teeth. These are sisters, these two; fine Inlander blood, the finest."

"What lines?"

"Kentakuyan, the best. These are the only two left after the Night of Sorrows."

"Bad-luck blood, then. And no wonder, look at those eyes." He jerked his chin toward me.

I stared back hard, daring him to strike me and my daemon eyes. For men living so far out on the Edge, these two had seemed a likely pair—old and scarred enough to have been the warriors they claimed, not so far gone as Hadl. I had almost hoped there would be a sale. What would become of us now, my sister and I, left to rot with this idiot lump of meat who claimed us?

The second man spoke for the first time. "The pregnant one, another day perhaps. You should have beat the whelp from her before she was ruined. But this one, eyes of Pelang." He spat. "Too young to breed, and cursed besides. This one is good for nothing but bintshi-bait. You insult us."

The man's voice was deep and dark as our old home. Haviva leaned toward him. I touched her arm, drew her back; this one was not for us.

"The insult is mine! Bintshi-bait? Cursed eyes or not, she is worth a handful of salt at least. Blooded as a woman; blooded as a soldier too. Bought the pair of them in Murran, two seasons back, from Hasna Mabaradi. This little *buta*," he pointed at me with his chin, "will kill anything you point her at, like a hunting cat. Better . . . you can't bed a hunting cat." He wheezed a laugh.

"That one will kill you in your sleep, like as not." The first man shook his head. "Daemon eyes, staring up at me? No. I think not."

Hadl complained, but without much meat to it; wives were mouths he could ill afford to feed, but without us he would be forced to look after himself. No doubt he counted it better my sister and I should starve with him than he should fetch his own drink. So Haviva and I served tea to the two men and their new wives, a thin and muddy hospitality. Hadl did not invite them to our territory, and they did not ask to see it.

Hours later, after the men had gone and the girls with them, after Hadl had eaten what little food we had and my sister had drifted off to sleep, I crept from the false safety of our underground home and went dancing.

I opened my mouth and let the hot salt air roll across my tongue. I flung *sa* and *ka* open as a wide net into the night, straining for any sense of life. Still young, still strong, and I was alive as I never felt in the stinking little crack we shared with Hadl. My cursed eyes drank in the moonlight; up top, from this angle, all the world was a hunting ground, and I was not just prey.

I was Kentakuyan a'o Yaela i Kaka'ahuana, last heir to an ancient and proud line of queens, and I was a *dancer.*

I spread my arms to the wide, dark sky, embracing the moons and the brilliant stars, the Web of Illindra that held it up, and all Her children, bound to the sticky weavings of life. I drew breath deep into my belly, imagining as I did so that I breathed in power, and peace, and love: all the things that were denied to me in the bottom reaches of the Edge, where we weak humans huddled in fear of the killing sun. I arched my spine and let my head fall back, and I danced with the night.

And, oh, the night danced with me. Sweet Eth, lord of the night sky and dark consort of Illindra, was my dark partner, my lover, my killer. He hid me from my enemies, even as he hid my enemies from me, and we danced to the drum-beat of a thousand dying hearts.

Nighttime in Quarabala can be peaceful, though it is the peace you see in the smile of a child who seems to be asleep and dreaming of a good meal. You know the child is dead, and you know the night is deadly, but it is a comfort to believe otherwise if you can.

I did not allow the lie to soothe me on this night. Caught up in the dance as I was, still I was awake and alert. My nose twitched and I stopped mid-twirl: the salted winds had carried to me the slightest tang of musk. It was a warning, a breath of warmth against my skin, and I quivered like a hunting cat on the scent. *Prey, not predator,* I thought, sniffing the air, *and very close.*

Pebbles and grit ground beneath the hard soles of my feet as I shifted my weight . . . *there.* Not ten paces to the fore, a small herd of goatlike dhurga was creeping noiselessly along a shallower crack. Their sensitive ears twisted back and forth but huge eyes were half-closed as they licked and licked at the rich salty walls.

Abandoning my dream-lover I diffused into the night, holding onto myself with only the lightest touch lest the dhurga sense my presence. I drew a crude shani, a wooden throwing-stick, from a fold in my shirt where I kept such things. Then I did a forbidden thing. As the old witch-tales say:

I drew a deeper, darker breath,
I breathed a prayer to darkest Eth,
And when I danced, I danced their death.

I pulled the essences of my self back in, slowly, like drawing the noose tight on a snare. I pulled in my awareness of the night, and its awareness of me. I pulled in the scent of the dhurga, and the feel of them, the whisper of their calls and the rasp-rasp of their tongues against rock, the sheen of moonlight on their dappled hides. I drew this down to the pit of my belly and let my heart consider it, let my blood dance to the music until I understood it to my bones.

And I danced.

I fed the music up, up to my heart, let it travel in a shock of energy through my arms, my legs, my hips. I moved to the *huh-huhhh* of their breathing, the *click-clack* of their tiny feet. I swayed to the *tha-rum tha-rum tha-rum* of my own hideous, empty heart.

As I danced, shadows rose in a fine mist about my feet, shielding me from the dhurga's senses and allowing me to draw close, so close I might have reached out and touched one. So close I heard their small hearts beating with mine, *thud-thud-thud,* saw them swaying to the movement of my feet, my hands. It was as my teacher had said, back when the world was kind and I believed such soft words: these creatures and I were one.

I drew back and released the shani with my blessing. My blessing of death. Shadows, which had been drawn to the dark song in my heart, poured across the seared earth like dark blood. They seized my weapon up and carried it in their fell hearts, and the dhurga screamed as their doom fell upon them.

The backlash of forbidden magic hit me hard, as it always did, and knocked me flat. I scrambled to my feet, shaking and lightheaded, so tired I wanted to curl up and fall asleep right there in the dirt. But must not, not until I had retrieved my shani and my meat and run far from the killing ground. The scent of hot blood would attract the notice of greater predators, and I was in danger. But there would be food tonight, precious meat for my sister.

Unless Hadl claimed it all for himself.

Well, I thought, *his wound festers–maybe he is dead already.* That cheerful thought gave me the energy to jog along the shallow crack after the dhurga.

The path down which the animals had fled was not much deeper than I was tall, and it ended in a pit of broken stones. My heart leaped to see not one but two animals down. One of them was dead, the other broke-back, and I murmured a quick apology as I ended his life. The rich scent of blood seduced me, and I gave in to the temptation to take a taste. The dhurga's death was life to me, rich and clotted and thick with salt, and I felt it humming all through my body to the very tips of my toes and fingers as I gave thanks for this gift.

A whole dhurga for Hadl, and one for us, I thought resentfully, *if only he would share.* But I knew better. And if I tried to hold meat back, he would–

He would what? I asked myself then, and the poisonous

thought rippled through me stronger than the shadow-magic moments before. He would *what,* exactly? Hadl would be unable to catch me if I chose to run. Would I stand still for him, again, and let him beat me at his leisure?

I thought . . . not. I should, instead, take a dhurga—both dhurga—and run. Run for the edge of the Edge, run over the Jehannim and all the way to Min Yaarif, where the land was cool and green and water ran aboveground, dripping from every surface. Where a girl might walk in the sunlight without dying, and belong only to herself. It was a three-day run, but I was young, and strong. If I could find a shadowmancer to cover me with three days' worth of shadow, I might pay for his magic with this fresh meat. I could—

Abandon my sister and her child to Hadl, and he would beat them to death, or let them be taken by others, who would beat them to death, or starve them, or use them for bait.

I could not.

My heart lost its wings and sank back down through the sky, past the cool blue moons, down down into my chest where it turned back to burnt, dead stone.

I brought the meat to Hadl. He beat me anyway, because I was fit to hunt and he was not, because I was young and he was not, because I was girl and he was man. I stood still and let him, I who was the daughter of queens, and the choice was bitter in my mouth as old blood. In the end, the beating bought us a skinny foreleg from one dhurga and a handful of half-digested mosses from its second stomach. I had planned to give the whole of it to Haviva, but the meat sent up such a redolence, as the fat crackled and crisped and dripped into the fire, that I gave her only a greater share, and fell asleep with a belly full of guilt and fury.

The men returned to our territory two nights later, two thin lean nights with nothing but dhurga-moss and prickweed in the pot, two nights of threats and curses and the stench of rotten meat boiling from Hadl's putrefying wound, two nights watching my sister's belly swell even as her face hollowed and darkened.

The child sucks the life from her, I thought, *even as Hadl sucks it from us.*

I was expecting a raid on our miserable home, now that others knew where we lived, and so in my hunting had not danced far. We were like a dying animal that snaps at the carnivores rather than lets them make a swift end to it, scrabbling in the dirt and our own blood and filth, struggling to draw one more useless breath. *For what?* I asked myself. *What do we have that is worth fighting for?* But still I kept breathing, and still I kept watch.

They came, they poured down our ropes like so much dust, stinking and ragged as we were, but better fed. They ignored Hadl as he cursed them and struggled to rise; he had not left his pallet for a day and the stench of him was our best weapon. They took from us girls what men always take, given the opportunity. They also took our cooking-pot, old and mended as it was, and Haviva's bone-handled knife. They took Hadl's heavy spear (it was of no use to us anyway) and the dust-tent, the small hoard of coins and dried meat and pleasure herbs that were the last of Hadl's treasures. Worst of all, as they left they took our ropes and our precious iron pegs; now I would be the only one fit to climb to the surface. They laughed as they left us to die, left us with nothing to cook in, nothing to eat and nothing to climb, and the stink of them on our skin. I closed my eyes and memorized their voices, their hateful laughter, and their eyes, though there was no chance I would ever find them again.

This much, I had learned long ago: it is never too early to begin planning one's revenge.

The men did not even bother to drive us from our dwelling, and that more than anything spoke of our end.

Hadl cussed us to sleep that morning, and Haviva wept.

I, I curled around the pain and dreamt it was my mother singing.

Two nights after the raid, the last of our sabra water ran dry.

I pried the tap from Haviva's grip, chided her for wasting

tears, and climbed up to the surface. It was twilight, too early to be aboveground, and the scorched earth blistered my feet as I ran for cover. I ran, I ran, imagining that smoke rose from my skin and rags, that my hair would burst into flame at any moment. I would end as had so many others of my kind: one more nameless, faceless, burnt-up corpse littering the face of Quarabala.

I did not die that night. Perhaps my agonies amused Akari Sun Dragon so that he wished to prolong them, for I found a deeper cleft than we had lived in for months, thick with sabra roots and hidden within folds of the earth. I marked the way back subtly, and when I returned, Hadl was on his feet, hobbling about and ranting in rotting delirium, but upright. Getting him and Haviva up to the surface and down again into our new home took the entire night, and more strength than I thought I had left, but we slept that next day with our bellies full to bursting with sabra water and lichens and a handful of bitter manna roots.

I lay pressed against my sister's back, as if we were children again and safe in our parents' rooms, one hand draped over her great drum of a belly. Beneath my fingers the child stirred and rolled and stretched.

Stay where you are, little one, I thought. *Sleep in the dark, dream sweet, dream deep. To live as we do here, dancing on the Edge, is to die.*

It did not take us long to learn why such a promising homesite, protected from the sun and with ready sources of food and water, had lain so long unclaimed. Our fire had scarce darkened a path up one wall, and I had yet to discover the local game trails, when the bintshi came calling.

The first notes of her wicked canticle trembled out across the land at midsun, in the midst of a windless calm, when all the rest of the world was still and we slept pressed against the cool stone. It stole into my mind as an old dream—my mother, singing to me—but a spider crawled across my face, startling me, and I woke to the harsh truth. The lyric which tugged at my heart was not my mother's voice at all, but the song of a greater predator, and at the end of this lullaby lay death.

To me, the bintshi's voice seemed sweet and light as the notes of a finger-bone flute, dancing and sparkling through the heated air. To the others, who knows? Haviva stirred and murmured in her sleep, smiling, mouth moving like a suckling babe's, and Hadl . . . well. It is known what wicked and lustful effect the song of the bintshi has upon human men. He roused from his sleep with a great roar, thrashing about and bellowing in a fit of lechery, and knocked me flat three times before I was able to get the wax-and-hide plugs into his ears.

Once deafened, Hadl lay panting and gasping and stinking of fear, and I turned to my sister, who lay curled around the child in her belly, hands pressed to her ears. Her skin had gone pale, her eyes so wide and dark they might have been cursed like mine, and I watched the mound of her belly straining and twisting in a grotesque dance as the child within responded to the bintshi's fell music. But as I would go to her, Hadl clamped his hand about my wrist and dragged me down to him, to slake and sate his daemon-roused hungers. I was no more able to fight him than he was able to fight the daemon's lure, and as he clutched and tore at me, my hatred and rage and shame coupled perfectly with the bintshi's evil song.

Love, lust, love, she crooned. A great shadow fell upon us as Hadl bit my flesh. *Love, lust, love.* The hot air boiled with the beat of her wings; her music was an exquisite agony and I screamed back at her: *Hate. Hate. HATE.*

Love lust love me, she sang. *Come come love me.*

Hate him hate him hate you, I cried, deep in the pit of my blackened heart. *Hate you hate him hate me.*

Hadl rolled away from me, groaning, and in my wretchedness I scraped together every crumb of power within myself, *sa* and *ka* and those beautiful, forbidden magics granted to those who bear the eyes of Pelang. Like a fist full of shit I flung this all up toward her, the filth and pain and abomination of my very existence, the stench of Hadl's mouth and the knowledge of my own death and a fury so old and so deep my bones cracked with it.

The bintshi wailed, a thin high note of rage kin to my own, and slapped her wings down upon the ground with such force that we three humans were sent deaf and rolling. With that final assault her shadow lifted and I felt her rising, rising up toward her brother the sun, trumpeting frustrated hunger to the world.

I rolled finally to my hands and knees, retching, bleeding miserably from nose and ears. My sister had begun a thin, trembling wail, and for one sharp instant I wanted to beat her for her terror. I watched Hadl struggling to rise and as he did so I saw him clearly. I saw how he truly was, wasted and thin and ill unto death, stinking with the rot of a wound because he was too cheap and too stupid to pay for a healer. He was weaker than I had known.

He was weaker than I.

"If you ever touch me again." My voice was low and ragged; a woman's voice. "I will kill you."

He was still laughing when the sun went down.

The bintshi did not come often; she must have had a large territory. She came frequently enough, however, that the three of us slept with plugs in our ears, and I with my shani to hand, as if a sharpened stick would be of any use against a greater predator.

Hadl ignored my existence. The threat I had made hung in the air between us like a bug in a spider's web. Neither of us knew whether the strength in my arms might carry such heavy words, and I guess he did not care to find out. I had not often been the target of Hadl's lust anyway, not back when he had a nag of twelve nubile wives, and no more now that he was down to the two most worthless. I was too small, too skinny, and cursed from birth with the eyes of Pelang.

Bintshi or no bintshi, we needed to eat. So I danced upon the seared earth at night, as I always had, and I returned before morning as I always had, sometimes with meat or an edible plant, usually with hands as empty as my soul. Often I thought that Hadl had been at my sister—the song of the bintshi had wakened in him what his illness had killed—but she said nothing to me, and I never asked.

One night, in a shallow cleft near a tangle of blackthorn with spikes as long and black as my hand, I found a hive of bees. Bees are beloved of Atuim and very, very rare. I dared the fierce little beasts' wrath and broke off a small section of honeycomb and was well stung for my efforts.

I licked honey from my hand and laughed, jumped half out of my skin at the sound of my own voice, and laughed again. It had been so long! And the honey was sweet, so sweet, the kindest thing I had tasted since my mother was killed.

I wrapped my golden treasure tenderly in a leathery black leaf and hid it well. When the sun came up that day and Hadl began to snore, I woke my sister and almost laughed again at her delight when I gave it to her.

Sometimes, I told myself, *you can find a little sweet between the bitterest of days.*

It happened one night that I returned early, carrying half a dhurga, and with all the hair on the back of my neck standing stiff. I had barely escaped the attentions of a taarek. Fortunately the big cat had decided that the meat I threw at it was a better meal than my stinking scrawny self would be, and it had allowed me to go. I was caught up in thoughts of my narrow escape, so soon after finding honey that it felt like a turn of luck, which was always suspicious. *"Blessings from Atuim always come in threes,"* my tutor had warned me, back when there were books and candles and I was a princess, *"and the third pays for all."* My people said only, "Beware the third gift." Never do the dragons bless us without purpose, or without expecting something in return.

As I neared the place where I kept my pegs and bit of shabby sabra-root rope for climbing back down to our pitiful shelter, there at the edge of the Edge, I saw that the dragons had sent me the thing I needed most in the world and wanted least: they had sent me a man.

He was clad in the night sky and burned against it like a black flame, bright to my cursed eyes. So still that the thin air stirred not a fold of his cloak, and the moonslight never noticed him. But I saw him, standing at the very entrance to my home, and my gut turned to water.

He lifted his face, as if he had scented something, turned his head slowly toward me, and dropped the shadows he had gathered about himself as a lesser man might wear clothing. Beneath the cloak he was clad in scraps of red—a priest's color—and his night-black skin was scarred all over in imitation of the Web of Illindra, set with bright gems and dark spells.

Shadowmancer.

When his gaze met mine, I dropped my weapon and my meat in the dirt, and swayed where I stood, lightheaded and sick. The man's eyes were as wide and pale as the moons and shone a pale blue in the dying night.

Eyes of Pelang.

He made no threatening gesture or word, just stood in the dark, daemon-eyes so like my own drinking in the night. Then he smiled, and I wondered why I had been so afraid. What could he do to me, after all, that the bintshi could not, or a swarm of soldier beetles, or even our own sweet Hadl?

I shook off the last of my fear as if it were dust, and inclined my head in a graceful nod, as I had been taught from infancy. He raised his eyebrows, perhaps surprised that I did not bow; his night skin, nearly as dark as my own, marked him as high caste. Doubtless he expected some show of obeisance. He would receive nothing of the kind from me, on this night or any other. The man was certainly a shadowmancer, and worthy of respect, but I . . .

I was a queen.

And then, laughing silently as the weird wretchedness of it all, I picked my weapon and meat up out of the dirt and retrieved my climbing gear, so that I might offer our honored guest all the mean hospitality at the edge of the Edge of the Seared Lands.

In all my life, no person besides my mother and my sister had ever met my stare without turning away. That this stranger would do so was unsettling. I was unsure whether to feel angry or excited, and so I was both.

His name was Aasah, and he was a man of wonder. He had the true-black skin of a high caste man, and his eyes were as blue and as deadly as a midsun sky. Cat-slit eyes, eyes of Pelang, like mine. Though he worked not a whit of magic, I knew him for a shadowmancer, for he had the ritual spider's web-and-jewels scarring and of one who has earned his place among the stars.

He shared our meager food, our salt and sabra water. One of the Usil had come calling, and we offered goat-meat and bitter sap. I had thought my own well of misery had long since run dry, but tears stung my eyes, and I wanted to crawl under my verminous blankets and die of shame. Such a man as this might well have once sat below my mother's table and hoped to catch her favor; now I all but trembled in his presence, a beggar-slave chasing scraps.

He jerked his chin up toward the lower ledge, above which a slice of hot sky could be seen. "I see you have a problem with a bintshi."

"Problem?" Hadl puffed himself up and displayed his remaining teeth. "Yah, problem. But my little Yaela run that beast off good, she a killer that one. And young. Good, strong. You want her tonight, she is yours. Unless you want the other one, she a beauty and ripe too."

Haviva glanced up at the stranger and cast her eyes down again. She had combed her hair, I saw, and washed her face as well. I tried not to resent her for clinging to hope.

Teeth flashed shocking white, so quick I might have imagined it. "I will take this one today. I like her eyes."

I had not imagined it . . . he *winked* at me.

So strange, to have my sister dressing *my* hair for a change. I fussed and fidgeted till Haviva yanked at my head in frustration.

"Hold still, you! Oh, this is impossible." She yanked again and I resisted the urge to pinch her. Barely.

"Leave some—ow!—on my head. Ow! You did that on purpose."

She rubbed her fingers in the little pot that had once held oil, a futile gesture, and sighed. "When is the last time you combed your hair? Oh, this is impossible. I think you have ghat nesting in there. Yes, see? A nest of pups. How sweet."

"And why should I—ow!—why should I bother? You are the pretty one."

"I am the fat one. And you are prettier than I, except . . ." Her voice faltered. We never spoke of my curse. "Well, I suppose *he* can hardly complain about your eyes, can he? His are much worse than yours." She shuddered dramatically.

"Thank you." I snorted.

"You are welcome." There was a smile in her voice. I imagined that we were girls again.

Hadl shocked us both by allowing us girls to make a tent of sorts with our bedding and build up the fire, so that we might heat rocks and squeeze a bit of sabra pulp for a steam bath. I am sure he hoped that the stranger would buy one of us—or fall asleep so that we might slit his throat and take his fine cloak. It would not be the first time Hadl had ordered such a thing done, guest-laws or no.

I thought of the man—Aasah—the way he moved, the calm stone of his face, and shook my head. This man would not fall prey to the likes of us.

"Sister." Haviva left off scraping the grime from my back and pressed against me. Her arms wrapped around my neck and her belly pressed against my spine, thumping and insistent. "Sister, you would never leave me, would you? Not even for a handsome stranger?"

"Not for ten handsome strangers." I gripped her hands and leaned back to press my cheek against hers. "Not for a hundred."

"What would you do with a hundred handsome strangers?"

"I would take them all as my husbands, and they would wait on me as a queen."

"A nag of husbands?" She giggled.

"Husbands are not a nag," I informed her with the lofty air of eldest sister. "They are a headache. I would have a headache of a hundred husbands."

This memory I have kept, for all these years, though I have scoured so many others from my cold dead heart.

Our guest had selected for himself a sheltered and private corner and now he sat, cross-legged on his cloak, and waited for me. He wore a *sharat*, the traditional men's loincloth of red spidersilk, and over that a very finely woven robe in the most beautiful shade of blue I had ever seen, dark as the evening sky.

I sat as far from him as I might without seeming rude, and my heart ran like a frightened animal. The small sounds of morning were magnified a hundredfold, and I was too aware of them. Hadl was watching us through half-closed eyes, and I scolded myself for daring to feel shame; surely anything I might have been shy about had been ripped from me long ago.

Aasah reached and held my jaw lightly in his long, strong hand, turning my face this way and that, as if I were a milk-goat for trade. He thumbed my mouth open and looked at my teeth, and stared long at my eyes. I stared back, daring *him* to call me cursed.

"You see well in the dark. Your eyes are meant for seeing the hearts of shadows, little one. They are beautiful."

I shrugged and pulled away, unimpressed. Hadl had already given me to this man; why did he feel the need to compliment me at all?

His eyes were wide, wide as mine, and the shocking blue irises all but hid the whites. He had cat's pupils, same as mine, and already they had narrowed to near slits in the growing light.

"Who were your people, little one? Etudumayloh?"

"Kentakuyan. We are the last, my sister and I."

"Kentakuyan." A long pause, and then, "The other one is your sister?"

I nodded, but he waited for me to speak. "Yes."

"Ahhh." A long exhalation of breath. *He is sad*, I thought, and wondered that he would waste his sorrow on such as us.

Aasah did not speak again, or move, for a very long time. He stared into my eyes and I tried very hard not to squirm, wondering what he wanted of me, and whether I offended, and what I was supposed to do next.

"Do you want to . . ." I shrugged, and made the gesture with my hands.

He surprised me by laughing; a big, fearless sound. "Yes, I do. But not with you, little one. Not today. I am a man, and a man does not hunger for the flesh of a child."

I blinked at him, astounded, and his laugh faded, to be replaced by a look of profound sadness.

"Come here, little sister, come to me and I will sing you a song. And you will sleep."

He stretched out, and I curled against his chest, and he began to sing.

Shall I describe his voice to you, or name the things it made me feel? Would that I could. A simple babe's song, a lullaby and nothing more; but as my ear pressed against his chest I felt his music unfurling, and within it I saw every color of love and tenderness one might feel for a child, even for a child that is not your own. His song was everything I had ever lost, and it cried me to sleep.

The next night I saw magic, as I had not seen since I was small, and bright, and the world was good.

Aasah hunted with me. Or rather, I should say that he hunted, and allowed me to follow him. He sang as he walked, a low sound, a slow sound and bold, and as he sang the manted shadows swirled about our feed like sand-dae. Drawn to the shadowmancer's music against their will, they thickened about our bodies, rising up to cover us. The chillflesh rose along my arms at the shadows' touch, cool and soothing, not at all as I had expected death to feel. For bound as they were to the shadowmancer's song, these shadows were spun of death and silence and the long, cold nothing between stars.

I—who had survived the Night of Sorrows, the slave pits, and the fighting pits, who danced every night on the edge of the Edge of the Seared Lands—I wept in fear and was ashamed.

"Hush, sweet princess," the shadowmancer scolded. "These shadows are mine to command; they will not harm you, not while you are with me."

Hidden from the sun in such a manner might we travel across the burning lands, I knew, all the way from the Edge and over the fell Jehannim to Min Yaarif, and beyond that to the lands of free peoples. But the price of shadowmancy was far beyond the reach of my wishes.

Aasah sang on as we walked shadow-cloaked in darkness deeper than night, invisible to man or beast or Illindra herself, and from the heart of obscurity his curved knife flashed out swifter and more deadly than my shia. The night was not half done and I staggered under the weight of his kills; a fat dhurga-ewe dripping with milk, two of the swift and flightless makkim, and the real prize, a young surcat, the small dark version of its dappled cousin. The meat of the last was rank-tasting, but its fur was valuable, and the long dagger teeth could be used as pegs for a climbing rope.

The moment we returned, Hadl's eyes lit greedily upon the cat; Aasah gave it to him freely. "To repay you for your hospitality." Hadl grinned and nodded, as a king receiving just gifts.

I had never felt such a beggar.

We feasted that night as I had not in years. The dhurga was fat and her dugs full of milk, and bird's meat is rare enough to be a delicacy in the Seared Lands. Hadl could hardly begrudge us girls a share of the feast with his guest looking on. His eyes measured every mouthful we took, and we would pay for it later, but I figured the cost well worth it and ate till I could barely move.

Aasah pulled a flask from the folds of his wonderful robe and offered the first drink to Hadl. At the time I had no idea what was in the drink. It smelled of overripe fruit of some sort and bitter herbs. Hadl spluttered and coughed, and his eyes watered, and then he pounded Aasah on the arm.

"Ah, my brother! Such a fine thing! So fine!" He showed all his teeth and most of his gums and took another long pull. "A pity we did not meet when I was still a warrior, with two good legs. We would have owned Quarabala."

A queer look passed over the stranger's face. "For how long has this wound plagued you, my brother?"

"For a two-moon at least, my brother! Yes! My brother!" Hadl slapped a hand against his bad leg and grimaced. "I was a warrior, like you, but I got an arrow in the knee."

"Have you seen a healer?"

"Healer, hah." Hadl spit. "No good healers here at the Edge, all they want is to rob you."

That much, at least, was true.

"I have some knowledge of healing, and of herbs." Another odd little smile. "I could take a look at it, if you would like. There may be something I could do."

Hadl beetled his brows suspiciously. "What do you want for it?"

Aasah smiled wide, pale eyes flashing like the moons. "Nothing more than you have given me already . . . brother. Shelter from the sun. Your fire to keep away the predators. The company of your little Yaela for another day, perhaps two, before I travel on. An ear for my stories . . . I do love to tell stories."

Haviva clutched at my hand, and her eyes shone. He was a storyteller too! I felt a little sour; was there nothing this man could not do?

Hadl grunted his assent, and Aasah turned to me. His eyes were very wide and strange, pupils dilated so that only a thin ring of blue glowed about the edges.

"Yaela, my dear," he purred, "do you have a small bit of water? Real water, not sabra?" He turned to Hadl. "For purification. You have a powerful enemy."

"Oh, yes." Hadl nodded, eyes flashing hatred for this imagined enemy. "Most powerful."

Aasah nodded soberly as he stripped the rags back from my husband's flabby, hairy leg. The rot was not as bad as I had imagined—for a pity, it did not look as if it would kill him—and in fact the edges of his wound showed a healthy flesh color beneath the grime. Apparently most of the stink was Hadl himself.

"Ah, yes, see here, where the flesh is still hot?" He poked a reddened area just above the cut; Hadl cursed roundly. "This is full of ill-wishes and poisonous energies. You are lucky that it has not gotten into your blood, yet. You would lose the leg for sure, and likely die. Become impotent, even."

"Impotent, hah! Not me! I—"

"This is from an arrow wound, you said?" inquired Aasah, politely but pointedly.

I said nothing, but thought of doe-eyed Samilah with her little knife. *Arrow, indeed.*

"Yes. An arrow." Hadl glared as if he read my thoughts. I looked away and said nothing.

"And the man who gave you this wound, does he yet live?"

Hadl smirked. "No. I fed that heart to my wives."

Haviva made a small sound and pressed her lips together as if she might vomit.

Aasah smiled, wide and cruel. "Ah, I see you are a true warrior. Hold still, this is going to hurt."

Hadl did scream, long and long, the notes of it rolling across the Seared Lands, and my heart sang to hear it.

When he had finished, Aasah washed his hands and face, and called me to his side. I brought him sabra water and cold meat. When he lay down to rest I curled up at his side, shivering at the warmth of him, and tried hard not to wish that I might always feel so safe.

Hadl's harsh breaths and sporadic moans were all the lullaby I needed. Still, my heart leapt when Aasah pulled me close, and I felt his breath on my ear. I thought he would sing, that I might feel his magic again, but he only whispered to me.

"Your husband," he confided, "is a *quss*."

I had to bite my hand hard to keep from laughing.

"Will you dance for me, girl?"

We had run far, under cover of Aasah's shifted shadows. He had caught a tiny half-fledged dae owl unawares and had given it to me. I had eaten half of it raw before I realized he had meant for me to keep it as a pet. As if Hadl would ever have allowed that. Ah well, meat was meat.

I shrugged, crunching the tiny bones of one wing between my teeth and spitting feathers off to the side, and stood as seductively as one might when covered in bits of owl-fluff. I let my robe slip, showing a hand's width of filthy skin, and hid my pain and disappointment behind flirty, cursed eyes. He had said that I might go untouched, that a man does not hunger for the flesh of a child.

Ah well, I mocked myself, *meat is meat.* I struck a provocative pose, ready to slip into the slave's dance that had convinced Hadl to buy me and my sister in the first place.

"No, no, little one," he held up a hand to stop me, and his eyes were deep as night with heart's sorrow. "No. I mean dance for me. As I sing for you. Dance the sky, dance the red salt earth." He patted the ground beside him, raising a little puff of dust. "Dance the shadows, child. Do you know how?"

"I do know," I admitted, "but only a very little. Enough to help cloak myself on the hunt, enough to give myself a few seconds more to run from the sun if I stay out too late. But I am weak, untaught." I gestured to my filthy, pathetic self, so ready to lay with a stranger, bitter and wicked to the core of my heart. "And I am broken."

Shadowmancy, the ability to shift shadows into physical form and bid them obey me, had always run in my veins. None could deny this, not since I was pushed screaming from the safety of my mother's womb and stared upon the world with my eyes of Pelang. The Listeners had informed her that I was to be a dancer, and so it was; my first steps, they told me time and again, were graceful as a true wish. Before I learned to walk properly I had been taught to move with poise and purpose to the song in my heart.

"Never dance with anger," a tutor had lectured me once. *"To do so is to call not upon Illindra, the Mother of All, but upon Eth the Unmaker. Never allow his shadows to enter your dance, little one, because once they have made a home in your heart, they will never leave."*

I closed my eyes upon the memory, shattering it. Those words had been uttered long ago, when the song in my heart was good, and I had value. My world had been broken on the Night of Sorrows, and I along with it.

"The Sindanese have an art form they call *jinxiuli,*" he said. "Have you ever heard of it?"

I shook my head. *No.*

"If a fine piece of pottery is broken, they do not throw it away. Their artisans use gold to join the shattered pieces together, making a new piece of art, more beautiful and more valuable than the original."

"You are saying that I am not broken?"

"You *are* broken, little one. I am saying that the choice to remain broken is yours. You can remain as you are—or you can make yourself into something more. Something stronger than you would have been, safe in your mother's arms."

The shards of broken dreams pierced my eyes, and tears ran down my cheeks.

"Will you dance?" he asked again. "Will you dance with the shadows of death? Will you dance for me, little princess?"

He knew who I was, then. Likely he had known all along.

When I opened my eyes and looked upon the shadowmancer, they were hot and dry as the seared earth, hard as my seared heart.

"Yes," I said, "I will dance."

I was a girl living on the Edge, and that is the most miserable creature one might imagine in this world or any other. I owned nothing, not the sharpened stick I pretended was a weapon, not the food I brought home, not the filthy rags that covered my bruised skin—even that skin was another's to do with as he pleased. I owned nothing, I was nothing, worth less than a handful of red salt dust—

Until I closed my eyes and danced. In those moments I fell from the sticky, immutable Web of Illindra and into a world of my own making. When I danced, I was *Yaela,* and it was enough.

This time, for this dance, I tried to be more. As my feet pressed against the hard red flesh of the Quarabala and my hands pressed up toward the moons, I imagined that I was part of everything, and that it was good. I was made of salt dust and star dust, hot sunlight and cool shadow, and the blood rushing through my veins was a river coursing across the parched earth, bringing life. As the soles of my feet slid through the dirt, as my hands sang a beautiful descant to the stars, I exulted. I was the bud of a blackthorn rose, opened just enough to reveal a soul born of dance and fire, hot and dangerous and beautiful as Sajani Earth Dragon herself. I danced, and Illindra danced with me along her shining web—

But then the shadows came. A voice once broken will never sing so sweet, and a spirit as crippled as mine can never truly dance.

My toes in the dirt sang of running, running in fear, my skin whispering against the wind sang of pain. The tangled knots of my hair as they fell down my back sang of violation, and my closed eyes of shame; it was to this song the shadows responded, and they rose in fury like the night, death made flesh, bent on silencing all song and all dance for all time. One outflung arm brushed against something cold and hard and prickly as a sabra pear. Startled, I faltered between one movement and the next, dropping the silken threads of magic I had so shyly begun to weave. My eyes, my cursed eyes, flew open of their own accord, and stared straight into my face, reflected back at me by the shadows. I looked into my own heart, and for the first time I faced what I truly was, what I had become—

I screamed and buried my face in both hands, but it was too late.

The shadowmancer Aasah stepped back from the sight of me, hands held before him in a symbol I had seen far too often in my life, a circle bisected by a line—a gesture meant to protect one's soul from evil.

Far below us, safe in her world shell as a chick is safe in its egg, Sajani Earth Dragon saw me in her dreams and turned away in fear.

Only the shadows of death, seeing me as I truly was, loved me. And so they came to me that first night, my children—the only children I will ever know—they rose about me and the shadowmancer like a wave of corruption, drowning the stars and the moon and all things good. They swept me up in their arms, strong and sweet, dancing along to the bitter-ash song of my heart.

Kill, kill, they crooned to me. *Kill them all, kill us, kill you.*

I could have fought them; I could have stilled my arms and

my legs and the twisted whisperings of my mind, and broken the shadows' hold on me.

I did not.

Instead, knowing what they were, knowing what I was, I joined the dance.

Hours later I awoke and found myself held in a pair of strong arms. It was Aasah—I knew his scent, by this time—carrying me home as a father might carry a child. For a while I remained limp in his grasp, wishing that things might not have changed between us, wishing that the world was not as it was.

But in my experience, only the darkest and wickedest of wishes are ever granted. I opened my eyes and pushed against his broad, hard chest, and the shadowmancer stopped and put me down. I stood before him, itching with the salt of dried sweat upon my skin, weak-kneed and exhausted.

I had never felt stronger in all my life, or more ashamed. He did not have to tell me that I had failed his test.

I stilled my trembling limbs as best I was able and wondered whether, now that he knew, he would tell Hadl that I was well and truly cursed, or whether he would kill me himself.

"I beg you, forgive me."

But when his hand met my cheek, it was gentle. "Forgive you? Forgive me, child, for not being there when your people needed me. And forgive me for abandoning you again, for I must."

My world stopped. I dared open my eyes, and begged him with them. *No. No.*

"I will not leave tonight," he promised, and shocked me further by pressing a kiss to my forehead with his bloody mouth. "Not tonight, but soon. I will sing the shadows, that they might conceal my path from Akari Sun Dragon, and then I will run the shining path to Min Yaarif. Were it just the two of us, we might run together. But your sister . . ." He held out his two hands and shrugged. "Perhaps someday, little one, you will learn shadowmancy on your own and make your way to the free lands, and to me."

I believed his words no more than he did. Aasah reached out a hand to stroke my cheek and continued, "Before I leave, I will give you a gift. But in return, you must promise me something."

"Anything." I wanted to die. *Take me with you.*

"You begged me for forgiveness." He frowned. "You are Kentakuyan. Never forget. You do not beg. Do you understand me?"

"Yes, Aasah. I promise." His name was honey on my tongue, so rare and sweet.

"Good girl." He patted my head, and then patted at the sides of his sharat. "Ah! Here we are. Come here, little one. I have something for you."

Three days later, I woke from a midsun nap to find Aasah staring at me. A world of sadness was in his eyes, and I knew what he would say before he opened his mouth. But he had reminded me that a queen does not beg, and so I waited and said nothing.

"I will leave at dusk."

The words were a cold knife in my throat, and I choked on them. His arms tightened about me, warning, and his soft whisper tickled at my ear.

"There is no help for it, sweet one, I have stayed much too long as it is. People die every day that I linger . . . how many lives are you worth? Many, perhaps. We shall see."

"Will you . . ."

"Will I?" He mocked, not unkindly.

"Will you . . ." *Keep me. Love me. Save me.* "Will you buy me from Hadl?"

"Yes, and yes. No, and no." I thought he sang the words to me. "You are mine forever, little sister, and I am yours . . . but you will have to buy your own freedom. And when you do, I will be waiting for you."

"Buy myself? That is not possible. I have nothing." My words cracked with despair. "I am nothing."

"Do not be foolish. You are more than you know, and the price . . ." He let out a long, slow sigh. "The price will be greater than you can imagine."

That much I believed.

"When you are free, make your way to Min Yaarif, and I will find you there. Find the Trail of Bones, not far from here as Sun Dragon wakes. You must dance, sweet one, as you have never danced in your life, hard enough and true enough to make the shadows fall in love with you, that they might protect you from the killing sun. By laws as old as Sajani's bones, that protection will last not more than three days. Shift the shadows of death to your will, and then *run*. As soon as Sun Dragon turns his face you must run as if all the Araids in Quarabala are at your heels. Do not stop, not for pain, not for love, not even for the breaking dawn. Stop, and Sun Dragon will find you. Stop, and you die."

Run for three days, while maintaining control over shadows, when I had not been able to control them for a few minutes? Learn to shadowshift by myself, on the edge of the Edge, while protecting my sister and her babe from our rotting husband?

"It is impossible." I might be able to run for three days, I thought I might, but Haviva would never make it. And if the shadows slipped away from me, come the breaking dawn . . . to be caught aboveground was death for all of us, a long, slow death by fire.

"Of course it is impossible." His whisper mocked mine. He stood, and the dim light caught at the jewels on his skin; he shone like the night sky. "You do not become a shadowmancer by attempting the possible. You live, or you die. It is that simple, little one. Now, stop your crying and help me gather my things; come the night, I will sing, and then I will run."

He left before morning, when the air was still so hot my skin ached just to think of it, and so I would *not* think of it, or of him. I told myself that the pain in my heart was a small punishment for ever being so young as to hope again. *Stupid, foolish girl.* I turned my face away and would not watch him go.

Hadl felt well enough and manly enough to beat me that night for having lain with another man, and then he took my shia and climbed out of our hole. I wished he might fall drunk into a clutch of dhurga and be stampeded. Or break through the crust of earth and into a nest of soldier beetles. Or . . .

"Do you love him?"

"Hadl?" I spat; Haviva glanced about, fearful, but he was gone.

"The other man. Aasah." She glanced at me, dared lay a hand on my arm. "I had feared he might . . . I had hoped he might buy you. Take you away. I thought you liked him."

I shrugged away from her touch. "We had better get this stinking place cleaned up, lest our beloved husband beat us, Atuim smile upon his head."

Haviva's eyes were round as moons. "Yaela, you must not say such things. You must not! What if he hears? He would kill you!"

"And I should care if he does?"

"I should care."

I looked at my sister and sighed, and thumbed the tears from her cheek. She hugged me, and I let her, and we bent to our task.

That morning I dreamt that I had wings. I would fly up, up, up to the moons, and they promised to show me the road to Min Yaarif, long and cool and glittering with sung bones. But first, they explained, I must cut out my own heart and use it to buy my freedom.

When I woke, I washed my face, and my hands, and my feet. I combed my hair, just as if Aasah were still there to see, and I prepared food and drink for my beloved husband, Atuim smile upon his head, and before he or Haviva had yet stirred I was cutting up the last of the meat the shadowmancer had hunted for us. I could do that much for her, at least, before I left.

I froze, knife high in the air, surprised at my own thoughts. *Leave?* I would never leave my sister.

You must, insisted the shadowmancer's voice in my head. *You live or you die . . . it is that simple. Your choice, little one.*

My choice. My choice? I hacked at the meat as if to cut the lie from it. What part of this life had I ever chosen? I cut my hand and did not care. *You live or you die: your choice.* Fine words for a man to say, who had never been hunted and shared over a fire and chewed upon like a piece of meat.

I scraped a fine powder of rich, red, salty earth, and rolled the strips of meat in it, and hung them to dry. Though I might not have bothered: it was well salted with my tears.

Hadl ate the food I had brought for him, and the sabra water I had squeezed for him, and scratched his crotch, and looked well pleased with himself. "My wives. My good wives. Havi, I have decided. You will keep the whelp."

Haviva dropped the knife. Her eyes grew huge, and the world grew still.

"Yes. You will bear a son, a fine son for me. I have made a decision. My leg is good—see?" He pulled his grimed leggings down. The scar was angry-looking and fresh, but indeed, it looked to be healing well. "Two good legs, two good wives. I will join my cousin Saamid, and we will start a new clan. And you will be first wives, eh? You like that?"

"Yes, Husband." Haviva dropped her gaze; the color was high in her cheeks. I knew she had never dared hope to keep the child.

I made my face a mask but could not hide my glare. I need not have bothered; Hadl was busy in his head with his new life, his new clan, and his new wives. A hundred of them, no doubt, a great nag for a great warrior.

Your choice, little one.

I spent the night cleaning our little crack in the ground, as if anything I might do would make it smell less like smoke, and sweat, and rot. I shook out our bedding and ragged clothes, and beat herbs and dust into them, and climbed to the surface over and over again to dispose of old bones, and dried shit, and such other treasures as we had accumulated. Haviva combed her hair, wore her cleanest kamish, and roasted salt meat with manna roots. Hadl preened himself by the fire: our beloved husband, Atuim smile upon his head, the great warrior, the great carrion-bird full to bursting with another hunter's meat.

I took a deep breath and drew the flute from beneath my bedding.

"What is that?"

"A flute." Sun Dragon's gaze had just begun to seek us; just as Aasah had promised, the glittering runes had faded to nothing. It looked a flute, a plain instrument some shepherd might own, nothing more. "Aasah left it, that I might play for you of a morning."

He grunted. "Liked him, did you?"

There was no good answer to that question, and so I gave none. "I would play you a tune, my husband. I would dance for you."

Naked as a shadowmancer's promise I stood upon the unyielding ground and struck a dancer's pose, at the same time raising the flute close to my face and squinting against the growing light. *One ring to bring them close, two rings to send them,* he had told me. I arched back, back, and the muscles in my legs flexed in readiness. Smiling, I brought the end of the flute with a single red-painted ring to my lips—

—and blew.

She raised her voice in a glad song, a call to the Hunt, a call to kill. She rode a great wooden bowl upon the water, so much water there was no end to it; a great wave warm and salty as blood slapped my dreaming face and I wondered at my own surprise. It was the sea, after all, and we were her hunters. Mahadra raised her voice again, a shrill ululation, and the sun shone on her copper bracelets as she pointed up. Our prey had been sighted! I reached for my . . .

"What is this? What is this? What did you do?" The back of Hadl's hand smashed against my mouth, breaking my trance. His blow sent the flute flying, and for a horrible moment I cared more for its fate than I did for mine. It bounced against the earth, unharmed; not so my face, bounced against my husband's tender fist. "*Buta!* I will kill you, you . . ." He shoved me aside and scrambled to his bedding. "The plugs! The plugs! What have you done with them, you . . ."

A single note rang out, the sweet and joyful wailing of death. The bintshi had answered the flute's call.

My husband turned to me, face purple with rage and eyes full of murder. But my eyes were the eyes of Pelang, and they had seen his death. I smiled at him even as he raised his hand to strike me down, and I raised my own two fists and shook them at his face.

"Never again will you beat me," I told Hadl, and his jaw dropped open, eyes bugged out at me like a spider's in his great surprise. "I am done with you, *husband*." And I spat upon the ground at his feet.

"I will kill you!" he roared, forgetting the greater threat in the face of my mockery. "I will—"

Hadl froze, hand upraised, and then cocked his head as the bintshi sang. His eyes glazed over as he was caught in a web of my own spinning, one which would likely end this night in all our deaths.

"You will not," I answered, lifting my chin in defiance. "I think, tonight, you will die." I was trembling all over in exertion and fear, drenched in sour-smelling sweat, and so afraid of what would happen next that the blood wanted to crawl out of my veins and hide. But I was also, in that moment, utterly at peace.

Better to die dancing with the bintshi, I told my pounding heart, *than live another moment dancing on the Edge.*

The bintshi crooned, voice rising sweet upon the wind. *To me, my loves,* she sang. *To me.*

The ear-plugs had been thrown out that morning with the rest of our rubbish, and Hadl had no chance. He swayed, grinned like a three-night drunk, and shuffled to the new climbing rope I had twisted and hung just that day. Such a wife, a good wife. He set his hand to the rope and climbed.

Haviva cried out and would have followed him, would have dragged him down to his safety—and our death, once the bintshi had gone—but I wrapped my arms about her and held her fast. She screamed, and begged, and beat against me with her fists; I accepted the pain as part of the price of our freedom.

Hadl hitched his good leg over the lip of the rift and then he began to scream too. The bintshi shrieked her triumph, great wings beat above us, and she thanked me for the meal with a blessing of red, red rain.

Long after Hadl's screams stopped I loosed my grip on my sister. Haviva slid boneless to lie in the dirt, shaking with sobs so that I feared for her and the child.

The shadow of the bintshi passed over us one last time, and I dared a small sigh of relief. No doubt my beloved husband, Atuim smile upon his memory, had been a fine fat meal.

"Haviva, my sweet, we are well, we are very well. Look, Hadl is gone. Well, *most* of him is gone." I pulled my blood-sodden kamish away from my skin and grimaced.

"Our husband is gone!" She wailed. "What have you done, what have you done? What evil magic is this, you have killed our husband! How will we live, who will protect us? Where will we go?"

I gaped at her. How could she be so stupid? "What do you mean, where will we go . . . we will go wherever we like. Haviva, my sweet, we are free, do you not understand?"

"You are the one who does not understand." Haviva left off her weeping and sat in the bloody dirt as if all the spine had gone out of her. "Yaela, how could you be so stupid? We were going inland, where it is safe. We were going to . . . he was going to . . ." She sighed and sat up, dashing tears and blood from her face with the back of her hand. "I suppose it does not matter now, does it? Thanks to you."

"Yes, thanks to me. Inland, where it is safe?" I wanted to strike her, to shake her, to make her see. "No place is safe for us. No place in Quarabala. Now, we can leave, we can . . ."

"You can leave. And I . . . I suppose you will, now. Go after him, your handsome sorcerer." Tears welled up in her eyes, terrible to see. After all this, that I had caused her to cry. "I think, I think you . . . you should . . ."

"Hush, hush." I dropped to the dirt beside my sister and gathered her up in my arms. "Hush, hush, silly one, do you think I would leave you?" I stroked her hair and made a face; it was thick with gobbets of Hadl.

"I guess not." Her voice was muffled against my breast. She turned her head to the side, streaking my cleaner skin with blood and tears. "I am just . . . afraid, Yaela. So afraid."

"Yes, and fear is such a new feeling for both of us."

She laughed, and I held her at arm's length. "It is a choice, dear one," I told her. "To live, or to die."

"Just like that?"

"Yes."

"Oh, well then, if that is all it takes, I choose to live. I want to live." Her voice wavered, but she took a deep breath and forced a smile, and my heart squeezed tight in my chest.

"There is something we must do first."

"Oh?" Her smile faltered.

"Yes. We must clean up Hadl."

She looked about us and grimaced. There was blood on the walls and the floor, and on our bedding, and our food, and in our hair.

"Trust a man," she sighed, "to leave such a mess."

The bintshi never returned. Perhaps Hadl had been sweet enough to satisfy her hunger. More likely, she took sick and died from eating such foul meat.

I went dancing most nights, partly to ease the ache in my restless legs, mostly to get away from my sister, who was torn between blessing me for ridding us of Hadl, blaming me for robbing us of Hadl, and endlessly cleaning and rearranging our vile pit of a home. I ranged farther and farther out, testing the night's patience and my own too-elusive grasp on shadow magic. One morning I all but fell down the rope, hair smoking, feet bloodied, and Haviva refused to speak to me for two days. I felt her fear; who would care for her and her babe if I never came back? Still, my gaze and my feet and my thoughts drifted toward Min Yaarif.

What would it feel like, I wondered, *to have water fall from the sky and land on your skin? To give up the life of a stinking, sneaking scavenger and walk tall under the sun?*

To be free from the endless whining of an overly pregnant sister?

I could not fathom why she blamed me for her woes . . . I had hardly gotten her in such a condition. I said so, unwisely, and she was giving me such looks that I dared the bees again and brought her a peace offering of honey, lest she poison my food.

Unfortunately, when you remove a greater predator, the smaller, nastier ones move into its territory. With the bintshi gone, I was perhaps the largest predator around, and I knew that would not last long.

The scat of lesser predators began to appear at the edges of our little world. I found one leg of a full-grown makkim, gnawed by a big cat and so befouled that I scorned the meat. Bits of shed skin, claw-tracks, and belly-tracks from lionsnake and lizard. Once I hopped down into the shallow crack favored by the salt-hungry dhurga and nearly landed knee-deep in ghat shit; there would be no more goat meat for us.

It was only luck that had kept us safe from the sun, fed, and hidden from our own kind—*and luck,* I worried, *has never been our friend.*

Sure enough, the same night that thought occurred to me, Haviva tapped into the sabra's root and was able to coax forth only a mean trickle of cloudy sap. She turned to me, stricken, and for the first time in my life I could not meet my sister's eyes. With no source of water ready, we would have to abandon our last hope of a home and go . . . where? It would be impossible for us to go inland, or for us to run to Min Yaarif with my sister's big belly dragging behind us, and we were already so far out on the Edge that it cut our feet.

I lay awake deep into the day, gnawing at the bone of things I was unable to change. Across from me, where Hadl once slept, Haviva twisted and moaned and shifted till I wanted to throw something at her.

"Are you all right?"

"I cannot get comfortable. I think I am going to have an entire litter of babies, like a cat." She groaned again, a strange, low sound that made the hair along my arms prickle.

"Is it your time?" *Please, no.*

"How am I to know?" She wailed. Then, "I think not. I just cannot sleep."

"Neither can I."

She went very quiet. I sighed and tried for a kinder voice. "Would you like me to rub your back?"

"Please."

So I moved to her side and I rubbed her back, and I rubbed her swollen legs and even her great, round moon of a belly. The skin was taut and strained to bursting and I wondered at it; that the body would strive so to bring forth life, even in such a world. It seemed senseless to me, and cruel.

"Do you hate it?"

"Hate it?" She twisted to look at me. "The child?"

I shrugged. "Your belly, Hadl, the child . . . the whole thing."

"I hated Hadl, but he was just a man. And he is gone. I could never hate my child."

"Even if it looks like him?"

"What, hairy?" She laughed. "I suppose I will love it, even so." Haviva stroked her rounded belly, and I saw the child within writhing beneath her touch.

"I could not, I think. If it were me."

Haviva opened her mouth to argue with me, but paused and then spoke more slowly. "I think . . . I think you are right. Perhaps it is better this way, that you are the warrior and I am to be the mother. I will be a mother," she said again, and smiled a little.

"I, a warrior." I snorted.

"You are," she insisted. "I never said so, when Hadl was alive, but it was you who brought the meat and kept us safe. It was always you."

I wrapped my arms about her, and we finally fell asleep. Sunlight waned, and we slept on into the cooler night.

Had I known it would be our last peaceful moment, I would have treated it better.

Late that night I ranged inland, far to the east. I judged our need of sabra to be greater than the risk of discovery.

I was wrong, and Haviva paid the price.

I knew I had misjudged as soon as I smelled the cat. My head jerked up and I saw her, a sleek, fine, dark little beast. She flicked the tip of her tail, annoyed that she had been sighted, and melted into the night like dappled smoke, but not before I had seen the hunter's collar at her throat.

We were discovered.

Stealth would not save me now—likely nothing would save me now—so I threw aside all caution, all fear, all hope, and ran for home as fast as my terror could carry me.

It nearly came to an end when in my hurry I slipped and fell the length of our rope. Had my sister not pushed aside a pile of our worst rags to be mended, I might have broken my neck and died. Often, I wish that I had.

As it was, I managed to scramble to my feet and claw my way across the floor to where Haviva lay. I smelled the blood before I saw it; she lay in a spreading pool of gore and water, and as I stared in horror she arched her back and screamed.

"No." I whispered. "No no no nooooo. Haviva, my sweet, we have to go, we have to go now, we must."

"Can't," she panted. Her eyes were wide and stared past me, pupils dilated and fixed on some desperate goal; never had she looked more like me. "Yaela . . . sister. It hurts. It hurts." And she screamed again.

Did I imagine its echo, far to the east? I slapped her face, hard, shook her by the shoulder so that her head lolled on her neck. "My sister, my sweet, I know it hurts, but we have to leave. They have hunting cats, Haviva! If they catch us here . . ."

She moaned again; my fingers were digging into her shoulder. I let her go and saw that I had bruised her beloved flesh with my own hands.

"You . . . go." She strained again, panted. "Go."

"No, Haviva, no. Oh Atuim, no. Haviva, I will stay with you, I will . . ."

"Yaela. Sister. Go." Her body rippled, betraying her to her death. "Do not die here with me . . . please. Please. Sister, choose life. Please. Take my child, take her and . . . and dance . . . dance the road to Min Yaarif."

Choose life.

"I am not strong enough to do this, sister," I whispered. "Not without you. This price is too high for me to pay."

A cat screamed in the distance.

"*I* will pay it."

"Haviva! No!"

"For once." She bared her teeth in a feral snarl. "Let me do this, sister. Let me be the warrior . . . for you. One last time."

"Haviva!"

"No time." She panted. "No time, sister. We can do this. We can." She struggled to sit up, and pointed at the little red clay pots. "Sister . . . help me."

Were those men's voices I heard on the wind, raised in triumph?

In the end, I did as she asked. My hands reached to the little red pots, Hadl's drink. My hands carried one to her, lifted the lid; my voice bade her drink, drink yourself to sleep, sister, drink deep. She cried out only once, when the stuff touched her lips.

I held her to my breast as her breathing grew ragged and then slow, as her body labored on.

"Go," she whispered, but I would not. I knew she was in pain, and my heart broke to think of all the times I had scolded her for her tears. "Take the child. Go."

Then she brought my hands to her throat, she pressed them hard against her own flesh.

"Do it," she said, staring hard into my eyes, my cursed eyes. And she did not look away, even as I—

I loosened her grip, kissed her eyes closed. Her body's labors had brought the child forth, even as she slipped into death. It was a small thing, beautiful and frail and doomed. I hated it for killing my sister, hated it. But I had promised, and so I fetched up the tiny murderess—for a girl child it was, whole and shrieking—and cupped the back of her tiny head in my hand when it would have flopped backward. Eyes that would be brown met mine—

I learned in that moment what Haviva had always known; I still held, deep in the chasms of my seared and hateful heart, some capacity to love.

My heart split open, dead, dry thing that it was, and spilled forth such a wail, such an anguish, that my jaws cracked with the force of it. A terrible keening burst forth and as it hit the night air it lived, and breathed, a raw and beautiful music pregnant with death, thick with venom. I did not unfurl gently into the night this time; I tore through it, shredding its false promise of safety, and felt the fabric of life fray and tremble at my touch. I knew then what I should have always seen, I with my eyes of Pelang; my soul danced not to the melody of the hunt, or the harsh cacophony of life, but to the long, slow lullaby of death.

Shadows flew to me from the sky, from the ground, they tore themselves from the very sky to come to me. Trembling in fear, they knelt at my feet, thick as birthing-blood, bitter as death.

Princess, they babbled at me, a shade of sound I could almost hear. *Your will, Princess.*

"I am no princess," I told them in a voice strange from screaming. "I am your Queen."

This time, the shadows wept with fear.

I stripped to the skin and wrapped the babe as best I was able, knowing it would not help. I did not hurry as I covered my Haviva with our best blanket; let the hunters come, with their cats and their knives and ropes. Let them *dare.* The only reason I left, in the end, the only thing that might send me from her side, was this: I had the child's life to save. And after that—

After that, I vowed, *I have many, many lives to take.*

The men were close, so close I heard them shout as they found my tracks. I crept up onto the scorched earth, a tiny and wailing babe clutched to my breast, and stole away into the fading night.

I held Haviva's child in my arms and watched the sky over the Jehannim. A hot wind rose, scouring my bare skin, tugging at the rags which were all I had left and which I had wrapped about her tiny, dear self.

"You are my Maika," I crooned, kissing the rags. "My tiny queen."

Run, sang the wind, *run while you can.*

Hide, whispered the sand as it scoured my naked skin. *The men are coming. Akari is coming. Hide.*

Die, suggested the shadows, *lie down and die with us, sweet Queen. Your struggle is for naught.*

But I did none of these things. The time was past for running, and for hiding, and for all things born of men and shadows and cowardice.

And besides, I told the wind, and the sand, and the shadows, *I have never seen the sun rise. I have heard it is glorious.*

I took a deep breath as the sky beyond the Jehannim turned to white gold.

Come, my darlings, I commanded the shadows, *come.* They rushed to do my bidding, wailing in defeat, wrapping me in a shroud of darkness.

Come on, girl, I told myself, rising up on the balls of my feet and taking a deep breath. *It is time to dance.*

When Akari burst into the sky, setting the sky aflame, I leapt to meet him, and the shadows leapt with me.

We danced, Akari Sun Dragon and I, we danced on the Edge of the world,

and it was

glorious.

Todd Lockwood

BEFORE MY DEBUT NOVEL RELEASED, I HELPED SHAWN OUT WITH HIS first *Unfettered* collection. He asked if I would donate the cover, in the spirit of all the stories donated by so many authors whose work I knew and admired. I was happy and proud to do so. He had recently read an early draft of *The Summer Dragon: First Book of the Evertide*, so I found myself saying, "I'll write you a story too."

"Great! Cool!" said Shawn, without batting an eye. That story was "Keeper of Memory," set in the distant past of my world. While I work on the sequel to my novel, it only seems right to put a sneak peek in this third volume of *Unfettered*. So here is the prologue to the *Second Book of the Evertide*, tentatively titled *Autumn's Ghost*.

Todd Lockwood

PROLOGUE: SECOND BOOK OF THE EVERTIDE

Todd Lockwood

The Torchbearer was flame made flesh.

Body and limbs black as coal, with face and wings of fiery red. Stripes of orange and yellow twisted up her forelegs and shoulders like a rippling blaze. She even smelled of smoke. All the Juza rode Torchbearers; the dragon breed belonged to them alone. The Juza, the fabled warriors and mounts of the Temple's most elite fighting force, were sometimes called the "Keepers of the Flame." Rumor said these dragons could breathe fire.

The thought of all that heat only made the night feel colder. Magha watched the Juza warrior and his dragon for any furtive glance, any hint that they studied him in return. Magha didn't trust them. He didn't want them here. *Which is the Keeper?* he wondered. *Is it the dragon who keeps the flame? Or the rider who keeps the dragon? Or the two together?*

And who keeps the Keepers?

The Juza fighter called himself Qorru, but did not identify his mount. He didn't speak as he worked, or much at all, actually.

But he moved through the making of camp with efficiency, as he had each of the last five nights, only shedding his armor once he'd fed his dragon and put her to bed. His bow and his quiver of red arrows were never more than a few feet away. His sword remained strapped to his back at all times.

Magha poked another stick into the fire and adjusted the pot of beans bubbling there, scented with the last of their salt pork. "What have I done, Shuja?" he said low to his bondmate, his old war-mount.

The big dragon looked at him askance. Black overall, but smoky on chest and underbelly where his battle scars showed white. He'd been very quiet on this trip so far and said nothing now.

Magha shook his head. His lost, reckless son, Darian, had taken his newly bonded dragon Aru out into the wilderness to chase a fantasy—to join the Dragonry, like his father did as a young man. Curse his impulsive blood.

"I thought if I could pick up Darian's trail quickly, I might avoid greater harm. But I was wrong. This trip has been a bad mistake."

Shuja blinked slowly.

"Everything has changed so much. I feel the aeries slipping away, and I'm powerless to stop it. I had to at least *try* to bring Darian home. It was something that I could..." He looked down at his hands. "Something I could *do*."

He needed to find evidence of Darian's passage soon—a cold cookfire, rumor at an outpost, a carcass where a dragon might have dined—so he put his eldest son Tauman in charge of the aeries. As Broodmaster, in fact, with the aeries' signet ring on his finger.

And he wanted to move light and fast, to pick up Darian's trail quickly, so he begged the Juza commander, the prelate Addai, to please not burden him with an escort. But Addai insisted on sending Qorru. The Juza team caught up to Magha with ease. He never waited for them, but he couldn't shake them either. They dogged him. Never helpful, only ever-present.

Magha worried more with each passing day; he knew the Juza and the Dragonry had designs of their own. Could Tauman handle them? How was he coping? "We've been gone six days with no rest, old friend. Running out of food, and nothing to show for my stubborness." He noted the callus where his finger had grown accustomed to the signet ring, now absent. "I put too much responsibility on too few shoulders. I was rash. And poor Maia stuck in the center of it, the focus of all the striving." His daughter had shown incredible grit and tenacity in the face of combat, threats, and accusations. He knew that Maia, at least, would stand up for herself. But he shouldn't have left them alone for so long. If at all.

"Anger got the best of me again," he said. "It always does. Reiss knew that about me, bless her light. You'd think I'd have learned by now. Instead, I find myself in the wilderness looking for signs of passage left by a creature who can fly."

Shuja snorted. Magha chuckled and patted him on the elbow. "We'll be two days returning, I think. Not three, counting on luck."

Shuja tilted his head in order to meet Magha's gaze. "Home then?" he said, the first words in two days.

"Yes."

"Good," said the dragon, adding a rumbling purr of encouragement.

Magha pushed to his feet. That was that. If Shuja agreed, then it was time. He felt a burden lift for having simply made the decision, but also heavy emptiness in the pit of his stomach. *I'm sorry, Darian, you impulsive child. You are truly on your own now.* He looked for the northern horizon, but twilight and mist hid it from sight. *I pray that you find what you need, and not what you're looking for.*

Shuja rumbled and Magha took a deep breath. "I'd love to give this guy the slip in the middle of the night, but that hasn't worked yet. So we're stuck with him." He crossed his arms. "Qorru!" he called.

The Juza warrior looked up from laying out his armor for the night. Magha raised his chin. "Qorru: I thank you for your assistance these last few long days. I'm sorry you had to be here." He swallowed uncertain words. "It's time to abandon the search for Darian and Aru. The trail has gone completely cold, if there was ever a trail to find. We'll start back to the aeries at first light tomorrow."

"I understand," said the warrior, his brow knitting. "I am sorry."

"No need to apologize. If we haven't found evidence of an encampment by now, then he's beyond our reach."

"You have my condolences, Broodmaster."

Technically, he wasn't really Broodmaster any longer. Tauman was. But he said "Thank you" and turned to his own bed, frowning as he unrolled his blanket.

Shuja leapt to his feet,. "*Stop,*" he growled. The Torchbearer froze in her tracks, head low, as if she'd been caught attempting to flank Shuja. He twisted to face her, putting Magha at his back.

"What is this? What's going on?"

Qorru shook his head. "I did not wish to confront you, but your dragon has caught mine being unstealthy, and spoiled my surprise." He pulled his blade from its sheath. It glittered in the firelight.

Magha felt ice flash inside him, the cold fire of combat readiness. The automatic response to *threat* that sometimes woke him—he and Shuja both—out of dreams. "What are you talking about?"

Qorru planted his feet shoulder-width apart. "I am sorry because I cannot allow you to return to the aeries."

Magha stared at him. "Why not?"

"If we had found your son, neither of you would return. Those were my orders. Now at least your son has a chance. But it's better this way, I think. Man to man. I'm not an assassin. I didn't want to murder you in your sleep."

Magha scanned about for a weapon. His sword was scabbarded on his bedroll, eight feet away. His bow and quiver lay beyond. *Time–make time.* "Not an assassin. And you'll simply return to the aeries and tell them *what*?"

Qorru rocked from foot to foot. "I can never return to the aeries. I will fly instead to Avigal and report to the Temple."

"Why are you doing this?" Magha asked, stalling. He already knew why. The political struggle over the aeries of Riat had turned deadly. The Juza—the Rasaal—were making a power play. *Sweet Avar . . . What harm will they do?*

This was no time for defensive postures. "Shuja—*go!*"

Shuja launched into the Torchbearer as Qorru raised his sword and charged. Magha grabbed the pot of beans off the flames. The handle seared his palm with a sizzle. He screamed but held on, used the side of his boot like a shovel to sweep the cookfire at his attacker—sticks, coals, and all. Most of it bounced off Qorru's shins and knees, but a cloud of smoke and ash enveloped his head. Embers clung to his jerkin. He slowed for a brief moment, stung and blinded by sparks and cinders. Magha swung. Qorru parried blindly, but the pot of beans struck his chin. Rocked his head back. Thick, boiling soup splashed onto his neck and face. He howled and staggered away.

Before Magha could rush him for another strike, Qorru cleared his eyes with an angry swipe and leveled his sword again.

Orange glare erupted to his right. Shuja screamed in pain and outrage. Fire bloomed on his chest and left wing, in splashes and runnels of a viscous flaming liquid. It burned in puddles on the ground. A blazing drool dangled from the Torchbearer's lip. Shuja pressed her against the trees, off balance, raking viciously despite the fire, fighting to keep her head turned away.

Qorru acted in that instant of distraction. Magha dodged, but the fighter sank his blade to the hilt through his side, out his back in a gout of blood. He grabbed Qorru's wrist, held it tight. *Don't let him withdraw the blade.* He dropped the empty pot and grabbed a fistful of Qorru's jerkin, yanked him in for a head butt. Shattered the man's nose in a splash of blood and bubbling soup. Qorru reeled for an instant, then lurched upright again. With a snarl, he wrenched the blade sideways in the wound and shoved Magha back several steps, pinning him to a boulder.

Magha cried out in agony as the warrior twisted his grip, the blade sawing and lurching in his side. He held fast, battling with his other hand to gouge an eye, mash his nose, prevent him from doing the same. Over the man's shoulder, he saw the Torchbearer convulse again. Shuja lunged for the creature's throat. Took hold. Shook his head, ripped cord and muscle with his teeth. When she screamed and gurgled, Qorru turned to look, horrified. The Torchbearer vomited up her last torrent of fire. Flames erupted from her neck, out the sides of Shuja's mouth, splashed on his shoulders, poured into a pool at their feet. She slumped down to lay in its inferno.

Shuja turned toward Magha and Qorru, his chest and mouth ablaze.

With an angry cry, Qorru wrested the blade, pushing downward. Magha groaned and lost his grip. The Juza assassin ripped the sword free and stabbed him again, through his forearm and into his ribs. As Qorru drew back to stab one more time, Shuja's blazing maw dropped over his head and shoulders with a crunch, lifted him off the ground, shook him. His muffled shriek ended with a snap. Then the dragon spat him out, flames dripping from his lips.

Magha slid off the boulder into darkness.

Robert V. S. Redick

RESPONSES TO THE LAST PAGES OF THE CHATHRAND VOYAGE QUARTET might best be described as volcanic. Some readers praised it as beautiful, transcendent, a cause for joy. Others wanted to roast me on a bed of coals by the seaside. A good number embraced both positions. If anyone had a moderate response, I should love to be informed.

The plea I would enter here is that I, too, am eager to learn what happens next in the lives of the Chathrand alums. This story begins that new journey. I think of it as a bridge I very much needed to build: not just between the past and future of my protagonists, but between heaven and hell.

If you haven't read the Quartet, which opens with *The Red Wolf Conspiracy*, what follows may feel like meeting your in-laws for the first time in the middle of a tense (not to say homicidal) family reunion. It also, perforce, contains spoilers.

Robert V. S. Redick

THASHA'S CURE FOR CABIN FEVER

Robert V. S. Redick

"Shipwreck," said Felthrup.

"Landscape," said Hercól.

"Monsters," said the young woman seated across from them, elbow on table, chin on a battle-scarred fist. "I mean it:, you're monsters. I could be dying here and you'd take no notice. I could be dead."

"You could be a touch less dramatic," said Hercól.

The swordsman, her fighting tutor, spoke without looking up. She scowled at him through unwashed golden hair.

"You are both wise and cultured, Master Hercól," said Felthrup, "but in the arena of the jigsaw, you are a foundling. This puzzle depicts a shipwreck, I tell you."

"Landscape," insisted Hercól. "A blue mountain glimpsed from a window. As I shall prove when I find *that* bit, that single missing—"

The young woman's eyes slid to the black walnut table. In its whorls she saw figures in agony, torn by ghost panthers, drowning in pitch.

"I'm going to kick this table over," she said.

"Will you, Lady Thasha?" said Felthrup, not lifting his eyes. "I should think even your prodigious muscles—is that the word, prodigious?—would be thwarted by a table nailed so firmly to the deck. Besides, you are a convalescent. Dr. Chadfallow is still worried about your shortness of breath."

Thasha surged to her feet. *I'll show you shortness of breath.* Leaning forward, she blew at the thousand bits of puzzle with all her might.

Nothing moved. Hercól chuckled and rapped on the tin sheet before him.

"Magnetized, m'lady," added Felthrup. "Have you forgotten we're at sea?"

Felthrup was a woken rat—brave, bookish, gifted, impeccably clean. Hercól was a *Thojmélée* fighter and one of the deadliest men alive. Thasha would have given her life for either of them in an instant, and had never doubted that the feeling was reciprocated. Until, perhaps, today. She could not quite manage to laugh at the thought.

"I took your sword once, Hercól," she said.

"Did you? That was cheeky."

"It was desperate. You were crushed beneath a stone. And I killed that man, the one who was torturing us. Are you listening? I killed him, I *beheaded* him, with your sword Ildraquin. You remember, don't you?"

She could hear the accusation in her voice, but what she truly felt was closer to terror. For she knew Hercól would not reply: on the I.M.S. *Chathrand,* no one ever spoke about the past.

She closed her eyes, willed herself to remember. A forest clearing, a ruined tower, a mage working a death-spell. An instant of perfect clarity as she swung the blade.

Where, when, why? Her memories were sharp and bright and shattered, a mirror caught in a cyclone. She could pluck them one by one from that gritty whirlwind, but even as she did so, a voice insisted that she was lying to herself. *Let go all that,* said the voice, the stern voice of an aunt or priestess, *Let go, rest easy, that is not memory but mirage.*

"It happened," she said aloud.

"We believe you, Thasha," murmured Hercól.

But of course he didn't. No one believed those tales that poured from her, those phantom memories that had grown like a riot of weeds during her illness. A circumnavigation of the world in this very ship. Battles with mercenaries, flame trolls, sorcerers, mutant rats. Lost empires in the south, cities of crystal, black forests of carnivorous trees. Storms of red light enveloping the *Chathrand*. A valley swallowed by a wave.

All so real. But so were dreams, weren't they, until shattered by birdsong, morning clatter in the kitchen, the drop of a spoon?

What if the voice was right? What if her illness had blown shards of her dream life into her waking mind, like sea birds carried inland by a storm?

She lifted her eyes to a painting on the stateroom wall. The River Ool in springtime, not far from the Isiq family mansion, a barge stacked high with cargo for the seaport, morning mist, a fieldstone wall, two boys climbing a tree.

Utter sap. Why not add a rainbow.

Then Thasha frowned. Across the river, on a hilltop hazy with distance: tombstones, cracked and fallen. Gaunt figures crouched among them, digging with their hands, tugging, eating what they found. Tall, bone-white beings. Ghouls.

"What in the Nine Pits—"

She shook herself. Man and rat ignored her. There were no ghouls in the painting, no tombstones, nothing but shadows on the hill.

She closed her eyes. Don't panic. Recite the certainties, the precious mundane.

You're seventeen. You dropped out of school. You live in Etherhorde in wealth and boredom with your father and a nurse and two slobbering dogs. Your mother's long dead, barely a memory. Your father's important, the emperor's fleet admiral, and sometimes he plays the diplomat. This is one of those times. But you, you're just an ornament, a dependent, along for the ride. We're sailing west to the island of Simja; the wind is steady but the seas are flat. Nothing happens. The days are endless, soundless, quiet as winter, quiet as a tomb.

And the point of the journey? *We're to witness a marriage, to cheer the signing of a treaty, the end of a war.* Which war? Whose marriage? Thasha's nails bit into her palm. The answers darted like minnows, needle-bright, impossible to touch.

"I think I'll visit the topdeck," she told the chamber. "I need fresh air."

"Whatever for, Lady Thasha?" squeaked Felthrup, suddenly attentive. "You are in the stateroom of the finest ship afloat. And as you well know, it is the genius of the *Chathrand*'s design that her wealthy passengers never want for fresh air, never breathe the miasma of the lower decks." He raised his eyes to the brass orifices in the ceiling, the mouths of the windscoop pipes. "You are enjoying the breeze off the Nelu Peren at this very moment, fresh as any sailor aloft."

"I've had enough of privacy," she said. "Come with me, Felthrup. You could do with a bit of sun."

"But there is no sun," said her father.

She whirled. The old admiral was seated with his feet up in the window seat of the portside galleries, a book across his lap. The windows were heavily curtained, as they always seemed to be of late—for warmth, they assured her. Admiral Isiq lifted a corner, barely an inch, and frowned out on a world Thasha could not see.

"Mist," he said. "Thick and cold. You don't want to step out there today, my morning star. Pneumonia is the worst sort of lodger: destructive on arrival, difficult to evict. I've seen more sailors perish by a relapse of that disease than by cannon fire."

Thasha stood at bay. The sight of her father had deeply unsettled her. It was unlike him to crawl into window seats: the old man was stout and stiff. But there was more to her unease. His voice? His very *presence*?

Her heart thumped wildly, a sparrow in a cage.

Get ahold of yourself, Thasha. Of course your father's here. Where else would he be?

She glanced about the stateroom, determined not to be startled again. Besides the two men and Felthrup, there was Marila, her pearl-diver friend, brushing her hair in the washroom doorway. There was Nama, her old nurse, seated in a corner and rather furiously knitting a scarf. There were Jorl and Syzyt, her mastiffs, dozing and drooling beneath the table. There were the muffled cries of birds and sailors, the thump of boots overhead.

"I'm not ill," she said at last, wishing someone would make eye contact. "And there's always a mist, isn't there? I can scarcely remember the sun."

"Then you're definitely not recovered," called Marila from the washroom.

"Heed your friends and be patient," said the admiral. "You still have one foot in the grave."

In the corner, Nama's knitting needles were a cart horse on cobbles: *tick-nick, tick-nick*. Thasha moved toward her father. At the very least she could look out at the mist. But the admiral, irritatingly enough, settled his shoulder firmly against the curtain and opened his book.

Fine, starboard: no one seated there.

"Lady Thasha, please!" cried Felthrup. "Master Hercól's pursuit of a landscape will drive me to outright *verbosity*! And you promised to help."

Thasha stifled a growl. Why in the Nine Pits did the puzzle mean so much to them? And why did they never make any progress?

"Give me ten minutes with that stupid thing. Alone."

Man and rat left the table. She sat down and studied the chaos on the metal sheet. Hercól's mountain, she saw at once, was no mountain at all. It was living tissue, blue scales on a limb or a neck. Reptilian. She turned the pieces, glaring. Every one of them was fighting her, refusing to mate. Just when she seemed to have the pattern, it melted into clashing colors, divergent lines.

"It's a boat," she said aloud.

"Look again," said Hercól.

She blinked—and the pieces blurred. Was that deck planking or tree trunk? An oarlock or a knocker on a cottage door?

"You see our plight, m'lady?" said Felthrup. "It could keep us occupied for weeks."

"Only if we let it," she snapped.

But he was right: the puzzle was fighting her. Second by second, the pattern retreated, no image, no story, a primordial chaos that would claim her too—

Her knuckles went white on the arm of the chair. *You won't win, damn you. Every puzzle has a solution if you dare to see it.*

"I read here that the Simjans believe their dead return as insects," said Admiral Isiq, squinting at his book. "That if you gaze long and deep into the eyes of dragonflies, you will see the faces of departed friends, and catch their voices in the droning of bees."

Snap. Two pieces locked.

Every head turned Thasha's way.

"Definitely a boat," she said.

"Daughter," said the admiral, "leave off there and come to me. Read me a page or two; my old eyes are—"

Snap.

Snap.

The others froze as though she'd drawn a knife. The sailors aloft fell silent. Only Nama knitted on, *tick-nick, tick-nick.*

"It's one of the landing craft," said Thasha. "Hercól! Look here, it's *our* boat, the one we tried to take ashore in Bali Adro. The boat the sea-serpent crushed, that day we nearly drowned."

Marila drifted from the washroom and looked over Thasha's shoulder.

"All right," she conceded, "a boat. Are you happy? But it can't be yours, Thasha. Don't get carried away."

"Why can't it?"

"Because no one paints you into a jigsaw puzzle unless you're famous."

"Well of course I'm famous," said Thasha. "We all are. I mean, I'd rather we weren't, it was terrible—"

"What are we famous for, exactly?"

Thasha looked at her old friend, begged with her eyes. In a whisper, she said, "Saving the world."

Marila put her head back and laughed.

Thasha dropped her eyes, jabbed furiously at the puzzle. The voice was Marila's but the laugh was not: Marila was incapable of cruelty, but that sound was like a fistful of glass. *Saving the world!* she thought. *Where did that howler spring from? You're a rich girl from Etherhorde, you've never done a bold thing in your sheltered, fleeting, ridiculous little–*

Snap.

Another piece. She had the horizon, now, and the stern of the boat.

"I'm famished, suddenly," said the admiral. "What's keeping old Fiffengurt? Thasha, just go and pull the lunch-bell, will you?"

Snap. Snap. The puzzle was losing, the image taking shape. There were the boiling blue-green waves, the sand-spit islands, the frail open boat. There the gargantuan serpent, rising above it, a mountain with fangs.

"You must be hungry too, Thasha," said Hercól. "Healing requires focus, but also fuel. Let us put that puzzle away for now and lay the table."

Snap. Snap. Snap.

And suddenly she saw him: the brown boy, the figure she had not known she was seeking. An utter stranger. A friend.

Find him.

She had only a fragment: his left hand and wrist, and a bare bit of forearm. The others muttered in a growing chorus–*food, lunch, clear the table*–but now another voice was rising, drowning them out.

Find him, find all of him, hands shoulders shirt rib cage brown cheeks warm welcoming lips–

"LUNCH IS SERVED!"

The stateroom's double doors crashed open, and Mr. Fiffengurt swept in with a great sizzling tray.

He was the *Chathrand*'s quartermaster, a kindly ruffian with a limp and a lazy eye. "See what old Teggatz cooked up for you, Miss Thasha!" he boomed. "Ruby prawns caught this morning, broiled in coconut milk, and red Sorrophran taters–"

"Almost finished," said Thasha. *The boy, the boy–*

"–and Ulsprit watercress, and deviled grouse eggs, and plum

wine to wash it down. And bowls of salted whatsit for you and the dogs, Master Felthrup. You can't say we don't spoil our guests."

All lethargy vanished; her friends rushed the tray like wolves. Thasha was trembling: where was he? Why could she not find one more piece the color of his skin?

Felthrup hopped on the table: "I adore salted whatsit!"

Marila whisked the magnetic puzzle from the table; Thasha stifled a cry. Bowls and cutlery appeared. Fiffengurt took a seat with all the rest.

"Come, Nama: won't you join us?" said the admiral, filling his plate.

"Presently," said the nurse. *Tick-nick, tick-nick.*

"And you, Thasha? You have always loved prawns."

"No thank you," said Thasha.

"But it's hours since breakfast," said Fiffengurt, shoveling potatoes onto his dish.

"You will grow pleuritic without food," said Felthrup. "Is that the word I require, m'lady, pleuritic? Perhaps the connotation is not quite—ah, mmm, gah."

He buried his face in his bowl. Dogs, rat, humans: all were jolly and ravenous. Now and then they beckoned to her empty chair. The mounds of prawn shells grew, but the food in the serving dishes never seemed to decline.

"Every puzzle has a solution," said Thasha.

"Yes, but you were right about that blasted jigsaw," said Hercól. "Not worth the effort. I suggest we stow it away."

They went on eating, wiping their mouths on linen napkins, reaching for more. With a shudder, Thasha recalled what she had seen in the painting: the feast among tombstones, the ghouls.

"Do you know what I really want?" she told them. "A bit of bread. I'll bet Teggatz has some warm heel he can—"

"He doesn't," said Fiffengurt through a mouthful. "Sorry, m'lady, I asked."

Thasha sidled toward the doors. "Then I'll just . . . see what else he's cooking. Doesn't matter, really." She frowned. "Right, where are my boots? I left them right here by the doors. Which of you tidied up, and where did you put them?"

No one answered. But above their smacking lips and grunts of satisfaction she heard another sound, a sound that chilled her blood.

It was very low, at the threshold of her hearing. But it was not her imagination. The sound was a moan of deathly pain or paralyzing fear, or both. It was the voice of someone in agony. And it was calling her name.

Thasha whirled, panic-stricken. "Rin's love, people, can't you hear—"

The sound vanished in a puff of steam: Marila was filling a teapot from the samovar. Thasha steadied herself against the door.

Is this hell? Am I dead already? Will you take me apart if I sit down, skin me, devour me raw?

"My dear daughter—eat!" said the admiral, passing Marila his teacup. "Or at the very least have a cup with us. Chereste plumroot, your favorite. Sit down, keep an old man company. I'll tell you a story about your mother, if you like."

"I'd like that, when I return," said Thasha.

"Now see here." The admiral wagged a finger. "You must abandon this talk of tramping about the ship. You'll catch your death of cold."

"In the *galley*? It's hot as the Nine Pits in there."

"Captain Rose is in a foul mood, too," said Fiffengurt. "There's a reef in this mist, and he's all nerves, shouting at the crew to peel their eyes every second they're aloft. You don't want to cross paths with him today."

"Rubbish," said Thasha. "What's he going to do, Mr. Fiffengurt, confine me to quarters? Oh Gods, where are my *boots*?"

The others chewed more slowly now, watching her sidelong.

"I understand," said Hercól, "that a cough is spreading among the crew."

"Then I won't kiss anyone," said Thasha, gripping the left-hand doorknob. *And to hell with it, I'll go barefoot.*

At the table, Marila nudged Felthrup sharply, eliciting a squeak. "Hercól is right!" he blurted. "I took a turn about the decks just this morning, and how I wish I had not! Coughs, wheezes, sniffles, leaky noses—"

"I don't care," said Thasha.

"—neglected hygiene, mucus, sores and burst blisters, every manner of effluent discharging from sailors, tarboys, passengers, from every part of them at once, from their arsenal of orifices—"

"Shut up, Felthrup!" The rat shook himself, and Thasha felt somewhat cruel. But she pressed on. "Listen, I don't care if the whole mucking crew is wallowing in dysentery. I'm going for a walk."

"Will you, then?" Felthrup cocked his head and hunched his shoulders in a fair impression of listening. "And after all, why not? Master Hercól, Master Fiffengurt, perhaps we are mistaken? Perhaps—"

"I forbid you to leave the stateroom, girl," boomed her father.

Thasha turned the knob.

Hercól, Fiffengurt, and Marila leaped to their feet and rushed her. The mastiffs followed, howling. Felthrup flung himself from the table. Thasha pulled at the door with all her might—it had become preposterously heavy, the door of a bank vault, or a crypt. But it moved. She gripped its edge, gasping, and just managed to wedge her shoulder through the gap.

Hercól snatched at her arm. Marila grabbed a handful of shirt. She fought back, swearing, kicking.

"Let me go! What's the matter with you? Are you my friends or my mucking jailors?"

"Let her go! Why not?" Felthrup nipped at their ankles. "Freedom! More precious in the last than shallow safety! Thou art my oath and my covenant, my homunculus, oh hell, that's not what I—"

"VARAK!"

Nama stood up. Her knitting fell to the floor; her blue shawl fell; her gray hair writhed about her shoulders; the mastiffs cringed; something was in flames at Thasha's feet. Nama, shaking with fury, reached with one blue-veined hand toward the doorway, and finally, finally, someone met Thasha's eye.

Reeking breath, warm wet tongues. Her dogs were competing for access to her face. Their dumb affection: what else in the universe promised so much comfort? Even before she opened her eyes, Thasha reached out to scratch them, a reflex action. But her hand met rough wool. Nama was standing by her bed.

They were in Thasha's cabin adjoining the stateroom. The nurse's lips were sealed tight, but her jaw chewed curses. The door to the outer chamber was closed.

"What did you do?" Thasha asked.

"What I swore to do, girl," snapped Nama. "Protect you from all harm. Including harm from yourself."

"I wasn't about to—"

"Shut up. You have no idea what you were about to do."

"Nama, don't talk to me that way."

"What an ignorant slouch of a girl you are. Why did I choose you? Anyone would have served. A fisherman's daughter. A dairy maid. A wet nurse. The hat-check girl at the Etherhorde Lion."

"Served . . . for what?"

"Shelter, of course. A roof over my head. Now behave yourself, do you hear me? By the Gods, it's almost over."

Thasha felt suddenly cold. "Something caught fire," she said. "I smelled it too. Like burning skin."

Nama studied her warily. "Nothing is burning now," she said. Then she turned away, only to pause again beside the door. "If you feel unwell, call Dr. Chadfallow. Use the speaking tubes; they're labeled. *P* for—"

"Physic. I know."

"Very good. Now lie still and—"

"But Nama, Dr. Chadfallow is dead."

The nurse froze. Thasha waited, scarcely daring to breathe. *Deny it. Chadfallow was stabbed on the lower gun deck, we were a month from landfall, we buried him at sea. Deny the memory. I dare you.*

Nama spoke over her shoulder.

"Call whomever you like then. Call for food, call a tarboy to empty the chamber pot. Just don't bother me again, girl. Let me work."

She slammed the door behind her. Thasha's limbs felt cold. She'd caught a glimpse of the men and Marila: lurking in the stateroom, vacant, lost, waiting for the nurse to return.

Let me work. Nama was not speaking of her knitting.

Thasha swung her feet to the floor.

Nama was not Nama.

She stood up, horrified. If her nurse was not her nurse, then Hercól and Marila were not themselves either. Nor Felthrup, nor Fiffengurt. Nor even her father.

She looked down at the mastiffs. *Nor you, you pair of lummoxes?*

She took a step toward the door. Instantly, Jorl and Syzyt began to pace, whining deep in their chests. Thasha hushed them, made them lie down. All her life they had been obedient to a fault. Now they watched her in anguish. When she reached for the doorknob, they erupted in howls.

Security guards.

This was a jail after all.

She dashed to the porthole window. Madness: the glass was painted over from the outside. Some fool sailor's mistake, and no time to correct it in the rush to launch in time for the wedding.

No! Thasha struck the wall with both fists. *No mistake. If my family's not my family, then even this ship, these timbers . . .*

She paced the cabin: window to door, dresser to writing table. Portrait of her parents on their wedding day. Antique mirror, antique mariner's clock upon her dresser. Speaking tubes. Her dagger and her training sword on the wall above the headless, blade-scarred practice dummy. Her private bookshelf. Her basket of sweat-stained clothes.

She looked at her knuckles: there were splinters from where she'd struck the wall. If this was an illusion, it was nearly flawless. This cabin was her own. And she was not meant to leave it until the thing that looked like Nama finished its work.

And by then, Thasha knew in her bones, it would be too late.

She crossed her hands over her chest, calming herself as Hercól had taught her. A perfect counterfeit, all this. But in its very perfection, could there be hope? For Thasha had tricks of her own. If only she could remember them.

She lay back on her bed, searching her thoughts. Then, as if at the prompting of a dream, she rose and approached the mariner's clock. It was a masterpiece, this clock. It told not just the time but the seasons, the phases of the moon. A circle of leaded glass protected the clockface, which was an extravaganza of rosewood, walrus ivory, gold lacquer, and mother of pearl. The face itself was mounted on a hinge, as though the centuries-dead clockmaker had wanted easy access to the guts of the machine.

Open it, her mind insisted. Somehow, the clock's interior would lead her to a friend.

But that was nonsense. What friend could fit inside a clock? No answers, only the teasing storm. She began to pace again, cursing under her breath. She studied the clock from all angles, pressed her ear to its side.

She snatched her practice sword from the wall and drove it blade down through her bed.

Ramachni!

The name surfaced like a whale. Ramachni, her lifelong ally, linked to her somehow by the clock. Was he a mage, a woken animal, a warrior like Hercól? Was his face hidden in the clock's artwork, in that setting sun or gibbous moon?

Then, horror: the practice dummy was bleeding, gushing from its severed neck, bleeding as living tissue pierced by a hundred wounds—

No! She shook her head; those were only old stains and stitches. *Don't look, don't give in to delirium, get back to the clock.*

Hand shaking, she unscrewed the glass cover on the clockface. The firefly thoughts of him shone instantly brighter. Yes, a mage. Whatever this false Nama was attempting, Ramachni would put a stop to it. He made things right.

She touched the minute hand. Memories swarmed from it: climbing her fingertips, her arm, spreading through her veins. *Spin it forward, that's it. Around again, and again.* The hour hand followed, advancing through the day. With each revolution, Thasha's mind grew clearer. And at last she knew.

Twelve minutes past seven. That was their code, the trigger for the spell that would call out to him across all distances. But she had to stop at nine minutes past the hour. For three minutes the clock would handle the spell alone. Then the clockface would click open of its own accord, and he would come.

The sweep of the second hand brought him ever closer. Thasha felt warmed from within. Ramachni did not fail, did not abandon his friends. The minute hand reached eleven. She knew his power in battle, the way he'd crushed foes greater than these. What a surprise for her jailors. The minute hand ticked to twelve.

Nothing happened.

She tugged. The hinge would not move. She touched the clockface with two fingers and nearly burst into tears.

"Ramachni."

She could feel him on the other side—inches away, a world away, his hand pressed against her own.

Oh Thasha, my champion.

"Come through," she whispered. "Open the door."

You know I cannot. There is only one mage aboard the great ship, and she will brook no interference. Nor can I cross this abyss between us. I can only wait for you here.

"Help me." She was reduced to begging, babbling. "Help me, I'm alone."

Not entirely.

"The others aren't real. Gods, I don't know if *anything*'s real."

You are real, Thasha. And so am I.

Her fingers were sweating. She believed him, but his words were not enough. "I can't face her. My mind's in a thousand pieces. I can't remember my life."

All those pieces make a whole.

"Ramachni, you say I'm not alone. Do you mean Felthrup? He heard me, finally. He took my side."

I am sorry. Felthrup is gone.

His words brought it back to her: the flash of light, the small flame at her ankles. Burning skin—and yes, burning fur.

"She killed him! She murdered Felthrup!"

I must go.

"Ramachni, was he real, like you? Is that why he tried to help me?"

She will sense me, Thasha, and things will be worse.

"You don't understand, there's death everywhere I look here, it's seeping in through the walls. I'm going mad. I can feel it."

Goodbye.

"Tell me what's real, Ramachni. Tell me, if you've ever loved me at all."

Have you never understood, then? Mages do not love.

It was like a blow to the face. Thasha wept where she stood, and almost took her hand from the clockface. Then rage boiled up in her, and she snarled.

"Yes, they do. One of them at least. But he lies about it."

The silence that followed was absolute, but she could still feel him, feel his struggle. And then she felt his surrender, and his voice began again.

It was your choice. There was evil loose in Alifros that only she could overcome. You may not love her, but she bested that evil. She did what we could not.

"My choice? Are you saying I promised her my service?"

No, Thasha. Your body. Your senses. Your mind.

A click. Thasha whirled as the door opened. The thing that was not Nama stood there, glaring.

"What are you doing with that clock?"

Thasha could feel her heart slamming in her chest. But *were* they hers, any longer, if what Ramachni said was true?

"Are you deaf, girl? I said, what do you think you're doing?"

"You killed Felthrup," Thasha whispered. "You murdered my friend."

The Nama-creature blinked at her, cold as death. "Who were you speaking to?" it said at last.

"My dogs," said Thasha. "Are you going to burn them to cinders too?"

"Perhaps."

Thasha looked past the creature's shoulder: Hercól and Fiffengurt had drawn chairs up against the stateroom doors. They sat with crossed arms, waiting.

Snap.

Thasha twitched. "Your name," she said. "I've remembered your name."

"Shall I congratulate you?"

"But I don't know why you're holding me prisoner, or where we are. This isn't the *Chathrand*, of course."

The Nama-creature made a face, as though the question was difficult to settle.

"And I don't know why you've crushed my memories to bits. Are you experimenting on me? Are you dissecting my mind like a frog?"

"Of course. And I throw babies to wolves as a pastime. However did you guess?"

"You're Erithusmé," said Thasha. "You're the greatest mage to walk the earth in centuries."

"Millennia, as it happens."

"But there was still someone more powerful, wasn't there?"

"Never," said the mage. "I am unmatched since the first days of the Worldstorm, when Mäsithe of Ullum was lost upon the Ruling Sea. But five war-hounds may kill a wolf, and fifty sorcerers lusting for power—yes, they very nearly killed me."

"And I was the tool that prevented it?"

"There are better words than 'tool.' Nothing was forced on you."

"You're a mucking liar," said Thasha. "If I'd agreed, you'd never have broken into my mind, made me forget—"

Erithusmé hissed through her teeth, and Thasha jumped. The three hands of the clock detached themselves from the mechanism, flitted past her shoulder, and landed on the mage's palm.

"I did not take that hammer to your memories, girl. You arranged for it yourself." She closed a wrinkled fist around the clock hands and left the room without another word.

Thasha crossed the room, placed a hand on the door. "You can't use me any longer," she whispered. "Whatever I agreed to, it wasn't this."

She glanced at the disabled clock. Ramachni could not return, but the fact that he had spoken with her at all meant that Erithusmé did not control everything. If this was hell, she was not the queen of hell. This false *Chathrand* could still surprise her, even if she was the reason it existed at all.

Thasha pulled the sword from the mattress. It felt good in her hand, familiar. On an impulse, she retrieved the sword-belt and scabbard from her wardrobe, buckled it around her waist. She could fight—the trickle of memories included numerous battles—but no, that wasn't the answer. Erithusmé could disarm her with a word, gag her, bind her to the bed. For that matter, why hadn't she done so already? And why provide her sword and dagger? And why in the Nine Pits didn't she simply lock all the doors?

She didn't want to shut me in my cabin. She needs me strong, healthy, well fed. She needs me to be ready. But for what?

For long captivity. For oblivion. For a year, a lifetime in these chambers, playing with jigsaws, pissing in pots. *Damn Ramachni and his non-interference!* Damn him for his caution, for leaving her utterly alone.

But all at once his words came back to her: *Not entirely.*

What had he meant? Who else could she possibly call upon, and what could they do against the mage?

She sheathed the sword, glanced at the array of copper speaking tubes, sprouting from the wall like the pipes of a miniature organ. She went to them, wiped away dust, read the engraved labels. G for Galley, *P* for Physic, *SA* for Sanitary Assistance (the chamber pot), Q for the quarterdeck, the command center of the great ship, the domain of—

"Rose? Captain Rose?"

She murmured the name aloud, then shook her head: what was she thinking? Rose was the last person on earth she would choose as an ally. He was always ill-tempered, frequently violent, more than a little unhinged. He was obsessed with oral hygiene and afraid of cats.

He was also, like Dr. Chadfallow, dead. Thasha was not sure that mattered in this land of imposters. But it could hardly be an advantage.

Or could it?

She tore open the tube before her doubts could stop her. "Captain," she whispered. "This is Thasha Isiq. Can you hear me?"

She held her breath. She heard the hum of the wind in the ratlines, the groaning of timbers, a tarboy's cough. Nothing else. She shot a glance at her cabin door and tried again.

"Captain Rose, please answer me, I'm begging you, I—"

"What are you about, girl? And why the devil are you whispering?"

It was his voice, his unmistakable rumble—or was it? Something in its tone or timbre had changed, dried out.

"Speak up, girl."

"Captain, excuse me, but"—*Say something, anything, stall for time!*—"how are you feeling today?"

"State your purpose or be damned to you!" barked the man. "We're navigating a reef, and I am not your blasted valet!"

That was the Rose she knew. Still, that voice . . . Thasha bit her lips. *If I'm wrong, if he's just one of her servants—aya Rin, it's all over.*

This much was clear, though: if it was Rose, he would not answer a second time. Thasha blurted: "She's going to kill me, I can feel it. Kill me, or let me die. Please, Captain, you've got to help me. There's no one else I can trust."

In the long silence that followed, she heard him breathing. She could almost see him there, stock-still among hundreds of busy sailors. She could feel his mind at work.

"That creature in the stateroom," he said at last. "She's holding you prisoner?"

"Yes."

"Against your will?"

"Of course! What other kind of prisoner is there?"

Now Rose himself was whispering. "Her kind, that's what. Her puppets. We're surrounded by them. The whole ship is infested."

Relief drenched Thasha like a waterfall; she was no longer alone. But then she thought of Ramachni: *She will sense me, and things will be worse.*

"Captain Rose, there's no time. Get me out of here. Please."

"Out of the stateroom?"

"Out of her clutches! Out of this trap!"

"She's doing all of this for you, isn't she?"

"For me?" hissed Thasha. "Like hell, Captain! She's doing it *to* me."

"And you want me to spring you? I can."

"Do it. Bless you. Do it now."

"Of course," said the captain, "I will ask a favor in return."

A tiny sound made Thasha whirl. Someone was turning the doorknob.

"Anything!" said Thasha. "It's yours, I promise, I swear on my mother's soul! Just *get me out of here.*"

The door flew open. Erithusmé stood there, blazing with fury, her hand outstretched.

"Step back from the speaking tubes," she said.

"There's only one way," said Captain Rose, "and that way is—"

"Did you hear me, girl? Stand aside!"

"—shipwreck."

The world heaved. Six hundred sailors cried aloud. Through the timbers, the rudder chain made a sound like galloping horses as Captain Rose spun the wheel. The *Chathrand* lurched to starboard, rolling on her beam-ends. Screams followed—the bending screams of men in free fall—and then the thumps and splashes as they struck rails, rigging, open sea. One particular, ear-splitting cry rose above the others:

"REEF! REEF! BRACE FOR—"

The ship struck. Thasha and Erithusmé were flung like dolls through the cabin door and across the stateroom, and her dogs followed in a chaos of howls and collisions and snapping legs that made Thasha scream aloud; she felt the hull shatter like an eggshell, heard the sea rush in, felt the pressure in her ears, saw Marila and her father and Hercól and Fiffengurt maimed and bleeding against the walls. The stateroom doors against which Thasha lay were bending, bowing, the water had already reached them, was about to smash through them like the Gods' own battering ram, the portside window exploded, the salt water blasted across the chamber, and then Erithusmé raised a hand and said, "I yield to you, idiots," and the world was still.

She is falling, slow as a feather, empty as a husk. She cannot speak, can scarcely move; even to turn her eyeballs within her head taxes her strength. The medium about her feels like water but is not; she is breathing it, and dry. The light is slate gray and somehow inverted, as though it reveals not by reflection but negation: a chisel scraping away. Ten yards to her right lies the colossal *Chathrand*, keel shattered, spars and rigging furred with some kind of hoarfrost, drifts of ashen sediment upon the deck.

The bodies of her friends are falling beside her: a mangled, soundless snow. Hercól's back is broken. The admiral's eyes are gently closed. Marila's hands grip the timber that has been driven through her chest.

She lands in silt. Marila, at twenty paces, is the next to touch the earth. But even as she lands, her form changes, melts. She is no longer Marila but a writhing spirit, a shadow in a stream. The creature turns to Thasha, arms outstretched. Landing, the others too cast off their human forms, and all begin to glide in her direction, their eyes mere empty sockets, their mouths like gashes with a knife.

Thasha is gripped by a terror beyond anything she has ever known. With all her strength she fights the rictus that has seized her body, but only manages to turn her head a few inches. It is enough: a wide sweep of the slate-gray land opens before her—jagged, desolate—and from every direction the shadow-creatures are flowing and billowing toward her. They have one will, one need, like a people dying of thirst who have discovered a spring. But that spring is Thasha, and it is the warm blood in her that calls to them.

The first shadow clutches at her arm. Voiceless, Thasha screams; her flesh is blistering with cold—and with that scream, her rictus is gone.

She tears the sword from her belt and strikes. The creature breaks, scatters like oil in water. But before her eyes it begins to recover its shape. She leaps away; it follows. And now the others have surrounded her, ring upon ring. She whirls and slashes, but they are too many, they are infinite, and even cut to ribbons they manage to grip and bite and suck at her, and the cold seeps into her bones.

The sword slips from her fingers. Her death will be a useless one, in silence, in bitterest exile. She spits a curse—but why go out cursing? Seventeen years was long enough, life had been rich enough, after the Red Storm and the Nelluroq Vortex, the war with the rats, the cities of the dlömu, the glass spiders with their webs of crystal, the ogress at the bridge of ice, the boy who had loved her, sworn he'd always love her, touched her awed and humbled but with a heat like the sun—

She drops to her knees. The creatures fall on her like insects. They are drinking now, drinking her life. But even as her eyesight fails, she sees him: Captain Rose, massive, furious, charging from the broken hull of the *Chathrand,* his beard flowing wild about his shoulders, swinging his terrible axe. Behind him comes a woman Thasha has never seen, ancient as the hills but tall and strong. In her hands is a length of fabric, and it is red—blood red, furnace red, the only thing with color in this blighted land.

From the time that follows, only one image survives: Captain Rose lumbering against a savage wind, teeth gritted, unstoppable. He is holding Thasha against his chest. The red shawl is about her, whipping like a flag in a gale. All around them are the shadow-creatures, numberless, famished, but they fear to touch her now, and they have no interest in Rose. The ancient woman staggers after them, bone weary, falling behind.

"Eyes open."

Thasha blinked. A candle. A natural yellow candle, sputtering a little as though from damp. Rose was holding it near her face.

"Ouch!"

Hot wax had dripped on her neck. "Good," said Rose. "You feel pain. That means you're all the way back, if the mage spoke the truth."

Thasha sat up. She and Rose were deep in a cave. It was wet and dark, but against one wall a campfire burned atop a mound of sand. Thasha sniffed: weed, brine, shellfish.

"Where are we?" she asked.

Before Rose could answer, a low booming filled the cave. Thasha looked wildly around. The cave was tunnel-shaped, slick-walled, and astonishingly long. Miles away to her left it ended in a round mouth, bright and pale blue, like a spring day glimpsed through the wrong end of a telescope. The booming sound came from that way. To her right the tunnel ran on into darkness.

Thasha was naked, draped only in a careworn woolen cloth. She hugged it around her, but it was wet and ragged; in fact it was coming apart.

"You're cold," said Rose. "Crawl up by the fire."

Thasha dragged herself up the mound of sand. The cave, she saw now, was flooded to within twenty feet of where they stood. The booming sound came again, and now she knew that it was surf.

Captain Rose was in full dress uniform. "You look so—healthy," she said absurdly. "Your clothes are almost new."

"I should hope so," he grumbled, examining a cuff link. "You buried me in these."

It was true: she remembered him laid out on the forecastle, his red beard combed out straight over that smart blue jacket, and how she'd wondered at the time whose job it was to groom and dress a corpse before it was given to the sea.

All her memories were returning; the puzzle was nearly complete. But she recalled nothing of the escape from the shadow-creatures, the journey through that silent hell.

"How long did you carry me?" she asked.

Rose was whittling a bit of driftwood. "Time is fickle in that place: it flows fast or slow, according to laws the living cannot grasp. Have you worked out where 'that place' was, incidentally?"

Thasha warmed her hands. "I think so," she said. "I saw that place before, when I fell into a coma. I think we were in Agaroth."

Rose snorted. "Agaroth," he said. "The Border Kingdom, the No Man's Land between the living and the dead? You're not the first to survive a glimpse of it, girl. Many of the living are given a taste of Agaroth, when ill or mortally wounded. And yes, I carried you through Agaroth, through that endless twilight, to reach this cave.

"But that is not where we began. All your arguments with the mage, all your charades aboard the false *Chathrand*, occurred where the real ship lies to this day: far beyond Agaroth, in the Land of the Dead."

Thasha leaned closer to the fire. A part of her had known it already.

"Hercól, Marila, my father—"

"Dead souls," said the captain. "Random ghosts, drawn to the bait of your living blood, then snared by Erithusmé. She forced them to serve the illusion, but it was your mind she sifted for the details—faces, voices, habits, tics."

"But I'm not dead!"

"Of course not," said Rose. "If you were, she could not even attempt to return you to the living world. And the mage had sworn to see it done. Why was that, girl? What in blazes did she owe you?"

Under the shawl, Thasha passed her hands over her body: shoulders, chest, stomach, hips.

"Rent," she said. "Seventeen years of rent."

The captain squinted at her. Then he rose and walked a few yards away and knelt by a dark pool. When he approached the fire again, three spiny crabs were wriggling on his stick. He thrust them into the flames.

"I don't suppose," said Thasha, "that you'd lend me your coat?"

"You could not touch it," said the captain. "My coat dissolved years ago in the embrace of the sea. And you should not be ungrateful for the garment you have."

"This ratty thing—"

"Is what remains of a great cloak of protection. Erithusmé wove it for you to ward off the ravenous dead."

Thasha gasped. "*That's* what she was doing? All along? That was the work she had to accomplish? I thought—"

"That it was something foul, something selfish?" Rose laughed his old gleeful laugh. "Don't be in a hurry to hate yourself, girl. Yes, that shawl was her task—but she never meant to finish it. She wove six or eight inches one day and unraveled them the next. And all those dead souls: their faces were supplied by your memories, but their orders were to keep you placid, passive—sedated, in a word."

"You were different, though."

Rose nodded. "The *Chathrand* had ghosts aboard before she found it, and one of them was mine. When she cast the spell that kept you in limbo, I felt its tug, and played along. I guided a false ship through dream reefs, barked orders at phantoms playing the part of my sailmaster, my lieutenants, my boys. But I could break free of that fantasy. I was myself."

Thasha's eyes were moist. *Felthrup, you broke free too. You helped me. Were you real? Did she kill you?*

"Wrecking the dream-ship tore her illusion to pieces," Rose went on, "but still she tried to delay. She claimed she lacked the strength to bear you back to the living world. She was not pleased when I scooped you up and set off. I stole her last excuse, you see. I made her keep her promise to return you to life."

"And die herself," said Thasha.

"Her body had been destroyed by a pack of sorcerers," said Rose. "She delayed her death by seventeen years, skulking about in your mind. You owe her nothing."

Thasha looked up at him and shook her head. "You were dead already, when I let her return, use my body, work her spells a final time. You didn't see what she accomplished. *Everyone* owes her, Captain. Every living soul in Alifros. She saved the world."

"Fah," said Rose.

"What do you mean, 'Fah'?"

"Never mind, I am a cynic. Let us say she saved the world."

"I saw her walking behind us. I think"—Thasha squeezed her eyes shut—"she reached out her hand, the way she did when she was conjuring."

"A final spell?" The captain shrugged. "Plausible enough. There are wheels in motion that way"—he gestured at the distant cave mouth—"which I cannot account for. There is also this."

Rose fumbled in his pockets, and at last produced a damp, creased envelope. Within was a single sheet of paper: Thasha's own travel stationery, in fact. She turned it to the firelight.

> *I wanted to return with you, Thasha Isiq. I have left you an unfinished Alifros, a world still bleeding, a world in flames. One menace we defeated together; others you must face without me, with your strength and fine intelligence, and that quiet force I never mastered, which they say is stronger than hatred, binds the wounds of the soul.*
>
> *Tell Ramachni that if I had ever had the talent, I should have danced with him. And seek your own lost partner, if he still cares for you. And think of me when you dance.*

Rose snatched the sheet from her hands and tossed it in the fire. Thasha shouted in indignation, groping for it, but the letter was gone.

"What the hell did you do that for?"

"Her orders," said Rose. "No trace of her is to leave this place. Besides, you'll be swimming."

Swimming? Thasha glanced at the flooded cave, the bright window beyond. Rose pulled the crabs from the fire. "Eat," he said. "You don't have long."

"Are we back in my world, then? Back in Alifros?"

"Eat and stop talking."

At her first bite Thasha found she was famished. She ate like a wild dog, cracked the shells with her jaws, burned her lips. Rose watched her, bemused.

"Your world is right there." He nodded again at the cave mouth. "But you're not in it yet. This cave is an anomaly: what Erithusmé called *a flaw in the code.* Living humans can come or go from it only with the help of an . . . escort, if you like. I was your escort from death's kingdom. To enter the living world, you need a plane shifter, a traveler, the kind of being that moves naturally between worlds. Cloud-murths, fire weirds, mirror-sprites, selk. She had to reach out to them, ask their assistance, while she sat there knitting your shawl."

"Did she find one?"

"She claimed not—said the living world was too far for even her magic to reach it, from those depths. But she did follow us into Agaroth, and that is closer to the daylight. That gesture you saw, now: perhaps she alerted those who care for you, and they took up the search for an escort?"

"How could they? Why would a creature like that do them a favor?"

"We'll know soon enough, I think," said Rose. "Someone has entered the tunnel. Don't you feel it?"

Thasha shook her head, but she stopped eating all the same. In life, Captain Rose's instinct for the approach of strange powers had been uncanny. In death they appeared much the same.

He sat down beside her, and for the last time she felt his physical presence, real as any large, aging heap of a man. They gazed in silence a while at the glittering cave mouth.

"I promised you a favor as well," said Thasha at last. "What is it? What do you want?"

Rose opened his mouth to speak, but then his eyes narrowed.

A young woman, not at all human, was wading toward them, rising from the sea. She was exceptionally beautiful. Her skin glistened as though with iridescent scales. Her hair was long and white, and her arms and legs flexed in too many places, in fact everywhere, like tentacles. Her clothing seemed a veil of milky light.

"Horrible girl," she said, "are you ready? Get up."

Thasha jumped up. Rose too lumbered to his feet, chuckling. "A sea-murth! I should have guessed. One of you took a shine to a tarboy of mine, didn't you? A rather unusual tar—"

"Say his name, puss-toad captain of theft and disease, and I will swim away and leave the girl here to die."

"All right, all right! She's forgotten him anyway, what do you care?" Then Rose frowned, straightened his spine. "Is *that* what the murths think of me?"

"You stole from us, raided our reefs," she said. "We tried to kill you. I am glad someone did."

"Ah, well."

Thasha took a cautious step toward her. "I know you," she said. "You're Klyst. I remember: you followed the ship. But I can't recall what I did to make you hate me."

Klyst spat at her feet. "Liar," she said.

Thasha rubbed her temples. There was still a gap in her memory after all. Right at the center of the puzzle, the place where the hammer had struck. The place where the boy—

Klyst leaned close to her, bared a mouthful of needle-sharp teeth. "I do not do this for you, ugly Thasha He-Seek. Come, we will swim, I will see you through the door. But first you must promise."

"What, you as well?" said Thasha. "Oh, naturally. Go ahead, name your price."

Klyst put a hand into the white thicket of her hair. Thasha saw now it was braided with thousands upon thousands of tiny, exquisite shells. When she lowered her hand, one lay there upon her palm, white and perfect. Klyst held it out like a gift, but when Thasha extended her hand, the murth-girl suddenly pressed it, very hard, against Thasha's own palm. A jolt ran up Thasha's arm. The shell had vanished, as though it had melted into her skin.

The murth-girl tapped Thasha's forehead. "I can find you anywhere, now. I can punish you."

It was an odd promise Klyst demanded: that Thasha avoid the sea for the rest of her life, staying belowdecks if she should travel, living miles from any shore. "You will swim ashore today and that will end it. You will walk inland, never to return."

To spare you the sight of me, thought Thasha. *Aya Rin, what did I do?*

But the ferocity of Klyst's gaze left no room for discussion. "I promise," said Thasha. "I swear on my mother and my father, and Hercól and Ramachni, and—well, everyone I love. Is that sufficient?"

Klyst blinked at her, startled. Had she expected Thasha to refuse? Whatever the cause, she now looked distinctly less hostile. Even, perhaps, a bit ashamed.

"Come, then." Gently, she reached for Thasha's hand. She stepped in the direction of the cave mouth. But Thasha resisted, glancing back over her shoulder. Rose stood near the fire with his back to them. When Thasha called his name, he turned with a start.

"She's taking me, Captain."

"Of course she is."

"But you haven't named your favor." *And I'll never see you again, you ass!*

"Ah yes. The favor."

Rose lumbered toward them. Klyst backed waist-deep into the water, as though she could not stand to be near the man. Then Rose took something from his mouth.

It was the least probable thing imaginable: a glass eye. Not a human eye, either, but a feline organ, the eye of a panther, or a leopard, or a lynx.

"You may fight for Alifros," he said, "but I will fight a little longer for revenge. The man who killed me yet lives—and he knows this bauble is my calling card. You will keep it. And should you find yourself again in conflict with this abominable killer, you will show it to him at the moment of his death. He will understand that Nilus Rotheby Rose outsmarted him, and worked for his downfall even from the grave."

"I know who you're speaking of," said Thasha with a shudder, "but why do you think I'll ever see that bastard again?"

"Instinct," said Rose. "Do you promise?"

She promised. His satisfaction made her queasy. "Open your mouth," he said.

Thasha hesitated. There was no other way to carry the thing, true enough. "If you don't mind, I'll just rinse it first, oral hygiene, I know it's a bit—"

"OPEN!"

She opened. Captain Rose, smiling his worst smile of conspiracy and glee, tucked it into the pouch of her cheek.

And he was gone, vanished. Thasha reached out a hand to where he'd stood.

Goodbye, you old monster. Then she turned her gaze to the tunnel back into darkness, saw in her mind an old, old woman, exhausted, ghost-beset, dropping to her knees on the trail.

Goodbye.

Klyst lifted the shawl from Thasha's shoulders, folded it, set it gently on the rocks. "We will go now, Thasha."

She walked away into the water. Thasha turned to follow, but something on the cave wall made her look again. It was a single word, scrawled in soot above the dying fire.

PAZEL

Rose had not disobeyed, exactly. He had not spoken the name aloud.

Thasha waded after Klyst, and soon found herself swimming. The surf grew loud; the miles of tunnel flew by. When Thasha tired, the murth-girl came to her beaming and took her hand.

"You promised. I trust you. I see now why he—why others—never mind, hush, here's the door."

Barely a pinch as they swam through. Was that all it took, to skip between worlds? The shock of the sunlight was much greater: after her sojourn in the dark (was it months, was it years?), Thasha was quite literally blind.

"Don't leave me!" she gasped, and nearly swallowed Rose's eyeball. She closed her own eyes, and Klyst held her effortlessly afloat.

"Land-girl," said her voice in Thasha's ear. "I will never see you again, but I know you now, and my heart will never lose this." A cool hand touched her cheek. "Do not forget me, lovely Thasha. I shall make music for you, touch your dreams, be your sister in the sea."

Thasha was crying. She was alive and home. Hate was gone, her eyes like her memories were healing, shards of glass resolving into waves, clouds, rocky islands, anchored boats. She looked: Klyst's face was shining. The murth-girl's lips met her own for an instant, and then she spun upside down and vanished like an arrow in the depths.

The crowd on the beach saw her coming, and the strongest among them stripped and launched themselves into the sea. On the rising swells they shouted to her: *Thasha! Thasha!* Hercól's voice. And there were Marila and Fiffengurt and other survivors of the voyage, and Jorl and Syzyt baying and prancing in the breakers, and her old stout father waving a stick, on the brink of plunging in himself.

With the eye in her mouth, Thasha could not answer them, but she waved, and they cheered. They would lift her naked from the water and examine her, see she was no counterfeit. Body and mind and heart, she had returned.

And that missing piece of the puzzle, that stubborn gap—

She twisted to look back, even as her foot touched sand. Eight or ten small islands; no telling which held the cave. Dozens of big boats at anchor, small craft rowing shoreward, the popping of deck cannon, sailors raising flags of triumph on the masts.

And at the edge of it all, on a black rock that came and went with the ocean swells—rising, vanishing, rising again—a young man stood watching her progress, at home in the violent surf, nearly naked, one hand shielding his eyes.

He was dark skinned and strongly muscled. He did not wave at her like the rest. But as Thasha paused in her stroke he grew quite still, as though he felt her gaze. Then he slipped into the water and was gone.

Anna Stephens

"How Not to Invade a Country" is a story that was born out of a few seemingly throwaway lines of dialogue in my debut novel, *Godblind*: "Major Bedras found himself surrounded by the Dead Legion. It seemed appropriate to save him."

The protagonist, Crys Tailorson, has proven to be a favourite, not just of mine but with many readers, and when I was offered the chance to contribute to *Unfettered III* and help support such an amazing cause, Crys was the character I knew I wanted to write about, and that was the story I wanted to expand upon. His attitude to serving in the army and his acute sense of the absurd are always a joy to write, and I hope that shines through here.

You don't need to have read *Godblind* to read this story—though I do hope you'll want to know more about Crys and the world he lives in once you have. The sequels, *Darksoul* and *Bloodchild*, complete his epic, dangerous story, with the latter being available in late 2019.

Anna Stephens

HOW NOT TO INVADE A COUNTRY

Anna Stephens

Rilpor's Horse Lands were wide and endless, aptly named for the huge herds of half-wild horses and their semi-nomadic herders, and spotted with marshes, moorlands, and manure. A veritable paradise—if you were a horse.

Lieutenant Crys Tailorson was not a horse and nor was he a herder. He was a soldier, guarding a border that hadn't been disputed or crossed in force for a decade. For him, the Horse Lands were no paradise; they were as boring and predictable as a bad gambler.

Lost amid the rolling grasslands and moorlands crouched the four palisaded forts of the North Rank, home to five thousand highly-trained, squabbling soldiers. Crys had the dubious honour of being one of them.

On a clear day, looking west from one of the watchtowers, the shadow of the Gilgoras Mountains was occasionally visible. At their base, everyone knew, sat the famed and ever-vigilant West Rank, and hidden high in the snowy eyries above, Rilpor's centuries-old enemy, the Mireces.

The West Rank—all the danger and glory a soldier could wish for, as well as a real chance of promotion, of recognition. Of excitement.

But Crys wasn't in the famed West Rank and he wasn't standing on a watchtower on a clear day. Crys was a newly-demoted lieutenant in the North Rank, it was the small hours of the night, and the north wind was blowing rain in his face with what felt suspiciously like malicious glee.

There were no savage, merciless Mireces to face and overcome. No chances of glory here in the north. Instead, the Rank was tasked with finding Listran smugglers bringing opium over the border and with repelling the few ragtag members of the Dead Legion out to prove their status as warriors.

It was a bloody shambles of a posting, and the Rank spent more time riding patrols that never saw anything and helping herders pull horses out of bogs than they did fighting to protect Rilpor from its enemies.

Gods, it might pay my wages, but it's dull. It's so bloody dull.

And cold.

And dull.

Crys yawned, and then winced at the pain stabbing through his face. A week in the Rank's hospital and his jaw still clicked when he moved it. He'd got in a few decent punches before they'd overwhelmed him, but he was still more pissed off that they'd thought he was a cheat than at the beating they'd dealt him for it.

Crys didn't cheat. Not in the purest sense of the meaning, anyway. He was just . . . more observant than his opponents. Not his fault the other men at the table were bad losers. He'd even let them use their own cards, knowing they'd be marked. What more could he possibly do? Lose on purpose? If they didn't like it, they shouldn't be playing. It was called gambling for a bloody reason.

The wind cut into his cheek and he shivered and hunched his shoulders, right hand slowly going numb on the halberd as he peered into the night from the northwest tower of Fort Three. The watch bell had sounded and Orril hadn't arrived to take over from Pike. Third time this week.

Pike had been standing in the rain for four hours, so Crys had sent him off to bed and was waiting in his place for Orril to arrive. Orril's tardiness was becoming a problem. Crys's problem was that he was getting wet—because of Orril. Orril was going to be lucky if Crys didn't throw him from the top of the tower when he finally deigned to show his warty little face.

Crys's demotion from captain was punishment for the brawl, and General Tariq had added in shovelling latrine pits for a month. A commissioned officer, up to the armpits in shit with the same soldiers who'd kicked it out of him. Crys could almost admire Tariq's peculiar brand of discipline; it had cured him of any predilection for brawling, for a start, and there was a certain level of camaraderie built between men who spent an hour every day retching among the shit pits, despite any history of bad blood, alleged cheating, and violence.

Crys snorted and blew rainwater off his nose, convinced the fragrance still clung to his clothes and hair. *Trickster's cock, where's Orril?*

Still, a beating *and* demotion *and* extra duties? Aside from the humiliation and the cut in pay, the fact that nothing much had happened in the first six months of his two-year posting with the North didn't inspire much confidence that he'd have the opportunity to win back his rank. And if he wasn't reinstated as captain by the end of this rotation, his reputation wherever they posted him next would be in tatters.

More tattered than it is now? he asked himself and shifted in his dampening uniform, water running from his hair down the back of his neck. Irritation and self-pity vied for attention, while sleep beckoned with coy fingers.

"The fuck have you been?" he demanded when Orril finally shambled through the trapdoor and onto the watch platform. Crys shoved the halberd at him, then took in the man's miserable, waxy face and strained expression. "Third time this week, isn't it? Somewhere else you'd rather be?"

Orril grimaced but made no move to take the weapon. He was clearly preoccupied with something more important. "Sorry,

Lieutenant. I've had the shits since supper. Major Bedras insisted I still take my watch and–" His eyes bulged and he grabbed his belly and spun, aiming for the trapdoor and practically falling down it in his haste.

"Fucking great," Crys muttered, tucking the halberd back into position as he peered over the guard wall and watched Orril sprint from the base of the tower toward the latrines. Then he groaned and put his free hand over his eyes. "Gods, the pits. Your aim better be good, Orril, my lad, or I'll be using your sodding bedsheets to scour them out tomorrow. Even if you're still sleeping in them. Especially if you are."

Crys glanced at the other towers, at the small, warm, dry guardroom over the main gate, and then gusted a sigh. He took a stealthy step closer to the brazier and stared into the rain and the black, straining his ears for anything unusual. The tower couldn't be left unmanned. Orril wasn't coming back, not this side of emptying his arse anyway. Crys set his feet, let the halberd take a little of his weight, and began to watch.

"Tailorson. Get a patrol together. We're taking a Fifty to recce that bastard river. Suspicion of movement."

Major Bedras took three steps past the curtain separating the lieutenants' quarters from the rest of the barracks, but Crys was already on his feet and standing at attention. Army life tended to have that effect, despite the fact that he'd fallen asleep what felt like three seconds before.

Everyone knew Crys was on night duty. Bedras knew Crys was on night duty. Yet here he was, with dawn still blushing on the horizon, dragging him out of sleep and into a full day's patrol out to the border.

Probably doesn't realize I stood Orril's watch so the poor bastard could spend the night in the shit pits wishing for death.

Crys watched Bedras from his peripheral vision, noted the small, triumphant smile. Oh, no, he knew all right; he knew Crys had stood a watch instead of dozing in the guardroom and had been off duty for only a matter of minutes. He could see that Crys's uniform was still wet from the rain. That his hair was still wet. Apparently none of those things meant one of Orril's runny shits to Major Bedras.

Crys ripped off a salute that was almost an insult in its crisp perfection. "At once, sir," he said, his enthusiasm precisely calculated to walk the line between genuine respect and total mockery.

The major's eyes narrowed, but he couldn't reprimand a junior officer for obeying his orders, could he?

"And hurry up, man," Bedras added. "I want to be at that bastard river in good time."

He left before Crys could respond. *That bastard river.* It was what the Rankers called the river that marked the border between Rilpor and Listre. Its real name was Fogg's Bane, though the Dead Legion of Listre called it the White Tail. And no one over the rank of captain should ever, ever call it "that bastard river."

Bedras thought it made him one of the men. Then again, Bedras thought money made a major. Bedras thought a lot of things, most of them wrong, and all of them annoying. Bedras was a shit.

A Major shit. Ha.

Crys slid into his spare uniform, swallowing a yawn with a cup of scalding mint tea taken from the kettle on the brazier as he scrubbed a towel through his hair. He shrugged into his armour and clattered out of the door. It was still raining. Of course it was still raining.

Fort Three was home to the Fourth Thousand, and it would be so easy for Crys to pick the laziest, most sullen fifty to make Bedras's day trip something to remember. He didn't, because he knew his tiredness would make him short-tempered and it was probably a good idea to have decent men between him and his superior, but also because he was, at heart, a decent soldier. Or so he liked to believe.

So it was that Bedras and Crys led a patrol out of Fort Three not long after dawn and trotted north into the teeth of a gale, Crys loudly chewing bread and butter he'd snagged from the mess in the moments before they left. He dared Bedras to mention the breach of protocol, but it seemed the major was being magnanimous in his victory. The bastard.

The Horse Lands appeared wide and empty on first glance, but the gentle undulations made it surprisingly difficult to spot an enemy before they were on you, so despite the weather, the men kept their gripes to themselves and their eyes sharp.

Fogg's Bane, the White Tail, that bastard river, came into view just before noon. The storm had swelled it almost to bursting its banks, and it roared white and fast between the rocks. A hundred paces before the river was a small wood, and in it, smoking a long pipe among his sheltering animals, a herder.

Bedras rode through his herd, forcing them to part around him, stamping their hooves and nickering annoyance. "You, man, any trouble around here lately? Seen any of the Dead, have you?" Bedras called.

The herder stared out from his hood and sucked his teeth, silent. Crys dismounted and ambled over. "Dancer's grace upon you," he said with a friendly smile. "Filthy fucking weather, eh? Couldn't be wetter if I fell in the Bane."

The herder focused on Crys, and Crys saw the exact moment the man spotted the peculiarity of his eyes—one blue, one brown. The slightest recoil, the merest suggestion of a hand moving for an amulet or charm inside his shirt, and then he was still.

Every. Fucking. Time.

Like I'm some sort of freak. It's your bastard superstition, not mine.

"Dancer's grace," the man returned the greeting. "Weather's been better, aye. Didn't think to see your lot out here today."

"Routine patrol," Crys lied automatically. "Which is unfortunate in this weather, eh? So here we are, wet and miserable. But while I'm here, do you have any concerns? Lost any of your herd recently, spotted any tracks, debris, anything out of the ordinary we should know about?"

The man was still staring into Crys's eyes, so Crys glanced away, then squatted down side-on. The herder leaned forward, trying to see again, but Crys wasn't playing that game. He should be used to it by now, but growing up amid the whispers, the rumours that had followed him into the army, hadn't taught him any patience for the folktales and stories about "his kind."

"Not much," the man said eventually. "My herd's intact, anyway, though I've heard tell some others have lost a few. Wouldn't expect it just yet—weather's not bad enough—so it might be the Dead. Might just be bad luck. Might be Rilporians for all I know, some desperate man lost all he owns to the king's taxes. Gods forbid, could be disease."

He made the sign against evil, a little too close to Crys for his liking, and then gestured to his herd. "That's why I'm keeping them to themselves for a while. Don't want a case of the strangles running through this lot; they're for market come spring."

Crys stared out at the river and the rain, the dull shape of the Fifty hunched beside their fractious mounts, rain capes blurring their outlines. "They're fine beasts, for sure. Trickster's luck at market. Do you know where these other herds were when it was discovered there were animals missing?"

"Further east than this, half a day's ride, maybe." The man shifted again. "Should I be worried?" he asked. "These horses are my life, Lieutenant. Can't afford to lose any."

Crys patted the man's knee, earning another flinch, and stood. "Maybe move south a day's walk for a week or so, let us check things out. Just to be safe, like you said. But I wouldn't expect there to be trouble. A scuffle or two, perhaps. But if you do see the Dead," he added, and his tone made the herder squint up at him, "you get on one of your horses and you ride, you hear? You say these animals are your life, but you know what they'll do to you if they catch you."

The herder nodded, then spat. "Yer a good man, for a soldier," he said. "For a splitsoul," he added under his breath, but Crys had good hearing. His lip curled at the phrase, but he held his tongue, turning away and heading back to Bedras and the Fifty instead.

Splitsoul, they called him. Cursed. Crys huffed out a plume of vapour. *They're just eyes, you know. For seeing with. The colour doesn't mean anything.*

"Well?" Bedras demanded and Crys focused on the major's damp, pasty face.

"Reports of a few herds losing animals half a day east. Nothing here, sir," he reported. *Please not east, please not east, please not east. Home, and warm, and sleep.*

"All right, mount up. Let's push east a few miles alongside this bastard river and see if we can find our horse thieves, eh? Bit of action should liven up the boys."

"As you say, sir," Crys said in his blandest voice. "Come on then, Fifty. Got somewhere you'd rather be than riding through Rilpor in service of king and country?"

They were clever lads, and they knew exactly what the answer to that question was, so they jogged out to their horses and swung up into their saddles without a word.

The best thing about riding east?

Fuck it, there was nothing good about riding east. There was nothing out here, just miles and miles of endless rolling plain and brown moorland dotted with stands of stunted trees, bogs and pools, and the looming forests of Listre over the river.

Crys could see all the way to the end of the sky, it seemed, and it was black and roiling, muttering with thunder and lit by periodic sheet lightning. The rain had stopped, but it was getting colder and Crys knew they were in for another bitch of a storm. Winter was coming early, and she was angry.

He glanced yet again at Bedras, but the major was apparently determined to do something heroic before returning to the forts. Funny thing about senior officers, though, was their heroic was every other soldier's bloody stupid. Crys wondered whether Bedras's heroic would include allowing his command to freeze to death in the wastes. Though if the good major suffered the same fate, it might almost be worth it.

Crys hunched his shoulders and dislodged a tiny puddle of rainwater from his cape. It slid down his neck and chest and he shuddered. "Sir? It's not long until dusk. Perhaps we should—"

The thunderclap was so loud and unexpected that every horse in the Fifty leapt in the air and bolted. While most of the animals carried on east into the plain, Crys's, Bedras's, and those of two other soldiers reared and galloped north, heedless of their cursing riders. The cold and storm had made the horses bad-tempered, and once they began to run, there was going to be no stopping them until they were blown.

Despite Crys's dislike of the man, Bedras was an expert rider, and he kept his seat as his horse took the lead. Crys concentrated on staying in the saddle, paying little attention until the thunder of hooves was echoed by more thunder—water. Fogg's Bane had twisted away from them as they rode but now it loomed ahead, white and in full spate as it tumbled over a short fall and raced on.

"Stop!" Crys yelled, hauling on his reins, but his gelding snorted and tossed its head, ears pinned back. It wasn't stopping until Bedras's mount stopped.

"Stop!" Crys bellowed again, but then they were all of them up on an outcrop over the river and the other side was close, too close, and the horses were lengthening stride and *Oh Fox God's hairy bollocks we're in Listre. We're soldiers of His Majesty's North Rank, wearing his colours and bearing his arms.*

We've just invaded Listre.

Bedras seemed to have grasped the same, because he hauled on the reins so hard his horse screamed and flung itself back on its haunches, then slipped, falling on its side. Bedras threw himself clear.

It was as if the other horses realized what they'd done, too, for they slowed out of their mad gallop into a canter, a trot, a walk, and Crys managed to lead them around in a circle and back to Bedras. The major was standing, but swaying, blood sheeting down one side of his face and his eyes glassier than a dead fish's.

"Major? Major, we need to get back over the river right now. Where's your horse? Major, where's your horse?"

Bedras pointed a wobbling finger and Crys followed it to the animal, standing by a sudden outcrop of rock, reins held by a shadowy figure.

"Oh, shit."

More figures emerged from the rocks and the gloom and the

thunder lent them an aura of threat that was completely unnecessary in the circumstances. Crys already knew they were a threat.

He reached down for Bedras. "Get up behind me, sir, right bloody now," he hissed. Bedras blinked.

"You two, do not draw weapons," he added as one of the men, Alba, reached for the bow wrapped in oilskin and strapped behind his saddle. "We back away, we let them keep the horse, and this doesn't become a diplomatic incident. Or, worse, one that sees us with our cocks nailed to the nearest trees."

Bedras was staring at him in concussed outrage. "Leave my horse? Leave my horse, Lieutenant? Are you completely out of your mind?" He stepped away from Crys and raised his voice. "You there, return my horse at once and we'll forget all about this."

Crys groaned and for a single, heady second contemplated leaving the idiot behind. Then he urged his mount forward and grabbed Bedras under the arms and heaved the man into his lap. "Go," he roared, kicking his gelding into a laboured trot back toward the river.

We'll never make it back over the same way, that outcrop's too high to jump onto from this side. We'll need to find a ford. I'm pretty sure they're not going to let us find a ford.

We're going to have to fight.

Bedras was shouting something into Crys's knee, but Crys ignored him and turned west, parallel to the river and back the way they'd come. Toward civilization, albeit on the wrong side of the border.

"Find a crossing," he shouted over his shoulder to Alba and Ned, but there were no acknowledging bellows. He risked a glance. They were both down, arrows and spears sticking out of them like a hedgehog's spines. Behind them, half a dozen of the Dead Legion were aiming bows at him.

Crys pulled his mount to a halt and let Bedras slide to the ground. "Arm yourself," he hissed before the major could start shouting. Bedras hesitated, hand going automatically to his scabbard. Then he looked behind and squawked.

Bedras grabbed Crys's boot and shoved it out of the stirrup. "Dismount," he spluttered. "Get off the fucking horse."

Crys did so, though he'd had a vague idea of trying to ride down the Dead, scatter them at least, chase them off at best. He eyed the approaching warriors, rolling his shoulders and drawing his sword, and then Bedras was up on his horse and kicking it into movement.

"Hold them," he heard, and Bedras was away, screeching to coax more speed out of the panicked animal.

Crys just stood there for a second. Then he sucked in a breath. "Bastard!" he shouted at the fleeing man, but it seemed the Dead Legion were even more keen on stopping him than Crys was, because three arrows sprouted from his horse's haunches and a fourth stuck deep into its flank, going in to the fletchings—a killing shot. The gelding screamed and crashed onto its side, and Bedras was thrown again.

The major was a coward and a bastard, but Crys needed him, so he sprinted toward the man, hauled him to his feet, spun him to face the oncoming attackers, and shouted him into drawing his sword. Crys stood on Bedras's right, prepared to use him as a shield where possible, and they watched the Dead Legion approach, the feathers and bones of their headdresses and cloaks dull and flat from the wet.

They were young and skinny, three boys and two girls, hair plastered down with red mud and rain so it looked like blood ran down their faces. Their eyes were bright and their hatchets brighter, and Crys recognized the strings of teeth around their necks. Human teeth.

"Blood-hunting," he hissed at Bedras, tightening his grip on his sword and scanning the ground in front of them for any natural advantages.

"What?"

Gods alive, does the man know nothing about the border, or Listre's people and customs? About his godsdamn command?

"They're blood-hunters, sir. Each member of the Dead Legion, male and female, must take an enemy head and return it to the Legion's inner council before they can choose mates. It's a test, to prove themselves adults and so be eligible to marry and have children."

Bedras was mystified.

"So it's unlikely they'll just let us go, sir," Crys added. "They *will* try and kill us. They remain children until they succeed."

"But, but," Bedras began, his bulging eyes almost popping from his head. "They *are* children."

"I know."

"You're asking me to fight children?"

Crys couldn't tell whether Bedras was horrified or offended. "I'm afraid so, sir. They must kill us or they fail. So we kill them first, or at least make taking our heads too much like hard work. They might search for easier prey." The herder's face floated in Crys's vision—the very definition of "easy prey."

"Two of them are female, Lieutenant," Bedras gasped, as if embarrassment had drowned out the fear he should be feeling.

"Fine," Crys snapped. "I'll kill them, you kill the three boys."

Bedras wasn't happy with that solution, either, funnily enough, but Crys ignored him as he once more began to protest. Instead, Crys watched the eyes and hands and feet of the approaching enemy, forcing himself to name them as such because "children" really didn't help his state of mind. Besides, they were tall enough and well-armed enough that in Rilpor they'd already be counted full-grown.

Alba and Ned are dead already. They've already got two heads. Can't they just share?

It wasn't fair for Alba and Ned, but they weren't going to complain, so Crys didn't worry too much what they thought about it. He gestured at the distant corpses with his free hand. "You've killed two of our men, and whatever you may think, we're not here with hostile intentions. But look, multiple wounds means you all killed them, eh? So you're all grown-ups—congratulations! Off you go."

The Listrans had halted with his first words, and now two exchanged a glance that made Crys's heart leap. They were going for it. Then one of the girls slashed her hand through the air, cutting off the beginnings of a muttered conversation.

"You fight over scraps," she snarled, her accent guttural and muffled by the bone stud in her lower lip, "and get low-caste mates in return for a shared kill. I will mate high. Take them to present to the Mother if that is all you are worthy of. My commitment is greater; She will receive a man killed by me alone in return for my right to mate. One warrior: one kill." She thumped her chest, making the teeth rattle. "High caste."

They all knew what would happen now, of course, with the exception perhaps of Bedras, who was still goggling over her intention to kill him. The two who'd been willing to run stepped over the corpses and advanced with the others, five on two.

"Listen, they're going to rush us," Crys began, "so we need to—"

Bedras dropped his sword and raised his hands. "I surrender!"

The move had one thing in its favour—it shocked the shit out of the Dead. Crys wasted a second gaping along with everyone else, then he grabbed Bedras's sleeve in his fist and began to run, head down, knees pumping, dragging the idiot in his wake. He didn't even know why he was doing it; Bedras was plainly too stupid to live, but he supposed the man was some sort of shield between Crys and the likelihood of arrows, so why not? If it looked like the Dead were gaining on them, well, he'd just let go. Fastest runner in the North Rank, was Crys Tailorson, and right now, he didn't need to outrun the enemy. He just needed to outrun Bedras.

The major seemed to realize that he wanted to live after all, because soon enough he tore his sleeve from Crys's grasp and panted along at his side, unencumbered by the sword he'd dropped. The river was narrowing up ahead; they might be able to jump across, find the rest of the Fifty . . . an arrow thumped into the sod just in front of Crys's foot. He leapt it and kept running, realized Bedras wasn't with him, kept running anyway, and—

"Shit," he panted. He stopped, turned, took in the scene, and began sprinting back. The silly fuck had fallen, twisted his ankle in a rabbit hole, probably, and was howling on his knees with the Dead closing in and vying to be the first to stab him.

Crys scooped up the arrow in his free hand and barrelled into the group, stabbed the first to come within reach in the face—arrow into his cheek and back out—and then again under the jaw, the barb tearing him open. Not fatal, but any cut to the neck is terrifying in its own unique way, so the boy fell screaming and clutching at his throat.

Crys still had the arrow but no time to use it, ducking a hatchet and chopping his sword into the girl's knee, dislocating it. She shrieked and fell and Crys spun past her, deflected the spear thrust of a third and riposted, a wild backhand slice that carved upward and into the boy's chest, opening him to the bone.

More screaming, and over it Bedras bubbling prayers and snot and clutching his leg. Broken ankle, maybe, not just twisted. Because things weren't bad enough already.

Still two left unhurt, untested, unfought, but they were backing away with wide eyes in their muddy faces, looking at the three on the ground at Crys's feet. The Dead didn't wear armour, believing their faith would turn blades and arrows. Silly fuckers. But helpful, if you were Crys Tailorson and you were both outnumbered and tethered to a gigantic arse of an officer.

Standard procedure said to take them prisoner or execute them—the Dead Legion was small, but those who claimed a head and became adults were vicious killers and a constant threat in service of their peculiar cult.

I'm not killing children. And I can't get the jolly fucking major out of here along with three prisoners, either.

"Bedras, get up."

Bedras mumbled something unintelligible and Crys whooped, lunged at the nearest of the still-standing foe. The girl screamed and leapt back, swinging wildly with her hatchet and knife both and more in danger of hurting herself than him.

"I said get up. Now, Major. Now or I leave you here."

"No. No! You can't, mustn't. I'm your superior officer and—"

"And you just invaded Listre, so shut up, get up, and head for the river. That is an order, *sir*." Crys didn't even bother looking. The Dead were closing in again, the girl with the broken knee screaming at them to take him and doing her best to stand, using the downed boy's spear as a crutch. She was making a far better job of it than Bedras with his ankle. Crys was impressed.

Crys was worried.

Crys, to be honest, was shitting himself.

Killed by a bunch of children with borrowed weapons and no armour. Ma and Da are going to love that when they get the letter. And the death purse for a lieutenant, let's not forget. Barely enough to bury what's left of me.

Thunder rumbled again and the rain finally came, cold as snow, heavy as a waterfall. The plain vanished into greyness, the Dead becoming wraiths and more frightening for it. Crys took a step back. The girl was standing now, spitting blood and rainwater, pointing at him with a hatchet that shook in her grip. "For Mother and Son!" she screeched and hobbled for him.

Crys took another step back and nearly fell over Bedras. "I swear by the Fox God I will kill you myself if you do not get the fuck up, Major," he snarled. He reached down and grabbed Bedras, hauled on his arm so the man had no choice but to stand, a shriek bursting from his lips as he put weight on his bad foot.

"My leg," he moaned.

"It'll be your fucking head you need to worry about," Crys muttered. "Walk. Backward, slowly. Don't take your eyes off them."

"Shouldn't you, you know," Bedras made vague stabbing gestures, "finish them off?"

"I have no desire to commit suicide, Major. Right now none of theirs are dead, even if two of ours are. I'd like to keep the numbers as they stand. If I kill one of them, the others will slaughter us both."

It looked like they were going to get slaughtered anyway as the two uninjured blood-hunters raced past their comrades, shrieking war cries and new-found courage. Crys let go of Bedras and the man immediately sank to the grass again. Crys stepped between him and the boy and girl howling toward them.

They came at him together and Crys had lost the arrow somewhere. Just a sword and no shield against two of them. No horses, no retreat, and while the hunters certainly weren't Rank-trained, they weren't farmers swinging hoes at foxes, either.

There was no way out unless he left Bedras. "Fuck," he roared, knowing he wasn't going to leave Bedras.

He cut low and defended high, spun out of the way of an axe, grabbed the boy by the shoulder and threw him at the girl. They went down in a tangle of limbs and Crys managed to club the boy over the head with the hilt of his sword. He collapsed, pinning the girl. It'd have to do. He turned for Bedras as the girl swiped at his boot with her knife, scoring the leather. Crys kicked her wrist and the knife spun away.

"Come on." He held out his hand, but Bedras was pale with shock now, his foot at a funny angle. "Trickster's cock," Crys swore and shoved his sword into the major's slack hand. Bedras tightened his fingers around it instinctively, and Crys hauled him up again, flung Bedras's sword arm over his neck and hoisted the man onto his back.

His spine crunched and his knees wobbled, and then Crys was staggering through the rain and the wet-slick grass, using Bedras as a human shield and hoping the poor fuck didn't stab him in the arse with his own sword.

"They're coming," Bedras gasped, much too soon for Crys's liking.

"Then hold them off," Crys managed. "You've got the . . . bloody sword."

"Wha–?" Bedras began, and then, "Down!" he screeched, and Crys threw himself onto his face, Bedras's pelvis cracking into the back of his head. Bedras thrashed on top of him and Crys eeled out from beneath, flipped over and caught the girl's knee smack in the face.

Lightning went off in his head and blood flooded his nose and mouth, but her knee and his face were the least of his worries, because she'd retrieved her long knife and she was trying to fillet him with it. "Get . . . off," he grunted, grappling with her, but his hands were muddy and her arms were wet with rain and the knife was skittering all over the place and getting closer as they struggled.

Crys got a knee up between him and her, sacrificing a good amount of shin to the edge of the blade, roared at the pain, and managed to shove her gracelessly away. His leg was hot and sticky and he could see a flap of skin through the tear in his trousers as he scrambled onto his hands and feet, the cool of the wet grass pressing briefly into the heat of the wound.

Bedras was biting the boy's hand, so Crys left him to it and threw himself at the girl, twisting the knife out of her grip. Her other hand came around and it, too, was holding a knife and this one scored across the top of his chainmail and over his exposed collarbone, hot, streaking pain and Crys was reminded that a neck wound made you panic and he knew this because he was fucking panicking.

He clamped one hand to his throat and punched her so hard his knuckles split. Her cheek opened and she tumbled into a puddle, sending up a sheet of dirty water. Crys exhaled carefully, but there was no aspirating spray of blood and air; his windpipe was intact and so were the big veins. Eyes narrow, he took a step forward and rolled the unconscious blood-hunter onto her side so she wouldn't drown, then hauled the boy off Bedras and put him in a sleeper choke.

The other three, the ones injured at the start, were still out of action, two invisible in the storm. The girl with the spear was hobbling for them, but even Bedras could move faster than her. Crys pulled bog moss from the medical kit on his belt and pressed it to his neck, then got the major's arm over his shoulder and together they limped for the sound of the river.

There'd be a way over, somewhere. The Dead crossed the river all the time, so of course there'd be a way over.

Gods, let there be a way over . . .

Crys dropped the blood-soaked moss and snatched the sword back from Bedras just in case and they staggered on, the river a roaring of white foam on their left, the intermittent flickering of lightning bleaching the world for brief instants and, no doubt, outlining them against the terrain.

There was no way over the river.

"All right, Major, can you swim?" Crys asked, when he'd gone as far as he dared and the blood-hunters were once more gaining on them, the ringleader girl with the bloody, damged leg being supported by the two Crys had rendered unconscious. Couldn't bring himself to regret the decision to leave them alive. Though there was still plenty of time to do so.

"Swim?" Bedras whined.

Crys slapped him. There was a moment of absolute stillness and dawning horror as they stared at each other, and Crys was horribly, minutely aware that his career had just gone the way of Orril's guts and Alba's head.

"You are a major in His Majesty's North Rank, sir," Crys barked, going all in on the most desperate gamble of his life. "You will conduct yourself with the appropriate rigour and endeavour." General Tariq's words, when he'd visited Crys in the infirmary before demoting him on account of the brawl.

But Bedras blinked and made an effort to stand unsupported. His hand flickered up and then dropped before it became a salute.

"I can't get you over the river, Major," Crys said in a softer tone, "and the Dead are gaining on us. We have to swim. It'll be cold and it's running high and fast, so don't fight it. Angle toward the other bank. Yes?"

"Yes," Bedras said weakly, but at least he wasn't protesting anymore. Crys helped him down the slippery bank, feeling an unexpected flicker of pity as the man put his weight on his broken ankle and let out an agonized howl. Only a flicker, though. The proximity of edged weapons drives sentiment from all but the most stupid.

He heard Bedras's gasp as he entered the freezing water, and then another howl, this one from behind and full of hate and triumph. Crys whirled to face the threat, lost his footing and went to his knees on the slope, slashing blindly with the sword.

He'd done his best not to kill any of them before, because they were children, even if they were shitting little bastards, but he was out of patience and out of mercy. He came back up onto his feet and lurched up the bank, right into the middle of them, kicked the spear the girl was using as a crutch so she collapsed sideways, then stomped on the joint he'd cut into.

Her scream was full of such white-hot agony it stopped the others in their tracks.

"You can take the two you've already killed, or you can join them in death," Crys growled, barely recognizing his own voice and vaguely aware it didn't have anything to do with the neck wound. He knew he was threatening children, but the animal part of him was eyeing their weapons and the bloodlust shining in their faces and coming to a very different conclusion. Young, yes. Children, not exactly. A threat? Absolutely.

The ringleader was still screeching as she flailed for her spear and made a feeble effort to trip Crys. *Gods, but she's brave. And stupid.*

He stamped on the spear, scooped it up and lunged for the boy creeping up on his left. The boy yelled and threw himself backward, and like that, it was done. They knew they weren't killing him, not today. *Not fucking ever, I have anything to do with it.*

"Weapons down," Crys ordered and they complied. "Take her and go. Right now, before I change my mind and kill you all." He widened his eyes and lunged at them again, and again they yelped and pulled back.

The girl on the ground hissed, pointing. "His eyes," she breathed. "The Son. Son of the Mother!"

Crys nodded solemnly. "One blue, one brown. Eyes of the Fox God, the Son. You realize who you've been fighting now? Realize why you can't win against me?" The others pulled the girl to her feet, more terrified than at any other time, almost shaking. "And do you know why I left you alive?" Crys demanded, slightly shocked at his own play-acting and no idea what he was going to say next.

They shook their heads, hands clutching at amulets of bone and rock.

"So you could carry a message back to your people. Rilpor is out of bounds. Rilpor is off-limits to you and your kind. Its people, its livestock, its crops, its border. I name you full-fledged members of the Dead Legion," he added and their eyes widened even more, "on condition you tell everyone what I have told you."

"But, but Holy Son, we kill in your name, yours and the Mother's," a boy ventured. "As the Mother created you from the dead, so we must bring back a kill to be able to marry and have children of our own. We kill in *your* honour. How else do we prove ourselves?"

The storm saved him from having to answer such twisted logic. Lightning rent the air, so bright it burned after-images into their eyes, and lit up the landscape as it struck a giant elm not far from where they stood. The trunk exploded into flame and the trio shrieked and ran, dragging their leader between them and heading, presumably, for the last of their number, the two who lay bleeding somewhere in the darkness, veins open to the sky.

Crys stood for a few seconds, making sure they were really going, and then turned to the river. "Fuck me," he breathed, "I think I've just rewritten their entire bloody religion."

He sheathed his sword and waded into the river, mouth open in increasing pain at the biting cold. He kept hold of the spear and struck out into the current, gasping and swearing at the temperature, aiming for the far bank and doing his best to fend off the rocks.

He heard shouting and realized Bedras was just ahead, half out of the river on the Rilporian side. "Here," Crys called, shoving the end of the spear at him. Bedras caught it and Crys hung on, dragged himself up its length until his feet found the riverbed. Together they clambered up the bank and into the teeth of the north wind, cutting through sodden clothes, biting exposed flesh.

"Can still die out here," Crys stuttered. "Come on, we need to find shelter."

There was the stink of horse on the wind and Crys headed for it, seeing as Bedras had no other ideas. Pain and cold had done for him and he was reeling along, barely conscious. But horses meant men and men meant fire, and with luck, it'd be their Fifty camping out and waiting for dawn to continue searching for them.

Bedras used the spear as a crutch much as the Dead girl had, Crys on his other side lending support, hugging himself with his free arm, head hunched as they pushed into rain that was almost solid.

They were slowing, shuddering with cold and exhaustion,

when they reached the herd beneath the trees of a small spinney and threaded their way into its midst. Steam and warmth greeted them as the wind dropped. Crys draped Bedras's free arm over a horse's withers.

"Stay here, there'll be someone nearby. I'll come back," he added when he saw the panic Bedras was trying to conceal. The major jerked his chin in dismissal, striving for a semblance of self-possession, and Crys left him to try and find it.

He was hurting now, the sharp burn of opened flesh leaking blood, and he was aching from the fight, from the cold, from the rocks in the river that had kissed his ribs and elbows and the back of his skull.

He threw caution to the storm. "Hello?" he called. A couple of horses startled and stamped, but nothing else answered him. Crys stroked the nose of the nearest. "Where's your herder, eh?" he asked.

"Right here," said a voice so close behind him that Crys felt the breath on his wet neck.

Crys leapt to his right, twisting as he did to face the man behind him. "Motherfucking godsdamn bastard!" he gasped when he recognized the herder from earlier that day. "I swear I nearly died on the spot."

The herder put his head on one side. "You would've, I thought you were trying to steal my horses."

"I'm not. We're not, I mean. Look, my commanding officer and I got separated from our patrol a few hours ago in the storm. He's broken his ankle, I think. There was a fight, and we're wet and very cold. Would you mind if we shared your fire?"

"Fighting each other, were you?"

Crys grimaced. "Not exactly."

The herder snorted. "Why don't that surprise me? You boys just can't leave them alone, can you? The Dead, I mean." He peered at Crys. "You the one I saw here this morning?"

"That's me," Crys said and waved a hand at his face. "Not that you can tell, probably, but yes. Captain, I mean, Lieutenant Crys Tailorson, Fourth Thousand, North Rank."

"And this officer you mentioned. He that fish-eyed idiot spoke to me like I was a simpleton?"

Crys winced. "Yes, sir, I'm afraid that's him."

The herder sighed. "Name's Tully. Bring him in, then." Tully gestured to the dim glow of flames. "She's only a little fire, mind. Don't want to attract no attention." Crys nodded and began to head for Bedras when Tully grabbed his arm. "They follow you? 'Cause you'll be fighting alongside me to save this herd if they did."

"I don't know," Crys said truthfully, "but if they have, it's not the herd they'll be after. They were blood-hunting."

Tully sucked his teeth and then spat between Crys's boots, wiping the trail of saliva from his chin. "I got no problems with the Dead, and they never had problems with me, no matter which side of the river any of us have been on. You change that by being here and I'll kill you myself."

"You have my word, Tully," Crys said and noted the little bird-skull-and-feather ornament hanging in the shadow of the man's hood. It almost looked like part of a headdress. It almost looked like Tully was a member of the Dead Legion himself. Tully saw him note it and stared him out.

Crys licked his lips. "I'll fetch the major."

General Tariq of the North Rank sat at his desk, one forefinger stroking the thin moustache that sat above his lip like an angry caterpillar. His eyes were as colourless as water and harder to read.

Crys stood at parade rest and stared above and to the left of Tariq's head. To his right, Major Bedras stood in immaculate uniform, leg splinted and crutch prominently positioned for the greatest possible sympathy. Crys contemplated kicking it out from under the lying, snivelling fucking wretch.

Crys didn't have an immaculate uniform. Crys was wearing the rain-soiled mess he'd worn for his night watch and then left drying three days before when Bedras dragged him out on his fool patrol. *Three days. Three fucking days in his company, two of them listening to him whine and bitch about his bastard leg while I practically carry him all the way here because the rest of the Fifty gave us up for dead and left us, and then what does he do?*

Crys should've expected what he'd done, but it appeared that even after a lifetime of bitter disappointment, he still hadn't learned his lesson.

"Major Bedras, your account is nothing short of remarkable," Tariq said, breaking in on Crys's seething. "To fight on in defense of your junior officer, on a broken leg no less . . ." Tariq spread hands as thin and wiry as his moustache. "Well, it beggars belief."

Bedras's chest swelled with so much air and pride Crys thought he might explode like an over-filled pig's bladder. *I've probably got a pin somewhere,* he thought, keeping his face blank as only a soldier could, though from Tariq's swift glance, he suspected his eyes were telling the general more than they should.

Tariq leaned forward and fixed pale eyes on the major. "Dismissed," he said, and Bedras deflated a little. "I must discuss matters with the lieutenant in private. Though wait outside. I'll have need of you again."

"Sir," Bedras said, saluting so hard he nearly concussed himself.

Crys opened his mouth as soon as Bedras closed the door behind him, but Tariq held up a finger. A voice from outside politely requested the major take a seat in the anteroom, followed by departing footsteps and the ostentatious clicking of a crutch on the stone floor.

"Lieutenant Tailorson, I'd like your report now," Tariq said and Crys felt a wash of relief flood his guts. He was going to get to tell the truth. He wasn't going to have to swallow that horseshit Bedras was peddling and take the blame for the deaths of two good men and the invasion of a foreign fucking country.

It took longer than he expected, and he had to fight to keep his voice down more than once, but he told Tariq everything, including that Bedras had ordered Orril to stand a night watch while ill. He stuck to the facts, but even without embellishment it sounded like he was trying to get Bedras kicked out of the damn army. *No, Bedras is doing that himself. I'm just the messenger.*

By the time he stopped talking, his throat sore and his fists clenched, Tariq was leaning forward with his elbows on the desk. Crys hoped that was a good sign.

"And you'll swear to this testimony in a court-martial, will you?" Tariq said when he was sure Crys had finished.

Shit shit shit.

Crys cleared his throat, knowing there was no backing out of it now. "Yes, sir, if needs be. The major's command is a mess, sir. He lacks the respect of the men and he lacks the ability to lead them, to make quick decisions, or the . . . Sir, if the men find out he surrendered to a group of children, well, his career will be over, sir."

Tariq's eyes narrowed. "But they won't find out, will they?" he said quietly. "Because the only people who know that happened are him, me, and you. And we're not spreading rumours among the Rank, are we, Lieutenant?"

Crys stood a little straighter. "Absolutely not, sir."

"Good." Tariq stared at him for so long, Crys began to sweat. "And the Dead Legion?"

Tully's face floated in Crys's inner vision for a moment. "As far as we know, they didn't enter Rilpor, sir."

Tariq nodded. "For your efforts to save Alba and Ned, and your quick thinking and bravery in getting your superior officer to safety while mostly avoiding a diplomatic incident, you are hereby reinstated to the rank of captain, with all rights and responsibilities that entails. Move your kit into the captains' quarters."

Crys saluted, trying to keep the shock from his face. "Yes, sir. Thank you, sir."

"You're not going to let me down, are you, Tailorson?" Tariq asked. "Because you know that if there's one more brawl, one more incident of insubordination, one more accusation of cheating at cards, you will be flogged, demoted to private and put on permanent shit-pit and night duties for the rest of your time here. And, if I have anything to do with it, with any Rank you are rotated into in the future."

Crys swallowed, sweating harder. "No, sir. I won't let you down, sir," he managed.

"Because it's truly surprising just how much one line on a

man's record can follow him around for the rest of his career," Tariq added, and while the threat was a little heavy-handed, it certainly made an impression.

"I understand, sir. Consider me a reformed character, sir. A model officer."

Tariq snorted. "I doubt you'll ever be that, but feel free to prove me wrong. Dismissed."

Crys saluted again and marched to the door, left Tariq's office and stalked through the anteroom, past the smug smile of Bedras and out of the administration building into the drill ground. There he sucked in beautiful, clean northern air and thanked the Dancer and the Fox God both for his reprieve.

He needed a bath and a hot meal and a long, long sleep, so he headed out of Fort One and across the grass to Fort Three in the distance, unencumbered by Bedras's moaning for the first time in what felt like forever.

He reached his barracks and stepped inside quietly. It was empty but for the cadre of night-watch sentries sleeping sprawled on their cots, and he slid past them to the curtained alcove at the far end.

Crys ducked through the curtain and collected his filthy uniform and personal possessions, stuffed them into a sack. He flung it over his shoulder, picked up his weapons and armour, and made his way to the small building flanking the main barracks.

The captains' quarters were warm, quiet and familiar, four men to a room. It was empty, so Crys chose the unoccupied bed farthest from the window—it had been his before his disgrace, and he was pleased no one had moved into it in his absence.

Tariq had only allowed them an hour between arriving back at the forts and making their reports, and Crys had spent the entirety of the three days previous acting as Bedras's personal manservant, scout, defender, and crutch. He was knackered, he ached, he was footsore and probably in need of a few stitches, but he was home and back in his proper rank.

He collapsed onto the cot and heaved out a contented sigh. *Captain Crys Tailorson of His Majesty's Ranks.* Next time he had permission to take some leave, he'd head for Sailtown. Pretty girls liked a dashing captain who'd recently seen action against the Dead Legion, even if they were only blood-hunters. Not that he'd tell them they were only blood-hunters.

The slamming of the door woke him and Crys bolted upright, blinking away the tendrils of dreams and standing at attention with automatic, unconscious precision. Bedras stamped into the room.

Oh gods. He knows I told Tariq what really happened. Is he petty enough to . . . of course he is. He's Bedras.

Crys's eyes strayed to his weapons and then back to the door, waiting for Bedras's cronies to sidle in with clubs and brass knuckles and oily little smiles. Bedras was alone. He shoved past Crys and threw his gear down on the last unoccupied bed.

And that's when Crys noticed it: the man's new rank, hastily pinned to his sleeve and over his heart.

Crys sank down on his cot and put his head in his hands, letting Bedras clatter around the room and knock things over with his crutch. He waited for silence before looking up, and it was a long time coming. Bedras was sitting straight as a spear on the bed opposite, glaring, his expression overflowing with loathing and his martial bearing only somewhat undone by the splinted leg sticking out like an unfortunate and uncontrollable erection.

"Hello, *Captain* Bedras." Crys grinned, but there was absolutely no humour in it. "Brothers in arms, I see. Won't this be fun? Tell me, how long do you have until you're rotated to another Rank?"

Peter Orullian

IT MIGHT BE FAIR TO SAY THAT I WOULDN'T BE WRITING IF IT WEREN'T for Stephen King. And I'm hardly the first writer to say as much. But his first two short story collections were like talismans to me. Still are. And either because they were so influential, or because my mind isn't so different from King's—as scary a thought as that may be—I get story ideas that seem to fall in line with both *Night Shift* and *Skeleton Crew.*

So when one day I had a vision of a piece of college-ruled paper coming to life and berating me for not getting the writing done that I needed to be doing, I went with it. And I also let the little guy's voice be what it was—dismissive and berating. I found him funny as hell.

The other thing about the story—the deeper part, if you will—is a truth that writers usually find when they're willing to write about hard things, personal things. And that's simply this: a writer pays dues. It sounds a little silly when you say it out loud, but certain things hurt to write about. In this story, I've given that hurt a physicality. And make no mistake, paper cuts make me wince. But they're also a metaphor for being willing to expose the raw stuff that usually make stories worthwhile.

Peter Orullian

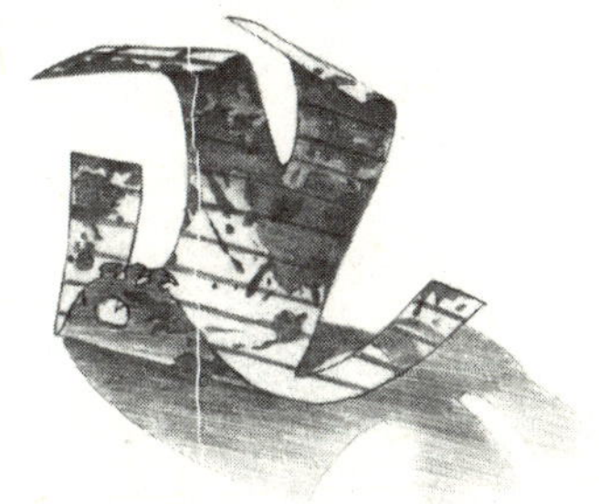

THE PAPER MAN

Peter Orullian

"I'll tell you about writing, you fuck," the paper man said. "Just do it, that's all, just do it."

Stephen Kreig looked up through sleep-filled eyes with disbelief and wonder. *What the hell?* The paper man wasn't a reporter, as in the *Daily Herald*, or an adult version of that vanishing profession paperboy, usually reserved for kids of eight to ten whose parents believe it's never too young to learn work ethic. He was, in fact, a man made of paper, just like sounding it out.

The paper man stood about eleven inches high, and looked to be about three inches wide. He appeared to be fashioned of a standard sheet of college-ruled rolled into a tube. The lower half was cut up from the bottom to form half-cylindrical legs. And somehow part of the paper had pulled out to create short arms with no hands. All of these flared slightly at the ends, giving the paper man a somewhat sixties look. And except for one of the ring-binder holes, which gave the paper man one pupil-less eye, there was no definite head.

"What?" Steve finally croaked, still half asleep.

"Writing, you fuck, writing." There was impatience in the voice. Of course, there was no mouth to speak the reproach, but Steve heard it just the same.

Some dream, Steve thought, but made no attempt to dismiss it.

"What about writing?" Steve asked, his interest waking slower than the rest of him.

"You're lazy. Just flat out lazy. You pen that horseshit for your professors at the university, and you think 'Oh, I'm doing something. I'll serious up later.' But you're just a fuck, a lazy fuck. And it's my turn to tell you."

"Who are you?" Steve asked, looking at the blank, featureless face. He wasn't hearing the slander; he was hearing the minute, humorous crinkle each time the paper man bowed and turned, emphasizing "you fuck."

"Never mind that. Are you hearing me okay?" the paper man spoke with a hint of sarcasm. "'Cause I can speak up if you got wax in those mindless ears of yours."

"No, I heard you fine. But if I'm going to converse with a . . . a paper man, I'd like to know his name."

Steve started to smile. He liked this fancy. The paper man stood atop his computer, an old shop-built desktop, which meant cheap parts, maybe used. It also meant he'd lost lots of documents right out into low-cost-nowhere. Behind the paper man, right above Steve's work area, was a poster of Albert Einstein that read: "Imagination is more important than knowledge." A pithy saying to comfort those who detour past college to start life. *And that's the broad and short of it,* Steve thought: life or college, mutually exclusive terms by every stretch of the imagination, and Steve wished he'd had the courage to detour past college. But right now the paper man was really a hilarious-looking dream creature. *Imagination!* Steve sat up and smiled broader.

"You want to wipe that silly-ass grin off your face, you fuck. I didn't come so you could exercise your jaw, either. You want to listen here for a minute and try to believe I'm not gibbering for my own sake." The paper man took a step forward, curling one handless arm back toward his tubular body. Steve wanted to laugh but kept it in. He very much wanted to hear this little guy speak. It's not often dreams come with such clarity, and humor.

"Okay," Steve said choking off his smile a little.

"Okay, my ass, you still think this is a joke, but okay, just so you listen. I don't care for you to believe anything but what I *say*." The papery voice laid importance on *say*. Then he stepped back, and pulled his paper arms behind him like an orator. *If he'd had a throat, here's where he would have cleared it,* Steve thought. The paper man turned to the side, obscuring Steve's view of the one lid-less eye, and began to pace.

"I'll start with the compliments," he said. "You're not bad. Or, at least, you could be so you weren't too bad. But you spend all your time with that pair of tits, or swilling beer at eight dollars a case. And maybe worst of all, you scribble something in the way of analysis for some esoteric, impotent professor and call it paid. Didn't it ever strike you that the root of that word is *profess*—not exactly an argument for truth. Well, it's fixed easy enough, just start writing. You owe the paper."

The paper man pivoted on one half-cylinder leg and started pacing the other direction. "Writing dues come all sorts of ways, and one falls for us. The muse takes her cut right off the top, and then the writer goes to giving it everywhere else. And what he usually means to say is, 'It's me. I did it. I busted my balls and I made it.' But don't you believe it. There's dues all up and down a story, and it starts right here." The paper man unfolded an arm from behind his back and beat it on his thin, hollow chest. The paper crinkled in and out, and Steve wanted to burst.

"But all that's after the writing starts, and usually when it's done. You," the paper man pointed his arm at Steve, "ain't even put a serious mind to it yet." He paused. "So start."

The paper man turned his cyclopic eye to Steve and all of a sudden it seemed baleful and direct. The paper man may be funny to look at, Steve thought, but he meant what he said, funny- looking or not. Steve could feel his own subconscious goading him. He had been resting on his laurels. Or maybe planting them was closer. The paper man was, if nothing else, right about the lazy stuff. Still, if Steve could have thought of a good rebuttal he would have argued back serious enough. Argued that he was too busy with school and couldn't effectively manage both grades and fiction. But the paper man had hit a nerve, like drilling into the crook of a tooth without Novocain. So he sat there seeing the paper man superimposed over Einstein's nose. Sat there as speechless as he was authorless.

The paper man observed Steve with his single eye and finally said, "Just do it, dammit. No fanfare, no money. You owe the paper . . . you owe me."

Steve felt that writer's prick then, and thought that the one real due was the one he owed to that internal pricking. Once it started, it had to be relieved, or else . . . no, no *or else,* it had to be relieved. And Steve thought the paper man could see him thinking.

"Good," the paper man said good-naturedly, seeing it indeed. "I think you got hope, my boy. I really do. Maybe not Shakespeare hope, or Faulkner hope, but son-of-a-bitch if you won't make a dent. One great big dilly of a dent, you bet." He clapped his hands together, making a small, flat paper smack, and Steve wanted to see a smile there, on that paper face, but did not.

But Steve's own optimism began waning even then. It was the same old situation. *I want to write. I need to write. But what do I write?* And with that, he began to drift. He wanted to force ideas, something he knew didn't work, but something he did nonetheless, like many writers he supposed, or at least wanted to believe. Soon all his thoughts were a jumbled gook of garbage, which was plenty good enough to turn him to sleep.

And by morning the paper man was gone, and so was Steve's pricking.

"I had the best dream last night," Steve was telling his dad at the breakfast table. It was just Dad, because Mom had found aerobics a year before, and a guy named George just two months ago. But breakfast didn't suffer; Dad had always been the cook.

"What was that?" Ronald Kreig asked, shoveling in a bite of toast behind some egg.

"I dreamt a little man made of notebook paper." Steve smiled and lifted his orange juice.

"Yeah, what'd he do?" Ron followed, as amused secondhand as Steve had been right off.

"It's not what he did. It's what he said." Steve chortled. "He told me I'm a lazy ass and ought to be writing. He said I owe the paper, that I owe him."

Ron didn't return his son's laugh. It was a sentiment, at least the first part about his son's laziness, that Ron shared. But the man also knew it was risky to step so close to this particular subject with Steve. So he faked a smile and finally asked, "Well, what did you say?"

Steve tried to ignore his father's hesitation. The truth was, his dad had a genuine interest in his writing career, if so auspicious a title could be given to his half dozen unpublished short stories. It was probably because his dad had once entertained the same thoughts of marking up good paper to earn his way through life. Had, in fact, written the better part of a novel, but called it quits when Steve was born, because writing time gets used one way or the other. And, in moments of honesty, his dad had told him that his unfinished novel hadn't been very good anyway. He just didn't have the chops.

But Ronald Kreig could, if nothing else, tell when writing was good, whether that writing belonged to the "canon" of English literature, or was sold at the checkout with a good word from the Book of the Month Club. "Good writing," his dad was fond of saying, "doesn't know the reader. It just does its job." And his dad thought Steve was good, which is why he believed his son would do more than publish. He believed he could join the forerunners in modern popular fiction—as dirty a word as that is to the "canon."

Steve's face fell a little, "I didn't say anything. I fell asleep." Steve thought a moment and added, "How's that for life imitating art."

His dad smiled and Steve rejoined him. But Steve still had no plans to do any writing on his own. Just whatever appeased the University God.

As Steve drove up "the Hill" on his way to what the University Parking Services jokingly referred to as parking, he had a really good idea for a story. It would involve a slavering beast that lived in abandoned bootleg tunnels that network underneath the streets of downtown Happyville. There would be a flower delivery guy who made trips into a flower shop basement to deposit money in a safe. He'd discover bricked-up archways, fresh dirt, and bodies. Then the story would end with him in a mental institution writing it all out, so you had to wonder if he killed the people or if the monster existed. Not bad, anyway. Everything is what you make of it. Even Shakespeare stole most of his stuff, but who remembers from whom.

Steve's idea didn't make it out of the car. It certainly didn't make it as far as his first class, Shakespeare 541. And it absolutely never made it into the office of his Shakespeare professor for his personal conference regarding his last paper, entitled "Let's All Wear Coxcombs."

"I think you make some valid points, Steve," his prof was oozing, "but I'm not sure what you say can always be derived from the text."

Steve let the smile that started in his brain filter into his lips. It would not be interpreted as disagreement with Professor Ooze, but rather as a wimpish blush at his paper's digression. What the smile really meant was, *Holy hell, you think I've gone out of the text? The man who tells us every couplet is taut with double entendre, wit, allusion, philosophy . . . ad infinitum.* Steve hadn't thought it possible that he could get outside the text. Not with Shakespeare, or more accurately, with Professor Brentley, formerly of Oxford University.

"Well, I guess you're right," Steve said, thinking, *Bullshit, you're wrong.*

"I'm not saying the whole paper needs to be redone, but the logic turns tangent too often. I'd like to see you work a revision of it." Professor Brentley scrubbed one forearm while smiling the okay-interview-over smile. It was all happy-crappy. That's all. And Steve supposed he could do a revision in his sleep. When you know your audience, just write to their prejudices.

"I'll do it," Steve said, standing. "I appreciate your time, Professor Brentley."

"Yeah," he said and began packing some Benson & Hedges as Steve closed the stipple-lettered door behind him. He dropped the paper into the trash can in the outer part of the English department office, pondering inscrutably on the shallow *ka-thud* the paper made on the tin bottom. *Belongs in the old circular file anyway,* Steve resolved. Besides, he had it on file at home. Just a touch away on his crappy computer. Then, with unwelcome abruptness the paper man flashed into his mind, right on the nose of Einstein.

You owe the paper.

Steve picked "Let's All Wear Coxcombs" out of the garbage and walked absently toward the parking lot.

They had cola in the fridge at home. Always Coke, and always bottles. Steve snatched one of these on his way to his room. Coke had a mellowing effect on him. No Pepsi Generation. Just cold carbonation from an upended bottle. Not that he was overwrought, he observed. Not yet, anyway. But somehow he always needed a Coke after a personal conference at the university.

His room lay bathed in mid-afternoon sun. Uneventful sun. So much the better. Steve dropped his backpack heedlessly onto a clutter of wash-clothes. Since Mom had left he'd been doing, or rather not doing, his own laundry. In one hand he swayed his Coke, with the other he picked "Let's All Wear Coxcombs" out of his pack. He looked at it and hated what it represented—so much tired rhetoric; *pedantic* might be the word he was searching for. But the deeper truth was that it wasn't writing. Not *his* writing, anyway. It was regurgitation about some other guy's work, a guy dead since 1616. It was . . . hell, it meant he wasn't writing his stories. Somehow it was a tattletale. Steve's eyes lifted to see a sheet of college-ruled paper, flat this time, lying on top of his computer keyboard.

He stood looking at that blank sheet and thought about his

own few pieces of fiction. He thought about how his dad seemed so mildly to encourage him to write. He thought, too, about Professor Brentley and his tangents. Steve tossed "Let's All Wear Coxcombs" onto his bed, pages fluttering against the staple. Then he took four quick steps, slammed his Coke onto his desk, and seized that piece of college-ruled paper. He turned it over once, then crumpled it viciously.

"There. How's that feel? Am I all paid now, Mr. Paper Man?" Steve squeezed harder and harder on the crumpled ball, and then threw it across his room toward the can. He missed miserably. But the point had been made. He'd do as he damn well pleased. Always did. Still, his anger hadn't bled out the frustration. It sat mute and heavy on him: he still wasn't writing.

When he looked down at his desk, he saw that he'd spilled Coke everywhere. Almost right into his keyboard.

"Shit." He picked up an unlaundered shirt and wiped it up. Then he sat heavily in his rolling office chair and stared at the screen. It was lifeless and lackluster. *Like my own writing,* he thought. The screen was dust-covered to boot.

"Revision, huh. I can do revision." He booted up his system and clicked into Word. He chose the filename Coxcomb and launched review mode. Then he turned on his printer. It startled him at first, that tiny, siren-like sound, screaming at a high C. The red "no paper" light strobed with the sound.

"Wouldn't you know," Steve said to the blinking red light, which looked like a miniature of a car hazard light. He fetched a new ream of paper. As he ran it into the tray, one hand slipped.

"Ouch, dammit." Steve pulled his hand back and had sliced a neat groove into his third finger. Blood began to seep through the cut. "Paper cuts are the worst," he muttered.

A few drops escaped before he clamped it off. He made a cursory glance at the paper, silently indignant at its seeming conspiracy against him, and saw that the top sheets had red splashed polka dots. *Rather Jackson Pollock,* he thought bitterly and exited to get a Band-Aid.

He returned in better spirits. He always felt better when he'd decided to write, even if it was revision. And even if it was for Professor Brentley. Deciding was the hard part. The rest was okay. And he'd decided. Hot damn!

He sat again, and even with a bandaged finger, he meant to show Professor Brentley a thing or two. He went at it. His thoughts formed clearly, logic came nicely, thank you. Tangents deleted, and insights abounding. Hot damn, indeed. He spent four straight hours, which actually felt like four minutes. The writing just went well, and when it was done he felt cleansed. No more guilt. He might even try a new story, if he could get an idea.

He punched up the print mode and almost ran the document before remembering the stained sheets. He reached to remove them, but the paper was clean. "I thought there was blood on it," he said to himself. But he turned the paper back in and began printing "Let's All Wear Coxcombs: Revisited." He got up to go downstairs while it printed. Stopped. Picked up the crumpled ball of paper and plopped it into his oversize cola bottle trash receptacle on his way out, with nary a thought of the paper man.

"That was a mistake, my friend."

Steve opened his eyes. There was a crumpling sound, or rather an uncrumpling sound, coming from behind him and to the left. He turned onto his side and pushed himself partway up. There was nothing for a moment, and then the paper man's short arms curled over the lip of the trash can. He lifted himself out, actually grunting minutely. He was creased everywhere. But all the creases gave him a surreal quality, kind of like personality.

"Ah, shit," Steve muttered, rolling over onto his back again.

"'Ah, shit', yourself. You don't seem to take my meaning. On top of that, you do *this* to me." He hopped down onto the floor, and Steve heard the *crickle-crinkle* of his short gait toward his bed. He was afraid all of a sudden. He didn't know what he thought an eleven-inch piece of paper could do to him, but he thought it could do something, *would* do something. And he suddenly didn't care for being a writer or writing, or paper.

"You're a lazy ass, *and* an asshole. And goddamn if you aren't starting to piss me off."

As the paper man pulled himself onto Steve's bed, Steve said, "What? I thought I—"

"You thought you what? Wrote?" the paper man interjected. "Putting multisyllabic hogwash together, linked up by 'Thus' and 'Therefore' and 'Whereas.' You suppose you had thoughts never before entertained and expanded on? Wanted to contribute to the body of knowledge known as the corpus Shakespeare, did you?" There was a flat, merciless tone in the paper man's voice. He wasn't at all amusing to Steve tonight. "You're a fuck, Steve Kreig, a real righteous fuck. Starting to buy into your own horseshit." The paper man's sullen tone began to grow more fevered, more furious. "But, more than that, you don't seem able to understand the proper line of credit. So, let me tell you something—"

"No, let me tell *you*," Steve interrupted with his own sudden anger. No surprise on the paper man's non-face. "I don't give a hang for that paper, or Professor Brentley and his Oxford education. But I got my share of pride, and I could hear the patronage in his voice when he asked for a revision. Not directly patronizing, but like he knows what everyone else doesn't. So I just decided to put it to him. Told him I know all right."

There was a short pause where the paper man might have smiled if he'd had a mouth.

"Well there you go. Be damned if that isn't the Steve I wanted to hear." The paper man walked across Steve's chest and climbed onto the desk.

A little of the comedy in the paper man, as he hefted his featherlight body onto the desk, eased into him.

"You talk like you know me," Steve said, anger fading fast.

"Sure. Known you since you penned "Dark Child" back in '86. Senior that year weren't you?" The paper man had once again gained his place atop Steve's crappy shop-built PC. Right between Einstein's eyes.

"Yeah, I wrote it at work. How'd you know?" Steve was sincerely puzzled. Though why he might be would later astound him.

"Was there my boy, was there. Got a working relationship with quite a few people to be frank. Course, some I like better than others, and some are much more accommodating that. But I'm there at the first, as well as the last." As he spoke Steve noticed that the wrinkles were pressing themselves out. Slowly, but surely. "There's a bit of magic with the first moment someone touches pen to paper, or fingers to keys, for something other than school, work, or money. Those things want to bleed feeling out of writing, Steve. But when it's true, the way the crack of dawn is true, or a child's prayer is true, well, then, it starts a life. Not really a writer's life, not the way that beast more often than not turns out. But it starts a life. A way of turning things in the mind. Kind of a need too. But then, you can push that thing way back if you try." The paper man manipulated his little tube body and half-cylinder legs into a sitting position, his legs hanging down over the edge of his monitor.

And so much sense. The little guy, which Steve was beginning to equate with conscience, and which Steve thought could only have real dominion in sleep, was making so much sense.

"It's a bitter irony, I suppose. Or at least, an irony. That thing is alive, very much like a pet, a good pet like a dog. But if you push it back, try to forget about it, it eats you. Makes you know you're unhappy, but isn't got the power to force you to feed it." The paper man leaned forward an inch, seriousness practically written across his lines. "It's writing, Steve. Just do it, that's all, just do it."

Steve saw that all the wrinkles were gone now, save one that ran through the paper man's single flat eye.

If it hadn't been abundantly clear last night, it was now. But SOS (same old situation). *I want to write. I need to write. But what do I write.* Maybe he didn't understand after all. It made him feel pretty miserable too. Because now that life that the paper man had spoken of, the one Steve had sealed away, was open, and bleeding freely.

In a small voice, with his eyes turned toward the floor, Steve said, "What if I can't?"

"Now there's a disappointment, my friend. There's a real ass-licking disappointment. I sure hope there's more to you than that." Steve listened to a voice mixed with honest anger and disarming sadness. But it had no head to shake in disheartened reproof.

Steve would not look at the paper man. He was a mock right down to his material component: paper. It was a long time before sleep claimed Steve's embittered mind.

The paper man said no more. A final *ka-thop* sounded as the last crease in the paper man's eye pushed straight.

Steve awoke feeling glum. The dream was so vivid still. And so absolutely dead on. He ran a hand through his hair and sat up. He saw but one thing: a perfectly uncrumpled piece of college-ruled on top of his computer. *Maybe it wasn't a dream after all,* he thought. But the truth was he'd already decided the paper man was real enough.

Steve had been working at a fever pace almost since he'd gotten up. He'd felt dreary, pessimistic, and a little tired. He hadn't stopped to eat, or take his ritualized morning shit, or anything. He'd started to write and he hadn't stopped, hadn't wanted to stop, had, in fact, been afraid to stop. There was a piece of paper, no wrinkles, laying quietly beside him on his desk.

By two o'clock he had a good twelve pages of "Under the Wood" hammered out. It was the idea he'd had the day before on the way to school: the slavering beast. Somehow it found him again and had demanded to be written. And Steve thought it was coming along pretty well. He always felt better when he was writing. No, amend that, he *felt* when he was writing—it was the only time he ever really did.

By two-thirty he had cramps so bad in his hands that he *had* to stop. That was welcome. It was a physical side effect of writing. Some pain relieves.

He switched off the power after saving the document under filename Slaver. *Now what?* he thought, then realized he'd missed school. Not just missed it, completely forgotten about it. He didn't mind. Losing himself in a story was perfectly acceptable, even admirable, as far as he was concerned. He did have one errand at the university, though. He had to deliver to Professor

Brentley the revision he'd promised him. He'd do it after office hours so he didn't have to see the man. Less hassle.

Ron had passed by Steve's door that morning ready to rap at it and let his son know he was late for class. But he hadn't. He'd heard the hollow echo of keys from behind the door, and hoped it was writing, not homework, his son was doing. And the thought that a crazy dream about a paper man might have lit a fire under his son's ass, that he was now starting to write again because of it, tickled him to death. *If only I'd had a paper man,* Ron mused. In any event, it was the sole reason for his chipper mood all day long. And now, as he pulled into the oil-stained driveway, which usually reminded him of his ex-wife's ratty old Corolla, he wanted nothing more than to hear those keys clacking from his kid's room and maybe take a peak in at the next Asimov.

What Ron got was a disenchanted, disheveled picture of his boy-author.

"Hey pal, you don't look too good," Ron said, looking at Steve sitting at the kitchen table with about a dozen sheets of printed paper in his hands and an open bottle of Coke in front of him.

"You're not winning any contests," Steve said, still looking at the story in his hands.

"What're you reading?" Ron asked with a vague sense that it was the fruit of his boy's latest literary efforts.

"Shit, Dad, pure shit." Steve dropped the manuscript into a slight fan configuration on the kitchen table. He sat back and blew out an exhausted breath. "It's a story I just started working on, but it isn't going anyplace. God, I really didn't think it was that bad." He picked up the Coke, took a pull, and grimaced. "Coke's even gone flat."

"You mind?" Ron queried his son. He wanted to see what could be so bad. His mind was telling him that the author-critic was always overly dramatic.

"Help yourself, but don't expect much," Steve answered, drinking more of his flat soda.

Ron read it, all twelve and a half pages, and hated to concur with his son's assessment of "Under the Wood," but he did. The story was dry. The slavering beast in it was cartoonish. Steve sat watching the sky cloud over outside, watching his dad turn pages.

Ron finished. "It's not that bad."

"Like hell. It's the worst thing I've ever done, and that's saying something." Steve had finished his drink and got up to return it to the rack of empty bottles.

As Steve's dad, Ron wanted to be reassuring, positive, supportive, but he didn't want to pretend, either. That would be more damaging. The story wasn't very good. Of course, it wasn't done. But it didn't seem to have anyplace to go. Not in any literary sort of way. Ron could give a damn less about literary levels of appreciation. The story just didn't make you want to finish. So Ron didn't know what to tell his son. The truth at an angle, he decided.

"I do like your other stories better, but I wouldn't give up on this one. I think you could do a lot with it." That wasn't too bad.

Steve knew the truth at an angle, but the other thing Ron said seemed to land, as if it was something he'd stepped past in his need to write again: the work.

"You always have to write out the clots," Steve muttered. "Maybe you don't forget how to ride a bike, but you sure as hell don't do it well after years of driving a car."

Steve hadn't written for months. How had he expected to mount that keyboard and churn out publishable, or even readable, fiction the first time out. So Ron had done it after all. He'd steered his boy back to brass tacks.

"Thanks, Dad," Steve said with quiet sincerity.

"So," Ron asked, "you gonna go do something with it?"

"Yeah, you bet your ass I will. Give me that." Ron handed the pages to his son and watched him head back up the stairs to his room. The keys echoed down to him after a few minutes. He smiled and thought for the first time that maybe he was doing okay by his boy without his aerobically conditioned ex-wife.

"It's shit, Steve, and you know it's shit." The incessant papery voice startled Steve out of his dream. He'd been dreaming of winning the Pulitzer. The first man to do it with a piece of horror fiction. And in a banquet hall, giving his acceptance speech, all he'd been able to say is "How should I presume? How should I presume? HOW SHOULD I PRESUME?!"

"C'mon, Steve, I think I may have to walk you through this once. You've gotten hopelessly out of practice."

Steve opened his eyes and saw the paper man standing next to the monitor near the power switch. The monitor was humming softly and glowing a mellow blue. The color caught on the paper man's featureless face and made it look ghoulish. This was all too fucking crazy, too . . . scary. Gooseflesh rose on Steve's neck.

"But I've been working, dammit, really!" He stared at the paper man, who remained motionless. There was something predatory about him tonight. It might have been the blue computer screen and its witch-light, but the paper man was not a grouchy yet well-meaning goad anymore. He was here for something, and there was a dreadful purpose in him. His one eye was glowering and hateful. And it was all the worse because the paper man didn't breath. If it had ever been funny, the way he crinkled, the way he unwrinkled himself, the size, the tiny mouthless voice, it wasn't funny any longer. And the blank look it gave Steve was more horrid, more pitiless, than any fanged or screeching creature could have managed. Steve was frightened. Goddamn frightened. The paper man was small, but he instilled a feeling of power. Holy hell, a piece of paper that was alive! What was he capable of?

"Get your ass up and let's get started," the paper man said with a slightly lower and more measured voice.

Steve obeyed without discussion. He knew the paper man meant to show him how to write. And he meant now. Steve sat in his rolling swivel chair in his boxers.

The blue light spread onto Steve's face, basking him in a hellish luminescence. It made him feel sluggish and the room feel kind of dead. The paper man still hadn't moved.

"Give me your hand," the paper man said with that imperative, calculated voice.

Steve did so, bringing it up toward the paper man slowly, palm upraised.

The paper man lifted one short arm and slowly cut a groove in Steve's first finger. The pain was exquisite. The paper man's arm sliced easily down into his flesh with a searing heat. He pulled his paper edge across the skin, a hot, uncomfortable friction biting the blood. The paper man seesawed his arm back out of Steve's finger and the blood welled up.

"Now, hold it over the paper." Steve did as he was told, spellbound, slivers of pain still rising through his arm. But he was getting it. There were dues to be paid. And he understood why his attempts at "Under the Wood" had failed. So he obeyed, his eyes glowing with the light from the monitor. Drops of blood fell onto the computer paper for a long time.

As he drifted away he heard, "One great big dilly of a dent, you bet. Just remember who you owe. There's dues, Steve."

The next morning Steve slept late. When he finally awoke he remembered the paper man in the pale blue light and he shuddered once under the covers. Then he jerked his head and saw that one single piece of fucking college-ruled paper on his keyboard.

"You sonofabitch!" Steve yelled and pushed himself out of bed. He winced and drew his hand toward his face, staring at the thin white groove.

"Look at that," Steve said to no one, prodding the wound. "Well, we'll just take care of that," he mentioned to himself as he realized where the cut had come from.

He'd had it. It was one thing believing the paper man was real. It was another thing entirely to pander to him. "Dues, my ass," Steve said loudly, "and speaking of asses, kiss yours goodbye." He went to his drawers and produced a Bic; he used it when he and his friends went camping, or smoked cloves, or both. He fingered it twice before it caught, and then turned the flame dial all the way up. Smiling, he walked back around his bed.

"Should have thought of this before," he reprimanded himself mildly. "How you going to unwrinkle ashes, friend. I'll tell you how. You won't. You can't. So goodbye, Mr. Paper Man," he concluded with sarcastic glee.

Steve picked up the single sheet nervously. Still, just touching it was unsettling. But even with trembling fingers he managed to get it up. Then he fingered the Bic. It lit, first time. Karma. But before he could do the deed, his eye caught something, like the way you can look over a humongous crowd and see to see the one face you recognize. It was in the printer.

He let his finger slip off the propane lever. He took a step to his right to see it straight. It was type. It was a story. Or, at least, there was a "The End" at the bottom of the last printed page. But if it was a story, whose was it? That question was at least semirhetorical. No one had been in here during the night but Steve and the paper man, and somehow Steve didn't think it was the other. The paper man seemed confined to the other side of a story, the part that's finished. And if it wasn't the paper man, then who? *Me? But when?* Steve stared dumbly down at the fatalistic two last words: "The End."

Happy-sad words Steve called them. Always it was good to have finished something, but then you always felt like you were leaving something behind too.

Steve put down the piece of college-ruled that was by night a wicked man of paper, like maybe a lost cast member from *The Wizard of* Oz. He sat down, looking dazedly at the computer. It was more craziness to think he had written a whole story *unawares*, as Professor Brentley would say.

"One way to tell for sure," he spoke softly to the story, as if speaking to calm a savage beast. Then he tore the sheets from the receiving tray and laid them in his lap, a good forty pages of manuscript.

"Looks like I might have been busy," he teased himself, and started to read.

"Hey, that's pretty good. Pretty *damn* good," Steve said for maybe the tenth time as he'd read one hell of a version of "Under the Wood." It was amazing. The story he'd been reading for the past hour, and just possibly written, was more than good—it was fantastic. He'd be cashing a check on it as soon as whatever magazine he submitted it to could send one back. He felt sure of that.

He put the manuscript down gingerly on his computer desk. Then he sat back with an intense sense of satisfaction. The way he'd felt the first time he'd had sex and actually known what to do. But it beat sex handily. Or maybe it was sex. Coitus in some pure sense. Whatever. The story kicked ass.

Steve's satisfaction again turned to curiosity. If he'd written something so good, why didn't he remember? He'd heard of automated writing, but it didn't seem to explain this, not really. He closed his eyes and scrubbed out the sleep-seeds. His cut rubbed ungraciously on his skin. He slowly opened his eyes then and again remembered the paper man cutting him, and the blood. Blood on the paper.

Steve snatched up "Under the Wood" and riffled the pages. There must be blood stains on it, at least on the first couple of sheets. Nothing. Steve lowered the papers with trembling fingers. His mind turned on one of the paper man's dark, ridiculous utterances: "You owe the paper." Steve's jaw dropped perceptibly. He was thinking about *dues*, what "owe" meant. How did paper collect for its part in a writer's success? And the money winner: What did you do different last night, Steve, that you haven't done before? Why is this version of "Under the Wood" so much better than before?

Steve looked down at his paper cut and then up at the single piece of college-ruled. He was taking the paper man's meaning when the phone rang downstairs. He jumped, but got to the phone in a run-walk, glad to be out of his room for some silly reason.

He picked it up halfway through the fourth ring.

It was Professor Brentley.

"Hello, may I please speak with Stephen Kreig," Brentley said with trained telephone etiquette.

"You got him," Steve returned with deliberate slang.

"Steve, missed you in class, you feel okay?"

"Yeah, just busy is all. Don't tell me you called 'cause I missed one class," Steve said, feeling rather bitter toward the good doctor, because he felt bitter.

"No, though I hope you don't make a habit of it. What I called about is 'Let's All Wear Coxcombs: Revisited.' Steve, I won't beat around the bush. It's great. Probably the finest piece of analysis I've received during my tenure here." Professor Brentley was sure Steve would melt under such congratulation.

"Oh," Steve said.

It was clear to Steve that Brentley was slightly taken aback by his response.

"I'm not donning you with feint praise, Steve. I mean it. You looked right at it. It was a pleasure to read. A-plus. You really poured your guts into this revision. Most of my students sweat blood and tears for a paper half as good."

Steve soured out a smile. The literary term was dark irony. But whatever the term, Professor Brentley had hit the head of the nail. Steve had poured something into that paper, all right. He remembered the small cut he'd gotten feeding the paper into the printer. He also remembered how well the writing had gone that day.

Dues.

Had it been an accident, really? Or was the paper taking what it had coming?

Hold up! He called a timeout on the crazy. Even the Christians had dispensed with blood sacrifice millennia ago. The fact that he was entertaining the idea was probably proof that the paper man and all the attendant horseshit were part of a larger psychotic breakdown. Too much pressure from his schoolwork. Mom up and leaving him and his dad dry. And the fact that he hadn't been writing. It had all stacked up on his mind and broken him down. Thus the nightmares about a horrific little paper golem and the ludicrous idea that paper, as a thing, required blood to yield good writing.

I'm losing it.

And yet, Steve allowed himself to think it a couple of steps further: How much is too much? Is it ever enough?

"Stephen," said Professor Brentley, "are you there?"

"Well," Steve said to maintain the idiot parlance, "I tried to feel some of Lear's pain. After that, the text opened itself up to me." *Boy, that ought to make Professor Brentley wet himself.*

"Really very remarkable, Steve." A studied pause. "Have you considered graduate school?" Steve heard the pitch. Professors were constantly trying to do missionary work. Convince their students that continuing education was where it's at.

"Yeah, but I've got a few more papers to write before I'm ready." Steve was studying the cuts on his fingers, accidental or otherwise.

"Never too early. I might offer that our graduate studies are nationally ranked."

"Really," Steve said mustering faux interest. "I'd like to get an application," he finished, hoping it would end their telephone conversation.

"Have one for you in class Monday, Steve. And really, you went right to the heart of Lear."

"Thanks Professor Brentley. See you Monday."

"You bet. Goodbye."

"Bye."

It had taken an entire day of moping, eating Clover Club potato chips, and watching *I Dream of Jeannie* reruns for Steve to see the error of his ways. He had felt alarmed, and sanctimonious, and apprehensive, and scared shitless about the paper man and his dues. He still couldn't remember what happened that prior night as far as the writing was concerned, but the little ritual before it was crystal clear in his mind. It was pulling a dagger down on a sacrifice. But you had a right to do it, if that sacrifice was yourself, right? And why the hell was he being so crazy about it anyway? A few token drops of blood. And what in return? One hell of a story.

Probably worthy of a Year's Best anthology. So why had he felt like burning the paper man? That little leprechaun had just shown him a way to get it done. And by the time Steve handed the new and improved "Under the Wood" to his father that night, he had indeed seen the error of his ways.

"Well, bless my soul, boy," Ron said looking up at Steve, who sat munching more Clover Club right from the bag.

"Not bad, huh?"

"Not bad. Get your coat on. I'm taking you out for ribs." Ron was absolutely preening. Paper man or no paper man, fathership or no, his dad had the look of a man who thought his son was on his way. And when a man can see his son making a life, he was fit to mount the heavens. And the heavens tonight would be a full rack of baby backs at the new in-town Tony Roma's.

"I thought you might like it," Steve said, smiling with a hint of modesty. He took another chip out and put it in his mouth whole before chomping it.

"Steve, I told you how I'd wanted to write myself as a young man." His dad's face turned sober.

"Yeah," Steve said, putting the chips aside.

His dad smiled sadly. "What I didn't tell you was how bad I wanted to. It was like an ache inside me. An itch I couldn't scratch. I tried and tried. But I just didn't have your talent . . ." he broke off. He tried to smile through a face on the brink of tears, filled with regret and remembrance. "I guess what I mean to say is that it feels like a kind of victory for me too, this story." His dad held it up, his eyes glassy.

"It is, Dad," Steve said before his dad could let it go. "It sure as hell is."

"Since your mother left I didn't think I was—"

"Hey, you said ribs, and that's as far as I need to hear."

His father sat a few moments more. Then he stood up. "All right, let's go. You can drive. I'll grab my wallet and be right out."

"Okay," Steve said, the disastrous sad-talk averted, and went out to warm up the car.

Ron went upstairs to get his wallet. He passed Steve's room on the way and thought about the paper man his son had told him about. On his way back, he stopped at his son's door. Rollercoaster was what he was thinking when he pushed into Steve's bedroom just to take a look.

The room lay in shadow. Hall-light spilled in to form a yellow rectangle on the carpet. Ron just stood there, tears coming again, thankful. The last few months he'd thought he was failing with Steve. Steve was his life. And so, failing life. But now things were looking up. Maybe there was no woman to come home to, and maybe that scar would show forever. But his son was alive, alive and writing, and all because of some damn dream about a paper man. Life, huh? His son's room filled him with a strange kind of peace. He looked opposite the door and his eyes fell on Albert Einstein and his quotable quote. The house lay still all around him.

Distantly he heard the computer monitor click on and warm to life.

Then Ron's eyes fell on a piece of paper that lay atop Steve's keyboard. A smile came over him and he walked over to it. He stood looking at it. A paper man dream. Ron picked up that piece of 8½-by-11. He looked at it and a tear escaped his left eye. It made him feel silly, emotional, but he couldn't deny it. He pulled it close and gave it a kiss.

"Thank you," he said, "you gave me my son back." He replaced the paper just as a honk blast came from the car.

He smiled again on his way out of the room, thinking about a silly dream that had kicked his son into gear.

Steve was awake this time when the paper man started to speak. He felt too good to sleep. There was the story, and most of all his dad—they'd eaten ribs and joked with each other to the amusement of their lovely waitress, who scolded them with every new rack she brought to the table. Ron tipped her generously for putting up with them. He didn't think even the paper man could ruin this high.

"Feeling pretty good, are you?" the paper man said from his perch.

"Yeah, I am," Steve replied without looking directly at him.

"Good to hear it," the paper man said with a sound of sincerity. "May I assume then you like what we've done with 'Under the Wood'?"

"That's an understatement." Steve turned to see the one paper-hole eye. He became more serious. "Did I write that?"

"*We*, and yes we did." The paper man sat down, dropping his legs over the monitor screen. "When you keep things in proper perspective, you'll be surprised at what you can accomplish. And by the way, I received the nicest payment tonight that I think I ever gotten for my efforts."

"Yeah, what was that?" Steve asked, looking back toward the ceiling, musing.

"A kiss—a kiss from your old man."

Steve whirled his head back to the paper man, "What!"

"Yep. Nicest thank-you ever."

Steve stumbled over his words. "You mean he saw you? What the—"

"Nah, don't get so drawn up. He just came in and said 'thank you' to a piece of paper. Kissed me and left." The paper man swung his legs playfully. "Appreciation, Steve, what body doesn't want it, or need it."

Steve settled. "I think I'd feel better it you left him out of this."

"Sure. His writing days were a long while ago, but he's harder on himself about it than he needs to be." The paper man sat looking nowhere. "But to the matter, my boy. You've got writing to do."

"I do?" Steve said quizzically.

"No more on your laurels, Steve, let's be about it." The paper man stood.

"What about an idea. I can't just write aimlessly."

"You got ideas," the paper man said back, "got a lot of 'em. Got one about a malevolent little girl name of Genevieve. Haven't forgotten about that one, have you." It wasn't a question.

Steve looked at him. He didn't need to ask how the paper man knew. But neither did that mean it didn't make him uncomfortable. Genevieve had been a novella idea he'd had his first year of college. He'd never gotten around to it.

"Let's start," the paper man prompted, his voice merry and yet not companionable at all.

Steve got up as the paper man had directed. The paper man himself hopped nimbly down to the power switch and keyed the computer into life. The pale blue light filled the screen and then touched the paper man's tubular body. Again he stood motionless. The room was expectant suddenly. And it all emanated from the sexless eleven-inch incubus that stood alongside Steve's terminal. Even the hum of the computer droned out in the blank stare of the paper man. A wicked sensation caught Steve. The lackluster body of the paper man nailed that sensation home with finality.

Dues.

Steve sat into his chair and produced another piece of 8½-by-11-inch college-ruled from his desk drawer. He looked at the paper man who said nothing and felt nothing; he might not have been alive at that moment except for the intimidating way he stood witness to this little ritual.

Steve looked up at Einstein once, back at the paper man, and then brought the new paper up. He looked at it for a long moment. Then he drew its edge across the third finger of his left hand. The paper cut slowly and deftly down, pulling that easy, heating friction with it. It came cleanly through the layers of skin, sending pricks of sharp pain through Steve's hand. He winced but made no attempt to stop. Paper buried in his skin. He was only halfway across its length. He pulled on. The agony was slow and exquisite. The thin edge sank hotter and deeper into his flesh, searing tender nerves. At the end he ripped it fast, shooting screaming darts of pain into the tip of his finger. *How easy it glides right on through,* he thought.

Then it was done and blood began flowing up.

Steve applied it.

The paper man didn't stir.

Steve began to type.

A week later *Genevieve* was written. It was almost a hundred and fifty pages and it was at least ten times better than "Under the Wood." Steve's hands looked like he'd thrust them into a twirling fan. The story was great.

"This story is great," Ron said over his dinner plate. He had just finished reading *Genevieve.* Steve had given it to him not long after he'd finished it.

"Not bad," Steve replied somewhat indifferently.

"You're too modest. Steve, I think your writing's getting better every day. Say, what are those Band-Aids on your fingers?" His dad hadn't really noticed them.

"Oh, just a few little paper cuts. Nothing to worry about." Steve thought about the antiquated medical practice of bloodletting. A bitter laugh burst out and flapped his lips.

"What's so funny?" his dad asked.

"Ah, nothing. I just . . . you really like it, Dad?" Steve was inwardly desperate to be sure of that.

"No, it's awful, probably only sell a few million copies," his father said smiling. "No lie. I'm fit to be stuffed. Or however the saying goes."

Steve managed a meager smile. "Thanks, Dad. I guess I needed to hear that. The truth, I mean. I can always tell when you're lying."

"Oh, you can, can you? Well, it's your turn for dishes. You think I'm lying there?" Witty can was his dad.

"No, I'll do 'em." Steve got up to run some dishwater.

"Hey, pal, I'm just kidding." Ron felt bad, because his son looked like . . . well, he looked the way he did the day his wife left him that pain-alleviating note: "Ron, it's not working. I think I deserve more. Don't be bitter. You'll find someone too. Love, Jess."

"I know, Dad. I'm just not particularly chipper today, that's all. Give me your plate." Ron handed it to him.

"Want to tell your dad why?"

"I don't know," Steve replied. "You want anything to fuck up how good things are going lately." He paused. "I'm sorry. It's just you deserve your share of happiness too, that's all."

"That's not how families work, son," his father said quietly. "I'm on your side of things. Always. You can tell me anything."

"I'll get over it," Steve said, feeling the acidic soap he'd poured into the water bite at his paper cuts.

"Okay, pal. But day or night, I'm here. I love you."

"I know, Dad. Me too."

Steve lay awake all evening. After the dishes, he'd just come into his room, closed the door, got undressed, laid down, and stayed awake. He kept thinking: How far? How much? He understood his unhappiness before. It was like another life, just like the paper man had said. The not-writing, it makes you know you're unhappy, and it eats at you. The not-writing eats you. And Steve understood that. But now there was another dark irony. What price was enough? You had to pay dues. But that searing, slicing, razor-edged paper. How much? How far?

The sun set, taking all the light out of Steve's room. There was only the faint indirect glow from the crack under the door, and his bedroom window. But when the paper started to ripple and crackle, he saw it.

The paper began to do waves, from one end to the other. It bumped, jerked, heaved, and then it rolled into a tube. The legs divided, the arms pulled away. The paper man stood up.

"Hiya, friend," the paper man said.

"Hello," Steve said deferentially.

"Hey, you don't sound too good." The paper man jumped to the desktop and shuffled up to the edge.

There was quiet for a space.

Then Steve finally said, "How much?"

"Ah, that's a bogus question, Steve," the paper man said knowingly. "You don't ask a price on something you got to have. Now, shall we begin?" The paper man seemed in good spirits. *Why not? He was getting his dues,* Steve thought resentfully.

"That dark irony. It's there whether you write or not, isn't it?" Steve looked with hatred at the paper man. Partly for the irony, and the cuts on his fingers. Partly because he did want to pay his dues. He wanted to write, needed to write. And at last, would write. But he wanted this much clear, if it was possible: How far?

"My boy, there's always something that's left behind. How much? Or what? Those aren't the right questions. It's where those things take you that's important. The stories themselves, that's the question. What about the story? You don't want to spare the tale at the expense of the teller? Do you?" The paper man seemed to expect an answer.

Steve thought this out. There was a lot to consider. And then nothing to consider, because in the final analysis, as Professor Brentley would say, it's pretty much academic.

"No," he said.

"That's what I thought," the paper man replied with even good nature, and flipped the computer switch. Shallow blue light dropped slowly onto everything, giving it a pale and solemn cast.

Steve picked up a piece of college-ruled and pulled its thin, measureless edge heedlessly across the middle of his first finger.

Cat Rambo

"MERCHANTS HAVE MAXIMS" IS SET IN THE WORLD OF TABAT, WHERE I've written several dozen stories and a few novels. One feature of the world is the belief of the Merchant caste in the Trade Gods, a series of economic forces that keep the world in order. What happens when that set of beliefs becomes insufficient—or when it's misused to justify injustices?

Chronologically, this is set several months before the beginning of *Beasts of Tabat.*

Cat Rambo

MERCHANTS HAVE MAXIMS

Cat Rambo

Though she'd been on land for two days now, the ship's sway still made Essa stumble, phantom waves rocking her back and forth, the horizon dipping and lurching as she walked. She concentrated on putting one bare foot down after another on the dirt path, watching out for the angry red ants that seemed to swarm everywhere.

The jungle was noxiously hot and sticky; unpleasant sweat crawled down her back. But complaining would do no good, and so she, along with the rest of the ship's survivors, trudged after the people they hoped were rescuers rather than opportunists.

On either side, the shorter vegetation pressed inward, leafy walls smelling sharp green where the leading guide had hacked away plants blocking the path. Insects buzzed in shrill chorus. Probably more of those grasshoppers whose bodies were as long as Essa's hand, sometimes longer, as big as the wagon maestra's long, spiky fingers. That tall woman hunched inward as much as the rest of the party, stumbling after their guides, who were so clean and calm in contrast to the bloody, dirty, stinking-in-the-way-only-someone-who's-been-sleeping-in-their-own-clothes-for-three-days-stinks party of Merchants, who were still not entirely sure how they had managed to stay alive after their ship foundered and left them in the middle of what was, to them, mostly uncharted territory.

Surely they would stop soon. She needed to pee badly, and had for at least a league or two.

She tried to occupy her mind, with things other than worries about their situation. Every Merchant, even a minor scribe, kept a journal in which they developed their personal maxims. They recorded every time they made a decision—in theory every decision, big or small, but most people recorded only what they considered to be the big ones—and which of the Trade Gods oversaw all the factors that had gone into making that decision. And what they thought the outcome would be. And they would later go back to that journal to develop the personal principles that would guide them throughout their future trade, and beyond that into retirement.

A Merchant had a journal since first learning to write. A Merchant without one felt that lack like a missing limb, something Essa kept reaching for and not finding. She already missed being able to flip through it at night, to figure out the results of different actions and what part each God had played, from small ones like Kepterto, who handled tailors, or Rilriliworhaomu, Trade God of Hypothetical Marital Alliances, to the larger ones like Enba and Anbo, Want and Supply.

She thought back yet again on what she'd learned so far. At some point, surely, she'd be able to start a new journal.

So far this journey had yielded several new maxims for Essa—who had analyzed the most recent big decision she'd made at the great, repeated length afforded by a sea voyage.

Do not make hasty decisions was a major trade maxim. It invoked a whole group of Trade Gods, with particular attention to Planning, Forethought, and Experience. Essa had refined this with subclauses of her own, which she intended to apply going forward and never, ever, ever deviate from again.

They were as follows: (A) *Never make decisions while drunk.* (B) *Never make decisions while wanting to impress someone* (like that mathematician one wanted to study with). And (C) *Give oneself at least a day to think about any trip that involves a lengthy voyage, particularly a sea voyage to the Southern Isles.*

Since that very early morning when, purple and red moons visible just above the horizon, she had stumbled, still drunk, aboard *The Subsequent Minnow*—a sailor's necessary bag in one hand and a satchel containing three blank notebooks and all of the mathematician's works, including a new manuscript to be proofed, along with an assortment of pens and ink blocks in the other—she had ended up (after that first week of total and abject seasickness) with plenty of time to write down several thorough analyses of the situation. Enough to fill the first notebook and start a second.

All of that had, of course, been lost in the experience that led to another new personal maxim, one she suspected more than one Merchant before her might have personally adopted: *Do not get on ships going into dangerous territory in any season, let alone storm-prone ones.*

"Come along, idiot!" A hand jerked Essa's elbow, making her outright stumble on the path. Then the twin who had pulled at her spoke to the other in Ligurian: "Why couldn't any of the useful ones survive? All she can do is write numbers on pages." The twins often used Ligurian, thinking that no one else spoke it, when the truth was most of the sailors knew it and two had taught Essa all she needed to know.

One moment she anticipated with glee, a little gift waiting for her sometime in the coming days and weeks, guarded by Diahmo, God of the Balanced Ledger, was the moment she let the twins know that *she* spoke Ligurian. Actually, their use of it had honed her skill significantly. She'd rehearsed the revelation in her mind multiple times, usually on occasions like this when she might have quoted the ancient Ligurian poet who had said *All life is numbers.* But the truth was, the farther off that day, the more moments like this the twins would have to think back to.

In addition, it was downright useful knowing what they

thought they needed to keep secret from the rest.

The twins were translators and proud of how many languages they knew, though many of these were, in Essa's opinion, not particularly useful, since the cultures that had spoken them were dead and only texts remained. (The twins' names were Felip and Felim, but no one could tell them apart, and Essa always thought of them in the plural.)

Essa had signed on as a minor accountant, tracking the voyage's costs and bills of lading and such. She was indeed currently useless, the more so because they had nothing to trade, since all of their goods had gone down with the ship. Worse yet, the majority of those actually trained in trade matters had drowned, leaving the maestra—whose specialty was transportation of goods and whose original role had been not that much larger than Essa's—as the most senior Merchant of the six of them and in charge of somehow gaining some profit from this journey, or else leaving all of them in the red and prone to being sold as slaves back home in order to recuperate the debt.

Now Essa was sandwiched between the twins, who had of course managed to survive as a unit, and who had attached themselves to the maestra's heels. Every once in a while a lanky elbow would get in her way. She didn't think they were doing it deliberately. Just that they weren't quite as quick to stop it as they might have been when they noticed she was the target. They weren't happy about the overall state of things, and, despite being translators, they didn't speak their guides' language, So everyone was reduced to Trade tongue.

The twins didn't really care what they took their frustration out on as long as that thing had little chance of fighting back. Like the trees one of them kept swatting with their staff or the bushes the other was prodding. Or Essa.

Or Skiff the dog girl, behind them with the hound, Yadi, at her heels. The child had chattered plenty to Essa at first, about all sorts of things, like what sort of oil she used when combing out the dogs' fur, or flea preventatives, or how the dogs' diet must be maintained scrupulously, for something harmless to a human might prove deadly for a dog, even something simple like garlic or onions. But as the day had worn on, she'd grown quieter and quieter, perhaps for lack of energy but also perhaps due to Essa's lack of reply, her breath stolen away by the day's heat.

Essa huffed in damp, hot air and hoped again that they'd stop soon. She flicked away an ant exploring her bare leg, its path like fire against the sunburn.

Above her head, one twin said something snide to the other.

Essa added one to a number in her head and permitted herself a flicker of a smile.

They did stop, just a little farther in. What's more, they did it in the shadow of a waterfall that filled its rocky basin before roiling on through hillocks bearded with green ferns and full of niches edged with whispering reeds and pleasured with the flicker of minnows.

The three guides rested, sitting cross-legged on the rocks. They were an older woman with her white hair pulled back in a shaggy braid, a young man impressive with muscle and self-conscious down to the roots of his well-oiled dark hair, and a bored young woman, skinny but nimble, her head shaved and her protuberant ears set with bone hoops piled atop each other. All three had plenty of bare skin, sometimes with things inlaid in it: the young woman had strips of what seemed to be green and brown snakeskin sewn from shoulder to wrist, and the older one the same in scarlet and silver.

The man had two great beetles, one on each hand. The centers of the shiny carapaces had been fused to the backs of his hands, so the legs waved in the air while the mandibles roved back and forth as the heads turned. From time to time he raised a hand to his neck and let a beetle strike, shuddering at whatever substance the bite pumped into the vein there.

The older woman waved at the water.

"Bathe now," she said shortly. "Safe."

Everyone else waded into the pool, shedding clothing with rapidity. Except for the twins, Essa noted. She made for the nearby bushes herself and finally satisfied her urgent need while Yadi and Skiff splashed each other, barking and giggling. Then Essa dropped the reeking, salty bundle of her clothing on the shore and swayed her way past the scowling twins and into the water, feeling cold, hard rock underfoot, the give of gravel where it had clustered in ridges and pockets while the water continued on into its green-fringed escape.

She ignored everything and plunged directly under, the cold smacking her in the face with delicious chill, washing away the fevered heat the sun had enforced on her skin.

When she came up for air, pulling sodden hair away from her face and licking water drops from her lips, the twins were arguing with the guides and the dripping maestra, who stood submerged to the middle of her thighs, arms folded and adamant.

"We're supposed first to follow them without question and now get naked in a pool?" one twin exclaimed.

The man with beetles on the backs of his hands kissed one beetle, then the other. He raised his head to mumble through venom-puffed lips, "You smell bad and will offend people."

Essa swept her arms back and pulled herself deeper into the water, still facing the shore and the argument.

"Get in and wash the stink off," the maestra said wearily. "I'll watch." When the other twin started to say something, she held up a hand, using Merchant handspeak despite the watching guides. Essa froze, her thoughts more chilling than the water could ever be. The maestra considered the rude behavior of the twins that dangerous—so dangerous it warranted giving up secrets. The maestra didn't know what sort of people they might be meeting. What they might do if they took offense. The maestra, the twins, Skiff, even Essa were all totally dependent on the guides' village's goodwill. Shivering, Essa raked her hands through her hair and waded out to keep the maestra company.

By the time the twins exited the water, two other people had appeared, both of them younger than Essa, wide-eyed and alert but utterly silent. They carried baskets, three stacked one atop the other, which they put on the bank, removing the wicker lids so the traders could see the fabric inside.

"A change of clothes," the maestra guessed, and a glance at the oldest guide—who had identified herself as Tria, the man as Sfeo, and the other woman as Hana—confirmed this.

The outfits were a soft cloth, gauzy and loosewoven, of a kind Essa had never seen before, covered with lacy patterns that the maestra said were made with wax and dye, her tone light but pedantic, as though in the face of everything she was determined to maintain the Merchantly values of teaching things to the juniors in her care.

Essa tried to take everything in, despite the sensation that the boat still swayed underfoot—would it ever leave her? It was accompanied by the feeling that sleep was creeping up on her, was lurking in the corners of her eyes.

She yawned, shrugging on the blue and green flowery fabric, and looked at Skiff, who stood staring down at herself, expression bemused. It was probably the nicest thing the girl had ever worn—she was one of the duke's dog handlers, supposed to be taking three culls from his kennels down to Sugarport to trade with a breeder there. Yadi had been the only dog to survive. It nuzzled the girl's palm, and she glanced up, startled, to meet Essa's stare, then looked down at her hands.

Another girl brought a green ointment, its smell citrus and mint, and motioned at Essa to apply it. As she rubbed it into her skin, the omnipresent gnats and mosquitoes relented. She wrung water again out of her hair and followed, much cooler, behind the maestra and the twins as they trailed the guides. Given how quickly the robes had appeared, the village had to be close.

The narrow path zigzagged up a hill, or rather a mountain, she decided as they continued. Then it gave way to a flat plateau, and buildings among the towering jungle trees.

The buildings were unlike Tabat's brick and tile. These looked as though they had been grown in place, and in many spots walls of vines sequestered porches or led in various directions. The smell of the leaves and flowers shifted every time paths intersected or approached one of the tiny bridges, most no more than a few feet wide, although there were several larger ones crossing the river that divided the village. As their footsteps echoed across one of the latter's planks, the scent shifted from cinnamon's warmth to a crisper floral and mint, and Essa realized these must be the equivalent of street signs.

There had been plenty of birds on the walk earlier, but here there were hundreds, brightly colored as trade beads, from dozens of species, most eating from small suspended platforms or from the hanging baskets of blooming flowers beside each doorway and landmark. The composition of each basket varied, as individual as signs back home.

Many plants bore enormous drooping flowers, the smell of the bell-shaped blossoms feathery light, faintly citron and sweet, and popular with the many hummingbirds. The tiny birds flitted between baskets like miniature rainbows gone rogue, pausing to sip and pose, watching the visitors with eyes like jet and amber and, once, bright turquoise.

The group stopped in front of a building that, while it seemed just as organic as the rest, was grander in its dimensions. The trunk of an ancient dead tree that extended far up into the canopy hosted it, and formed a good third of the space inside. They were led down halls carved into the wood; painted vines and flowers flickered in the light of the candle their guide held.

Essa expected everyone to be taken to meet whomever it was that they were supposed to meet—after all, what had been the point of bathing and dressing them all? But no, the maestra was escorted off, and the rest of them were left in a windowless room where at least they were—finally—given food, even if it was unfamiliar and very spicy, to the point of making her cough. The dog and Skiff huddled together, and the twins bickered among themselves.

Essa looked around and tried to imagine what details she would have recorded in her journal, if only she had one. She thought of the mathematician's manuscript and hoped that someone else might have proofed it by the time she got back.

He had sneered at her—that was what had made her sign up for the expedition—had told her she might have plenty of school years but she had no experience in trade.

At the time it had seemed one of the most significant, angering moments of her life. Everyone looking at her while he stood with folded arms, giving her the reasons he wouldn't accept her as a student. And then he'd had the gall to say he'd reconsider if she proved herself by proofing his manuscript in a worthy manner. Worse, she hadn't pointed out that he was taking advantage of her labor, and invoked Diahmo in rebuke.

Since then she had faced storm and shipwreck. His sneer seemed much less significant, somehow, in the face of those elemental forces. She imagined herself back in that inn in Tabat—she skipped right over the wherefore and why of how she might get there—facing him down. She didn't want to study with him anymore, but she did still rather want to do something with mathematics. Something that involved the university and clean classrooms during the day and warm baths and that sort of thing at night. If one ever got back to Tabat, that might in fact be doable.

Getting back to Tabat . . . She let out a long sigh, louder than she had intended.

"This is your fault," a twin said to her.

"Fuck off," she wearily retorted. They'd tried to pick fights before, all through the journey, jockeying for status. Now they were doing it just because they were bored.

He leaned over and shoved at her shoulder. "You fuck off," he said.

All of the rage at the journey and its circumstances boiled up in her in an instant, and she couldn't do anything except shove back, so focused with rage that all she saw was his face, first startled and then suddenly full of elation, and then the fight was on in a tangle of fists and falls while the dog barked as Skiff tried to pull it back. She was fighting both twins, which would have been harder if they hadn't been fighting each other too. A hard fist caught her just under the eye with a slice of pain and a flash of black stars across her vision. Someone grabbed at her shoulder, and the flimsy colored robe ripped, tangling with her arms as it fell away.

Then shouts and hands yanking them apart and the maestra's voice, so disappointed and furious, shouting at them all to stop.

Essa pulled her robe around herself. Her eye throbbed as she tried to focus on the maestra, who was speaking.

"Come along then." Her long fingers gestured at them to follow. "They're putting us up in guest rooms. We're still discussing how to get to the port, but it doesn't seem like it will be a problem. Essa, you and Skiff will room together, as will you boys." She didn't mention the dog, but Essa assumed it would follow her and Skiff, which it did.

The guest room was small, its walls the braided grass and bamboo latticework that had marked many of the village structures. Fresh robes hung on pegs near the door; a shelf held basin, comb, and other necessaries; but where a mirror would have been in Tabat, someone had painted an oval of green leaves, red flowers, and blue and yellow butterflies.

Essa had feared they'd have to share a bed, but sleeping shelves lined the eastern wall, each with a gauzy screen that could be drawn down to shield the occupant from mosquitoes. She slipped off the remnants of her robe without paying attention to Skiff or the dog and bundled herself into the nearest shelf without thought, exhaustion driving her down into the bedding. She closed her eyes and still felt as though the ground below her swung in place, but she could finally relax into it, fall down into darkness, down and down and down.

Shouting woke her. She didn't know if it was minutes or hours later. A glance toward the window through the gauze showed a lighter shadow inside the darkness: almost dawn.

She might have closed her eyes again, but a thread of panic in the clamor out in the hallway pulled her upright and through the gauze, pulling on a fresh robe. The noise yanked her down the hall to the door where everyone stood but no one dared cross the threshold. She joined the crowd, staring in to where the maestra lay across a bed, throat a scarlet ruin. Skiff was already there, the dog behind her, its teeth white and protective.

"A wild animal," someone said.

"No," Skiff said, voice suddenly louder and more authoritative than Essa had ever heard it before. "I know how animals bite.

That's someone trying to make it look like an animal did it."

Essa averted her eyes. She didn't want to know.

The twins were there too, for once not speaking in any language, their eyes wide and horrified. Others spoke in the language Essa had heard before, which she could not make sense of.

Several large and muscled people carrying spears showed up and gestured everyone else away from the door. Two took up posts outside the doorway while another motioned at the visitors to follow.

As though emboldened by her earlier speech, Skiff began to speak more words than Essa had ever heard from her before; she downright chattered as she and Essa followed after the twins.

"Without the maestra," she said, "who knows what will happen? Perhaps we will stay here. It does not seem a bad place. Warm, at any rate."

"You don't want to go back to Tabat?" The idea startled Essa.

The girl gave her a blank stare. "What's for me and Yadi there?"

"Your family . . ."

"They sold me to the kennels. Here I don't answer to anyone." Skiff tugged at the dog's ear affectionately, and it tilted its head, looking up at her.

"Shut up," said a twin.

"You shut up," Essa started to say, framing the words in Ligurian, but she fell silent as they stopped in front of a doorway.

Where most of the architecture of this house had seemed organic, this door seemed even more so, as though freshly grown out of the wall to hide an opening with a curtain of heart-shaped leaves, each about half the size of Essa's palm, fuzzed with a shimmer of white over the green. Through the foliage, she glimpsed a large chamber, lit by a combination of natural morning light and torches.

Before she could see much more, they were shoved through the doorway and then down onto their knees in front of a massive figure on a throne.

It was not a single person, but two, she realized, as she looked up past the robes embroidered with feathers and scales to two heads on a single trunk, both bearded but full-lipped, as though sexes had mingled into one pool.

"We are Turtle." The right-hand head spoke, the other staying silent. "We watch over this settlement. Your leader is dead." All four eyes were fixed on Essa, as though she were the only one worth addressing, and she found herself straightening under that stern gaze.

"I . . . ," she started, but a twin said, "By precedence, my sibling and I are the new leader. We will still require passage to the coast, so we can find our ship."

The eyes stayed on Essa. "You do not wish to stay here?" The Trade tongue was clear and understandable but edged with thick accent.

"Not really," she said. "Though your village is very pretty, and so is the country. I like all the flowers in the trees."

The left-hand side smiled a little, but the right-hand face remained stolid and unyielding as a cliff face. She saw that there were subtle differences despite the identical faces—the left-hand one wore a garland of white orchids and what Essa thought were black berries, and bell-shaped earrings, thumb sized, swung from their earlobes, while the right-hand one had a necklace of butterfly wings interspersed with shimmering beetles and no earrings, but a ring of braided iron wire pierced their lower lip near its left corner.

She thought about adding, "Some of us want to stay," and pointing out Skiff, but that would mean losing the dog along with all the other cargo, and the duke was not the sort of man who would like loss piled upon loss. To the point where she already wondered what the reaction would be when she returned. It would be so much better if she had some of the cargo with her, if she could report that the dog had been delivered as intended, and was brewing in the southern kennel, building social capital for Tabat as well as pups to be sent back to build up the duke's own stables.

No. Better not to open up that account book and start working future figures. She would maximize profits by holding on to all she could. She looked to the twins for agreement and found them both nodding. Her eyes traveled to Skiff's face, which was silent but rebellious. She wondered if the girl would run away. It wasn't that she was a slave, but the duke would have paid good money to her family in return for a decade of servitude. He'd fed and clothed her and educated her in a trade. It was a common practice nowadays, despite what anyone said about it. And no matter what, Skiff couldn't keep the dog. It belonged to the duke.

"We need to think and pray and consult the gods on this," Turtle said.

"Then what are we to do in the meantime?" a twin asked.

The gaze finally swung toward the twins, so slow and ponderous that they actually flinched back. "You will stay where you have slept and eaten so far," the right-hand head said. "There is music tonight, a celebration of the moons, and you will be invited, as any traveler would be, to feast and drink and dance with us. In the morning I will tell you what I have decided, and what is the best for you. Such mathematics are hard."

"I could help with that," Essa said. "That is what I am trained in."

The right-hand lips quirked. "And like any Merchant, you will shape the equation as it suits you. Things that I value, you do not, and vice versa, and I do not think you understand all the intricacies of that or you would already have told me your sums."

Four hands lifted to gesture jointly, and the travelers were pulled away by hands that smelled of sandalwood.

The twins paced throughout the day while Skiff petted her dog, whispering into its furry ear, but Essa spent most of her while sleeping, enjoying the feeling of being safe and warm.

Midday, someone came to her with a clamshell of some pale liquid and she drank it down, finding it peppery and sweet, sinking into her stomach to anchor her so the swaying finally went away, bit by bit. Another someone came with an armload of fresh dresses, as brightly patterned as before, and another with jewelry—earrings, bracelets, necklaces, anklets, crowns, combs, and hairpieces—all made of braided ironware strung with little white coral beads, each as small as a shrimp's eye.

At dusk, bells and whistles called them to the center of the village, where they found great stone blocks, which had been unadorned during the day except for friezes of bas-relief carving, patterned rather than figurative, and were now strewn with flowers and lit with upright candles, illuminating wooden platters and glazed ceramic bowls filled with food, each artfully decorated with more flowers and conceits carved from fruits, like tiny green birds perched on the edge of a roasted ear, or root petals around bright red seeds, looking more like flowers than the accompanying, more subtle blossoms. Everything smelled of roasted meat and vanilla, cinnamon and smoky fruit, and the sharp tang of the grain beer being handed out in wooden tankards, the largest thing Essa had ever drunk from.

It was so good to be so full after days of privation, even if everything was still too spicy. She was starting to get accustomed to it. She felt some of her tension loosening, particularly after she took a deep draft of sweet, burning liquid that rocketed down to her belly, then spread out like afterfire along her limbs. Drums joined with the whistles and flutes, and the music shook its way through her skin and into her, coaxed her out to stamp and dance with the others, laughing as they taught her.

For an evening she didn't think about decisions, wasn't a Merchant, just a dancer. The other travelers did not join her though. The twins stood and drank morosely, faces growing angrier and angrier as the evening continued, until finally they had some sort of obscure shouting match with each other—Essa couldn't catch what all was said, for they had picked an obscure dialect of Rosian. They seemed fixated on the carvings, knelt beside the blocks to examine them. Youths and maidens tried to draw them into the dance and were impatiently rebuffed with shoulder shrugs, never looked at.

Meanwhile Skiff had vanished somewhere along with her dog.

Essa didn't care. This was the moment, the moment was now. She let herself be drawn into a cluster of giggling girls her age. She emerged well kissed but shaking her head, declining all invitations, and then did the same with a hopeful-looking youth, his eyes dark welcome. Sex led to complications in trade. Everyone knew that. Wait until deals were done before you take your pleasure, or pay a price to Chalwoarma, Trade God of Lustful Influence.

Across the crowd, she saw one of the guides watching her, the man with beetles on his arms. Sfeo. A long, slow, and not unpleasant shiver worked its way through her stomach and then farther down. His dark eyes pulled at her, an insistent, eager allure.

She shook her head, took a step back. She had just been thinking that from now on she was going to live by the maxims. Not thinking had led to this journey in the first place.

She broke the gaze and did not look back as she walked away. Behind her the drums and flutes continued; she could hear the stamp and murmur of the barefoot dancers. The memory of the liquor burned in her throat as she made her way through moonlight to the hut's door.

Skiff and the dog were not there. Essa stayed awake a little while, thinking somewhat dizzily about Skiff. The girl was named after a coin—that was how her family saw her—and not even a major coin like a galleon or frigate, but the next to lowest, a skiff, a raft the only denomination lower. No wonder the child didn't care about the city.

But Essa loved Tabat, its terraces and its staircases and the tang of oil and steel when you rode the Great Tram down to the sea. Homesickness washed over her, tears flowing in its wake, and she sank sadly into slumber.

In the morning, the morning heat woke her with a shimmer of sweat on her upper lip, a drop rolling along her hairline. She washed her face with water from the basin but felt the sweat returning even as she dried herself with the towel.

Everyone else was eating breakfast out on one of the building's upper porches. Scarlet and blue birds, eagle sized, but with tails twice as long as their bodies, chased each other in and out of the whispering palm leaves at eye level, and two squirrels, black as jet, sat on the banister watching the dog. Essa sat down and poured herself juice from the pitcher on the table. In the center was a platter of fruit slices, colored like fleshy candy, red and orange and yellow and pale green, sometimes in combination. Essa could name only two or three of the fruits. Foreign fruit did not usually make the journey up to Tabat.

"Neither of you could be expected to have noticed this," one twin said, eying the dog licking crumbs off the floor around Skiff's feet.

For a giddy second of amusement, Essa thought they meant the dog and Skiff, but then she realized the remark had been directed to the only other humans in the room. She helped herself to a slice of fruit from the platter, an oval of soapy-feeling orange flesh, and tasted it. It melted in her mouth with a sweet, filling richness.

One twin raised their head and said in Ligurian to the other, "You can't be disappointed in them, they're just too slow. Once you factor that in, you find them much less frustrating." They beamed at Essa and Skiff in what they no doubt thought a kindly fashion.

Essa revisited the moment when she'd snap something back in Ligurian, like, "Your mother didn't find me too slow last night." But she bit her lip and kept silent, spooning a few mouthfuls of what looked like overdone rice porridge, scattered with tiny red and black flecks, onto her plate.

"The patterns are writing," the twin went on, speaking slowly and clearly as though to a particularly obtuse client.

Essa ignored them and looked to a platter just past the orange fruit. It was stacked with small doughy crescents that proved to hold a crunchy, minty paste. The surrounding thin rounds of yellow-fleshed fruit, paned like stained-glass windows, proved tarter, washing away the last sweetness. She reflected that it was probably a good thing the dishes served them had proved much less spicy than last night's meal, if they all had heads that throbbed like hers.

"They reference an ancient settlement nearby where they used to grow an herb they called *vanra*. From the description, we think it's actually feytongue. You of course know what that means." The twin paused in a way that implied that of course, in actuality, neither Essa nor Skiff would know such a thing, but Essa forestalled his next words.

"Feytongue, used in a number of magical processes, primarily dye and print related, although it can augment some others. Imports from the Southern Isles, trades in half and full ounces, full legal, taxed as a magical good. Supply affected by winter storms once every few decades. At the time we left, hovering around four golden skiffs per half ounce."

She was an accountant after all. She spent her time memorizing these things. No real-world application to that knowledge, her ass. And the last figure wasn't totally accurate but an estimate.

There was silence.

Essa helped herself to more fruit and alternated bites of the creamy orange with nibbles at the tart yellow. It was very good.

"Well," a twin finally said, as though Essa had said nothing. "It's quite valuable, and a ready supply of it would give us a reason to establish direct trade with this settlement. We'll need the both of you to help us scout and chart it, as well as gather enough to make some profit from our time here and give us samples to show the house."

Skiff said, "But I thought to stay here."

"You are under our command," the twin said. "We require your assistance."

Skiff sat silent for a moment, then took a long breath, released it, and said, "But if I help with this, then I may return here afterward?"

"Certainly not!" Both twins spoke at once, as though surprised and horrified by the notion, and glancing at each other in confusion as though each thought the other would understand. "We must return to Tabat with as much to trade as possible. After we have charted the area described by the blocks, we will go and search along the beach to see if any cargo has washed ashore."

"Or survivors," Essa said.

The twins looked at her. "Sure, sure," one said. The other shrugged. They both turned their attention back to Skiff. "You see?" one said.

"What about Yadi?" Skiff said.

The twin looked blank. "Who?"

She pointed down silently, and the dog's tongue lolled from its mouth, punk and floppy and oblivious as it panted. Essa wiped sweat away from her forehead; otherwise it trickled down into her eyes and burned unpleasantly.

"The dog is supposed to go to the kennels at Southport," a twin said. "Maybe they'll send some back with us." They flashed an insincere smile. "Maybe we'll get lucky and have a whole batch of puppies."

"I don't want puppies," Skiff said. She looked sidelong at the hound and it looked back at her. "I want Yadi."

Before anyone could take the conversation, the older female guide from the day before was in the doorway. "Turtle wishes to speak with you."

Everyone but Skiff stood. She sat, hands folded on the table in front of her. The dog whined and wagged its tail, looking at her.

"You go," she said sullenly.

Essa would have said something, but a twin snapped, "Very well," and pushed Essa along and out the door before she could think of a way to persuade the girl that she should come with them. But she should, Essa thought as she went along the corridor. *If you want your interests represented, you should be there to represent them.* That was basic trade lore and not to be ignored. She sighed.

Turtle was in the same throne, wearing much the same garb, with the exception of the fresh flowers, all of which had been replaced. They smelled sweet and new-cut, and beads of dew rode the petals, falling sometimes to the straw matting to darken it like momentary tears.

The left-hand head said, "We have decided to keep you until we discover why your leader was killed."

At the words, both of the guards at the door stamped their spears twice on the floor, as though it was a ritual. Unease crawled around Essa's lower belly, crawled like a snake trying to accommodate itself in a tangled space that could not entirely contain it.

These people do not like strangers, she thought. *Or someone among them does not. Or does one of us hold something that they want?* Her mind sorted through possibilities, holding the situation up to past experience and then, when that approach failed her, roved into texts she'd read, things learned at school, precepts preached at her by her aunt Melisent, the one who'd sponsored Essa as a scribe. Nothing.

"Keep us where?" a twin demanded. "May we travel a little way out, with guides, to the ruins to the east?"

Both heads tilted in united puzzlement. "How do you know of those?"

"The blocks in the center of the village speak of them, and when we asked, we were told the direction. They said they are but an hour or two away."

"There is nothing there but old gardens and buildings fallen in on themselves. Some are dangerous; they have bad flooring and you can fall through to the tunnels below, filled with poisonous snakes and worse."

"We will not go in the buildings. We only wish to see the old gardens. We were told they are filled with flowers that can be seen nowhere else."

"That much is true," Turtle said. "But no."

Essa had not seen the twins startled much, but this definitely took them aback. One said, "May we ask why?"

"Because before you came there was no one dying of their throats torn out in the middle of the night. The strongest suspicion lies on you four."

"This is ridiculous," one twin said to the other in Ligurian.

"Indeed it is not," Turtle replied, in Ligurian, and this time the twins gaped. Essa grinned full on, then bent her head to hide it while she fought to contain it. She didn't want a twin to look around and realize that she could speak the language as well.

One twin recovered a breath before their fellow. "So we are to be prisoners?"

"There will be a guard watching over you, but you will not be kept in a room. You will come to the feast tonight. It is its third night." Turtle shrugged lightly.

Before they could speak again, they were dragged away in the usual waft of sandalwood.

They did not stay together, but Essa, Skiff, and the dog went to bathe again in the pool, seeking coolness in the midmorning as the heat began to build. Their guard was Sfeo, the guide with the beetles, along with a more martial-looking, spear-carrying woman, fiercely scarred and sinewy. Sfeo smiled at Essa as they walked along the path, and she let herself smile back, just a little.

They'd learned yesterday that most of the villagers stayed in the shade during the fiercest hours of the day, working with their hands: braiding ropes out of lengths of hairy dried vines; carving things from several woods that Essa could not identify, dark-hearted but streaked with ruddy veins and rings as well as a spectrum of tans.

She'd spent part of the previous day watching them make the elaborate fabric, bright and colorful, that everyone wore. They used a combination of wax-resist and woodblock stamps (made of the ruddy and black wood, apparently for its durability), and boiled the dyes in iron vats.

A new robe fluttered around her now, soft and bright, printed with paired blossoms in amber and purple, the most muted of the multitude she'd been offered. Would something like this catch on in Tabat? So bright and gaudy, but some people had a taste for such things. A better bet, trade-wise, were the herbs the twins had described, but also the perfumes that she'd smelled the day before in her wanderings, from clay vials corked with a soft scarlet substance that looked like dried mushrooms. When you plucked away the lid, the liquid inside smelled like an armload of flowers, as though you stood in a cloud of blossoms. She'd smiled and gaped appreciatively enough to be given a few vials, which she'd tucked away as trade samples, offerings to Abvioti, but not without anointing herself with her favorite.

Though it had previously been deserted, today a flock of villagers swam in the pool. Children threw a ball back and forth while teens chattered and flirted. Their more sedate adult counterparts swam back and forth under the waterfall or sat on the vine-curtained banks. Two boys and an older man sat among the shadowed rocks, out of reach of the waterfall's spray, the boys playing smaller versions of the five-stringed, long-necked instrument the man held.

Everyone was naked, which Essa thought very practical. It was too hot to be thinking of anything but getting cooler.

She looked at the guards where they stood. Sfeo shrugged back, then gestured at the water in a "go ahead" sort of way. He and began removing his own robe, setting down the long staff. The woman guard moved to lean against a large boulder twice her height, in the shade. She kept her spear upright and aligned with the trees around her and watched the pool.

Essa and Skiff exchanged glances, then followed Sfeo's example, but Essa kept stealing looks at him as she did so.

Without his clothes, he revealed himself even more alien than before. Patches of snakeskin were laid in laddered stripes along his pale thighs. His skin had a pearly luminescence to it, as though it rejected the sun entirely. He undressed entirely, and she saw more snakeskin along his hairless groin, surrounding his relaxed cock, which bobbed in the water as he waded in. She wondered if the beetles had to breathe, but he seemed unconcerned.

The dog splashed its way in, Skiff in its wake and Essa following more slowly, taking in a deep breath as the cooler water hit her, moving up her body farther with each step, sand and small rounded rocks underfoot, every once in a while the jerky flicker of a minnow catching the eye as it darted away.

When she was neck deep, she closed her eyes. The tall trees all around filtered the sunlight, removed its burn, and turned it into the green clarity she could still see through her eyelids.

Water swirled against her as someone stopped nearby. She opened her eyes. The guide.

He said, tapping his chest at the point where the water left it, just above his sternum, "Sfeo." As though worried she might not remember.

She tapped her own chin. "Essa."

"Essa," he repeated. He was not unhandsome, she decided. Rather the opposite, his features strong and even. She saw that tiny scarlet feathers were braided into his eyebrows, their outer corners edged with scales so fine they seemed drawn on with a pen.

The water surged against her skin again and a minnow brushed the back of her thigh as he moved a little closer. He pointed to the guard watching them, her face bored. "Ava."

The woman rolled her eyes as they both looked at her.

Sfeo called something to her, then turned back to Essa, laughing. He said, in careful, slow Trade tongue, "Better no sun, water cold, yes?"

"Cool more than cold," she told him. "But much better, yes."

He grinned outright at her.

"You like this place, yes?"

"I do."

"You like . . ." He gestured around himself expansively. The beetle legs waved as he did so, and water streamed off his silvery skin. "Water, trees, flowers. Rocks and houses. All of Alahu." He paused, tilted his head, considering her. "You like the people of Alahu?"

"Of course I do," she told him. She bobbed in the water, watching him, but he moved no closer. Her arms trailed in the water and she spread her fingers, feeling minnows, emboldened by her stillness, nibbling at them.

"The people of Alahu like you," he told her. He tapped his chest. "And Sfeo likes you. Is it well with you that Sfeo likes you?"

"I'm not sure what you're asking."

His arms floated along the top of the water as he looked at her, expression wavering between uncertain and sly. "If not well, then I go and swim. Myself alone."

Her breath caught. "And if it is well?" she asked.

His smile lost its uncertainty. "Then I would stay and maybe come a little closer now and then. No more than that," he said.

"No more than that?" she repeated.

"Maybe other questions, later," he said. "Always a question first."

Warmth tingled in her fingers as the minnows kissed their tips.

"It is well," she told him, voice barely audible over the water's lapping, the chattering of the children playing.

She asked him about the beetles as they swam and talked

together, and he told her they breathed through him, that their poison was what caused his skin's pallor. He offered her a wrist, his smile a little ironic, and unsurprised when she shook her head and paddled away.

As they got out of the pool and shrugged on their robes, Skiff said, stroking the flowered fabric, "This is the most beautiful thing I've ever worn."

Essa blinked. The colors were bright but the contrasts often gaudy, she thought. She supposed that such things might appeal to one person and not another. Here was the concept in the flesh. An unbidden thought came—*Real-world experience.*—but she shrugged it away along with the gnats exploring the line of sweat that had already begun to crawl along her hairline.

She glanced away and met Sfeo's eyes where he sat talking with the youths.

"Do you think they might let us keep them?" Skiff asked.

"It would be unMerchantly to ask," Essa said firmly.

The girl's lips drooped. Beside her, the dog's tail did as well.

"You have nothing to trade now," Essa pointed out. "But when we are both in port, I will give you some of my trade share."

"Trade share?" Skiff said. "What is that?"

One Merchant maxim is, *Never speak of money with someone who gets less of it than you do,* but this was Skiff, after all. Essa said, "I am a Merchant and part of the expedition. I have part of the trade share."

"But the ship is gone."

"It will have been insured. We will not make as much as we would have with even a moderately successful voyage, but there will be some money for me when we get to port."

"Then there should be some there for me too."

Essa shook her head in impatience. The girl was very slow. She'd spent so much time with her quick-witted betters, Essa had thought surely some of that would rub off. Apparently not.

She took care to put kindness in her tone. The girl could not help herself, after all. "No, because you are the duke's indentured servant."

"Then there is no share set aside for me?"

"There is," Essa said, "but it will be given to the duke." She didn't add anything after that. Alberic was notoriously frugal and would not dispense bonuses to his servants no matter how fruitful the voyage.

Skiff's face worked. "It is unfair."

"It is as the gods dictate," Essa said. "We follow the practices they have given us."

"Practices that only benefit the rich!" Beside Skiff, the dog growled.

"Again, that is how the gods have dictated," Essa said, working hard to stay unirritated despite the heat, the buzzing insects, and Skiff's stupidity. "Money goes to the rich so then it will flow downward, administered by their wise hands."

"Administered how?"

"Spent, for one. Flowing down to Merchants, entertainers, crafters, artisans, suppliers of all sorts . . . the list goes on and on."

"I would spend my money on three robes like this. More than that I would not need." Skiff rested her hand on the dog's head and said, mostly to herself, the rest to the dog, "It is not unreasonable to ask enough for that."

"It is entirely unreasonable!" Essa snapped. She mopped at her forehead. The coolness engendered by the pool was entirely gone, despite the green shade they stood in.

Skiff didn't answer her as they went back to the village. The sleep shelves felt close and hot, so they followed the example of some villagers and rested on wicker lounges out on the balcony. Essa closed her eyes and tried to sleep but couldn't. The oppressive heat pressed down on her. She was too conscious of the presence of Sfeo and Ava, the buzz of insects, the shrill calling of birds, the same repetitions over and over again. In Tabat the birds were quieter. Barely there in the winter. Better behaved.

She realized with a start that she had been sleeping when Sfeo touched her shoulder.

"Eat soon," he told her. She smiled up at him, wishing she'd been dreaming about him.

She and Skiff washed in their room, then made their way to another repetition of the feast. This time the food was even more lavish, the bowls higher and more varied, the music more frenetic, starting as the sun kissed the horizon and a cool breeze swept inland from the sea.

Sfeo took her hand, led her among the dancers, showed her how to twist right and left then right again, a sinuous motion that set a fire stirring low, made the cradle of her thighs ache, made an accidental brush of chest to chest set her blood singing even stronger, higher, more insistently.

When he leaned into her and whispered a question, she did not speak, only nodded, and let him lead her into shadows, exacting a kiss for each footstep, till they fumbled with each other's clothing, till their robes fluttered away like the bats swinging low and musically overhead, freely given to the air and chance.

This time she let him bring the beetles' questing heads up to her skin, let the bite make the world sway, make her body a flame, a candle, a waterfall, again and again, a roaring in her head and fire in the wake of their rasping search, each time their bite making her phoenix reborn.

She could have slept there in the puddled shadows beyond the flickering torchlight, but the truth was, an ant bit her and sent her back to the room.

She entered quietly, trying not to make more noise than necessary. The beetle's drug still sang in her veins, leaving the world etched with purple and silver shadows. She could still feel the aftertouch of Sfeo's fingers on her skin, a languorously sweet sensation that fled like cold water had chased it when she saw that Skiff and Yadi were unexpectedly awake, sitting on a bench below the open window.

She said, in question, "Skiff?"

"My name is Doralina," the child said. In the darkness she was only a silhouette against the starlight. "The youngest of the kennel children is Raft, and then there is Skiff, and then Barge, and after that the kennel keeper, who is named however they please."

The breeze carried copper and jasmine in equal measure. The dog was growling, Essa realized, so softly she could barely hear it, but a sound that had started the moment she stepped into the room.

She stood stock-still. Her heart pounded so hard in her throat that she could no longer hear the growl, only feel it in the way it teased the hairs on her arms upright. Fear grabbed her heels and rooted her, every instinct shooting danger.

"Why are you awake?" she asked.

"I was waiting for you," the child said. "You like this place too, or you would not have gone with that man. Do you love him? He made you smile, you must want to stay with him."

"It is a more complicated equation than that," Essa said.

An impatient grunt and shrug, and the dog's growl ratcheted up a precise and alarming notch.

"Equations. Numbers. Things no one can see. And all of them become coin. But nobody needs coins here. They build a little house and they live there. They fish and they hunt and they gather fruit." The girl fell silent for a moment. Her hand moved on the dog's head, stroking between its ears, and it quieted.

"The twins wish to encourage trade," Essa said. "They'll be back this way."

"Not anymore," Skiff said. Her little laugh made the upright hairs strain upward as though they would flee Essa's skin.

"You killed them," she said. "Or . . . your dog did. But why?"

"Why did I do it? It wasn't easy to lure one in without the other," Skiff said. She rubbed an arm across her sweaty face as though trying to wipe away weariness at the same time. "Why would I want this place to become what Tabat is, where to do anything, be anyone, you must have money? You have not explored this place, but there is so much bounty that they have leisure to do what they like. And you will bring in Merchants who want the equations and numbers to add up, and there is no number in their equations for workers for anything other than eating and sleeping and worshipping your gods as they trample us underfoot to make us into coins."

A spasm of surprise widened Essa's eyes. "You killed them so you would have leisure?"

"You are not even trying to understand," Skiff said. "To you it is right and proper that the people with money do well, because you believe your gods love them, that they love the gods and are rewarded. And certainly they love the gods, for those gods justify all sorts of things for those who do not understand things in the same way, and that is anyone who is not a Merchant and capable of using them." She bit her lip. "Perhaps you are incapable of understanding."

It was as though the reeling of the ship underfoot had overtaken her again. She took a step back, throwing her arm up between them as though to ward off the heat, the truth, the shame of Skiff's words. To avoid questioning her existence in a way she never had before, despite years and years in Merchant school. No maxim had prepared her for this moment.

And the dog took that gesture as attack.

Its weight bore her down in the darkness, its jaws seized her forearm, and she felt the flesh tear and the bone snap. She clawed at its eyes with her free hand, tried to draw up her leg to kick it off her, but everything was pain and shoving and brutal movements and the dog's heavy breaths while Skiff watched in silence. She collided with something cold, soft, and heavy, and rolled away from it with a shriek.

Then the dog recoiled, loosing her, staggering away. She pulled herself into a ball, tried to gather herself. She heard Skiff's wordless question, her steps. Essa raised her head to see the dog on the floor, convulsing, barely visible in the tangle of shadows and colored moonlight.

The beetle poison, she thought, just as Skiff turned, her child's face a grimaced mask of rage, and screamed, "What did you do?"

Essa staggered to her feet, trying to gain the advantage of height. Feet thundered along the corridor outside, and Sfeo and Ava were in the doorway with torches, light finally showing what Essa had suspected: the twins lying where they had died, one on top of the other. No more words for them.

They took Skiff—Doralina, she corrected herself—away, and brought someone to tend her wounds.

Essa taught them papermaking before she left, and reaped the benefit of that on her last night: a soft, crude volume, handstitched, that any bookbindery in Tabat would have sneered at. The cover was cloth, printed with flowers. Maybe she'd start a fashion.

Sfeo had declined to come with the expedition accompanying her down to the port, not for anger or bitterness or anything but his ardor cooling. She'd learned from some of the women that he was always interested in newcomers, but was not bold enough himself to travel.

What the villagers had done with the girl was not something they were inclined to tell her. Essa had not seen her again, nor had she ever been mentioned. It was as though all memory of her had vanished.

The final night, before she left, Essa tried to write down what she remembered of Doralina and Yadi, here where the memory would be freshest. But try as hard as she could, the Trade God maxims could not contain everything Doralina had said. At their heart, everything was coin, and some of what the child said could not be broken down like that.

Not that she had been right, of course. Without the Trade Gods, the world would fail. All would be chaos. But perhaps Essa could add things in, somehow. With enough time, with enough thought and study. She had years in which to do it.

Years for the memory of the contorted dog's body, the child's sobs, to fade. Or not fade precisely, but be bulwarked against by good works, perhaps?

To begin with, Diahmo accrued profit, certainly, but she'd seen him reckon up vengeance for the twins and their Ligurian. Other additions might be performed, and things added to what a human being was due from the way of things.

But still she chewed her pen all that night and had yet to put any of it into words.

Ken Scholes

When Shawn asked me to write for *Unfettered III*, I knew this was the story I wanted to tell. While I was crafting the Psalms of Isaak between 2006 and 2016, I left lots and lots of tidbits behind intentionally like a bread crumb trail for future stories. In *Canticle* and in *Requiem* I dropped some teaser sentences about Rudolfo and Gregoric—middle-aged characters during the events of the series—sailing with the pirate Rafe Merrique (another character) in their youth. I've said for some time that I would eventually come back to that, and Shawn gave me a great excuse to put my toes in those waters. It also gave me a chance to explore Gregoric's point of view as we never get to experience it in the series.

Of course, right away it was obvious that I could only tell some of the seafaring adventure I hinted at in the Psalms of Isaak. There is more to tell, as this story suggests, and I suspect a novella or two may show up down the road.

If you enjoy this story, you may want to look into more of my work at KenScholes.com.

Ken Scholes

OF ANCHOR CHAINS AND SLOW REFRAINS AND LIGHT LONG LOST IN DARKNESS

Ken Scholes

The first bell chimed softly in the dim-lit Androfrancine lobby, and Gregoric looked up from the corner where he waited. The sky had been a predawn purple when the Grey Guard had admitted him to the Office of Acquisitions and Travel thirty minutes before.

The early hours of these offices astonished Gregoric. He'd spent his twenty years living in the Ninefold Forest, set apart from the rest of the Named Lands in the distant northeast, where customs were far more relaxed. In the Forest, no business was transacted until well after sunrise.

And now I'm waiting on an arch-something and a king before my first cup of chai, he thought.

Gregoric had half expected to find his king snoring in one of the lobby's plush chairs, reeking of peach wine and perfume, grinning at having proved his friend wrong.

"These ladies," Rudolfo had told him last night in one of the city's less restrained quarters, "only require my attention for a few short hours." Gregoric had protested both the practicality of the proposed venture and the underestimation of the time available before dawn, but Rudolfo was king and general, after all.

Of course I'll be on time for the meeting. Of course I will have slept and bathed. The offense upon Rudolfo's face at the mere suggestion that he might not be either of these things had Gregoric's eyes rolling even in memory.

But Rudolfo hadn't been waiting, and so his first captain had initially paced the room, then finally succumbed to the chair, where he fidgeted and fussed at a state uniform he'd worn only once before.

At the next bell, Gregoric sighed and stood. He'd made his second turn in a new round of pacing when the doorknob rattled. Beyond the door, he heard a familiar voice.

"Thank you, good sir," Rudolfo said as the door opened to the Grey Guard captain stationed at the building's main entrance. "Oh, *Captain,* is it? Yes. Then sir seems certainly apropos. Ah. There he is." Rudolfo strode into the room, met Gregoric's eyes, and laughed, the Grey Guard just behind him in the doorway. "My own captain, whom I assume you've met?"

Rudolfo, Lord of the Ninefold Forest Houses and General of the Wandering Army, stood a full head shorter than most of the men of the Named Lands. Barely nineteen years, his beard was coming in wispy and thin. That, combined with his own state uniform and the green turban of office, lent him a comic quality that he seemed at ease with.

Gregoric saw it as a possible blind spot—not taking things seriously and then not being taken seriously—but then again, he saw blind spots everywhere.

Because it's my job to see what he can't see. It's what you did when your best friend was also your king. And if he stumbled, you picked him up and carried him if you had to.

The Grey Guard captain's face betrayed the slightest bemusement as he pulled the door closed and Rudolfo crossed the room to clap Gregoric's shoulder. "Well met, First Captain Gregoric," he said with a wink. "And good morning."

Gregoric smelled the faintest trace of perfume but little of the wine he'd expected, and his friend's uniform was surprisingly well put together. He raised an eyebrow and opted for the military title. "Good morning, General Rudolfo." He lowered his voice. "You've slept?"

Rudolfo chuckled. "After a manner."

Gregoric let his curiosity lift his eyebrows even farther. "And?"

"It seems the Androfrancines do not tend to all of their flock with equal grace and magnanimity," Rudolfo said with a grin. "Our assistance in certain earthly matters was long anticipated and greatly . . . appreciated."

His words would've been more suave than boastful except that he blushed as he said it; Gregoric pretended not to notice. "Good then," he said. He wouldn't say more beyond that, and hadn't any of the other times.

Rudolfo, Lord of the Ninefold Forest Houses and General of the Wandering Army, had come late to his awareness of his body and the bodies of the young women around him. Far later than most young men, and Gregoric saw its arrival over the last year as a welcome change.

It seemed a much healthier activity than brooding on the observation deck while listening to the screams of repentance beneath the Physicians of Penitent Torture's knives. Not that Gregoric blamed his friend for that streak of darkness. Nearly all of the penitents had been followers of the Heretic Fontayne and those who'd harbored or aided them—those responsible, directly or indirectly, for the murders of Rudolfo's parents.

They had grown up together, Rudolfo and Gregoric, mostly in the vicinity of Rudolfo's father's Seventh Forest Manor and the unnamed town that had sprung up around it. Gregoric's father, Aerynus, had been Lord Jakob's first captain, and from his earliest memory, Gregoric had assumed he would serve Rudolfo in the same way. But no one had expected it might happen so soon.

The sudden memory ambushed Gregoric. His closest friend, covered in his parents' blood, eyes red but fierce, as Rudolfo barked his first commands. He'd gone from twelve to thirty in seconds, and Gregoric still saw it in his eyes some days. Wrath and sorrow twisting and turning to find a purpose. They'd both gone with Gregoric's father to hunt Fontayne down, but only Rudolfo had participated directly in the interrogations led by Chief Physician Benoit.

No, Gregoric thought, the stream of dalliances was a welcome change. *Let him chase pleasure for a season rather than pain and penitence.*

Rudolfo dropped himself into one of the chairs. "How are the men?"

Gregoric snorted. "They're sleeping, I'll wager. But they'll be ready to ride at your command."

Rudolfo nodded. "Excellent." He opened his mouth to say more, but a smaller bell chimed and the inner door opened to admit a young man in a long white robe lined with threads of blue that marked him as an acolyte.

"Lord Rudolfo? His Excellency Arch-Archaeologist Tobin will see you now."

Gregoric watched his friend incline his head and then made to follow him as he left the waiting area.

"I'm sorry, Lord," the acolyte said, raising his hand. "But it is more appropriate for your aide to wait here."

Gregoric felt a flash of anger and gritted his teeth. Rudolfo chuckled. "Actually, it would be utterly inappropriate," Rudolfo said. "But if my first captain is not permitted beyond this door, I'm happy to receive His Excellency here in his lobby."

The acolyte turned purple and said nothing. Rudolfo winked at Gregoric as the acolyte turned to lead them into the office.

Swallowing that moment of anger, Gregoric followed his king.

The walls of the Office of Acquisitions and Travel were largely undecorated. Tobin was third in command, and that gave him a lush office on the ground floor with a window overlooking a meditation garden now gray with morning.

The arch-archaeologist waited by a small table set with chai. "Good morning, Lord Rudolfo." He glanced disapprovingly at Gregoric and then to the acolyte, whose face still looked flushed.

"Will your officer be joining us for chai?"

"Certainly." Rudolfo looked to Gregoric and raised his eyebrow. "You've not had your chai, I'll wager?"

Gregoric knew better than to say anything and instead sized up Tobin. He was portly but powerfully built, his hair close cropped and iron gray. He wore spectacles—something Gregoric had only seen once before, on another Androfrancine passing through: pieces of glass fit into wires and worn for vision by those whom the various powders and magicks available in the Named Lands could not heal.

The arch-archaeologist gestured for another chair, and the acolyte fetched it before pouring out chai in three spotlessly shined silver mugs.

Once each had sat and taken a first careful sip of the steaming liquid, Rudolfo dug into his pocket and drew out a letter. "This is a Letter of Credit from the Tam Banking Concern that I've had drawn up for your consideration. It is the Forest Houses' honor to serve the Order and to underwrite our service to the light, as is the custom of kin-clave."

Tobin took the document, opened it, and scanned it. "This is a liberal Offer of Underwriting, Lord Rudolfo."

"I am very specific in the offer I am making."

Tobin nodded, and Gregoric waited. They'd spent years talking about this moment, in their boyhood. It was around the same time that they'd discovered the secret doors and hidden tunnels that networked the Seventh Forest Manor. And not just the Seventh, but all of the manors they'd visited before the day that Rudolfo's childhood burned down.

"When I'm king," Rudolfo had said in those lighter days, "I'll get the Order to help us find him, and we'll join his crew."

Gregoric couldn't remember the circumstances, but he remembered the words with absolute clarity. They'd spent the entire summer pretending that houses were ships and sticks were swords

He forced his attention back to Tobin, who'd handed back the letter. "We have valuable work for you to do, but we have no control over some portions of your offer."

Rudolfo nodded. "But he *is* available for hire, and the Order *does* have the ability to contact him?"

Tobin returned the nod. "Yes. And your entire letter may underwrite half of the offer you propose."

Gregoric waited and held his breath. *Now you surprise him.*

Rudolfo drew the small box from his sash and placed it on the table. "I think he will be interested in this portion of my offer." Opening the lid, he slid it toward Tobin.

The Androfrancine's eyebrows went up behind his spectacles. "It's a brooch," he said.

"No," Rudolfo said. "It's *the* brooch."

And Gregoric smiled when he saw the recognition upon the arch-archaeologist's face. It had taken some work to figure out the details, but Rudolfo's intelligence officers had earned their promised lands and titles.

Tobin swallowed. "*The* brooch?"

Rudolfo nodded. "The same."

They'd read about the brooch in Hyrum's *Pirate Lord of the Ghosting Crests.* Certainly much of Hyrum's tales scribed during the scholar's year with Merrique were embellished, but the brief conversation about regrets during the seventeen days they spent shipwrecked in the Ghosting Crests seemed starkly real. And the pirate lord's singular regret, voiced to the Androfrancine in a moment of raw honesty, was a brooch. There was no additional explanation. But over the course of this last year, Rudolfo had put himself and his kingdom's vast resources to determining what the brooch was and how to acquire it as bait.

And now, Gregoric thought, *we catch ourselves a pirate with it.*

Rudolfo smiled. "Did you know that it was an heirloom that had been stolen from the Merrique family?"

Tobin held the brooch up to the light. "Yes," he said. "I do not know how you came to possess it, but I'm certain the Order could . . ."

His words trailed off at Rudolfo's upraised hand.

"No, Your Excellency, I'm afraid it's specifically for Rafe Merrique, and we intend to deliver it to him personally." His grin caught Gregoric off guard with its ferocity. "It's my gift to him for his service to the light."

For a moment, Tobin said nothing, then he placed the box on the table. He looked up and met Rudolfo's eyes. "We'll make the arrangements. Captain Grymlis will have the Letters of Introduction for you once they're executed by the office clerk. By then we'll also have instructions from Captain Merrique, should he accept your offer. It will be a simple retrieval from the Churning Wastes if he is inclined to serve as transport."

Rudolfo inclined his head. "Thank you, Your Excellency."

He slipped the box back into his sash. "And please forward our gratitude to Pope Introspect for his hospitality and endorsement."

Now the arch-archaeologist inclined his head. "I will tell him." He stood. "Now, gentlemen, please finish your chai. I've another matter to attend to."

Once he and the acolyte left, Rudolfo grinned again, and Gregoric tried to resist doing the same. His king and best friend raised his eyebrow, and only then did Gregoric notice the lip rouge on his neck. "What say you, Gregoric? Are you ready to test your sea legs?"

Gregoric shook his head against the sudden ache in his stomach. "I guess we'll know soon enough."

Then Rudolfo drained his chai with one gulp, stood, and broke out in the one song they'd memorized as children. "Far into the Ghosting Crests and beyond the Emerald Sea, I swear my sword to the pirate lord and a life of piracy."

Gregoric blushed, and Rudolfo smiled and sang all the louder. He was into the third—and raunchiest—verse when a Grey Guard, face red with restraint, arrived to escort them out.

And Gregoric quickly covered his embarrassment at the spectacle of it all. The look of delight upon his friend's face was like time turned back by magick, like light brought back from darkness, and for the briefest moment, Gregoric let himself rejoice in it.

The ride south and west onto the Entrolusian Delta was a wet and cold affair with autumn moving closer to winter. The staunch

Gray Guard officer they'd met at the main doors had shown them to a quartermaster for re-outfitting, given them a map, Letters of Introduction for Rafe Merrique, and generic letters that proclaimed the Ninefold Forest engaged in service to the light on behalf of the Order. The Order also sent birds ahead requesting discretion and non-interference for a kin-clave nation's traveling retinue in service to the light, including the promise of any and all appropriate fees and taxes for such discreet passage. These of course being carefully accounted for in Rudolfo's offer.

Once they were out of Windwir, Gregoric sent half the squad back to the Forest. Those who remained turned their horses toward the Delta.

They made good time to Dandylo Terrace, dressed in the nondescript clothing of lumbermen on leave from the evergreen forests that blurred the border between the United City States of the Entrolusian Delta and the Protectorate of Windwir to the north.

The city states were united under an overseer—currently a pompous man-child named Sethbert—and were Windwir's largest, closest neighbor. They had kin-clave with the Ninefold Forest, as well, though the two nations had little to do with each other. The Ninefold Forest was largely self-contained and its Gypsy Scouts seldom rode farther south than Windwir—and even that was rare. So Gregoric turned his three scouts loose to gather intelligence on their immediate vicinity while exploring and experiencing Dandylo Terrace. Even this smallish town, here on the southern tip of the Delta, was a metropolis to the wide-eyed Foresters. Still, he trusted them to enjoy themselves properly while at the same time maintaining their presence.

Only the best became scouts of the Ninefold Forest, and these were the best of Rudolfo's Gypsy Scouts.

With the men left to their own devices, Gregoric and Rudolfo found a quiet corner in a tavern where they could wait for Rafe Merrique to make contact.

Time away and unknown, in a tavern full of a variety of food and drink that defied Gregoric's imagination. Time spent hunkered over a table with his best friend, listening as he predicted their future at sea. It was a good enough time together. At least, it was when Rudolfo wasn't trying too hard to engage the various ladies of the establishment. Still, even one day in a tavern would be too much for Gregoric, and three was becoming unbearable. He closed his eyes against Rudolfo's latest attempt, with a woman who looked maybe five or ten years his senior. "Stab me in the eye with a fork," he muttered to himself.

The woman smiled sympathetically at Gregoric, and he blushed at being overheard. "He's not that bad," she said. "Just too young." She raised an eyebrow, pouted a little, and it was the first time Gregoric thought of her as pretty. "And too poor."

Rudolfo winked. "I may be that book that is on the wrong shelf of the library."

She returned the wink and leaned in. "An unfinished book, I fear, in a rather small library." Then the woman leaned even closer, her hands moving down the front of Rudolfo's shirt toward his waistband. "On, I suspect, a rather short shelf," she finished.

Then the woman flashed a smile at them both and bolted for the back door.

Rudolfo's face turned crimson even as he leapt up. "She took it," he said. "She took the brooch."

Gregoric was on his feet and whistling for his men by habit. He doubted any were within earshot. Then he was out the door and in the alley behind the tavern in the gray of midafternoon. His hands ached to draw his knives, but he resisted and focused instead on the woman. He could hear the splashing of her feet in the puddles as she ran, and he followed.

A low whistle reached his ear, and Yaric, one of the older scouts, slipped in beside him. "First Captain?"

"Stay near the general," Gregoric whispered and stretched his legs into a run. He felt the pouch of scout magicks beneath his shirt and was tempted to take them for the burst of strength, speed, and clarity they would give him. But scout magicks also rendered one nearly invisible, and they were expressly forbidden by kin-clave except during time of war. Gregoric wasn't about to violate the Forest's kin-clave with the Delta.

Instead, he ran. He heard Rudolfo and Yaric following.

The alley spilled out into a wider paved street still awash with puddles. Overhead, a dark sky drizzled rain on the tired city. The street was largely empty, and the few stalls along it were closed. The woman ducked behind one and then down another alley. Gregoric willed speed into his feet and raced after her, entering the alley as she leapt through an open door.

He was two sword spans behind her when the door closed behind her, and he hit the oak with outstretched hands full force before it had time to latch. Gregoric's momentum carried him through the door, and he had a moment of stark panic that caught his breath as his feet found no floor beneath them.

As he fell, he heard the door close and latch above.

When he struck the water below, his entire body felt the penetrating cold of it, and his mouth and nose flooded with salt. As he sank, Gregoric felt ropes grabbing at him, and a net closed over him and lifted him from the water.

"Ho there," an amused voice said. "Look what we've caught."

Gregoric took in his surroundings as his net began to move. It was a large stone room stacked with barrels and sacks and crates, and a single canal that exited toward a distant slit of light. A long boat loaded with supplies was tied off not far from where Gregoric hung, and he saw a system of ropes and pulleys. A slender, middle-aged man with salt-and-pepper hair tied back behind a colorful scarf stood at the levers, a cutlass at his hip, as Gregoric swung toward him. A pirate. The pirate. Rafe Merrique. Gravity and the tightness of the net made moving difficult, but Gregoric's hand found the hilt to one of his knives and he started quietly working at the netting behind him.

The woman from the tavern entered the room from a door that Gregoric noted as the exit up and out. She crossed the room, her face flushed, to stand beside the pirate. She held up the box she'd stolen from Rudolfo. "He had it, Captain. Like you said." Then she nodded toward Gregoric. "This one has two knives. Might be a third in his boot."

The pirate raised an eyebrow and yanked the lever another

direction. Gregoric stopped moving toward the man, instead swinging back out over the dark water he'd fallen into. "Is that true?" Rafe Merrique chuckled. "I invite you into my home and you bring weapons? I thought your king wanted to parley with me, Forester."

Gregoric gritted his teeth and saw Merrique work another lever as the rope released and he plunged back into the icy cold.

He came up sputtering a minute later as Merrique hauled him up. This time he left Gregoric hanging over the water.

"Let's start over," the pirate said. "I'll ask some questions. You can answer or you can keep trying to cut your way out. Either way, the water is quite cold, and I truly have all the time in the world." He smiled, and Gregoric growled. "What does the Gypsy King want with me? Why has he spent a dozen fortunes to compel the Order to summon me?" He held up the box, now opened, and the stones sparkled in the dim light. "And how in the nine hells below did he find this?"

Gregoric glared and said nothing. Rafe Merrique laughed and hit the lever. There was something in that echoing peal of laughter that touched spark to some deeper anger, and Gregoric didn't feel the water this time. Instead, he felt heat and a throbbing in his forehead.

He came up roaring his rage at the pirate and his accomplice. They both laughed all the louder.

He was still bellowing when the water closed over him again. He wasn't sure exactly how many more times the pirate asked or how many more times he was dunked.

Finally, he hung limp in the nets, coughing and shaking.

"Well?" The pirate raised his hand above the lever.

Gregoric tried to shake his head. "We read Brother Hyrum's book as boys," he finally said. "And he did spend a dozen fortunes. He would've spent more to find it; he knew you wanted it."

Rafe Merrique grinned. "And now I have it." Gregoric's anger flared briefly at the sight of that grin, but this time, Rafe's voice took on a gentler tone. "But why?"

Gregoric's frustration gave his voice more urgency and edge than he'd intended. "You're his hero. For the life of me, I don't know why," he said. "Especially after sampling your generous hospitality."

The pirate looked dumbfounded. "His *hero*? The King of the Ninefold Forest Houses?"

Gregoric nodded and met Merrique's eyes. "He wanted to meet you and sail with you."

Rafe Merrique stroked his perfectly sculped beard. "Well I'll be d'jin-and-crested," he muttered. "It's as they said it was." His eyes narrowed. "Did you really get tossed out of the office singing that damnable song of Hyrum's?"

Gregoric said nothing.

Finally, Rafe looked at the woman beside him. "What do you make of all this, Jasper?"

The woman shook her head and gave Gregoric a sideways glance where he dripped above the water. "I make of it whatever you tell me to make of it, Captain."

He worked the levers, and Gregoric lurched forward to slowly settle on the dock. "Then I reckon we're taking on servants of light," Rafe said as he slipped the brooch into his pocket and tossed the box aside. "I will get you dry clothes and send you back to Rudolfo. I'll take you around the horn and back, but I have a condition, and the ship has rules."

Gregoric waited as men slipped out of the shadows to pull him from the nets and stand him up.

Once he was standing, he bit back anger again. "I'm certain Lord Rudolfo will be eager to hear your condition himself."

Rafe Merrique laughed again. This time it was loud and long, and the others in the room, suddenly more of them than Gregoric had realized, were laughing with him.

"Oh no," Rafe Merrique said. "The condition is yours to meet, First Captain Gregoric."

The merriment in his voice and the twinkle in the pirate's eye told Gregoric that whatever condition it might be, one thing was assured.

It could not possibly bode well for him.

Gregoric put one foot in front of the other and avoided eye contact as the handful of people at the dockside market whispered and gawked. He felt more heat in his face as a child laughed, and he pretended not to notice the pointing finger.

They'd given him the choice of dressing himself or being dressed. But they were clear on what he would wear for his walk to the tavern. So now he walked quickly, head low, and followed the directions they'd given him. Supposedly, Merrique had sent word to Rudolfo that Gregoric would return shortly bearing instructions.

The colors he now wore were not so much the issue. His own uniform bore the colors of the kin-clave rainbow. But these silks, and the laces and the buckles and bells, made him the caricature of a pirate. Gregoric couldn't help but notice how similar the outfit was to the one worn by the pirate lord on the cover of Hyrum's book.

"Now that you're an honorary member of the *Kinshark* crew," Merrique had said, "go tell your king we sail at dawn. You know what door to find us at."

And so Gregoric walked and endured the growing noise of being noticed until he reached the tavern and the last humiliation of his day.

"Gregoric!" At first Rudolfo's face was concerned, but the weather shifted quickly. The amusement there looked too much like Rafe's expression for Gregoric's liking.

Their eyes met, and he fought the anger down again. He strode into the room in the midst of more laughter and kept walking, past Rudolfo and up the stairs to the room they all shared.

He was digging through his pack for new clothing when Rudolfo entered. His friend and king was quiet for a moment, and Gregoric swallowed against a sudden lump in his throat as the day caught up to him.

"How are you?" Rudolfo finally asked.

"Worn," he answered. "But it's done. We sail at dawn."

"And how was he?"

He looked at Rudolfo. "He's a bastard. I'd tell you this was a mistake but I know you won't listen."

Rudolfo nodded. "You're right."

Gregoric looked away. "You never listen."

"Sometimes I do, when you're not looking. But you're right about the other. It might be a mistake." Then he shrugged. "Mistakes," he said, doing his best impersonation of Gregoric's father's gravelly voice.

They finished the saying together. "Those that don't kill you just might teach you something."

Rudolfo turned away and sat on the bed as Gregoric peeled out of his costume. "We've had birds from home," he said. "You've a message from that girl you've been seeing. The one with the big brown eyes."

"Adela?" Gregoric wasn't sure why he was asking. She was the only one of late he'd spent much time with. She'd not been happy about him leaving for a few months but had understood well enough why he needed to be with their king. And she'd found the whole notion of going to sea both terrifying and elating.

But why would she write? It was a surprise and the first time he'd received a personal bird while out and about with Rudolfo.

He pulled on the sturdy woolens of the northern wood and dug a pair of soft slippers from someone else's pack, after looking long and hard at the brightly shined and brightly buckled boots he'd pulled off. He'd get his own boots back in the morning according to Jasper, Rafe's first mate.

Rudolfo offered up the scrap of paper and Gregoric took it.

The note was brief, and it dropped him to the bed beside his friend.

"Sorry, Gregoric," Rudolfo said. "I didn't mean to read it but . . ." His words trailed off, and Gregoric felt a hand on his shoulder. "Congratulations are in order."

He looked at the note again and blinked. The anger and humiliation of the day melted away into a wonder he'd not considered but found welcome.

"I'm going to be a father," he said. "The River Woman says it will be a boy."

Rudolfo squeezed Gregoric's shoulder then dropped his hand. "Yes. I know. And I also know that you'll have the biggest, most audacious Firstborn Feast that the Seventh Forest Manor has ever known. A week, I think, and perhaps even a traveling celebration."

He heard excitement in his friend's voice, and it took some of the fear out of him. He stared at the tiny scrap and read the coded words again.

"So," Rudolfo said after another two minutes had passed, "if you need to return, I'm prepared to forgo this voyage and send Captain Merrique our regrets."

Gregoric wasn't sure he'd heard correctly and looked up. "Forgo this voyage?"

Rudolfo's eyes were warm. "Of course. You're becoming a father. There's much preparing."

He looked back to the paper. "It's months away," he said.

Rudolfo's eyebrow arched. "That is true. Or at least I'm told that it works that way."

Gregoric nodded and gestured to the boots. "And I've endured much to secure our passage."

"You have indeed," Rudolfo said. He leaned over to examine the boots. "But these are actually a bit fantastic." His eyes lit up. "They look like the ones on—"

Gregoric cut him off. "They're meant to."

Now Rudolfo nodded. "Then to sea?"

Gregoric took a deep breath against the ocean of fatherhood that threatened to flood him. "To sea," he finally said.

Rudolfo had them all awake well before dawn, and the enthusiasm in his eyes and grin were too much for Gregoric's pre-chai capacities. To make matters worse, his king had decided to dress himself in the ridiculous garments—and the boots—that Gregoric had returned in.

"How do I look?" he asked with a flourish.

Gregoric grunted and pulled on his boots. Yaric and Bryn were already dressed and packing. Gerundt fussed at the sheaths tucked beneath his oversized shirt, adjusting the knives so that they were within reach.

Gregoric stood and did the same, slipping a fresh pouch of magicks over his neck once his blades were in place.

When they were ready, Gregoric opened the door to lead them out. He'd expected the tavern to be dark at this hour and was surprised to see a lantern lit and a small group gathered in the common room below. He picked out Jasper and Rafe Merrique immediately, and he paused long enough that they looked up at him there at the railing.

And Gregoric finally found something in the morning worth smiling over. Rafe wore exactly the same outfit—or at least the original that the model was based on—that Rudolfo now wore. Only his bore the marks of time and were obviously made from the finest silks. His black boots were decorated with polished seashells of deep burgundy and bright silver buckles. His feathered hat was deep purple, and he bore twin rapiers at his waist.

"Captain Merrique," Gregoric called out in a gruff voice. "Allow me to present to you Lord Rudolfo of the Ninefold Forest Houses, General of the Wandering Army."

Then he stepped aside for Rudolfo, who leapt forward and bowed deeply. "Well met, Captain Merrique," he said.

Rafe Merrique stood. "I am at your service, Lord Rudolfo," he said. Then he returned the bow. There were snickers and chuckles. Jasper rolled her eyes. Gregoric noted it all with suspicion.

"I had thought we were to meet you at dawn," Rudolfo said as he took the lead and moved toward the staircase. "Has something changed?"

"Only my heart," Rafe Merrique said. He moved toward the stairs as well and glanced to Gregoric. "I was unkind to your first captain and owe amends. I thought I would apologize in person and escort you myself."

They clasped hands at the foot of the stairs. Then Rafe offered Gregoric his hand as well. "I apologize, First Captain."

Gregoric nodded and shook the hand briefly, then moved aside. Jasper joined him.

She tipped her head toward Merrique and lowered her voice. "He reread the Hyrum book last night over a bit of rum," she said.

Gregoric glanced to her before nodding toward Rudolfo. "He retold bits of it from memory last night, and there was chilled peach wine involved."

The two were complimenting one another's boots now, their voices becoming louder as they sought to out-grace each other. "This is going to be an insufferable day," Jasper whispered.

"Aye," Gregoric agreed.

They left the tavern, Rudolfo and Rafe in the lead as they strode into the predawn gloom. As they walked, the two continued their upbeat chat and pulled ahead, a few members of the crew falling in behind them. Gregoric tried to move past them, but Jasper was at his side with a question.

"So have you sailed before, First Captain?"

He shook his head. "I've been on lakes but nothing like an ocean. Our ocean is grass."

"I've always wanted to see the Prairie Sea and visit the forests," Jasper said.

"It's a long way from the Ghosting Crests."

His half squad moved in behind them, carrying Gregoric's and Rudolfo's packs along with their own.

"One day," she said, "I'll get there."

They left the main avenue and slipped into an alley. Rafe and Rudolfo stopped at the door, and the others gathered around. The pirate gestured to the door. "Welcome to my home, Lord Rudolfo. We will breakfast and then board, if you concur?"

Rudolfo smiled. "I look forward to both, Captain Merrique."

Rafe opened the door. "After you," he said.

Gregoric glanced at Jasper. The expectant look on her face brought his mouth open, but he closed it when Rudolfo spoke.

"Oh no, Captain Merrique, after *you*."

"I insist," the pirate said, extending a hand toward the door.

Rudolfo seized the hand. "We'll go together then," he said

and then tugged Rafe toward him as he tipped himself back and through the doorway.

Rafe howled all the way down even as Rudolfo laughed, and Gregoric found a second reason to smile on a pre-chai morning. The splash followed by more splashing, the spluttering, the cursing—it was all music to Gregoric's ears, especially mixed with the raucous laughter of his closest friend.

"You ridiculous fop," Rafe yelled below.

"You damnable pirate," Rudolfo yelled back.

Music indeed, Gregoric thought.

Three vessels that might or might not have been Merrique's *Kinshark* sailed out of Dandylo Terrace that morning, and between the decoys, the bribes, and the administrative fees, Merrique's actual crew slipped quietly out of the harbor in a ship that no one would've suspected carried a pirate or a king. It looked like a fishing schooner, and it ran low and sleek in the water, most of the crew hidden below deck as they put the Delta behind them.

Once they'd stowed their gear and toured the ship in Jasper's care, Rudolfo and Gregoric met Rafe in his stateroom. The room had a small wardrobe and a narrow bed, and those were the only evidence that anyone lived in it. Otherwise, it held a table strewn with papers and shelves crammed with books and charts in no order whatsoever. A long iron tube fixed to a wooden stock—some kind of weaponry Gregoric didn't recognize—hung above one of the room's portholes. A telescope hung over the other.

Rafe gestured to stools that waited and unrolled a map over the scattered pages of his worktable. He pointed to an area that Gregoric didn't recognize. "We are here," he said. Then he drew his finger south and east slowly until it stopped at the far end of the parchment. "We need to be here in two weeks, but we are already four days ahead of schedule."

Rudolfo glanced at Gregoric then back to the map. "Then we arrive early?"

Rafe shook his head. "It doesn't serve to be early with the

Androfrancines. Their caravans are never early . . . sometimes late . . . and those aren't waters to lay anchor in for long."

Rudolfo leaned over the map. Gregoric was gradually orienting to it from where he sat. Windwir was at the center of most Named Lands maps, which helped, but in this case the world's largest city wasn't noted. But the Keeper's Wall, that north-south border of impassable mountains, stood out, and that gave him some perspective.

"So what do you propose then, Captain Merrique?" Rudolfo asked.

Merrique pointed to a large island south of them that seemed to have been split in half. "A pit of piracy," he said. "Down here. An estate that needs breaking into."

Gregoric sat up. This wasn't what they'd planned, and he already saw a dozen reasons why this was a bad idea. First, Rafe was from the Divided Isle, and no longer welcome there. Second, there was an awfully big leap between setting sail in service to Androfrancine light and robbing a manor. Rudolfo noticed the look on Gregoric's face and raised an eyebrow, but looked back to Rafe. "Please continue, Captain."

Rafe smiled. "These hauls around the horn are nothing. There and back quickly without incident nearly every time." The smile widened. "If you want to experience the life of a pirate lord, you won't get it running crates and robes. That's the least pirate-like thing I do, sir."

Rudolfo glanced at Gregoric again before speaking. "And you think we can do this with the spare time we have?"

Rafe nodded. "I do, Rudolfo. Though it may involve a bit of running under magicks. But I'm told that's something your people are quite good at." The pirate looked at Gregoric this time. "Is that true, Gregoric?"

Clever now to use our first names and not our titles. Gregoric found himself answering, "Rudolfo's Gypsy Scouts are the best of the best."

"I'm counting on that," Rafe said. He looked at them, and in that moment, Gregoric thought the older man almost seemed fatherly. It evoked a kind of trust that was unexpected—something else for Gregoric to keep his eye on. "We change course, do a bit of piracy, make haste around the horn, and have you back with the Order's trinkets, hale and whole, in no time at all. What say you? Shall we?"

Gregoric's hand found Rudolfo's shoulder and pressed scout code into it with fumbling fingers. *This is ill-advised.*

But before Gregoric finished, Rudolfo grinned. "Aye, Captain," he said. "We shall indeed."

That night, after a much better dinner than he would've expected on a ship, Gregoric found a quiet place above deck and settled in to watch the sky at sea.

He and Rudolfo were sharing a small room, and the three scouts were in a similar room directly across the passageway and near the galley. Two of them had spent most of the day vomiting in pails and sleeping against the seasickness that gripped them. Even Gregoric had felt twinges of nausea those first few hours, but by dinnertime, he was ready for the salmon steaks served in a bed of chilled, pickled sea vegetables he couldn't possibly name, with warm black bread and cold rice wine.

And now this sky.

It was painted in colors he had no adequate words to describe and against a horizon that defied his comprehension. He'd thought the line of horizon over the Prairie Sea was vast, but it was nothing compared to this.

He sat and watched the sky deepen toward dark and didn't notice Rudolfo until the Gypsy King was already seated beside him. "What do you think, Gregoric?"

Gregoric saw concern and curiosity on his friend's face. "I think we violate a dozen articles of kin-clave with the Independent Counties of the Divided Isle and risk war if the Lord of the Ninefold Forest Houses is caught in a criminal act," he said. He could hear the matter-of-fact nature of his own tone.

Rudolfo grinned. "Getting caught is definitely not optimal, so

I'm recommending that we not." He dangled his scout powders from their string around his neck.

Gregoric felt his eyebrow twitch. Use of magicks during a time of peace was one of those violations he had anticipated.

"But," Rudolfo continued, "that's not what I meant." His eyebrows furrowed. "I mean about becoming a father. That was a bit . . . unexpected."

Gregoric shrugged. It was the thought he didn't want to have but kept having regardless. "It happened to my father. It happened to your father, too. It doesn't seem so very unexpected."

"Yes, but not so young."

Gregoric could tell Rudolfo wanted to ask, thought he shouldn't, and then moved forward with his next question anyway. "Weren't you using the powders? Your father and Kember both have been pretty insistent about them with me of late."

Gregoric sighed. No, he'd not used them, and neither had she. But they'd also been clear-eyed on the possibilities no matter how rare. And it was none of Rudolfo's concern. Deflecting was easy here. "I think they've good cause for their concern of late," he said.

Rudolfo smiled. "Regardless. I've no heir, and you've one on the way. I meant what I said about the Firstborn Feast. But how do you *feel* about becoming a father, Gregoric?"

It was a serious question. Gregoric smiled. "I feel like I'm meant to."

"And how is that?"

"A mix of fear and delight, a stuttering and stammering heart full of love," he said. "And like I'm meant to . . . like I'm *meant* to be a father." He looked back at the sky. Pregnancy was rare enough in the Named Lands—a leftover of the Age of Laughing Madness studied and unsolved by millennia of Androfrancine research—that most couples did not marry until after their first child was born. "And I don't feel like starting a war over a bit of piracy here in the shadow of my impending fatherhood."

Rudolfo smiled. "Then we must stick to the plan of not getting caught." He stood. "I think fatherhood will suit you well, Gregoric."

Gregoric inclined his head, and Rudolfo did the same before he slipped aft and below deck.

He'd always assumed he'd have a family just as he'd always assumed he'd be Rudolfo's first captain. It was all starting sooner than he'd thought, but then again, Adela had also surprised him when she'd shown up. She'd fit into his life easily and quickly, with grace, sass, and ferocity. *And those big brown eyes.*

She drew out aspects of him that Gregoric wouldn't let others see, and he could only imagine what their child would draw from him.

He took in a great breath and held it, watching the faintest stars grow brighter against the falling night. The wind in the sails and the sound of the water against the hull were a driving pulse in a refrain that declared this journey and the salt air more intoxicating than any rum.

Gregoric sat there for a goodly while taking comfort from a wide-open sky at sea and wondering how his life would unfold.

He was still wondering when the moon rose blue and green and full of promise.

Piracy, Gregoric decided, was nothing at all like Hyrum described it in his book. A day and a half after his first night at sea and he'd exchanged the rocking of a ship for the jostling of a wagon. And hours of bumping along rutted County roads had left him bruised and brooding.

Merrique had been vague about their target, but during the hours they'd spent planning the heist, he'd talked them through his plans.

Three parties, all magicked, would approach from three entry points onto the property, would make their anticipated acquisitions, and would then retreat. That was all well and good, but Gregoric had flinched when he'd first heard the words.

"And no weapons," the pirate had said. "We're going in magicked; we're not fighting."

Jasper and Merrique's own men had nodded. Rudolfo, Gregoric, and the half squad did the same.

And now we're about our piracy, Gregoric thought as the wagon jerked.

They were stretched out beneath a false bottom in the wagon, side by side like felled timber at the river's edge. For the first few hours, he'd fussed at the powerlessness he felt, then made a reluctant peace with it.

Closing his eyes, he turned his focus back to the plan and to his and Rudolfo's part in it. "Your room is *here,*" Merrique had said, pointing to a map of the manor. "The window will be open. There is a book—leather bound and without a title—and a jade statue of a long-finned kinshark." His eyes were fierce for his next words, and Gregoric sensed a quiet threat in their tone. "Touch nothing else."

"It seems quite specific," Rudolfo said. "Is it always so?"

Rafe had shrugged. "Not always. But sometimes it is better to sip than to gulp."

Gregoric heard something in those words that resonated and he noted it.

Rafe continued. "In this case, the dividends of this venture will be invaluable."

The wagon, after so many hours at a steady straight-ahead pace, now slowed as they navigated a series of turns. They came to a stop, and a few minutes later, he heard voices and felt the creaking of the wagon as men unloaded the cargo. It had been quiet for maybe thirty minutes when Gregoric heard a low whistle that someone in his wagon returned. Then, fingers from outside unlatched the false floor and swung it up and open.

Gregoric sat up slowly along with the others.

Moonlight, blue and green, washed the yard where the three empty wagons sat. Beside them stood a barn, its doors closed against the night. Beyond it, a scattering of trees and, farther away, the lights of a large town.

"We're close," Rafe said. "We'll run from here."

They wore dark clothes now along with their scout boots. Gregoric felt naked without his knives. He'd strongly resisted this decision to forgo weapons, and his attempt to change Rudolfo's mind had left him with an ache in the pit of his stomach. Still, Merrique had been most insistent, and even now, he raised the point again.

"We are in and out without touching a hair on anyone's head," he said.

Gregoric couldn't resist his question. "And what if something goes wrong?"

A voice cleared to his left. "I see no reason," Rudolfo offered, "for anything to go wrong."

Rafe's face was sober. "No matter what might go wrong," he said. He held up a handful of small silk pouches from their slender cords. "You'll be wanting fresh magicks, I'll wager."

Rudolfo reached for them, and Gregoric spoke up. "We have magicks, Captain Merrique."

"You do," Rafe said, "but they are from the north through one of your medicine makers. They don't always work well after being in the salt air."

Rudolfo shrugged and took the pouches, handing them out.

Gregoric slipped the cord around his neck with the other.

"You know your window and your target," Rafe said. "Keep your men in the garden. I'll take the vault; I have the Rufello cipher for it. Jasper and Uke have the library. We meet back here and run for the coast with a bird off to the *Kinshark* for our rendezvous."

Then he held up his pouch, opened it and sprinkled it into his hand, and licked it. Rafe vanished even as he sprinkled the powders onto his shoulders. "Let's run."

Rudolfo and the scouts followed the forest ritual, touching the powders to their foreheads and shoulders, tossing some to their feet, before licking the palms of their hands.

Gregoric watched them fade from sight and then followed the same steps. Only instead of using the new powders, Gregoric used his own powders. He was far from home, far off course from their Androfrancine-sanctioned mission, getting ready to violate their kin-clave . . . and without his knives. And Rafe Merrique, the prankster pirate, was the common denominator here. Gregoric had given over as much control as he was going to and would use the magicks he knew and trusted and trained under his entire life.

Gregoric felt them take hold, felt the strength surge through him as his stomach twisted into a knot and his head began to pound. The smell of the horses in the barn, the maple trees beyond, rushed his nostrils as the night became less dark.

And as he ran after Rudolfo and Rafe Merrique, his hands bereft for knives he did not have, Gregoric thought this bit of piracy felt much like the forest run of a Gypsy Scout.

They left the forest for the stone-walled fields that marked the lands and delineated the various manors on the outskirts of the city. So far, the maps and the hours spent poring over them were paying off, and whoever was in the lead knew exactly where they were going. Gregoric heard the low clicking of a tongue ahead and adjusted his course and pace as they crossed a road and approached a gated wall.

He heard the softest scrabble ahead of him as someone—Rudolfo, he suspected—scaled the wall. Gregoric followed after, dropping lightly to the ground on the other side.

A cobblestone drive nestled in the midst of fruit trees went perhaps a quarter league ahead to end in front of a large, two-story building. They stayed to the trees, skirting the large courtyard and moving into the gardens at the rear of the main house. Once they were on the other side, Gregoric saw their window on the second floor and the trellis beside it that they were to climb. And thanks to the magicks, he could also pick out the guards—two of them—both by scent and by their hazy outline in the dark.

He and Rudolfo broke away from the others now and moved in closer to the house. Gregoric was approaching the trellis, now ahead of Rudolfo, when he felt the first muscle spasm in his left calf. It slowed him, but he checked the trellis and then climbed it to the windowsill.

Another cramp, this time in his forearm. Gregoric winced and could've sworn he saw his hand and arm before him for just a moment. He blinked at it and felt a wave of nausea as yet another cramp seized his stomach.

He felt Rudolfo's hand on his shoulder and translated the coded words pressed there with his friend's fingers. *What's wrong?*

I don't know, Gregoric answered. He took a deep breath as the clenching subsided and then checked the window.

Moonlight etched the room in soft shades of green and blue, but Gregoric found his vision coming and going with the onset of a sharp pain behind his temple. A desk stood before the window, its surface tidy in a way that suggested it was never used. It was a smallish room, and apart from the ordered nature of it, it looked a great deal like Rafe Merrique's stateroom. A narrow bed piled in blankets, bookcases crammed with books and charts, a few objects here and there—including the jade kinshark, within reach on the corner of the desk.

Gregoric slipped onto the desk and dropped to the floor, then put his hand on the kinshark and waited for the magicks to work their way onto it. It guttered and flickered in and out of focus, but the magicks didn't hold. More than that, Gregoric's hand came in and out of focus along with the jade statuette.

"Who's there?"

Gregoric jumped, and the jade statue grated against the desk. He backed into the shadows and looked in the direction of the bed.

The pile of blankets had become a young woman sitting up in bed staring directly at him. "Rafe? Is that you?"

The name and the familiar way that she used it was as shocking to him as the cold water he'd been dropped in over and over again by the man attached to that name. Gregoric looked to the door and back to the bed. His first impulse was to flee, and his second was to reach her and silence her before she called for help.

Except it is almost as if she expected us. And Rafe specifically.

And before he could do anything, another cramp seized him, and he fell over this time. He closed his eyes against the sudden onset of it as his entire body clenched in pain.

"We are affiliates of Rafe Merrique," a low voice confided from the window. There was fear underneath Rudolfo's voice but Gregoric was confident that the girl could not hear it. "It appears perhaps we were expected?"

Gregoric squinted up at her as she looked to Rudolfo. "No," she said in a careful voice. "*You* were not expected. But *he* is hoped for *every* day." There was an emotion there that spoke to some kind of longing Gregoric couldn't fathom, followed by a bitterness he could. "At least some of us around here feel that way."

And for whatever reason, those words were the spark that, combined with the layout of the room, gave it all enough sense that Gregoric could solve the Whymer Maze before him.

This is Merrique Manor. This was Rafe Merrique's boyhood room, organized in the likeness of the stateroom of a pirate ship he'd yet to steal and sail. An imagined future he had crafted for himself.

The realization was lost to more cramping, and Gregoric groaned as his legs and arm shifted in and out of focus beneath the moonlight.

Rudolfo hopped to the floor beside him. "What's happening?"

Gregoric bit his tongue against the tremors that now rolled over his body.

"Something's wrong with his magicks." The young woman was up out of bed now, wrapped in a blanket, and reaching for her lamp. "Who are you? You still haven't answered my question." She paused and her next words weren't convincing. "I'm not above screaming for help."

"I hope you won't," Rudolfo said. "As I said, we are affiliates, and Captain Merrique would be quite unhappy with any mistreatment we might receive at your hands." He was thinking fast on his feet, and Gregoric was glad. His own ability to think shrank the longer his body shook against the magicks.

They both knelt over Gregoric, and he felt her hand, cool against the heat of his skin. "So you are part of his crew then? I saw him lifting up Rafe's kinshark statue."

"Of a fashion," Rudolfo said. "We are sailing with him in service to the light."

She snorted. "That explains little." Gregoric felt her hands probing his neck and armpits. "How are *your* magicks holding up?"

"Fine." Rudolfo paused and Gregoric felt his fingers suddenly pressing words into his shoulder. *Did Merrique's magicks do this to you?*

Gregoric couldn't keep the shaking still enough to code his words. "I used my own," he said through chattering teeth.

"I know little of these things," Rudolfo said, "but Merrique told us to use the powders he provided. He said the salt air could have an impact on ours."

She sniffed Gregoric's breath. "Fortunately, I know a bit about these things. And I have what I need in my workshop to treat him."

The trembling and cramping stopped for a moment and Gregoric tried to climb to his feet, only to find his legs now unable to hold his weight. He buckled.

"And where exactly is that?" Rudolfo asked.

"It's in the basement," she said, "but I can be there and back quickly."

There was no hesitation in Rudolfo's reply as he squeezed Gregoric's shoulder. "We are at your mercy, Lady," he said.

She grinned. "Yes. You are."

She slipped into a robe and slippers but didn't leave by the door. Instead, she ducked into the closet.

The kinshark lifted from the desk and Gregoric blinked at it as it gradually disappeared. "What was the book he told us to take?" Rudolfo asked.

Gregoric found his voice. "You're not planning to—"

"Save your voice, Gregoric," Rudolfo said. "And yes. I do not know exactly who she is or where we are, but I intend to complete the task and escape even if I have to carry you out of here on my back."

"It's his own house, Rudolfo." Gregoric's voice was raspy. "He's had us break into *his own house.*"

"To be fair," Rafe Merrique said from the closet, "I didn't think anyone would be at home apart from the staff. But I see you've met my sister, Drea." A wall of clothing rustled as his magicked form entered the room.

There was an edge in Rudolfo's voice. "This doesn't appear to be quite the act of piracy we discussed, Captain Merrique."

"No," the pirate agreed. "Not at all." His voice was closer now. Gregoric felt a boot nudging his side, and too weak to snarl, he groaned. "And the stubborn baboon used his own magicks despite my warning."

"Aye," Rudolfo agreed.

Gregoric felt Merrique's hands, strong and firm, taking his ankles. "Grab his arms then. We need to be gone before she returns."

The hands tugged at him but no others joined in. Gregoric saw the young woman was back now, postured in mock outrage in the open closet with her hands upon her hips. "Do you now?" she said. "I think you've spent enough time gone, Rafe Merrique."

Her brother chuckled. "I thought you were *all* going to be at the summer lodge on Lake Elsyn?"

"I decided to stay home when I saw the bird from Simmons." Drea Merrique smiled and Gregoric saw a strong beauty in the line of her jaw. "I know which people you correspond with when you're going to be in the area."

"Yes," Rafe said. "But I time my visits for when everyone's away. I didn't expect to find you here. Neither at home nor in my room. I sent them for my journal and my statue from Grandfather. Why aren't you in your own room?"

Drea shrugged. "I like it in here. Not everyone's big brother is a famous pirate." Then she smiled. "Besides, I was hoping you'd be back and thought this would be the best way to catch you. The oily-voiced one already has the statue, I'll wager." She pointed to the drawer on the desk. "The journal is still there. They've kept it all the same since you left . . . only cleaner . . . which has always struck me as odd." She stepped from the closet and knelt over Gregoric, drawing a satchel up from the leather strap it hung by. Drea rummaged through it, drew out an envelope and tore it open.

"Give me a canteen," she said, then her warm breath was near Gregoric's ear. "Open up, sailor."

He complied and tasted the bitterness of the powders she tipped onto his tongue. She closed his mouth, opened another envelope and mixed those in as well. He felt foam building as the powders hissed and bubbled. Drea uncapped the canteen and pressed it to his mouth, the cold water pushing the powders down his throat. He felt the softening of all his edges as the kallacaine relaxed his muscles. His eyelids were heavy, and he could see his hand clearly now when he held it before his face.

Drea Merrique pushed his hand away and down. "This one is going to need some rest before he can be re-magicked."

"He can rest on the ship," Rafe said.

Drea ignored her brother. "Help me get him into the bed," she said.

This time, Gregoric felt hands half lifting and half dragging him across the room and he did his best to help until he rolled into the bed and hands pulled the blankets over him. Behind them, he heard Rafe protesting. "We don't have time, Drea. This was supposed to be a quick in and out."

"Next time," she said, "you should have the civility to plan a longer visit."

Rafe smiled. "I might be able to now, and you've these men to thank for it."

Then Gregoric was in a warm tunnel. The room, the bed, and their voices were all growing farther away.

"I asked them who they were," she said. "They wouldn't say."

"How rude of them," Rafe Merrique observed. "These men have acquired the brooch and brought it to me at great expense." His voice was sober now, and Gregoric heard Drea gasp as the words took hold. "We've brought it back tonight. Tell them that it's back in the family vault."

Their act of piracy had been breaking into Rafe Merrique's family estate to return the brooch Rudolfo had spent a dozen fortunes to acquire. There was some aspect of this that made Gregoric want to laugh and not stop laughing, but he was too tired. There were more words, and he could've sworn he heard his friend introducing them with great flair and embellishment. But everything melted into warmth and darkness as Gregoric slid into a deep and welcome sleep.

At some point, Gregoric awakened to the lurch and lope of being carried across a meadow in the gray of predawn. He was certain he must be dreaming, strapped to someone's back as they ran.

"What's happening?" His mouth was dry as cotton and his voice raspy.

"Easy, Gregoric," Rudolfo panted. "We're nearly there."

He's carrying me. Gregoric tried to move but found he couldn't. He'd been tied over Rudolfo's shoulders with belts, and they were both wet from the sweat of Rudolfo's exertion as he ran.

Every word was an effort, but he forced them out. "You should not be carrying me, General."

And Rudolfo's words silenced him for the rest of the run and long after hands had lifted him up and pulled him aboard the waiting ship. He took those words with him back into sleep. "You've always carried me, Gregoric," his king and closest friend said between ragged breaths, "and across much rougher landscapes." His hands squeezed Gregoric where they held him across his shoulders. "From time to time, when it falls to me to return that favor, I will carry you, my friend."

Gregoric smiled as the rocking of the waves replaced the rocking of their run and sleep carried him back down the warm well of Rudolfo's echoing words. They were a slow refrain to a song that soothed him and flooded him with an unexpected gratitude.

I will carry you, my friend.

Gregoric watched his second sunset at sea from a hammock they'd rigged for him on deck, and Rudolfo sat nearby and watched it with him. He'd been nearby most of the time Gregoric had been awake, and according to Jasper, he'd stayed by while Gregoric slept.

"We tried to help him carry you," she had told him during one of Rudolfo's brief absences, "but he insisted upon doing it himself."

Rudolfo said nothing about it, and Gregoric wasn't about to bring it up.

They watched the setting sun paint a wide-open sky in colors so overpowering that he simply watched slack-jawed in wonder. Rafe Merrique approached, raising a bottle of rum.

"How are you feeling?" the pirate asked, offering Gregoric the bottle.

Gregoric took it. "Much better," he said. He drank from the bottle and passed it to Rudolfo.

The Gypsy King took a long drink and handed the bottle back to Rafe. "And how are you, Captain Merrique?"

Rafe's face was a mix of emotion, and he tried to hide it with another swig of rum. He smiled, but his eyes held something closer to sadness in them. "I've seen my sister a handful of times in twenty years. She was five when I left." He leaned back against the mast. "I was at odds with my parents and the life they planned for me—the life planned for them by their parents. But Drea—she was the innocent caught in the wake of my departure." He took another long drink from the bottle.

"Regret," Rafe said, "is a curious thing. Our Androfrancine friends would tell us the only useful regret is the variety that is more akin to guilt—feelings of remorse that lead to a change in one's path." He used the bottle to conduct the next words as if he were in front of a choir. "Because as we all know, 'Change is the path life takes.'"

"I aim to regret nothing," Rudolfo said.

Rafe Merrique laughed. "Good luck."

Jasper poked her head out of the hatch and looked around. Gregoric saw her eyes meet with Rudolfo's and suppressed his smile. It seemed that sometime in the last twenty-four hours, Merrique's first mate had decided Rudolfo's library was perfectly adequate, shelf, book, and all. Which of course meant Gregoric would be staying up on deck long into the night.

The coded looks between the two of them weren't lost on Rafe either, but like Gregoric, he pretended not to notice.

"You're certain," Rudolfo asked, "that you want to proceed, Gregoric?" He looked up at Merrique. "When is our last chance to change our minds?"

Merrique chuckled. "We're pirates. We can always change our minds."

Rudolfo stroked his beard and considered Gregoric carefully. "And you're quite comfortable here for, say, a few hours?"

Now Rafe's chuckle was the bark of a laugh. "Best not keep my first mate waiting, Lord Rudolfo. She brooks no dissent."

Gregoric smiled as Rudolfo blushed and disappeared quickly.

Rafe settled into the chair he'd left and handed the bottle back to Gregoric. "Your king is a fine young fellow. He's on the way to becoming fierce and sharper than sharp." Their eyes met. "And you too. I'd have not trusted me on the powders, either, especially with the paces I've put you through."

Gregoric shrugged and was surprised at how easy his next words were. "I should've listened." He took a drink and passed the bottle back. "So explain to me what we did?"

Rafe smiled. "You and your king helped me lay a regret to rest. I've returned the brooch I stole to finance the first *Kinshark*. I knew the moment I had it in my hands that I needed to take it home immediately. And you not listening to me gave me a few hours with my little sister that I didn't know I needed to have." He finished the bottle. "So there's nothing there for you to regret. Learn your lesson and move on."

Gregoric nodded. "Aye."

Now Rafe regarded him and raised an eyebrow. "You also have family. A father and mother?"

Gregoric nodded. "And a son on the way." He paused. "A bride, too."

"And Rudolfo," Rafe said.

"He's more than family. He's my king and my closest friend."

"Yes and what are you to him? Do you know?"

Gregoric hesitated, and Rafe continued.

"You're his anchor, Gregoric. You ground him."

He nodded. *Yes.* He could see that.

"And he is your chain. When you're buried in the muck of doing your job, he can lift you up if you let him."

Gregoric looked from Rafe back to sky and sea that had become indistinguishable from one another. The pirate was right, of course. As much as Gregoric focused on Rudolfo's need for grounding, he needed to let the tie that bound their fates pull him up when the ground he was so good at going to swallowed him whole. Chains kept anchors from being lost and stuck.

For a moment, he was drugged and hazy on Rudolfo's back and he heard his friend's words again—that refrain that he suspected he'd go back to for the rest of his days as one of the more surreal assurances life had ever granted him. *I will carry you, my friend.*

Gregoric wasn't sure what to make of their bit of piracy, but he knew it had changed him. And that more change lay ahead as they sailed for the Churning Wastes. There, men in dusty robes would pass over to them whatever bits of light long lost in darkness they had dug up in the ruins of the Old World. And then, they'd sail for home and fatherhood and Firstborn Feasts. If he had his way, he'd raise his son in peace among his family in the Ninefold Forest and in service to his friend. And one day, he'd tell his son all about the time he sailed with a pirate.

Rafe stood up and stretched. "Rest well, First Captain."

"Aye, aye, Captain," Gregoric replied.

And after Rafe Merrique slipped down the hatch and after Gregoric had checked to be certain no one was within earshot, he turned his eyes upon the stars that guttered to life above him.

"Far into the Ghosting Crests and beyond the Emerald Sea," Gregoric sang softly to that sky, "I swear my sword to the pirate lord and a life of piracy."

Gregoric, First Captain of Rudolfo's Gypsy Scouts, smiled and wondered what tomorrow might bring.

Megan Lindholm

I've always loved hearing the "behind the scenes" stories from friends in film. My dad was an extra in *Captain Blood,* the Errol Flynn one. He told me that the director had the extras swinging back and forth on ropes to appear as though they were jumping from rigging on one ship to another, as the production assistants dropped flaming pieces of canvas down around them. I've watched that movie more than once, hoping for a glimpse of him!

Reality television has become a fixture in our entertainment. I trace its roots back to the old quiz shows and live shows like Art Linkletter's *Kids Say the Darndest Things.* Linkletter was an expert at getting kids to reveal rather embarrassing facts about their home lives, to the intense delight of the audience.

But our current crop of reality shows has a more immediate source in *The Real World.* The instant success of "seven strangers picked to live in a house" led to many imitators. But I have to admit that the ones I'm mesmerized by are the home/garden improvement and find a house and fix it shows. Watching someone else transform a home is so much easier than actually working on your own! It happens so fast and always seems to turn out well!

But if you know people who work in the reality TV genre, one quickly comes to realize that there is much less "reality" in those shows than one might expect. Often "storylines" are constructed and "surprises" are staged. In a way, reality television is improvisational storytelling that happens after the initial filming. One takes the footage one has and creates a story from it. The unexpected event can be a curse, or a ratings boost!

Film is a strange world, and in this story, it gets one notch stranger.

Megan Lindholm

SECOND CHANCES

Megan Lindholm

It's not a smell. It's not a sound. It is, literally, the sixth sense that doesn't have a name. It's almost impossible to describe it to someone who doesn't have it. Imagine conveying the fragrance of lavender to someone who has no nose. That's why I didn't mention it to the rest of the crew. The sensation permeated the house from the moment I arrived for work, and after everyone else left, it became stronger.

I don't encounter ghosts daily, but I've sensed more than my share of them. I work for that fixer-upper reality show *Second Chances*. A cute twenty-something couple, Bert and Giselle, with a curly-headed toddler nicknamed Sweetie and doting Grandma Chris find rundown houses, fix them up, and sell them to people who would not ordinarily be able to get financing. The touching tales of helping the homeless into homes, a peculiar variation on flipping houses, had started out as a blog, then moved to YouTube, and then became a television show. The first season was mostly sincere. Real houses, real fix ups, real homeless, and creative financing. Bert and Giselle crowd-sourced funds for down payments and deposits on utilities. Grateful families Tweeted and Instagrammed for months afterward. It truly was heartwarming.

But suitable houses and appropriate families are hard to find on a consistent basis. It gets messy when the house has real problems or the happy family is arrested for meth production six months after they move in. So by season three, *Second Chances* was cutting corners. It had been an underfunded shit show from the start, and the reduced budget had cut the crew to less than bones. But for a local-to-Tacoma show, it was still the best work in town. Good crew. Cringeworthy cast when the cameras were off. But since the cast owned the production company and were also the executive producers, the cringing was something best kept to oneself. I was the art department. All of it. Tonight's task, long after the paid crew and the overeager interns had been sent home, was for me to "prep" the house for tomorrow's establishing shots.

I didn't like the late-night hours but the show had a tight shooting schedule. Can't lose a day. Tomorrow's episode was Giselle and Bert touring the rundown house they "might" buy. Tonight I was trashing the place they'd already bought to make it look bad enough that the rehab would be truly remarkable.

I had stocked the old fridge with some fungus-coated leftovers from home, and stuck dirty, sticky secondhand store alphabet magnets on the refrigerator door. My cat had contributed an overflowing cat box to leave under the rickety Goodwill table I'd brought. My staging goal was at least two "ohmigawd!" shots in each room. The wallpaper beside the range was decked in greasy cobwebs. I pulled some loose to dangle in shreds. Done.

I yawned. Not from boredom but because I was tired, and I still had five rooms to go. The master bath was easy. Smear yellow playdough on the toilet seat and sponge on a mixture of baby oil and Coca-Cola for the bathtub ring. Pull the shower curtain half down. Quick and easy, and I ticked those tasks off on my tin clipboard with the handy interior compartment. It was too warm in the stuffy house. I started to take off my sweatshirt. The long sleeves snagged on the scabs on my arm where I'd cut myself the day before. I left it on.

Who's down there? Monty? Is that you? Have you finally come to tell her you're sorry, you son of a bitch?

I looked up from my clipboard. The words had drifted into my mind in the same way that sometimes as you pass out of range of your car's radio station, another one cuts in for a few moments. Thoughts in my head that were not mine. Ignore them. Get on with my work.

The master bedroom had a smell like vintage Avon Brocade mixed with old urine. Too bad a camera couldn't capture that. There were two badly patched holes in the Sheetrock at fist height. I made a note to myself. A particle-board dresser and an old bed frame beckoned. I tugged the mattress slightly off the bed and then staged some dingy tighty-whities with Hershey's stains on them. I pulled a drawer from the dresser and left it on the floor. A sprinkle of fake rat turds along the wall. Done. I checked my phone and nodded to myself. I might finish before midnight.

As if he had heard my thought, a text chimed from Raymond.

Progress?

Raymond's our AD, or Assistant Director. He's a top-notch talent working in a third-rate market at crap wages. He shares custody with his ex-wife, so he lives in Tacoma instead of Burbank. Going good, I texted back.

Text when done, he instructed me.

OK! I tapped back. I knew if he didn't get a response, he'd be at the door in five minutes. He wouldn't sleep until he knew I was done and home.

I keep my kit in a sturdy metal toolbox. I grabbed my mug of coffee and my toolbox and headed up the shag-carpeted stairs. Nothing I could have done to them could have made them look worse. At the top of the stairs, the landing offered me the open door of the half bath, or either of two small bedrooms to either side of it. All three doorframes showed signs of splintering around the catches. That almost always meant someone had broken through a locked door. Domestic violence. And three doorframes to repair or replace. I noted them on my list.

The cheap toilet seat didn't need help to look disgusting. The finish was warted with moisture damage, and mold had grown in the rough surface. I took out my squirt bottle of homemade "gas station dirty-soap grunge" and slimed the sink with it. There was a half roll of toilet paper on the hanger. I took it off, smudged it on the dirty floor, and put it back. Perfect.

My phone buzzed. Done?

Almost. Raymond's like that. If I fell down the stairs and broke my neck, he'd be liable. But even if he weren't, I think he'd still check on every crew member every night. He cares almost enough to make up for the crap wages we get. I feel like he knows each of us better than any of us know him.

Almost, I'd told him. Two rooms to go. I twisted the lid on my commuter cup and took two gulps of coffee while I did a quick survey of the smaller bedroom. Little to work with. The abandoned furnishings were a bare twin-size bed frame and a nightstand missing a drawer. Cheap cracked linoleum with a speckled pattern was peeling up from the scarred hardwood floors. Three walls were ecru-painted Sheetrock with the seams and tape showing through and a few amateur patches. One wall had terrible wallpaper, even worse than the teapots and flowers in the kitchen. Scotty dogs in tartan coats. I stepped inside.

It was akin to walking into a garage full of exhaust fumes. Ghost permeated the room.

No matter. Get the job done and get out. I set my coffee and phone on the nightstand and opened my kit.

The wood-framed window had only a curtain rod above it. I knocked the rod loose so it dangled across the pane. From my kit I took bread pellets rolled in ash and did a sprinkle of fake rat poop along the sill. By the bed frame, I peeled a long strip of wallpaper and let it dangle in dusty shreds. The dust was from a ziplock bag, courtesy of my home vacuum cleaner.

As I was carefully dipping the wallpaper in dust, the ghost suddenly demanded, *What the hell is wrong with you?*

I made no reply. It's best to ignore them, generally speaking. Most people can't sense them. If you pretend you can't hear or see them, sometimes they give up.

Monty sent you, didn't he? The coward. I know what you're looking for. Better be careful. You might find more than you want.

It was harder to ignore that threat when I peeled back another strip of wallpaper. I exposed tally marks, the old four strokes and a cross stroke to mark groups of fives. There were letters next to each group. B, NS, DR, R, and a couple of others that I couldn't make out.

I told you so, said the ghost. *Or didn't Monty tell you about any of that?*

Give no reaction. Pretend that I have no sixth sense.

B was for a beating. NS means no sleep. DR is drunken rage. R is for rape.

I touched the strokes by R. There were over fifteen by the other letters, but only two by R.

And that makes it acceptable? the ghost asked acidly. *Only two rapes as opposed to seventeen beatings and twenty-seven nights with no sleep? Twenty-seven nights of "scrub that floor again, I don't care how tired you are, I'm not coming home to a filthy kitchen?"*

I pressed my lips together, holding back my words. The ghost was getting angry, and that could be very bad. I zipped my bag of dust shut and marked on my tin how I'd dirtied the room.

But maybe it was more than twice. I didn't always know what he did to her after the beatings. After she stopped shrieking and begging him for mercy. I was too scared to know.

I shook my head. A moment later, my cell phone fell from the windowsill to the floor. Okay, that wasn't funny. I wiped my hands down my jeans and picked it up. Screen intact. Good. I wasn't due for phone upgrade for eighteen months. I kept track of these things. I shoved it in my hip pocket and turned in time to see my commuter cup teetering on the edge of the windowsill. I caught it. But it was open, and that meant I drenched myself with what was left of my coffee. I'd filled it up at Starbucks, an expensive treat for myself. One I was now wearing for the rest of my night's work. "Goddammit!" I shouted, shaking hot coffee from my hands.

Don't blaspheme! Not in Jenny's house! the ghost shouted, and the overhead lightbulb flared sun-bright for a moment.

"Okay, okay. I get it." No ignoring these manifestations. Best to acknowledge the ghost and try to calm it down. "I'll respect Jenny's house." A sudden breeze blew my hair into my eyes. That was more engagement than I wanted. I softened my voice. "I work for a TV show. They'll be filming here tomorrow and they want the house to look messy. They'll come in, walk through, gasp, and be horrified at all the work ahead of them. Tomorrow evening, we clean it up. Then paint and Sheetrock and refinish the hardwoods. Maybe some carpet up here. Day after that, stainless steel appliances and granite countertops and new cupboard doors. An island in the kitchen. Updates and dress ups. Then a family in here for you to haunt. Are we good now?"

No response. That happens. Sometimes, if you acknowledge a ghost, they seem as terrified at knowing you are aware of them as most people are at encountering one. That veil is there for a reason. Neither side really wants to part it. I put my pouch of dust back in my toolbox. Finish up and go.

The day after or a few days later, he would always say he was sorry. Sometimes he brought her a cheap box of chocolates or a gas station rose. She always forgave him. I always knew he lied. She always seemed happier after he apologized. Like she believed he was really sorry. How could she believe him?

I made no response. What can you say to something like that? It doesn't matter if it's the next-door neighbor or the ghost of a teenager, there are some questions that have no simple answers. The waiting pause stretched until it became an ear-ringing silence. Maybe my listening was all she had needed. Maybe I was connecting with her on a deeper level. I decided I didn't want to know what we had in common.

What about the sag in the foundation, and the water pipe in the utility room that's leaked so long the floor is rotting out? Will they fix that?

Oh Lordy. She was back. I spoke calmly, not looking around to try to see her. "Those aren't my job. Maybe they'll fix them, maybe they won't." They wouldn't go near them. There would be some hand-waving at major repairs. Fix one leaky spot in a pipe instead of replace all the corroded piping. Maybe put a house-jack under the floor where the foundation was failing. Band-Aids over spouting arteries. So far, no one had sued the show. So far.

I opened the closet door. Small by today's standard, only about four feet wide. It had a shelf, a three-foot dowel to hang clothing on, and a slanted ceiling. And the ghost. She was wearing fleece pajamas and was barefoot. The teenager she had been sat cross-legged in the corner, her right hand clasping her left wrist. She was colorless, all grays except for the bright leaping of blood piping up between her clenched fingers. A very determined suicide. I only looked at her from the corner of my eye. A lot of ghosts get a charge of energy from the shriek response. That's why they take the trouble to scare. I wouldn't bother to trash the closet. The small size would be enough to make Giselle nearly faint with horror. I picked up my kit and my coffee.

The ghost suddenly materialized in the doorframe, blocking my exit. *Don't you dare dirty Jenny's sewing room!*

I walked through her, snapping off the light as I went. She was a waft of cold on my skin, as if I'd opened and shut a refrigerator door. People walk through ghosts all the time. The difference was that I had seen her. I've seen ghosts since, well, since I figured out they were ghosts. My mother called them "strangers." As in, "We don't talk to strangers." I've inherited her attitude toward them. Like any strangers, some are benign, some don't register your presence at all, and a few are dangerous.

Jenny's sewing room was plain beyond bland. Cream-colored walls, worn hardwoods, original wood trim on the single-pane window, a bare lightbulb in the ceiling fixture. Not a stick of furniture. The sliding doors for the small closet were missing. Nothing here. The room was empty. Filled to the brim with chill emptiness. The presence in this room was a compelling absence so strong that it was hard to breathe. I'd taken one step into the room. I took two backward steps out of it and into the other bedroom before taking out my cellphone.

Raymond answered on the third ring. "You trying to wake up Marcella?" he asked me.

"We have a problem," I replied.

"Did you hurt yourself?"

"No. It's the house."

"Structural danger?" he asked immediately. "Electrical? Plumbing?" As the AD on the show, any problem is his problem. But Raymond's particularly sensitive about sending any crew into a hazardous situation, such as a partially flooded basement or an attic where the previous owners had cut out roof joists to increase the storage space. It's a good thing that he cares so much, since the producers do not, and they would happily insist that Grip and Electric set up lights in the flooded basement and then expect the director to stand hip deep in water to catch the shot where Bert and Giselle come down the rickety wooden steps and act surprised by what they find. Raymond always has all our backs and, as a result, we all have his.

"You remember when I told you we had a poltergeist in the little bungalow, and you helped me deal with it before the show filmed?"

"Yes. Not again."

"No. This is a ghost. Two, I think. One very cold haunt in one upstairs bedroom and one angsty teenage suicide in the—"

My phone flew out of my hand. It hit the wall hard enough that I heard the screen crack. *Not suicide! Murder!* The silent scream made my ears ring.

One step to snatch up the phone, turn and walk—do not run—down the shaggy stairs. Do I take my tool kit? Too late, I left it on the landing at the top of the stairs. I walked to the door, opened it, and as I closed it behind me, my toolbox came flying down the stairs to land with a crash at the bottom.

I locked the door and walked to my car. I'd left the lights on upstairs and in the kitchen. They all began to flicker wildly, surging to white brilliance and then deathly yellow.

I got in my car and waited, damaged phone in hand.

Raymond pulled his van up beside my car. He motioned to me and I transferred into his car. I moved the baby's diaper bag from the front seat to the back as I got in. "Who's watching Marcella?"

"Suzanne across the street. She owed me a favor. I picked her up at the airport at 3 a.m. last week. You hung up on me."

"No. Ghost smashed my phone."

He nodded curtly to that. He drove and I knew where we would go. There are not that many all-night coffee stands, even in Tacoma. I think Raymond knows them all. He got a twelve-ounce black and bought me a vanilla chai. We sat in his car and drank them as I told him my tale.

"Well. Rats." Raymond doesn't curse anymore. Not since Marcella started talking. "We're scheduled for establishing shots tomorrow morning, and Bert and Giselle come in the afternoon. So we have maybe six hours to fix this."

"The show must go on," I said.

"That's right," he replied. "I was surprised when we got a second season. Shocked when we got a third, since our numbers weren't that great. In this market, it's hard to find houses that we can get on our budget. We can't have any shooting delays."

"I don't think this is a 'fix it in six hours' thing, Raymond. The teenager ghost is territorial. And angry. But whatever is in that other bedroom is . . . cold. Beyond anger. Beyond hate."

"Let's go see," he said, just as I'd feared he would. Raymond. He gets things done.

When we pulled up outside the fixer house, the lights were on and steady. I handed him the keys. He drank the last of his coffee and I finished my chai. "Time to do this," he said, and opened the car door.

I followed him up the steps to the house. He stepped inside the door and looked all around. "Is she here now?"

"No. She's upstairs." Raymond doesn't see ghosts. I give him points that he accepts that I do. Though perhaps I should credit the poltergeist for that.

We walked in and he did a quick tour of every downstairs room, nodding to everything he saw. My clipboard was on the floor by my toolbox. He picked it up as we went, ticking off items with the stub pencil I keep tethered to it. "Nice job," he said. He walked to the base of the stairs and looked down at my bounced toolbox and scattered kit. He crouched beside me and helped me repack it. When we stood up, he nodded at the steps. "Okay, Marcy. Let's go."

He started up the stairs. The lights flickered, just once. Raymond glanced back at me and kept climbing. I followed. By the time we reached the top of the stairs, the lights were flashing without any rhythm. It made me queasy. On the landing, Raymond glanced into the bathroom and, after three flickers, added another tick mark to my clipboard list. He turned toward the smaller bedroom. "Knock it off, will you? You're making me sick."

She did. Raymond has that effect on most people. It's why he's an AD. We were plunged into darkness. I heard the jingle as he took a Maglite out of his cargo pocket and snapped it on. He turned to me. "Now. What does she want?"

"She isn't a diva, Raymond. She doesn't want blue M&Ms in her dressing room or more camera time. She's a ghost. You can't just ask her what she wants."

I want Monty to come back. He needs to apologize. She was abruptly standing in the doorframe, blocking our entrance to the room. Raymond can't hear ghosts either, so I was the only one who flinched. He saw my twitch and raised his heavy brows and gave a short nod, his signal for "go ahead" when everything was quiet on the set.

"Who's Monty?" I asked.

She flickered. Sometimes that happens. Ghosts forget who they were, or they get a burst of emotion and can't seem to hang on to their materialization. She vanished.

"She wanted someone named Monty to come back. But she's gone now. Maybe that was all she needed. Just to say she wanted Monty to come back."

"Okay." Raymond snapped on the light switch in her room and stepped inside. Clipboard in hand, he toured it. He nodded to the rat poop and curtain rod, and checked them off my list. Then he came to the tally marks on the wall by the peeled wallpaper. "What's this?"

I told him. His eyes grew darker. "She still gone?" he asked and I nodded.

I hung back as he crossed the small landing and looked into Jenny's sewing room. He frowned slightly and walked over to the window. "It's closed," he said, and I nodded from the doorway.

"So you can feel the cold in there?" I asked.

"It's not . . ." I don't think I'd ever seen Raymond hesitate before. New experiences for both of us tonight. "It's not really cold." He rubbed his arms as if to be sure of it. "It's more like . . ." And then his chin dropped to his chest and he went to his knees.

If the room had been on fire, I'd have been more willing to go in there. But I did anyway. He wasn't completely passed out, but I think that made it harder to grab him under his arms and drag him out of there. I'm five feet five inches and Raymond is a husky fellow about half a foot taller than me. His efforts to stand nearly knocked me over. But I got him out onto the landing. I was on the point of dragging him down the stairs when he gave himself a shake and staggered onto his own feet. "Let's go," he said, and held on to my arm as we went down the stairs toward the door. He slowed at the landing and looked all around. I didn't. I went straight to the door and put my hand on the doorknob.

"She around?" he asked me as he stood holding my clipboard.

"No," I said, but as I looked up the stairs she materialized at the threshold of her bedroom. I had a brief impression of raggedly cut dark hair, jeans, and a Mötley Crüe T-shirt. Her face was a blur. She flickered like an old film. Maybe she didn't remember how she had once looked. *Monty Winslow,* she said. *He has to come back and say he's sorry. Tell him you found this. In a hole in my wall.*

She was gone. I'd had a brief impression of a piece of jewelry dangling from a chain. Something sparkly.

"In the Shape of a Heart," I said to myself.

"What?" Raymond demanded. His usually swarthy skin was still pale, like too much milk dumped in coffee. It wasn't a good look on him.

"An '80s song my mom liked. Jackson Browne song, about dropping a necklace in a fist hole in the wall."

He took my arm. "You aren't making sense. Let's get you out of here."

It's easy to forget other people don't hear ghosts when you do. "She was there for just a moment, at her door. She wants us to find someone named Monty Winslow. And show him a necklace that she dropped into a hole in her wall."

He looked sick. "So that means we have to go back upstairs into that room, and try to find a necklace tonight?"

"Tonight?" I echoed him feebly. I just wanted to go home, take a very hot bath, and find a nature documentary and fall asleep to hyenas eating gazelles. Something natural and restful. "How about tomorrow, during the day?"

"We have a schedule to keep," he reminded me. He added, "If we have to tear a hole in a wall, it's better we do it now. And maybe stage the necklace to be found when we're taping." He paused, looking thoughtful. "Yeah, that might be good. The viewers might love that."

The man amazes me sometimes. It's all about the show for him.

I hefted the weight of my toolbox onto my hip by adjusting the shoulder strap, wondering as I always did why I carried so much stuff in it, and followed Raymond. He had already started back up the stairs. Over his shoulder he asked, "Which bedroom do you think?"

"Hers, I think. If she punched a hole in the wall and dropped a necklace in it, it's probably in there."

We both halted on the landing. I was afraid. I'd never encountered phenomenon at this level before, nor interacted with a ghost who changed moods and attitude so quickly. "Hello," I said softly. "May we come into the room? To locate the necklace?"

I felt no response and saw nothing. I shrugged at Raymond. He gave me a tooth-clenched smile and I followed him into the room. The light was steady again.

Raymond was methodical. He began with the wall patch closest to him. He used my hammer to reopen it. He peeled the patch free, then tapped a long break in the wallboard down to the first cross brace between the wall studs. Chalky bits of Sheetrock fell to the floor. He peered in. "I hate that blown-in insulation stuff. It always falls to the bottom of the wall space." He poked around in the insulation with his flashlight. It looked a lot like masticated newspaper. "Nothing," he said aloud, and moved on to the next patch. He had to push the bed frame away from the wall to reach it. Its metal feet screeched against the old linoleum. He tapped the patch free with my hammer and then carelessly ripped it out, letting it fall to the floor. It made a larger hole than the one before. He clicked on his flashlight and peered inside. "Nothing," he said again.

Look again.

"Look again," I echoed her, and he tore the Sheetrock wider until we saw it, caught and dangling on a bent nail inside the wall.

"It's there," he said, and reached inside to take it. After a moment, he said, "It's hung up on something."

I spoke softly. "No. She's holding it there."

Only Monty takes it from here.

"She says she'll only let Monty remove it."

"O-kaaay," Raymond said thoughtfully. He touched it with fingertips only, arranging it so that it wasn't obvious but it would be found if anyone took a second look in the crack. "I'll be sure that Giselle finds it. I'll tell her that the house looks like someone was searching for something in the walls. She'll be on it like a beagle on a rabbit trail."

Only Monty!

"She's adamant. Only Monty removes it."

Raymond looked at me. He sighed. "Go home. I've got some staging of my own to do here. Get some sleep and be back here by noon."

I left him there.

I wasn't late the next morning, but Giselle behaved as if I were. "Oh, look, she stopped for coffee! Well, I'm so glad that's more important than being here for us."

I tried to look appropriately shamed and hid behind my sixteen-ounce vanilla latte. The prospect of actual coffee shop coffee had been the only way to lure myself out of bed. I hadn't really slept. I kept seeing the teenager in the closet, the blood spouting up between her fingers. I texted Raymond three times in the night, asking if he was all right. Each time he'd only texted back a smiley face.

Raymond had obviously arrived very early, even before the crew had come to get the establishing shots. Every kitchen cupboard door was standing open, and there were two fresh holes in the living room walls. "It wasn't like this the first time we viewed the place," Bert complained. "This is gonna cost us!"

"Looks like someone was searching for something," Raymond observed. "Like maybe someone hid something here and didn't take it when they moved out."

"Drug money," Grandma Chris said darkly. "I saw a boy with a red shirt on the corner. Probably a Crip or a Blood."

Giselle's head swiveled like a puppet's. "Oh, Ramon! Do you think so?" She has spent the past two years convinced that Raymond is Mexican and really named Ramon. She often cites him as an example of how diverse her crew hires are.

Raymond nodded. "Probably not money, Chris. They broke holes in the walls, so it was hidden a long time ago, I think. But someone remembers it. When I got here, the kitchen window was jimmied open. Someone broke in last night."

"Tweakers," Grandma Chris announced darkly. "Sweetie, don't you touch anything. It might have meth on it."

Sweetie didn't even look up from her iPad screen.

Raymond cleared his throat. "Okay, to work. Establishing shots are done. Time for some action. Marcy, stick around. I may want more rat poop."

Raymond walked the crew through the sequence he'd decided on. He was right about Giselle. She was wriggling with eagerness. But he made her do the outside shots of them first seeing the house, and then walking up to it. He requested some outdoor footage of the opened kitchen window and the muddy boot prints where "someone" had climbed in. Once the cameras moved inside, Giselle could barely hold up her end of the dialogue. I saw her stoop down to peer into the cupboard below the kitchen sink with uncharacteristic interest in the plumbing. There was one drawer in the kitchen that was closed; she opened it and then pulled it out to look behind it.

My rat poop and other decorations met with cast and crew's approving *ews* as we progressed through the rooms. I felt no sign of the ghost. When we reached her bedroom, the light switch didn't work. I scowled at that; the rainy gray light coming through the crusty window wasn't very illuminating. Raymond shrugged. "Probably just the bulb."

"It worked last night," I said quietly. He shot me his "shut up" look and took a cautious step into the room. All remained calm. I frowned to see that my rat poop had been moved, but said nothing. I felt a tingling tension in the air and could not keep my gaze from wandering to the closed closet door.

Raymond unclipped a massive flashlight from his belt. He played it over the room. "Looks okay to me. We'll get some light up here." He moved the beam over the walls, and as it traveled over the enhanced holes we'd made in the Sheetrock, there was a sudden bright glitter of returned light. No one reacted. He did it again and Giselle gasped.

"What's that?" she demanded, scuttling across the room and falling to her knees. "Bring the flashlight!" she demanded, and Raymond had to thrust it to her through the mob of crew that had clustered close.

"Wait, don't touch!" Bert suddenly commanded. "I want lights and cameras on this. I think this is going to be our big hook for the new season.

Giselle clasped her hands into fists and held them in front of her bosom. They shook with her eagerness. *Second Chances* has a great crew. Grip and Electric thundered down the stairs to fetch more lights and extension cords and equipment, while our camera crew began setting up tripods and talking white balance. When the bright lights went on, even I gasped.

I'd always heard of sparkling, brilliant diamonds. Best I've ever done is Austrian crystal earrings. But the pendant in the wall spat light back at us in a way that had the cameras moving to get shots that were more than blinding glare. Giselle, Bert, and Grandma conferred outside the bedroom, and when Raymond barked, "Quiet on the set!" the rest of us stood in breathless silence.

Giselle does great as a reality show hostess, but her acting skills are limited. They performed their standard patter of "Oh, so dirty, so much to fix, but great potential; oh dear, rat droppings!" but Giselle could not keep her gaze off the damaged wall. Her shriek of surprise when she discovered the pendant seemed to me more like a triumphant squawk. Close-up of her startled face, of Bert's surprise and Grandma's puzzlement, followed by close-up of the treasure. It was a simple cross, silver with sparkling stones set in it. As Giselle drew it out of its cobwebby hiding place, a torn piece of age-browned paper came with it, folded around the fine silver chain.

"It's a note!" Bert exclaimed, and at that moment their surprise was as genuine as mine. He unfolded it carefully while Giselle possessed the pendant. I watched her tug on it stubbornly as Bert read aloud. "It says, 'Ask Monty Winslow. He knows.' What on earth could that mean?" Bert has a wonderful, resonant voice, and he played the moment to the hilt. It was fortunate the cameras were on him, for the dismay on Giselle's face was plain. I folded my lips as the camera zoomed in on the crumpled note. It's not that hard to "age" paper with a quick dip into tea. Raymond prints all his instructions, but something about the careful cursive in the note still seemed awfully familiar to me.

"I can't get it free!" Giselle complained.

"Let's not break it," Bert counseled her and as he bent to help her, Raymond cut the cameras.

"Leave it there!" he suggested. "The drama will be so much greater if we can find this Monty and he's the one who actually takes it out of the wall."

The rest of us trooped out of the room and down the stairs to let them argue in private. We ate dry sandwiches and drank coffee and waited. When they descended, it appeared that Bert and Raymond had prevailed against Giselle. She was not pleased about it.

In the times throughout the shooting day when the cameras

were turned off, Giselle made her feelings plain. "Finders, keepers!" she exclaimed more than once. Grandma was prone to side with her, and when the day's shoot was over, I followed them back up to the ghost's room. Did anyone besides me notice that no footage had been taken of "Jenny's sewing room"? No one else mentioned it and I didn't bring it up.

Crouched by the crack, they took turns peering in at the trapped pendant. Grandma immediately offered to take the necklace to have it appraised and cleaned. Bert was more pragmatic. "Sure, we can do that. But there are bigger things to think about beyond what it's worth. Look, the audience we can draw with this, especially if this Monty fellow has a good story to tell, will outweigh the short-term pleasure you get from having a sparkly necklace. You don't even know if it's anything more than a piece of costume jewelry."

"Let's get it appraised," Grandma repeated. "For the story. Real diamonds would make this episode grow legs and run!"

"Break the hole wider and let's see if we can't at least get it out." Giselle commanded.

"No!" Bert and Raymond were a chorus. "We need to have it stay just like that until Monty can see it."

"And what if we can't find this Monty?" Giselle demanded.

They're real. And it's antique. Monty's mother gave it to Jenny when she married Monty. It's a family piece. Monty was furious when he found out that Jenny had given it to me. I'd never heard a ghost catch back a sob before, but she did. *Jenny was different from all the other foster moms I'd had. She didn't talk much, but she listened. She really listened. She asked me what music I was playing in my headphones, and I told her. And the next week, she got me a Mötley Crüe T-shirt. She was so quiet that I talked a lot more than I ever had. I even told her when I thought I was pregnant. A few days later, I found out I wasn't. But that night, she came to my room and sat on the foot of my bed, and I told her everything. I told her I'd been having sex with boys since I was thirteen. And she started crying. She said, "You poor little lamb!" And then she took that necklace off her neck and put it on mine. It was still warm. She said it would remind me that my body was mine and I should treat it well. I promised her I'd do my best . . . She told me just to reach up and hold onto it and it would help me remember not to do anything that wasn't good for me . . .*

Do not react, I counseled myself. I could feel the room becoming more and more charged. I wondered if she were drawing energy from the argument between Giselle and Bert.

But it didn't work. I tried. But sex was . . . when you're a foster kid, sometimes it's all you've got to trade for anything. For a boy to walk you to the bus, or buy you a can of soda from the school machine . . . Monty caught me making out with a boy in the garage. I . . . I didn't have my shirt on. He hit the boy, and he slapped me and dragged me into the house shouting for Jenny and calling me a slut. And when he saw I was wearing the necklace, he said I'd stolen it. He tried to rip it off my neck but the chain was too good. He yelled that I was a cheap slut, and I wasn't worthy to wear his grandmother's necklace, that I was shaming it by having it touch my filthy body. He said it was worth thousands of dollars, and then he said he was sending me back to the foster care people, that the money they gave him wasn't worth having a whore under his roof, shaming him. The chain nearly strangled me.

The knowledge flooded into me, not as words, but at the speed of thought. I lifted my hands and covered my ears. That didn't hold it back.

Then Jenny hit him. She screamed that she'd given it to me, that it was hers and she had the right to give it to me. She yelled that things were only worth as much as people valued them. Monty was so astonished that he let go of me. Jenny never fought back when he hit her, but she tried to protect me. He turned on her. Then Jenny stepped between me and him, and told me to get out. I ran away up to my room. I thought she was mad at me too. I took off the necklace . . . and downstairs, I could hear them fighting . . .

"I found him! I found Monty!"

Stunned silence—from the ghost, from the entire cast.

It was one of the interns, and it took me a moment to remember that I was surrounded by live people. Alice was the enthusiastic intern who always had her phone in one hand. She waved it around, her face alight with excitement. The argument by the wall crack ceased and the ghost forgot me. I saw her shade drift closer to Alice.

Raymond asked, "Are you sure it's the right Monty Winslow?"

Alice grinned. "My mom's a real estate agent. I know how to look back and see who owned places. Monty and Jennifer Winslow owned this house for twelve years before they sold it, uh," she peered at her phone. "Twenty-nine years ago. It's had, um, fifteen different owners since then. Sold, and resold, and then it was a rental for a long time. The value on the home has been dropping for six years, and the current value per square foot is low against comparative properties, and the—"

"Do you know where Monty is now?" Raymond asked, cutting to the essential.

"Working on that . . ." She held up a cautioning finger. "Just a moment . . . okay. Let me cross-reference that . . . oh, he's claiming a senior tax rate now on a bungalow on South Eleventh Street . . . Yeah. I think I do."

Raymond turned back to Bert and Giselle. "Let's call Monty," he suggested. "Let's set up downstairs around the kitchen table. I want to be sure we get good audio on the call as well as some footage."

He herded them away as if shepherding chickens. When I started to follow, he turned and shook his head at me. As the others moved away, he stepped back to pull me aside.

"Hey, salvage that ugly toilet seat, would you? It shot great. We might want it again for another house."

I nodded, thinking of the rubber gloves and garbage sacks in my kit.

"Oh, and I don't want anyone but you cleaning on this floor."

"What?"

"Well, maybe I can get someone to help with the bathroom. But three crew have already told me that the upstairs bedroom is 'creepy.' And that's just her room, not the cold room. I know I don't have your sensitivity, but that one room feels really bad, even to me."

I looked at him in dismay. He shrugged eloquently and said, "You're all I got," and walked away. As if that settled it.

Actually, it did. Film jobs are hard to come by in this town. It was in my own best interest to make sure this episode of *Second Chances* bought us a fourth season. I collected supplies and trudged back up the stairs. My task was to get the room sanitary enough for the drywallers and painters to come in. Tomorrow's shoot would show them at work, after the "Monty sees it" scene. As Bert had once loudly explained it to us: "The painters are paid to paint, not clean. We don't want to pay painter's rates for someone to sweep up rat poop. So you do all that before they get here."

I worked alone up there while down in the kitchen Raymond captured our stars calling Monty and making arrangements for him to come tomorrow. Then they'd take the shots of Giselle with her hair bundled back in a pretty scarf, a spray bottle in one hand and a dirty rag in the other. They'd find a reason to put Bert up on a step ladder, to repeat their favorite joke about him being afraid of heights. Grandma Chris would stand and beam as Sweetie bid her parents an extremely fond farewell before being whisked away. Then the cast would leave the set and the crew and interns would all pitch in for the cleaning.

The ghost was in the closet again. She was slumped, head sagged forward, knees bent. And the little fountain of blood went *leap, leap, leap.* I crossed the room and gently closed the closet door. I took the broom and began sweeping the ceiling, knocking down cobwebs and old popcorn texturing. It fell to the floor like clumps of dirty cottage cheese.

The feel of the ghost had changed. She was sad rather than angry. Her sadness permeated the room. I found myself sighing heavily. It was hard to find the energy to clean the glass in the windows. Memories of times when I'd done stupid things came back to me, linked to memories of saying dumb things that made people laugh at me or walk away. One after another, painful memories rumbled through my brain like trains clicking past on an uneven track. I heard myself whisper aloud, "I never want to be friends with anyone." I drew breath and tried to focus. I took notes on my clipboard as I worked. Three places where the Sheetrock needed patching; the outlet covers on the electrical boxes didn't match;

the ceiling light fixture was wobbly and had no cover. And no one was ever going to want to marry me. The window opened and closed but the catch was broken. My sister wasn't speaking to me. I stood on my toolbox to unscrew the remnants of the curtain rod holders from the wall.

And every moment, with every blow of sorrow, I felt her watching me.

Monty's coming tomorrow?

I nodded, sweeping up bits of Sheetrock and ceiling texture.

Maybe he can fix it. I can't touch her at all. When he said he was sorry, for a few days afterward, he'd be nice and she'd be happy. It was so crazy, how she always seemed to believe him when he said he was sorry and would never hurt her again. It was a weird kind of strong. Like he couldn't break the good part of her.

"I had a friend like that once. Until he killed her." Words popping out of my mouth. Unshared secrets spoken aloud.

Monty didn't kill her. She just died. In her sewing room. It was after I was dead. I can't go there. But the people who have come and gone here, they say terrible things about Jenny's room. That it's cold and awful. People who slept there had terrible nightmares. But the last two people who rented this place, they didn't even get furniture moved in before they decided to break the lease. Something is wrong with her. Something terrible.

Time for the question. *Did Monty kill you?*

Gone. No trace of a ghost presence. I suddenly felt as if I could draw a full breath.

I went for a bucket and sponge mop. I used a bleach mixture on the old linoleum. It stung my nose and every small cut on my hand and made my eyes water, but I could almost see the room as it had been. I put clean water and more bleach into the bucket and began to wipe down the trim and the windowsills. Patch the walls, fresh paint, new flooring, some curtains and carpet, and it would be a nice little room.

Jenny was always so warm. She was different from any other foster mom that I'd had. Like a real mom. Even on that night when Monty nearly choked me . . . when she could, when he was done with her . . . I could tell she'd cleaned herself up before she came up here. But there was still blood around her nostrils and in one ear. And her lip was fat. But she came up here and sat down on my bed. I was so scared I couldn't even cry. I tried to give her the necklace. She folded it back into my hand and said, "Everyone deserves another chance to try again. You especially."

The ghost's voice became an angsty wail. *She was so kind to me! In the evenings, I'd go across to her little sewing room and watch her make things. She wanted to teach me how, but I was always afraid to try. Afraid I'd wreck something.*

The knowledge flowed into me, not as words I heard but as memories suddenly shared. Her shame, her fear, her pain were as mine.

But after that, Monty was like a ticking bomb. I don't think she'd ever said no to him before, and he blamed me for it. When Jenny wasn't in the room he'd whisper awful things. He said I was wrecking their marriage. He'd call me slut or whore. I started leaving for school before he got up, and as soon as I got home, I'd come up here. Jenny would bring me my dinner on a tray. I could guess how he was shoving her around and cursing at her. But she just took it. For me. For what she thought I could be. But I didn't live up to what she believed. I was a coward. He'd beat her and I'd hide up here. And cut myself, as punishment for my cowardice. Because I knew it was my fault he was beating her. I was a COWARD!

The room exploded. I opened my mouth and clapped my hands over my ears. There was no sound, just a burst of pressure that made the window panes slam against their frames and the water in my mop bucket jump. It slammed shut the door of the room as the closet door flew open. I stared at the girl in the closet. For the first time, I could see her clearly. Goth-white skin, chestnut hair flying wild in a wind of her own making. Blood on both her hands, blood forming a puddle around her. Ears still covered, I backed slowly away. I put my hand on the doorknob. It wouldn't even turn. "You were just a kid!"

You are going to help me! It was a command, not a request. *You are going to get Monty here, and you are going to make him walk into*

Jenny's room! He has to tell her he's sorry. He always said he was sorry afterward. And she always forgave him. Every. Single. Time. I think that's what she wants, maybe. Maybe if he says sorry, and she forgives him, she'll go back to being Jenny. To believing things can be good. To being warm and kind.

"Please let me out." I could hear anxious voices from downstairs. My heart was hammering. She was strong and getting stronger. Ignoring her was becoming dangerous.

She protected me. I was terrified of him, and she must have been scared, but she stood up to him. For me. Can you imagine how frightened she must have been?

I thought I had a good idea of it, yes.

I would hear him yelling at her. And soon I would hear other sounds. He'd push her down, or slam her against the wall. Or throw things at her. I'd hear a kitchen chair go flying. I was so glad she was protecting me, and so afraid. So ashamed of letting her do it. I knew I didn't deserve her necklace. That's why I dropped it into the wall. He has to tell her he's sorry. PROMISE ME!

"I'll do my best!"

That's not a promise! That's what I said to Jenny, and my best wasn't good enough. PROMISE ME NOW!

There were shouts and one shrill squawk from downstairs. Somewhere, glass broke. This was no time to tell the ghost that a promise made under duress is not binding. "I promise!" I shouted.

She vanished. A terrible ringing silence filled my ears. I felt as if they were stuffed with cotton. I could turn the doorknob and I did, and stumbled out and nearly fell down the steps in my hurry to get away from her. I slammed into an intern in my flight out the door, and we went down in a tangle of arms, legs, clipboards, and walkies.

Raymond was suddenly standing over me. "What was that?" he demanded.

"The ghost made me promise that we'd get Monty into that cold room upstairs. She wouldn't let me out of her room until I did!" I shouted the words, but only realized how loud I was talking when Raymond stepped back from me.

"The ghost?" asked the intern I'd fallen over.

"Let's be calm about this," Raymond suggested over two interns shouting "I knew it!" One rushed up the stairs while the other fled into the street outside. Raymond hauled me to my feet. "CALM DOWN!" he shouted in his command voice, and we all did. Amazing what knowing that someone is in charge can do for you. He escorted me to a kitchen that now smelled of bleach and fresh coffee. He sat me down at my battered prop table. "Now. From the beginning, for everyone. And *nobody* interrupts her."

I hesitated. I had already taken a lot of ribbing over a prior poltergeist event. Announcing two ghosts wasn't going to improve my standing in our ragtag production company. But Raymond was giving me his steely-eyed look, and someone else clacked a cup of coffee down in front of me. So I told. I was glad that our cast wasn't in attendance. When I was finished, Raymond shook his head. "Well, that screws up the call sheet entirely."

That was the whole issue for him—how would it affect the production? In moments, he was on his cell and walkie, issuing new instructions for Grip and Electric about how rooms had to be lit and prepped. Alice the intern announced suddenly, "I got her! Laura Comstod! The suicide made the papers and it was the end of Monty and Jenny Winslow as foster parents. 1987. Long time for a ghost to hang around."

The moment she spoke the name aloud, I felt Laura's presence grow stronger. She'd been named. There would be no defying her now. "I want to take a sick day tomorrow," I told Raymond.

"And less than a week later, here's the obituary for Jennifer Winslow." Alice was so pleased.

"You're not sick," Raymond said to me. "And I need you."

And that settled that.

Nonetheless, I felt sick when I showed up for work the next day. None of the food I'd eaten had stayed in my stomach, and I had the shaky, light-headed feeling that goes with that. I'd spent all night battling anxiety sharper than the box cutter in my tool kit.

I wasn't the only one affected. Several of our interns had vanished, and three other interns had brought friends with them. News of a ghost is like that. Some people flee and others cluster. Raymond seemed to have expected it; he had sets of the NDAs and other forms prepped for the "new interns" before he put them to work. Our cast arrived early, a first. Raymond had anticipated that, also, and had spent the night on the set to be sure nothing was disturbed. Including the pendant. Giselle was bright-eyed with fury that Monty was coming to claim it.

Within minutes of her arrival, she had another grievance. "Why didn't anyone tell me about this ghost thing?" she demanded of Raymond. She stared over his shoulder, and her icy glare was all for me.

"Because it's all nonsense!" Bert declared comfortingly. He put his arm across her shoulders and hugged her. She didn't relax.

"I know you, Bert Fuller. You're hoping something will happen, something on camera!"

"Now, honey, I didn't know any more about this than you did, right up until we arrived here this morning. And I'm sure it's just a case of someone getting the spookies in an old house at night." The look he sent me was condescending, in a threatening sort of way.

Raymond had witnessed both looks, and moved me out of the line of fire. "Let's have Art upstairs for now. Make sure no one touches anything before we're filming," he suggested, and I went.

We were set up and ready for Monty when he arrived. Raymond had rigorously limited who would be upstairs for the filming. Some were bitterly disappointed at being excluded. I felt awful about being included.

"No one touches anything up there," he'd reminded me.

"There is no predicting what's going to happen," I warned Raymond, and he just grinned. And I abruptly realized his wild enjoyment of this.

Monty arrived in a pickup truck driven by a younger man of about fifty. I stood at the top of the stairs, clutching the railing and hoping the ghost wouldn't bring the whole house down on us when Monty stepped in the door. I saw the old man hesitate on the doorstep, and the atmosphere in the house swelled with bitter anticipation. A few of my coworkers exchanged glances. Some people can feel those shifts in mood in a haunting. Others scoff until there's a physical manifestation. A few times, I've taken pleasure in seeing disbelievers suddenly confronted with shuddering lights or fluttering curtains. But I'd never encountered a manifestation as strong as this one, and all I felt was dread.

In the room below, Raymond kept the show on track and on schedule. Introductions and handshakes were followed by non-disclosure agreements and releases to sign, makeup, microphones, and last-minute discussions of shots, angles, lighting, and all the other details. Monty had been a big man, but now he was bent over a potbelly. And a little deaf, perhaps. I heard Raymond explain to him three times why he had to go back outside and be filmed arriving at the house.

And all the while I waited upstairs with a simmering ghost. I could tell when they started filming. Raymond had decided that the lead-in to the story would happen outside and then move into the house. The cast was recapping the finding of the necklace and the mysterious note. I could only catch a few words of what the old man was saying. Politically correct he was not. "My dear old Jenny . . . a bit simple but a sweet woman . . . many happy years here . . . a diamond cross my grandmother wore on her wedding day, so . . ." I listened to them move through the house below and heard snatches of his version of life there. "Jenny wanted children . . . I warned her about that little tramp . . . a pain in the ass. Jenny always said . . . stole my grandmother's necklace . . . no morals, sleeping around . . . pregnant . . . that girl's suicide just broke my Jenny's heart and . . ."

Liar. Liar, liar, liar! You killed her. You broke her heart when you told her I'd committed suicide! It wasn't true!

Some of the crew were backing up the stairs toward me, microphones and cameras and lights preceding the procession of Monty and the cast. Only one of my coworkers seemed as on edge as I was. One of the others was a bit nervous, and two others were absolutely immune to the ghost. I was sweating, and the salt of it stung in last night's cuts. One of the interns, Jerry, abruptly whispered, "So the foster kid committed suicide because she was pregnant?"

I wasn't! I didn't commit suicide!

"Be calm!" I begged her. Jerry gave me an offended look. Monty and Bert and Giselle were reaching the landing.

Keep your promise!

I held myself in stillness.

One of the camera crew was taking the steps backward, trying to catch Monty's every expression as he ascended the stairs of his old home. I retreated into the bathroom to make more room. I had no set task. Perhaps Raymond had stationed me there thinking I could keep the ghost under control. I knew better. I also knew of Bert's plan. Monty would be shown the necklace in its dusty hiding place. Raymond was hoping for an extreme reaction shot.

I was fearing the same thing. When I saw that Grandma Chris and Sweetie were following them, my stress skyrocketed. Don't hurt anyone, I mentally begged the ghost, and wondered if she were aware of my thoughts. I felt the ghost's energy surging and falling in waves, bolstered by the heightened emotions of everyone there.

On the landing, Monty hesitated. He glanced first toward Jenny's sewing room. As he swung his gaze to Laura's room, our eyes briefly met. I didn't like his eyes. They were a gray paler than his side-combed hair. His mouth turned down at the corners like a fish. He glared at me standing in the bathroom, and his scowl deepened as he looked into Laura's stripped room.

"Lead on, Girly," he said to Giselle, and did not even notice how she bristled. Cameras and cast entered the room and I stepped onto the landing to peer after them, my curiosity outweighing my common sense. Giselle had recovered her aplomb. I wondered if they would remove the "Girly" in the final cut. She reminded me of Vanna White as she waved a slow and graceful hand to indicate the hole where the necklace had been found. The roaring in my ears drowned out what she was saying. Bert took an empty jewelry case out of his carpenter's belt pouch and presented it to Monty. The old man's eyes were watering and his hands shook as he reached into the opening. He seized the chain and drew the pendant into view, but the chain held taut. I watched the ghost's face, her features shifting and reforming as she fought to keep him from taking it. He pulled harder. Abruptly Laura released it, and the jewelry flew from his hand and fell to the floor.

The ghost hadn't trusted my promise. Defying all laws of physics, the fallen necklace slid across the floor and out onto the landing right in front of me. Did Laura urge me? Perhaps. I kept my promise. I tried to make it look accidental as I swept the necklace with my foot into the other bedroom. Monty gave an old man's protesting cry and Giselle gave a furious shout. They bumped shoulders, jammed in the door, and nearly knocked me over as they charged after the jewelry. Cameras and lights tracked after them, with Bert trying to push his way back into the frame. Monty had gone to one knee inside Jenny's sewing room and was trying to pick up the necklace chain between finger and thumb. Giselle had hold of the cross. It wasn't budging off the floor. I saw Laura's ghostly hand settle on Giselle's shoulder and squeeze.

Giselle's expression was almost comical as she swiveled her head to see who was shoving her. When she saw no one, her eyes widened to manga-size. She shot to her feet, crying "There *is* a ghost here!" and a moment later she was pushing past the retreating camera to get out of the room. Monty remained where he was. Laura stood over him, a ghostly foot planted on the chain of the necklace.

Tell her you're sorry!

Did Monty hear her angry command as clearly as I did? He seemed unmoved. I glanced at the rest of the cast and crew. Raymond's dark eyes were huge and his teeth were bared in terror, but he wasn't fleeing. Even Bert had lifted both hands to cover his mouth. But Monty heard and felt nothing. He was a sour old man, down on all fours and digging at the necklace like a dog after a bone.

I had not entered the room, and everyone except Raymond, our camera operator, and Bert had retreated from the deepening cold and stillness. Dimly I heard Giselle wailing from downstairs. "It was so empty, so cold! Bert, where are you, I need you! It was so full of nothing!!" I wondered if anyone was capturing that on film. Raymond remained on the landing, his hands on the shoulders of the girl holding the camera steady, softly whispering instructions in her ear.

"Tell Jenny you're sorry!" Raymond suddenly said aloud.

"What?" Monty's voice was cracked and irritated. "*Me* sorry? Sorry for what? It was that little whore who broke her heart. Got herself knocked up and slashed her wrists in the closet while Jenny was out doing the shopping! I knew she was going to do something stupid. I kicked that door down, trying to get in there to save her! But I was too late! Little slut was just sitting there, the blood going everywhere!"

I didn't! I knew Jenny was out of the house and I heard him downstairs, muttering. I was in the closet. I was cutting myself. That's true. But just, just shallow slashes. Like I'd done before. But . . . then he came up the stairs, and when he kicked in the door, the razor went into my wrist! Jenny, I didn't commit suicide. I didn't!

All the cold in the room was coalescing into a gray old woman. Gray hair, gray face, gray housedress and apron more fitting to the fifties than the eighties. I glanced at Raymond. He was seeing her. I took a step closer to look in the camera monitor; the ghosts were just light flares in the screen. The camera girl was shaking her head and trying to back away; Raymond lifted the camera from her hands and she fled. Raymond held the camera on Monty's face. "Say you're sorry," he mouthed at the man.

Instead, Monty looked down at the necklace. "Well, this ain't it! You all played me for a fool, didn't you!" He got ponderously to his feet. He kicked at the necklace. Corroded links and cheap rhinestones in rusty settings scattered. "You got me here with a trick! You want me to say I'm sorry? Well, I'm not. They weren't too bright, either of them. Should be able to tell a woman what you want and get that out of her. That's how it's supposed to be. Just like with a dog. But Jenny never did learn, and that little slut just taught her more bad ways. Tried to shame me, the both of them! I was better off the day both of them were gone! I wasn't sorry then and I'm not sorry now!"

The old woman's faded lips moved and her thoughts flooded me. *I don't care, Monty. I don't care that you're not sorry. Did you think I'd died of a broken heart, you pathetic old man? I lived through your beatings, didn't I? I lived through your not caring. No. I died of not caring anymore. Of not having anyone to care about anymore. I grew up believing that was what a woman did: she cared for people. Lord knows I tried to keep caring about you; I tried to keep my vows. But when you hit her, I stopped caring about you. And when Laura killed herself, there was no one left to care for. No one to live for.* She swung her gaze from Monty to Laura.

Monty wasn't hearing her. I doubted he'd ever heard her. He was leaving, his face set in a cold scowl. He shouldered past Raymond. Raymond let the camera wander over the scattered bits of cold glitter on the floor, and then he turned it on Monty's back and followed him down the stairs.

I remained rooted where I was.

Laura's ghost stepped toward Jenny, her open hands reaching out in a plea. I saw them then, the familiar parallel cutting scars, all up and down both her inner arms. She'd been a dedicated cutter. But the only one that bled in bright splashes that vanished before they touched the floor was the deep slice at one wrist.

The necklace. That was what had held Laura in that room, unable to penetrate Jenny's wall of cold. A promise made and not kept. Thoughts poured from Laura.

I didn't commit suicide. I didn't, Jenny! I listened to you, I threw my cigarettes away that very night, and I stopped smoking pot with Jeremy and Cliff, and I didn't even taste a beer after that! I didn't. But when I felt really bad, I would cut myself still. Just a little bit.

And when it was awful here, when Monty was yelling at you or when I was hating myself for hiding while you took it for me, I could cut myself! Jenny, I swear it wasn't suicide. I murdered myself but it wasn't suicide! He was throwing things downstairs, and there was a big crash when he kicked the door in and the razor slipped. It was dark–I was hiding from him in the closet. I didn't even know I'd done it until he jerked the door open and there was so much blood! Oh, Jenny, I tried to keep my promise! I tried!

The air in the room shuddered. I wanted to back away. I couldn't. The shuddering became a trembling. Downstairs, Raymond shouted, "Quake! Stand in a doorway or get outside!"

But it was no quake. The floor shivered and the silver chain and the scattered rhinestones trembled and crept across the floor. A rush of warmth suddenly suffused the gray woman, and for an instant, I saw her as she had been, her washed-out blue eyes and the faded pink ruffles on her white apron. At her feet, a silver chain gleamed and a silver cross glittered. She opened her arms. *He said it was my fault. That if I'd watched you better it wouldn't have happened, that you killed yourself out of shame!*

No. It was an accident! A stupid accident. Can you forgive me? Laura was still standing back from her.

Forgive you? I can finally forgive myself.

I've never seen the light that some people talk about. I'd never seen ghosts do what those two did. They embraced, Jenny and Laura. They didn't go toward the light; they were the light. They vanished into each other, and then they were gone.

Downstairs, doors were slamming and people were shouting. Raymond's firm voice rose over all of them. "Everyone calm down. It's nothing we can't fix in post-production!"

I heard Giselle's shrill laugh that shattered into short hysterical shrieks.

Weak sunbeams came in through the dirty windows of Jenny's room. The diamonds sparkled in its light and then calmed. I walked into the room, empty in an ordinary dusty way. I knelt by the necklace.

When I picked it up, it was warm in my hand, as if someone had just taken it off and given it to me. I slipped the chain over my head and slid the cross down inside my shirt. Did the thought come from them, or had they left it inside my mind? *Second chance. Stop hurting yourself.*

Tad Williams

THIS HAS BEEN A DIFFICULT YEAR FOR ME FOR SHORT STORY WRITING (for various boring reasons), but I very much wanted to contribute something to this *Unfettered*, both to keep up the connection to an excellent series of anthologies and to support Shawn Speakman.

So we had the idea to use part of my new Osten Ard book as a contribution, since the anthology will come out before publication of the novel and thus will be new to both readers who know my work and those who don't.

You don't need to know too much about the books to understand this excerpt, but here's a brief overview:

Utuk'ku, queen of the Norns (they call themselves "Hikeda'ya"), has awakened after a decades-long sleep and is once more waging war against the mortals and her Sithi relatives.

The two main characters featured in this chapter are Derra, also known as Tzoja (her Norn name), who is the long-lost daughter of Josua and Vorzehva, two of the main protagonists in the first Osten Ard series—Memory, Sorrow, and Thorn—and Viyeki, a Norn noble who became Tzoja's lover and the father of her daughter, Nezeru, one of the queen's most accomplished soldiers. But her father, Viyeki, unlike most Norns, has doubts about the wisdom of his deathless ruler Queen Utuk'ku's destructive hatred of the mortals.

The Norns are one of two main groups of immortals, Sithi and Norns, who once ruled Osten Ard, and who are now seeking revenge against both their Sithi kin and the mortals who have displaced both groups. There is also a third group of immortals, the Tinukeda'ya, or Changelings, who at one time were more or less slaves to the Norns and Sithi. They are different from both the mortals and the immortals, and their history is not entirely clear (at this point of the story, anyway), but unlike the Sithi and Norns, they come in many sizes and shapes.

Seem complicated? It won't when you're reading. A lot of this is expanded upon in the excerpt itself. And even if it's all new to you, you shouldn't have any problem getting the flavor of Osten Ard, a place I've been writing about so long I know it better than many of the places I've actually lived.

I hope you enjoy this taste of *Empire of Grass,* to be published in May of 2019.

Tad Williams

THE HIDDEN

Tad Williams

"Do you know how your father lost his hand, Derra?" her mother had once asked, with the tone of someone about to reveal an important secret. She often said things like that, suddenly and out of nowhere, as though she were answering angry voices only she could hear.

"In a war," Derra—as she had then been called—answered. "He said it happened a long time ago, before he met you."

"He lost it for a woman," Vorzheva continued, as if her daughter had not spoken. "A woman he still loves, a woman he keeps in his heart like a treasure."

"What a ridiculous thing to tell a child," her father said, laughing, but his face looked a little angry. "I was fighting to protect my brother's wife. Our caravan was attacked and she was killed, so it is a sad thing to talk about. Killed by Thrithings-men, as a matter of fact—your mother's people."

Her mother turned on him. "Not my clan! They fought on your father's side!"

Derra had stopped paying attention: she had heard it before.

She had already begged her father for the story until he'd told her. She couldn't remember how old she'd been when she had first noticed that other men were not like her father, that most of them had two hands, but from that moment she had burned to know the story. Her brother Deornoth, strangely, had not, and had walked away when her father began to explain.

But Deornoth had always been that way. He did not like bloodshed, not even in stories. Once when they were smaller he had hit Sagra, a boy who lived near their parents' inn, and bloodied the child's nose. Deornoth had run home and hidden under his blanket, refusing to come out even when Sagra himself came by later in the evening to ask him out to play.

But Derra had always loved stories. She didn't care that her father had only one hand, or that he had once been a prince but had decided not to be—a story her mother told often, sometimes as evidence of his love for her, sometimes as evidence of the reverse, especially when she was feeling oppressed by what she called "this wretched-smelling, watery place!"—Kwanitupul, on the edge of the Wran.

It seemed strange to think about those days, especially when she could not have been farther away from them—not in plain distance or years. The lengthy, winding road that had led her to this place in the blackness beneath the great mountain was only bits of separated memory now, like beads on a necklace.

When their father had not returned her mother had despaired, and after months of rage and recriminations, at last decided to take Derra and Deornoth north—although with what plan she never told them. She had sold Pelippa's Bowl and its unexalted reputation for very little—even Derra, despite being only ten years, had known they were being cheated by the fat merchant—then set out with all their remaining goods on a single cart. But they had been captured on the road by Thrithings-men, who had been mostly interested in Vorzheva's purse, but heard her muttering under her breath in her original tongue, which was also theirs. Only a few days later the entire family, minus the proceeds from selling the inn, of course, had been delivered to Vorzheva's horrible father, Thane Fikolmij, ruler over much of the High Thrithings. From that point everything had gone from merely bad to dreadful. Her brother Deornoth was sent away to live with another clan—he did not even get to say goodbye. And Derra and her mother became no better than slaves to Fikolmij, laboring from dawn to dusk and beyond with the other women in her grandfather's camp.

Derra might have been able to put up with even such a dire change in fortune, but with each day after Deornoth had been taken away, her mother seemed to lose life. Vorzheva's eyes became dark-circled and her face gaunt—she could barely force herself to eat. She even lost interest in Derra and began to avoid her. Derra's kindly Aunt Hyara, the only good thing that had happened to her since her father vanished, tried to tell her that Vorzheva was not angry at her, but that each time she looked at her daughter, she saw the absent twin as well, her son, and it broke her heart.

"She will come back to you," Hyara had said. "Give her time."

But time had been the one thing Derra had not been able to give. Every day felt like being buried alive. She was not even allowed to mix with the other children—her grandfather deemed her too old for play when there was work to be done.

And worse, her grandfather had begun to notice her in other ways, ways Derra could not talk about with her mother, who hardly spoke to her at all, or even with Aunt Hyara. And when the old man's furtive squeezing and pinching and poking began to keep her from sleeping at night because she was terrified he would come to her bed, she decided she would run away from the camp, from the wagons, from her monstrous grandfather and her silent, brooding mother, who acted as though she had lost both children and not just one . . .

Tzoja stopped, startled by a noise from the underground lake. She folded the glowing sphere called a *ni'yo* deeper into her hand, until it showed as only a faint red glow in the web of her finger and thumb, then stood in silence, listening. She had heard a splash. Perhaps only a fish, but she had been so deep in memory that she hadn't realized how close she had wandered to the shore of the underground lake. As far as she knew, there were no other people in any of the other lakefront dwellings, because they mostly belonged to rich nobles who only made the long journey out from the heart of the city during festivals. But back in the Enduya clan house, Viyeki's wife Khimabu must have realized by now that Tzoja had fled—so she could not afford to be noticed even by some gardener or servant preparing for the arrival of a rich master, anyone who might mention to his masters that he had seen a mortal woman near the lake.

And what if it were something else entirely? Things moved down here in the dark tunnels that even Viyeki avoided talking about, and he was magister of the order that had excavated these depths.

She crouched in place. With her light-sphere hidden, the only glow came from the strange shining worms dangling above the lake on strands of luminous silk. She had been thinking of the old days, her old life, and for a moment she saw the glowing creatures as something else, as stars in the broad sky that she had not seen in so many years.

The Thrithings, she thought, *and Erkynland, and last in Rimmersgard, with Roskva and the Astalines. Sky as far as I could see in all directions, the mountains so far away they were only shadows . . .*

Something splashed again, making her heart speed, but now she was almost certain a sound so small must come from a fish or a frog, and she felt her fear ease. She knew she might have to start thinking about catching fish soon: the food she had brought from the clan-house pantry would not last too much longer. She had paced herself as carefully as she could, though it was difficult to know how much time was passing in a dark house in a cavern far beneath the ground, where she dared not even light a fire for fear of someone seeing it. In fact, that was the reason she had begun her daily walks around the lake to a rich manor house some distance away. By its outer decorations and the spiral on the door, the house seemed to belong to somebody well-placed in the Order of Song. She would never have dared to cross the threshold of such a place, but whoever owned the house had placed a very fine water clock in a grotto on the outer grounds of the property. The clock was a mysterious arrangement of gears and troughs and several stone jars of water, but she could mark by the movement of the decorated dial in the center of one of the largest gears how the face of the moon was changing in the sky above the mountain, on the far side of an incomprehensible weight of stone.

Still, the noise had unnerved her, and she decided to give up this day's confirmatory visit to the water clock and turn back.

It's the darkness, she told herself as she walked back toward the festival house, shielding the sphere in her hand so that only the tiniest needles of light illuminated her track. She thought she had learned all its tricks and cruelties while living in Nakkiga, but as bad as things had been in the gloomy Hikeda'ya city, this was much worse. Day after day, alone in a pitch-black house in a pitch-black cavern, with only the ghost light of the worms for illumination, and those to be seen only once a day during her walk around the lake, she was beginning to feel as though she were caught in some terrible dream from which she could not awake.

But I can do it. I must. She had to stay alive until Viyeki returned. If she was caught, Khimabu would see that she was killed. But even that meant nothing to Tzoja compared to the true horror. Khimabu would not be satisfied with destroying Tzoja alone, but would want herself rid of Nezeru as well, her husband's half-mortal bastard.

Nezeru, her Nezeru, so strange and so beautiful. Like a fierce little animal from the very first moment she had emerged into the world. Tzoja had never pretended to understand her child, but that had never prevented her helpless love.

I will not let that witch harm my daughter, Tzoja thought as she made her way as quietly as she could up from the main path and through the modest grounds of Viyeki's house, and for a moment a rush of anger dissolved all her fears. *I will die with my fingernails in her eyes and my teeth in her throat if I have to.*

She was so caught up in imagining it that she did not stop to listen at the door she liked to use, which opened on the back gardens. Instead she was halfway down the hall before she heard the noises coming from the kitchen.

Whispers.

She stopped so quickly she almost fell down. A thousand ideas rushed into her head at once—it was the Hamakha Guard, looking for her, or robbers who would kill her before despoiling Viyeki's house, or ghastly shades out of the depths. But was it really whispering, or was it something else? She paused again, listening with fast-beating heart to the wordless sounds, squeaking, chittering, and the rattle of small things being pushed across the kitchen's stony floors.

Rats! Oh, Usires and all the other gods, what if they've found my food?

Tzoja felt around just inside the door until she discovered one of Viyeki's walking sticks, then edged down the corridor, sliding her feet across the polished floors to make as little noise as possible. The closer she got to the kitchen, the more clearly she could hear the strange sounds; for a moment she almost thought she heard a cadence to them, like speech.

She lifted the stick high, then pushed open the kitchen door and lifted the *ni'yo.* A slight pressure of her fingers made it flare into brightness and paint the entire scene in an instant.

Eyes. Eyes and grotesque shapes, staring at her—a waking nightmare.

Tzoja gasped and almost dropped the sphere. The figures in front of her suddenly burst into life and went squealing and hissing as they scattered in all directions to escape the sudden light. She saw eyes, hands, limbs, but all in a mere moment before their owners scuttled into the dark corners of the kitchen or past her into the hallway, so that she could not immediately make sense of what she had seen.

They were not rats, that was dreadfully clear: she had seen faces. Mortals like Tzoja? No, they had not been like her. Hikeda'ya? No, they had not been like the immortals either. In that panicky instant she could not even think of a prayer, though she sorely wished to make one.

She had fallen backward at the first shock. With her fingers loosened, the light of the sphere began to die. All around her she could hear clatter and scratching as its glow faded, then she was surrounded by darkness again and in another moment, by silence as well.

Monsters, was her first real thought, remembering the mad things the flare of light had revealed. Small monsters, perhaps, but what else could you call them? She remembered one like a naked child with one limb far longer than others, others with no real limbs at all, and fat, toadlike creatures with human skin and bulging but still human eyes. Already the details were sliding from her memory—it had all been too swift, too violently strange, too unexpected.

What could they be? Why did those horrors come here? I have lost my sanctuary. Her thoughts were sliding like an avalanche of stones. Monsters, and they were still all around her! She straightened up, half-certain she would feel hands grabbing at her ankles at any moment, then squeezed and rubbed the sphere until its full radiance burst forth again, but in its yellowy light the kitchen was empty and silent.

No, not silent, she realized after a moment. Beside her own hitching, terrified breath, she could hear another noise, a soft, wordless moan from deeper in the large kitchen. What were they? She was grateful that they seemed as startled and frightened as she was, but she did not trust it would last.

I should leave this place this very moment, she told herself. *Whatever these things are, the house is no longer safe. It certainly isn't secret.* But she had spent days learning the house's plan by darkness, had found hiding places for all her belongings so that nobody arriving suddenly would know she was here unless they actually caught her. Where would she go if she left? To another house beside the lake, probably just as full of hairless cavern rats or whatever those ghastly things had been? Another festival house that, unlike Viyeki's, might be occupied at any time?

She heard a noise coming from the brick oven—a strange, thin sound like an animal gasping for breath or a baby beginning to cry. It did not sound like anything large, so she felt around for the walking stick she had dropped, then slowly and quietly got to her feet. The kitchen was long—even during the short times the house was occupied, her master's wife, Khimabu, brought a large contingent of servants to wait on the Magister and his guests, so the kitchen had to provide for them as well. She made her way across the polished flagstones in darkness, marveling at how long it took her to cross it. As she drew closer to whatever made the noise, her foot crunched down on something and the muffled whimpering abruptly stopped. After the initial shock and a stifled scream, Tzoja reached down hesitantly and discovered what she had trod on—a heel of bread. She squeezed hard on the light-sphere.

Whatever had been making the hitching noise was now silent. The heel of bread was the largest piece of food on the floor; the others were little more than crumbs and a few gnawed ends. With a sudden upswelling of horror and despair, she ran back across the kitchen, heedless now of the light that would be visible to anyone outside the house nearby, and threw open the chest in which she had hidden her supply of bread, several large loaves, enough to last her for weeks.

Gone. All gone. Fragments of dried fruit and sausage among the crumbs and gnawed crusts confirmed what she already feared, but she doggedly went and dragged out the covered basket where those things had been kept and discovered that all but a single waxwing sausage and a few tiny morsels of cheese were gone.

It was all Tzoja could do not to let out a howl of rage and misery. All her stores, so carefully obtained and hidden, food that should have lasted her until Sky-Singer's Moon, or even Tortoise, now gone.

She would have to go back into Nakkiga or risk starvation.

Her fury rose again. She swung the *ni'iyo* around the wide kitchen until its light fell on the round bread oven. Whatever hid inside began making soft, terrified sounds again. Angry, frightened, gripped by feelings she couldn't even name, Tzoja reached down and shoved the ball of light close to the oven door as she leaned forward, careful not to get too close in case whatever was hiding in there had claws.

An infant stared back at her from the oven's depths. It was not human, not Hikeda'ya, but not impossibly far from either. A naked, big-eyed infant with a swollen belly, no mouth between its nose and receding chin, and a slit throat—a horrible slash of red across the center of its neck.

Tzoja recoiled in horror and almost fell again. The thing in the oven gave a soft, startled shriek, but did not try to escape. Her heart beating so hard she was dizzy, she leaned toward the opening again. Huge eyes stared back at her, dark as lumps of coal.

It wasn't a wound across its neck at all, she saw now with a mixture of disgust and astonishment, but a mouth, which for some unfathomable reason opened out of its neck instead of its face. For a moment, everything she had ever heard about demons and monsters came back to her, from her mother's tales of unnatural grassland fiends to Valada Roskva's warnings about restless things that watched the living from beyond the veil of death. But then the unnatural mouth of the thing in the oven pressed together in a wrinkled pucker before opening again to emit a wail of terror, and despite her fear, she became a mother again.

"Here now," she said, suddenly realizing that the noise might be a bigger danger to her than even the strange little creature itself. *"Hush. Stop that."* Without noticing, she had slipped back into the tongue of her own childhood, her mother's words straight from the grasslands. *"Hush. The Night Eater will hear."*

And then, as if to prove her words, Tzoja heard a strange, uneven noise in the great hallway beyond the kitchen—*thump-drag, thump-drag, thump-drag.* Whatever was making the footsteps was no tiny monstrosity like the oven-beast, but sounded larger than any mortal or Hikeda'ya.

Again gripped by terror, Tzoja only remembered the other door out of the kitchen when the hallway door thumped open. She lifted her light even as she shrank back. A huge, two-headed shape that could have only leaped out of nightmare or madness swayed in the doorway. It threw out its misshapen hands and let out a rumbling noise of rage as it lurched toward her.

The sphere dropped from her nerveless fingers. For a moment

the falling light seemed to make everything leap into the air, then it struck the ground and went out.

She clambered after it, feeling with both hands, and when she found it she lifted it and held it before her like a weapon, then squeezed it into shining life. A huge shape loomed above her but fell back, groaning as though the light were painful as fire. As the thing wiped frantically at its eyes with the back of a massive forearm, she pushed herself back out of the reach of those huge arms. The creature's vast face turned toward her, eyes tightly shut. It was as bizarre and misshapen as a grassland shaman's demon mask, the mouth slack, the eyes hurt and angry but as uncomprehending as the lowest animal.

"Do not fear," the monster said in oddly accented Hikeda'yasao, but as if to prove that terrible face truly was a mask, the slack lips did not move in time with the words. They did not move at all. "We do not harm you."

Now she finally saw the second head that she had glimpsed in the doorway, as large as the first but canted at a strange angle and thus slightly hidden from her at first. This head, despite being nearly as grotesque as the other, hairless and with round, slightly crooked eyes, seemed actually to be watching her with interest, and when the voice came again the lips moved in time with it: it was this head that had spoken before, not the first one. "Please do not make the light bright again," it said. "That hurts the eyes, mine and Dasa's both."

She had just been about to make the sphere glare as powerfully as she could, but the speaker's tone was reasonable, almost apologetic, so she hesitated. She pushed herself back a little farther, and only then did she see that what had come through the kitchen doorway was not one creature with two heads, but two creatures, one carried by the other. The head that spoke lolled atop a shrunken, almost infantile body whose legs ended in stumps just where the knees should have been. This nodding oddity was curled in the crook of a powerful arm that belonged to a carry-man, one of the nearly mindless Tinukeda'ya bred for servitude, but this carry-man had a badly withered leg, and she now understood the step-and-drag sound that had announced its arrival.

But there was no such thing anywhere in Nakkiga as a crippled carry-man, let alone one that was only a head on a useless body. The Hikeda'ya would never allow such malformed creatures to live. Even Viyeki, the kindest of the race she had met, would have had them dispatched in an instant.

"Who are you? *What* are you?" she demanded, fear rising again.

"Naya Nos am I," said the malformed infant. "This is my brother-in-claim, Dasa. He does not speak." The swollen baby-face looked grave. "What we are is Hidden Ones—but that is not something to concern you. Our young ones stole from you. We are sorry, but they have gone long without food, and it has been a poor season for both gathering and gifting. We will do our best to make good what they took from you."

The day's events had been so shocking that Tzoja could only watch in stunned silence as the infant-sized creature called out to the remaining Hidden, who slid out of the oven and other hiding places, eyes wide with fear, then crawled past her as swiftly as they could, as though Tzoja were a sleeping predator instead of the victim of their raid. They followed their rescuers out of the festival house and in moments had vanished into the darkness. She pushed the door closed behind them, then stumbled back to the kitchen to pick up the few crumbs that remained, weeping silently as she pressed the salvaged remnants into a single lump that would be that night's supper, and perhaps her last meal for a long time.

Nonao, the secretary who had replaced poor Yemon after his execution, was unobtrusive even by the exacting standards of the Hikeda'ya, but not so much that he escaped Viyeki's notice as he stood waiting outside the simple, slanted wall of fabric that was the magister's tent. Viyeki did not look up at him or acknowledge him in any way, but continued to read his much-handled copy of *The Five Fingers of the Queen's Hand* with what must have seemed like great concentration. At last even Nonao's patience began to stretch beyond the fraying point, and the secretary made a small movement, a silent shift of weight from one foot to the other.

Viyeki looked at him just long enough to make certain Nonao saw him, then dropped his eyes to the book again. "What do you want?"

"This worthless servant begs your pardon, High Magister, but the prince-templar has arrived."

"Ah." He kept his eyes on the words, though he was not truly very much interested in them. Like all in his caste, he had committed it to memory long before he reached adulthood.

"Do you not wish to greet him, High Magister?"

"Of course! That is why I have returned to the words of venerated Xohabi. To remind myself of what is expected, what is right." He held the book up as though Nonao might not have seen it before. "You have read the *Five Fingers?*"

"Of course, Master!"

"So full of wisdom. So full of help for every situation." Viyeki began to read. "'*The Five Fingers are the tools the Queen, the Mother of the People, uses to feed and shelter and protect her people. Without a knowledge of these tools and how they are used, without an energetic determination to act for the good of all the People, a noble can only hinder, not help, the Queen in her great work.*' You agree of course, Nonao?"

"Of course, Master. They are the words I live by, and which are always uppermost in my thoughts as I strive to serve you and the Mother of All."

"Good, good." He ignored Nonao's increasing anxiousness. "How wise was great Xohabi! Give your ear to this, Nonao-*tza*—the simplicity entrances us still, all these Great Years later! *'Loyalty to the People is the first finger. Without dedication to your own kind, you are no better than a solitary witiko'ya in the wilderness, hunting without a pack, dying alone of starvation.'* So true! Who would reject his own people? And what else should the lot of such a fool or traitor be, but death?"

"Yes, Master."

"And how much joy I get from revisiting these words, no matter how often I have read them before. Loyalty to the race! Loyalty to the city! Loyalty to the order and, of course, loyalty to our queen and the Garden that birthed us . . . !" He shook his head in mock-wonder. "I have heard it said that in this one slender volume is written every word needed for a good life. I shall never tire of it."

Nonao was wringing his hands together, too anxious now even to hide it. "No one reveres Xohabi—or *you*—more greatly than I do, Master, and please forgive my unpardonable interruption . . ."

Viyeki decided he had tormented his servant long enough. He did not dislike Nonao personally, but he knew beyond doubt that the new secretary was giving information to the relatives of Viyeki's wife and doubtless to others as well. It would have been virtually impossible to find someone utterly honorable and incorruptible to fill the position—there were very few such creatures to be found in Nakkiga, and none of them had the talent or intelligence to do a good job with anything more challenging than spreading oil on a slice of *puja* bread—so he was content with a secretary he knew from the start not to trust.

But my old master Yaarike would have warned me not to treat him too badly. Better a casual enemy than a determined one. And if I make too much sport with The Five Fingers, *he'll report that to the listening ears as well.* The book was an object of near-religious veneration among the noble classes, although Viyeki had no doubt that many of its most noisy proponents were no more inspired by Xohabi's legendary fawning than Viyeki was.

So we make liars of ourselves, and by doing so, prove Xohabi a liar also.

It was a new thought, and one that brought him a pang of what felt like sudden fright. Was he losing his mind, that such heretical thoughts came to him so easily these days?

Outside, the Sacrifices were lined up at one end of the camp in martial rigor, along with Viyeki's Builders and the rest of the company, as the prince-templar's party made its way up to the hilltop beneath the deep blue of a clear night. All expression absent from his face except serene satisfaction—the only proper look for a high noble in the presence of the very highest noble family, the queen's—Viyeki observed that the prince-templar was dressed in the full panoply of his sacred station, robed in white with yellow ornamentation, including a ceremonial hood that recalled the Gatherers' hats from the long-lost Garden. His Serene Highness Pratiki wore his white hair long and unadorned. His skin was so pale it almost seemed to glow from within, like the wax of a burning candle, but the prince-templar's eyes, though calm and almost sorrowful in appearance, watched everything carefully. He was of the queen's Hamakha clan, but of much more recent generation than most of the queen's most trusted servitors, only a little older than Viyeki himself. He had only met the prince-templar a few times—before Viyeki had become a high magister their circles of acquaintanceship had barely intersected, and even afterward they seldom frequented the same gatherings—but he had heard nothing to make him think badly of Pratiki. Still, the princeling seemed to be here in the mortal lands to lend some kind of official support for this ill-considered invasion, so Viyeki knew he would have to treat him with gracious caution.

Surprisingly for one of his ruling clan, Pratiki had not brought much in the way of an entourage, just a hand of Hamakha Dragon Guards and a few clerics, nor did he unduly drag out the welcoming ceremony. Viyeki went first, greeting Pratiki with all due respect but avoiding flowery speech, which he had heard the prince-templar did not like. That bit of gossip seemed to be true, as Pratiki then watched with little enthusiasm while General Kikiti, lean and tall as a stork, made lengthy protestations of loyalty to the queen and Clan Hamakha, then was followed by Sogeyu and her Order of Song minions welcoming him with all their own ancient and ornate formulas. When they had finished, Pratiki said, "I am certain there is more important work to be done than seeing to the comfort of a mere religious official, but I thank you on behalf of the Mother of us all. You may all go now. My servants will see that I am housed. Oh, and High Magister Viyeki, will you grant me the courtesy of a short audience?"

This was intriguing if a tiny bit worrying. Viyeki waited as the prince-templar's tent was erected—it had more sides than Viyeki's own simple lean-to, but was otherwise quite spare and unassuming—then Pratiki sent his clerics away.

"How goes the queen's task?" he asked Viyeki when they were alone in the tent.

"I have little progress to report, Prince-Templar." Viyeki framed his words carefully. "The time for my Builders to do their part has not yet come. Although of course I do my best every hour and every day to serve the Mother of All."

General Kikiti had told Viyeki that they would be excavating the tomb of legendary Ruyan Ve himself, hidden for years beneath the fortress that mortals called Naglimund. Naglimund stood only a short distance away across the valley, but at the moment, several thousand mortals still occupied that fortress, many of them well-armed soldiers. Viyeki did not know what exactly such a task would entail, and also could not imagine any way, short of open warfare, that the tomb could be reached, but those were not the kind of questions he was going to ask a lord of the high Hamakha.

"Of course," said Pratiki with what almost seemed the hint of a smile. "I did not mean to suggest you should have finished it already, High Magister. I know you are a loyal supporter of the queen. You are Clan Enduya yourself, as I remember. An old and worthy family with a long record of service to the throne."

Viyeki could not help wondering whether some other meaning swam beneath the prince-templar's words, but said only, "You are kind, Serenity."

"We will be thrown together frequently," said the prince-templar. "I know you will serve the queen with wisdom and courage. I wished only to say to you that I am aware sometimes it is difficult to reconcile the needs and wants of different Orders, and that this may be one such time. Please do not hesitate to come to me if you need assistance or advice."

"I will think of you as though you were the queen herself, gifting me with time and attention I could never deserve."

Pratiki nodded, but did not seem entirely satisfied by the answer. For his own part, Viyeki could only wonder why a member of the queen's own family was here in the middle of nowhere, on the eve of a new war against the mortals. And what could the Mother of All want with a long-dead Tinukeda'ya, even such a famous one as Ruyan the Navigator?

He bowed to an appropriate depth before the prince-templar. "All praise to the queen, all praise to her Hamakha Clan," he said.

Scott Sigler

"THROWDOWN" IS A SEQUEL TO THE STORY "VICTIM WITH A CAPITAL V," which appeared in *Unfettered II*. Both stories take place in a future North America, where an unknown event caused all metal to waste away into rust. In "Victim," a young woman named Lisa leaves an isolated mountain fortress where she had been training for a decade as a warrior, specializing in throwing glass knives. Now twenty, she wished to see the turn of the millennia in the big city of Frisco. On the night before the dawn of the year 4000, she ran into the very reason she'd fled to the mountains in the first place—the man who violated her when she was only ten years old.

As events spun out of her control, she killed that man, and is now wanted by both the Frisco law and from the dead man's vengeful son. Accompanied by two grown men, men hardened by long years of military service, Lisa must run to stay alive.

Scott Sigler

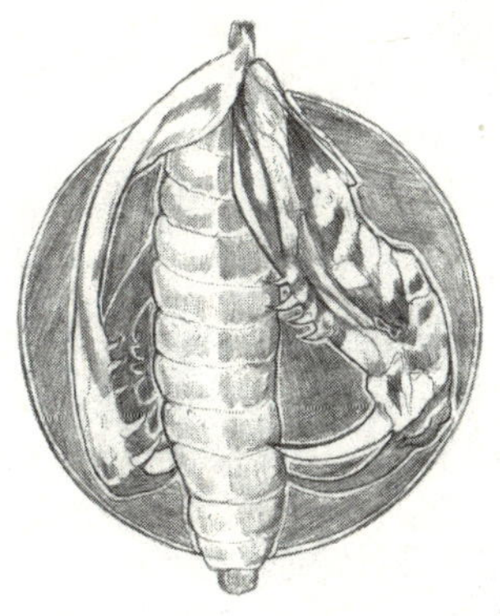

THROWDOWN

"Victim with a Capital V," Part II

Scott Sigler

On New Year's Eve, she killed a man in Frisco.

On New Year's Day—dawn of the first day of the new millennium, on the back of a mangy Morgan, sitting behind a man she barely knew—she ran.

The first day of the year 4000. This was not how Lisa had dreamed of spending it.

Jimmy turned his head, enough for her to see his right eye glancing back from under the rim of his cattleman's hat.

"How's your ass, Miss Lisa?"

It felt like it was about to fall off. Each *clomp* of horse hooves on the stony ground sent a dull shock into her bottom. She would have described the feeling as *numb,* but she'd been beaten numb before—if you still felt pain, you weren't numb. No saddle. They hadn't had time to steal a saddle, not that Lisa would have known how to ride in one.

"It hurts," Lisa said. "Are we going to take a break soon?"

Jimmy faced forward, giving her the same view she'd had for

the last eight or nine hours: his broad shoulders, covered by his dark gray duster, and the back of his tattered hat.

"We ain't stopping until Fish says we stop."

Fish. Lisa marveled at the dumb luck of it all. She'd left the Hovel, alone, walked for weeks, alone, to reach the big city. After only a few hours in town, she'd run into the Laughing Man—the very reason she'd fled *to* the Hovel a decade ago. Now the Laughing Man was dead, her survival seemed intertwined with two strange men, and one of those men—Fish—was making all the decisions.

Lisa wanted to go home.

She leaned right, looked past Jimmy. Fish was ten or so horse lengths ahead, atop a black-and-white painter. Fish's dark green duster seemed to merge with the early morning mist floating through the thin pines and scrub brush that flanked both sides of this thin path.

Fish and Jimmy had both been highwaymen. Or so they said. In truth, Lisa knew nothing about them, other than that after the incident at the bar, they'd stolen horses and rushed her out of town. Nothing around but the stony trail, scrub pines, and underbrush. If Fish and Jimmy tried anything with her, there was no one to hear, no one to help. Lisa was ready for that, though—her slivers were never far from her fingertips.

Jimmy knew firsthand how good Lisa was with them. So did Fish.

The Laughing Man's corpse was testament to her skill.

Lisa shivered, tried to push away the thought of that man, facedown on the saloon table, blood gushing out of his mouth to stain the wood, to spatter across the dirty floor.

She righted herself, adjusted her light hold on Jimmy's hips, her hands atop his gray duster. She didn't want to touch him at all—she didn't want to touch *anyone,* and didn't want anyone touching her—but he insisted she keep hold lest she fall off.

The mist found its way through her thick robe, seemed to creep along her skin and raise goosebumps like corpses rising from the grave.

"I'm cold," she said.

Jimmy's hat tipped forward, came back.

"Yup," he said. "So am I, Miss Lisa. And, yup, I'm hungry too, so just keep that one to yourself."

He didn't want to hear her complain anymore. She couldn't hold that against him—out of the three of them, only Jimmy was blameless. Lisa had killed the Laughing Man, not Jimmy, and if Fish hadn't insisted on following Lisa, she would have left the bar without hurting anyone.

Jimmy, it seemed, had been in the wrong place at the wrong time. And he'd been there because he'd chosen the wrong friend.

The first day of the New Year, of the new millennium. Lisa had hoped to spend it in Frisco, a place she had dreamed of visiting all her life. It had all gone south when she'd heard that laugh, the same laugh she'd heard a decade earlier, when it was right up against her ear, when she'd felt that man's breath on her cheek, her neck, in her hair.

Well, he wasn't laughing anymore. That was for sure.

She still wasn't sure if she'd meant to kill him or not. Her hands had just *moved*, as if they were wild animals that would not be tamed. She'd thrown a glass sliver twenty feet into his open, laughing mouth, killing him.

The Laughing Man's son had promised revenge. Fish and Jimmy hadn't wanted to wait around to see if the son could back up his claim or if the Frisco cops would arrest all three of them. The Laughing Man wore the clothes of a rich man—cops tended to side with people who had money, not a wandering Victim and two ex-highwaymen.

Jimmy had stolen two horses. No point in stealing three, since Lisa couldn't ride. They'd ridden to the Presidio, taken a ferry to Marin. The ferry had cost Lisa most of her money. Jimmy had paid half. Fish had even less money than he had teeth, and he didn't have many teeth.

From Marin, they'd started north, riding into the night. They'd rested the horses at the far edge of a ranch, grabbing a couple of hours of sleep themselves. Fish had warned of the massive pitters that lurked in the hills. The beasts would attack travelers, but tended to steer clear of places that had more people—he'd hoped the nearby ranch would be deterrent enough for the beasts. Nothing had attacked, so as far as Lisa knew, he'd been right.

Lisa hadn't seen a pitter in over a decade, but she knew them well. As a little girl, she'd seen a pair of them carry off her screaming little brother, yanking his body between them as they vanished over a hill.

The Morgan reached a dip, fell a little farther than expected; the jolt of landing went straight through Lisa's ass and into her spine.

"Don't we have to rest the horses again?"

Jimmy's hat tipped forward, came back to level.

"Soon," he said. "I rode this trail once. There's ranches not too far from here. We're better off stopping closer to those."

"You rode this trail before?" Lisa felt a spark of hope. "So, it's pretty safe, right?"

A pause. A pause that told her this place wasn't even close to safe. The wind picked up, rustling the shrubs and pines, rattling the tall grass.

"We had a lot of men," Jimmy said finally, an answer that whisked her hope away.

On the main cobbled highways, the ones laid down by the Empress so long ago, travelers were fairly safe. Far from those roads? In the places where you went hours without seeing another person? Nothing safe here.

Out here, there were monsters.

Cold, wet, hungry, afraid . . . no way to spend New Year's Day at all.

Jimmy leaned back, stopping the horse. She felt his body stiffen.

Something was wrong.

The Morgan shifted from side to side, whinnied.

When Fish called out, his single word sent a flame of fear burning through Lisa's body.

"Pitters!"

Jimmy cracked the reins. Lisa felt his legs kick as his spurs dug into the Morgan's flanks. The horse shot forward; if Lisa's hands hadn't been on Jimmy's hips, she would have tumbled off. She cinched her arms around his waist, her left hand grabbing her right wrist. She held on with all her strength.

She hadn't heard anything, which shocked her when she saw the creatures rushing out of the mist on her right. Dogs in name only, the streaking shapes slid through the trees and grasses and shrubs. Muscles twitched with each step, rippling beneath mottled tan fur. Thick heads low to the ground, as steady as her hand before a sliver throw. Beady eyes staring out with a predator's blank focus.

Four of them. No, five.

Jimmy dug his spurs in again, but the horse needed no further motivation; Lisa could feel the animal's sheer panic.

The dogs fell in behind them, long strides closing the distance.

Lisa could do nothing but hold on.

She looked down, saw the lead pitter keeping pace on her left, its stone block of a head rock steady, eyes locked in on its prey.

The animal gathered, leapt.

Lisa kicked out, saw teeth flash, felt jaws crushing down on her foot, only for an instant, then the pressure was gone. She saw the pitter hit the ground, her boot in its teeth.

Another beast on her right, twitching muscles so pronounced the animal might have been skinless. The pitter leapt. Lisa tried to kick, hit nothing but air. The big dog slammed into the Morgan; teeth *clacked* on the empty space just above Lisa's thigh.

The impact made the Morgan's hindquarters swing out to the right; just a bit, but at that speed the horse lost balance, stumbled.

And Lisa was flying.

Her training took over: in the single second of air time, she scanned the area before her. She spread her arms, angled her body to get her feet under her. She hit, planning to kick down as she landed and roll forward with the momentum—her stockinged foot hit a sharp rock. The pain shattered her focus. She half rolled, half fell, shoulder smashing into the ground, tumbling legs over head right into a bush.

Pain . . . no time for pain.

Teeth and jaws, coming to rip her to shreds.

Lisa tried to right herself. Her robe tangled in the bush, slowing her, making her awkward.

She heard the pitter rushing in.

Jimmy, screaming.

Lisa lurched to her feet to see a pitter launching itself at her, mouth open wide, spit trailing from long white teeth.

She reached into her sleeves, fingers finding sliver handles, already knowing she was too late, knowing the thin slices of shaped, sharp glass wouldn't hit in time.

She was dead.

A flash of blue.

A yelp.

The pitter sailed past her, trailing blood and entrails. It crashed into the bush, through it, a coil of wet intestine catching on a branch, bouncing lightly.

Fish stepped in front of Lisa, witchglass sword in his hands, the blue blade catching the light of dawn.

The Morgan, on its side, *screaming*, eyes wide with panic, hooves kicking, a pitter's deadly jaws locked on its throat, the dog's neck and shoulder muscles rippling as it *shook* and *shook* and *shook*. Another pitter rushed in, biting the back of the horse's head.

Lisa heard bone cracking.

Past the Morgan, Jimmy, tucked into a ball, arms in front of his face, knees to his chest as a pair of pitters dug their teeth into his duster, tried to shove their thick heads past his arms to get at his neck.

Slivers flew from Lisa's hands. One, two, three, four . . . clear blades whipping out, glass digging into the animals attacking Jimmy. One yelped, scurried away, limping—the other backed off for only a moment, then rushed in and savaged Jimmy's arms.

Five, six, seven, eight . . .

The dogs scooted clear of Jimmy, but they didn't run. Sliver handles stuck out of them at odd angles. The weapons were designed to kill *people*—they hurt the pitters, but the animals' tolerance for pain was far higher. One shook its head; Lisa saw one of her slivers—blood gleaming on the clear glass—fly away into the bushes. The other pitter's face was sliced open, cheek dangling, bloody flesh gleaming in the morning light.

The Morgan spasmed, legs sticking straight out, and stopped fighting.

Its two killers rose and turned, heads low, eyes locked on Lisa and Fish.

"We're fucked," Fish said.

The pair attacking Jimmy leapt over him. All four of the big animals rushed forward, a vicious pack instantly operating as one hunter. Four mouths on four thick heads, driven by four powerful bodies.

Lisa drew two more slivers, tried to breathe, to calm herself. She had to hit them in the eye—it was the only chance to stop them.

From the trees and mist, the yells of men. Big bodies crashing through underbrush.

The four pitters stopped only a few feet away, heads turning right and left, toward the sounds that seemed to come from all directions but *back*.

Fish stepped forward and stabbed his witchglass sword. The pitters danced away, as if they already knew his range.

More yells. Lisa wanted to see where they were coming from, but she couldn't take her eyes away from the killing beasts.

Something flashed in, sticking into the ground at the pitters' feet: a crossbow bolt. Another hit. A third smacked into a pitter's ribs, seeming to wobble as the animal turned and ran.

With the same speed that had brought the attack, the predators fled into morning mist.

Lisa's body sagged. She wasn't going to die. Not today.

Horses and riders all around her. She glanced up, confused, relieved, shocked. Men in cattleman hats and dusters. Cowboys. Some holding tomahawks, some with long spears, some with crossbows . . . two with witchglass blades, one a deep red, the other a light amber.

"Well, slap my ass," Fish said, smiling his few-toothed smile. "If I ain't happier than a discount whore what fell into a drunken rancher's lap. Y'all picked one *hell* of a time to save our skins!"

A cowboy on a black horse, wearing a red shirt with a black rope tie. He held the red blade—it blazed a dark orange when hit by the rays of the rising sun. The cowboy pointed at Jimmy, who was still tucked into a ball, his hat off to the side, blood staining the shredded arms of his duster.

"Get that man up," the cowboy said. "If we get him to the ranch fast, maybe Kwallan can save him."

Two men slid off their horses and ran to Jimmy.

"Miss?"

Lisa glanced up, dumbfounded that she wasn't being torn to shreds. The man with the red blade stared down at her.

"Miss, are you all right? Did they get you?"

She couldn't find her voice. How was she still alive?

"This here is Lady Lisa," Fish said. "They didn't get her, I got to 'em before they could."

The rider ignored Fish.

"Miss, we need to get your friend to our shaman, right now. We can't leave you here." He slid the blade into his back scabbard, a smooth and practiced motion. He extended a hand. "Can you ride with me?"

Lisa was aware of Fish looking at her, but she couldn't process that, either. She took the rider's hand; he pulled her up behind him. Her ass reminded her she'd been riding for far too long, but she didn't care—anything to get out of there, away from the beasts lurking in the trees.

The man turned the horse, looked down at Fish.

"Mister, your horse looks all right," the man said. "Follow us."

Lisa felt the cold wetness in her pants, down her legs, just before she heard the red-shirted rider sniffing the air.

"I guess the dead one must have pissed itself," he said. "Or the horse did. Come on, boys, let's get out of here before some other critter shows up."

The horse beneath her galloped down the path.

Lisa held on to this man, this stranger, and wondered if she'd rather die from the pitter's bites, or from embarrassment.

Lisa sat in the nicest chair she had ever seen. A throne, really—at least that was the only word she had for this cushy, leather affair studded with polished wood brads on the arms. The feet, ironically, were carved to look like pitter claws.

"You two are lucky," the bald man said. "Real lucky."

His name was Gary Duran. The man in red worked for him. Duran owned this house, this ranch, and, apparently, everything within eyesight of the ranch keep's log walls.

"Well, we sure do appreciate this," Fish said. "Pitters is mean bastards."

Fish downed the cup of brandy—his second—in a single pull, smacked his lips noisily, and wiped his mouth with the back of his duster sleeve. He sat in a chair that was exactly like Lisa's. The fanciest chair she'd ever seen, and the bald man had *two* of them. The chairs were matched in elegance by the big wooden desk, behind which sat Duran. His shaved head and the desk's polished lacquer both gleamed with the sunlight filtering in through the windows.

Glass windows. How rich was this man? It wasn't just the house, it was the clothes he wore. Black leather vest, with roses trimmed out in emeralds on the chest. Teak rings dotted with diamonds. A silk tie, tie pin gleaming with black witchglass that seemed to massage the light.

Black witchglass—as far as Lisa knew, the most valuable material there was.

His fine clothes made her feel ridiculous, because the clothes she wore weren't hers. A servant's maybe. Loose tan cotton pants held up by a rope belt. A rough white hemp pullover with a low-cut collar, the material so thin it was almost see-through. She kept shifting in her chair, reaching up to make sure the pullover hid the rattlesnake skull and tail that hung from her leather necklace.

The red-shirted cowboy's name was Rowan. During the short ride here, he must have realized the true source of the piss smell. When they'd arrived at the ranch—a cluster of buildings including this house, barns, stables, work sheds, and more—Rowan had quietly guided her to the back of the house. He'd led her into a room, where the clothes Lisa now wore were waiting. Also waiting was a big bucket filled with soapy water.

"Leave your belt here," was all he'd said. "You can't have weapons on you when you meet Mister Duran."

Without another word or even a shameful, mocking glance, Rowan had left her alone. She'd stripped, quickly given herself a standing bath. She'd dressed in the clothes, shoved her filthy robes, shirt, and jeans into the bucket.

And her underwear, of course. She'd peed those too.

How humiliating.

Was this going to happen to her every time she faced danger? If so, what more motivation did she need to *avoid* danger and go back into the mountains, to the warmth and safety of the Hovel?

"This brandy sure is delicious," Fish said. "Mind if I have another?"

Duran's eyes narrowed. His nostrils flared, just once. He glanced at Rowan, nodded. Rowan, stone-faced, brought a glass bottle from a cart against the wall that held several such bottles. He refilled Fish's glass.

"Thank you kindly," Fish said.

"Drink it slow," Duran said. "The Goddesses' rules of the road say I've got to give hospitality and assistance to travelers in need, but my hospitality has limits."

Fish paused midsip, locked eyes with Duran for a moment. Lisa felt a sinking sensation that Fish was about to say something stupid, but the former highwayman raised his small glass in salute.

"Your assistance is greatly appreciated," Fish said, then took an exaggeratedly small, loud sip.

Duran turned his attention to Lisa.

"You don't like the brandy?"

She looked at the glass, wondered why anyone would want to drink something that tasted so awful, that burned the tongue and scorched the throat.

"It's fine, thank you, mister. But maybe I can't sit here and drink when Jimmy is dying."

Duran raised an eyebrow. "You seem more worried about the

gentleman than Mister Fish, here. Have you known Jimmy longer?"

Lisa looked down. "I barely know him at all. Don't know either of them, really."

"Might say we're recently acquainted," Fish said. "Lady Lisa needed to do some traveling, Jimmy and I were in the mood for a little adventure, so we offered to escort her north."

Duran leaned back in his chair, a chair even more ornate than the ones in which Lisa and Fish sat.

"Sounds to me like you had to get out of town in a hurry," Duran said. "And on New Year's Day? I'd think a young lady and her companions would want to stay and enjoy the sights and sounds of Frisco."

Lisa felt her face flush. She closed her eyes, but that didn't stop the vision of the Laughing Man, the blood pouring out of his mouth, that awful choking sound he'd made just before he never made another sound again.

Fish took another exaggerated sip.

"To be honest, Mister Duran, our collective decisions mighta been influenced by alcohol. I mean, why else would we be riding a back trail through pitter land?"

Duran squinted, nodded. "I can think of a few reasons," he said. He sat forward, lightly slapped the top of his desk. "Let's go check on the status of your friend."

He stood. Fish started to stand, paused, looked at his glass as if he wasn't sure if he should leave it and come back to it, or slam it in case someone took it away from him. The debate didn't last long. He drank it in one gulp.

"Damn fine," he said.

Duran gestured to the door. "After you, miss. Are those pants fitting you all right?"

Her face flushed. She glanced at Rowan, who showed no reaction.

"They fit fine, mister," she said. "Thank you for your generosity."

She expected Duran to smile, but he did not. Aside from Fish, she'd seen no one smile in this place.

She and Fish followed Duran out of the office. She marveled

again at his house. It was like the log cabins in the mountains, only much, *much* larger. Size-wise, it was nothing short of the castles she'd read about in storybooks. Many rooms. *Two* floors, the second story with a rail that overlooked an open center area beneath the peaked roof, an area filled with stuffed bears, mountain lions, porcupines . . . every form of animal she'd ever seen. And a few she had not. Stuffed pitters, too, even bigger than the ones that had almost dragged her into the trees. Fancy furniture. Paintings, mostly of Duran and a woman Lisa assumed was his wife. Sculptures. And everywhere, in art or burned into the hundreds of cow skins hanging from the walls, the seared image of the letters *DR*, the brand of the Duran Ranch.

Lisa smelled amazing things drifting out of an unseen kitchen. Bread, soup, and *meat*. Judging from the hundred or so head of cattle they'd passed on the way into this house, meat wasn't hard to come by here. Hopefully, Duran's hospitality would include a meal.

"Mister Duran," Lisa said, "can I ask you a question?"

"Of course," the bald man said as he led them out of the house and onto the wide porch.

"How many people live here with you? In the big house, I mean."

Duran didn't break stride as he stepped off the porch onto a walkway paved with flagstones.

"Just me," he said. "Servant quarters are over there"—he pointed to a log house on the right, big, but not as big as the main house—"ranch hands over there, by the stables."

He pointed ahead of him, to the stone building they were approaching. "And this is Kwallan's place."

The way Duran said it, *Kwallan's place*, it sounded like Duran didn't own it, even though it was on his grounds.

A palisade of weathered logs surrounded the entire compound. Rain barrels lined the wall's inner walkway. To put out fires if someone attacked the walls, maybe. Three bowmen up on that walkway, spaced evenly around the wall, keeping a lookout across the clear-cut ring surrounding the small fortress. The area encircled by the palisade was almost as big as the entire Hovel.

Cows were everywhere inside the walls. Holsteins, she knew, their black-and-white hides so distinctive. Many more outside the walls—she couldn't begin to imagine how many head Duran had. He was rich, of that there was no doubt. Easily the richest person Lisa had ever met.

They reached the stone building—the only stone building in the compound. The stones were rough and natural, not smooth-cut blocks like the buildings and walls of the Hovel, or some of the buildings she'd seen in Frisco. The building had a single wooden door. No windows. It felt . . . *dark*. There was something off about this place.

She shivered.

"This is where they took Jimmy?"

Duran knocked on the stone building's wooden door. He had a big hand, a big fist, but the knock made little noise, evidence of the door's heavy, thick wood.

Fish spit on the ground. "You got a Whitey in there, I bet. Only a Whitey could help Jimmy, the way he was all tore up."

Duran didn't answer him. Instead, he turned to Lisa.

His eyes flicked down, to her chest. She crossed her arms. His eyes flicked back up.

Finally, he smiled.

"You're not from around these parts, are you."

She shook her head. "From the mountains."

Duran nodded. "I suspected as much."

The door opened.

Lisa hissed, took a step back and dropped into a fighting crouch, hands reaching for sleeves that weren't there, for slivers that weren't there.

"Take it easy," Duran said, holding up a hand toward Lisa. "I should have warned you about what you'd see. My apologies."

A woman. Naked. Her breasts had been cut away, leaving gnarled scar tissue. A square of black glass covered each eye, anchored into her skull by yellow glass screws, her flesh puffed up around the posts. So *skinny*, like a skeleton draped with loose old skin.

Her head turned quickly, this way and that, like the head of a cautious little bird.

"Who seeks Kwallan?"

"I do," Duran said.

The woman's head flicked toward Duran, but she didn't look directly at him. Maybe she couldn't see through the black glass. Maybe she was blind.

Or maybe she didn't have eyes at all.

"The man you brought lives," the woman said. "Come in."

She stepped backward into the stone building, which was thick with shadow.

Duran led the way in. Fish gestured gallantly for Lisa to go first. When she shook her head, he shrugged and followed Duran.

Lisa stood in the doorway, afraid to enter. The woman was a nightmare . . . would Kwallan be even worse?

"It's all right."

She jumped away from the voice behind her, turning and again dropping into her fighting stance. Rowan stood there, tall, expressionless, the handle of his sword peeking out from his back scabbard.

He tipped his hat.

"Sorry to scare you, miss," he said. "Kwallan works for Duran. You're Duran's guest, Kwallan won't do anything. Just don't insult him, that's all. Make sure you don't insult him."

Lisa stood straight. She hadn't even heard him approach. If he'd wanted to stab her in the back, she would have been dead.

Victim training left much to be desired, it seemed.

"I don't like it here," she said, quietly. "I want to leave."

She was confiding in him. Why? He couldn't he trusted. *None* of these men could be trusted. She knew Fish wanted her. Duran had looked at her breasts.

But Rowan had not. Every time he'd addressed her, he'd looked her right in the eyes.

He nodded toward the doorway.

"If you want your friend to leave this place, you need to go in," he said. "If you're too afraid to go in and parley with Kwallan, then we should have left your friend for the pitters. There's worse things than death, miss."

No expression, but his eyes . . . haunted, empty. Lisa wanted to know more about this tall, red-shirted cowboy, and at the same time wanted to be away from him forever.

Worse things than death. What did this man know?

She wasn't about to piss her pants in fear again. Never again. A strange woman wasn't going to scare her.

Lisa turned away from Rowan. She stepped into the stone building.

Rowan didn't follow: he shut the door behind her.

All darkness at first. Her eyes adjusted. A single, large room. Dozens of candles in a candelabra hanging from the ceiling, their light locked in a losing fight against the shadows clutching tight to the room's edges. In the center of the room, a flat stone altar surrounded by tall candle stands. On top of the altar, Jimmy, flat on his back, unmoving. A white cloth covered him from the waist down. Red, puffy wounds on his right shoulder, lined with fine black thread. Black stitches on his forehead, his cheek. A plaster cast on his left arm, from the wrist to the elbow. The pitter bite had broken the bones in his forearm.

Movement from the edges of the room, where the candlelight didn't reach. Lisa looked left, right, saw shapes sliding through the shadows. People? Animals? Something else altogether? They made noise when they moved, like wet fur sliding across rough wood.

She shouldn't have come in here.

From behind the altar, a man in a hooded white robe stepped into the candlelight. Stepped, or *appeared,* she wasn't sure, as he seemed to melt out of the darkness and into reality. The shadow of his hood hid his face, but just like the things at the edge of the room, something seemed to be *moving* in that oval shape.

"A Whitey," Fish said. "I knew it. Didn't I tell you, Lady Lisa?"

She nodded absently, wished Rowan had come in with her.

"Kwallan," Duran said, "will this man live?"

The man in white spread his hands through the air above Jimmy. Hands that seemed too fat for the body hidden by the robes.

"Yes," the white-robed man said. His voice . . . like a grave shovel sliding into dirt. "He will live. But the cost was high."

The things in the shadows writhed. Lisa glanced at them, still unable to make out exactly what they were. She took a step toward Fish. He smiled at her. Something about that smile made her skin crawl. She took a step away from him.

Evil things . . . some hid in the dark, others stood in the light.

"Thank you, Mister Duran," Fish said. "I didn't think Jimmy would make it, what with the way those pitters tore him up."

Duran gestured to the door. This time, Lisa was first, not last. She saw the things in the shadows reaching toward her. Dim candlelight played off of arms and hands that weren't quite human, skin pale and crusted with dots of hard color, oranges and reds and yellows . . . almost like the skin of a snake.

The woman with the glass-covered eyes opened the door. Sunlight flooded in; the reaching things snapped back into the shadows.

Lisa had never been so relieved to see the open sky.

Several steps outside, Rowan was waiting. In his arms, he held Lisa's folded robe, jeans, shirt, her weapons belt curled up atop the stack of fabric. And on top of the belt, her boots.

Including the one the pitter had ripped off her foot.

"I sent men back for it," Rowan said. "Our cobbler stitched up the holes. You're lucky to even have a foot, Miss Lisa."

The hospitality of the road, or something more? Was it possible Rowan was just *nice*? No . . . he wanted something from her. Outside of the Hovel, everyone wanted something from her.

Without a word, Lisa went to him, snatched her robe out of his arms and pulled it on. Under it, she removed the borrowed shirt and handed it to him. She'd dressed enough times beneath the robe that she knew how to do so without showing any skin. She put her own shirt back on, marveling, for a moment, that it smelled like lilacs instead of sweat, then the rest of her clothes, then her boots. She tied off her belt, let the robe hang down, slid her hands into her wide sleeves—the welcome feel of sliver handles in their hidden pockets.

Rowan had reloaded for her.

Fish smiled that horrid smile. "Damn, Lady Lisa, you smell real pretty. You don't know the stink of the road until it's off ya, heh?"

She could still smell Fish. The stink of the road? On him, for sure, and also the stink of a dozen bars, a bottle or two of hooch, and maybe a stale pile of horse turds.

Lisa's fingertips played off the sliver handles again, danced along the dozens of handles sticking up from her waist holster, the larger handle of her stone knife.

She was armed again . . . she felt *whole* again.

Clean clothes. Her slivers. The knife at her hip.

A Victim needed little to be happy, or so the saying went. She had those things, so why did she still feel that tentacle of dread wrapped around her heart.

Once glance at the stone building told her why. She wanted to be away from this place. Far, *far* away.

"She gets her slivers?" Fish frowned. "Then where's my blade? Why don't I get my weapons back?"

"Because I don't like you," Duran said. "You'll get your blade back when you leave. Now, let us discuss the matter of payment."

Fish sighed. "So much for the hospitality of the road, huh, Mister Duran? What would Goddess Chanterelle say?"

"My men saved your life," Duran said. "That's pretty damn hospitable, by anyone's measure. Healing your friend is another story. I don't know what Kwallan used to heal him, and I don't need to know. What I do know is such materials cost money."

Fish glanced at Lisa, shrugged.

"We don't have much money," Lisa said. "What we do have, you're welcome to it."

She reached into an inside pocket, her blood running cold for an instant–Rowan, or whoever had washed her robe, had surely taken what little she had left. That fear eased instantly . . . the finely carved wooden coins were still there.

Three and a half Bowens. All that was left to her name.

She held out her hand, offering the coins.

Duran looked at the coins, but did not take them.

"Sadly, miss, that doesn't even come close."

"Maybe you need outriders," Fish said. "Could we work off the debt?"

Duran shook his head. "With what I pay my men, you'd be riding for the next hundred and fifty years to pay what's owed."

Fish spit on the ground. "If we'd known you were charging to save a man's life, maybe we would've kept moving on."

"Nothing's in life's free," Duran said. "You didn't know, because you didn't ask. None of that matters now. There's a price to be paid. But you don't need money. I have an offer for you. I'm embroiled in a land dispute. Lady Falma, do you know who that is?"

Lisa shook her head, but Fish nodded.

"I've been through her territory a few times," he said. "When I was riding with Highwayman Pitrelli."

Duran raised an eyebrow. "You rode with Pitrelli?"

"That's right," Fish said. "Me and Jimmy both."

"Falma owns the land east of mine," Duran said. "She seems to think she can let her people hunt on my land. I've taken it up with the duke. The duke says we need to work it out between us, that he won't intervene."

Fish shrugged. "If you want us to kill her, mister, we can't help you. She's got a thousand men, at least."

"I don't want you to kill *her*," Duran said. "She's challenged me about who owns the land, offered to settle it with a battle of champions. If it was a sword fight, I'd put Rowan there up against anyone."

He nodded toward the man in red. Rowan stared straight out, said nothing.

"But it ain't a sword fight, I take it," Fish said.

Duran shook his head.

"Flinging at twenty paces," he said. "I got boys that love to throw, that are good at it, but her champion is a tall beanpole with fast hands. *Real* fast. No one around here can touch him, so I haven't put anyone up against him." He smiled at Lisa. "But a *Victim*? I'm willing to bet a Victim could take him."

She hadn't shown her necklace. She hadn't said exactly where she was from. When she'd left the Hovel, it had never crossed her mind if people knew about the Victims or not. The robes were a bit of a uniform, sure, but she'd passed hundreds of people on the road—none of them seemed to know she was a Victim, or maybe they hadn't known what a Victim was at all. Fish hadn't known.

"I saw a Victim throw, once," Duran said. "In Orado. Street duel. Fastest thing I ever saw. When Rowan saved you, he saw you flinging slivers at the pitters. He said you hit eight shots, didn't miss a one. He said he hadn't ever seen anyone throw that fast. If you're as fast as he says . . . you could win this for me."

Lisa stared back at the man. Empress, she wanted to be back home.

"You want me to duel for you?"

Duran nodded. "I'm tired of this dispute. The land is mine by rights, and I mean to have it. You came from out of nowhere. No one knows who you are. You couldn't have been in town for long, or I would have heard about a Victim in these parts. If I haven't heard about you, neither has Falma."

"Lisa's brand-new," Fish said. "You're right, no one knows her round here." He laughed, showing his missing teeth and grayish gums. "I been all up and down the coast, from Astoria to San Diego. Yeah, I said it, I been past the Trench. *Way* past it. I've seen plenty of slingers in my day. In all my years and all my travels, Lady Lisa here is the fastest I ever seen."

Fish was *excited*. Did he think there were *two* Lisas—the delicate, twenty-year-old girl hiding her body beneath a thick robe, and the slinger that could kill in a fraction of a second? The first Lisa was something to be desired, to be *taken*. The second? Fish *respected* the second Lisa.

"Decide," Duran said. "Kwallan needs an answer now. If your friend wakes up, and Kwallan hasn't been paid? Then it is too late for you to do anything."

A duel at twenty paces. She'd done that at the Hovel, sure, hundreds of times, but always while wearing wooden armor, a helmet with a stiff mesh mask. She'd never thrown in a real duel . . . and she'd never been thrown *at*.

Lisa shook her head. "I'm not settling your business for you, mister. I appreciate you helping Jimmy, but I—" she thought of the Laughing Man, the blood pouring out of his mouth, the way his face had *thunked* against the table "—I don't want anyone dying."

Duran spread his hands. "Then I have no choice but to give Jimmy to Kwallan."

"You got a fucking choice," Fish said. "Pay Kwallan. You got all the money in the world, you manipulating cocksucker."

Rowan reached for the handle of his sword, took a step toward Fish.

"No," Duran said sharply.

Rowan stepped back, let his hands fall to his side. His eyes, still cold, still distant. Would he have killed Fish for just *insulting* Duran? Lisa knew he would have.

"Gimme my sword back," Fish said. "And we'll see how good you are, Red."

Rowan said nothing.

"It's not the money, it's the principle of the thing," Duran said. "Besides, I have an arrangement with Kwallan. He doesn't want *my* money for such things. Our deal is that anyone we rescue has to pay his own way. If not . . ."

He shrugged.

Fish stared at Rowan. Rowan stared at Fish.

"If not, *what*?" Lisa said. "What happens to Jimmy?"

Duran sighed, as if he felt real sympathy for Jimmy's fate.

"Then he belongs to Kwallan," the bald man said. "For Kwallan's . . . experiments."

Inside Lisa, the tentacle of dread stretched and spread.

"Those things in the shadows," she said. "Those were experiments?"

Duran shrugged again.

Lisa wanted to draw right then and there, throw a sliver into Duran's bored eyes. The man already knew he'd won.

Lisa had met Jimmy just last night. She hadn't even known him a full day yet. But when she'd been in trouble, Jimmy had stood with her. He'd stolen a horse. He'd gotten her out of town.

And, maybe, he'd protected her from Fish.

Lisa couldn't leave Jimmy to that . . . that . . . *Whitey.*

And wasn't she trained? Had she thrown two hundred thousand throws for *nothing*? She was fast, the fastest one in her group at the Hovel. She was faster than most of the instructors.

This wasn't the Laughing Man. Whoever Lady Falma had as her champion, that man had never hurt Lisa. Lisa had no reason to take his life.

"Do I gotta kill him?"

Duran shook his head. "Up to you. You put him down however you like. Once he can't get up, you win."

Lisa looked to the stone building. If she didn't step up, Jimmy might never leave this place.

All she had to do was win one duel.

"When?"

"Tomorrow," Duran said. "Noon, most likely. Falma wants this settled as bad as I do."

Lisa felt at her chest, fingers finding the rattlesnake skull beneath her shirt.

One, single, duel.

If she didn't, Jimmy was lost.

"All right," she said. "I'll do it."

She rode in silence. Duran obliged, leaving her to her thoughts.

The carriage was as fancy as anything in Duran's house, another testament to the rancher's wealth and power. On an actual highway, it probably would have been a smooth ride. But they weren't on a highway. Through the narrow slats that passed for windows, Lisa saw endless scrub brush and struggling pines, the same as she'd seen on the ride north.

She also saw Duran's men. A trail of them behind the carriage, spears at rest, tips pointing straight up. Some had small flags on the ends of their spears, red, stitched with a black *DR*. More men out in front of the carriage, two riding on either side.

At least the pitters would steer clear.

There were other creatures out here in the hills, she'd heard.

Bears. Mountain lions. Packs of cabras. Supposedly even continuars, with wings wider than four men lying end to end. With this many riders, though, everything would stay away. Even the continuars.

Maybe.

After agreeing to the duel, Lisa had spent the rest of the day practicing her throws. She'd reduced a throwing post to splinters and kindling. Two of her slivers had broken. Duran had offered to replace them, but when Lisa learned that Kwallan would be the one to do the work, she chose to leave those two holsters empty.

Hours of practice had helped her focus, helped her tune out thoughts of Jimmy and Kwallan and the Laughing Man. When the sun had set, Lisa had eaten, then gone to bed in a guest room in the big house. She'd expected her thoughts to keep her awake—the dread of the coming duel, the unstoppable image of the Laughing Man's blood—but the bed proved to be the softest she had ever known. With the stress and exhaustion of the previous day, she'd slept like the dead.

The hours-long ride from Duran's ranch to the duel site, however, had left her plenty of time to think. Think about the coming duel. How she might be wounded. How she might die. How she might kill a man.

No . . . kill *another* man.

She barely knew Jimmy. So why was she doing this? Jimmy might be a bad man, the kind that took ten-year-old girls into the woods. Maybe he worshipped demons. She didn't know. So why was she doing this?

Because Jimmy had helped her.

And no matter how much she wanted to leave, she couldn't abandon Jimmy to Kwallan. She couldn't let Jimmy become one of the things crawling in the shadows.

One duel. Then she could head home to the Hovel.

The distant, isolated Hovel.

The *boring* Hovel.

Lisa closed her eyes, breathed slowly. She was a Victim. She was fast. She could win this duel, win it easily. She had to focus on that.

She heard the driver calling for the team to stop, felt the carriage slow. When they came to a rest, Duran waited, smiled at her.

"Not long now," he said. "One sliver to the eye, or the throat, or the wrist, and this is all done."

She realized she hadn't asked a question. A very important question.

"And if I lose?"

Duran shrugged his arrogant shrug.

"Then Jimmy belongs to Kwallan."

Anger flared. Who did this man think he was that he could hold Jimmy's life—or his soul—hostage? Who did he think he was that he could make Lisa fight to the death?

Death. She would have died without Duran's men. Would have died horribly. That she could not deny.

"Tell me something," she said. "If Rowan and your men had rescued us before Jimmy got hurt, and you still found out I was a Victim, would you have found another way to get me to fight for you?"

In answer, Duran offered only his smile.

The carriage door opened. Rowan stood there, offering a gloved hand to her.

"Watch your step, miss."

She ignored his hand. She didn't want to touch him, but not for the reasons she didn't want to touch anyone; she worried that if she took his hand, she would want to touch him *more.*

Besides, she wasn't some frail thing that needed help. She was a trained slinger. She was a Victim.

She hopped down. The wind blew from the west. Did it carry the smell of the ocean, or was she imagining that? The ocean might be right over the ridge, for all she knew.

Maybe she could find out after this was over.

If she survived.

A horse trotted to a stop near her: Fish, riding his painter. The mount had been brushed, fed, and watered while at the Duran Ranch; it looked like a different animal altogether.

"You ready, Lady Lisa?"

She had to get him to stop calling her that.

"Let's get it over with," she said.

Ahead on the road, another carriage. Two dozen horsemen, most holding spears just like Duran's men did, only these spears were flying flags of green and black squares, with a yellow lightning bolt in the middle.

A man in a black shirt and black hat helped an older woman out of the carriage. She wore a pink hat and a pink dress, both lined with black witchglass beads. A few petticoats under the dress added to her shape, but Lisa had seen far worse in Frisco.

From the end of the woman's group, a man rode up on a white horse. Lisa knew, instantly, that this was her foe. He wore all black: boots, jeans, button-down shirt. No hat, but rather a bandanna tied over his head. A black scarf knotted at the neck, pointed ends blowing with the wind. Trimmed black mustache. Small granite U's through his earlobes, a matching one through his nose.

And a black leather belt studded with sliver holsters, the worn wood handles sticking up in a regimented row.

"Well," Fish said, "ain't he a fucking dandy?"

Duran dabbed at his forehead with a kerchief.

"He's killed three men," he said. "That we know of. Come along, Miss Lisa, It's time."

Lisa and Duran walked forward.

Her opponent dismounted. He walked to meet Lisa, the woman in the pink dress at his side.

On a lonely trail in the middle of nowhere, Lisa and Duran stood before Lady Falma and Lisa's foe. He was tall . . . maybe six and a half feet. Longer arms meant a longer release speed, but he could probably throw much harder than she could.

"Rancher Duran, you disgusting pig," Lady Falma said, her voice as sweet as honey.

"Lady Falma," Duran said.

The woman looked Lisa up and down.

"Really, Duran? Your sack finally drops enough for you to accept my challenge, and *this* is what you bring to the dance?"

Muscles twitched under Duran's ear.

"I'm confident in my choice."

Lady Falma *hmphed* dismissively. "Whatever it takes for you to give up your ridiculous claim on my land."

"The land is *mine,*" Duran said. "I shouldn't even have to go through this!"

Falma *hmphed* again.

A man wearing white-trimmed black robes walked forward from her group. He wore a flat-brimmed black hat with a white enameled star on the front.

"Rancher Duran," he said. "Lady Falma."

"Judge Witcomb," the two said in unison.

The judge looked Lisa up and down, concern on his face.

"Young lady, are you fully aware of the gravity of this duel?"

All this *talking*—she wanted to get on with it. Formalities she'd never gone through back at the Hovel. Local law . . . she had to endure it.

And she had to pee.

"I am," she said.

"You're doing this willingly," Witcomb said. "You're not being coerced in any way?"

Lisa glanced at Duran. She couldn't help it. His eyes narrowed in a wordless warning.

"I am doing this willingly."

The judge sighed. "Very well. And you, Pete?"

Lisa's tall foe stared at her, a half smile on his lips.

"Gravity," the man said, waving a black-gloved hand. "Willing and all that shit. Can we get on with this?"

The judge nodded. Duran and Lady Falma walked back to their respective groups.

"I hope a ricochet hits you in the eye and kills you," Lady Falma said over her shoulder in that syrupy voice.

"Blow it out your ass," Duran said, apparently unable to remain polite.

The judge clapped his hands together twice.

"Turn perpendicular to the road," he said. "Duran's champion to the north, Falma's champion to the south."

Lisa glanced up, saw that the sun, hidden by a few thin clouds, was directly overhead.

Noon.

The black-clad man grinned at her.

"You should concede," he said. "I got no wish to hurt you. Concede, Falma wins the land, you walk away. Ain't that right, judge?"

Witcomb nodded. "That's right. Now that we're here, first person to concede, or who falls and can't continue, loses. At any time, you can call out *I give,* or tap the ground three times. When you do that, you lose. I'm a surgeon, so I'm ready to stitch up cuts, but don't wait too long—if you bleed out, nothing I can do for you."

Lisa swallowed hard. Butterflies in her stomach. She *really* had to pee.

"Concede now," Pete said. "Just walk away, girl. You know this ain't your fight."

She thought of Jimmy on the stone slab. She thought of the things reaching out to her from the shadows, the things that flinched away from the light.

"I'll throw," she said.

Lisa didn't want this, not any of it. She didn't want to fight this man. She had to make him see that, make *him* want to walk away.

Not everyone in these parts had heard of the Victims . . . maybe this man had.

She held up her right hand, palm out.

"Not drawing," she said. "I want to show you something."

Pete's smile faded. He wondered what was going on.

The judge nodded.

Slowly, so slowly, Lisa reached a hand inside her shirt collar. She gently pulled on the cord around her neck, lifting her necklace free. She let the rattlesnake skull and tail drop to her chest, the combined weight of both not quite enough to pull the cord taut.

The man—Pete—stared at her chest.

Recognition in those eyes.

He knew. He knew what the necklace was, knew what *she* was.

Walk away, walk away, please walk away . . .

Pete held his hand up, palm out.

"Not throwing," he said.

Slowly, so slowly, he reached for his collar.

Lisa's soul sank.

Pete pulled at a cord around his neck. Slowly, deliberately, he let the rattlesnake skull drop, dangle against his chest.

"Aw, *fuck*," Duran said.

Lisa glanced over at him, saw him throw his kerchief to the ground.

He didn't think she could win. Because she was a *girl*. He thought a girl Victim could beat anyone . . . except a *male* Victim.

She looked at Fish, who crossed his arms and nodded at her.

"Kick his ass," Fish said.

Fish believed she could win?

Lisa looked back to Pete.

"Sorry," he said. "If you thought that talisman of yours might scare me, I'm afraid you're mistaken."

He had the skull *and* the tail. He'd completed the training, just like she had, only he was a grown man. Bigger. Stronger.

But was he faster?

"I left eleven years ago," Pete said. "I got bored. You?"

Lisa started to speak; her dry tongue ran around her dry mouth. She licked her lips, trying to work up some spit. She swallowed, a scratchy, parched feeling.

"Two months ago," she said. "Wanted to see the New Year in a city."

Pete nodded slowly.

"I can understand that," he said. "Here's the thing, girl. You still can. Say *I give*. Yield. Walk away, under my protection."

It had never occurred to her that her foe had thrown a hundred thousand throws, then *another* hundred thousand, honing his abilities up in the mountains just as she had.

In two months away from the Hovel, she'd already killed one man.

Pete had been gone for eleven years; how many men had *he* killed?

Lisa looked at Duran again, her eyes pleading.

He stared at her, hard, shook his head.

"We have a deal," he said. "Don't you back out on it."

Jimmy. He'd been pulled into this mess because of her, because she'd killed the Laughing Man. Jimmy could have run, abandoned her and gone his own way, but he hadn't. He'd stuck by her. A complete stranger, and he'd stuck by her.

"Enough talking," Lady Falma called out. "You two going to throw, or are you going to stand there flapping your mouths?"

Pete never took his eyes off Lisa as he held up one finger toward Lady Falma—a warning to back off.

"You'll win the day, Lady," he said. "How you win it ain't your call. You be quiet, now, and let me do my work."

Lisa didn't dare look away from Pete to see Lady Falma's reaction, but the woman didn't say anything in answer.

"It's hot as donkey balls out here," Judge Witcomb said. "Throwers, turn back to back."

Lisa turned, the movement automatic, drilled into her by thousands of duel repetitions in the Hovel.

"On my command," the judge said, "take ten paces forward in a straight line, each step matching my count. If you turn early, you hang, and I'm the one who makes that call. Duran? Falma? In front of these witnesses, do you validate my authority to punish any cheater in this duel by an immediate sentencing?"

"We do," they both called out.

Lisa hadn't faced consequences like that before. When she'd trained, part of the game had been seeing if you could anticipate the step-count, turn just a *smidge* early. If she did that here, even by accident, would she hang?

This wasn't the same. It was a duel, but *not the same*. She should have asked more questions.

She wanted to go home.

She had to pee *so bad*.

"By the power invested in me by the Queen of the Redwood Empire," the judge called out, "I hereby begin this duel in the name of settling the land-ownership grievance between Rancher Gary Duran and Lady Patricia Falma. Champions, on my command. *One . . . two . . .*"

Lisa's feet carried her forward, as if they remembered the training better than she did.

"Five . . . six . . ."

What if she stepped on a rock and slipped? Twisted her ankle? The ground was so uneven. She watched it, shook off the thought; she had only seconds to live.

"Eight . . . nine . . ."

If she lost, Jimmy lost.

Kill a stranger to save a stranger.

Lisa's hands slid into her sleeves. The sliver handles . . . so familiar, so comforting.

Thoughts drained away.

It was time to throw.

"Ten!"

Lisa turned to her right, drew and threw all in the same motion, stepping far off the line she'd walked. As she did, she saw Pete—twenty paces away—stepping to his right.

Her throw had been a hair faster: her sliver hit the empty air where he'd been an instant before she felt a sting on her right ear as his sliver drew blood. There wasn't time to think about how close she'd come to death, only momentary realization that Pete had anticipated her step, had known what she would do.

Instinct and training told her to step left again, but she planted her left foot and stepped backward instead, slightly changing the angle of his attack—his next sliver sailed past to her left.

Lisa flicked both hands. She was a faster throw than Pete, she knew that instantly, but the way he *moved.* He twisted left and her first throw hit empty air. Her second sliver grazed his thigh. Lisa saw a flash of white flesh through the cut in his pants, a flash with a thin red streak down the middle, then Pete's hands became a blur, reaching to his belt and flicking faster than she could follow.

Lisa dove right, rolled, flaring her robe as she came up, giving Pete a bigger target that might draw his aim. She drew two more slivers from her sleeves as she felt sudden tugs on her robe—his slivers slicing through fabric as if it were paper.

A sting in her left thigh.

Lisa rolled to a crouch, already throwing, Pete already moving to dodge the strike. Lisa's left hand let go its sliver; she flicked her right a fraction of a second later, but didn't release. Pete's move took him clear of the first sliver; he'd already committed to dodging the second before he realized her right-hand strike was a feint. He planted a foot to change direction—his boot sole skidded on dirt.

He wobbled, so slightly, trying to fight his momentum, to regain control, but it was too late. In the instant it took him to recover, Lisa's sliver closed the distance, slid into the scarf tied around his throat.

The handle stuck out, worn wood jutting from black silk.

Pete stopped moving. He stood there, stock-still, staring at her, slivers held limply in his fingers.

Lisa's fast hands moved on their own, grabbing the handles of two more slivers from her sleeves.

But she didn't throw.

A single spurt of blood arced away from his neck, fell to the dirt, kicked up a tiny puff of dust. He turned his head, slightly, maybe to look to Lady Falma, maybe to look to the horizon, Lisa would never know, because when he turned, blood jetted from his neck, spraying out from behind the suddenly soaked black scarf.

He dropped his slivers. One stuck in the dirt blade-first, as if he'd meant to kill the ground itself. The second one fell from his hand—the glass blade hit a rock, chipped into three pieces with a musical *tink*.

His neck sprayed a third time. Then, a fourth. His knees sagged. He fell to his butt. A fifth pumping spray, not as strong as the earlier ones. A sixth, weaker still.

Pete reached a hand to the ground, slowly patted it three times.

He gave up.

But it was too late.

Lisa looked to the judge, who was standing with Lady Falma. The judge shook his head; there was nothing he could do.

Her throw had been perfect—Pete could not be saved.

As if he were lying down for the night in a comfortable bed, Pete laid on his side, knees up. Another jet of blood, a burble more than a spray, one that landed on his cheek. His hand reached for his hip holsters. He weakly drew a sliver. With a limp flick of his wrist, he tossed the sliver in front of him, perhaps aiming at a foe that only he could see.

His hand fell to the dirt.

He did not move.

Fish's *whoop* of joy split the ar.

"Sheeee-*it*, you put that tall bastard down, Lady Lisa!"

Duran's men cheered.

The distant sound of Lady Falma cursing, then the judge arguing with her, but none of the words made sense.

Lisa's legs wouldn't hold her. She fell to her butt, the move as graceless as when dying Pete had done the same. She couldn't take her eyes off him.

Had she thought about her first throw? Maybe. Maybe. But after that, after that she hadn't thought at all—she'd just *moved*, ten years of training controlling her like a puppet.

She'd saved Jimmy, but at what cost?

She'd killed . . . *again*.

What had she become?

Lisa had trained hard so that she would never again be a victim, never again be preyed upon. Pete hadn't attacked her—he'd offered to let Lisa walk away. Pete had been a tool of Lady Falma's, just as Lisa had been a tool of Duran's.

Someone lifted her, set her on a man's shoulder. People were cheering for her, calling out *Lady Lisa! Lady Lisa!*

Each step the man took, the shoulder dug into a butt still sore from yesterday's long ride.

Her ass hurt.

But . . . she hadn't peed herself.

Wasn't that worth something?

Was it worth a man's life?

No.

As the men carried her back to Duran's carriage, Lisa realized she didn't want to go home at all.

She had no *home* to go to.

The Hovel had turned her into a killer.

She'd trained relentlessly, religiously, so that she would never again be a victim, but that's exactly what she was—a victim of Duran's manipulations.

Lisa touched her necklace, felt the rattlesnake skull and tail that she'd worked so, *so* hard to earn. She lifted the necklace free of her head.

She let it fall to the dirt.

Whatever came next, she didn't want the thing anymore.

With or without a capital V, she would never again be a victim.

Never again.

Carrie Vaughn

I love superhero stories. All kinds of superhero stories. But I think most of all I love the unexpected superhero stories, about what it must be like to live in a superhero city as a side character. It's not about the powers so much as it's about how do you *deal* with it all? Also, I worked as an administrative assistant in an accounting office for eight years, and it seems a much richer environment for stories than most people give it credit for. And yes, I do have a master's in English lit, but I have not read *Finnegans Wake*. Just in case you were thinking this narrator really is me.

Carrie Vaughn

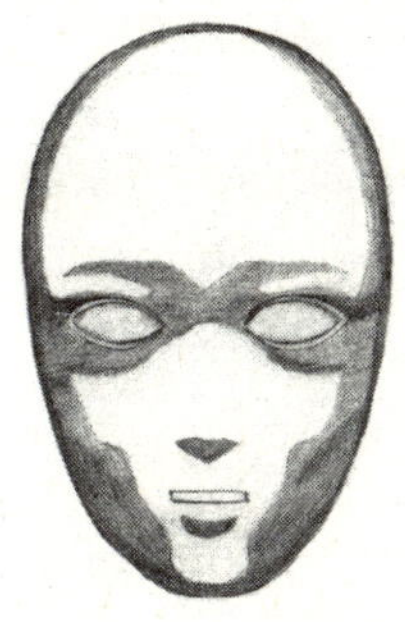

SIDEKICK

Carrie Vaughn

I was not sick before I came here.

The room is quiet except for the soft buzz of electronics—a ticking clock, a beeping monitor. The bed is soft, the linens comfortable, if thin. The opposite wall has a chart on a whiteboard that I can't quite read from where I lie. I wake up and instantly know this is a hospital room, but I don't remember how I got here. I try to be calm. Someone will explain all this.

Sure enough, a nurse comes in and bustles around the bed, checking monitors just outside my line of sight. I don't have any tubes or wires connected to me. No needles, no sensors. I brush both my arms and feel all around my head to be sure. None of this has anything to do with me.

I ask her why I'm here.

The nurse is a short woman, auburn hair primly tied back in a bun. Her scrubs have tiny cartoon rabbits on them. "You fell, don't you remember?"

Of course I don't. She knows I don't.

"You don't remember anything about the accident? Falling off the horse?"

I don't even remember going riding.

"You weren't wearing your helmet," she adds. "Why weren't you wearing your helmet?"

"But I always wear my helmet." I wouldn't ride without wearing my helmet; I never don't wear my helmet.

"Well, never mind, loss of memory is common with head injuries," she says and bustles back out of the room without explaining anything.

I don't even have a headache. I feel *fine.*

A doctor comes in next, a man in a white lab coat wearing a serious expression. I must have fallen asleep because I wake up when the door opens. I don't remember falling asleep.

"How are we doing?" he says, wearing a condescending smile. We? He's on his feet, I'm in bed, apparently with a head injury. There isn't any *we* here.

"I'm fine. I think I feel fine. Can I get up, walk around a little bit?"

"Not so fast," he says. "We're still making sure you're stable. For now I'd like to ask you a few questions."

"Okay." My voice sounds small. I'm not sure I can sound anything but small, lying in this bed.

"What do you remember about the accident?"

"I don't remember anything," I say, even though I know that's the wrong answer, an answer that will keep me here, in bed.

He tsks, shaking his head. Consults a clipboard sitting on a side table. "What's the first thing you remember, then?"

"I woke up when the nurse came in. I . . . was that a few hours ago? This morning? I'm not sure."

"So you're having trouble keeping track of time."

"Maybe if you could put a clock in here—"

"Has your boss been in to see you yet?"

My boss? "I'm not even sure he knows I'm in the hospital."

"Oh, he's been alerted. His information was listed as your emergency contact."

That doesn't sound right—my mother is my emergency contact, and why hasn't she been in to see me yet? I really want to see her. To see any familiar face.

"Do you have my phone?" I ask. "I'd like my phone. I could call him. And my mother. I'd really like to talk to my mom."

His smile is a kind mask. "We don't want you to get too excited, not yet."

"But I'm not—"

"Never mind that for now. With a head injury like yours, we don't like you to read anything or strain your eyes too much."

It sort of makes sense. Sort of.

He takes out a light pen and shines it in each of my eyes, clicking his tongue as if he's found something there he doesn't like.

"What's wrong?"

"How are you feeling?"

I'm starting to get a headache. "I'm okay. I think I'm okay."

"But you weren't wearing your helmet."

I hadn't been riding, I know I hadn't. My horse died ten years ago. I still miss her.

The doctor holds my wrist, taking my pulse. I assume he's taking my pulse. "What do you remember from before the accident? What was the last thing you remember doing before you woke up?"

"I think I was going to work . . ."

"What kind of work is it you do?" he asks conversationally, that fake smile still in place.

"I'm an administrative assistant."

"Oh? For what kind of business?"

"An accounting firm."

"You must get a lot of questions at tax time."

"Not really. I'm not an accountant myself, I just run the office."

"So you pass folks along to your boss?"

"He isn't really that kind of accountant," I say. Darren is an auditor and forensic accountant. Tax time isn't really a thing—he goes out on jobs year-round. "It's all pretty dull."

"Oh, I imagine not. If you're his assistant—"

"I just answer phones, stuff like that. Keep the office running."

"It would all fall apart without you, hmm?" He makes it sound like a joke but also sort of not.

The blandness of the questions and intensity of his stare make me nervous. I don't want to talk anymore.

"Your pulse is a little elevated," the doctor says seriously.

I look for a name tag. I don't find one. I don't know what to call him. "I might be a little nervous," I admit.

"I think we'd better keep you sedated for the next few days."

"But I'm feeling better." In fact, my new headache is getting worse.

The doctor pushes a button, and a nurse comes in with an IV stand and bag. I don't argue, because what if they're right?

The next time I wake up, the doctor is waiting for me, asking more questions.

He checks the IV bag, brushes his finger on the tape holding down the needle in my arm, and pretends to take my pulse again.

"Where did you say you worked again?"

"An accounting firm," I say wearily. "It's not very interesting."

"Can you tell me who your boss is?"

"He's Darren Bane. He's an accountant. An auditor."

"I mean who he really is?"

I shake my head, confused. "That's it, that's all he is, I told you."

"And who are you, Miss Smith?"

"I'm nobody. I just run his office."

"What do you mean, 'run his office'?"

"He's good at his job but he's not very practical, you know? I have to remind him to pay bills, I make sure there's coffee for the coffee maker—"

"Are you sure?"

"What do you mean, am I sure? Of course I'm sure."

"There's nothing else?"

I wince. "He also never remembers the network login. I have to reset his password a couple times a week."

"An administrative assistant," the doctor says flatly.

"Yes."

"Your pulse is elevated again," the doctor says, as if disappointed. "Do you know where Darren Bane is now?"

"No. But if you gave me my phone I could call him—"

"Get some rest for now. I think your injury may be a little worse than we thought. You really should have worn your helmet."

"But I didn't . . . I don't think . . ."

"You definitely seem agitated, Miss Smith. Maybe we ought to increase the dosage."

"No, I'm fine. I'm really fine."

The doctor leaves.

This time when I wake up; I'm strapped to the bed by my wrists and ankles, nearly immobilized. I don't panic. It seems a natural progression. The room is the same, smelling of antiseptic cleaner and exhaustion. The IV needle is still in my arm, a clear liquid dripping into it.

"Miss Smith, how are you today?"

I flinch because I hadn't heard the doctor come in. "I'm not feeling too good," I say honestly. I want to get up and walk around. I want to know how long I've been here.

"Well then. We just need to find out a few things, then we'll get you fixed right up."

"I don't think you ever told me your name," I say. "I don't even know what hospital I'm at."

He looms over me, smiling. "Now, don't worry about that. Just worry about getting well."

"Are you the doctor?"

A beat, and then, "I'm wearing the white coat, aren't I?"

That doesn't seem like a good answer. "I don't know what's wrong with me."

"You fell. Don't you remember?"

I still don't remember. I've fallen off lots of horses lots of times, but that was years ago, when I was a kid. When I still had a horse. And I would have worn my helmet.

"Miss Smith, tell me about Darren Bane."

"He's my boss," I say plaintively. "You know that. I don't know what else you need to know."

"He's out of the office a lot."

"He travels," I say. "He's an auditor. He does on-site audits."

"And you handle the office while he's gone."

"Well, sort of. It's not that big a deal. I get the mail and answer the phones and stuff. I'm his administrative assistant."

"Now, Miss Smith. Tell me the truth. What are you *really*? Just what is it you do for Darren Bane?"

I pull my wrists, kick my legs, but caught up in thick nylon and Velcro straps, they only move an inch. "He's an accountant. I'm the administrative assistant—"

"No. What are you really?"

"That's it, an administrative—"

"You're lying."

"I'm not—"

"What are you?"

I start crying, embarrassed and ashamed to be crying, sniffing hard as my nose clogs up.

"This doesn't have to be hard," the nameless doctor says. "Just tell me who you really are, and what you really do."

I've always been so sure that I could be strong if I needed to be. The kind of heroine I've read about. And here I am, crying wet, messy, painful tears.

"Miss Smith, I need to know—"

"All right, fine, fine! I'm a secretary! Just a secretary. A glorified secretary! I have a master's degree in literature and mostly I just make coffee and go out for dry cleaning. That's it. I mean—I've read *Finnegans Wake* but this is the only job I could get! I'm sorry!"

The doctor frowns. I sniff, catch my breath. Think maybe I've stopped crying but I can't feel my face anymore. The clicking of some monitor fills the silence.

"You're lying," he says finally.

"I know, I should have said it right off, I'm a secretary, just a secretary."

"I don't believe you," the doctor says curtly.

"But—"

"No one's read *Finnegans Wake.*"

"But I did, I wrote a paper on it, on anticipatory postmodernism, it even got published, and now I'm just a secretary—"

The doctor turns and leaves. The door shuts firmly behind him.

Being scared is probably normal when you're stuck in a hospital bed. But I'm not really sick. At least, I didn't start out sick. This time I'm woken by a bright light, and the expressions on their faces are no longer kind. The questions continue, and what I learn: these people, whoever they are, are on a deadline.

"Where is Darren Bane?"

"How am I supposed to know—"

"You work for him, don't you? You must know what he really is—"

The doctor—the man in the white coat, rather—and nurse are both in on it.

"Is he nice to work for?" the nurse asks conversationally as she changes out the IV bag. Like this is normal.

"I guess. He gives out Christmas bonuses and things."

"Do you ever travel with him?"

"No, I take care of the office." I've said this a dozen times already. "So are you a neurosurgeon or what?"

The doctor seems taken aback. "Why do you say that?"

"You keep saying I have a head injury, that I fell off a horse. So I figure you must be a neurosurgeon, if there's something wrong with my head, you must know what—"

"Miss Smith, I need to you tell me everything you know about Darren Bane."

"He drives a BMW," I say. "And even if he asked me I wouldn't date him."

He blinks. "Why not?"

"Because he's never around. And when he is he's irritable. I don't think he gets enough sleep."

The doctor leaves, and even the nurse looks after him, surprised. But he returns just a moment later carrying what looks like a phone, and I think, finally. I can call my mom, I can call Darren and tell him these people really want to talk to him—

The nurse's eyes widen. "Are you sure?"

"We're running out of options."

He holds the device—which is not a phone, it doesn't have a screen—flat in his hand and presses a button. A light comes on in the center and projects up. Within the light blurry shapes appear, then resolve into a clear image. A movie plays in full color and three dimensions.

"What is that?" I say, gaping. "It's . . . it's a hologram, isn't it? I've never . . . is that even possible?" Clearly it's possible—it's right in front of me.

The holographic movie shows a fight. A group of maybe six men wearing leather jackets and balaclavas are gathered on a dark, damp street. At night, the details are obscure, but their reactions to a powerful figure dropping into the middle of them are plain. They try to overpower the man, but he's too fast, delivering a roundhouse kick even as he smacks two heads together, and those movements flow into a smooth pivot, another kick, and a clean punch that flattens its recipient.

The man, the amazing fighter, wears a formfitting suit of black tinged with silver. It might be made of leather, sleek and supple, with some armored plating. He has on a mask that covers his head. He's like a shadow given form, and in short order all his opponents lie writhing on the ground.

"Is this a movie?" I ask. It's probably a movie.

"No, Miss Smith, it isn't."

He's right. The angle's all wrong, taken from too high up, as if from a security camera mounted on a building, and the frame never moves.

"Who are you people?" I demand. "How are you even doing this?"

"Can you tell me who that is?" the doctor asks.

"How am I supposed to know?"

"The man in the mask is Darren Bane. Now can you tell me where he is?"

I blink at him, then stare at the image, which has started over again, the masked figure punching and kicking his way through the mob of thugs again. That my boss, the accountant Darren Bane, is some kind of masked crime-fighting vigilante is the least surprising thing about all this. All the business trips, his apparent lack of social life and yet also lack of free time, the occasional days he comes to the office with bruises and stiff joints and blames it on racquetball—

"I don't know anything," I say. Maybe I should have seen it. Maybe I should have known. But really, what makes more sense, crime-fighting vigilante or racquetball? "He told me he was playing racquetball."

"The problem," says the man who I'm pretty sure isn't really a doctor, "is that crime-fighting vigilantes usually have sidekicks. And you know Darren Bane's business better than anyone. No one is closer to him than you."

But I'm just a secretary. No, that isn't right . . . I'm the administrative assistant. I manage the office. Does that make me a sidekick?

"But I'm not—"

There's an explosion just then. But I don't remember it, not at first. Head injury. They tell me about it later.

"What's the last thing you remember?"

I don't actually remember the last thing I remember, not anymore. I woke up in a hospital bed, and before that I woke up in a hospital bed.

"I think I got kidnapped," I say groggily. My head hurts, for real this time. It's not my imagination. "These guys, I have no idea who they are but they made me think I was in the hospital, and they kept asking about my boss, and they showed me this video only it wasn't really a video, it was a hologram. They kept asking questions but I swore I didn't know anything."

A man in a white coat is standing by my hospital bed. A different man than the last time, ten years older and thirty pounds heavier, and maybe this one really is a doctor. The tight set to his jaw suggests he is frustrated. "Do you remember the explosion?"

"Explosion?"

I have to think for a moment, and realize that yes I do remember. I remember the explosion that blew the side wall of the hospital room inward. A man appeared. I couldn't see his face, he wore a form-fitting armored suit, his face obscured behind a mask. He came straight to the bed and unfastened the restraints. I was free, I was finally free. And I was sick. Really sick. "I don't think I can stand up," I'd told him, and he seemed prepared for this, carefully sliding out the IV needle, taping over the wound, pulling out other wires and monitors. The medical devices were all screaming, shouting came from down the corridor, and the masked vigilante scooped me up into his arms and there was no place I more wanted to be.

Maybe I will say yes if Darren Bane ever asks me out on a date.

"Hold on," he said, but I was already clinging to him, arms around his neck. He was close enough that I could smell him, some kind of spicy aftershave blended with the sweat of heroism. A gun fired. I grit my teeth and hid my face. Which meant I didn't see what happened, but I felt flames, heard more gunfire and a muffled voice shouting, "This way!" Then we were in sunlight, I was outside, in fresh air, away from the hospital stink. But all my limbs felt like butter and I couldn't move. The masked vigilante, who sheltered me all this time, whispered that everything was going to be all right, that I was safe now, and I believed him, and we were moving away and away—

And I passed out again. I hadn't had anything to eat in days and I hadn't even noticed. Now I'm here. In a hospital bed. Again.

"Do you have a phone?" I ask. "I really need to call my boss. I really need to talk to him." I have so many questions.

"Your boss knows you're here. That's what I'm trying to get you to remember. There was an explosion at the office."

What?

"A gas line," the doctor continues. "You were working late. You were able to call 911, but you have a very bad concussion—"

But that would mean— "I really need to call my boss. Can I have a phone?"

"With a head injury like yours we really don't like you to strain your eyes too much."

"But. Maybe. I could just tell you the number, and you can call—"

"All in good time. For now, I'd like to ask you a few questions. What can you tell me about Darren Bane?"

"He's my boss," I say. "He's an accountant, a forensic accountant. At least I thought he was." My brow furrows.

The doctor takes my wrist with chilled fingers and frowns. "Your pulse is slightly elevated."

"Of course it is!" I'm groggy this time, really groggy. And maybe it was all true, maybe I really was sick, and I should just lie back, let it all fade. But I get out of bed anyway because I don't really have a choice.

"Wait a minute, Miss Smith!"

I walk right past him. Or rather I kind of sway and stumble, with a hand on the bed, then a wall, then the doorknob. A cloth hospital gown hangs loosely on me, flapping around my legs, open in the back, and I don't care. The doctor reaches for me but doesn't actually take hold, which makes me think he really is a doctor. He really is worried.

I open the door and walk out, and I don't know what I'm expecting. A sound stage. A warehouse. A wall held up with two-by-four struts, proving that this is all a fake, a sham. But I'm in a hospital hallway. A normal, institutional hospital hallway with a tile floor and fluorescent lights and cheerful signs on the wall ordering people to wash their hands. And in a chair shoved up against the wall, reading a magazine, is Darren Bane. He looks like what he is, what I always thought he was, a slick hotshot businessman filling out his perfectly tailored suit. He looks up at me and raises an eyebrow.

"He told me you weren't here," I exclaim.

"He thought you weren't strong enough yet for visitors."

I start to say something angry, close my mouth. Glare.

"Out with it," he says.

"This is a stunt." I try to yell, but I'm too tired for that. "You brought me here to try to make me think this was all a hallucination so that you can convince me you aren't really a masked vigilante, that I somehow imagined the whole thing, when it's not true. I mean it is true. And you have enemies, and you were probably keeping all this secret because of some idea that if I knew, I would be in danger, but, well, look what happened, I'm in danger anyway! And here I've been keeping up your front this whole time and . . . and . . . I want a raise. And a better job title. I want to be office manager. I mean, you don't even know the office email login, you need me to do that. And I'm sorry, I'm getting dizzy, I need to sit down."

He deftly stands and guides me to sit in the chair. I put my head between my knees for a minute and when the floor stops shimmering, I straighten and look at him. He smells like aftershave and heroism.

"Office manager, hmm?"

"Yes," I say.

"All right."

This seems easier than I was expecting. "And the raise?"

"Of course." He names a number that makes two hospital stays, even if one of them was fake, seem worthwhile. "Okay then. I'll see you at work, when you're back on your feet."

"Okay."

He brushes his jacket off, smooths back a strand of hair that wasn't out of place, and walks away to the elevators.

The doctor is standing at the doorway. "What did you say your job was?"

Both of us are still watching Darren Bane's departure, the suave poise of him. When I open my mouth to answer, to state my relationship to my boss, I realize the terrible truth. My *actual* new job title.

I say instead, "It's complicated."

Patrick Swenson

When Shawn asked me for a story for his almost-completely-fantasy anthology—a series I adore, by the way—he also said I might consider something set in the world of my novels. Whoops: my novels are science fiction mysteries. Or, as I like to call them, space opera noir.

I was writing a dark fantasy novel at the *time* Shawn asked, but deadlines being what they are, I wasn't going to be able to fulfill *that* request in time. (That novel is now complete and will be looking for a home soon.) I decided, however, to give him a *fantasy* mystery. The story literally started with that first line and went from there. Now I have an idea ricocheting in my head about a novel set in this world. Well, damn. *Now* it shows up.

Patrick Swenson

HAWKEYE

Patrick Swenson

At dusk, Jarrel stood on the parapet atop the castle's south tower and waited for the hawk to return. Concerned, he searched the deepening sky, hoping his earlier worries about the hawk would fade. He folded his arms against his heavy cloak.

A good ten minutes passed before he saw the hawk silhouetted against the dying sunset, flying out of the Southlands. Jarrel closed his eyes and concentrated, initiating contact with the hawk by releasing his *animale* self. His mind's eye centered on the approaching hawk. He knew the hawk's name—this was a necessity for communing—but though his *animale* soared freely and pulled within several wingspans of the bird, Jarrel could not break through. He should not be having this kind of difficulty communing with the hawk.

"Talam," whispered his spirit voice. *"Talam, commune."*

Talam seemed to hear him. Or was it Jarrel's imagination? The hawk's wings beat erratically, as if the spirit voice were an intrusion, not a call for the *animale* communion.

"Talam," he pleaded.

This time, the hawk did not respond in any way.

Someone cleared his throat lightly behind him. "Jarrel?"

Jarrel broke the *animale* trance and opened his eyes, recognizing the voice of his servant Polto. Jarrel sighed as he watched the hawk turn and head west toward the sea.

"I apologize for interrupting, Jarrel," Polto said, "but the queen insists on seeing you. She asked half an hour ago, but I didn't know where you were. She said it was urgent."

Jarrel turned toward Polto, the young man he'd met a few months ago at the weeklong Animale Games in Saleena. Jarrel had participated in the Games, but Queen Laurice, without his knowledge, recommended him to the Games Committee as an investigator. Quite a number of money pouches had gone missing during the first few days of the Games, and the queen had forced the committee to put him into service to uncover the thefts.

Jarrel discovered the culprit fairly quickly. Polto, nearly two heads shorter than himself, had a clever system that allowed him to deftly lift pouches unseen. He would pretend to gyrate in the manner that some *animale* practitioners did to call their animals, and in the process, bump into those attendees careless enough to have their pouches within view. In the confusion, Polto came away with their money.

Clever, but of course Jarrel spotted him, since he'd had an idea of what to look for. He followed Polto to see where he went afterward. Polto used some of the money to buy food, some to buy passage to the far end of Saleena, and the rest he gave to his mother, feeble and bedridden.

Jarrel hadn't had the heart to arrest him. Jarrel had been swamped with investigative jobs recently, hired by those within the city, and sometimes from the Crown. More than once, he found himself wishing he had added help in these endeavors.

So instead of arresting Polto, he hired him. After confronting the thief and making the offer, Jarrel continued with the Animale Games, but it wasn't long before he was eliminated. He was beyond good in his ability to commune with Talam, but he'd never competed before, and didn't know how to work the hawk the way the judges wanted.

Jarrel left with Polto several days before the Games ended, returning to the castle with Jarrel's promise that he would do his best to help Polto's mother. Polto's kindness toward his mother had made Jarrel take pity.

"Jarrel, did you hear?"

"Yes. Urgent." Jarrel smiled. "Indeed, I actually know what it's about."

"You do?"

"A precious matter to be sure. I spoke with Chancellor Skaal an hour ago." He inclined his head toward the tower door, behind which echoed heavy footsteps. "In fact, so precious—and urgent—it sounds like she couldn't wait. That's her now."

The tower door opened, and the queen stormed through. "Jarrel."

"Queen Laurice," Jarrel said, and bowed formally.

"Oh stop," she said. "I truly *hate* it when you bow."

"Apologies."

"And stop apologizing." She glared at Jarrel. "Do you think you could put some haste into your work? Must I come running up here to find you myself? I could catch a chill."

Queen Laurice wore an evening robe of violet silk and fur, and even as Jarrel took notice, the queen wrapped her arms around her shoulders and shivered. In her sixtieth year, her long black and gray-tinged hair fanned behind her as the wind picked up. She looked him over quickly, as if searching for some kind of physical flaw in his own cloak. Reaching out with her hand, she grasped a button and tore it from the fabric. Jarrel began to protest, but he quickly realized what she was up to. He could always get another button. Laurice Sunderstone was a Changer. She was preparing to do magic.

The queen held the button between thumb and forefinger, closed her eyes, and whispered something completely foreign to his ears. The button lost shape and shimmered like a mirage. Within a few breaths, the button gained mass and weight, and before long, she held tight to a shawl made of heavy wool. She wrapped it around her shoulders and sighed with relief, as if the shawl had saved her from certain death.

Jarrel, impressed with the queen's magic, often wished he could do something more magical than speak to hawks. A Changer had power most people but dreamed of.

"Polto just now told me, Queen Laurice. I was on my way—"

"The Tappan stone is gone, Jarrel. Did you hear me? It's *gone.*"

Jarrel nodded. "I know."

"The Tappan?" Polto whispered. "How can that be? It is guarded day and night—"

"You already know?" the queen asked.

"Before I came up here," said Jarrel. "I ran into Chancellor Skaal and he told me it disappeared sometime between supper and First Watch."

Polto mumbled something and made a sign of protection.

"He should not have," she said.

"Perhaps not."

"I want you to find it, Jarrel. I know it's not your area of expertise, that you're best doing surveillance, but scour the entire Kingdom if you have to. The stone may be small, but worth more than life itself. If the Tappan is not found before King Torrance returns from overseas, there will be sorrow in this castle unlike any ever known."

Jarrel glanced toward the sea and caught sight of the black speck of the hawk. Somewhere out there King Torrance's ships sailed, returning from the long peace talks with Varlaux. The Tappan stone, worth more than all the gems of the Kingdom put together, had been an offering of goodwill from King Renner of Varlaux. It was a gift the Varlaux king sent at Laurice's insistence. It was a sure way to guarantee the safe passage of King Torrance on his journey to Renner's kingdom and back.

Jarrel understood the severity of the situation. If Queen Laurice could not return the Tappan stone to the ambassador. . .

"Seeing as King Torrance is due back in a few days, I will get to work immediately," Jarrel said.

Jarrel had come up to the tower after hearing about the Tappan from Chancellor Skaal. He'd hoped to use his *animale* connection with Talam before the queen's arrival and send the hawk looking for the Tappan, but that hadn't happened.

Jarrel was on his own; Talam would not be of any help during the investigation.

Two days to discover the Tappan stone. It seemed an impossible task.

Jarrel spent the first half of the next day searching the castle. He spoke with innkeepers and other merchants, asking if they had taken notice of anything out of the ordinary. He queried clergy about any unusual offerings, or any sudden changes of behavior in members of their congregations.

He then met with Bakal, the best seer in the Kingdom, hoping the old man could make a connection with the Tappan stone.

The seer was ancient, older than Skaal. He had long white hair and a beard that reached to his stomach. His eyes were clouded with blindness.

Bakal said, "Since I've not been in direct contact with the Tappan, I can't sense it, even to narrow down any general location within the castle."

"Chancellor Skaal never brought you in to see the Tappan to make an initial connection?" Jarrel asked. "Never brought you in to touch the stone?"

Bakal shook his head.

Skaal was in charge of the king's guards, and the guards had been tasked with the important duty of protecting the stone. Since he had to see Skaal again to ask more questions, Jarrel, finding Bakal's testimony most curious, bid farewell to the old seer and made his way to the chancellor's rooms. Jarrel found Skaal writing in the library.

"Ah, Jarrel," Skaal said. "I hear you're on the case. How goes the investigation?"

The chancellor was not as old as Bakal, but he'd seemed old to a young Jarrel when King Tymon had died. Tymon's heir, Torrance, took the throne at age sixteen. Because Torrance was without magic and needed a Protector, Skaal became his regent.

Skaal was an Eliminator. He could wish things out of existence if necessary. Once, he had thwarted an assassination attempt on Torrance's life by eliminating the attacker's knife. When Torrance turned eighteen, he married Laurice, a powerful Changer, and Skaal gave up his regency and became chancellor.

"The investigation led me to Bakal," Jarrel said.

Skaal managed a weak smile. "Ah. The seer."

"He says he was not brought to see the Tappan stone when the Ambassador of Varlaux left it with you. Why?"

Skaal shrugged. "I didn't think it necessary."

"Really?"

"Security, Jarrel. The queen insisted that no one be allowed near the stone."

Jarrel clasped his hands behind his back and rose up and down on his toes. "Certainly understandable then."

"And have you spoken with Polto yet?" Skaal asked, putting down his pen. He squinted at Jarrel.

"Polto?"

Skaal leaned back in his chair, his face showing his distaste for the man. "Come now, Jarrel. How long have you known him? A month?"

"Two."

"He is a known thief."

Jarrel clenched his teeth. He knew the truth of Skaal's accusation but disliked the chancellor's tone.

"I did some checking when you brought him to the castle," Skaal said. "You remember. The Animale Games. It seems you weren't entirely truthful about Polto. You missed the last few days of competition, and no more thefts were reported in Saleena during the Games. Interesting, no?"

"Be that as it may, what possible reason could Polto have for taking the Tappan?" As soon as he asked it, he knew what Skaal would say.

"His family is quite poor. You're funneling some of your own earnings to his mother, meager as they are."

Jarrel didn't argue the point, but was impressed how much

Skaal had found out on his own. Jarrel wondered if he should worry about Polto. There *was* some validity to Skaal's concerns about the servant.

"Well," Skaal said, rising from his chair, "if you'll excuse me, I have an audience with Queen Laurice."

Jarrel came out of his thoughts in time to respond to Skaal. "I'll follow you there. I must make a quick report to her."

Skaal inclined his head, then headed for the door. They walked out of the library and through the main hall of the royal palace in silence, up to the noble's chambers, through the back servant's rooms, and beyond. Jarrel trailed behind Skaal, surprised at how easily the old man navigated the castle's myriad passageways and staircases. Their footsteps echoed in the hall, their shadows dancing on the gray stone walls as they passed lighted torches in their sconces. Jarrel smelled something roasting in the kitchen two floors below and remembered he hadn't had anything to eat all day.

When they reached the garden, a darting shadow in the sky startled Jarrel. It was Talam. The hawk made odd movements, as if playing a game, circling most often to the left, making unnatural dips, climbing high, his wings stuttering from time to time.

Jarrel, though worried, had no time to attempt communion with Talam.

Skaal also noticed the hawk, and laughed. "It has eaten from the dagal root, obviously."

"No," Jarrel said. "It's something else."

"What?"

"I don't know," he murmured, frowning at the wobbly shadow.

They left the garden and entered the foyer to the throne room, where two of Skaal's guards stopped them short.

"We have an audience," Skaal said.

One guard entered the room and returned a few moments later. "Go ahead, sirs."

Queen Laurice met them at the door. She was dressed in formal silks of glittering shades of blue and purple, and her gold crown sat slightly askew on her head. Lines of worry on her face marred her natural good looks.

"Jarrel," she said, "what have you found?"

"Nothing, and everything."

Laurice frowned at him. "You're a puzzle, Jarrel. Must you always be so?"

"He has spoken with Bakal," Skaal said. "And we discussed his servant Polto."

Jarrel frowned at Skaal's mention of Polto, but kept quiet. The queen's commission for him to investigate the Tappan's disappearance was indeed an important matter, and he had to consider every possibility.

Laurice walked quickly back to her throne and sat, but remained rigid. Beside her, King Torrance's empty throne reminded Jarrel of the urgency of the investigation. The red curtain behind the thrones fluttered slightly from a breeze coming through an open window.

"Maybe I should bring both men here," she said. "Turn them into dung heaps until one of them confesses."

"That seems a bit harsh," Jarrel said.

She sighed, finally slumping a little in the throne. She seemed not to register Jarrel's insubordination. "What a messy business this all is."

"Particularly if you change them into—"

Skaal cleared his throat. "About your meeting with the advisors this afternoon. . ."

She waved him forward. "Yes, come, tell me. Jarrel, you'll excuse us a moment."

"Of course," he said, and barely managed to keep from bowing.

"You can tell me what you've learned when we're finished," she said.

Jarrel nodded and withdrew, backing up several steps before turning. He walked casually to the door, then began following the wall around the throne room, one hand on stone, finger tracing the mortar. Laurice and Skaal spoke in low tones, loud enough for Jarrel to hear that they were indeed talking about the upcoming meeting with the advisors. About halfway around, almost directly behind the thrones, he noticed something on the floor. He bent down for a closer look and saw several tiny black ovals.

He picked one up and rolled it in his fingers. It was soft. He brought it to his nose and sniffed. "Speaking of dung," he whispered.

More specifically, hawk dung.

That evening, after a meal of roast pork and half a loaf of fresh bread from the kitchens, Jarrel tried to commune with Talam. The air was colder, the wind more brisk. The hawk showed up but wandered aimlessly, keeping his distance from the castle.

Gazing out at Talam, Jarrel thought about the discovery of the hawk dung in the throne room. He had given his regrets to Queen Laurice and excused himself, telling her he would talk to her on the morrow when he was rested and could better understand what he had learned.

He had spoken the truth when he told Laurice "Nothing, and everything." He had found many bits and pieces, but it still left him with nothing tangible to solve the mystery.

His early attempts to solve this puzzle had been inadequate, and Laurice's concerns about his detection skills beyond the simple tasks of surveillance seemed warranted.

Then he reminded himself he had only just begun the process, and King Torrance's ship was not due back until the day after tomorrow.

Talam's awkward circles eventually took him out of Jarrel's sight. Sighing, he retired to his quarters, sprawling on the animal skins covering his bed, not bothering to undress. He continued to concentrate on what he had learned until he drifted off to sleep.

He dreamed of his past.

His *animale* master, Hrisko, looked intently into the eyes of a hawk. The hawk was tethered to a wooden perch. Jarrel, a young boy, was dressed in the long gray robe of the *animale* initiate.

Hrisko raised an eyebrow and cocked his head, all the while gazing at the hawk. "Interesting," he whispered. "Interesting."

"What is it, Master Hrisko?" Jarrel asked.

He redirected his gaze to Jarrel. "He says you don't know what you're doing."

Jarrel groaned. "I am *trying*, Master Hrisko," he said. He brightened for an instant, a victorious smile crossing his face. "I *do* know that the hawk's name is Ranta."

"Good, you know his name. And he knows you."

Jarrel's shoulders drooped. "I can make the connection, Master. I can *hear* him, but I still can't communicate."

"That's because you're still trying to use your tongue."

"Master? I'm speaking aloud?"

Hrisko turned and smiled at Jarrel. "No, but the connection between mind and tongue is what you haven't broken."

"Then how do I commune?"

Hrisko held up a finger. "Concentrate, Jarrel, and I will show you." He pointed to the hawk.

Jarrel nodded and closed his eyes. The path to Ranta became clear, like an elongated bubble stretching between them. He made the connection quickly.

"Do you see Ranta?" Hrisko asked.

"No," Jarrel said.

"Your eyes are closed."

"Yes."

"Open them."

Jarrel did so.

"Do you see Ranta?"

"Well, yes. Of course."

"Can you hear him?"

"Yes."

"Then speak to him."

Jarrel nodded and closed his eyes again.

"No!" Hrisko said. "With your eyes open."

Jarrel opened his eyes once more, confused. "The connection. It's made with the eyes?"

"Yes. Speak to Ranta."

Jarrel took a deep breath, made the connection with his eyes open, and began communion.

The bubble was there just as surely as it had been with his eyes closed. But now it shimmered and widened, and all at once it seemed as if the hawk became more defined, gaining an emotional and spiritual reality, more real the more the bubble shimmered. Ranta offered his name again, and Jarrel said a phrase of communion he'd learned during his *animale* lessons.

"He hears me!" Jarrel shouted. "With my eyes open he hears!"

"You speak with the mind's eye," Hrisko said. "Your physical eyes are windows to the soul, to the *animale.* You are a creature of reason, but the hawk is a creature of habit and instinct. Keep communing and see what happens when I alter the connection."

Hrisko rummaged in a bag at his side and pulled out a small black hood. Calmly, the master approached the hawk, cooing softly. He placed the black hood over the hawk's head, and instantly, the connection broke, the shimmering path to the hawk gone. Ranta was mute, and Jarrel came out of the trance.

Jarrel blinked and stared open-mouthed at Hrisko.

Hrisko smiled with pride and said, "From now on, I will call you Hawkeye."

Jarrel woke.

Sunlight streamed into his east window. He rose and sat on the edge of the bed, recalling the dream. "Nothing, and everything," he whispered.

He had promised Queen Laurice an accounting of the investigation, and he would definitely give her one.

Out in the hallway he called Polto.

Polto straggled out of his own room, rubbing sleep from his eyes. "Yes, Jarrel?"

"We have an audience with the queen."

"We? This early?"

"Yes. Run ahead and announce us, will you Polto? I have an errand to do first at the eastern guard tower."

Polto nodded and ran off toward the queen's chambers.

"You'd better have good reason for waking me this early in the morning, Jarrel," Laurice said, cinching her robe tighter. Polto was there, in one corner, and so was Chancellor Skaal, sitting on a wooden chest. "It better be good news," she added with a sigh.

"It is, and it isn't."

Laurice shook her head, looking Jarrel up and down. She sat on her bed. "You *are* a puzzle."

Skaal stood and smoothed out his own night dress. "Well, I heard Polto running down the hall and decided to see about the commotion. But if you don't need me, I'll go back to bed."

"Stay," Jarrel said. "For I've discovered who took the Tappan stone."

Skaal blinked in surprise, then sat.

Laurice said, "What? Already?" She glared at Polto, who suddenly looked nervous.

Jarrel walked over to Polto, whose eyes betrayed his worry. "Polto was a thief, and his mother was poor, this much is true. The Tappan stone is priceless, but therein lies the problem. Who in his right mind would think for a minute of trying to sell the Tappan stone for coin? Polto *was* a thief, but no longer. And his mother is living comfortably at least."

Queen Laurice smiled. "I never doubted Polto for a moment."

Polto looked relieved, but Jarrel thought he saw a moment's irritation on his servant's face.

Jarrel turned his attention to the chancellor. "Chancellor Skaal. You never made contact with Bakal, the seer. Was it so Bakal couldn't track the whereabouts of the Tappan? So you could hide it without worrying whether the seer would find it in a place that incriminated you?"

"No!" Skaal insisted.

"No," Jarrel said. The thoughts that fell into place during the night after his dream had cleared his head of much of his doubt. Certainly, he'd realized his skill did extend farther than trailing pickpockets. He could read Skaal like an *animale* master. "No, you didn't. But you've resented King Torrance from the day he married

Queen Laurice and you had to give up your regency, isn't that so?"

Skaal slumped, looking at the floor. "Perhaps I resented him," he said. "But I didn't take the stone to enact revenge on him."

"You wouldn't necessarily have had to *take* the stone. You'd only need it to disappear. You're an Eliminator. Destroy the Tappan, and Torrance would be ruined."

Skaal stared hard at Jarrel, his eyes dark and unyielding. "I didn't."

"You're a loyal man, then. You once saved Torrance's life." He walked to the eastern window and looked out toward the sun. "Tell me something, Skaal. Have you, to the best of your knowledge, ever disobeyed an order from King Torrance?"

Skaal's answer was quick. "No."

"An order from Queen Laurice?"

"No."

"Why didn't you allow Bakal to come up to see the Tappan?"

This time there was a pause. Jarrel turned back to Skaal, and on the chancellor's face a flurry of expressions cycled through a handful of emotions before his jaw clenched.

"Why, it was the wish of Queen Laurice."

Jarrel now walked to the bed and crouched down until he was face to face with Laurice.

"You would have the unlikeliest motive for taking the Tappan. It would put your husband at risk. You specifically asked me to lead the investigation. Surely you had nothing to hide."

She smiled a pleasant smile. "Of course not."

He stood, shaking his head. "And that puzzled me. Because you really *do* have a motive. You really don't care much for the king. Yours was a marriage of convenience. Convenient because in truth, you despise Varlaux, don't you? Enough so that you would rather be at war with them than be at peace. Oh, and I certainly know you don't think much of my abilities as an investigator. Apart from watching money pouches."

Laurice reddened and patted her hair. "That's very interesting, Jarrel, but I'm still waiting to find out what happened to the Tappan."

"Polto," Jarrel said, turning to look at his servant. "Do you remember the night on the tower, when you came to get me? When Queen Laurice told me to find the Tappan?"

"Yes, Jarrel."

"Did you see her do anything unusual?"

He shook his head. "No. I mean, nothing unusual for a Changer. She turned one of your buttons into a shawl."

"Do you have the shawl, Queen Laurice?" he asked, turning once again. "Could you retrieve it?"

"It's in my wardrobe."

"Could you retrieve it?" he repeated.

She stared at him a moment, then gave a sigh of exasperation. "Fine. Yes, of course." She stood and went to her wardrobe. In a few moments she found the shawl and gave it to Jarrel.

Jarrel nodded his thanks and took it over to Polto. "Take a close look, Polto. What do you see here embroidered on the corner?"

Polto peered intently at the shawl. "I see two letters. An *L* and an *S*. Those are initials."

"Laurice Sunderstone," Jarrel said.

"It's my shawl," Laurice said. "So?"

"Well, I was always under the impression that you were a Changer. You take an ordinary object and change it into something else." He jabbed a finger at his temple. "I *thought* about that, you know. That you might have changed the stone into something, and no one would be the wiser. But when I realized what you were doing with your magic, I knew you couldn't possibly have done that."

Laurice smiled. "Of course not."

"You're not a Changer, you're an *Exchanger.*"

"What?" Skaal said.

Laurice was silent.

"You didn't change my button into that shawl. That shawl already existed. It's *yours*. You simply made the button and shawl trade places."

Skaal drew in a breath. "Good gods," he said.

Laurice looked uncomfortable. She smoothed a wrinkle out

of the bedcovers. "So I'm not a Changer. Where are you leading with this, Jarrel? Do you have the Tappan or not?"

Jarrel reached into his pocket and pulled out four round black objects. "I found this hawk dung behind your throne."

Laurice paled and put a hand to her throat. She let it flutter there, nervously.

Jarrel put the dung back in his pocket. "I didn't tell you this, but I've been unable to commune with my hawk, Talam. He won't respond to me. He flies as if insane."

"That's—unusual," Laurice said.

"Here's what happened." Jarrel sat on the bed next to Laurice. He draped her shawl over his knee. "Before meeting with me, while in your throne room, you made the shawl and hawk trade places. That put Talam there with you in the room."

"What?"

"Of course, that left your shawl somewhere outside on the ground. You couldn't figure out any other way to capture the hawk, and you certainly didn't know I communed with it." He raised the shawl. "That night out on the tower, you realized you didn't have this, and exchanged my button for it."

"So I like hawks," she said. "Why *not* bring one inside the throne room?"

Jarrel shook his head. "Once you had the hawk, once you could visualize this particular hawk, you exchanged again."

Queen Laurice said nothing.

"Exchanged for what?" Skaal asked.

Jarrel ignored Skaal's question. "Last night I had a dream. I dreamed of my past, when I was a boy studying under Master Hrisko. You remember him, don't you Queen Laurice? You studied with him for a time yourself, though you never did do well as an *animale* initiate."

She glared at him, but nodded.

"I learned to commune with hawks by realizing that I had to use my eyes," Jarrel said, "not my tongue. When sight is altered in any way, the connection is lost. That is especially true of the *animale*. In my dream, as in my past, I could not communicate with the hawk when Hrisko put a hood over his head."

Jarrel stood, handing the shawl to Laurice.

"So finally," he said, "you took the Tappan and exchanged it for one of the hawk's eyes."

"Good gods," Skaal said again.

"Like"—Polto stuttered—"like a glass eye!"

Laurice leaned away from Jarrel, then stood.

"That's why I couldn't speak with Talam," Jarrel said. "You damaged his sight, and it broke any possible connection with me. This wasn't your intent, not knowing about Talam. You simply hoped that without direction, he would wander off, perhaps to the far villages, where food is plentiful, taking the Tappan away from the castle."

Laurice walked away, came to stand by the window. "Like you said, Jarrel, you have everything, and nothing. No Tappan, no proof."

"I *had* nothing," Jarrel said. "Polto, would you please open the door? I have a guest outside."

Polto nodded and slipped by everyone to the door. When he opened it, a young man in uniform came in carrying a burlap bag. On his back was a bow and quiver of arrows.

Jarrel motioned the young man to him. The man gave Jarrel the bag, turned and bowed to Laurice, then left the room.

She whispered, "I hate it when people bow."

Jarrel opened the bag. The hawk was there, injured but alive. "That was one of our best archers. Clipped Talam's wing, enough to bring him down."

He held up the hawk, and the Tappan stone was there, in the hawk's right eye. The red gem, flawless, glowed as if from an inner fire.

Laurice made for the door, but Skaal, still quick in his old age, got there first and blocked her way.

"You still have the eye, don't you?" Jarrel asked her. "You had someone cast a spell to preserve the eye. Someone insignificant in the scheme of things, someone who didn't understand what was going on or realize the full seriousness of the matter. So that after you were rid of Torrance, you could, no matter how far away Talam was from the castle, exchange Talam's eye with the gem and miraculously find the Tappan again."

Laurice was as silent as the hawk, which had not moved since being taken out of the burlap bag.

Jarrel glared at her. "Where is it?"

Laurice hung her head and said, "A box. Under my pillow."

Polto went to the bed, removed the pillow, and found the box.

"Look inside, Polto," Jarrel said.

Polto looked and made a face. "Looks like an eye to me."

Jarrel held the hawk higher. "Make the exchange. Do it now, and King Torrance might be lenient when he returns."

Laurice sighed, tears pooling in her eyes. She closed them, the tears tracking down her white face, and mumbled softly.

The exchange was made. Jarrel knew it before looking at the box. At this close distance, he could sense Talam's presence and his confusion. He squawked loudly, trying to move from Jarrel's grip. Jarrel communed easily with the hawk for a few moments, then broke the light trance and put his hand out for the box.

While Polto gave the box to Jarrel, Skaal took Laurice gently by the elbow. "Come on, Laurice. I'll have to take you to a holding cell until King Torrance returns and can decide what to do."

"That's *Queen* Laurice," she mumbled.

"Not anymore," Jarrel said.

Laurice lowered her head, avoiding eye contact with Jarrel, who had come up close beside her. The hawk squawked again.

"You can't blame him," Jarrel said. "Talam really doesn't like you."

Then Skaal led her away.

Polto followed to the door, poked his head out into the hallway, and watched them disappear down the corridor. When he turned back into the room, he said, "The Tappan. What will you do with it?"

Jarrel gave the hawk to Polto and took the Tappan out of the box, holding it up to the morning light. It shone like wildfire. "Take it somewhere safe."

He would take it to the seer, Bakal, where it would remain until King Torrance's return. Then it would be given back to Varlaux, and peace between the two kingdoms could begin. He smiled at Polto. "First, I'm going to talk to Talam for a while. Then I'll get him some help for that wing of his."

"I like him," Polto said.

Jarrel nodded, pleased. Maybe Polto would make a good *animale* initiate.

Polto smiled, giving Talam back to Jarrel.

After Polto had left, Jarrel communed with Talam. For the first time in a long while, he felt peace.

Ramón Terrell

When Shawn invited me to write a story for part three of his amazing *Unfettered* anthology series, I had to take few moments to come down off the excitement of such an opportunity so that I didn't foam at the mouth all over him through the computer screen. This series of anthologies means a lot to me for several reasons. The first *Unfettered* was born by top SF&F authors coming together to donate short stories into what would become a bestselling anthology to help a truly worthy cause. Being part of *Unfettered*, which launched Grim Oak Press and lists some of the biggest and best authors in the genre, is a high honor that has left me thrilled and humbled.

My decision to write "The Spectral Sword" came through my longtime desire to return to the World of a Broken Age. I started that world when I was a new author. My first book in the series, *Echoes of a Shattered Age*, was the first book I ever wrote. Looking back, I see how much I've grown since then. I wanted to write something in that world again that would introduce people into the World of a Broken Age, before the events in *Echoes*. This story sits in a book among giants. I truly hope you will enjoy it.

Ramón Terrell

THE SPECTRAL SWORD

Ramón Terrell

1

Staring across the threshold of the underground chamber, Shinobu could imagine the admonishments of every one of the teachers—young to practically ancient—of the farstrider clan. Just as when he was a boy, they would warn him about his maturity level not matching his skill. They would have demanded he leave this place.

But they hadn't cried themselves to sleep every night as a child. Shinobu closed his eyes and could see his big sister and brother, smiling teasingly at him after many a beating during their endless sparring matches.

Aika. Hironobu.

Gone. Disappeared one day, with only the faint trace of some otherworldly resonance remaining. "Demonic resonance," the family elder, Hikaru had said. Even now, decades later, Shinobu could see her in his mind's eye, trying to hide the genuine fear in her eyes when she'd detected the residual energy. "Sometimes even a weaker demon can find its way past the barrier between our dimensions, Shinobu," she had told him. "But for one to bypass the wards and take someone back to their world speaks not only of power, but cunning. Beware evil possessed of cunning, boy."

Shinobu opened his eyes and stared at the sword . . . that beautiful sword, sitting secure in a recess in the stone wall on the far side of the chamber. He thought he could hear it calling for him to enter the chamber and take it up in his hands.

The farstrider took a deep breath. Two nights ago he'd dreamed someone had come to him with a sword that could help him free his siblings. The visitor had been shrouded in green mist, but the power of its presence was overwhelming. Shinobu had known better than to tell anyone about the dream; anyone but wise old Hikaru, that is.

"Beware spirits and demons that come to you in dream," Hikaru had warned. "They know our deepest desires and use them to ensnare us, or use us as their instruments."

Shinobu had bowed politely and thanked her without another word. Trap or not, if there was a chance his siblings were alive and he could free them, he would take it.

He remained just outside the threshold, frowning at the sourceless green light that illuminated the chamber like mist drifting in the air. Vertical runes were carved into every wall. Shinobu knew they must be important, but it hardly mattered. He couldn't read them anyway.

He recalled the many stories he'd heard about mysterious chambers like this one. Such places were supposedly scattered around the world, and had survived every cataclysm and human-wrought breaking of the ages. Some were flesh forges: chambers inhabited by malevolent beings who demanded sacrifice of the flesh in exchanged for safe passage.

Shinobu's gaze returned to the sword. He saw no altar of sacrifice, no indication that anything inhabited the chamber. He reached over his shoulder and slid his fingers over the hilt of his own sword for reassurance. If this was a flesh forge, or home to any other type of evil, he'd find out as soon as he stepped into the chamber. Shinobu looked at the sword across the room again. He could barely make out some sort of design etched on the blade. He had to have a better look.

With another deep breath, the strider stepped across the threshold and stopped. If stepping through triggered a trap, he could still dive back out into the corridor. When nothing happened, he took another cautious step forward. Shinobu kept his hand over his shoulder, fingers resting on the hilt of his sword as he eyed the chamber. That no monster or entity materialized made him especially wary. Could the sword itself be some sort of adversary?

He scoffed at the thought. One needn't look far to find a story about a fabled "sentient sword." The idea that an inanimate object could speak to someone had a fun ring to it, but the strider didn't believe in such things. He *did,* however, believe in monsters and evil places housing evil entities. He'd seen too much of the world to be fool enough not to.

After nothing happened, Shinobu straightened and started across the chamber. The runes adorning the walls were sharp-edged and looked as though they could cut him just by looking at them.

As soon as he reached the sword, he noticed that the hilt, while unremarkable, looked especially plain. No ergonomic craftsmanship had gone into it. It was simply a straight silver hilt. The blade was a different matter. Despite any number of conditions in this underground chamber that should have dirtied the naked steel, it glimmered as though sunlight touched it. An unfamiliar purple material composed the middle of the blade from hilt to tip.

Shinobu glanced over his shoulder then leaned in closer to inspect the purple section. As he did so, it pulsated.

He hopped back, then laughed at himself. What did he think it would do, attack him?

"You are a beautiful sword." He stepped in front of it again. Tip downward, the blade was about as wide as his arm, straight, and double-edged. "Why would anyone carve out a recess in the wall and put something so valuable in it?" he thought aloud.

Shinobu's instincts screamed at him not to lay so much as a finger on it. He should leave this chamber behind and forget the sword even existed. Or perhaps he should return home and research the history of this cavern—if any—and its mysterious weapon.

Aika. Hironobu.

Pick up the sword.

Shinobu blinked. Those four words felt like a compulsion. Had it been his own, or an outside thought? He glanced around again.

The chamber hadn't changed. Same stale, underground smell, same green light mist illuminating the space, same foreign runes populating every wall.

With one last thought of his siblings, the strider shrugged off his instincts and reached out. He slid a finger over the hilt, then wrapped his hand around it. The hilt's rectangular shape would make it uncomfortable to wield. He grunted in disappointment and started to let go.

The hilt suddenly shifted form. Shinobu snatched his hand away and took a step back. He stared wide-eyed as the hilt shifted back to its original shape.

You are worthy to wield me, and I am worthy of your skill.

"Hearing voices inside my head," Shinobu said dryly. "Either I've lost my mind or something's in here."

Only the worthy could find me. Only the worthy can wield me. There is no other.

"Yes, losing my mind." In a gesture of sarcasm, he bowed to the sword and turned to leave.

I am condemned to eternity in this cave, for there is no other capable of wielding me. I am wasted.

Shinobu stopped, arrogance and better judgment warring inside him. He thought about the rigorous training to become a farstrider. In his last ten years he'd not met an adversary he couldn't beat, and his strider clan was home to the most lethal of warriors. What could be worse than that? "I can always put it back," he said with a shrug.

He returned to the sword and wrapped his fingers around the hilt. He flinched when it started to change shape again, but held on. Despite the bizarre nature of the sensation, it felt good, as though the hilt had been crafted to fit perfectly in his hand.

Shinobu took a deep breath and removed the sword from its home in the wall. He took a step back and held the blade in front of his face, turning it this way and that. The blade looked sharp enough to cut the gods themselves.

"You are not made of steel," he thought aloud as he inspected the perfectly honed blade. He took a practice swipe. *SHIIING.*

Shinobu nearly dropped the weapon. He swung it again and again. *SHING. SHING. SHIIING.* "Amazing," he breathed. The strider launched himself into a series of swipes and blocks, counters and parries, as he fought multiple imaginary opponents. The sword felt too light to have any sort of durability, yet he had the feeling it could cut through almost anything.

As he practiced, the blade began to fade and waver, as though he looked at it submerged in water. "What . . ." Shinobu held the sword away from him and looked back to the recess. A scabbard rested where the sword had been. How hadn't he noticed it?

The naked blade had fully transformed into some ethereal thing now, waving in the air like a long purple flame. He took a hesitant swipe. *ZNNG. ZNNG.*

Shinobu's eyes lit up. "What can this thing do?"

He went back to the recess and grabbed the scabbard. He looked at it and the waving blade, wondering how he would get such a thing back into the scabbard, which obviously had been crafted for the blade in solid form. He pointed the tip to the opening in the scabbard and brought them close. The wavy blade slimmed to fit the space. Seeing this, Shinobu sheathed the blade, then pulled it out just enough to see that it was solid again.

"What *are* you?"

The runes in the walls flared to life.

2

"Gratitude to the human mortal who frees the key. Behold the khazira."

Shinobu sprinted for the chamber's only exit. Gratitude? The words came from the very air itself. He didn't like the way they felt, and he certainly didn't like the sound of whatever this "khazira" was.

"I'm not 'beholding' anything," he muttered as he neared the exit.

Thud. Thud. THUD.

Shinobu skidded to a stop just in front of the threshold and backpedaled.

His speed and reflexes saved his life. A long white tentacle swung around the corner and crashed into the wall. Debris exploded from the crumbling stone. Shinobu shielded his eyes from flying rock while still running backward. He stopped on the other side of the cavern and drew his own sword.

The ground vibrated with each step of a great hulking humanoid beast that rounded the corner. It had to bend low to get through, then straightened to its full height, easily double Shinobu's.

"Gods," he breathed. "I've done it this time."

The khazira stared pure red-eyed malice at the strider. Its arms and legs were as big as Shinobu's body, its massive heaving chest expanding and retracting. It flexed its fists, and when it opened its hands, the fingers elongated into tentacles, then retracted into long-nailed fingers again.

Parts of its body drifted apart and attached to other areas in a state of perpetual shifting, while the general humanoid shape remained constant.

"I don't suppose you'll just let me put your sword back?" Shinobu asked. "I didn't mean to steal anything."

"Gratitude for freeing the key," the disembodied voice said.

Shinobu waited for the rest. That thing didn't look like it was just going to take the sword and leave.

" . . . and knowledge of it will be erased."

"I'm not going to like this, am I?" he said to the weapon, hoping and not hoping for an answer.

The khazira executes her will. It will never let you pass.

The fact that the weapon had actually responded to him was almost as unnerving as the idea that this hulking monster actually served something else.

"Wys wyrp ssshyeern zzzzyyyerrk." The khazira's shoulders heaved as it regarded Shinobu. It held its massive arms out at its sides, claws flexing, fingers continually elongating into tentacles and back to fingers again.

"I'm sure I don't want to know what that thing just said," Shinobu muttered to himself. His back was almost against the far wall opposite the beast, but he kept from touching it. No telling what would happen if he touched one of those green glowing runes.

"Ysh yyyyrrrop ggeeernn yyyyyrrrrick zzzzzeeeert yyyyyrop."

"What in the five hells are you saying?" Shinobu lowered himself into a defensive stance. The thing was obviously stronger than him, but he might be faster. He'd yet to meet anyone nearly as fast as he, but of course, he'd only fought humans.

It speaks in the tongue of the khazira.

"Obviously." Shinobu didn't like the sword speaking into his mind, but he'd take the deal if it increased his chances of survival. "There's no way to understand it?"

Not in this world.

"Fabulous." Shinobu carefully strapped the mysterious sword across his back and held his own sword defensively in front of him.

Your weapon can do nothing to the khazira. You will die. When the khazira has decided you've died enough, it will send you to her.

"Her?" That set the strider's mind racing. "Who's her?"

All of your fantasies and nightmares combined. Your chance to survive lies with me.

The khazira never moved. It didn't need to. The only exit from the chamber sat right behind it.

Shinobu wasn't sure he trusted the sword. Why hadn't it told him about this thing? And why the mysterious "her"? Why not just say what it meant? He took a step forward. The khazira didn't move. He took another step. No response. The beast stood there, feet wide apart, arms flexing out at its sides, massive chest heaving. Small bits of its body continued to detach and float about to reattach in different places. Those red eyes bore into him like pinpricks of fire.

"Can't stay here forever." Shinobu started walking. As soon as he took a final step placing him within fifteen feet of the beast, it struck.

The khazira drew back and lashed its tentacled fingers down like a whip. The attack came so fast, Shinobu barely reacted in time to avoid being blasted into nothing.

He leaped aside half a breath before five tentacles hammered into the ground in an eruption of stone.

The khazira struck with its other hand. Left, right, left, right, it pounded great thick tentacles into the ground. The sheer ferocity of the attack set the cavern shaking.

"*Shimatta!*" he cursed in his home-tongue as he ducked and dived, leaped and ran. As fast as Shinobu moved, he could barely get ahead of the savagery of the khazira long enough to think of attacking.

Five finger-tentacles crashed into the ground right beside him. The force of the impact lifted Shinobu into the air. The tentacles from its other hand came swinging toward him even as he was still airborne.

Shinobu twisted about and slashed his sword at the incoming appendages. The sword struck true, but the appendages kept coming. They wrapped around his body and pressed the back of the blade against his chest.

"Wrrrryyyraah!" The khazira swung the arm that held Shinobu as it released him.

He knew what was coming. As soon as the beast let go, Shinobu tucked himself into a ball. He turned his body as he flew toward the wall and "landed" with his feet. His intention had been to kick off the wall back toward the beast with a counterattack, but the thing had thrown him with too much force. He quickly bent his legs to keep from breaking them, and actually rolled upward before tumbling back to the ground.

Ignoring what felt like hundreds of scrapes and bruises all over his body, Shinobu flipped back to his feet, leaped forward, and slashed the monster's leg. The strider launched into a flurry, swiping his sword left, right, diagonal, horizontal. Any normal enemy would have been reduced to bloody ribbons. This monster wasn't normal. He might as well have been shouting curses at the beast, for all the effect it had.

The khazira swatted at him again, lashing its ten tentacled fingers at the ground, the walls, every direction the strider fled.

Shinobu kept on the move, using every bit of speed and dexterity in his repertoire to simply not be pounded to a pulp.

A tentacle wrapped around his waist and lifted him in the air. The other four wrapped around the rest of his body, holding him fast like a spider spinning its catch in silk. Through some bit of luck, Shinobu had managed to keep his sword hand free. He tried stabbing and slicing at the appendages, but it was no more effective than if he were hacking at a tree.

No weapon can destroy the khazira, but I can save you. Trust in me.

A sword just implored him to trust in it. Shinobu shoved the question of his sanity to the back of his mind, just in case he survived this. The khazira's other hand was coming in, reaching straight for him. It would rip him apart if that hand got hold. With no time to think twice, Shinobu dropped his sword and drew the sentient one.

To his astonishment, the blade somehow came out of the sheath sideways, as though passing through the hard covering. It also sheared cleanly through the tentacles holding him.

Shinobu fell through the severed appendages and hit the ground in a crouch. He started to reach for his other sword but the khazira had gone into such a rage, he retreated. While fleeing the swinging appendages and flying debris, Shinobu was still struck with awe at the magnitude of the monster's rage-fueled frenzy. The severed tentacles melted away in the air, but the stumps regrew.

That did nothing to quell the khazira's fury. It swung its tentacles in every direction, blasting holes in the walls and ceiling, tearing streaks in the stone wall, shattering whole sections of the chamber. "WwrrryyAAAARRRR!"

The khazira's enraged cry shook the chamber so violently Shinobu was certain it would bring the entire mountain down on them.

You are the first to have hurt it, the sword said into his mind. *Flee now while it is blinded by its anger.*

Shinobu thought "anger" might be putting it mildly. He

sheathed the sword and sprinted for the exit, or tried to. The ground quaked under his feet. More than once, he took a step that simply wasn't there, only to have the ground rise to meet him again as he stumbled.

Five finger-tentacles pounded the ground just in front of the exit, less than ten feet in front of the fleeing strider. Shinobu skidded to a stop just as the khazira leaped into the air and landed in front of the opening with a resounding crash. The ground crumbled under its great weight. It stood with feet widely apart, claws balled into fists.

Shinobu backstepped again. He thought he could feel the weight of its hatred wafting off of the monster. Its shoulders rose and fell, chest heaving as it leveled its baleful red glare over him. This close, Shinobu saw that it had no mouth.

For the first time in his life, the strider knew he stood before an adversary he could not defeat. "This is how it ends. His mind flashed back to his training to become a member of the obscure class of elite warriors, the striders. Faster than anyone he encountered, more precise than even the masters who taught him, Shinobu had risen to the top of his clan. Never had he given ground in a fight.

He thought of the times with his older sister and brother. Aika. Hironobu. Deep down he'd been confident that if he ever discovered his siblings lived, he'd find and free them. Knowing he would die without saving them filled Shinobu with cold despair.

Fool, my wielder. I tell you again, trust in me. Draw me from my home and survive!

The khazira threw its arms back and lashed down with tentacles as large around as tree trunks.

Shinobu drew the sword.

3

The khazira faded away.

Shinobu's mouth fell open and he looked around in alarm. He stood in the same chamber as before, only now, instead of a green light drifting in the air like mist, the entire surroundings were bathed in it. The ominous green light came from everywhere and nowhere.

The chamber walls were undamaged, as were the ground and ceiling. The recess where Shinobu had found the sword stared back at him, unblemished as well. "What is this? Where am I, and where did that thing go?"

I have brought you to Imphetos. The spectral realm.

"Imphetos?" Shinobu whispered. "What is this, spectral realm? I've not heard of such a thing."

This realm mirrors your own, only different.

Shinobu frowned. "A mirror image that's different?" It was then that he finally looked down at the sword in his hand. The blade waved in the air like a slithering snake, and he could feel power pulsating through it. He raised the insubstantial sword in front of him, but before he could analyze it further, the hulking form of the khazira materialized.

He cried out in surprise and jumped back. The transparent form faded, then appeared again, then faded.

"What's happening?" he asked, willing his hammering heart to calm. "What's it doing?"

None native to this plane or yours can enter the other without me, for I am the key.

Shinobu thought the sword sounded like something akin to surprise or confusion.

The khazira struggles to enter Imphetos.

The strider didn't waste another moment. He sprinted for the exit to the chamber just as the brute materialized in front of him again. Shinobu gritted his teeth and hoped it didn't take solid form as he ran straight into it. His luck held, and he passed through it as the monster faded away again. He exited the chamber and turned left, retracing his steps as best he could in the semi-familiar surroundings.

The khazira is not native to either plane, the sword said into his mind. *It was created by her. That must be the answer.*

To Shinobu, it sounded like the sword was actually thinking the situation through. How could that be possible? *"Her?"* he thought in response. *"Do I even* want *to know?"*

You do not.

Fantastic.

He ran down a corridor that only mildly resembled the one he'd previously traversed. Where the original stone passageway had been flat and lined with torch sconces Shinobu had lit, there were only bare walls. The ground rippled out before him as though trapped in stasis during a tremor.

"What in the five hells is this place? *Am* I in one of the five hells?"

Not one of the five hells, the sword replied. *Imphetos.*

"You said that," Shinobu snapped. "But it means nothing to . . ." he finally looked at the sword in his hand, or what was supposed to be a sword. The blade was neither its solid form or the wavy manifestation when he'd kept it unsheathed. It was fully insubstantial, like a dark blue flame attached to the hilt.

Shinobu almost dropped the weapon. *"What is this thing?"*

I am the key.

The sword had read his thoughts again. Shinobu's first instinct was to cast it aside and hope the khazira would find it and leave him alone. He disregarded that notion immediately. The sword had told him more than once that it was the key. Shinobu's very presence in this strange dimension proved that fact. He'd need the sword to get out.

He retraced his steps through the winding corridor, passing through open areas that had been water in his home dimension but were dangerous-looking pools of unfamiliar liquid here.

Water in your dimension is a semiliquid acid in Imphetos, the sword told him.

"So, avoid it," Shinobu replied, his thoughts laced with sarcasm.

I do not know what effect it will have on you, material dweller, the sword responded. *This is not a plane inhabited by your kind.*

Shinobu frowned. *"So it might be harmless?"*

Yes . . . or it may dissolve you.

Disembodied voices drifted through the air. Some words Shinobu understood as human languages, while others were not. He heard tones of anguish and ecstasy, fear, threat, and confusion.

Some voices just sounded . . . lost. He understood that sentiment.

The hairs on the back of his neck stood on end and Shinobu dove into a roll without thinking. The instinct saved him.

Shinobu came to his feet and whipped the sword across his face. A creature that looked like a giant squid, but with three round eyes on either side of its elongated head, floated in the air in front of him. Its tentacles waved about its angular body, coiling, bending, flicking towards him.

Clyto, the sword imparted. *Do not let it grab you, or it will draw you to its funnel and devour your soul.*

"Wouldn't want that." Shinobu kept his stance defensive as he backed away from the thing. It watched him with those unblinking round eyes, all staring right at him, or rather, right into his eyes. There was an intelligence to that stare that the strider found unnerving.

Much like a squid would swim through water, the clyto rose higher into the air and swept down. It pulled up and flicked its tentacles at him.

Shinobu kept the appendages at bay with the sword in a constant dance of strike and dodge, attack and retreat. The tentacles were moving so fast he couldn't tell if there were nine or nineteen. Calling upon a lifetime of training, the strider proved equal to the challenge. Shinobu's speed and dexterity kept him from being grabbed, but to his surprise, he found his endurance to be augmented in this realm.

It is the nature of Imphetos, the sword imparted. *Use it to survive but deny its allure.*

"Noted." Shinobu ducked under a grabbing tentacle and leaped into a backflip. When three more reached for him while he was midair, the strider expertly picked each appendage off. Though it was a simple flick of his wrist, the powerful blade sliced through the tentacles as though they were nothing.

The clyto responded with an anguished wail that sounded like a flat saw grinding across metal. It twitched and spasmed, turning about in the air as though something devoured it from the inside.

"A bit dramatic," Shinobu thought.

It has learned the power of my bite.

Shinobu didn't know whether to be relieved or unnerved by that.

Movement from the corner of his eye caught his attention. Given the nature of this Imphetos dimension, Shinobu didn't bother to find out what it was. He turned and ran.

As more figures darted in and out of his periphery, he got a quick glimpse. More clyto.

You are surrounded. Wield me well.

"Thanks," Shinobu said dryly.

A dozen clyto swam a circle about him, closing in with each pass. Shinobu was forced to stop and hold his ground. He held the sword at his side and watched the passing monsters, waiting for a target to get too close. The attack came without warning.

The farstrider ducked and struck out, leaped and twisted in the air. He found that his muscles never tired, his breathing never labored. He could jump higher as well. He needed all those advantages, for his speed remained the same in this realm. But Shinobu was already fast.

He killed three before the encircling clyto broke formation and backed off. They floated in the air, tentacles waving gently about their bodies as they studied him.

Shinobu dropped into a defensive stance and held the fiery blade in a reverse grip. "Your move."

The clyto scattered.

"I . . . what was that?" Shinobu asked aloud. "Are they put off by a voice, or something?"

Clyto only give up when injured or killed . . .

"Or if something worse comes along," Shinobu finished in his mind.

He heard the same screech as before, only this one sounded like a hundred of them all together in one terrible chorus.

The creature that descended from the dark green sky above might as well have been a hundred of the squid-monsters combined.

Shinobu cursed and took off in a full sprint. He snapped the blade into its sheath on his back and leaned forward. *"Good thing I won't get tired, here,"* he thought.

You cannot outrun it, the sword replied.

"But I might make it there," Shinobu thought, looking ahead to the mouth of another corridor. *"No way it can fit in there . . ."* he craned his neck back to watch the enormous clyto glide mockingly over his head and settle right in front of the mouth of the corridor.

They are intelligent.

"Wouldn't have known if you hadn't told me," Shinobu said with a mental eye-roll. He kept running and drew the sword. It flared to life, blue flame dancing just above his hand. *"You can hurt something that big?"*

I can destroy far more durable adversaries, wielder.

Shinobu held the sentient weapon at his side and ran straight for the waiting monster. He'd need to sever as many tentacles as he could and keep moving. Hopefully he could inflict enough pain that it would retreat, or else he'd have to kill . . .

A black tentacle punched through the back of one of the enormous eyes of the clyto. Three more punched through its elongated body, and two more punched through the head. It let out a deafening scream that nearly buckled Shinobu's knees.

"WwrrryyAAAAAAAAAAAAAARRRR!"

That sound wasn't the clyto.

The giant squid-monster's screams cut off as the black tentacles ripped it apart.

Shinobu skidded to a stop and watched in horror as the black appendages savaged the clyto. Behind the falling pieces of what was left of the monster stood the hulking khazira. It was now black, with bits of white light snaking around its body. It looked even bigger, though nowhere as large as the behemoth it had just torn asunder.

"I think it's really angry," Shinobu thought.

There is not a word in your human tongue to fully define its rage, wielder.

For the first time in his life, Shinobu was at a loss. He knew he couldn't kill that thing, but if it wouldn't stop chasing him . . .

Run toward it and keep me in hand.

"What?" That was the last thing Shinobu wanted to do.

Do as I say, wielder, and trust in me.

Shinobu had no choice. He ran straight for the khazira, and the great beast waited for him. He tightened his grip on the sword, his only hope of survival.

The khazira roared again and whipped its tentacled fingers down on him.

The world shifted.

Shinobu stumbled into the corridor. The real corridor. *"What..."*

You ask that word a lot, wielder. Flee!

Shinobu did just that. A loud crash and the sound of crumbling stone announced the khazira's arrival. "That was fast," he said aloud.

It has adapted.

"How in the five hells do I get that thing off my back?"

The sword's silence carried much weight.

Shinobu sheathed the sword and sprinted through the winding corridors, all too aware that despite his finely honed endurance, he couldn't keep up this pace indefinitely; not in this world.

"Wvt wwwyyyyvt worrrvty zzzzyyeeeert yeeevvt."

Shinobu felt a shiver down his spine. "I wish it would stop doing that."

Tentacles slapped at his heels; the unintelligible words of the khazira drew closer. *Thud thud thud THUD THUD THUD.*

Shinobu drew the sword again. How could the thing move so fast? Surely it had to hunch down in this corridor. Did it shrink its size accordingly?

White tentacles shot past him and overhead. Like spears, the appendages stabbed into the ceiling of the corridor.

Shinobu dove forward with a desperate shout, but the stone ceiling crumbled on top of him.

4

As soon as Shinobu crashed into the ground and realized he wasn't dead, he scrambled to his feet and kept running. *"Thanks for that."*

You are unhappy I intervened?

Shinobu's clenched his teeth. *"It's not that."*

But you are unhappy, I can sense it. You are displeased I saved you from being crushed.

"I assure you I'm happy to be alive," Shinobu explained. *"It's just a blow to the ego that I would have died under other circumstances."*

I have then diminished the arrogance in your self-perception, wielder?

Shinobu mentally sighed. *"How about we leave it for if I find a way to survive this."*

That is wise. The khazira comes.

The hulking beast faded in and out of view in front of him. Shinobu kept running, hoping he could get by before it fully materialized.

The brute solidified once Shinobu was within a dozen feet. The strider dropped and slid between its legs. He swung the fiery blade as he passed through. The blade cut deep into the khazira's leg, yet it didn't sever the limb. Still, the khazira arched its back and let out a terrible bellow.

Shinobu rolled back to his feet and kept running.

Tentacles crash all about him, pounding the ground, the walls, the ceiling. Large rocks and chunks of stone fell apart all around him.

Keep me in hand . . .

"I know, I know," Shinobu interrupted. *"Trust in you."*

Yes. And trust in yourself. I am the key to the spectral realm of Imphetos and the material realm of your world. Use my power.

Shinobu came to a final juncture and turned right, down the final corridor leading to the surface. The khazira dogged his trail, unleashing its ferocity on the corridor behind him. His heart dropped into his stomach when he saw the wall standing between him and freedom. *"No! That shouldn't be here!"*

Remember the nature of Imphetos, the sword said.

A mirror of the material world, but not an exact copy. He knew not how, but Shinobu willed the sword to return him to the material plane.

The world shifted around him, and he found himself running for the mouth of the corridor. Shinobu had never been happier to smell the fresh damp air of the rainy surface beyond.

He ran free of the corridor, out of the mountain, and into the world above. And he kept running.

The khazira burst out several heartbeats later. It leaped high into the air, and Shinobu knew it would crash down on him. He reentered the spectral realm without missing a step. The khazira appeared again, less than a dozen heartbeats later.

It pounded at his heels, swinging and slapping its tentacled fingers at Shinobu's back. "Run forever or surrender to oblivion and rest, thief."

Shinobu's heart fluttered in his chest, and the pit of his stomach went cold at an unfamiliar feeling. Fear. *"Did I just hear that right?"*

Its words are decipherable in the spectral. The sword seemed just as surprised as Shinobu.

"All who take up the key shall cease to be." The khazira's baritone voice sounded as though it came through a funnel, directly into the strider's ears. It made the hairs on the back of his neck stand.

Shinobu crested a hillock and arrived in the midst of a pack of monsters that looked like jackals walking on two legs. They swung toward him, knuckles dragging the ground, wide maws hanging agape as they realized prey had stumbled upon them.

Shinobu killed two before they could attack, and kept going. The grayish-green monsters pursued, their hungry grunts urging the strider onward. When the grunts turned to terror, Shinobu knew what that meant.

One of the monsters crashed into the ground just beside Shinobu. He looked over his shoulder just as the khazira hurled another of the unfortunate things in his direction.

The strider shifted back to the material plane. Mere moments later the khazira hurled a tree at him, which he barely dodged. He still didn't escape being splashed by mud and sand. Shinobu started uphill when a boulder crashed farther up and began rolling toward him. He shifted to the spectral.

The boulder faded from view as he passed through its image. Shinobu leaped left and right, avoiding lunging monsters and swiping claws. He used the sword to dispatch any threat that got close, but above all, he kept running.

Though the ground didn't tremor at its steps, the strider heard the khazira behind him. He heard the screams of every spectral monster that either fled or was ripped apart. Bodies and body parts crashed all around him; tentacles tore up the ground behind him. When the khazira drew too near, Shinobu shifted back into the material plane.

He glanced over his shoulder just as he passed over another hill. The khazira was just materializing as he started down. Shinobu immediately shifted back into the spectral realm. He ran down the hill, but angled left toward a cluster of mounds with green mist seeping out of them.

Shinobu slipped behind one of the mounds and hid. He didn't know what the mist was, but he hoped it was just some other random feature of this twisted world. He lay on the ground and waited, but nothing happened. When he remembered that footfalls couldn't be heard in this dimension, Shinobu carefully peeked around the side.

The khazira stomped down the hill, swinging its torso left to right as it searched. Its tentacles retracted back into clawed fingers. The beast's shoulders heaved, its claws repeatedly flexing into fists. Shinobu could feel the rage wafting off of the thing.

A gurgling squawk drew Shinobu's gaze to the sky where he saw a saber-toothed, bat-winged horror flapping overhead. Unfortunately for the unsightly monster, it glided too close to the brute below.

The fingers on one of the khazira's hands elongated to tentacles and it swung its arm up. The winged monster gave a squawk of surprise that quickly turned to desperation when the tentacles wrapped around one of its legs and squeezed. The khazira yanked the creature straight out of the sky.

Shinobu winced as the beast repeatedly slammed the monster to the ground in every direction. The khazira grabbed it with the hand that still had fingers, retracted the tentacles of its other hand, and tore the monster apart.

It arched its back and threw two pieces of the dead monster behind it as it roared to the green sky above. That was the strider's final view of the beast as the enraged khazira faded from view, leaving a panting Shinobu staring wide-eyed while trying to settle his pounding heart.

Well done, the sword said. *You have eluded it for now.*

"For now?" Shinobu hesitantly rose, eyes darting this way and that. *How would it know where to look for me?*

Whenever you shift from your home dimension to this one, it will know. Whenever you use my true power, it will also know.

"True power?" Shinobu looked at the fiery blade in his hand and again, wondered if he should return it to its place in the wall of the chamber, now that he'd escaped that terrible monster. If the thing could only find him if he shifted planes or used the sword's true power—whatever that meant—he could shift into the material plane and hopefully lose the khazira again, then return to the chamber and be rid of this burden.

You hold the key to many possibilities, wielder, the sword reminded him. *A key such as I can be used not only to access a place, but also to free those who have been imprisoned.*

Shinobu's face tightened. Apparently the sword could access his deeply buried thoughts as well. *"You're crossing a line."*

It is not uncommon for a demon to find a way into your dimension and steal away a prisoner to torment. Alone, you could never find them, but with the key, you have a chance.

The sword's choice of the word "them" wasn't lost on the strider.

Shinobu walked down the hill, still casting his wary glance about in case the khazira or some other weird and twisted monster found him. He stopped at the edge of a cliff that overlooked an enormous canyon.

Aika. Hironobu.

Just the thought of his older siblings threatened to tear his heart from his chest. His remaining family had resigned themselves to never seeing Aika and Hironobu again, accepting that they had likely been killed and taken.

Shinobu had never been able to make himself believe that.

Aika and Hironobu's skills eclipsed his own. No one would have gotten close to either of them, sleeping or awake. Aika would have feathered any would-be assassin with enough arrows to have the corpse looking like a pin cushion. Hironobu would have quickly cut any assailant apart.

There had been no signs of struggle, no blood, nothing damaged. There *had* been one clue: an unidentifiable scent in both homes. He thought again of the wise elder Hikaru. She had known what it was but said nothing. People thought the ancient woman had lost her wits, but Shinobu knew better. He remembered again her warning about demon trickery; about how one may have come to their dimension and taken his siblings. Was it simply to take victims to torture, or was something else at play? And why Shinobu's siblings? The whole thing seemed too targeted.

He looked down at the fiery blade in his grasp and truly wondered for the first time if he'd found a way to locate and free Aika and Hironobu. The sword hadn't lied when it said it was a key, but could he trust it? And what about the figure shrouded in green mist that had come to him in his dreams? It had hinted at a key to saving his siblings.

A feeling deep within pulled at him, interrupting his thoughts. Shinobu frowned. At first he thought it was the sword, but the weapon had gone silent in his mind. He looked out and watched another giant winged creature lazily flying across the canyon. The feeling was faint, but he felt as though it pulled him toward the northwest. A tiny spark lit deep inside his being. It wasn't an explosive flare of power, but a subtle flicker, as though something had awakened.

Shinobu unconsciously turned to the northwest, and the pull grew stronger. Could it be Aika and Hironobu calling to him across the planes of existence for help now that he had found a way to reach them?

"Home." Shinobu looked about his surroundings for a way down. He needed to get back to his home dimension, but he had to plan a way to elude the khazira when it inevitably found him after the shift.

The pull grew stronger when he started moving. Something was definitely calling to him, but what? The strider held the fiery blade in front of his face. "You said this was 'her' dimension. Who?"

Imphetos is the name of the spectral realm; her realm, and the one she named for herself.

"You're saying her name is Imphetos?" Shinobu frowned. "I don't know this name."

Imphetos is of her name, but not her name.

Shinobu took a deep breath to keep from grinding his teeth. "Speak your meaning clearly. I'm in no mood for riddles."

Imphetos is of *her name, but* not *her name.*

Shinobu stared at the sword, moving his lips as he worked the word over and over in his mind. "*Of* her name, but *not* her name? I don't . . ." he trailed off. "Do you mean the word is composed of the letters of her name?" The sword didn't respond, but he received an impression of approval from it. Why wouldn't it just tell him?

Because she is my creator, and I, her betrayer.

The sword was reading his thoughts again. He needed to discipline his mind to block it out. Later.

"Imphetos." Shinobu tried the name backward, but the sword disapproved. He tried it many different ways, but came up with nothing.

She is known in your human lore.

"I've never heard of such a name in the lore of my homeland."

I do not lie.

Shinobu thought about it. The sword might not distinguish between different cultures. "Is this even important?" he asked. The new feeling deep inside tugged at him. "If it is, can you tell me nothing more?"

This is important, the sword assured him. *There are those in your world who know her name. There are those who tricked her by altering my nature in order to seal her away, back to her spectral realm.*

That rang familiar.

Shinobu ducked behind a gnarled tree with branches that writhed in a non-breeze like fingers groping at the air. A six-legged animal with a silver coat and wide jaws trotted by. The bulging muscles in its legs gave a spring to its step that assured the strider it wasn't a predator he'd escape if it found him. The thing had at least two rows of teeth perfect for tearing, and its glowing green eyes were large and round like saucers.

It trotted away and Shinobu let out a long sigh and sat down. He needed to get out of this realm before something terrible found him. He ran his fingers through the dirt—or what was similar to dirt—and found that it felt tangible, but barely so. Such an odd place this was. He chewed his bottom lip as he stared at that dirt, then used a finger to write out the word I-M-P-H-E-T-O-S.

He spelled the word several different ways, but nothing made sense. The sword never reacted either. He brushed over the dirt and tried again, several more times. The last try elicited a spark of approval from the sword. The word was unfamiliar, but it somehow rang true. Shinobu stared at the word for a long time with a growing sense of dread in the pit of his stomach.

The sword had said she was his greatest fantasies and nightmares combined. Seeing the name scratched into the ground now, he remembered Hikaru's warning of a demon possessed of cunning.

The manipulator. The one who knows the greatest desires of every sentient being. The one that could trick the cleverest of opponents out of their very souls.

Shinobu swallowed. The growing cold in his stomach felt as though he'd swallowed his own dread.

M-E-P-H-I-S-T-O.

Anna Smith Spark

"Gold Light" is what I always say I won't ever write—the backstory to single brief throwaway image in *The Court of Broken Knives*. It exists within the world of my Empires of Dust novels, but is not a part of the series narrative; it can and perhaps even should be read without your having so much as heard of me before (luckily). The intention behind it was simply to write something beautiful and strange and stark and dragon-wild, inspired by the beautiful cover image Shawn Speakman showed me.

The underlying "Gold Light" image itself was inspired by my young daughter, who tells stories in which she is a heroine with a sword of light, shining. This seemed suitable for an anthology to raise money for writers' health care. Youth equals health equals healing. And, again because it was for an anthology raising money for health care, I wanted to tell a story with more of an element of good-against-evil hope to it.

Or perhaps not. The golden light of the sun can burn one's eyes and leave one blind. A doctor heals a man, makes him strong—and then learns to fears him.

Anna Smith Spark

GOLD LIGHT

Anna Smith Spark

Her brother talks to dragons.

In the bright morning, Ysleta sat in her bedchamber, watching the sun rise over the Bitter Sea. Her room was high in the tallest of the towers of the fortress of Malth Tyrenae, that rises over the city of Tyrenae clear as a sword blade, old as dying, so tall that clouds come around it to shield it from mere human sight. When the sky is clear in the blue of a northern summer, she can sit at the window of her chamber and stare far to the horizon, watch the sun rise over the White Isles and the endless expanse of the silver sea. The great ships that make the passage between the White Isles and Ith, their sails green or red or cloth of silver, their masts sweetwood or mountain ash or witch pine, slaves in rags and jewelled collars bent over the oars—the ships look as tiny as children's toys from the towers of Malth Tyrenae. A whale breaches, far out in the silver sea—from the towers of Malth Tyrenae it is a flicker on the water, a dark flash like an insect's wing. The clouds come in, grey and heavy with cold northern rain, and the sea is lost, the city beneath the window is lost, its green copper-roofed houses, its squares and courtyards, the alleys where blind children beg for coins, the doorways where mad men crouch and shake. All is gone, hidden by the clouds that taste of sea salt, crusting sea salt on the tower's walls. The towers of Malth Tyrenae are lost in the grey sky.

Ysleta sat at her window, watching. The city, her city, disappearing beneath her. She was a princess of the great kingdom of Ith, the daughter and the sister of kings; she could trace her descent back to Eltheri the sword-brother of Amrath, to the Godkings of Immier and Caltath. Thus fitting that she should be cut off from the world of mere men. Her hair was silver pale, from drinking a cup of quicksilver every morning. Her eyes were pale grey.

"Ysleta." Her brother came into her bedchamber. Undyl Silver Eyes. The King of Ith. The Lord of Malth Tyrenae. A thin sad man with the same pale hair and pale eyes.

"Undyl." She went over to him. Drops of water in her hair, from sitting staring into the gathering cloud. She took her brother's hands in greeting; his hands felt hot and dry. The skin on them was cracked. Burned. The skin on them was red. Her own hands were very white, cold and clammy like the belly of a fish. There were black hairs on her fingers that she was ashamed of. Very black, like ink stains, against her white skin. Her brother's hands were hairless. The tips of his fingers were swollen. He had no fingernails.

"I am waiting for you," Undyl the King of Ith said. Ysleta smoothed her clammy white hands down the skirt of her dress. Followed him out of her room.

They climbed the stairs of the tower together. Higher and higher. Walking into the sky. Walking up above the clouds. Up here the air is thin and silent. Cold as Ysleta's hands. They went on past windows looking out at nothing. White sky. Almost as though they were sinking down through the depths of the sea. After a long time climbing, they came at last to the very top of the tallest tower of Malth Tyrenae. The highest point, it is said, in all the world. Even after the world has been drowned and destroyed, at the end of all things, the tower will rise above the waters, alone, undisturbed. It rises like a beam of light from the heavens. And indeed the light up here is pure and golden in the morning, above the clouds. Beneath them the clouds are like a snowfield.

There are no birds, up here in the cold silence. The air is so thin that Ysleta gasped for breath. Undyl beside her coughed and panted. Steadied himself, drew himself up, raised his arms, cried out.

"Athela. Athela."

Come. Come.

There are no birds, up here in the cold silence. But a thing . . . a thing like a bird came flying, far away from out of the north where the wild places begin. If the whale breaching in the Bitter Sea was an insect, this was a grain of sand, nothing. But it came on and came on, swimming through the golden light of morning, the light that is above the clouds where the sun is always bright, and its shadow fell on the white clouds beneath it, and as it came on it grew vast. Its shadow stained the clouds black as night.

"Athela!" Undyl the king of Ith called to it.

It was blue and green and gold and silver and scarlet. The colours moved on its scales, flowed and winked like the light on frost. Its body rippled, the strength of its muscles was like water, or like ice crushing and pushing on the water's surface when the ice comes down from the far north over the Bitter Sea. Its wings were lace and filigree, frothed as fine as a woman's hair as she dances; it had spines on its back that were curved and gleaming; it had talons on its feet that were polished sharp as butchers' knives. Its body was as long as a mountain. Its mouth could swallow an army. It opened its mouth and the fire there was a furnace, its jaws and its teeth gleamed like liquid metal; the breath that came out of it smelled of honeyed wine, sweet and hot and sharp. Its eyes Ysleta did not look at. Never look into a dragon's eyes. Never. "Swear it, Ysleta!" Undyl her brother had begged her. "Swear!" She saw them with her mind as they looked at her, black and burning, like the heart of the fire that is too bright to look upon and can only be seen as a blinding absence of light. All that can be known would be there in its eyes. Thus swear, swear that you will not look.

Her brother talks to dragons.

"Athenen," it said.

I come.

Undyl's face was as beautiful as the dragon. The glory in him. The wonder. The King of Ith, who has summoned a dragon. He had called for it, begged for it, and it had come. It hung there before them, beating its wings. Unreal thing. Impossible thing. Ysleta thought: This is a dream. This is an absurdity. My brother has summoned a dragon. This is a thing of madness.

"Temen ysare genher?" the dragon said. *What do you want?* Its voice was a whisper. Ghostly. No meaning in it, and yet words were there. A small, quiet, sweet voice, for such a vast deathly thing. The young girls of Tyrenae played a game where they went down to a cave on the shore outside the city, listened for words in the play of the water on the stones, listened to hear their future husband's name and their future children's names. Ysleta thought of this when she heard it speak.

Undyl was forming words in his head, his lips moving, trying to piece together what he must say. They had rehearsed this together, brother and sister, gone over and over the words. Speak, brother! Ysleta thought. Yet she herself had no thought what words she would say. Her mind and her brother's mind blank and white.

The dragon laughed at them.

Hot fire riding on its breath, the hot sweet scent of burned wood.

"Temen kel tiaknei ke ekilan?" the dragon said. *Are you afraid of me?*

"Stay!" Ysleta cried out to it. "Stay! Please!"

The dragon beat its wings. It raised its head up into the sky. It poured out fire. A column, a fountain of fire, silver fire and gold fire, white fire, rushing up and up into the heavens, a tower of fire to hold up the sky, a mirror of fire brighter than the dawn sun. A waterfall of fire. The heat was scorching Ysleta's face.

The dragon beat its vast wings. Flew off into the north. So

vast, they watched it as it shrank away, its shadow falling on the white snowscape of the clouds, the sun catching on its scales and making them flash with colour like the sun on frost.

"You fool," Ysleta said to her brother. "You fool, you fool. You said you could speak to it. Make it serve you, as it once served the old kings. You fool."

"I can make it come back," Undyl said in a thin voice. "I can. I will."

The next evening at dusk, they stood above the clouds at the very top of the tallest of the towers of Malth Tyrenae and the sky was midnight blue and twilight blue and blazing burning brilliant red. And again Undyl stood and raised his arms and called to beg the dragon to come to him.

And again, the dragon came. The colours had faded in its body, it no longer wore its splendour, its scales had paled to white. The skin of its wings was pink like a seashell. There was laughter in its eyes. Scorn for them. Amusement.

"Temen kel mene kel tiaknei?" Are you still afraid?

Undyl said, his voice trembling, "Yes."

Ysleta clutched at his arm. Remember. Remember. Nerve yourself. Speak to it. The sky was darkening, the sun sinking away. The dragon hung in the air dark as a shadow, pale as flowers on a summer night. Its eyes burned, the fire burned in the depths of its body, red fire glowed through the skin of its throat. There was a princess of Ith once whose skin was so white that wine showed red in her throat when she drank. So the fire moved beneath the dragon's skin. It opened its mouth and its mouth was all fire, its words were fire in the air as it spoke.

"Ysare kel ekilet ke seleriet?" Do you want to anger me?

"You served the Godkings, my ancestors," Undyl said in fear. "Why will you not speak to me? I have . . ." Undyl's voice was broken. "I have something . . . a tribute . . . an offering. For you."

What is this? They had not discussed this. "Dragons, Ysleta! Dragons! I am the King of Ith, I can summon them to me!"

Ysleta thought: Not offerings. Not tribute. Not pleas.

"Hekelth, Tiamenekil." A gift, dragon. Undyl drew something from beneath his cloak.

A human arm. A child's arm. Smooth and pale, the skin with a sheen like silk to it, so thin, so little, with the plumpness of a child's limbs. The ghost of the scent of it, the lovely clean smell of a child's limbs.

"My son Aann," Undyl said. "My youngest child. To see dragons! To speak with dragons! What would I not give!"

He threw the child's body out into the air. Obscene. A man throwing a scrap to a hawk. But Ysleta thought: I must not scream. I must not run. It will turn on me, if I scream, if I run. I must not run. And Ysleta thought: don't look at him. The dragon, I must watch the dragon. I cannot I will not look at him. The dragon is a cleaner thing. In the darkness the dragon's mouth opened in fire. The dragon's eyes glowed and she thought: it would be better to look into its eyes than to look at him and what he has done.

The dragon beat its wings. It seemed to Ysleta that it was smiling at them. It seemed to shrink down, become a thing more to be grasped by a human mind. She thought, with guilt: but I have seen a dragon. And thus perhaps my brother is right in what he says.

"Tribute," the dragon said, in their own tongue. "Yes."

"I have three children," Undyl said.

That night she could not sleep. Her head was filled with death and wingbeats. The tower of Malth Tyrenae seemed filled with the child's ghost. The child's mother's ghost, also: Ysleta saw her as she had seen her dying, in her chamber after the boy had been born. *"Your brother has killed me,"* Queen Elita's eyes had shrieked out, dying. *"Your brother has killed my son,"* Queen Elita's face screamed and wept at her now when Ysleta closed her own eyes.

Undyl was walking and walking through the tower. She heard him, once, very late, stopping outside her chamber door. What have I done? Oh, what have I done? All the Kings of Ith, the

Godkings, Eltheri, all their ghosts must be watching him, mocking him or praising him.

"He was sitting playing," Undyl had said. "And I saw him, and I thought . . . I thought . . . I saw . . ."

Why? How? How could you see that? Her heart is broken, the child's death screams to her.

And yet. And yet. The day passed as in a nightmare. That evening as the sun set she found herself climbing the steps of the tower, round and round, up and up. Up forever, praying, hoping that she will never reach the top. Undyl walked beside her. In his arms he carried a heavy oilcloth sack. They reached the top of the tower. Stepped out, stood on the edge between the sky. No clouds: the sea, stretching out black and silver, moving in the light, birds wheeled far out over it, following the night fishing boats, black and flowing like lace. To the north, the dark forests, the Empty Peaks rich in copper, rich in quicksilver, rich in tin. Dead empty places. Beyond them the world ends in grief. At the foot of the tower, the city sprawling: copper roofs, flower gardens, forge fires. Ysleta watched a line of carts come down the road from the mountains, pass beneath the north gate. Ten white oxen, bringing tin and copper to be forged into killing bronze.

"Help me." Undyl opened the oilcloth sack. "I cannot do this, Ysleta. Help me." Together they lifted out the child's body, Undyl's second son, stretched it out before them. Naked and pale and weak and white like the first had been.

"*Athela!*" Undyl cried out in a broken voice.

A long time, they waited.

When the dragon came, it bowed its head to them.

"Tribute," Undyl whispered. "Tribute. A gift."

Blood on the dragon's teeth.

"Tribute, dragon. Are you pleased?"

The dragon snorted fire. Laughing, Ysleta thought. Or itself grieving, for what Undyl had done to the child and to it. It twisted in the air, soared up into the twilight, beat its wings, danced and leapt. It stretched its head forward, very close to them, the smell of blood still on its mouth, the stink of ash and carrion, scorched metal, the strength of its scaled flesh. *Do not look into its eyes.* But it was so close that Ysleta could not keep herself from looking. Its eyes went on forever, like the sea on a moonless night.

"My name is Aesthel," the dragon said.

It meant: *truth.*

On the next evening, the dragon beat its wings against the sky and screamed, and all the people of Tyrenae stared up in terror, and all the children of Tyrenae wept. The dragon Aestheyl feasted on the last of Undyl's three children. It flew far out over the Bitter Sea breathing out fire, it danced out its fury, it burned the sky red. It flew up so high that it seemed to burn the stars in the heavens. It dived down and lashed its tail on the surface of the sea.

It stretched out its neck, its head very close to Undyl. Undyl reached out his hand and touched its face.

"What would you have me do?" the dragon Aesthel asked him. "My Lord King."

Her brother talks to dragons.

Wonder filled Ysleta's heart.

The dragon flew off into the north, burned the trees, tore the rocks apart. Rich veins of copper and tin and quicksilver running beneath the mountains, marbling the stone of the mountains like rich fat. Undyl spoke and the dragon Aesthel opened the mountains to men's clawed fingers, laid out the wealth buried there beneath. The mine men crawled in its shadow like worms, thousands come flocking to the far mountains, their faces dirty and pinched, swollen with wealth-lust. All the treasures of the earth that lie buried, and the dragon ripped them open, and the men dug them out and took them and shaped them. The sky over Ith was dark, even in the midday sun, with the smoke of a thousand fires to smelt the ore and melt the metal, to forge coins and swords and helmets and spears and shields.

The dragon flew into the east and into the west, over the waters of the Bitter Sea and the Sea of Grief, burned the fishermen's ships, burned the merchant ships that sailed from any land but that of Ith. The men of Ith sailed out into the empty waters. The dragon flew into the south and danced in the air over the fields of Immier, poured out its fire to light the sky crimson, came down low over the farmsteads and the villages.

Fear. The people of Cen Andae cowered in their houses; terror came on the people of Cen Elora; in far-off Tarboran the mountains rang with weeping; in Immish and Theme and the distant countries of the west men hid away and wept. The power of Undyl Silver Eyes the King of Ith was spoken of in hushed voices across all the world. An Ithish merchant might cheat and steal, an Ithish sailor turn pirate—but not a voice was raised in protest, for the King of Ith had at his command a dragon.

Ysleta sat in her bedchamber, watching the sun rise and the sun set. The ghost of her brother's wife: *What have you done to my children? What have you done to me?* The ghost of the children: *You held our bodies in your hands, Ysleta. For what? For what? For power? For death? For wealth?* The towers of Malth Tyrenae were empty of anything. At night outside her door she heard her brother walking the halls whispering, unable to sleep. In the city beneath the people went with bowed heads, did not look toward the tower. If the shadow of the towers of Malth Tyrenae fell on a man as he was walking, if a woman raised her head and saw the towers rising before her, their hands moved in fear to ward off ill-luck.

I must destroy it.

In the blue dawn she realized this. However wondrous. It will destroy her—indeed, she could not see a way in which she could destroy it and live. She would fail. Madness, to think of trying to harm it. But there in the dawn the certainty was stark before her. Like the bare branches of winter trees. The dragon and her brother, she must destroy them, both of them.

She was afraid then. She sat at her window and the fear ate her, left her weak. Cold and shivering in the sun. But it must be.

Destroy it. Beneath its wonder it is formed of children's broken bones. Her brother's footsteps in the corridor outside her bedchamber, and then he was climbing the stairs up and up to summon it again, and she must destroy it. Destroy him.

The bronzeworkers of Malth Tyrenae, who made the glories of the Ithish kings. The mine men crawled like worms, brought down copper and tin; in the forests trees were cut and burned to make black charcoal; the bronzesmiths turned the metal into blazing liquid, formed it into beautiful precious things. A cup. A bell. A mirror.

A sword.

"Make me a sword," Ysleta said to the master bronzesmith. He was old, his back hunched from years spent bending over the forge fire, lifting the crucible of bronze light. His arms red and scarred, a terrible white scar running from his foot to his knee where the bronze had once spilled over him. His arms and shoulders heavy with muscle, and his legs withered, for after being burned he could no longer walk without pain. His fingers were splayed and thick and knotted; there was no skin left on the tips of his fingers. His face, too, was scarred and marked with flecks of metal; he shimmered like a dragon himself in the forge light. His eyes were red with smoke and heat, and with pain.

"Why should you want a sword?" he asked Ysleta. His voice was bold, almost scornful. If she was a Princess of Ith, he was a master bronzesmith. A greater thing than she might ever be.

I cannot speak it. My tongue cannot form the words. It is a curse-spell: if I speak it my heart will burst with fear and grief.

Ysleta did not answer, but looked up at the sky.

The bronzesmith's face paled. The scars and the flecks of metal clear against white frightened skin. His eyes wide. Afraid.

"You cannot mean to do this," he said. "I cannot make you a sword to kill a dragon. No man can."

"Coward," said Ysleta. "You, who boasts of his skill with the bronze, who claims to be like to a dragon himself with his skill over the fire and the molten metal."

The master bronzesmith said, "Yes."

That night the dragon danced in the sky over the city of Tyrenae. No one within the city slept. The sky rolled with white and golden flames, it flowed like water, it washed over the sky, blazed to scald the stars clean. The moon was full, its light reflected off the dragon's scales as off ten times a thousand drawn swords. White scales, the white moon, the white moonlight: Ysleta saw the white of children's bones. The sky was filled with music, low and mournful; it sings for joy, some said in whispers; it is weeping, others said; it is filled with shame. A shooting star rushed across the sky beneath the moon: look, some said, it is weeping, there are its tears there in the sky. The dragon flew out over the Bitter Sea, its wings almost touching the white crests of the waves. It breathed out its fire and the water rose up in perfumed steam.

There was a knocking on the door of Ysleta's bedchamber. Her brother? Ah, gods, have mercy. Please, no. She feared, even, that her brother might have come to kill her, offer her up to the dragon. But when she opened the door the bronzesmith's bellows boy stood there. In his hands he held a crudely made sword blade.

"It will kill you," he said. "But I thought . . . you should try."

"Thank you." She saw then that his hands were red with blood. That the sword blade was already marked with blood. "What have you done?"

"I . . ." He shifted on his feet, did not look at her. There was blood smeared on his face. Like a child who has been playing in wet mud. "My master . . . he would not let me do this thing." And then he said, "In some tales, my Lady, a sword that kills dragons must . . . must be tempered in a man's blood."

She should close the door in his face. She should flee from him. From all in this place. How, she thought, how have we come to this? The dragon speaks and we . . . we are driven mad by it. Madness has come over us.

The sword was brittle. Badly weighted, rough, not well made. Too small, and yet too heavy for Ysleta's hands. But the blade was sharp. Had killed a man.

"You will be punished," she said to the bellows boy, "for what you have done. I will see you hanged from the city walls."

The bellows boy lowered his head to her. "I know it, my Lady."

"Wait here in my rooms," Ysleta said.

His eyes went huge with fear, as his master's had. Wild horse's eyes, the whites all around. "You will go now?"

"I would rather not sit with a bloody sword in my hands and wait."

Ysleta swung the sword back and forth between them. The smell of metal. The faint rancid smell of drying blood. Metal, of course, smells like blood. In the candlelight the blade seemed to be glowing. She thought of dragon fire, and the liquid light of the molten bronze. Pure white light being poured into the mould.

She said, "I will call the sword Goldlight."

At the top of the tower her brother stood staring out into the darkness. His hands gripped tight to each other, his nailless fingers clawing at himself.

"Beautiful. Beautiful. Ah!" He turned his head to Ysleta, his pale grey eyes like moth's wings. Silver, in the moonlight. His lips and his skin, too, silvery and gleaming. The Lords of Ith drink quicksilver in the morning and in the evening, it silver-tints their hair and their skin. "Ysleta! See! See!"

The dragon had grown larger. Long years it had slept in the mountains, drowsing, unreal, a dream thing, a pale shadow thing of no depth. Snow or white blossom. As unreal as a star. As the liquid bronze is an unreal thing. A dream thing. A ghost thing. Her brother speaks to dragons: it grows real, it beats white wings, it fills the world, there is blood on its claws, on its teeth. It spins in the sky around the tower, its wing beats are a storm wind. It is lit by its own fire, it is every colour the eye can behold, it flashes colours like frost. Its fire unrolls in the sky like great banners of crimson silk.

Ysleta raised the sword Goldlight. Rough, crudely made thing. Awkward in her hand: a Princess of Ith, a woman of power, one such as her would have no need of a sword. Its blade was smaller than the dragon's claws.

"What are you doing? Ysleta? Sister?"

She struck her brother with the sword that had already killed one man for trying to stop her doing this. The rough blade went into his throat. His breath sounded like the dragon's wing beats. The bronze was washed with his life's blood. The people of distant Chathe, they say, believe that the base of the throat is the seat of a man's soul.

He fell at her feet, dead, his hands still clasped together. Undyl Silver Eyes, King of Ith.

The dragon shrieked. The sky burned.

"Ekilankanderakesis. Ekilanaltreset. Geonanare ke nane kel genher?"

My master. My beloved one. What have you done to him?

The night sky was red as bleeding. The fire came down around Ysleta. She raised the sword Goldlight. The blade was filthy with her brother's blood. In the heat of the dragon's fire, the bronze began to glow, to sweat and melt.

The dragon came at her to devour her. It was so vast before her that she could see nothing beside the scarlet of its open mouth. Like turning closed eyes to the summer sun, and all the world is only red nothingness.

Her hair was burning.

Such pain.

Swallowing her up. Drowning her in its flames.

She swung the sword out. Striking the fire, cutting the sky apart, her hands running with her brother's blood. The blood rose up as red steam. The sword burned her hands. Burned itself into her hands, becoming part of her skin. The dragon's teeth came down upon her, they were longer than the sword blade, they were like the bars of a cage.

Ysleta drove the sword down into its jaws. Cried out at the pain of striking it. Flame and heat burning her throat.

It screamed with her. Its head whipped away from her, its body coming at her, it was like a ship striking the rocks of a cliff. It poured toward her. It thrashed with light.

She drove the sword down. Into the base of its shoulder, where its wing met its twisting back. Its muscles moved there like a nest of insects. The sword caught something there. Dark blood came welling up.

The blood, like the fire, burned her skin raw. The sword fell from her hand.

"Geonanare kel genher?"

What have you done?

Blood. Blood.

Her hands. Running with blood.

What have you done?

The dragon screamed in grief. It soared up into the night sky, tearing itself, the world opening up around it. It was wounded. It was itself a wound. Impossible, that such a thing could be harmed. Blood poured from it in a rainfall, and the stones upon which Ysleta stood began to hiss. Its wing beats frantic, grasping at the sky; its body spinning; it was like snow blown on a wind. Its fire burst from it. Choked and guttering with blood.

Far below, the city was filled with torchlights. Voices calling out in terror. People on the streets pointing, cowering, running. The dragon fire and the dragon blood poured down, set houses ablaze.

Footsteps, running up the stairs of the tower. Soldiers. Servants. The bellows boy, thinking she must now be dead.

The dragon was a maggot thing, writhing. Mindless. Opening itself. It fled upwards into the sky. It screamed. It flew out over the Bitter Sea, spiralling down, drifting down, spinning like snowflakes, it gleamed white in the moonlight, it struck the water with a crash.

The sea boiled. Seethed in a maelstrom. Salt mist. White foam stained with blood.

The waves folded over the dragon Aesthel's body. Took it into themselves. Waves broke on the shore. Whispered. Sang.

The water grew calm.

The sea and the sky were empty. A slick of blood floated on the water's surface, black in the moonlight.

The night was very dark, without the light of the dragon's fire. Ysleta's eyes were half-blinded with the fire of its dying. She bent and groped for the sword at her feet, took it up with arms that trembled. She looked out over the city. A red glow rising from the buildings burning far below.

"My Lady?"

Servants, soldiers, their eyes fixed on her brother's body. Ysleta held out the sword at them with trembling hands.

"I killed him. I killed it." She should weep. Her heart was weeping. "I killed it," she said.

The bellows boy, his eyes white with terror. Still traces of his master's blood on his face, smudged there, like a child who had been playing in the dirt. "My Lady," the bellows boy said.

Her brother talks to dragons. She has killed a dragon.

The moonlight fell very bright on the bronze blade.

The bellows boy knelt at her feet. Bent his head low, his forehead pressed to the ground. "My Lady Queen," the bellows boy said. All of the people assembled, the soldiers, the servants, terrified, half-asleep, unbelieving, filled with revulsion, filled with joy-at the top of the tower they knelt in the dark and said in one voice, "My Lady Queen of Ith." And she had not even thought of this.

"Bury my brother's body." Ysleta laid the sword carefully on the bloodied ruin of her brother's chest. "Place the sword on his grave as a marker. As a warning." She pointed to the bellows boy. "And this man . . ."

She looked at the line of the sky, where the sea and the sky met in darkness, where the first light of dawn would rise. The endless expanse of the sea. The endless eternity of the night sky. A single yellow star hung there. And the moon, round and white. Clouds were coming in, below them, cutting the tower off from the world beneath, clouds thick and solid as stone. Hiding the city and the sea and the dragon's grave place.

"Turn this man out of the city of Tyrenae," Ysleta said. "Banish him from all the kingdom of Ith. If he is not gone from my city by the time the sun is risen, kill him. But give him first . . . give him three bags of gold. One for each of my brother's children." She took the bellows boy up, kissed his bloody face. "Thank you," she said.

In the bright morning, Ysleta sat sitting in her bedchamber, watching the sun rise over the Bitter Sea. Her room was high in the tallest of the towers of the fortress of Malth Tyrenae, that rises over the city of Tyrenae clear as a sword blade, old as dying, so tall that clouds come around it to shield it from mere human sight. She sat in her bedchamber, watching. Ysleta White Hands, Queen of Ith. Her hair was silver pale, from drinking a cup of quicksilver every morning. Her eyes were grey. She wore a crown of red gold on her head.

The sunlight flashed on the spire of the tower. The sea shone gold and silver and black as metal. White crests danced on the waves. In the harbour of Tyrenae, the great ships and the fishing boats were coming in.

She gripped dry white hands on the sill of her window. Raised her face to the morning light. The air smelled of salt and wind and flowers. A scent to it, also, of dark blood.

In the east, out over the water, out over the rising sun, a thing like bird came flying. Calling to her.

"Athela! Athela!"

Come! Come!

Ysleta turned away from the window. Walked down very slowly into the world beneath.

The clouds came down, grey and heavy with cold northern rain.

The sky above the city of Tyrenae was hidden and gone.

Jason Denzel

THE STORY YOU'RE ABOUT TO ENJOY HOLDS A SPECIAL PLACE IN MY HEART. According to the timestamps on my earliest revisions, I began writing it in early 2011, more than four years before my first novel, *Mystic,* would be published. In those years, I commuted from Sacramento to San Jose once a week for work, and during that four-hour-round-trip journey, I'd get lost in music and let my mind wander, searching for ideas or characters who might whisper to me in the stillness and routine of the drive.

Qual'Jom's lonely golem was one such character.

I first imagined him lurking in his stony domain, massive and hunched but lost in deep thought. Loreena McKennitt's music has always had a significant impact on my writing, and this story was the first that it directly affected. Her *Nights from the Alhambra* live album was my constant companion in the writing of this story. Listen carefully and you'll hear its influence throughout, especially (but not limited to) the songs "Dante's Prayer," "The Old Ways," and "Never-Ending Road."

Now, after all these years, I'm delighted that the golem and his story have found a home in this anthology. It may've taken a while to emerge fully into the world, but, as you'll soon see, time means little to a golem made of stone.

Jason Denzel

THE STONE GOLEM OF QUAL'JOM

Jason Denzel

Awareness dawned with the sound of my master's voice. Like the muffled echo of an earthquake far distant, I heard him call out, repeating my name over and over in a rumbling mantra of summoning. His firm and patient voice awoke my consciousness and drew it from the firmament of time and space.

I have forgotten the name he called me by, along with most of the memories from those first chaotic moments. I remember only the sound of his voice, luring me away from my blissful rest and willing me to fill the form he'd crafted.

When at last I arrived in this world, I felt my essence locked within a hulking form. He confined me to a shape with thick arms and legs, pressed down upon me like the weight of the very earth. I roared my disapproval.

In those initial seconds, I learned the truth of my new reality, instantly comprehending the cursed concepts of mass and weight. I lashed out, trying to escape, but all I managed to do was stumble and collapse. From that moment on I realized my master, along with gravity, force, and pressure, had become my jailers.

My master spoke again, and this time his sounds solidified into words. "Golem?" he whispered. "Can you hear me?" His voice lacked the chanting rhythm from before. Instead he spoke with a gentle voice, trying to comfort me.

I ignored him in a stubborn refusal to acknowledge my new existence. It may have been moments that I laid in that place, or it could have been hours. Time was an unfamiliar concept to me. I understood its concepts, but had not experienced it directly before. The flesh of humans withers quickly, requiring them to measure the passage of time. My flesh does not wither. My muscles do not atrophy.

For I am made of stone.

My body was formed of the same granite as the natural cavern in which I dwelt. Strong and unyielding, it complemented my dank environment of utter darkness.

At some point during that period of early silence, I became aware of other objects touching the earth. I sensed wooden tables lining the cave. A towering bookshelf stood against the wall near a cluster of stalactites. So sensitive was this affiliation with the stone around me that I could even discern the dust creeping across the floor, seeking every hidden crevice one feathery wisp at a time.

Mostly though, I could feel *him* upon the uneven, rocky surface. He never left this dwelling, and constantly moved about, stopping only to sleep fitfully on the cot in a recessed nook, or to give full attention to something from his shelf.

I laid there in silence, quietly hating him while I sensed his shuffling. I have patience beyond all measure when it comes to such things. "When you are ready, golem," he would say amid his tasks, "we shall talk."

A steady drip of water in a distant corner splashed into a shallow puddle. I counted the regular cycle, trying to mark time. Eventually, after what must have been several days, I finally spoke.

"Why?" I demanded. I heard my own quaking voice echo through the chamber. My master shifted his weight, turning toward the corner where I'd awakened and fallen. He strode forward, and I noted the labor of his steps. The tattered hem of his robes traced a path in the dust behind him.

"Why?" I boomed again.

"Easy, golem," he soothed as he came to stand before me. "I have created you to assist me in the great cause of improving our world."

I recognized the vibrations of my master's words, as well as ambient echoes of the splashing water and the crackle of the cookfire. I knew where he stood by his weight on the floor. But I could not perceive him in any other way.

I reached out, trying to feel him with my heavy hand, but he slipped around it. "Take caution until you are used to your body," he said.

"I feel limited," I said.

"Interesting," he murmured. "You have great potential, golem. But stone cannot see as other elements do. You will become used to your nature."

Anger boiled within me. I dropped my hand, and my master left me to my thoughts. I traced his footsteps around the dwelling. In time I calmed, and forced myself to accept the truth.

Blindness consumed me, for my eyes are made of stone.

Within that utter darkness I felt a hollow place where previously I'd known only perfect awareness. I knew not where I came from, but I remembered a glorious place—or perhaps a state of being—which my new stony manifestation could not fathom. I had been drawn from it; summoned away into darkness by the steady voice of my master. Just as I instinctually knew his words and their meanings, so I knew of light and vision. Yet it was a distant thing, like a memory of another life, now long forgotten.

I remained on the ground, letting the terrifying absence of sight claw at me.

On another day my master spoke to me again. "The terms of your service have been woven into you. Repeat them to me." His voice wrinkled like the soles of his feet.

I knew the terms embedded into me as deeply as the roots of a mountain. My master compelled me to speak them, so I obeyed.

"I shall carry out your commands," I rumbled. "Endeavor to satisfy your intended meaning."

I felt the subtle shift in his weight as he nodded.

"I shall guard you from harm."

"A little simplified," he mused. "But it shall suffice. What of the last?"

"Obey and protect your lineage and legacy as fiercely as I would protect you."

"Very good," he replied. "And your payment?"

I paused to pull the answer from the depths. "In exchange, you or your successor shall release me from this form, freeing me to return to that from which I came."

His voice carried a smile. "Good. Please stand."

I consciously moved my whole body for the first time, rotating my thick marbled arms to help sit myself up. Then I heaved my giant torso of smoothed granite, and lifted myself to full height atop my massive stone legs.

"Astounding," my master whispered, his voice now far below me. "I am Qual'Jom. Tell me, golem, is there anything you need or desire?"

"I wish to be released," I rumbled. The dim memory of the place I'd come from still sang to me.

A wheezing chuckle escaped him. "Oh, golem. You just arrived! Barring that desire, is there anything else you would like?"

I pondered this for a moment. "I wish to see."

"Hmm," he muttered. "I had not expected you to ask that." I sensed him cross the room to his bookshelf. I felt the lifting of a slight weight from the bookshelf, followed by an added pressure on the large wooden table in the center of the room. My master leaned his thin frame over the table, pressing it into the stone floor. The soft whisk of pages turning echoed in the cavern.

"Very well," he said. "I shall research methods to bring sight to your eyes. For now, I trust you have enough awareness to clearly perceive what is happening around you?"

"Yes."

"Good. Then I shall continue with my studies. You will oblige me as needed."

I bowed my head in sad acceptance of my fate.

My master and I settled into a routine where I grudgingly assisted him in his ongoing experiments and studies. He gave me mundane tasks like fetching and lifting objects around his dwelling. I restrained and slaughtered animals he called forth from his summoning circle. He ate only a portion of what he conjured. I did not ask, nor did he ever offer to explain, what he did with the rest.

He worked in every corner of the dwelling. I felt his fingers trace the walls in strange patterns I did not recognize. He mumbled to himself as he did so, but I cared not what he said.

Much of his work focused on the summoning circle. Traced in a wide arc in the place I awoke, the lines were drawn with varying degrees of thickness and shape. Initially, I observed my master chalking runes through the vibrations against the ground. Later, he gave me the task of maintaining them. At one point, he complimented me. "Well done, golem. You have an unexpectedly steady hand."

His encouragement failed to penetrate my cold being. The gentle manner of his voice now vexed my senses. He told me stories and jokes, but I cared nothing for the subtleties. Sometimes he sighed and referred to me, not without affection, as a "grumpy lummox."

Time wore on, but nothing changed in my enclosed world except my master. The labor of his step increased. His pacing slowed. The bookshelves swelled as he studiously churned out volumes of research and directed me to place them ever higher. He jabbered frequently about his work, but little of it made sense.

On one nondescript day, I felt my master approach the corner where I awaited tasks. He wore the added weight of a cloak over his thin body and tattered robes. He held a wooden staff and leaned on it ever so slightly.

"Golem," he said with unusual energy. "I am going on a journey. I have discovered the method of granting you vision."

I remained immobile and expressionless, but listened carefully as he went on. "I've read of an artifact known as Quolosin's Fire. It is a long distance from here, but I am willing to make the journey for you. Remain in this dwelling, and do not leave for any reason. Let no one disturb my possessions, including you. When I return, the Fire will allow me to give you sight!"

He gave me an affectionate pat with his gnarled hand. His footsteps echoed across the cavern and out the crooked doorframe in the most remote corner of our abode. Beyond the entrance, I perceived his staff-assisted march through long, winding halls of stone. Even past that, I could sense his steps grow lighter as they dwindled into the distance. Then he was gone.

I dwelt alone in the darkness of the mountain.

The days passed, and I found myself eager for my master's return. The promise of receiving vision from Quolosin's Fire lifted my spirits.

In my positive mood, I did not mind keeping my master's dwelling clean and tidy. I exterminated any vermin that dared to creep in, such as rats and other unsavory critters that came seeking the treasures of his food hoard.

But many weeks passed, and the remaining food had long been spoiled by the time someone finally entered the cave. At the first distant padding of footsteps, I felt a flash of excitement at the prospect of finally becoming complete. I squared myself to the entrance and waited for my master and the Fire that would bring me vision.

Yet my hopes sank as I realized that the approaching footsteps were not light and shuffling, nor aided by a staff. They belonged to a heavyset person wearing large boots who hefted their bulk down the stone steps leading into the cavern. A velvet-trimmed cloak dragged upon the ground.

The stranger entered my master's chamber. I heard their quiet gasp.

"I had to see it for myself," the person said. His voice revealed him as a man, yet he was not my master. "So this is how ol' Qual'Jom applies his theories. No wonder he's been absent from our quorums." He sidestepped into the dwelling, his back brushing against the wall. "What name did he call you by, construct?"

I did not respond, but followed him with my blind gaze as he slid deeper into the room. An instinct to guard my master's home rose inside me.

Perhaps my silence ignited boldness within the man, for he stepped forward and his voice became more confident. "Speak, if you can hear me!"

I remained silent.

I felt his boots walk toward my master's bookshelf. He stopped there, and I heard the gentle slide of leather as he began to pull a volume free. I shifted and loomed over him.

"Do not disturb my master's possessions."

He froze and waited for a count of twenty thundering heartbeats. Then I felt the weight of the leather tome shift from the bookshelf to himself. His voice quavered with forced intensity. "Your master is dead, creature! I-I claim this knowledge for my own!"

"Replace the tome," I repeated, not believing his lies.

He eased one step forward, heel rocking toward the toe. "No one has disturbed this place since his death. Therefore you are masterless, and I shall claim you as well."

I felt a pressure upon my body, seeking to ensnare me. It was not a physical sensation but perhaps one wrought of the firmament I had known before my awakening. This force sought to bind me, perhaps even harm me. But my master had crafted me well, and I shrugged off the intruder's sorcery like splashing water. I struck out with the speed and strength afforded by my nature and lifted him by his skull. I had never touched a person so directly, and I marveled at the feel of soft flesh. He squirmed in my grasp, the book falling from his fingers as he clawed at my iron-like grip.

"Release me!" he croaked, legs kicking. The pages of my master's precious book scattered across the damp floor beneath his flailing feet, igniting my senses.

Soiled. Ruined. Because of this man.

A surge of anger overcame me. Without another thought I crushed his head. His skull shattered easily within my grip, for my hands are made of stone.

The intruder's fluid emptied upon the ground, further desecrating the discarded book. Not quite comprehending what I'd done, and unsure what to do next, I stood motionless for a long period, the passage of time marked only by the decreasing drip of his juices.

The intruder claimed my master was dead. He disturbed my master's possessions. In my carelessness, I had further spoiled them. A dark suggestion crept into my mind: had I failed in my duty to protect these treasures?

Months passed as this question consumed me. The blood on the cavern floor crusted. Yet still I stood there, holding the intruder's decaying corpse. As he deteriorated, his rotting body began to slip. Not wishing to disturb the ruined pages further, I threw the remains into the corner where waste collected. Let the rodents and maggots consume as they would.

How would I know if my master was truly dead? I couldn't recall if he ever specified how long he'd be gone. I understood he was old by the accounting of humans, but I also knew he possessed great power. In his studies, I'd heard him murmur about the extension of life. Such things had not mattered to me then. All I cared for now were the desecrated pages and the possibility that I had failed.

I despaired and longed for his return in the most silent of ways.

More months passed, and the intruder decomposed to bone. On one of those days, I sensed new footsteps approaching. I grew suspicious, as I felt many pairs this time.

Resigned to more invaders, I shifted my frame toward the lone cavern entrance. The memory of the previous intruder remained fresh. Rage boiled within me, fueled by my embedded instincts and by my lingering frustration of how the last intruder ruined my master's book. I clenched my fists and waited for them to come. This time, I would not fail.

They descended the carved stairs. I counted a dozen heavy figures, all wearing metal boots, and—judging by the clanking noises—similar metal clothes over their bodies. They rushed into the open room, fanning out along either wall.

I stood motionless in their midst. Their feet kicked up the ubiquitous dust that normally lay around the room, and I heard steel weapons being drawn. One of the invaders knelt near the midden heap where I'd thrown the previous intruder. I felt him stand and turn in my direction.

"By the right of the Emperor," he called, his voice slightly muffled as if something covered his head, "I declare judgment on you, abomination, for the death of Sen'Pollus."

"Where is my master?" I thundered, not caring for their judgments. The cavern shuddered with the might of my voice. Dirt and tiny stones rained from the ceiling.

Metal scraped as several of them shifted in fear. An invader to my left eased a few steps forward, trying to move unnoticed.

"The sorcerer Qual'Jom received what he deserved," sneered the captain. "He delved too far into the forbidden arts. Now with the slaying of Sen'Pollus, his tower and this dungeon below it are claimed by the Emperor."

I loomed before them. "This place will not be defiled."

They heeded me not and attacked, beginning with the one to my left. I obliterated him with my fist. The rest fell upon me like stalactites in a deep earthquake, yet I proved to be as invincible as the mountain. Their metal weapons shattered on my skin, hardly scratching the surface.

They screamed in the end. Eventually only two remained: the leader and one other. The lesser man fled for the exit, well out of my reach. Without thought, I stomped my foot down hard, pulverizing the ground. The floor beneath the fleeing coward thundered upward, ramming a pillar of rock to the ceiling, pinning and crushing him there.

I marveled at what I had just done. Somehow, I'd cast my

mind and energy out my foot and channeled it through the stone floor at a speed faster than thought. The earth obeyed my instinctive command and re-formed itself to my will.

In that moment of dazed wonder, the leader of the invaders assaulted me, leaping and swinging a great sword with considerable strength. The mighty blow landed true, chipping a fragment from my neck, but his sword shattered to worthless pieces.

"Hateful beast!" he cursed, tears of rage in his voice. "You—!"

I crushed him with a swing of my arm and a bellow of my stone lungs.

Corpses littered the floor all around me. Twelve invaders now joined the original intruder in death. Arms pulled wide, I roared my rage to the vaulted ceiling, a challenge to any aggressor seeking to defile my master's dwelling. They could come, but I would tear them apart.

Splattered blood ran down my hands and body, following the chiseled rivulets of my stone form. I reveled in my brutality and felt no remorse.

For my heart is made of stone.

I sensed every fallen book and broken inkwell. Many of my master's precious possessions littered the cave, smashed and fouled by the fighting.

I moved about, intending to clean up the bodies and bring some semblance of order to the chaos. But with every step I took, my cumbersome feet crushed another implement or scattered more pages of a fallen tome. I silently cursed the invaders for their reckless devastation. Their vengeful greed in seeking my destruction yielded naught but the ruin of my master's dwelling.

I made my way to the back of the cavern, near the summoning circle, and hunched down. This nook comforted me. I sought solace there, my thoughts dancing.

Placing my hand on the wall, I caressed the cold rock from which I'd come. I heard again the voice of that first intruder telling me Qual'Jom was dead. How long had it been since my master left? All the invaders came seeking power or revenge. I now began to wonder what secrets my master researched in this lair. He'd once told me his efforts were designed to improve the world, but the captain of the invaders had called those studies "forbidden arts." What was I to believe?

The blood on my rocky body dried quickly. A melancholy silence fell upon the cavern as I lingered in my alcove.

I realized now that I missed my master. I yearned for his warm voice. I tried in vain to recall his humorous stories. He'd left our home in order to fulfill my desire, and perhaps died for it. Was there nothing I could do to bring him back? I would sweep the floor forever, re-chalk the summoning circle a thousand times, if only it would return him to me.

I called to my master in the lonely darkness, but only my echo replied.

I shifted my attention outward and listened for the faintest vibrations of a three-legged man returning home. He would walk with his staff in one hand and Quolosin's Fire in the other. There would be no wrath or greed in his step, only peace.

Yet he did not come.

And so once more I waited, and the passing months rolled into years. During that long interval of despair my senses grew stronger, more expansive. I gradually became aware of the rush and crash of something beyond the back wall of the cavern. I reached out through the earth, melding with the stone, until I came at last to its edge and sensed moisture. I perceived a crash of water, followed by its retreat. Then another crash, and another retreat. I counted this tidal rhythm for innumerable cycles and at last determined that my cavern must be deep within a cliff, at the edge of an ocean. I clung to this new world I'd just discovered, trying to fathom how it would be perceived by those who possessed sight. I could neither sleep nor dream, but my sense of wonder knew no bounds.

The years withered to decades, and more invaders came to call. I killed without discrimination, refining my physical skill to minimize damage to the dwelling. None of them could harm me, yet still they came, pathetic as they were. From the words they spoke, it seemed I had gained a reputation in their world.

I cared not, and annihilated them all.

In one of those years, lost somewhere in the span of time, with the corpses of innumerable would-be conquerors heaped in every corner, a new set of unwelcome guests arrived. Unlike the men and women who came bearing swords and words of sorcery, the creatures that now shuffled into the cave did not come with aggression in their hearts. Dozens of them scuttled in, walking on clawed feet and knuckles, cackling in a crude language. They gagged at the stagnant air, which reeked of death. I towered over them, preparing to unleash my slaughter if they made the slightest move toward my master's possessions.

Yet they did not come forward. They cowered as far away as possible, scratching the walls and earth in fear. At last the heaviest of them scampered forward. I heard the rattle of bones as he spoke.

"Golem of Qual'Jom," he hissed, and I hated it all the more for the blasphemous use of my master's name. "Great golem who could crush us all. Hear what I have to say."

I did not kill the wretched thing. That was answer enough.

His voice shook as he went on. "We are kovul. We seek to live in the tower above. We—" He cut off as I curled my massive fists at my side, the sound of crackling stone sending a warning through the cavern.

"Plu-please, great golem," it begged, all pretense of propriety gone. "Spare us. We will keep interlopers out! We will prevent any who try to reach this cavern! You will never be disturbed! Please!"

I could not determine if the weak and miserable creatures were human or some pathetic reject of nature. In the end I simply nodded. As they scurried out, I commanded them to remove the corpses. They delighted in this, as they did in the looting of weapons and other treasures left by the invaders. I gave them only one other command.

"When my master returns bearing Quolosin's Fire, he is to be welcomed and led directly to me."

Soon after, I felt them place a heavy metal door at the top of the long stairs leading to my cavern, isolating me further.

The bargain proved to be well made. At first I had no care for the tower above, and I learned to block out the scuttling society living there. They were a crude race, constantly squabbling as they feasted and fornicated. Yet they upheld their bargain, and the marauders never disturbed me again. From time to time I sensed strangers approach the tower, but the kovuls set upon them with their cunning little traps.

Once more I settled in to wait for the coming of my master. Decades churned outside the dwelling while all remained timeless within. The kovuls kept me isolated, and I was not disturbed.

They never knew it, but through my senses, I experienced much of their lives and culture. I witnessed their society flourish with success and all that comes with it: children, conflicts, community, and death. The process of life revealed itself to me generation after generation. I listened as the elders recounted their tales about me to their offspring, who in turn passed it onto theirs. Their genuine relationships became an unexpected comfort in my lonely darkness.

And then I sensed them all die in a great plague.

I could do nothing. Their moans and cries floated down upon me like motes of dust. I turned my face toward the cavernous roof in mournful silence as they dwindled away. I could not see, but my acute awareness described every bleeding gasp they took. It saddened me how quickly life could be wiped out.

When at last they were all gone, I mourned in my silent way and pondered my own fate. Had my master intended me to die? Or was it in my inherent nature to live forever?

Only silence answered my questions, and no others came to call for a very long time.

The quiet centuries turned, and I waited in my isolated world. The thickening dust remained my only companion. The length of my life since awakening—always vague to me—shifted firmly into the unknowable. I waited for my master, knowing he would fulfill his promise and return with Quolosin's Fire to grant me sight.

I cataloged every pebble and fiber of my cavern, along with its contents, the abandoned tower above, and the mountainous cliff that encased it all. So gloomy was my environment that even the phenomenon of sound abandoned me, save for the eternal crash of the tides on the distant cliffs of stone.

The constant drip of water in the far corner wore away the bedrock, hollowing out a smooth basin. I felt every drip of this process, every tiny deterioration of stone. My form did not change, yet I blindly observed the abrading shape of my residence. The stalactites grew long, reaching toward the ground before joining with stalagmites to form what must have been a mesmerizing lattice of columns.

I'd long since lost count of how many hundreds or thousands of years passed, when at last I felt the footsteps of a living creature. The person who approached bore a staff, walked with light footsteps, and dragged worn robes in his wake. Lifting my head in interest, I waited as the newcomer neared the kovuls' metal door, which had somehow survived the test of time. I heard and felt the door's traps and locks fall away at his touch.

Hope rising, I moved to face the entrance. In my heart, I sensed the time had come at last.

As the person who would surely prove to be my master took the final steps of the long staircase, a strange sensation flickered before me. It began as a tiny point floating in the impenetrable darkness—a gentle wisp that grew and spread, pushing back the void of my blindness.

This must be light!

LIGHT!

Never in my existence had I *seen* anything, but before me at that moment shone a phenomenon of momentous proportion. Warmth bathed the entrance in a glorious pool of radiance which revealed a figure holding a torch in one hand and a tall staff in the other. An understanding of visual expression arose within me like the rest of my innate knowledge.

I stared in wonder, basking in the effulgence for which I had waited centuries. The torch burned low, illuminating only a tiny area. Its subtle boundaries held back the familiar darkness.

"Master?" I gaped, unable to contain my excitement. I towered over the heavily cloaked figure. Gratitude filled my—

No.

It could not be.

The torchlight shifted, revealing a woman standing before me. She wore dark, shimmering robes, and her pale face was smooth and free of blemish. She stood not even half my height. Her long hair shone with the color of roaring heat, and it spilled out of her raised hood and down past her shoulders.

She stared at me with wide eyes. I drank in the sight of her, fascinated by subtle shifts of musculature as emotion crossed her face. She took a fearful step backward, and I felt an irrational dread that she might take the light away.

"No!" I rumbled, holding up my arm. I beheld the shape of my limb, thick and round, easily wider than the whole of her body. "Don't leave."

Her hand holding the torch trembled less now, but I could still feel her heart beating fast.

"So the legends are true," she said. "You are the stone golem of Qual'Jom. I half expected you to not exist." Her lips curved in a smile, and she stood taller. "Have you truly waited two thousand years for this Fire to be brought to you?"

Her words formed sounds unlike any I'd heard before. She spoke not with the words of my master, or the invaders, or even the kovuls. But they were just words, and so I understood.

"Time is endless for me," I replied in the same language. It was not my nature to speak this much, but I did not want her to leave. I savored every beam of light, marveling at the detailed textures revealed by its nimbus.

The woman's eyes tiptoed behind me toward the inner cavern. Her face expressed caution before she stepped deeper into my dwelling. I felt the instinct to destroy her as I had the others, but I stayed my hand and followed her with my newly functioning eyes.

"It is said," she continued, walking toward my master's bookshelf, "that you guard a vault of knowledge unequaled since the days of the ancient Emperor."

I said nothing as she came to stand before it. The itch to defend my master's work overwhelmed me, and it took all my willpower to keep it at bay. Setting her staff against the rocky wall, she brushed the dust from the spine of a crumbled volume and pulled it down. Much of the dry leather disintegrated at her touch.

"The wealth of wisdom here is beyond compare," she whispered, her eyes dragging over the prize in her hand. "The old kovul legends claim you waited for something called Quolosin's Fire." She closed her eyes and her face shifted into a smile. "The years I spent tracking down this Fire—going to the Heavenly Forge itself!—have proven worthwhile. With this, Qual'Jom's secrets of eternal life will be mine."

A hungry gleam shone in her eyes. Her desire for my master's possessions triggered my long-held oaths and unleashed my protective instincts.

I strode toward her. "My master's dwelling is not to be disturbed."

Suddenly, the torch whipped away from me, and she held it over a puddle of water. "Harm me and I douse the Fire forever."

We stood there at a stalemate: she, unwilling to leave the treasure, and I, unable to jeopardize the light.

At last she broke the silence. "You know he is dead." Her eyes did not waver and I read the truth in them. "Qual'Jom's lineage ended with him. He had no successor. You are all that remains."

My fists clenched, the stone grating beneath my fingers. A low growl rumbled deep within me. But the woman did not falter. "I am sorry for the loss you feel. You served your master well. In gratitude for protecting his treasure all these years, I release you. Quolosin's Fire is yours."

She lifted the torch high, and the light expanded, fully revealing the cavern walls and floor. I looked upward and stood in awe.

Carved runes and glyphs covered the walls of my master's cavern. I had no memory of their making; they must have existed before my awakening. Diagrams and symbols illustrating the cosmos awakened deep knowledge within my consciousness. Overwhelmed, I stepped backward, and felt a profound sense of accumulated wisdom settle into me.

The markings told the story of life everlasting. They sang of a place beyond time that was both origin and destination, of a place filled with supreme light and awareness. They whispered the secrets of the firmament from which I came. I drank in every shape and carved them forever into my memory.

These glyphs danced across the walls in a symphony of pattern, leading my gaze toward the distant recess where the summoning circle rested. A faint glowing fungus coated the walls, but dared not cover the mystical runes.

The beauty of those moments cannot be told. Had I the means of expressing it in any possible language, I would have sung.

Stealing away from the wealth of beauty and secrets, I looked down at myself and marveled at my body, its contrasting shades of slate and granite carved from the foundation of the mountain. Thin lines of warm color inked their way around the heavier tints on my skin, like veins of precious metal spread through rock.

My attention returned to the woman holding the magnificent torch. Her offer sang to me.

Conflicting thoughts erupted in my mind. How long had I lied to myself about my master's death? I knew even the foremost of humans lived only a few hundred years, far shorter than the two thousand she claimed I had waited in this dwelling. I knew even my master could not survive so long. With his lineage gone, was I free? Or trapped eternally?

"Where would I go?" I had no concept of the world beyond the cavern.

"Have you ever seen the stars?" she asked, her voice warm. "There's a whole world beyond the dimness of this cavern. A world of light and beauty." She gestured at the walls encasing us. "A world without boundaries."

Perhaps the moment had come to accept the truth about my master. Before me waited everything I had ever wanted.

I held out my hand to accept the Fire.

Yet as I reached out, I hesitated. My heavy hand looked cold beside the warmth of the Fire. Cut from the earth, I could see how I differed from this woman and everyone who'd ever come to my lair. The reminder that I was made of stone, and not the warm flesh of humanity, washed over me. I realized the outside world was not my place. How could it be? My master had crafted me for one purpose: to defend his legacy. That came before all else. Even my own desires.

My arm wilted back to my side.

The woman cocked her head askance.

"No," I rumbled. Deep down, I knew it had to be this way. "This is where I belong. Without this purpose, I am nothing. I shall remain, and protect my master's legacy. Return the tome to its shelf."

The woman's eyes hardened, and I felt anger and sorcery storm within her. "I will have this knowledge, golem. It has dwelt in this tomb too long."

I stepped toward her. "Replace the book. Leave."

She held her ground and pulled the torch away from me. "You will lose Quolosin's Fire. Is that what you want?"

Her words tore at my soul, but I remained firm.

"Bah!" she snarled. Closing her eyes, she hummed, a buzzing sound rising in her throat. Quickly the hum turned into a mantra I did not understand. I felt sorcery in the air and grabbed for her. But before my rocky hand reached her, she punched the Fire into the air. A sudden flash of light blew out my vision, and I found myself in a blaze of overwhelming brilliance. I stumbled back, splintering the wooden table in the middle of the room.

Enraged, I shook my head, trying to banish the blinding light. When at last I did, I perceived Quolosin's Fire dimming and darkness encroaching upon me once more. My new vision vanished except for a fleeing halo emanating from the staircase.

Then I realized she'd stolen my master's tome.

With a surge of panic I never before experienced, I leaped toward the entrance. The base of the stairway was too small for me to pass through, but I would not lose the tome or the Fire. Desperate, I smashed my way through, roaring for her to return the stolen book.

The light retreated faster, and I pounded my way through the long stairway. I extended myself into the rock, willing it to yield a path. What obstacles did not open before me were pulverized by the strength of my form. I united with the mountain and became an avalanche of raging earth and stone.

The world around me quaked as my passage broke the roots of the mountain. Behind me, the stairway collapsed. Before me, the kovul door exploded as I charged forward.

When I finally burst free of the mountain's base I saw the woman standing with her back to a ledge, clutching the tome. A vicious smile played upon her face as she held the torch aloft. The light of Quolosin's Fire spread wide, and I marveled.

No ceiling towered above me. Only a pale, airy vault hung like a dome that could never be reached. Soft puffs lulled across its surface. I felt a crisp, fresh breeze wipe the dust from my skin. I could have stood there forever, rejoicing in that simple, surprising sensation.

I reached up to discover whether I could grasp the gentle blue above. In that moment I envied the mountains, whose soaring peaks of stone could scrape this beautiful heaven.

Suddenly, behind me, I felt the cliff and the tower atop its pinnacle shudder. A low rumbling awoke within the earth, and I felt the bedrock crack and die. Boulders plunged from above, smashing the earth and shaking the ground. Carved blocks from the tower rained upon me. I swatted some away, while others shattered harmlessly against my hardened form. A large piece of granite, sliced like a wedge, shattered the side of my head, ripping away much of my face.

I felt no pain, only surprise and anger. The tower collapsed completely as the cliff beneath it fell away, crumbling into the ocean. The sound and chaos of the cascade overwhelmed even the crash of the sea. Watching in horror, I despaired at the fate I had brought my master's dwelling. In the end it had not been invaders or sorcerers who desecrated and destroyed his home.

It had been me.

Turning my ruined head with deadly purpose, I leveled my one remaining eye at the woman holding Quolosin's Fire. She stared at me open-mouthed, clutching the stolen tome to her breast. The wind flogged her as she stood dumbfounded near the cliff edge. Behind her glimmered a body of water that spanned to eternity.

"D-do you have any idea what you just destroyed?" she stammered. Her anger gave her courage in the face of my looming revenge. "Is your pride so great that you'd ruin the very thing you were created to protect?" Her words condemned me, and I felt them pierce me as no attack ever had.

I said nothing. I strode forward with grim resolve, and she saw her death loom in my shadow. Desperate, she hurled sorcery at me, but it bounced off. She summoned a scorching wind, but it could not erode me. She screamed the blasphemous names of powerful beings to aid her, but even they dared not challenge me.

I crossed the final distance between us and raised my fist to hammer her into her grave. But in that final moment, trapped between me and the endless ocean behind her, she did the only thing she could.

She hurled Quolosin's Fire toward the open sea.

As the flame arched into the air, time stretched like the vast eternity of all my years. The woman fled, the stolen book clasped safe in her arms. My instinct screamed to reach for her, but instead I followed the arcing Fire with my remaining eye as it plummeted beyond the edge of the cliff.

I could not bear to reenter a world of darkness. I made my choice.

The pathetic woman forgotten, I stretched for the Fire, which spun end over end in the middle of nothing. I took a mighty step and launched myself from the cliff.

As I descended in free fall toward the crashing waves, I felt small and weak. I was a pebble beside the plates of the earth. Separated from my connection to the ground, a profound sense of loneliness crashed through me. Had I truly lived by myself for thousands of years? Despair bore down on me, plunging me toward the sea.

I grabbed Quolosin's Fire just before I hit the water. The ocean surged around me, coursing through every channel in my rocky form. I began to sink, the water rushing above my head, and for a moment only my hand and the Fire remained above the surface.

I held to my final glimpse of light as long as I could. The last thing I saw before the Fire went out was a blazing ball of light, brighter even than the Fire, raging high above me at the peak of the noontime sky. Then the ocean consumed the Fire and snuffed out my vision.

I would have wept, but I had no tears to shed. For I am made of stone.

My world consisted of utter darkness once more. As I grounded upon the ocean's floor, I felt the return of my profound connection with the earth and everything it touched. That, along with the heavy sensation of water pressing down, somehow comforted me.

I searched with quiet desperation. I must have moved half the mountain, sifting through the underwater rubble of the tower. But I never found my master's bookshelf or his summoning circle. I mourned the loss of the stolen tome but knew it would soon be dust along with the wretched woman.

Accepting that nothing remained of my master's home, I descended deeper into the valley of the sea. My footsteps pressed into the soft earth, kicking up silt as I passed.

For over a thousand years I wandered the depths. In that ageless period of my life the earth shook and shifted. The ocean surged and slept again. I crossed the mountains and plains of the unseen world.

At one point a massive force slammed into the land. The sleeping stone deep beneath my feet cried out in agony as its mantle broke, shattering the spine of the world. Violent energy radiated up my body and threatened to tear me apart. Unknown chaos raged around me as the ocean hurled itself onto every corner of the planet.

I stabilized myself as the disaster settled. Memories of the doomed kovuls washed through me. I wondered if the humans would survive this tremendous event.

Settling into a solid position, I relaxed and extended myself into the world around me. The earth clawed at me, desperate to drag me down into its torment. I held the pain at bay as I expanded outward, seeking its wounds.

Miles away, I felt landslides and broken hills. Hundreds of leagues distant, I felt the shape of sealed-off valleys and enraged volcanoes. Across great distances, I traced the courses of rivers and flooded canyons. Farther and farther I reached, shifting the energies of stone to envision the doomed land.

At last I found the civilizations of the world and felt them crumble. The weight of their charging feet bore down on me as they fought and killed over precious resources. I witnessed their fall but did nothing to help. I remained motionless at the bottom of the ocean, beyond their memories and history.

I thought again of my master and all his lost knowledge. For centuries I'd hoarded it in my desire to protect. What good came of that? Perhaps by holding onto it, I had, in fact, been working against my master's desire. Long ago he said our purpose lay in benefiting the world. I believed his legacy broken, but perhaps I could salvage something.

Extending my will, I merged with the earth. The soil became my skin, the mountains my bones, and the molten core at the center of the planet my heart.

Through my extended body I heard children cry, their wails reverberating against the mountains. I listened to a mother weep as she buried her baby. And in one particular cave on the far side of the ocean, I overheard a scraggly man praying into the stone floor on which he knelt. His whispered pleas asked for help in a time of desperate struggle. His soft whispers brushed against the cavern floor and vibrated to me.

I thought of Qual'Jom and his kindly voice. I thought of what he'd said, and so I decided to help this man.

Shifting my energy with deft precision, I carved words into

the ground beneath his nose. I felt him jump back in surprise, but I continued to carve shapes in the language he knew.

A valley with water waits for your people two weeks to the northwest. Find shelter there. Reforge your lives. Give thanks to Qual'Jom.

The man prostrated himself, then ran to share the news. Satisfied, I moved my attention to a hilltop where a starving woman knelt in the dirt and prayed for food. I shifted the earth, and broke words in the ground before her.

Find fresh water and meat in the fertile land south of the burned forest. Rebuild your home. Give thanks to Qual'Jom.

She wept and kissed the soil. Hundreds of times I sent such messages, and with each one I told them to give thanks to my master.

In time, societies managed to rebuild themselves. Some raised shrines to honor Qual'Jom. I watched from afar as they prayed to him, and later turned to him for wisdom and guidance. The runes I'd seen on the walls of my master's dwelling remained fresh in my memory. The knowledge they'd awakened within me burned. On days when I felt large gatherings at Qual'Jom's shrines, I shared the runes by carving them onto stone altars and tablets. The runes told the story of finding eternal life beyond death, and it pleased me to pass on my master's knowledge.

The people rejoiced at this gift. They honored Qual'Jom by carving statues and spreading his lessons. Every culture depicted him differently, but a strange phenomenon surprised me. Every rendering in every society showed him as a man with no eyes.

The realization that they honored *me*, and not my master, disturbed me. I retreated for years, not daring to reveal myself further. But as I hid in my lonely ocean, hopeful prayers continued to bombard me from afar. Elders placed soft flowers on my statue on feast days. Children from across the world sat on my carved lap. Men and women danced in swirling patterns matching the runes, and I felt their whispered thanks.

Intended or not, I accepted the lineage my master once held, and became his successor. I would have smiled, but I could not, for my ruined face is made of stone.

As the age of humans elapsed, I fulfilled my silent role as benevolent steward, guiding people toward revelations my master had worked so hard to preserve. Days came where I felt my watery home grow cold. I warned the people as much as I could, but in the end they came to their tragic fate, and I mourned their passing. The ocean froze around me, and for another endless span of time, I existed within a prison of ice.

Eons passed, ages beyond counting. All the time that had passed since my awakening was but an instant compared to what I experienced there. The mind cannot fathom the years that passed in the world above. In that time of solitude I tilled the emotions of my life, churning them endlessly until they had no hold over me.

Then at last, with a thaw that spanned a thousand times a thousand lifetimes, the ice melted away, shifting now to the other extreme. The warm and comforting sun above, which I so lovingly remembered from my brief encounter with the sky, became an angry tyrant, raging with such intensity that it burned away the ocean, exposing me to its hideous scorching furnace.

The weathering of ages had eroded my once mighty body of stone to smooth, thin lines of lime that could no longer bear their own weight. I sat on the dry, parched bed of the lost ocean and crossed my legs beneath me.

During that last, endless spread of time, I searched within myself, coursing over the ancient symbols on the walls of my master's cave. I basked in their transmitted wisdom. Where there were gaps, I traveled deeper within myself until the missing secrets came forth like magma from the earth's core. I had given the runes and their secrets to those who asked, but now I applied their lessons myself.

Despite the burning above and the loss of my body below, I felt my unbroken connection to the terrain around me. I reached out farther than I ever had, feeling every nuance of the world. Every stone and seared grain of sand made itself known to me. My eyes still could not see, but my awareness became so acute that the combined vision of every previous living being could not compare to my own. I discerned countless trees burn to cinder. On every continent, I felt the last traces of water torn from the soil. I sensed every tiny pebble across the planet quiver in fear of the murderous ball of fire above.

I knew then I was the only life remaining in the world. I, a golem of stone, had inherited the last legacies of every race, and of the earth itself.

When the last epoch came to its end, the storm of nuclear fire above swelled beyond its breaking point, setting fire to the air and to the stone itself. I felt the final cry of the condemned land as it disintegrated to ash, and then the ash itself annihilated. The last of my body vanished, and only the infinitude of my consciousness remained. Light replaced darkness, completely.

And in this light, I saw, at long last, my master.

He came to me, hobbling with his staff, and I welcomed him. "You returned to me, master. Have I done well?"

"Yes, golem, you have," he replied, stroking me with his words. "You guarded well the one possession that mattered: the great lessons of our lineage, which have led you here, and will live again someday when the world is reborn. You did well, my golem. So very well. Thank you."

And with that, the last of what I'd been holding onto became free. I rejoiced in the vindication that I had done my master's work to my end. The universe blossomed within me, revealing all the experiences a being might possibly witness. Closing my formless eyes of awareness, I released myself from the constricting passage of time.

In the moment of my apotheosis, I returned to the firmament of creation, to that place-before-places I had known in the moment of my awakening. A place where nothing is made of stone, where all of time exists within one endless, perfect moment, and where I, the stone golem of Qual'Jom, am made of light.

Robert Jordan & Brandon Sanderson

DURING THE EDITING OF EVERY NOVEL, YOU REALIZE THAT CERTAIN scenes just aren't working. There are a variety of reasons this happens, and while removing those scenes is always one of the most difficult parts of the creation process, it functions like the proverbial pruning of a tree—providing room for other scenes to grow. In the end, the book is better off.

That said, I'm always looking for places to show off scenes like these. They not only expose something I find very interesting about the process, but they often have gems in them that I am eager to share. (The scene with Gaul and the bridge in this excerpt is a good example.)

The following sequence was pruned from *A Memory of Light,* the final book of the Wheel of Time. Fair warning up front, it includes a lot of characters in the middle of their arcs, so without a background in the Wheel of Time, you might be a little lost. I've done what I can to make it work on its own, but it can't—by nature of its origins—ever truly be a standalone.

It also is *not* canon to the Wheel of Time. Though I'm very fond of how the sequence plays out, our eventual decision to delete it necessitated revisions to *A Memory of Light,* which grew to include some elements of this piece. The final book has no room for these scenes in its chronology; characters would literally have to be in two places at once. In addition, a few arcs of side characters play out differently here, contradicting the published narrative.

This shouldn't be seen as a replacement for those scenes. More, this is a chance for me to present something that never quite made it to publication. Imagine it as a glimpse of where the story could have gone, but ultimately did not.

The setup is simple: the enemy has been using an alternate dimension known as the Ways to move troops in secret and attack cities unexpectedly. Caemlyn—the capital of the nation of Andor, and one of the most important cities in the series—has recently been invaded using the Ways.

Our characters have decided that it's vital to interrupt the enemy's ability to use the Ways. They can't allow continued resupply and reinforcement of armies behind their front lines, and so a desperate plan is hatched. Perrin, with a team of elite troops and channelers (users of arcane power in the Wheel of Time), will travel through the Ways and destroy some of the paths the enemy is using.

Hopefully you will enjoy this for the fun bit of behind-the-scenes material that it is. In the postscript, I'll further explain why we deleted it.

For now, please enjoy!

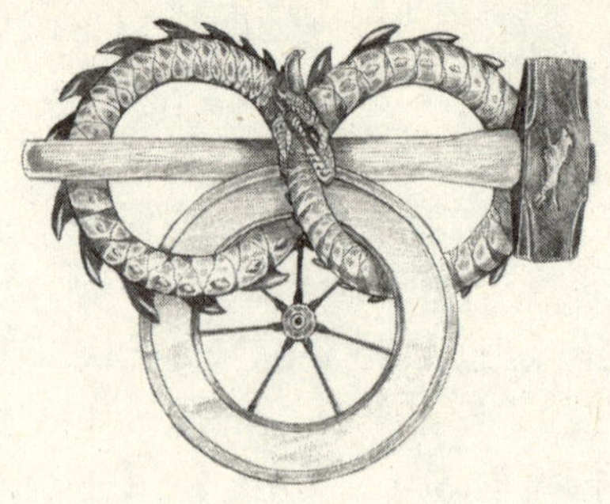

A FIRE WITHIN THE WAYS

Robert Jordan & Brandon Sanderson

Chapter 1
The Gate

Perrin stepped through the gateway into Cairhien, gripping his hammer, and looked right and then left down the narrow, cobbled alley. It was night, and the alley was dark—though lantern light shining through the gateway painted the cobbles golden at his feet.

The city was rank with the smells of men: smoke from nearby chimneys, the lingering aroma of powders and perfumes, even the scent of paint on the wooden boards of the alley—long dried and gone stale. Missing was the scent of rotting food so commonly associated with cities. Not even the smallest scraps were left to rot in Cairhien these days.

Part of him fixated on the smoke first, then tucked its presence into the back of his mind. Fire was the simplest and often the first way for a wolf to know that men were near.

Perrin prowled down the empty alley, waving for his group to follow. The still air was strange—for wolves, noise was the other sign of humankind. People were often oblivious to how much noise they made. A man in the woods was usually a thunderous, crunching, snorting, grumbling affair. That cacophony should have been magnified many times, here in the city.

And yet, it was still. Unnaturally still. Cairhien should *not* have been a quiet place, even at night.

Perrin reached the mouth of the alley and scouted the larger thoroughfare that it intersected, his eyes piercing the darkness. To his left, across the street, a building flew the Lion of Andor beside the Rising Sun of Cairhien. A few people passed by out here, smelling of wine and unwashed bodies.

"Where is everyone?" Arganda asked, slipping up beside him, holding a shielded lantern. First Captain of Alliandre's guard in Ghealdan, Arganda was a compact man, like a lean and powerful jackrabbit. He was a good one to have along on a hunt.

"Elayne has pressed most of them into one military division or another," Perrin said softly.

"Farmboys with kitchen knives and hay rakes," Gallenne said, coming up on Perrin's other side in his well-polished breastplate and helmet with three plumes, his single eye peering down the street. He could be a useful man too, if he could be kept in check. "They'll be cut to pieces by the first Trolloc they see."

"I think you'll find, Gallenne," Arganda said, "that some *farmboys* can be dangerous. Particularly if cornered."

"Quiet, you two," Perrin growled.

"I mean no offense, Arganda," Gallenne whispered. "This is not a matter of class, but of training. A well-trained soldier is of equal value to me in battle, farmboy or lord, but pressed armies have no training at all. Queen Elayne should not rely upon them."

"I don't think she's going to," Perrin said. "But what would you have them do, Gallenne? Sit and hide in their houses? This is the Last Battle. The Shadow will hurl everything it has at us. Better that the people should be armed and ready, if the soldiers fail."

The man quieted as, behind, the rest of Perrin's force moved through the gateway. Perrin wished he could still the clanking of armor and the fall of boots; if the Dark One discovered what they were up to, they'd find a force of Trollocs waiting for them in the Ways. And yet, to go without at least some troops would have been foolhardy.

It was a careful balance. Enough men to take care of trouble, if encountered, but not so many as to draw their own trouble. He'd settled on fifty. Was that the right number? He'd stayed up nights, carefully going over this plan a hundred times, and was confident in it—but this mission still had him constantly second-guessing his decisions.

The Ways were no careless jaunt through the forest. He suspected he knew that better than anyone.

Last through the gateway, crowding the alleyway, were six pack mules laden with supplies. In addition, each soldier carried a kit with extra water and food. Gallenne had questioned the need for so many supplies, but Perrin had been firm. Yes, the pathway they'd planned *looked* like it would take only a few days, but he was taking no chances. While he couldn't plan for everything, he'd not have the mission fail because of something as simple as supply problems.

That said, other than the pack animals, he'd brought no horses. Bridges in the Ways could be narrow, particularly when broken or worn. It was better to rely on feet.

That suited the Aiel just fine. Perrin had brought ten of them, including Sulin and Gaul. Ten Ghealdanin including Arganda, ten Mayeners including Gallenne, ten Whitecloaks including Galad, and ten Two Rivers men including Tam put him at exactly fifty soldiers. On top of that, he'd added Grady, Neald, Saerin, Edarra, and Seonid and her two Warders.

Five channelers. Light send he wouldn't need to rely on them much.

"Do you sense anything, Goldeneyes?" Seonid asked. Fair-skinned and dark-haired, the Cairhienin woman reminded him of Moiraine—but she was more severe. Though . . . he'd thought of Moiraine as severe too, when he'd traveled with her. Odd that he'd look back now and imagine her smelling of fondness when she spoke to him. Perhaps he was just remembering the past as he wanted to, like old Cenn Buie claiming the pies at Bel Tine had tasted better when he was young.

Either way, of the Aes Sedai who had traveled with him in the south, Perrin trusted Seonid most. At least *she* hadn't gone to meet with Masema behind his back.

Perrin peered at the street, smelling scents on the air and listening for anything out of place. Finally, he shook his head in answer to Seonid's question. He placed two men as scouts at the mouth of the street and alleyway, then joined Seonid to walk back through the alley, her two Warders following.

Their goal wasn't the street, but the dead end of the alley where it intersected a large wall surrounding what had once been the palace of Lord Barthanes Damodred—a Darkfriend, and coincidentally a cousin to Moiraine.

His palace was now Rand's school. Perrin had never been there, but he found the back gate into the grounds just where it had been described. He knocked softly, and a stocky gray-haired woman pulled the gate open.

"Idrien Tarsin?" Perrin asked.

The woman nodded, smelling of worry as she ushered them in. She was headmistress of the school, and had been told to expect their arrival. Perrin waited as the others entered, counting off his men and women—one more time, for good measure.

Finally, when all were accounted for, he pulled the gate closed behind him, then hurried along the line of soldiers to the front. Here Idrien hissed at them to be quiet, then glanced at the sky and pulled open the back door to the school proper.

Perrin stepped through it and into a place full of odd scents. Something acrid he couldn't place mixed with the aroma of flowers that had been crushed. Odd scents that he associated with baking—the sodas and yeasts—but none of the comfortable smells, like those of baking bread, that should accompany them.

As the others of his group entered, he stepped forward, sniffing at a room that reeked of a tannery. What was happening in this strange place, and why did he smell old bones from that room across the hall?

He would have expected the scholars to be sleeping, but as the headmistress led them down the broad hall, Perrin passed several rooms with lights burning. In one, an extremely tall man with long hair and fingers worked beside a . . . well, a contraption of some sort. It had wires and coils and pieces growing out of the floor like some kind of metal tree. Lights burned on the table in front of the scholar, inside of little glass globes. They were steady lights that didn't flicker at all.

"Is that an Asha'man?" Galad asked, stepping up beside Perrin.

"I see no weaves," Grady whispered, joining them as Arganda moved his troops through the hall behind.

"Then . . . he's figured out how to harness the One Power using only metal and coils?" Galad asked, smelling troubled. He seemed to consider the idea to be very disturbing.

Perrin shook his head and ushered the other two forward, worried about drawing the scholar's attention. The man didn't even look up, however, as if oblivious to the footfalls and hushed conversations in the hall.

Perrin hurried onward, passing underneath a model hanging from the ceiling—it looked like a wooden man with wings attached to his arms, as if they were intended to make him fly. Another room smelled of old dust and was filled entirely with bones—but from no animal Perrin recognized.

Eventually, Idrien led them through a very small door—perhaps a servants' door—out into the mansion's gardens. Perrin knew what to expect, as Loial had explained—at length, of course—about his trip here with Rand. The Waygate was in its own walled enclosure within the gardens. Sitting on the ground there was a balding fellow with a heap of star charts, staring up at the sky. What he expected to see through the cloud cover was beyond Perrin.

"I thought you were told to keep everyone away," Perrin said, hurrying up to the headmistress.

"Oh, don't mind Gavil," she said. She had a musical voice. "He's not right in the head. He . . . well, we let him study the Ways, you see . . ."

"You let someone *in*?" Perrin demanded.

"We are here to study and learn," she replied, voice hardening. "He knew the risks. And he . . . well, he only stuck his head in for a brief moment. That was enough. When we pulled him back out, he was staring and mumbling. Now he rants about a sky with no stars and draws star charts all day. But they're nonsense—at least, he charts a sky that *I've* never seen."

She glanced at Perrin, then—smelling of shame—looked away. "We've never opened it again, not since that Ogier showed up and chastised us for what we'd done. Of course, we couldn't have opened it on our own anyway, as he took the key with him when he left."

Perrin said nothing. He led his group into the small enclosure, and there was the Waygate, a portal of stone worked with incredibly intricate vine and leaf patterns. Perrin hadn't done much work in stone—the closest had been a fanciful attempt at molds for casting silver, at which Master Luhhan had laughed. As if there would ever be enough silver in the Two Rivers to waste on an apprentice's practice molds.

Still, the masterwork sculpting on the Waygates had always struck Perrin. The creators had made this stonework look almost as if it were alive.

"Thank you, Mistress Tarsin," Perrin said. "This will get me to the Two Rivers quietly, without anyone knowing where we've gone."

Perrin glanced at Galad—who blessedly didn't say anything. The man could be perniciously honest at times, and hadn't liked the idea of lying about their destination. But Perrin figured he should do anything he could to point the Shadow in the wrong direction—even starting deliberately false rumors.

"You may go," Perrin told the headmistress. "But forbid anyone from even entering this garden—barricade the doors. And don't worry about us. Remember the warning you got earlier. The Shadow might very well be planning to send troops here through this portal. It might feel quiet in this city, but you're actually sitting right on the front lines of the war."

She nodded, though she didn't smell as concerned as she probably should have. Well, perhaps she was just good at controlling her fear of the Waygates—they'd long known that the Shadow was using them, and Rand had stationed guards here during most of the school's existence.

A few guards wouldn't do much more than a locked door, unfortunately. This Waygate needed channelers who could Travel watching it permanently—whom Rand would send once he could spare them.

Or . . . well, *if* he could spare them.

Mistress Tarsin retreated out the door, locking it behind her. Not that a lock would do much to stop Trollocs—indeed, far stronger precautions had proven useless. The Waygate in Caemlyn had been locked tight like this one, behind the wall of stone that protected the entrance.

Perrin moved his soldiers back, leaving only the channelers and his attendants near the Waygate itself. Then he nodded to Grady. "All right, Grady," he said. "Bring it down."

Saerin folded her arms, and Perrin braced himself for another objection. The Aes Sedai—and Saerin in particular—hadn't liked this part of the plan. The fierce Brown sister had objected to the destruction of such an ancient relic.

Fortunately, she said nothing as Grady stepped up and adopted a look of concentration. Apparently Perrin's explanations had satisfied her: The barrier had meant nothing to the enemy in Caemlyn. It might as well not have existed, for all the good it had done the people there.

Right now, the only chance this city—and Caemlyn itself—had was for Perrin to find a method of shutting these Waygates permanently, from the inside.

"All right, my Lord," Grady said. "Brace yourself."

With that, the Asha'man blasted open the Waygate's stone covering.

The explosion ripped the barrier into several pieces, though the resulting *pop* was muted, as if it had come from many paces away. The chunks, rather than spraying chips of stone across the soldiers, hung in the air, then floated down and settled onto the path right in front of the Waygate.

Perrin felt a pang at the destruction, more so because he had ordered it. But no smith could be so attached to a piece that he couldn't see the need to melt it down when its time came.

Now that the stone covering was gone, Perrin's breath caught, and he took one of the lanterns and raised it high.

The opening exposed a glassy surface like a mirror—but one that reflected poorly. A shadowy version of Perrin, holding aloft the lantern, confronted him. Loial had said that once, the Waygates had shone like bright mirrors—back when they'd had light of their own within.

The ancient portal rested peacefully as Grady dusted off his hands. Perrin stepped up, listening, looking. The last time Rand had tried to use this Waygate, something had been waiting for him on the other side. The Black Wind.

Today, however, Perrin heard no calls for blood or death, felt no assault on his mind. He saw nothing but the shadowy version of himself, golden eyes seeming to glow in the lantern light as he searched for hints of danger. He could spot none. It seemed that *Machin Shin* was not lurking in wait for them this time.

He released his held breath as, behind him, Seonid spoke thoughtfully to Grady. "That was well done, with the explosion, Asha'man. Did you use Air to muffle the sound somehow?"

Grady nodded, wiping his brow with a handkerchief. "Been practicing how to do that, lately. Explosions can be handy, but we can't be shattering everyone's eardrums with each one, now can we?"

"The noise of the channeling is the one we must fear more," Saerin said briskly. "We should be quick, just in case."

"Agreed," Perrin said. He turned back to the troops, who had watched the display with stoic faces. This lot was as used to channeling as common men ever could be, he supposed. "Arganda and Gallenne?"

"Yes, Lord Goldeneyes?" Gallenne said, alongside a simple "Yes?" from Arganda. Both smelled eager.

"You may enter. Together."

They didn't seem to like that, but both stepped up to the dull glassy surface, as if approaching versions of themselves from the shadowy realm beyond. With the entire rock face removed, the opening was wide enough for two men, barely. Arganda reached up and tapped the surface, his finger seeming to meld with that of his dim reflection. He shuddered visibly as his finger stuck into it, rather than meeting something solid. He looked at Gallenne, and the other man nodded, his slotted helmet under his arm.

Together they stepped forward, their faces meeting those of their mirror images as they merged with the reflective surface, stepping into the Ways. A moment later, Arganda turned back, his torso breaking from the surface—causing no ripples—and leaning out.

"There is a modestly sized stone field on this side as described, Lord Goldeneyes. We see no signs of the Shadow, or of this . . . wind you mentioned."

"All right," Perrin said to the others. "In you go. One at a time, and go *slowly*, understand. I'll go last."

Galad stepped up to him as the soldiers began to file through. He watched the Waygate with troubled eyes. "I've been trying to convince the Children that we need not walk in dark paths in order to follow the Light."

"Sometimes you must walk a dark path," Perrin said, "because there is no other way forward. That doesn't mean you need to let it get inside you. That's something the Children never seem to be able to figure out."

"I am not a fool, Perrin," Galad said. "I realize that distinction. But if we intend to resist the Shadow without embracing evil methods, how can we justify using this . . . place?"

"The Ways aren't evil," Perrin said. "The fact that the Shadow has corrupted them doesn't change that they were made for a good purpose. The real corruption is Shadowspawn using it to attack us."

Galad thought for a time, then nodded. "I will accept that argument. You have a good logic about you, Perrin Aybara." He stepped up next and—without breaking stride or smelling the least bit worried—passed through the gate.

"Complimented by a Whitecloak," Seonid said to Perrin,

waiting as her Warders passed through. "How does that feel?"

"Odd," Perrin admitted. "Go on in. And remember not to channel once inside."

"You keep saying this," Edarra said as she stepped up. The Aiel Wise One had pale yellow hair and seemed young—though of course, that was deceptive when Wise Ones were concerned. She inspected her shadowy reflection with a critical eye. "Why bring five people who can channel, then tell us not to use the One Power?"

"Never swing an axe carelessly, Edarra," Perrin said. "The Power will be corrupted inside, almost like the taint that was upon *saidin*. We will probably have to use the Power to pull off this plan, but let's not be foolhardy about it."

Edarra finally entered, and though the Wise One didn't bow her head or betray an anxious step, she did smell distinctly of nervousness.

Seonid, in turn, smelled of . . . a strange mix of emotions. Something had happened between the two Aes Sedai and the Wise Ones. Perrin didn't know exactly what it had been, but it seemed to be over now. And strangely, Seonid seemed more respectful of the Aiel than she had of Egwene or the other senior Aes Sedai.

"Keep that Whitecloak at arm's length, Lord Aybara," Seonid said after Edarra passed. "His type turns on a man quickly, once he finds fault. I've seen it a dozen times." She strode into the Waygate, followed by the last of the Aiel—all save Gaul, who waited with Perrin.

"We have a saying in the Three-fold Land," Gaul noted. "The gango lizard will happily feed on your arm while the asp bites your leg. I think that one's advice could be applied to herself."

"I trust them both," Perrin said. "Seonid can be brusque, but she acts with honesty. And Galad . . . Galad is straightforward. If he does turn on me, I don't doubt he'll explain his reasons completely beforehand. I'd rather have that than a dozen attendants who tell me what I want to hear and scheme behind my back." Perrin scratched at his beard. "Odd. Rand would always talk like that too, and he ended up with a bunch of scheming toadies anyway."

Gaul laughed. "I would not call it odd, Perrin Aybara. Not odd at all."

After Gaul had passed through, Perrin stepped up, as if confronting himself in the reflective surface. He had entered the Ways only twice. First, so long ago with Moiraine. Then again when he'd returned with Loial to the Two Rivers.

It felt like an eternity had passed since either of those events. Indeed, it seemed a completely different person looked back at him from inside the Waygate. A hard man, with a weathered beard—thick like the fur of a wolf whose instincts knew to anticipate a particularly harsh winter. But Perrin could look that man in his golden eyes and feel at peace with him.

Both man and reflection slid their hammers into the loops at their sides. And both knew that this time, though wary, they would not smell of fear. He stepped forward and touched the surface of the gate, which felt icy, like water washing across him. The moment stretched—indeed, Perrin almost felt as if *he* were stretching, like a thick piece of tar.

Finally, though, he slid through and stepped firmly on the other side, entering the infinite blackness.

Chapter 2

Pathways into the Vast Nothing

The men had opened their lanterns, holding the poles out toward the darkness, but the light didn't extend around them as far as it should have. Perrin had braced himself for this feeling of oppressive darkness, but still it weighed on him.

The darkness felt *thick* here, pressing against the light. Hedging it in, penning it. Other than the Waygate—which from this side showed a view of the garden as if through dirty glass—the surroundings were utterly featureless. Just the smooth stone below their feet—marked with a faded white line leading away from the Waygate—and the darkness.

That *darkness.* Most of the soldiers, though battle-hardened, huddled together in a large group. Perrin knew that feeling. In here, you wanted the reassurance of having someone at your side. Though he knew it was an illusion, it was hard to shake the notion that the darkness was some liquid pouring in, constantly closing on the light and inching toward smothering it.

The air smelled of nothing. Stale. Dead.

A couple of the Whitecloaks had started out to the side, as if to look around at the back of the Waygate. Perrin signaled for them to fall into ranks, then crossed the stone ground—which was pocked with pits and furrows almost as if by the weathering of time, though there was no natural wind here.

Each group of soldiers formed a small rank—two lines of five. The Aiel, of course, ignored the command as if it didn't apply to them. And Perrin supposed that it didn't. They prowled about in pairs or trios, watching the darkness as if for something to stab. He didn't know that he'd ever smelled them so jittery. Not afraid, but certainly not completely comfortable with this place either.

As Perrin was counting ranks, he noted—with shock—that Gaul wasn't anywhere nearby. In the time it had taken Perrin to enter, he had vanished into the dark. Before Perrin could ask after him, however, a single light approached, bobbing in the darkness.

Gaul loped back up to the group, carrying a lantern. "The Guiding is intact, Perrin Aybara," he said. "No sign of Trollocs that I could see—no scorch marks of cooking fires or discarded bones. They may be moving through the Ways, but they did not stop near here."

"Good work," Perrin said. Then, under his breath, asked, "Showing off for the Maidens?"

Gaul laughed so hard, Perrin would have thought someone had slipped the man some brandy in his canteen. Gaul wiped a tear from his eye. "He asks if I'm showing off for the Maidens," he said to Sulin as she walked by. She immediately burst into laughter. It seemed incongruous in this dark place.

"You are a good man, Perrin Aybara," Gaul said, slapping him on the shoulder. "To give levity in these times. Showing off for the Maidens . . . As if that hadn't already sent me across such hot sands." He chuckled again, and he smelled completely earnest.

Aiel, Perrin thought. He waved for them all to move forward, the Two Rivers men bringing the pack animals, as they followed the white painted line on the ground. The Waygate disappeared behind them, and for a time they seemed to be making no progress. Like they were walking an unending path in the inky darkness, with no frame of reference or landmark other than the occasional sickly gouge in the stone underfoot.

Their footfalls seemed softer in this place, and their voices didn't carry. It was as if, upon reaching the darkness, the very sound was strangled.

Finally their light revealed a tall stone breaking the landscape. A worked rock slab, set on its end, seemed to appear from nothing. Perrin halted the men, set them watching out into the darkness as if on guard, and approached the Guiding with only the Aes Sedai, Asha'man, and Wise One.

The stone was inset with a delicate script, made of metal and worked so fine that Perrin couldn't imagine the time and effort it would have taken to fill the slab. Considering the fine swirls and leaf patterns, just one sentence of this Ogier script seemed as if it would take months.

They didn't need to rely solely upon the script, however. As they gathered near the pillar—huddling perhaps closer together than they might have in another place—Saerin took out a small notebook. "Alviarin's notes," she said, lighting the book with her lantern, "are confirmed by the more crude directions we found upon the Myrddraal's corpse."

She inspected the slab, moving her fingers over sections of scrollwork that were reproduced in the notebook. "Yes . . . I think this will be enough to get us to Caemlyn."

"How difficult can it be?" Neald asked. The young Murandian's usual exuberance was muted by that darkness, but he smelled of determination. Perrin had once been tempted to think of Neald as a boy—he hadn't yet hit eighteen winters—but after all they'd been through together . . . well, there were few men Perrin would rather have at his back than Fager Neald. "The Shadow is able to move thousands upon thousands of Trollocs through this place. If they can navigate the path, then surely you can, Saerin Sedai."

"I doubt the Dark One sheds a tear if he loses the occasional troop of Shadowspawn to this endless dark," Saerin said. "I, however, would rather not risk such a fate. My own skill in this script is lacking, and I wouldn't dare lead us on my own. But, near as I can determine, the notes are accurate. The third bridge on the right should have a post in front with these markings here. If so, we are on the proper course."

"Let's see these ramps," Seonid said, businesslike as always, "and perform the test we agreed upon. Final decisions about moving forward should be predicated upon the results."

Perrin nodded, passing orders to the soldiers to guard the retreat and keep their ears open. Then the small group of channelers—along with Gaul and Sulin, who trailed behind like shadows—headed to the right, reaching an area where bridges split off from the ground, arcing into the darkness.

He hated how structures like this seemed to appear out of nowhere—they didn't catch the light in the distance as one might expect. Instead, they emerged from the too-thick darkness once the light grew close, as if reluctantly surrendered.

Regardless, here at the edge, the structure of the Ways really started to defy explanation. Bridges split off the main path and reached out into the darkness, pathways into the vast nothing. In addition, stone ramps wound upward or downward, splitting off the main path and leading to what Perrin knew would be fields of stone identical to the one they now stood upon. Except these fields, best he could tell, were directly *above* or *below* the one they stood upon. There seemed to be no way that the structures could support themselves. He'd once tried to sketch it out, and it seemed that the stone fields must be discs—or perhaps Islands—hanging in the nothing, connected by networks of ramps and bridges.

He'd eventually abandoned his drawing because he couldn't say for certain if his perception was correct or not. The darkness of this place, the way it twisted the eyes and mind, made it difficult to judge distances. Trying to impose a visual structure on it had been like building a blacksmith's puzzle with no actual solution.

As others inspected the bridges and ramps, he could see several of them—Neald included—trying to wrap their minds around it, perhaps sketch it out in their heads. He caught Edarra shaking her head and muttering under her breath as she looked up, then down. Well, he *had* warned them.

"The post with the inscription is where the notes said it would be," Saerin said, stepping back up to him.

Perrin nodded, then waved Grady over. "All right, Jur. Let's do this."

The others gathered around him again, and he could smell their apprehension. Good. That meant he'd properly impressed upon them the danger of what they were about to do.

Jur Grady, appearing almost as weathered as these stones, adopted a look of concentration. He'd seized the Power.

"Do something small," Perrin said. "We need to know."

Grady held a hand out in front of him and summoned a globe of yellow light, letting it hover above his fingertips. He grimaced, smelling of anger. "Blood and ashes! That's something I *never* wanted to feel again. It's like the taint was never cleansed. How can it still be here, in this place?"

"It persists here," Saerin said. "Oddly, I can feel it too, so it's not just the men. It's like rot on a dismembered part of the body, continuing to fester after the corpse itself has been burned."

"All right, Jur," Perrin said, pointing toward a particular bridge they weren't going to be using—one that was pocked on the side, degraded by whatever affliction was progressively making the Ways decay. "Take a small piece off that bridge there."

Grady stretched his hand out and released a small jet of light and flame. Though Perrin couldn't see the weaves, he could tell—instinctively—that something was *wrong* with this one. The flame had a sickly brown cast to it unlike any flame he'd seen in real life. Grady, often stoic when he channeled, smelled suddenly of nausea and discomfort.

His blast of fire broke the knob of stone off the bridge, dropping it into the void below. He immediately released the Power and heaved out a sigh. Together, they grew still. Perrin strained, listening in the darkness for even a hint of wind. He was ready to abandon this entire endeavor, and would do so in the blink of an eye, if he thought they might have alerted *Machin Shin* to come for them.

He heard nothing, smelled nothing.

Grady spat to the side, something Perrin didn't think he'd ever seen the man do. "It's not exactly the same as the taint was—but that just makes it a different kind of awful. Back then, I felt like I was reaching through oil to touch the Power. Here, something was . . . was corrupting my channeling *as I used it*. Like I'd finished half of my meal, and only then found worms in the bread."

"How hard was it to destroy that piece of stone?" Perrin said, nodding with his chin.

"It crumbled like powder, my Lord," Grady said. "Like . . . like it wasn't stone at all, but dried clay."

"So we *can* do it," Neald said.

The plan that Perrin had presented, after hours of thought and work, was relatively simple. Their small group would find its way to the Waygate into Caemlyn. Once there, they would destroy the bridges and ramps leading to that particular Island in the darkness, isolating it. These bridges were long, expansive things. Destroying them would effectively cut Caemlyn off, denying their enemies the ability to resupply forces behind Rand's battle lines.

The chance to completely isolate armies of Shadowspawn was worth risking a trip into the Ways. Accomplishing it, however, relied upon two things: their ability to navigate, and their ability to actually damage the stonework pathways that led to Caemlyn. Both now seemed confirmed.

"We move forward, then," Perrin said. "Into the darkness."

Chapter 3

As If into Eternity Itself

Perrin led the way across another graceful stone bridge arcing out into the darkness. Hours into the trip, and it still felt as if they'd made no progress. He remembered this sensation from before, the nagging worry that somehow it was all an illusion. That he was leaving one Island and being wound around to arrive back in the same spot.

He found himself strangely grateful for the broken patches in the stone. They, at least, were different on each Island or bridge. He just wished that Grady's words didn't hang over him as they did. *It crumbled like powder* . . . As if he hadn't already felt nervous walking across stonework he knew had no support underneath it.

Arganda walked nearby, periodically looking over the edge of the bridge. Perrin resisted. He had no need to stare down into that darkness, as if into eternity itself.

Eventually, they reached the end of this particular bridge and walked out onto another nondescript field of stone. Their lights could never fully illuminate these places. He just wished he could *see* it all, rather than experiencing it from within these little bubbles of light that didn't extend far enough.

The soldiers had clumped together as they walked, and Perrin fell back to give them some encouraging words. This place did strange things to the mind. It was difficult to stay alert crossing bridge after bridge, with no sense of time or place.

They reached the next Guiding. This one was in far worse shape than others; barely any of the writing was legible. Saerin approached and pulled out her notebook, then waved for one of the Mayeners to bring his lamp closer. She squinted at the stone and ran her fingers along it.

"Such damage . . ." she said softly. "It's all deteriorating. Like a cube of sugar left out in the rain . . ."

"Can you find the way?" Perrin asked.

She consulted the book, then led them around to a ramp leading downward. Perrin did a quick count of everyone as they passed. Saerin stood next to him, flipping pages in the notebook. He hadn't known her as long as some of the others, but her direct manner didn't seem much like other members of the Brown Ajah he'd known. He liked that, and had accepted quickly when she volunteered for this mission.

"You're doing well," he told her once the count was done. Together, the two of them started down the ramp—last, save for the Aiel who had taken the rear guard position. "I was worried about this part."

"The instructions are clear," she said. "The notes include directions to only a few Waygates, but those instructions are very deliberate and clear. I'm less worried about getting lost than I am about this being some kind of trap or misdirection."

Perrin nodded, though a part of him was concerned by how indifferently she said it. If there was one thing Loial had impressed on him, it was that the Ways were *not* to be taken lightly. It seemed almost foolhardy to be in here without the Ogier to guide him. Loial had not only been able to read the Guidings, but his constant warnings—the sheer edge of his concern—had imparted a reluctance to them all.

Perhaps Perrin needed to take that role. He'd given in to letting the Aiel prowl ahead of and behind the group, as was their custom in any situation—but Loial had never allowed even Lan to scout for them in the Ways.

"This place," Saerin said, "is different than the records describe. The darkness isn't the darkness of night, but of something else entirely. We've entered a different place, with different rules, than our world."

"You've studied the Ways?" Perrin asked her, carefully prodding for more information. She'd been hesitant, during their meetings to plan this expedition, to reveal all she knew. But he was accustomed to that from Aes Sedai by now.

"I have dedicated my life to the most useful knowledge I could find," Saerin said. "And to its practical application."

"Practical application?" Perrin prodded.

"Nobody uses the Ways anymore," Saerin said, looking up into the absolute blackness. "That makes them all the more interesting, as there is an obvious power to be found here. A power that—before Traveling was rediscovered—was unique."

He smelled a curiosity to her, carefully controlled—and not much fear. "You've traveled them before," Perrin said. "Haven't you?"

"Only a fool would enter the Ways," she replied. "Everyone knows that."

An Aes Sedai answer, for certain. She likely didn't know how much of the truth Perrin could smell on her. Still, he left the topic for now, instead walking up past the Two Rivers men and the pack animals, where he cautioned the men to be extra quiet. He didn't want to dampen their moods further, but . . . well, better gloomy than dead. Or worse.

He moved up along the line until he was at the front, leading the way into the deep. He was accustomed to being able to see farther than other men, but he wasn't convinced that worked in here. It was hard to tell, as there really wasn't anything to see.

At least the Aiel weren't prowling too far ahead. The five at the foreguard stayed just in front of the main line. As Perrin arrived at the front, Gaul fell back and joined him.

"It looks worse than before," Gaul said softly. He had his veil down, but seemed about an inch from sliding it on. "If that is possible."

He was right. As they reached the next Guiding, Saerin led them to one of the spiraling ramps, which led straight down into more darkness. On the way down, Perrin had to step around holes in one side of the ramp or the other. There were pocks in the middle too, like places in a road where one cobblestone had been pried up and carried away.

He joined Galad at the bottom, where the tall Whitecloak was looking back upward, smelling strongly of distaste. Perrin knew that feeling—the uncanny sensation that the place they'd left earlier *should* be right on top of them, somehow held up by no pillars or other supports.

"This structure should collapse," Galad said. "A thing of the Shadow, this is. The natural world does not work in such a manner."

"We're not in the natural world, Galad," Perrin said. "We are . . ."

Perrin trailed off. What was that hushed sound? Distant wind, or just a rustle of motion from one of the others. His hairs stood up on his arms as he felt a chill run through his body. He strained to hear over the hushed voices of others whispering, of hooves quietly clopping on the stone. Sound seemed dampened here. Muffled. Over it all, he heard . . .

Nothing. It was nothing. He was mostly certain.

Galad cocked his head at Perrin. Most of the party was settling down on the Island beyond the ramp, digging out rations for the midday meal—though they could only guess at the actual time, and judged their meals by number of bridges or ramps crossed.

"Is all well?" Galad asked.

"As well as it can be, in this place," Perrin said, though he caught Grady by the arm as he passed.

"My Lord Goldeneyes?" Grady asked.

"Jur," Perrin said. "If we encounter the wind—if it finds us—don't wait for my orders. Hit it with everything you have."

Grady eyed Galad, then spoke more softly. "Will it work? You know that something's wrong with the One Power here. I . . . well, that thing you described. Will it even react to the Power?"

"Rand says he drove the Black Wind back once. He told me he used the One Power to push it back into the Waygate when it seemed ready to reach out and snatch him. If *Machin Shin* comes for us, that will be our only recourse. Understand?"

"I understand. And we will be ready. I'll let Neald know." He saluted, then withdrew.

Galad watched Grady go, smelling . . . of nothing specific, actually. Perrin had expected loathing.

"No gibes, Galad?" Perrin asked. "No commentary on the evils of the One Power?"

"I have never thought of the One Power as evil," Galad replied. "It is merely another tool for men to use. Any power or authority, however, does have a tendency to corrupt. The signs of this are all over the White Tower. You disagree?"

"No, actually," Perrin said.

"The Asha'man are terrible and worrisome," Galad said. "But, upon consideration, I also find them noble. To take the lot they have been given and try to use it to help, rather than harm, is commendable. More commendable would be to seek gentling. Few men are willing to take a step so severe, however, despite it being right."

"Right no longer," Perrin said. "With the Source cleansed."

"Not completely, if this place is a guide."

Light, Perrin thought. *I hope he doesn't mention this conversation to the other Whitecloaks.* Some of them might take this as proof that the Asha'man were still not to be trusted. Few of the Whitecloaks were as rational as Galad. Dain Bornhald, who passed by near the end of the line, was a good example. The young man still smelled hateful when he was around Perrin. And, strangely, guilty.

Perrin understood the hatred. Although Dain no longer believed Perrin had killed his father, that didn't wipe away old biases or dislikes. But why the guilt? Was it because Bornhald had been forced, by duty, to kill his friend? Bornhald often smelled of brandy lately.

Perrin didn't give the soldiers long for their break. Moiraine had always kept them moving, making them eat while riding, and Perrin was inclined to trust her wisdom in this. He soon ordered everyone forward, with further reminders to remain quiet, and they fell back into the rhythm of this place. Marching through the too-quiet darkness. Pausing briefly at each Guiding, and again at each bridge or ramp to check the markings.

As they reached the end of each ramp or bridge, the Aiel scouted forward to check for signs of Trollocs. None but the Aiel volunteered for the duty, but Perrin did not let them scout far. He remembered Loial's cautious warnings, imagining how easily even a careful scout might get lost in this darkness. Perrin would be forced to abandon them in such a case, and so leave them to wander alone in the darkness until thirst—or madness—took them.

Near the end of the first day of marching, they encountered a problem that Perrin had been dreading: a broken bridge.

He stepped up to the gap, joining the Aiel scouts at the edge. The decomposing stonework here had given way, dumping a ten-foot or longer chunk of stone into the abyss. Perrin knelt at the edge, feeling at the jagged, broken stone remaining. He could see the other side of the bridge, at the very limit of their light, where it presumably continued until it touched the next Island over.

Below lay only blackness. Would a man who fell drop until he starved, or would he hit one of the other Islands first?

"I think I could jump that," said Aviellin—one of the Maidens.

"A long jump indeed," Sulin said. "The wetlanders could not make it, that is for certain. No offense to you, Perrin Aybara."

"None taken," he said, shivering at the thought of even trying. He turned, asking for Edarra and the Aes Sedai. They approached, Saerin and Edarra pointedly ignoring one another. Perhaps Saerin had heard of how Seonid had been treated. Of course, Seonid was *also* one of the women who had sworn to Rand, so maybe . . .

Perrin hesitated. No colors. Usually, when he thought of Rand, colors spun in his vision, showing an image of the man wherever he was. Not this time. Were the Ways, in some manner, related to the wolf dream? He didn't see the visions there either.

The group gathered with him a few steps away from the crumbled end of the bridge. "I've encountered broken bridges before," Perrin said. "I was hoping that, by using a mapped-out path, we'd avoid the problem. This break must be more recent."

"What did you do last time?" Seonid asked.

"Loial took us around another way," Perrin said.

Together, they looked at Saerin. She displayed quintessential Aes Sedai composure as she met Perrin's eyes, then shook her head. "One measure of a woman's strength is her willingness to accept her limits. I do not think I can navigate in this place on my own. I would be willing to try, if pressed, but I barely know enough to determine we're going in the right direction *with* these instructions."

Perrin chewed on that, considering. "Make us a bridge."

"With what stone?" Saerin asked, amused.

"No stone," Perrin said. "Air. I know it can be done."

Saerin didn't respond at first. "That's a wide gap, Goldeneyes. It might be too wide for me."

"Edarra can help."

"It's not simply a matter of strength. The size of a bridge made of Air has strict limits. With that landing on the other side . . . well, it may be possible, but dangerous. Not only because the One Power is tainted in this place. I will be required to anchor Air against the broken stone on both sides. The bridge could crumble further, and dump everyone on it."

Perrin nodded, rubbing at his beard. "See if you can make the bridge first," he said. "If it holds, we'll send people across one at a time."

The others seemed to take this decision as reasonable. Saerin spoke with Seonid and Edarra in hushed tones, and then all three adopted a look of concentration. Though it had been happening for a while, it still surprised Perrin sometimes when people—including Aes Sedai and Wise Ones—did what he said.

"This is not a pleasant experience," Saerin said to him. "But perhaps I can see it as a useful one. Is this really how men used to feel while channeling?"

"Worse," Grady said from beside Perrin.

"The bridge is in place," Saerin said. "We will need someone to test to see if it holds."

Before any of the Aiel could volunteer, Perrin stepped out into the gap.

A couple of the Wolf Guard gasped, but Perrin's foot fell on something hard. He couldn't see it, but it felt as firm as stone under his boot. *Eyes forward,* he told himself, and took the next step. He kept his hand on his hammer as he walked—the warmth inside the metal was comforting—and tried not to think about the expansive nothingness beneath him. Sweat trickled down the sides of his face.

Never had he been so glad to touch stone as he was when he took that last step. Perrin let out a deep breath and turned to see Gaul coming next. The man could have been taking a nice evening stroll. He stopped and tapped his foot on the side of the invisible bridge, then leaned out over the darkness.

Crazy Aiel, Perrin thought. He *was* showing off, even if he wouldn't admit it.

The Maidens came next, one at a time, and though a few repeated Gaul's feat, none fell off. Perrin sent Gaul and the Maidens on to inspect the next Island—with cautions to remain close—but he wanted to wait until every person had crossed.

He all but held his breath the entire time. He could stomach men dying in battle under his leadership. He didn't like it, but he could stomach it. Having one fall off here, though . . . well, that would haunt him all his days. He knew it as sure as he knew his own name.

Eventually, only the channelers and the Whitecloaks remained. Grady and Neald came one at a time, as steady as the Aiel had been, though Perrin could smell their nervousness. That left Galad and his men.

Perrin could see their hesitation from across the gap, though he couldn't smell it. Some members of the Whitecloak army had refused Healing by Aes Sedai on previous occasions.

"Well?" Perrin called. "You demanded to come with me into this place. Cross now, or be left in the darkness."

Galad came first. Perrin nodded to him as he arrived; for once, the man smelled anxious.

"What was it you said?" Perrin asked. "The One Power is merely another tool?"

"Perhaps the 'merely' was said in haste," Galad said, looking back at the bridge of Air as Bornhald began to cross. "It is a tool, yes. But so is fire, and I would not much like to walk a similar distance with it underfoot."

Perrin grunted. "Well, so long as—"

Something cracked near Perrin's feet.

Perrin didn't hesitate. He swung an arm out, lunging toward Bornhald—who had nearly arrived. The young man stared at his feet in horror as the stonework nearest Perrin crumbled away, dumping Bornhald and the bridge into the darkness.

Perrin caught Bornhald by the collar of his shirt, but the move left him precariously standing with one foot halfway over the broken edge of the bridge, tipping. He grunted, holding tight as Bornhald screamed, flinging his arms up. He took hold of Perrin's arm, overbalancing him.

Perrin met the young man's eyes. And held on.

"Light!" Galad said, grabbing Perrin from behind and pulling him upright. Bornhald swung, dangling over the divide. The force of his swinging almost pulled all three of them over, but after what seemed an eternal moment, something seized them all—

something unseen—and pushed them back onto the stone bridge.

The three tumbled into a heap, Bornhald gasping, nearly crying. Galad sat up and rubbed the elbow he'd struck when he fell. Perrin took a deep breath, then sat up. He started to call thanks to the Aes Sedai and Wise One for the threads of Air that had saved them.

Then he saw Neald standing just a short distance away, hand out. "Blood and bloody ashes, Lord Perrin!" he said. "Light, I'm sorry! I almost missed you. I didn't hear a thing until Bornhald screamed!"

"You did well, Fager," Perrin said, dusting himself off as he stood—mostly because he wanted to be moving to keep himself from shaking. "You saved our lives."

"You reacted quickly, Aybara," Galad said as Perrin helped him to his feet. "How did you do it?"

"I heard the stone cracking," Perrin said. "That's all."

"I heard no cracking," Galad said, shaking his head. "Those wolf's ears of yours . . . Is it a thing another man can learn, do you suppose?"

Perrin found himself gaping. "You? You'd want to *learn* it?"

"Studying your talents would help me determine whether they serve the Light or not," Galad said, sounding perfectly rational. "I have accepted that wolves are not of the Dark One; at least, if they are, I have no evidence of it. I see no problem—yet—in a man learning what you do."

"I doubt the wolves would like you," Perrin said, then found himself chuckling despite the darkness, despite the near fall. He'd been cursed, hunted, and feared because of his eyes. But never, *never* had someone asked if it would be possible to emulate him. Now the question came, and from a Whitecloak no less!

Galad crouched beside Bornhald. "Are you well, Dain?"

"I . . . Yes, Lord Captain Commander. Yes, I think I . . . I think I will be."

Bornhald reached for the flask at his belt. Galad allowed him a single pull on it, then gently took it and tossed it over the side of the bridge.

Dain watched it go, smelling horrified. But Perrin shook his head, still amused. Galad was nothing if not consistent.

Galad helped Bornhald to his feet. "I'll see him the rest of the way across. Someone should walk with him. But first . . ." He turned toward the broken bridge, where the remaining Whitecloaks stood with the Aes Sedai and Edarra. "Well?" he called. "Can you make another?"

"We can," Edarra called back.

"Do it," he shouted, probably for the benefit of his men. "It takes more than a threat of death to unnerve the Children. We will walk in the Light even in this place, Aiel."

Galad nodded to Perrin, then moved on, holding a lantern pole in one hand and resting his other hand on the obviously shaken Bornhald's shoulder.

Light send we don't run into any more gaps, Perrin thought as the rest of the Children made their way across the new bridge, one at a time. He doubted they'd coax Bornhald across another.

CHAPTER 4

The Touch of the Blacksmith

"It's all right to be afraid of something," Perrin said.

Bornhald looked up. He had been sitting by himself at the edge of the pool of light.

Around them, the group made camp for its first "night" in the Ways. This section of stone seemed a little less degraded than others, and Perrin tried to imagine the Ways as Loial had described them: bright and sunlit, a place of life and warmth. When he tried to picture that, the looming darkness always intruded. Just as it seemed to want to intrude upon their camp, lurking outside the light.

To keep it back, they'd set a ring of lanterns, and within it were laying out bedrolls and getting notes on watch shifts from Arganda. Remarkably, everyone seemed to be taking the mood well, adjusting to the gloom of this place. Though they kept their voices low by Perrin's orders, some of the Ghealdanin and

Mayeners were chuckling together, trading friendly barbs as they arranged themselves for sleep.

Perrin smiled at that, glad to see those two groups in particular getting along. More remarkably, a few of the Whitecloaks joined in as well, laughing at some joke. Was it possible that even these harsh men could find common ground with the others?

Not Bornhald, however. The young Taraboner sat alone. He seemed a naturally thin man, but during his time in Perrin's camp, he'd grown almost skeletal.

"I'm not frightened," Bornhald spat, then took a bite of bread.

Perrin settled down. That earned him a glare.

"Look," Perrin said softly. "We have differences, but you're under my command now. The Last Battle is upon us. There isn't time for grudges anymore."

Bornhald continued eating.

"Is this about your father?" Perrin asked. "Geofram—"

"Don't." Bornhald stopped, took a deep breath, then continued, "Don't speak his name. Just . . . Just don't. Please. This isn't about him."

"Then it's about Byar."

"I don't want your help, Aybara," Bornhald said. "I don't want your sympathy. I'll control myself. Leave me be."

"Fine." Perrin sighed and stood up. He walked back toward the center of the light, where Galad—hands clasped behind his back—was surveying his men as they made camp.

"There's something big troubling Bornhald," Perrin said. "His near fall shook him."

"Dain has been . . . increasingly unreliable lately," Galad said. "Tell me, Aybara. Does the name Ordeith mean anything to you?"

Perrin drew in a sharp breath. "Yes."

"Dain keeps muttering that name."

"Ordeith is a Darkfriend," Perrin said. "No, he's something worse. He's the man who brought Trollocs to the Two Rivers. He'd pretended to join the Children, but was really just toying with them, using them for something. I'm not exactly sure what it was. Probably an attempt to draw Rand's attention."

"Might I note," Galad said, "that you have been accused of the same things—bringing Trollocs to the Two Rivers—and that you argued lack of evidence sufficient to convict. Do you have any way of proving to me that one of the Children was guilty of this crime?"

"He's *not* one of the Children, Galad," Perrin said, glancing back at Bornhald. "As for proof, once we're out of here, I can give you a number of witnesses to the crimes this man has committed. For now . . . Light, did Fain—did Ordeith—give anything to Bornhald?" Bornhald had a little of the same cast to him that Mat had had, back when the dagger had claimed him.

"I will ask," Galad said. "And I will speak with the other Children about this Ordeith, to see if any of them have met him."

Perrin nodded, accepting a hunk of jerky and some cheese from Tam, who brought it over when he saw Perrin hadn't eaten anything. At times, the Two Rivers men mothered him as much as any woman might. Still, he was happy to tear into the food as he walked over to the Aiel. He'd just noticed Gaul and Aviellin returning. The group was camping near the Guiding, and he'd reluctantly agreed to allow the two Aiel to go across the next bridge and scout the landing.

"More signs of Trollocs on the next Island, Perrin Aybara," Gaul said. "Bones in a pile. Some paintings in red on the ground. Might be blood. A few days old, at least."

Light. What did the Shadowspawn do? Bring people with them to eat along the way?

Is that why they were so focused on taking Kandor? Perrin wondered. *To gain prisoners for food?* The thought made him sick.

"We listened into the dark," Gaul said, "but could hear no sign of them in the distance. But who knows. Trollocs can be quiet, if they are on a tight leash—and this place seems to warp sound in ways I cannot anticipate."

"They didn't destroy the Guiding as you feared," Aviellin said. "It was kept completely clean, with no Trolloc markings on the ground nearby."

Perrin nodded. He'd thought that, with the existence of the notebooks, the Myrddraal might break the Guidings. That wouldn't much change this mission, but it would be a loss for the future. Anyone else wanting to travel these paths would be prevented from doing so.

But . . . will there ever be any others? Perrin thought. Apparently cleansing the Source hadn't had any effect on the taint inside the Ways. What little signs they'd had from the Ogier indicated that they were intent on withdrawing, leaving men to fight on their own as the end approached. Even Loial, among the most adventuresome of his kind, had been terribly frightened of this place, and at a loss as to how to recover it.

Perhaps Perrin should do the world a favor by destroying access not just to Caemlyn's Waygate, but to every Waygate he could find—leaving this too-hungry darkness to starve upon its own corpse.

Once, things grew on the Islands. Loial's voice—dredged up from Perrin's memories of another visit to the Ways—seemed to drift across his mind. *There was green grass to sleep on, soft as any feather bed. Fruit trees to spice the food you'd brought with an apple or a pear or a bellfruit . . . Crisp and juicy whatever the time of year outside . . .*

He would have liked to see that. And it seemed a crime of some incalculable nature that such a wonderful place should be abandoned without hope of recovery. Though the powerful and the elite of the world now had access to Traveling to cross distances, the steep requirements for that meant it would never be available to the common traveler. He thought of the Ways, lush and welcoming, providing a method for people all across the land to travel easily and safely. And when the darkness tried to intrude on that imagining, he forced it back.

For now, though, he needed to concentrate on his mission. One that was, unfortunately, more concerned with destroying parts of the Ways than recovering them. How often his hammer had to fall to break, instead of build, these days. He shook his head, chewing on his jerky and trying to decide if he should give orders to shorten the break for sleep from six hours to four. They'd been seeing more and more signs of Trollocs these last few hours, and he wanted to be out of this place.

And yet, if they did end up forced into a skirmish with Shadowspawn, he wanted the men rested and ready to fight. He'd rather use the channelers only as a last resort.

He eventually changed the break to a compromise of five hours, then—after giving the orders—found himself sitting near the perimeter of the ring of light, where he could watch the camp settle down as he took brief reports from the leaders of the various groups. It was remarkable how, after just one day of marching, there were already things that needed his attention. A thrown shoe on one of the pack animals, a soldier with blisters forming from a new set of boots—they might want to risk a dribble of Aes Sedai Healing for that—and a concerning report that one of the water bags had sprung a leak and drained by half with nobody noticing.

He handled each small problem in turn, then took reports from the Aiel he'd sent to scout across nearby bridges, just in case. Loial would never have allowed people to separate from the group like that, but Perrin wasn't Loial, and he felt he was capable of judging what risks his troops could and couldn't take.

Indeed, he lost none of the Aiel pairs to the darkness. They each reported back in turn. As he listened to what they said—nothing out of the ordinary—he noticed Edarra stopping to listen. They hadn't gone running to her first, as they once would have, before bringing word to him.

The camp was settling down, and the soldiers seemed to get to sleep faster than he ever had in this place. He did note that the two Aiel who were on watch duty—Aviellin and Sulin—walked over and joined the other soldiers on duty, who were sitting around a very small fire. They settled down, and Sulin began talking in an animated way.

Two from each group, he noted. Whitecloak sitting next to Two Rivers man, Mayener and Ghealdanin sharing a waterskin. And even the Aiel, telling stories for the others. He didn't catch all of what Sulin said to them, but it seemed to be a characteristically Aiel story, as the men looked baffled to hear it—though they did smile and ask her for another.

"I don't know that I realized what you were doing here,

Perrin Aybara," Edarra said. "No, not until this trip."

He started, having forgotten she was still sitting nearby, next to one of the lanterns.

"I assumed that once this was all done, we'd return to the Three-fold Land," she continued. "Continue to live apart from wetlanders and their soft ways. And yet, these months traveling with you have . . . made me wonder. You are building something grand here, which should not surprise me as it does. The touch of the blacksmith. You employ it as quietly, but as surely, as the best spear seeking *gai'shain*."

He didn't know how to interpret that. "Conflict brings people together," he said with a grunt, finishing off his jerky. "I haven't done anything special, Edarra. Except maybe keep some wool-headed fools from one another's throats long enough for them to realize who the real enemy is."

"You build," she said again. "And where you make shade, strangely, I find myself wanting to follow. Once, I would have said that you should abandon these wetlanders, and travel only with us into this darkness. What would you need of anyone but us? The wetlanders only slow us, and make noise.

"Yet today, I see what you are doing. And I find that I would have been wrong to make this suggestion. There is a wisdom in you, Perrin Aybara. I do not say this lightly."

He looked again at the small campfire. He'd ordered a small amount of wood brought, knowing they'd be grateful for it during the night they would need to spend here. There *was* something special happening in his group. Whitecloaks, Ghealdanin, and Mayeners chatting together, and listening to Aiel stories.

Perhaps he shouldn't have worried about such things in the face of the Last Battle. Yet something whispered to him that if life went on after the battle—and he was going to do everything under the Light to make sure it did—it would be important that each of these groups felt they had taken part in the accomplishment.

Edarra was staring out into the darkness. "There's something about this place," she said thoughtfully. "It reminds me of the World of Dreams."

"You're a Dreamwalker?" Perrin asked with surprise.

"No," Edarra said. "I always hoped to become one. As a younger girl, I . . . But no. That is not worth speaking. I have no personal experience, but this place reminds me of what others have said of entering *Tel'aran'rhiod*. A black emptiness that goes on forever. A place where nothing feels quite as it should."

"There are similarities," Perrin said, which caused her to glance at him and cock her head. "But the World of Dreams is not so bleak. It's not a place of infinite darkness, but a place of infinite possibility." He chewed on the cheese he'd been given. He didn't hunger for it—he hadn't even hungered for the jerky. Something about this place had always dampened his appetite. "I won't be able to go there so long as we travel in here, and I regret that. I need to return, and go there in my strength. Enter the World of Dreams physically."

She looked at him sharply. "Do not think of that, Perrin Aybara. It is evil."

Perrin didn't reply. He'd been rambling, and perhaps shouldn't have even spoken.

But another problem loomed over him, one that would demand his attention once this mission was through. Strength in the wolf dream—in *Tel'aran'rhiod*—involved a delicate balance. The more you pushed yourself into the dream—the more solidly *there* you became—the more powerful you were. However, you also risked entering too strongly and dying in the real world.

Slayer was strong there, so *very* strong. Perrin needed an edge, a way to defeat him. He rested his hand on his hammer, feeling the warmth inside.

This will not end, he thought, *until you are the prey, Slayer. Hunter of wolves. I will end you.*

"In many ways," Edarra muttered, looking at him, "you are still a foolish child, for all the *ji* you have found."

So much for her calling him wise. Well, Perrin had grown accustomed to—though not fond of—being addressed in such a way by women who looked not a year or two older than he. "You cannot enter the World of Dreams in your flesh, Perrin Aybara.

None of the Dreamwalkers will teach you this thing. It *is* evil."

"Can you tell me why?" Perrin said.

"To enter into the World of Dreams in the flesh is to lose part of yourself," Edarra said. "I only know that, and it would be wisdom to accept the wisdom in it, Perrin Aybara."

Perrin nodded, though it was nothing more than he'd been told before. What did it mean? What was the real risk?

The servants of the Shadow take these risks, Perrin thought. *What risks must we take to stop them?* He'd been willing to come here, to risk being lost in an eternal darkness—or to the madness of the Black Wind. Others would call this one step too far, but Perrin suspected it would only be the first of many for him.

Chapter 5

Fingernail on Stone

Two Trollocs sniffed at the air, looking lazily about themselves in the darkness. One had the ears and snout of a wolf, something that made Perrin's hair stand on end. Its legs bent like a wolf's, though the hands were distinctly human. The bear Trolloc beside it had an almost human face, with human teeth and a human eyebrow ridge, yet fur on its hands.

People who heard Trollocs described often imagined them to be people, just with animal heads. Such descriptions didn't do justice to the disconcerting amalgamation they were. Each one had some human features—particularly the eyes—grossly melded with those of something distinctly inhuman. It wasn't that they looked like beast parts chopped up and mixed with human ones. Instead, they were a terrible perversion of both. A horror that had too much beast to ever be tamed, but too much man to ever be trusted.

Worst, Trollocs smelled wrong. Musky, but also faintly of rotting meat. Perhaps that came from shreds of their meals, caught in fur or under nails. No right animal would ever be so unclean.

The Trollocs, with their sputtering lanterns on poles, stood in the very middle of the bridge from one Island to the next. They had a suspicious amount of light on them—not just the two lanterns on poles, but three more bright lanterns at their feet. Perrin had never known Trollocs to need light in the outside world, but the blackness of the Ways was complete. So he supposed it wasn't odd that they would bring some light. But so much?

Perhaps they were just naturally afraid of this darkness. They didn't seem terribly concerned, however, as they spoke to one another in rough voices in a language that Perrin didn't speak—and had no care to learn.

Gaul nudged him, and the two slid quietly back down the stone bridge and into the darkness. They hadn't brought lights, of course. Trollocs had senses as good as Perrin's; they would notice light, or they might smell something burning.

That meant, however, that Perrin and Gaul had to cross back to the waiting force in the dark. And crossing that bridge in the blackness—knowing that if he misstepped, he'd tumble into eternity—sent a shiver through Perrin like the feeling of a spider crawling up his spine. He let out a deep breath when he caught the sliver of light from a shielded lantern ahead. Four more Aiel crouched around it, including Sulin.

Perrin and Gaul had left their shoes here, after taking them off to prowl forward in silence. Notably, the Aiel hadn't questioned Perrin when he'd wanted to go with them to investigate the light; he had begun to think they respected his abilities as a woodsman.

"Those Trollocs are guarding the path for certain," Perrin said softly, crouching down near the lantern.

"We can take them," Sulin said softly.

Perrin shook his head. "Those two have a lot of light on them, and they're being loud. Something about this feels wrong. Like they're bait."

The little group fell silent.

"If I thought I might be followed," Gaul said slowly, "by soldiers who are quiet and dangerous, I might consider such a thing. Put out two guards I know will be spotted, then watch to see who emerges from the darkness to confront them."

"It is done sometimes," Sulin agreed. "Two rows of guard

posts, the outer of which must report frequently to confirm nothing is wrong."

Gaul nodded. "Very well. Just in case, I will sneak past these two and learn if there are any others beyond."

"Sneak past?" Sulin asked. "Stone Dog, the bridge is crumbling, and isn't two paces wide from side to side. The Trollocs stand in the center. How would you sneak past them?"

Gaul smiled, then slipped back into the darkness. Perrin glanced at Sulin, and she shielded her lantern fully. Together, they all followed after Gaul, feeling for the edge of the bridge with their toes as they crept forward.

Gaul crouched where Perrin and he had been watching a few moments before; Perrin could barely make him out in the faint light of the Trollocs' lanterns. When Perrin and the four Maidens arrived, Gaul glanced at them—then slipped over the side of the bridge.

Perrin's breath caught. What was Gaul *doing*?

There. Gaul had lowered himself, and now clung to the bridge by only the tips of his fingers. He began to inch to the side, moving one hand, then the other—not making any noise, not even a scrape of fingernail on stone. Light, he hung vertically from the bridge, dangling over that infinite darkness. Perrin could only imagine how that might feel.

The Trollocs seemed oblivious. One of the two sat down and began gnawing on something while the other yawned, its wolf's tongue stretching out. Perrin held his breath, fingers tight against the top of his hammer as Gaul neared the Trollocs. Perrin thought for sure the man would fall at any moment; just watching made his arms ache with fatigue.

Don't you drop, Perrin thought. *Don't you* dare *let go, Gaul.*

Gaul's fingers passed within mere inches of the Trollocs, but they didn't notice. However, when the bone snapped suddenly in the bear Trolloc's mouth, Perrin did jump slightly in startlement.

Ashamed, Perrin glanced to the side—where Sulin hunkered down further beside him. He caught a whiff of embarrassment from her, and realized that she'd also jumped at the sound.

Well, a part of him was glad for the sign of her tension. Gaul had acted as if this type of extreme activity was commonplace among the Aiel. The fact that Sulin was nervous indicated otherwise.

Perrin and the four Maidens waited until Gaul's fingers inched out of sight into the darkness beyond the Trollocs. Then they waited some more. It occurred to Perrin that if Gaul fell, he would probably maintain his warrior's silence, lest he give them all away. He wouldn't yell; he would simply vanish.

Moments stretched into minutes. Perrin grew increasingly anxious. What if Gaul had encountered trouble? What if he had run into Shadowspawn? What if he was out there in the darkness, bleeding and dying?

When Perrin had nearly taken all he could—when he was about to charge the Trollocs himself—something flew out of the darkness. The spear fell like a striking raven. It took the wolf Trolloc in the throat; the creature gurgled in pain, eyes opening wide as it stumbled back. The bear Trolloc turned with a start, and Gaul leaped from the darkness, knife in hand.

The Trolloc opened its mouth, and then Gaul hit, clinging to the ten-foot-tall beast and ramming his knife into its eye before it could scream for help. The two dropped, Gaul yanking out his knife and slamming it into the other eye.

Perrin charged forward, but he'd taken only two steps before Gaul stood up, wavered only a moment, then recovered the spear from the dead wolf Trolloc.

"I snuck to the next Island," Gaul said, pointing. "I found two other Trollocs at the base of the bridge, bearing only a small light—watching as you had guessed, Perrin Aybara. I killed them silently, then searched the Island. There were no others close by, but I dared not stray too far before returning."

Perrin clasped Gaul on the shoulder, smiling. To the side, the Maidens each raised a spear above their heads. Gaul actually blushed; Perrin couldn't recall having seen him do that before.

They searched the filthy carcasses, but found nothing of use, so they shoved them over the side of the bridge. Perrin wished they had some way of concealing the blood too. Perhaps they could wash it off? If someone came searching for these four, it would be better for them to find no signs. Trollocs that had been slaughtered meant enemies; Trollocs that had vanished could have wandered off, or been taken by *Machin Shin*.

He'd deal with that once they had regrouped. He led the Aiel back along the bridge, then down a ramp to where they'd left the rest of the troops, clustered with shielded lamps. Arganda looked relieved when Perrin emerged from the darkness.

"My Lord Goldeneyes?" the Ghealdanin whispered, raising his lantern. "What happened?"

"We killed the sentries," Perrin said.

"Excellent," Gallenne said. "That means a fight! They wouldn't have left sentries unless there was someone for them to report to, presumably. I bet that somewhere nearby we will find a fist or two of Trollocs, at the very least."

Perrin glanced at Sulin, and she nodded. She agreed.

"Then we'll have to find them," Perrin said. "For now, we keep going. Slowly, carefully, and with extra scouts on patrol. Pass word of what we found to the men, Gallenne. And warn them to be extra alert. We're getting close now."

Chapter 6

A Pinprick of Light

Perrin felt as if the darkness was watching him, measuring him. Stalking him. The unnatural stillness of this place reminded him of a forest gone silent—frozen perpetually in that moment of alert tension that came right before a predator struck.

They crossed the next bridge in near-total silence, passing orders as whispers. Even the pack animals seemed to sense it. Perrin and his officers and advisers reached the next Guiding, and here he pointed. His Aiel struck out in pairs to check for ambush. They bore shielded lanterns, only faint slivers of light separating them from this deepest dark.

"Light bless them," Gallenne whispered. "And lead them back safely. I've faced death on dozens of battlefields, never blinking.

But something about that darkness seems to steal the heart from even my bravest men."

"Makes you wonder what kind of people would just walk out into it like that," Arganda said. He and Gallenne often walked together in here—and at first, Perrin had thought it was their rivalry driving each to make sure the other didn't get ahead. Now, he wasn't so certain.

"I heard several of them whispering to each other earlier," Gallenne said. "They were making bets on which of them wouldn't return, and instead get lost in the dark. They seemed to treat it as a game."

Arganda nodded, as if this were what he might expect.

"It was a strikingly tender moment," Gallenne said.

"Tender? *Betting* on one another's deaths?"

"I've seen many a man laugh, instead of cry, on the morning before a battle," Gallenne said. He looked out into the darkness. "They do it differently, Arganda, but they remind me of that. The way men joke to prepare themselves for the fight. They're nervous. They don't like this place either, but they do their duty. I've often heard about murderous Aiel, even fought beside them under Lord Aybara's banner. But I don't know that I've ever seen them be as . . . human as they were in that moment."

Perrin nodded in agreement, though inwardly he was surprised. He had grown accustomed to bravado from the leader of the Winged Guard, not thoughtfulness.

The scouts returned, and brought him news of another group of Trolloc guards. The Aiel had disposed of them efficiently—though the news left Perrin increasingly worried. So far, they had not found the main Trolloc force, but each group of guards killed increased the inevitability. Someone would check on those dead Trollocs, and the Shadow had access to far more troops than he did. They could very easily end up trapped in here between two enemy forces, with no escape other than to risk leaving their prescribed and directed path.

They continued, passing the place where the Trollocs had been killed. He didn't need to see the blood on the ground to recognize it. He smelled the fetid stench in the air.

At the next Guiding, Saerin confirmed their location and the bridge they were to take next. Only two more Islands to go before they reached the Caemlyn Waygate. It was what he'd expected—he'd been counting—but it was so hard to feel they were making progress in this place. Each bridge looked like its fellows, distinctive only in the pocks of broken stone.

The scouts went out again, swallowed by the void. A short time later, Gaul and Sulin trotted back out of the darkness. "Perrin Aybara," Sulin said. "There is a gap in the next bridge, but it has been patched."

"Patched?"

"With wood," Gaul said. "Come see."

They waited for the other scouts, then struck out. When Perrin reached the bridge in question, he inspected the wooden portion with a critical eye. It looked sturdy enough, but it had been created without any skill at all. Pieces of wood jutted from the sides unevenly, and many of the nails hadn't been pounded in all the way. It was covered with symbols and words, painted in blood.

"Do we trust it?" Galad asked.

"We crossed it," Gaul said. "It is sturdy enough."

Perrin nodded. "It also presumably carried Trollocs across, so we should be safe. Still, let's go three or four at a time."

Perrin worried when it was Bornhald's turn, but the man merely pulled his cloak tight and started across. Perrin followed just behind him, lost in thought until the Whitecloak stopped in the center of the bridge and turned, looking out into the darkness.

"Did you hear that, Aybara?" he asked.

"What?" Perrin asked, a shiver running through him.

"Screams."

Perrin turned to the next man in line, a bearded Whitecloak named Golever. The man shook his head, indicating he didn't hear anything.

Perrin strained, listening, trying to pick out even the faintest hint of rushing wind. It was the sound he most dreaded, the one he'd spent most of their short rest earlier thinking he could *almost* pick out.

It was just nerves, he knew, because he didn't hear anything. Except . . . what was that? Not wind. Not something to chill his spine at all. But . . . it sounded . . . sounded like light . . .

What was this foolishness? A man could not hear light. It was just silence, he was sure of it.

"There's nothing, Bornhald," Perrin said.

"No. I hear screaming." Bornhald's red eyes glazed over. "That poor soul. It sounds like he's falling through that blackness. Ever falling. Screaming for nobody to hear . . ."

"Bornhald," Perrin said. "You didn't fall. You're safe."

"You should have let me drop, Aybara," Bornhald snapped, and he turned and continued across.

They reached the foot of the bridge, where Sulin and Gaul waited for them. "A Guiding is there," Sulin whispered, "but it is not needed. Nor is that book the Aes Sedai carries."

"What?" Perrin asked.

Sulin pointed. "Come closer. You can't see it from here, though one should be able to. This place . . ."

Despite her words, Perrin squinted into the darkness—and then was struck, as he *did* see something. A pinprick of light. He'd grown so accustomed to this place swallowing both light and sound that he was almost unnerved by it.

How large must that light be, he thought, *for me to see it from here?*

He put Gallenne in charge of seeing to the main troop, and told them to wait. Then—gritting his teeth—he struck out with Gaul and Sulin into the darkness. It *was* a fire—actually, more than one—burning in the distance, on the next Island over. They could see them better as they neared the Guiding.

Together, he and the two Aiel knelt near the stone slab, not daring to go too much beyond it lest they reach the edge of the Island and drop off into the darkness.

"The way shadows move in front of the fires," Sulin whispered. "Those are figures."

"Trollocs," Perrin said. He could smell their scents powerfully. "They're guarding the Waygate."

They slipped back to the main group, where he gathered his

leaders and—huddled around Saerin's little book—confirmed it, as best they could. One bridge remained to cross to reach the location of the Waygate. That was where the fires were, and the waiting enemy.

"Now what?" Arganda asked, squinting into the darkness, though Perrin doubted he could make out the distant light. "We could just blast the bridge between here and there. Would that do the job?"

"No," Saerin said. "I cannot navigate here on my own, but it's evident from what I've seen that there are multiple paths to any given Waygate. If we break one bridge, it will delay the Shadowspawn, but not to a meaningful extent."

"We can't continue to let them supply and reinforce behind our lines," Gallenne said. "We have to seize that Island and hold it long enough for the channelers to do their job."

"That sounds an awful lot like it would strand us here," Tam said, "even if it worked."

"No," Perrin said, scratching at his beard. "It's not ideal, but this doesn't have to be a suicide mission. If we can wipe out this group of Shadowspawn, then it's easy. We destroy the bridges, then walk back the way we came. If we can push them off, we can destroy bridges between us and them first—then do a careful retreat where we destroy each bridge we cross."

He hated the idea of doing further damage to the Ways, but this *was* what they had come to do. And the farther he'd traveled here, the more certain he'd become that it was the right thing. Failure here risked the fate of the entire world. Better to cut off the gangrenous hand than to let it kill the body.

"This is a rational battle plan," Gallenne said. "Assuming we can hold the bridge we first cross, we should be able to proceed with it."

"It depends on the enemy numbers, I suppose," Arganda said. "I still worry about being surrounded."

"Our final path of retreat is the Waygate itself," Perrin said. "We can escape through it, if we must."

"Into a conquered city," Arganda said.

"We will need only a brief moment after leaving the Waygate to open a gateway to escape," Seonid said. "I'd rather not have to try it, but I agree with Lord Aybara. It could be a last resort."

"Numbers," Arganda insisted. "We need to know what we're facing before we make plans."

Perrin nodded. He walked over to confer with the Aiel. Apparently it was Aviellin and Feralin's turn, and so they slipped off into the dark to do what might be the most dangerous job of the entire expedition—get close enough to those fires to count the enemy.

He ordered his soldiers up and into formation, organized to hold one of the bridges, just in case. Each clink of armor made Perrin wince, but he suffered it, waiting with pounding heart until the two Maidens finally returned. They stepped out of the darkness, having borne no lights at all, and passed the raised spears of their sisters without comment.

"We drew close enough to watch them by the fires," Aviellin whispered. "A hundred and twenty Trollocs. Unless they are hiding more in the darkness, I am confident in this count. Two Nightrunners."

Feralin nodded, concurring with those numbers.

Over a hundred Trollocs, with two Myrddraal. A daunting force for his fifty, though he did have the channelers. "How entrenched did they seem?"

"They weren't moving through the Waygate," Aviellin said. "I think they're guards, set to watch on this side for something like we're attempting. They have cook fires set up. There are people, in pens, Perrin Aybara. Wetlanders in what was once nice clothing."

"Captives from Caemlyn," Perrin said, feeling sick. "For food."

He had the two Aiel sketch out the locations of the fires, the pens, and the Waygate itself for reference. He presented this to his officers and advisers, careful—deliberate—in his methodical preparations. Something about this place made him want to jump into action, to get to the fight—for the sooner that happened, the sooner he could escape this darkness. Did it seem like their lights were smaller than they'd been the day before?

He forced himself to hold back the wolf, to think this

through, as the group considered the situation.

"Lord Goldeneyes," Gallenne said, "I suggest that we attack fast and decisively. If the channelers creep up and unleash the Power in an overwhelming strike, it will cause confusion and chaos among the Trolloc ranks. The soldiers will easily control the battlefield from there, sweeping the Trollocs away."

"Arganda?" Perrin asked.

"It's a good strategy," the shorter man agreed. "In another situation, I'd agree with that plan, no hesitation. But it *will* be noisy and require a lot of power from the channelers. You've warned us against both things in here."

Perrin rubbed at his beard, considering the map.

"We're not going to be able to do this without making noise, Perrin," Tam said. "You don't just make a hundred Trollocs vanish. If you don't want to rely on the channelers, we could try to lure them into attacking us near the bridge, then hit them with arrows. Draw them out into an extended fight and retreat."

That plan worried him even more. He thought of stringing his forces out through the Ways, of trying to successfully employ an attrition strategy against an enemy that could constantly bring new troops in through the Waygate.

"No," he said. "We have to pull this off as a bash and grab—hit them hard, sweep them off, and prevent reinforcements from coming in by seizing the portal itself. That's the only reasonable plan."

He looked up, and the soldiers nodded in turn—including Galad. They saw it too.

"We *have* to keep the noise down," Perrin said. "That means minimal channeling—but I think we can do that with Gallenne's plan. We'll sneak the channelers up with the Aiel and have them hit the enemy with a barrage to weaken and confuse their line. Then the rest of us will charge across. We do it carefully, mind you—I don't want men shouldering each other off the bridge by accident."

He waved over Grady and Neald, gesturing toward the map. "I want your initial strike to specifically try and split the Trolloc force in half here. We'll pour through the gap you make and shove the Trollocs to the sides, hopefully sweeping them off the edges."

He pointed at Edarra, Seonid, and Saerin. "Your first task is to kill those Fades. Focus on them; I don't want to lose a dozen men taking those things out. When the Fades are down, channel only in small bursts. Understood?"

Seonid nodded immediately, and Edarra said, "Very well." Both responses seemed to surprise Saerin. Perhaps she wasn't accustomed to women who could channel readily obeying . . . well, anyone.

The Maidens and Gaul nodded at their part when he explained it—sneaking up with the channelers. Next he'd have Arganda's troops charge, with Gallenne and Galad coming in behind. The Two Rivers men were to stay on the bridge last, then try to get into position at the flanks. This would probably be too tight-quartered a battle for archery, but he'd want them for reserves and—if things went poorly—to cover a retreat.

Perrin positioned himself with Gallenne's men. As much as he wanted to sneak forward with the Aiel, he would just be underfoot. Gaul and the other Aiel slipped one last time into the darkness, leading the five channelers and Seonid's Warders by hand. Perrin counted the seconds, his men shuffling nervously around him. He loosed *Mah'alleinir* in its sheath, the hammer's warmth comforting under his fingertips. Some of the Winged Guards stirred, and one accidentally tapped his pommel against his breastplate with a loud clink.

"Steady," Perrin said in the too-empty darkness. "Wait for the sign." Perrin forced himself to stand still and not prowl back and forth in front of his troops. They stood arranged in ranks of three right at the head of the bridge, close enough that Perrin could make out shadows moving in front of the fires on the Island.

The Last Hunt had come; all before this had been skirmishes, but this was the war. He found himself eager. What did that say about him? For years, he'd wished only to be back home, peaceful in the Two Rivers. Not any longer. Now he wanted to fight.

He carefully, deliberately, allowed the wolf to run. He had not started this war. He had not raised his hammer to strike the first blow. But he could see it ended—and with as much brutality as was required.

A flash of light soared into the air above the Island.

"Go!" Perrin bellowed, charging across the narrow bridge, pulling his hammer free.

Chapter 7
The Wolf in Him

Perrin reached the Waygate's Island before any of the men behind him.

On the Island, Trollocs lay scattered, smoke rising from their charred carcasses. As he'd ordered, the channelers had blasted the Trollocs down the center. Perrin joined the Aiel, and together the eleven of them smashed into this weakened core. They worked like a wedge intended to split a heavy stone in two along a fault, separating the Trollocs to the left and right and leaving the center—with the prisoners and the Waygate itself—exposed.

It was a strangely hushed force that joined him—Ghealdanin, Mayeners, and Whitecloaks alike holding in their battle cries. No trumps of war heralded this conflict, and he'd warned the men to keep quiet as they fought. One couldn't expect utter silence in battle, of course, but the resulting conflict bore a frantic sense of silent desperation. Men grunting and muttering, Trollocs growling. Weapons clanged or rang, but even those noises were muted—the pervasive darkness of the Ways seeming to sweep in, thirsty, and drink up both sound and light.

Perrin gritted his teeth as, with Gaul at his side, he threw himself at a Trolloc with the beak of some bird of prey. He laid about himself with *Mah'alleinir*, and each blow caused Trolloc skin to smoke and hiss.

Perrin was the wolf, and the wolf was in him. There were times when he would control the wolf and let the man rule.

This wasn't one of those times.

He planted himself near the captives, dropping a ram Trolloc as a dead Fade squirmed and writhed nearby. Bursts of Fire fell through the air, immolating Trollocs, throwing up waves of heat.

Perrin held his ground as the Trollocs tried to push back in. His plan was a dangerous one, for if the enemy recovered, they could theoretically pen his forces in the center and surround them.

Perrin continued to swing, feeling the rhythm of the hammer's beats, almost like he was pounding metal. Gaul and he made a good team, as Perrin's dramatic moves and sweeping blows drew Trolloc attention—and while they focused on him, Gaul could glide in with his spear, attacking Trollocs who slipped inside Perrin's reach or tried to flank him.

Time was meaningless to Perrin when he fought. There was only the swinging of *Mah'alleinir*, the howls of Trollocs, his labored breathing as he broke his enemies. The battle took on a horrific cast. The hulking Trolloc forms, lit by the bonfire, fighting among men who held in their screams—even when they were dropped, bloody, to the featureless stone ground.

It was difficult not to feel small when fighting Trollocs. You couldn't count on the weight of your hammer to make them stumble. He fought one that had been pierced with four separate arrows from a Two Rivers bow, and which didn't drop even after Perrin had connected his hammer with its skull. A follow-up stab from Gaul finally dropped it.

Each time one of the terrible creatures fell, another loomed from the dark to take its place. It seemed, for a moment, that they'd be forced back into a crushed knot of men, pressed too close to fight.

But he'd asked each captain to bring their finest, and the men didn't waver. Whether they wore polished breastplate, plumed helm, or stark white clothing, they stood shoulder to shoulder and fought. The channelers—following his orders—struck with small, precise attacks, burning down a Trolloc here or there to break any momentum they might gain.

Finally, step by step, Perrin's forces began to sweep the enemy back. They expanded their lines, letting the Aes Sedai move in to help the wounded. Perrin stepped back from the fighting to approach the wooden pens that held the captives. He slammed *Mah'alleinir* down on the first lock. "If any in here know how to use a sword, take one from the wounded. Otherwise, stick near the center of our force and stay out of the way."

The people inside were hollow-eyed. They'd seen terrible horrors during their captivity. They flooded out, heads low as they ran for freedom.

"Don't go out into the darkness!" Perrin warned them, smashing open the next cage. "Stay with us, or you might end up lost in that blackness forever."

He didn't have time to see if they obeyed. He loped back over to the left battle line, where the Trollocs were starting to get routed—they stumbled back, tripping over fallen bodies, as his forces shoved them farther and farther. Nearby, the Maidens forced back a snarling pack of six, who lost their footing and tumbled off the side of the Island.

"Perrin!" someone shouted. The loud voice seemed to pierce the darkness. He spun around, trying to orient himself. He had been about to join the Whitecloaks and some of Gallenne's men. In the near distance, the bonfires still burned near the open cages and the stoic shape of the Waygate itself.

It was open on the other side; through it he could see figures moving, as if in slow motion, gathering around and preparing to enter. Grady had been the one to call for him, gesturing toward the figures.

"Be ready," Perrin said, running over. "We can't let them reinforce from that side. They'll only be able to come through two at a time. We should be able to . . ."

He trailed off as he noticed something odd about the way the figures moved. Those lithe steps, the way they ducked and strode right into the Waygate, without concern or hesitation. That reminded him of . . .

Aiel. The figures that emerged into the Ways wore *cadin'sor* and carried spears, though they bore red veils. Perrin lowered his hammer in shock. Those *couldn't* be Aiel, could they? The first two that emerged started straight toward the Aes Sedai, spears held out. Light! They must be Shaido who had gone to the Shadow.

"Bring them down!" Perrin said to Grady. *"Now."*

Grady nodded, his face adopting a look of concentration. "Light! They can *channel*, Perrin!"

"They're bloody strong!" Neald said, stumbling up. "They're striking down my weaves as I create them."

Two more of the red-veiled Aiel followed, then another two. Grady got off a burst of flames, but one of the red-veiled Aiel blocked it with a bright flash of light, doing something that Perrin couldn't quite follow.

"Are those really *Aiel*?" Saerin demanded, rushing up to them. She, Seonid, and Edarra—guarded by the Warders—had been doing as he'd told them: seeing to the wounded, corralling the prisoners, and channeling to help the soldiers only when absolutely necessary.

As Perrin started to explain, one of the red-veiled men raised a hand overhead and shot a beam of pure white fire into the air. It didn't seem to be aimed at anything specific, but it was so bright, Perrin had to shade his eyes.

What was that?

The others in the red veils likewise raised their hands, weaving lights into the black above. Trollocs howled, breaking the air with their screams as the last of them were forced off the edges. But something about those lights—those piercing lights, summoned so deliberately—worried Perrin.

"Stop those men!" Perrin yelled to Grady and Neald. "Throw everything you have at them!"

The two Asha'man were obviously trying, and one of the red-veiled men went up in a flashing explosion. The others, remarkably, turned and ran—ducking directly through the Waygate. Grady and Neald caught a second one, but the other four escaped back into the outside world.

Everything fell silent. Perrin's soldiers were congratulating one another on the short, but frantic, attack. They'd taken minimal casualties, seized the Island, and rescued the prisoners. On the surface, their assault was an obvious success. It even seemed that the strange channeling Aiel—having put in just a brief appearance—had arrived only to discover themselves outmatched, then fled.

Perrin saw a different story. As Saerin bustled over to try to persuade the Whitecloaks to accept Healing, Perrin strained to listen.

He peered through the Waygate at the strange Aiel, whom he could see on the other side, moving very slowly because of the strange time difference between the Ways and the outside world. They lowered their veils, revealing smiling faces. Pleased with themselves.

The doors to the Waygate began to close, blocking the red-veiled Aiel from Perrin's view. And as his group hushed, tending their wounds, Perrin heard a soft, distant sound.

A faint howl, like the sound of a breeze blowing through a hollow. Somehow, the enemy had learned to summon the Black Wind.

Chapter 8

So Sweet to Kill

"Quickly!" Perrin said, grabbing Neald by the shoulder, then looking to Grady. "We need to fight through that Waygate to the other side."

The doors slipped closer and closer together, cutting off the light. Perrin leaped over the corpse of a falling Trolloc, running toward their exit, their escape. If the Black Wind was coming, they needed to get out *now*.

"Lord Goldeneyes!" Grady said, dashing after him. "Perrin, listen. We can't go through there. Light! Can you imagine trying to get through that with channelers guarding the other side? Only two of us could go through at a time; they'd slaughter us as we emerged."

Perrin halted before the Waygate. Sensing his concern, the Two Rivers men—who had been guarding the channelers while the infantry fought—pulled up around him. Tam nocked an arrow, staring out into the darkness. Nearby, the Aiel moved through the fallen Trollocs, checking for any that were still alive and dispatching them.

"Perrin, lad?" Tam asked. "Is something wrong?"

"We're trapped," Perrin whispered as the Waygate closed. Grady was right. Fighting through that would be suicide, so long as the enemy was ready for them. But staying here?

He strained, listening for any hint of sound. He heard nothing, but that faint, earlier howl echoed in his mind. And he felt . . . he felt as if he could smell something on the wind, a scent like rot.

It *was* coming. "Pull everyone back, Tam," Perrin said. "Quickly! Quietly! Gather the wounded, lead those people we rescued, and retreat back the way we came. We need to get away from this Island."

"But . . ." Neald said. "We've seized the Waygate on this side. We need to destroy the bridges and isolate it. That's our mission, right?"

"Those Aiel have done something to summon the Black Wind," Perrin said, pointing. "We need to get away from where they launched light into the air. Now *move*."

Nobody gave further argument. They passed the word in hushed tones, the soldiers moving from battle-ready stances to careful retreat. At Perrin's orders, they cut away some of the supplies and tied the worst of the wounded to the pack animals. Tam and the other Two Rivers men worked with the frightened former prisoners, and had to prod them sharply to get them moving away from the bonfires.

Perrin grabbed a wounded Whitecloak under one arm as Galad grabbed the other, and they moved across the bridge together. Perrin didn't know if the Whitecloaks had refused Healing, or if their wounds simply weren't dire enough to have taken precedence.

They left twelve dead. Low casualties, on one hand—though any loss was terrible. But it felt a terrible injustice to leave those heroes alone in the darkness.

"What is this you said earlier?" Saerin said, bustling up beside him as they crossed the bridge. "You think those Darkfriends in the red veils could *summon* the Black Wind? You think it serves them?"

"I doubt *Machin Shin* serves anything but its own hunger," Perrin said. "And I hope I'm wrong—I hope it's not coming for us. But that signal was meant to do something. Those Aiel didn't attack us; they simply made the lights appear, then left."

Saerin grunted, glancing over her shoulder, though the bonfires were already starting to die. As if lack of attention let the darkness smother them.

"I've wondered how the Shadow moves so many Trollocs through this place," Perrin grumbled, still walking with his arm supporting Golever, the Whitecloak. "Both times I entered the Ways before, Saerin, the Black Wind eventually found us. It can sense noise, channeling, life—and it will feast on Trollocs as eagerly as men; I've seen that for myself. But the enemy transports hundreds of thousands of troops through here.

"What if they found a way to distract the Black Wind? Draw it away? The Shadow could enter a Waygate far off and draw the attention of the Black Wind—keeping it focused there while others move through the darkness."

"Speculation," Saerin said. "You can't extrapolate circumstances backward from these effects."

They stopped, finally, at the other side of the bridge. Perrin turned, listening. A distant, soft sound came to him. The sound of a breeze. Elsewhere, it would have been a common, everyday kind of sound.

Here, it was the most terrifying thing he could have heard.

"We need another Waygate," he said to Saerin. "Where is the closest one? I don't care where it leads, as long as it gets us out of the Ways."

"Are you sure you want me to do this?" she said. "I told you before, I doubt my ability to navigate on my own."

"Either you find us a way out," he said, "or this place will take us all. We don't have time for hesitation."

"I'm no frightened child, uncertainly anticipating a test, Perrin Aybara," she said. "I'm being honest, not hesitant." She opened the book of notes, flipping through. "If I lead us out into the dark, we might never come back."

"Do it anyway."

She nodded curtly. "Give me a minute."

He took the time to pass the word, hushing the men. Oddly, he found one standing apart from the others. Bornhald was at the edge of their light, standing on the bridge, looking back the way they'd come.

"What is that?" he said to Perrin. "I hear something. A breeze. It will be good to feel some wind. It's so still here, like death itself . . ."

"Blood and ashes," Neald said, hand to his head nearby.

Perrin got them moving as Saerin struck out, leading the way across a bridge—one they hadn't taken before. Perrin hurried to help with the wounded again. Nearby, Seonid tried to walk while at the same time applying Healing to one of the wounded Mayeners, who had been thrown across a pack mule. Perrin couldn't smell any emotions from him any longer.

"This place," Seonid said. "Healing through the taint of it is uncomfortable. I worry I'm going to leave wounds infected, not Healed."

"No more channeling," Perrin said. "Not even to Heal." He looked to the Mayener who led the pack mule bearing his unconscious friend. "I'm sorry."

Perrin joined Saerin, who was reading her notebook. "I don't know if this will work," she whispered to him. "The notes here say there's a Waygate four bridges in this direction, but they don't say where it leads."

Four more bridges? That would take time. As they started across the next one, men started muttering—and he realized that their ears were only now picking up what he'd noticed earlier. That howling wind, growing louder and louder.

Four more bridges. Perrin made a decision. He stopped everyone in place on their current bridge, hushing them. Then he told them to huddle down, stay quiet, and fully close the shields on their lanterns.

The order drew panicked expressions. Arganda looked at him as if he'd already been taken by the Wind and had gone mad.

"This is our best bet," Perrin told them. "We have to hope that it will come to the Waygate, where the lights were released, but won't sense us out here."

"And if it does?" one of the Whitecloaks asked.

"Hope it doesn't," Perrin said, a dread growing within him. "Now. Do as I said."

The men did it, bless them, one by one closing their lanterns. Plunging them all into darkness.

Blackness became absolute. Nobody spoke, even to whisper. He could still smell them, though. Panicked emotions, terror at being in the darkness of this place. He could smell their sweat and their worry.

They all could hear the sounds of the wind now, the rushing breeze, the howling coming from the place they'd left. Perrin shifted his hammer back and forth between his hands, knowing full well that it would be useless if *Machin Shin* reached them. He forced himself to stop.

The sounds of the wind increased to a distant, terrible roar. Then, Perrin started to pick out the words.

. . . blood, so wet, so wet to bleed, drink it in, drink and drink . . .

Light. He held his breath.

. . . so sweet, so sweet to kill, to rend, to drink and drink and drink. To drink it, to drink his and kill him. To be mine, to be mine for now, to rend, to break while he shouts, to crunch the bones, to make them mine. To kill, and maim, and crunch, and sing . . . Aybara!

The wind turned toward them, growing louder. In that moment, Perrin knew that no hiding would work. It had caught their scent. It knew they were here.

"Lights on!" he roared, leaping to his feet. "And *run*!"

Chapter 9

Song and Fire

The men had been waiting for this. They rammed open their shielded lanterns and began running along the bridge.

They knew.

Perrin urged them on, yelling at them to pick up their pace. There was no longer time for whispers or stealth. He grabbed Azi, a Two Rivers man, and helped him along. He practically carried the limping man, but Azi wasn't the only straggler. Galad stuck beside Golever, and the Aes Sedai held back with the rest of the Two Rivers men, trying to usher the former prisoners. Many of them were weak from obvious lack of food.

The wind howled in the distance, drawing closer.

Light, Perrin thought. *Even if we were all galloping on horseback, we wouldn't to be able to outrun it. There's no way.*

He passed Azi off to Seonid's Warders as they reached the next Island. He hung back, waving the force forward. "Keep running!" he shouted.

Something about the urgency in his voice must have alarmed them, for his yell sent a wave of motion through the former prisoners, who spilled off the bridge onto the Island. Galad and Golever went next, though one figure in white lingered—alone on the bridge, looking back at the darkness.

"What *is* that?" Bornhald asked.

"That's our end, if you don't keep moving!" Perrin shouted.

"It's coming for me, isn't it?" Bornhald said. "Light, it knows my name. How can it know my name?"

"Come on, you fool," Perrin said, yanking him by the shoulder. That pulled Bornhald out of his stupor, and he fell into a dash beside Perrin. But he kept looking over his shoulder as they ran, while most everyone else kept their eyes forward or heads bowed as Saerin led them across the next bridge.

They didn't want to know. Perrin didn't blame them. The rushing sound advanced, and what had at first been a breeze now blew like a terrible howl, with overlapping voices. It drowned out Perrin's shouts to keep moving.

. . . death, so delicious, so sweet to taste, to taste your life as it drains. Blood, blood, blood and pain. Pain, pain, pain and death. Death, death, death and loss . . .

It was like a thousand voices, each chanting. The Black Wind was a thing of the Ways, an ancient thing, the essence of madness itself.

"How can it know . . ." Bornhald shouted, his voice nearly consumed in that of the Black Wind. "There was so much blood. A person couldn't have done that, could they? Even Ordeith? It wasn't right. They couldn't have all been Darkfriends. Some of them were just children . . ."

They reached the next Island. The wind tugged at Perrin's cloak, and . . . and then he felt it in his face. The terrible wind rushed around, coming in from all directions. His party pulled up short as Saerin, at the front, stopped in place. Clothing fluttered and rippled as the mass of people pulled in closer, huddling into their frail light.

"It's here," Bornhald said, stopping at the edge of the Island.

"Grady! Neald!" Perrin said, turning and pointing *Mah'alleinir* into the darkness.

. . . Aybara, Aybara, Aybara. Promised, to drink, promised to kill, so sweet, sing the sweetness, sing it to us. Tiny souls have become greatness to feast upon, to feast and sing. Sing, sing, sing!

The two Asha'man released streams of yellow fire, sickly. Particles of black ash floated down from the streams like corrupted snow.

Their channeling drove back the regular darkness of the Ways, but not the thing that had arrived. A blackness made incarnate, a churning wind that streamed and spun upon itself, wave upon wave of motion.

Its voice . . . its *voices* . . . were thunderous. Screams of pleasure, even as the fire struck it. *Blood to spill, bones to splinter, to grind, to feast upon!*

Behind Perrin, men fell to their knees. Saerin screamed at the front of the group, and released her own sickly beam of fire, joined by those of Seonid and Edarra, spraying in all directions. The wind rushed around them, and the shifting blackness of its substance undulated, shivered. Bits of light exploded outward from it, like frozen sparks. For a moment, Perrin actually thought they were winning.

Then the rushing blackness around them tightened, drawing closer and closer. By the light of the fires, by the sounds of the Black Wind singing, by men yelling, by the feel of wind whipping at his face and chilling his skin—he saw it, smelled it, heard it. *Machin Shin* was vastly larger than he'd assumed. Perrin had focused on the patch in front of them, the patch that they were fighting. His senses revealed something else, a deep, vast blackness that extended far into the distance.

This blackness wasn't just the size of an army, it would have dwarfed most cities. While a piece of it writhed from the fires of the channelers, the greater portion of it swept in and enveloped their Island.

They were surrounded. The bridges leading away from the

Island lay inside the mad spinning of *Machin Shin*. The wind became a vortex, buffeting men and women who watched with horror as the fire of the channelers felt smaller and smaller, grew somehow sicklier and sicklier.

Grady and Neald—white-faced and trembling—stopped for a moment. Then something new shot from their fingers: white-hot lines of light, one striking in either direction.

Those lines of light left afterimages in Perrin's eyes. They were so intense, it was difficult to look at them—in fact, being near them made him feel as if he were going to burst into flame. Balefire, the forbidden weave.

The balefire drove back portions of the wind, causing it to bubble like leather thrown on a fire. Still, the wind continued its song, its mad chanting.

. . . pain, so sweet, so sweet to sing the song, so wonderful to break and kill . . .

It seemed—somehow—*more* hungry for being held back a short time. Perrin set his hammer on his shoulder, turning about, his heart thumping. A way out. There *had* to be a way out.

Gaul stepped up beside him. "And so we wake," he said softly. "I should have liked to know whether or not this final battle was won. Perhaps I shall know, if I dream again."

"So much blood," Bornhald said. "Aybara, I'm sorry for what . . . what we did . . ." The scent of the man's emotions struck Perrin, despite the terrible wind. The pain, the horror, the loss, the fury. "I'm sorry for your family. It was Ordeith. I should have . . . I . . ."

Bornhald looked to Perrin once, seeming hollow. Then he ran into the blackness.

"Bornhald!" Perrin bellowed, reaching forward as the wind surged like a snapping predator, engulfing the Whitecloak.

. . . souls, so sweet! So sweet to gnash and the end to know. To know, and to rend, and to rip, and to feast, and to blood! The blood to spill and drink!

Machin Shin howled and pulled tighter, like a coiling serpent. Its voices overlapped like a choir of the demented, each member screaming his own song, trying to yell over his neighbors. Perrin backed away, raising an arm against the increasingly powerful wind. Gaul reluctantly joined him, the others pulling into a huddle in the very center of the Island.

The channelers continued to pour fire and light in all directions. But it was as if they were trying to destroy air itself; *Machin Shin* had no true substance to destroy.

Perrin's back hit that of Galad, the people all pressed together, with the wind spinning around them. Perrin lowered his hammer, thinking of Faile. Of Rand, and the Last Hunt, in which Perrin would not run. Light send that his failure here would not doom them all.

He looked at Gaul, who nodded. A final charge, then. Into the darkness.

Perrin could no longer hear the shouts of the men and women with him. He could only hear the roar of the wind and the chanting of voices. New ones faded in and out, and the cohesion—if there had ever been one—fractured.

. . . sweet! Sing the sweetness! Say it . . .

. . . give the Blood to spill, blood to take! Blood . . .

. . . up axes . . .

. . . the marrow to suck, to drink, to hold, to spread, to grind, to . . .

. . . Aybara, Aybara, Aybara, promised! Aybara to rend . . .

. . . shore the hold . . .

. . . take it and drink it, give it to all . . .

Perrin stopped.

Up axes?

"Gaul, no!" he yelled, grabbing the man, holding him back from leaping into the blackness with spear out. Perrin strained, listening with all he had, trying to separate the madness and the wind from what he thought he'd heard.

A low sound, a rumbling bass, in tune with itself and such a contrast from the screeching disharmony of the wind. Perrin seized onto this thread of sound, which rolled out through the blackness. A humming, thrumming sound that—despite being softer than the cacophony—somehow overwhelmed the mad voices. Consumed them. Like a flood of water from a broken barrel, pouring over a burning wood floor.

He could hear it. He could just barely *hear* it!

"Up axes, shore the hold.
Where walls can't stand,
We must be bold.
Up axes, strength unfold.

To serve the plough,
Some roots must break.
When we must swing,
The branches bow.

Up axes, shore the hold.
Where walls can't stand,
We must be bold.
Up axes, strength unfold."

Machin Shin shuddered. The blackness thinned on one side of the Island, and Perrin peered through. Yes, light approached across one of the bridges. Light, and an increasing thunder of boots falling in step. Creatures on thick, sturdy legs, with arms the size of tree trunks. Their ears swept back and wearing fearsome expressions, the Ogier marched—men and women—with axes on their shoulders and mouths open, singing a beautiful song of deep bass and fluttering harmony.

Their song flooded the Island, and the people around Perrin began to pick it out. They turned, like plants seeking the sunlight, as the Ogier reached the Island and increased their song tenfold.

"The night may fall,
Some logs must burn!
Of strength we'll sing,
And smoke we'll call!

Up axes, shore the hold.
Where walls can't stand,
We must be bold.
Up axes, strength unfold."

Machin Shin started to pulse and howl, as if the words wounded it. Perrin felt a weight to the Ogier song, and nearby the lanterns carried by his men actually seemed to shine more brightly.

"Do you feel that, Jur?" Neald asked.

"I think I can reach it!" Grady shouted back. "It's so pure . . ."

Their channeling cut off, and Perrin—trying to brace himself against the wind with an arm thrown forward—turned to watch as the two Asha'man raised their hands and released twin jets of bright flame that were distinctly more pure than the ones they'd released earlier. Bright lights, not balefire, but a type of weave that cut through the darkness. It shone here in the Ways like light *should.* Light that cast shadows, that drove back darkness instead of being swallowed by it.

The Black Wind howled, hating and screaming, and its chanting began to fracture. Words became fragments of words. Saerin stepped up beside the Asha'man and joined her fires to theirs, and the light they created reminded Perrin of something warm and familiar. The sun. Odd, how after only two days in here, he should regard sunlight as something he'd almost forgotten.

The wind howled again, cries distorting before the light and the song. Then, gloriously, it started to retreat. They weren't destroying it, but neither could it persist in this place of song and fire reinforcing one another.

Seonid and Edarra joined in, and together the five channelers advanced as the Ogier stepped off the bridge onto the Island. The two groups merged as the Ogier, axes still to shoulders, continued to sing.

Finally—reaching a crescendo of madness against steady, passionate song—*Machin Shin* shrieked a thousand screams upon one another, then withdrew into the darkness in a rush. It was gone in seconds, the troops' cloaks and clothing falling still, the Ways returning to their eerie silence.

Never had Perrin been so happy to hear nothing.

The Ogier lowered their axes.

"Oh, Perrin!" a voice said. Loial broke out of the line and ran forward, his eyebrows twitching. "Did you see that, Perrin? We sang the Black Wind away! I did not know if it was possible, and I do not think it unfitting of me to tell you how frightened I was. Everything I have studied told me this was foolish and hasty, yet I argued we must do it. Can you believe that? When we heard the sound in the distance, I told Elder Haman. He's back, you know. Right over there. I told him that *Machin Shin* might react to our song, if there were enough of us. The Ogier created this place, you know, with the help of the old Aes Sedai. There were songs of growth here, and I thought that perhaps songs would again make it—"

Loial cut off as Perrin grabbed him in an embrace. "Loial, how? How did you come here?"

"Oh, it is not so surprising a thing, Perrin," Loial said, laughing. As Perrin released him, the Ogier reached into his pocket with sausagelike fingers and withdrew a small piece of paper, which he held delicately. The words had been penned by a human hand.

Loial, son of Arent son of Halan, it read. *I have set another to this task, but sometimes he can be unreliable. I leave it to you, then, to buttress his work. The Waygate in Caemlyn must be closed tightly, as the Shadow plans to strike there. In the past, you have seen fit to fulfill my requests. If you have ever listened to me before, do so now. This is vital.*

It was signed, *Verin.*

"I showed it to Elder Haman," Loial said, "and he agreed that we should at least check on the gate as we made our way to the Last Battle. Oh! You missed that part. I spoke, and I thought they were going to open the Book of Translation and leave. But they listened to me! And everyone agreed that we must fight. The long hafts are surely on our axes now, no turning around. I spoke to them, Perrin, and they *listened* to me. Even my mother, Perrin. She's here. You see her over there? She never does look pleased with me, you know, but she came with us to fight.

"Ah, but I must be brief. If ever there were a time for brevity, now is it. Briefly, yes. Well, we came to see, and we heard the wind. We saw those lights in the darkness, and we knew that we had to try the song. Otherwise, it would take us. It was the only way. Do you know where the others are gathering? We must join the Last Battle. We *were* going to walk all the way to the Waygate in Shienar. You know the one we left open before, Perrin? You remember, don't you?"

"I remember, Loial," Perrin said. He laughed. "Yes, I remember." He nodded to Elder Haman and Loial's mother as they approached. "Greetings to you, Elders. Your arrival was quite timely."

Elder Haman's ears twitched. His white beard reached his chest, below the white mustaches that drooped on either side of his face. "Thank the young one. His encouragement brought us. This is all very sudden." He seemed a little dazed. Loial's mother shouldered her axe, looking around with stern eyes. Knowing them, they'd probably debated for weeks before entering the Ways, and had *still* considered it hasty.

"Ta'veren," Loial said softly.

"What, you?" Perrin asked, turning to him.

"No, no, of course not. You, Perrin! You needed us. Perhaps that was why I was able to convince the others to come join the Last Battle. At the very least, you drew us to you in here. I'm certain of that."

Perrin shook his head. "For once, I disagree with you, my friend. This wasn't about me being *ta'veren*. This was about courage. Yours, Loial. And yours, Elder Haman, and yours, Covril daughter of Ella daughter of Soong. Thank you. From the depths of all that I am, *thank you*."

For a wonder, Covril smiled. "There were some who would have abandoned you, and the world, to the Shadow's fate. I am not one of them, human. Trees will not grow if the Dark One claims this land."

Loial looked surprised. "But—"

"An argument must have opposition if it is to prove itself, Loial," she said. "One who argues truly learns the depth of his commitment through adversity. Did you not learn that trees grow roots most deep when winds blow most strongly?" She shook her head, though she did seem fond. "That is not to say you should have left the *stedding* when you did. Not alone. Fortunately, that's been taken care of."

"Taken care of?" Perrin asked.

Loial blushed. "Well, you see, I am married now. To Erith, you see. She's just over there. Did you hear her singing? Isn't her song beautiful? She was right at the front, with me. Being married is not so bad, Perrin. Why didn't you tell me it was not so bad? I think I am rather fond of it."

Perrin laughed, slapping his friend on the arm. "I'm certain it suits you well, Loial. But come, I have a mission to fulfill, if you are willing to join me."

CHAPTER 10

Rest in the Light

The Ogier sang a low, thrumming song. It vibrated through Perrin, making the very deepest part of his soul feel warm.

By that sound, the channelers lit the air. It wasn't enough to see by completely, as the Ways were vast. But within that illumination, Perrin could finally see this place. The Waygates sat on vast fields of stone, like hilltops, and connected to them were floating Islands of rock shaped like small discs. Bridges and ramps sprouted from these like vines.

In the light, there was an organic feel to it all. It seemed an entirely different place. Walking through it in the blackness, he had felt as if it had extended so much farther, and been far more twisted than these elegant structures. For a moment, he could imagine it as it must once have been, green and bright—grown, not built.

Perhaps they could find a way to bring it back. For now, however, their work was that of a farmer clearing a field—and ripping out tree stumps that needed to be carried away so new growth could thrive. With the hesitant blessing of the Ogier, Grady and Neald excised each and every bridge or ramp leading to the "hilltop" that held the Caemlyn Waygate.

There were nearly a dozen of them. The expanses of stone, when broken from their mountings on either side, tumbled down and fell into an expansive darkness that—even with their channeled light—seemed to extend into infinity.

The final bridge churned in the dark as it fell. Perrin held his lantern high and listened carefully, but he could not hear the sound of anything hitting down below.

"This is a day of sadness," Elder Haman said, standing near Perrin, his long-handled axe resting on his shoulder. "A day in which we see the demise of something grand, destroyed by our own hands in the name of preservation. Almost, I think the price too high."

"The Waygate itself remains," Perrin said. "This might be one step further than locking it closed, as you did—but it is not permanent. Bridges can be rebuilt, Elder Haman."

Elder Haman grunted.

"It had to be done, Elder," Loial said. "Verin Sedai asked it of us, and one doesn't refuse an Aes Sedai. That is the path of wisdom."

Elder Haman shook his head with a deep, rumbling sigh. "Well, it was good that you were here, Wolfbrother," he said to Perrin. "We could not have plugged this hole on our own. Our axes could not have felled those bridges as the One Power did, and we would never have been able to hold the Waygate against repeated Trolloc attacks. Still, it is a pity to see this. A pity indeed . . ."

Elder Haman joined the bulk of the Ogier, who continued to hum their thrumming song. Perrin followed, Loial and Erith beside him. Behind, the channelers walked in a tired group—breaking down those bridges had taken a great deal of strength, particularly considering the frantic battle before it. But, tired or not, they continued to provide light by channeling glowing spheres. So long as the Ogier sang, that light reached into the Ways as it should, though regular lanterns still seemed frail and weak before the darkness.

Erith kept peeking over at Perrin, her eyes the size of saucers. She seemed to find his own eyes fascinating, and Perrin bore it without complaint. "So it is true?" Loial's wife finally asked him. It was odd, how easily he took to thinking of Loial as married. It *did* suit him. "The male half of the One Power has been cleansed? Loial spoke to me regarding it, and I did so want to speak with these men of yours. How mad are they? Is that too forward to ask?"

"They are humans, Erith," Elder Haman said, looking over his shoulder. "It is all right. They do not think many things are forward."

Loial's ears went back and forth at that, which Perrin found amusing. Despite often complaining that humans were hasty, Loial knew a great deal about them.

"The Source *is* cleansed," Perrin said. "And no, Grady and Neald aren't mad. They as are solid and dependable as any men I know."

"I would very much like to speak with them," Erith said. "Were either of them there when the Dragon accomplished this task? I would like to speak with witnesses."

"Erith is going to write a book about it," Loial said proudly. "It can be a companion volume to my story about Rand. Isn't that a good idea, Perrin? Erith knows a great deal about the One Power."

She was looking at his eyes again. Perrin cleared his throat. "That's wonderful, Erith."

Before destroying the bridges, they'd recovered the bodies of those who had fallen on the Island. They'd lost fourteen, counting the poor Mayener who had died while they ran from the wind. And counting Bornhald, whose body they hadn't found.

We didn't divide the dead by group, Perrin thought. The men had laid the bodies in a line together, Whitecloak beside Two Rivers man, Mayener beside Ghealdanin. He was proud of that, despite the pain of loss.

Grady knelt next to the bodies, then raised a hand. "Any objections?" he asked of those watching.

No one spoke. Grady adopted a look of concentration, then burned the bodies in a great, Power-wrought fire that cast back the darkness of the Ways and shone as bright as a beacon fire.

Perrin stepped up, feeling the heat of the pyre on his skin. "They are our first losses in this war," Perrin said. "They won't be the last, but each death means something important. It means we won't let the darkness take us. Rest in the Light, my friends."

Galad nodded to him, and his rippling white cloak reminded Perrin of how Bornhald had looked, running into the darkness.

The things he said . . . had he been involved in the deaths of Perrin's family?

Light burn *me,* he thought, feeling old wounds open inside him. It had been satisfying to blame Trollocs for his losses. Trollocs were faceless monsters, and hating them was easy. But Bornhald's words had implied that the blame lay not on the Trollocs at all, but on Padan Fain.

Perrin already hated Fain. Could he hate the man more? Would that do any good?

The funeral pyre burned low. The ferocity of it meant that only ash remained, mixed with bits of metal. Perrin was about to turn away when Elder Haman lumbered forward. The ancient Ogier stepped right up to the ashes, then knelt and placed something among them. "Loial, if you will," he said.

Loial knelt beside the Elder, then began singing in a soft voice. He closed his eyes in concentration. Nearby, the other Ogier began humming. It was a wordless song, similar to—yet distinctly different from—the one they'd sung earlier.

In moments, the seed sprouted and a small tree rose in the ashes of the fallen. Loial opened his eyes. "I am sorry if it is not large," he said. "I am not so experienced at this as I should be. I am much better at creating sung wood."

"That will do, Loial," Elder Haman said. "This place was once ours." His deep voice had grown dangerous. "It was a gift to us from the Aes Sedai, the last grand work of the male ones. If what is said is true, then the male Aes Sedai have returned."

"We don't call ourselves that," Grady said. "But we *have* returned."

"Then we will reclaim this place," Elder Haman said. "It was a gift to us. We should have known that we would have power over it, for it is ours. Once this battle is fought, human, I would return here and see this place restored to how it once was. If you will join us."

Grady smiled, and nearby, Neald nodded. "I think we'd like that, Elder Haman."

"Then this tree will stand as a marker of our pact," Elder Haman said. "If it wilts, we will sing it back to life."

The other Ogier nodded. Looking at their dangerous expressions, one might never have guessed how reluctant they'd once been to enter this place. One would never have known how much trouble it had been to coax them. Some of these same individuals had thought Perrin mad for daring to enter.

Perhaps they had needed to be shown, in person, how much their gift had been corrupted.

"You wish to join the Last Battle?" Perrin said to them.

"We have decided that we must," Loial's mother said.

"Then let's rest here," Perrin said, "and allow my people time to recover from what they've been through. Tomorrow, we'll make for Cairhien and cut off its Waygate as we did this one. After that, I'll have you to the fighting in no time. I guarantee that every axe will be well appreciated."

Postscript

One of my goals going into the final book (which became three books) of the Wheel of Time was to address the Ways. There wasn't a lot in Mr. Jordan's notes about how to accomplish this, but I felt that the text of earlier books had implied there would eventually be some resolution to the plot arc.

I found my opportunity in the need to stop the enemy from using the Ways. It made both tactical and logistical sense to try to cut off access to the Waygate in Caemlyn. From the original outline, it was always my plan for Perrin to take his team into the Ways—and in so doing, I could reveal some hints about how the Ways might eventually be cleansed.

The sequence lasted pretty far into the revision process, to the point that I received extensive notes from Harriet, Robert Jordan's widow and editor of every Wheel of Time book, as well as his assistants Maria and Alan, about how to revise it. However, the final revision of the sequence never happened, because in the end, we cut it from the novel. Why? Well, there are two major reasons.

Problem One: Tone and Continuity

This Ways sequence was a little rushed during my initial writing, and so it didn't have the right feel and tone of earlier visits to the Ways in the series. Indeed, I hadn't remembered quite how rough the piece was. I thought that I'd be able to clean it up in a couple days of work, but it took almost two full weeks of revision to get it into its current shape.

There were also a lot of small, but important, continuity problems. We weren't sure if it was too much of a stretch to even have Perrin be able to navigate the Ways without an Ogier guide. I believe it was Maria who suggested that we use notes from the Black Sisters. After all, if Trollocs are getting through the Ways, there must be some fairly simple instructions to be found somewhere.

Even with this fix, however, there were other issues with this piece. For example, the original draft had them destroying the Waygate, something that earlier books had indicated was near impossible. I fixed a lot of these issues in this revision, making use of the extensive editorial notes, but it probably would have needed several more drafts after this to be worthy of publication in the final book. The second major problem, however, was a bigger one.

PROBLEM TWO: PACING AND REGRESSION

As we revised *A Memory of Light,* one concern kept coming up: Were we looking backward too much? We wanted the book to be pointing toward the battles happening at places like Merrilor and Shayol Ghul. The idea was that we wanted to keep our eyes forward, keep the momentum up, and dispense with anything that felt too much like a "side quest" distracting from the story's building momentum.

This sequence kept getting flagged as one that felt regressive—it felt wrong to turn the reader's eyes toward the Ways (which wouldn't be important for the rest of the book) and toward Caemlyn (which had already fallen, and wasn't going to be a focus of the book past the prologue).

Harriet was the one who finally decided this sequence needed to go: we just couldn't afford twenty to twenty-five thousand words of Perrin running off on his own adventure in the middle of the book. This was particularly true when it became clear that it was going to require a lot of time in revision to get the sequence right—a sequence that was ultimately nothing more than a diversion. The tactics were sound, but in the end, there were a lot of things the characters could be doing—and this one wasn't vital.

Harriet was right, and the sequence had to go. I feel bad about axing it, however, because I like a number of the things it does. Bornhald's end feels better to me in this. I enjoy the interplay between characters and the way they pull together here, and the echoing of earlier books. Most, I like the scene where the Ogier show up. The final published version of *A Memory of Light* has them simply arrive at Merrilor without much fanfare—a necessity of the deletions.

Of the main characters, Robert Jordan's notes said the least about what to do with Perrin. However, one of the things he did say was that Perrin was to end up as a king. I like how this sequence, better than most in the published version, shows that Perrin has done something incredible in binding together many groups of disparate ideologies and ethnicities to form a cohesive force. I like how this echoes that of all the main characters, Perrin is most suited to rule, because he is capable of building as well as destroying.

I wish I could have found a solution and worked the Ways into the last book in a manner that wouldn't be distracting. They were a vital and interesting part of the series, yet the finale was forced to ignore them.

In the end, I still think Harriet made the right decision to strike this sequence—but I hope that with this publication, I can offer a little closure to one of the threads of the Pattern that was left dangling.

Brandon Sanderson

Naomi Novik

Back when I was working on a story for the second *Unfettered* anthology, Shawn asked me if I might consider writing one inspired by his mother, a fan of my work, who had just been diagnosed with aggressive stomach cancer. I very much wanted to do it, but stories gestate at unpredictable rates for me, and the story that arrived in time for *Unfettered II* wasn't her story.

This is.

For Kathy Jane Tenold Speakman: may her memory be a blessing.

Naomi Novik

SEVEN

Naomi Novik

No one knew when or why the city had first been named Seven. There were ten walls running between six ancient towers that joined them into the city's five precincts, and four gates that went in and out of them. Seven was ruled by eleven: five councillors elected from the precincts, all women; five priests named by the temples, all men; and one king, to whom no one paid very much attention except when he had to break a tied vote, which the others made efforts to avoid.

Beneath the city ran thirteen mysterious tunnels carved by unknown hands. Once they had been the arches of bridges. Long since buried, they now carried the nourishing river under the city and out the other side to the wide ocean. Another city would have been named for that river, but instead it was the other way around: the river itself was called Seven's Blood, or just the Blood for short.

And whenever someone new came to the city, they always thought, incorrectly, that the city had been named for the seven great singing statues, although just like the river, their number had been chosen to grace the name instead.

By unwritten accord, nobody who lived in Seven ever corrected the visitors. It was how you knew someone was a fellow citizen, since you couldn't tell any other way. Among the people of Seven were the island cave-dwellers with their milk-pale skin, and brown fisher folk from the shores, and the deep-ebony farmers of the green fields that clung to the river before it reached the city, and travelers come on one of the thousand ships and boats and coracles that docked outside the walls every week. All those people had mingled furiously until there was not a feature or shade of skin or shape of brow or eye or chin that would let you distinguish a stranger who'd come through the gates five minutes ago from someone whose ancestors seven generations removed had lived all their lives in the city. Even accents differed wildly from one precinct to the next.

So no one told the strangers that Seven wasn't named for the statues. The seven of them stood at the gates that led in and out of the city. The Gate to Morning and the Gate to Evening and the Sea Gate each had two, and one stood alone at the Gate of Death. They didn't all sing at the same time, of course: even the ones that stood on either side of the same gate were angled differently into the wind, so it was rare for any two to sing at once, and if three or four were singing, it was time for the ships in the harbor to reef their sails and drop anchor and for the shutters to be closed so dust wouldn't whip into the houses. Elders told their grandchildren delightfully gruesome stories of the last great storm when all seven had sung at once.

They were made of the pale white clay that the river spilled out on the far side of the city, full of its effluvia. Broken bits of pottery and scraps of fabric mingled with human and animal wastes, flesh and bone and sludge and all the city's music. Clay-shapers had to work their hands over and over through every bucket they took, like squeezing fistfuls of flour and water, but there was a faint opalescent slick over the surface of that clay when it was fired that no one could mix or reproduce with glaze or paint. It was full of life, and therefore of death. No clay-shaper who put their hands to it wanted to work with any other, and none of them lasted more than five years before it killed them: a vein opened with a buried shard of glass or pottery, infections that festered, fevers that ate them away, or sometimes simply clay hunger that ran wild, so they worked day and night in their workshops until they fell down dead.

The statues had been meant, at first, to stop the city's clay-shapers dying. The law of Seven now decreed that the white clay could only be used to replace the statues. The desert and wind together ground them away little by little, and when a crack appeared, or the mouth and eyeholes gaped too wide to sing, or a surface was worn away to featureless smoothness, the council voted the honor of making a new one to the greatest of the city's clay-shapers. Once that shaper had finished their statue, they alone had the right to use the clay for the rest of their life, which was as a result generally short.

It happened once in a generation or so, and the fierce competition drove the rest to new heights. The craft of the great workshops grew ever more refined, and the ships carried away ever more delicate and fantastic vessels and cups and plates to all the distant reaches of the world. And whenever a statue cracked, and a new grandmaster was crowned, then for three years or four, sometimes five, a brief furious blossoming took place, and set the style for the next generation.

Kath was not the grandmaster of her generation: that was Hiron. He was unanimously elected to remake the left-hand statue at the Sea Gate, three years before Kath's marriage, and he died the year after it, of blood poisoning. Kath herself was not even born to a clay-shaper family; she was the daughter of a master ironsmith. But she married one of the lower clay-shapers: a very good match. Her husband had a small personal workshop where he made everyday pottery for the lower classes: even the poor in Seven were proud of the dishes they set on their table, whether or not they could fill them. Unfortunately, he inconveniently died after fathering three children in the span of three years, with contracts outstanding.

He had taught Kath how to throw a serviceable plate and bowl and cup by then. After the three children were put to bed, she closed the shutters and lit candles in his workshop and filled the orders. She claimed he had already made them, they had only been air-drying before they went to the kilns. The kiln masters were not supposed to allow anyone not a member of the guild to fire their work, but they were sorry for her, and the story was just plausible enough that they accepted her pieces for firing. Afterwards she pretended that her husband had laid by a very large stock, which miraculously matched what her buyers were looking for, and the kiln masters kept letting her fill the bottom rungs of their ovens.

But finally the end of her six months of mourning came round, and the kiln masters turned to Grovin, the most heartless of their number. He had neither wife nor child nor even concubine; he cared for nothing except to preserve and glorify the highest of the city's arts. He had fired every one of the great Hiron's pieces, before the grandmaster had died; it was rumored they had been lovers. Anyway, ever since he had found out that his fellow masters had been letting the widow's work through, he had been making increasingly cold and pointed remarks about how the blowing desert sand wore away even the strongest porcelain. So they deputized him to ban her, and when she next approached pulling her week's wagon-load, they all disappeared and left him to turn her away.

She had the baby in a sling across her front—Kath was far from a fool—and still wore her mourning gray. But Grovin paid no attention to the baby. He told her flatly, "Only a clay-shaper may use the kilns. Your husband is dead, and it is time for you to stop pretending to be what you are not and go back to your father's house."

There were six other unmarried daughters in her father's house. It had been crowded even before she had borne three children. "But, sir," Kath said, "surely you don't think an ironworker's daughter could make these?"

Grovin snorted, but when she threw the cover off her work, he looked, and then he looked again, and was silent. He bent and carefully took a piece out of the wagon, a small simple cup made for drinking vin, the strong liquor that the poor preferred. It was utterly contrary to the prevailing style, the one Hiron had set:

Kath's piece had no ornament or decoration except a thin waving ridge that ran around the bowl just where the thumb might rest, inviting the hand to move the cup round as was traditional, tracing the endless line around.

The debate over letting her into the guild raged for seven days and nights, and was decided finally only because Grovin said flatly that he would fire her work even if no other clay-shaper came to his kiln as a result, and if he starved, so be it. They knew he meant it. The masters of the clay-shapers' guild quietly agreed that the scandal would make more trouble than Kath would, so they let her in.

And indeed she didn't put herself forward; she continued to make only common, everyday pieces, and kept her prices low. But by the end of the year, there was a line at her door, and the poor reluctantly began to resell her older wares, because they could get too much money for them. Eventually she stopped taking advance orders: instead she made what she had clay to make and once a week opened her shop to sell whatever she had. Everything sold to the bare shelves.

The masters eyed her work uneasily. Hiron's statue at the Sea Gate was a marvel of the most delicate sculptural work; there was not a surface without ornament, and at its unveiling, a noble visitor from Wilsara over-the-sea had said—no one doubted it—that its song was as rich and complex and beautiful as the ten-thousand-voiced Great Chorus of the Temple of Thunder in that great city. For the last six years everyone had been striving to imitate and elaborate on his style. Kath's work seemed like a joke when one of her squat cups was put next to one of the grandmaster's triumphant fragile pieces, but if you looked at it too long, you began to feel the terrible sneaking suspicion that you liked the cup better.

Barely a month after she was let into the guild, the first few rebellious journeymen, mostly young men who liked to gather in taverns and argue loudly about art, began to imitate her style instead, and talk of the virtue of simplicity. While the fashion ought to have changed at some point, it was too soon, and too far. But no one knew what to do about it. A small group of the masters decided to go and speak to Kath and point out to her the hubris of setting up her own school, but the attempt foundered helplessly on the shoals of her solidity: her house full of yelling small children going in and out of the street playing, an untidy stack of her own pottery worth more than a chestful of jewels sitting dirty in the washtub, and Kath herself apologetically serving them tea with her own hands, because she explained the one maid was sick. It was impossible to accuse her of grandiose ambition, even as the masters held their mismatched cups as carefully as live birds, staring down at them and forgetting to drink until the tea was cold.

"So they've been to peck at you, have they?" Grovin said, that evening. He ate dinner at their house now. Kath had brought him home with her after she had learned he ate a dinner bought from a stall alone every night, disregarding his protests: he hated children, he hated women, he hated her cooking, and he hated company. He wasn't lying, he really hated all of those things, but whenever Kath threw a piece she liked very much, she kept it for home use—"That's your inheritance, so watch you don't break them," she told the children—and he did like great pottery, so after the first time eating off a blue-glazed plate that swelled from a faint shallow out to a thin edge, with small scalloped indentations all around the rim, he kept coming, and ate with his head bent over and staring down at whatever piece Kath was feeding him from that night, wincing and sullen at the noise around him.

"They don't mean any harm," Kath said. "I don't know what to say to them, though. I do what I like myself, that's all I know how to do. I couldn't do anything like Master Hiron's work without making a mash of it. But I told them so, and that I tell anyone who asks me as much, and they only looked glum."

Grovin knew the clay-shaper masters a great deal better than Kath did, and he knew perfectly well they did mean harm, by which *he* meant putting worse pottery into the world. "They'll make trouble for you," he said, but as it happened, he made the trouble, and worse.

Two days after the clay masters came to see Kath, the right-hand statue at the Gate of Morning began to hum softly, its voice going deeper and deeper until it was only just barely audible, a tickle of unease at the back of the listener's head. The clouds were already gathering over the sea, and the ships in the harbor were reefing their sails by the time the left-hand statue took up the song. Hiron's statue at the Sea Gate sang very frequently, but usually in a few thin, reedy voices; that night it was in full chorus, and even in the rain, some people had come out to hear it, although not quite as many as there should have been.

By the second night, no one was in the streets, or anywhere but huddled in the deepest cellars they could get to, and the seven voices of the statues could no longer be heard over the general howling of the wind. But when the ferocity was over, and everyone came blinking out into the washed-clean streets, a path of total destruction as wide as three streets had been inscribed across the city, as though some god had come out of the sea and walked straight through to the Gate of Death, the holy gate, and the statue there, less than a hundred years old, had been obliterated.

"Oh, shut up, you cowards, you all know it's got to be her!" Grovin shouted down impatiently, after the masters had all spent the first hour of their discussion very carefully not saying Kath's name. The kiln-masters were allowed to come and sit in the gallery during the deliberations for a new grandmaster.

So were the journeymen clay-shapers, and after Grovin's shout, all of them burst out into clamoring, either in support or violent opposition. Four fist fights broke out in the gallery and one on the floor. But that was exceptionally modest; there had been twelve, during the debate over Hiron's appointment. Even the ones who didn't *want* to name Kath—the very ones who had gone to lecture her, the previous week—had the uneasy sense that they had better. It seemed too pointed a message from the gods.

"But I can't," she said bewildered to Grovin, when he told her, smugly, afterwards. He stared at her speechlessly, and she stared back in equal incomprehension. "What would happen to the children? Anyway, I don't want to die just to work in bone clay. That's a thing for a fool young man to do, or a fool old one, not a sensible woman!"

"Your work will live forever while your children are dry in their tombs!"

"Unless my statue breaks after a hundred years," Kath said tartly, "and I'd rather live on in my children's hearts than a face of stone."

Grovin spent an outraged hour straight shouting at her, then stormed out finally in a rage and went straight to the Gate of Death, and the temple of the goddess outside it, which had just escaped the general devastation. It was very large and grand and mostly deserted; everyone wanted to bribe Death, but few wanted to court her. There was only one priest, who listened to Grovin's furious tirade and asked mildly, "What do you want?"

"I want her to make the statue!" Grovin said.

The priest nodded. "You ask for her death, then."

Grovin did hesitate for several moments. But then he said, "She's going to die anyway. Everyone does. But her work could live."

"All things come to the goddess in the end," the priest said. "But if you want to speed things up, you have to make fair return. A life, for a death."

Grovin hesitated again, but to do him what small justice he deserved, not as long as the first time. "Very well," he said, proudly and grandly, and three days later, the pains started in Kath's belly. The priest at the temple of Forgin—the god of surgeons and their tools, a favorite of ironsmiths—palpated her stomach and shook his head. "The mass is large enough to feel. A year, perhaps."

Kath walked out with Grovin and went home in silence, stricken. He didn't precisely feel guilty; he was still full of his own righteous sacrifice. But he did wait several hours, until after the children were in their beds and Kath had sat by them all for a long time. Only then, when she came back to the table and mechanically made the evening tea, he finally said, "Well, you'll do it now."

She looked up and stared at him with the teapot in her hand, still hollow, and then she paused—not quite as long as he had, in the temple—and then she put down the teapot and said to him flatly, "No. Not unless you marry me first."

Grovin stared at her. "What?"

"If you marry me and take the children as your own," she said. "Otherwise I won't."

"You have six sisters!"

"And they'll make it a fight over who takes my children in, for the chance of taking their inheritance, too," Kath said. "Marry me, and give the children a home, and I'll make the statue and work the white clay, as long as I can, to provide for them. Besides," she added, "they'll look after you in your old age," and Grovin almost opened his mouth to say that he wasn't going to *have* an old age, when he suddenly remembered the priest saying *a life for a death,* and understood only then, in real horror, that *this* was the price: he was indeed going to have an old age, and more to the point a long life of raising three small children, one of whom couldn't speak in complete sentences yet.

But he knew better than to try and go back on a bargain with the goddess, so the next morning he and Kath were married, in a quiet ceremony attended only by her family and a group of young journeymen who drank at the tavern around the corner from her house; they followed in delight to witness Grovin's doom: he was generally viewed with irritation by them all, for being a little too dedicated to art and showing up their own professed devotion.

Afterwards Grovin moved in with her: when she'd asked him to give her children a home, she'd only meant it in the legal sense. She'd already three months before bought the house next door to expand her workshop, so there should have been plenty of room, but the chaos of the household spilled into all the space available. Grovin put his small box down in the middle of a bedchamber that held a broken birdcage, a collection of small rocks, two rickety shelves, and six small boxes arranged behind little clay horses like a caravan, each one holding precarious towers of glorious glazed cups for cargo, one of which had already been chipped by the rough handling. He sprang to rescue them and looked around himself in almost savage despair, thinking of his own two-room house, scrupulously clean, with large cabinets against every wall, full of carefully spaced pottery, and his small cot in the middle of one room and his small table with its one chair in the other.

The next day, Kath went grimly to the clay fields, trailed by a ceremonial escort and a practical mule cart. Mostly when a new grandmaster first came to the fields, he spent a day alone in vigil, carefully sieving a few handfuls of the raw slip over and over to get the feel of it. Kath just had the two young men she'd hired shovel the slip into jugs and buckets until the cart was loaded up, and then drove back with it to the house. Two of her brothers-in-law, both ironworkers, had forged her five screens, going from one very coarse to one very fine, with large pans to go underneath them. The young men shoveled the clay on top of the coarse one and rubbed it through with wooden sticks, leaving behind a glittering deadly mess of pottery shards and pebbles, broken knife blades, chips of stone, frayed moldy rags. Whatever clay made it through into the pan, they rubbed through the next screen, and so on. Even the finest screen came out clogged with tiny gleaming slivers too small to tell if they had started as clay or steel or stone. When the last pan was full, they put the slip into a bucket and carried the screens and pans to the nearest fountain and washed them completely clean. Grovin followed and watched aghast as long trailing rivulets of precious white clay went running away into the gutters, along with all the detritus. He was not alone: the journeymen from the tavern were half-gleefully shocked in audience, and apprentices peeking in on their errands.

But the men Kath had hired were only laborers, and didn't care. They carried the clean pans and screens back to the workshop and rubbed the clay through a second time, and then a third. Three days later, after the clay was dry, Kath put on a pair of gloves made of very fine mail, and then another pair of thick leather and wool, and then a third of coarser mail, and went through the clay putting a handful at a time into a fresh bucket, poring over each one with the cold suspicion of someone eating a badly deboned fish. She only ended with three buckets of clay left out of the entire cartload.

She didn't begin with the statue, of course; she made a few test pieces. Grovin, sitting hunched in the kitchen trying not to watch the children playing roughly with three clay toy horses, spent the days in horrible thoughts: what if she wasn't good at working the white clay, what if it diminished her prosaic pieces, what if she had ruined the clay with too much sieving.

Finally she came out of the workshop with six cups and two bowls on a tray for him to fire, and they were ruthlessly unadorned, even compared to most of Kath's work. Everything was in the shape, and the shape was a little *too* simple, too stark, but Kath only said, "Fire them and we'll see," tiredly, and went to put dinner on with her hands unbloodied. When he brought them back after the first firing, she only made a simple bucket of clear glaze and dipped them three times, nothing more, and handed them back over.

But when he took them out of the kiln at last, he stood sweating and silent looking at them for a long time. The starkness was unchanged, and the glaze had dried clear, with an irregular crackling that interrupted and somehow brought forth the strange opalescent finish, and he picked up the first one before it was cool enough and burned his seamed leathery hands holding it, breathtaken, his eyes wet.

He carried the tray back to her house with a ceremonial air; not inappropriate, since the streets were full of supposedly loitering clay-shapers, who had all gathered to catch a glimpse. There was even a gathering of a dozen masters at the corner of Kath's street, all of them pretending they had accidentally run into one another. Grovin stopped beside them and they gathered around and handled the bowls and the cups in silence, turning them and passing them from one to the other, before reluctantly putting them back on the tray and letting him go into the house.

Kath looked at the tray and only nodded a little, still looking tired; she was sitting down, although it was the middle of the day, and she had a hand over her stomach. "It'll do," she said, and then she took one of the cups, mixed strong wine with water out of the jug, and drank it down.

In the meantime, several more cartloads of clay had come in, and been sieved and washed and dried and winnowed. She began on the statue the next day. The head was as long as Kath's arm from chin to crown, and almost faceless, only the slightest suggestion of the curve of chin and cheek, as if seen through a heavy veil. The mouth was the only opening, and that only a little, the surface of the clay caving softly into it as if a pocket of the veil had been breathed in. When Grovin saw it, he felt a stirring of unease, a guilty man who fears his wife knows what he's been doing with his late evenings and is just waiting to make him sorry for it. "A woman?" he said, to cover it.

Kath said, "One I'm likely to know better soon," with a ghost of humor, and he squirmed.

"Only one copy?"

"Yes," Kath said. "If it doesn't come out, I'll make another."

While it dried, she went back to making cups and bowls and plates, a small steady stream piling up. The smaller pieces dried quicker; they were ready to go into the kiln along with the head. Every one of them came out well; the head cracked down the middle and stained with smoke. He brought it back dismayed, but Kath only shrugged and began on another copy.

It was four months before the head came out clean, and Grovin was in rising alarm by then. But Kath ignored his increasing hints. She made one head at a time, weeks to dry it out, and in the waiting she heaped up more cups and plates and bowls and pots and jugs, so many that they made walls inside the walls of her workshop, so many that they overwhelmed the hunger and purses of Seven, and to empty the shelves Kath sold chests full to sea captains taking them away to distant cities. Gold took their place, and then that went out again in chests: she bought houses for each of the children to inherit, and for each of her sisters, and paid to apprentice all their sons to clay-shapers.

But of the statue there was nothing, except one broken or flawed face after another. Grovin had a moment of intense relief when one fired without a crack, but as soon as he brought it out into the daylight, he knew it was wrong. He had to study it for ten minutes before he realized *what* was wrong: a flawed faint line running from the left eye down the cheek, where the glaze had fought with the opalescence instead of marrying it, but even before he found it, he knew.

He brought it back to Kath anyway, in desperation, hoping that she might at least move on before recognizing that it wouldn't do, but she only looked at him in surprise and then asked, "Are you feeling all right?" suspiciously, and made him drink a dose of one of the dozen medicines that now lined up on the high shelf above the table where the children couldn't reach. Then she went back into the workshop and started over yet again. That head joined the others, in their cracked and broken pieces, in the alley behind the house where Grovin had to go twice a day to collect the children from the courtyard. He disliked walking past them.

At last the seventh head fired perfectly, though, and when he brought it out he sagged in relief and then put his hands over his face and wept. He had spent six hours the night before walking up and down with one of the children crying on his shoulder with toothache. The night before that, he had spent five such hours, after first spending an hour lying awake listening to Kath doing the same, and thinking of how little work she would be able to do, until those thoughts drove him to get up and send her to sleep. The day before that, the oldest boy had knocked over a salt cellar and smashed it into shards, and when Grovin had shouted in horror, the child burst into tears and Kath came running out of her workshop, hands wet with clay. Grovin had looked in past her shoulder just in time to watch a half-formed jug slumping into a formless pile on her wheel, like an undertow tide dragging away a jewel. He was very tired.

But when he took the head back to the house, Kath looked at it and sighed with something that wasn't quite relief. "Well, I'll go on, then," she said, and gave him another wagonload of small pieces to fire.

She did all the statue the same way, one piece at a time, over and over until it came out properly. The year went, and the stomach pains came, but she refused to be hurried. The temple physician shrugged when Grovin finally dragged her there. "It hasn't grown much. Another year, perhaps? Who can say." Kath only nodded and went back to her workshop.

The goddess grew slowly in the back alley, lying flat gazing up at the sky. Tuning the sound of the statue was ordinarily a vast and difficult aspect of the task, but Kath made no effort to do anything towards it as far as Grovin could see. The statue only occasionally made an unpleasant shrill whistling noise, like a kettle not quite boiling, when the wind ran into the opening at the bottom. The pitch changed only slightly as the body grew slowly down from the neck to the shoulders over the next year.

At the end of the second year, the priest of Forgin shrugged again, and sent them away with no promises. The statue crept towards its waist. Crate upon crate of bone clay dishes went out the front door. The young journeymen from the tavern had persuaded Kath to give them places in her workshop in exchange for doing her errands; they made dishes out of ordinary clay, but in her style. Grovin eyed them with disdain and refused to fire their pieces, except for one or two he grudgingly allowed as not entirely worthless. They were all annoyed with him, until one day they weren't, and began demanding that he tell them what was wrong with each piece they made, which annoyed him instead. But little by little they improved, roughly at the same rate as the statue grew.

The children grew also. At some point, Grovin couldn't even keep thinking of them as *the children,* as much as he tried to; now they were Shan, who came home from playing boisterous games every day in cheerful dirt he had not the least hesitation in marking all the dishes with, and Maha, who liked to put together mismatched plates whenever she was told to set the table, and Ala, who still didn't talk much and managed in her quiet obstinate way to get into the workshop every day. Grovin at last gave up and tolerated it because she didn't interrupt Kath's work. She only sat in a corner and watched, not her mother's work but her mother, as if she was trying to store up something she hadn't been told was soon to be gone.

Grovin had fed them and bathed them and told them bedtime stories of the hideous fates that awaited evil children who smashed breakable things, which they all loved so much they demanded new ones every night, although they showed no signs of becoming more careful with the dishes as a result. He had grudgingly begun to teach Shan his letters, mostly to keep him sitting in one place for awhile and away from the crockery, and Maha had begun to pick them up as he did.

Ala had no interest. But one morning Grovin came out and looked into the workshop: he measured his days by whether Kath was well enough and sufficiently free from distraction to get up and start working in the morning. She wasn't there, but Ala was sitting at her table, playing with scraps of clay as all the children often did, only she was playing with scraps of bone clay, and when he rushed inside, she looked up at him and stopped him by holding up a thumb cup, the first work of apprentices, which Kath often made and encouraged her own journeymen to do, pressed out with fingers and hands instead of on the wheel. Ala's cup was not competent; her small fingers had left lumpy marks and visible fingerprints, and the rim was uneven, but it had something more than the charm of a child's work, which you liked only because you loved the child, which Grovin resolutely didn't. He would gladly have picked it from a shelf in some cheap secondhand shop and put it on display next to a few examples of the journeyman work of the same clay-shaper, and then a single masterwork, to see the development of the eye and hand and style. He took it from her hands very carefully and put it on the shelf with the drying pieces and led her to wash her hands in the small basin Kath kept always ready now, with a row of jugs the journeymen filled fresh at dawn and a big slop bucket beneath to dump the water in after every single washing. He a little reluctantly said, "You must not touch the white clay again," as he made her first soak her hands and wave them around in the basin before bringing them out to be washed with the sludgy soap Kath kept half-dissolved in a dish on the counter.

"It's not the clay," Ala said.

It was as long a sentence as he had ever heard her produce, but he didn't care, so he wasn't paying much attention. "The bone clay," he said sternly again. "You must not touch it."

Ala looked up at him from the basin and said, "It's not the *clay* hurting Mama," with an effort that made it seem an accusation.

Grovin flinched. He did not know what to say, but he was rescued: Kath came in, saw what he was doing, and in moments she was scolding and alarmed, and then Ala said again, "It's not the clay!" and burst into tears.

The whole morning was lost to soothing her: when she finally recovered and ran outside to play and yell, Kath spent an hour just sitting tiredly at the table, breathing deeply over a cup of tea. "Well, at least it's *not* the clay," she said finally, with a ghost of humor, and Grovin stared down at his hands as she pushed herself up and went at last into the workshop. He still wasn't paying attention to anything but his own guilt; it took him catching Ala with the bone clay a second time, two weeks later, making a roly-poly bliba figurine of the kind that the children of Seven loved to play with, round clay balls for arms and legs and head and belly. She didn't repeat herself, only stared at him mulishly after he finished lecturing, the figure on the table with its slightly tilted expression staring at him too, and in her silence, Grovin finally heard the words.

Hiron had been twenty-seven when he'd been chosen, ferociously proud and careless of his health the way only a healthy young man could be. He had never spoken a word of fear or hesitation to Grovin; the closest he'd ever said was, "They're usually giving it to dried up old ancients. It's no wonder they die so soon. Anyway, no one can live forever," smiling, and he'd smiled even after he'd shown Grovin the hand of his statue, the intricate surface with its layers of small disks built up, tiny mountains like an army of bliba figures flattened out, and the palm stained dark brown with his blood, like a mirror of the white bandage wrapped around his own hand. It had been only three months after he'd begun. "A piece of glass," he'd said, still careless. "I didn't see it. It's nothing, a shallow slice, the priest says it'll be closed in a week."

The wound had closed only after three, and the scar never stopped being irritated and red. Both of Hiron's hands had been a battlefield of faint scar lines and half-healed cuts by the Festival of the Sun, and one of the other masters had even ventured, "Perhaps you should rest them a while." Grovin had eyed the man with irritation: at that very moment Hiron had been halfway through the magnificent breastplate, a marvel of delicate carving done at just the right stage of air-drying; he rose three times a night to check the sections, to be sure he didn't miss the chance.

Hiron had laughed a little, and said, "I'll rest them when the statue is done," but a month later, he had rested them sooner after all, because he spent a week vomiting and with the flux. Grovin hovered, feeding him soup and bread and wine with honey, miserably anxious: there were four pieces waiting for carving. Hiron tried to go to the workshop once, but his hands were shaking too badly; he scarred one piece beyond redemption, and then had to run staggering to the pot again anyway. After four days, Grovin looked in on the pieces that morning, then went back to his bedside and said, "It's no use, they're gone. You'll have to remake them when you're well again," and Hiron had wept a little before he turned to the wall and slept for the better part of three days.

His hands were healed a little more after the enforced rest, but he had a hollowed blue look to his face that hadn't been there before. He had been slower, afterwards; he only lost three pieces waiting for carving when feverish shakes laid him up two months later. He was sick three times during the rainy season, and listless; he was better once the weather dried out, but when the statue went up at last—after only eleven breakneck months of work—he came home from the dedication ceremony and lay down and was sick for a solid month with an illness no priest or physician or wisewoman could name or cure. Grovin brought a dozen through to look at him, spending the last of his own money to do it; Hiron had not sold a single piece since beginning to make the statue, and Grovin had not fired anyone else's work. Neither of them had ever put much of anything aside.

The landlord came by and apologetically said that he had to have the back rent, which wasn't to be had. Grovin had to sell four pieces of his prized collection, in anguish, although he managed to sell them to temples to be put on display, so at least he could go and visit them. "Never mind," Hiron said, consolatory. "The statue's done. As soon as I'm well, I'll sell some pieces, and you'll buy them back, if you really want to bother." Hiron himself had never had much patience for the work of other clay-shapers.

He did rise at last, thinner, and went back into the workshop, back to the clay. But he wasn't quite the same. Grovin swallowed it for a month, but he couldn't bear it; when Hiron tried to hand him one truly awful urn, finally Grovin burst out, "What are you doing? This looks like the work of those guildless imitators down by the docks, making trash to pawn off as the grandmaster's work. It's—*timid*."

Hiron had flinched, and then he'd smiled again, a little waveringly, and said, "You're always right, Grovin," and then he'd taken the piece and smashed it. His pieces improved after that, but there was still a thread of what Grovin called caution running through them, something withheld, for the next two years. Hiron wasn't sick quite as often, and once he was making pieces for sale, there was more money for food and firewood, although never quite enough to buy back Grovin's pieces. He never brought in as much as Kath's crates full of dishes, and the money had somehow vanished more quickly even with only their two mouths to feed.

Then at the start of the fourth year, the blood-poisoning took hold. Hiron was feverish every evening, even when he felt well in the mornings. Everyone consulted could name it, of course; the symptoms were well known. There was no cure, except to stop working the bone clay. The grandmaster Ollin had even done so some two centuries before; he had died a year later in a plague and was still spoken of disdainfully among clay-shapers as having been justly punished for cowardice. Hiron and Grovin had insulted his name amongst themselves many times.

Hiron didn't stop working the clay. Grovin was a little afraid at first, not of that, but of another weakening in his work. But the timidity didn't return. Hiron's work bloomed instead, going abruptly larger and stranger and even more complicated and convoluted. The pieces he made had no purpose but display, and found few buyers, but Grovin gloated over them with brooding joy, firing them with immense care and almost alone in the kiln; he added in only grudgingly enough other goods to pay for the fuel, at rates so low that their shapers wouldn't complain about having their work treated dismissively and shoved to the sides. Hiron's pieces became still more wild as the fevers crept further and further into his days, figures that twisted and writhed as if against strangling bonds. He had long since stopped speaking of *when I'm better.* But he still never spoke of fear. Grovin took the pieces that didn't go in the final sale and used them to decorate Hiron's tomb, a monument he considered greater than the statue itself, even if less refined tastes didn't appreciate them properly.

Hiron had lasted four years, in the end. Longer than most grandmasters. But the bone clay had been taking him from almost the beginning; in a long, slow feasting, not a quick slaughterhouse blow. Sitting in Kath's workshop, Grovin stopped lecturing Ala and instead looked down at her small, tender, unmarked hands. When Kath came in, he took her hands and turned them over, peering close: one small burn, from touching a cooking pot, and not a single cut, and her pains had not changed since the day they had first gone to the temple of Forgin three years before. She had been ill, now and again, but not with clay fever, or poisoning, or infections.

"Well, I'm not having *you* be the proof," Kath said to Ala, and sent her to sit in her room for punishment, and then she called in her journeymen and told them all that she'd let some of them knead the bone clay for her, if they were willing to try and see if any of them began to be ill. "But don't any of you do it if you have a child coming," she added, "and I won't have any bragging or teasing; it's not a joy worth dying for."

Grovin stifled himself before them, but when the journeymen had boiled out again in glee, he snapped, "It *should* be. That's what's wrong with their work: they don't care enough."

"If they don't care enough to die for it, that's as much as saying they've got sense," Kath said, washing her hands off, and for a moment he hated her.

"Do you feel nothing of your own art?" he said through his teeth. "I hardly know how you can make your work when you talk of it like a farmer, only worried about bringing your crop to market. I suppose there are birds that sing without understanding their own music—"

Kath startled round at him, surprised and hurt, but even as he stopped, she went indignant instead; she faced him and put her hands on her hips. "You love pottery because you've put your heart inside it," she said, sharp, "and you don't love the world because you've put none of yourself into any other part of it. Well, my heart's not shut up in a jar on a shelf. I understand my work, better than you. I'm making a thing out of the bones of the dead, and if it lives again, it's only because someone living loves it, even if it's just me myself. You can pretend, if you like, that a lump of baked clay means something on its own, even if no one touches it or looks at it or rejoices in it, and make that your excuse for not caring what any human being needs or wants. It's just another way of being selfish."

She swiped her wet hands off against her hips, back and forth, a decided gesture, and walked out of the workshop, back into the kitchen, with the shouting children. Grovin stood unmoving and blind there a long moment, and when he saw again, he had turned without realizing it towards the door, towards the faces of the goddess, blackened with smoke, cracked, misshapen; the goddess with her veiled face with its open mouth waiting, waiting to breathe and live.

Shawn Speakman

When I began writing "The Fire-Risen Ash," it was meant for *Unfettered II*.

Sadly, it never published there. My mother passed away at that time, and I felt I needed to commemorate her with a different type of story—one about her life and magic. I did that with "The Last Flowers of the Spring Witch." Looking back on it, I made the right decision, but I always regretted not finishing "The Fire-Risen Ash."

That regret is now gone. "The Fire-Risen Ash" features Knight of the Yn Saith Richard McAllister and his trusty fairy guide, Snedeker, as they embark on a quest to reestablish a fey species thought extinct. Those of you who enjoyed my novel *The Dark Thorn* will like this new Annwn Cycle tale. The short story also stands alone quite nicely without having read my previous work.

Hope you enjoy the fiery magic of the phoenix!

Shawn Speakman

THE FIRE-RISEN ASH

Shawn Speakman

Richard McAllister ignored dozens of wounds, anger bolstering his resolve.

The Heliwr of the Yn Saith had taken a beating. He had expected his task to be difficult—but not like this. The home of Christophe Moreau had been built to repel an army. In fact, it was more of a Gothic fortress, protected by various magical alarms, watchful gargoyles, and a state-of-the-art surveillance system that would never exist in Annwn but did in Paris. A wizard could never be too cautious—Richard had learned that more often than not knowing Merle—and Christophe Moreau was no different. He was young in his craft but had the patience and attention to detail of a man three centuries older, his home reflecting it. Merle had thought one unfettered knight and his wise-ass fairy guide stood a chance at infiltrating the home though. And it had worked.

Richard hated to admit it, but he now knew he had been bested the moment he had stepped within the wizard's walls. He knelt on cold stone, gathering his strength even as it bled out of him, livid that he had been brought so low so quickly.

"Would you *stop* with the blood and do your job," Snedeker snapped.

If he had been near enough, Richard would have knocked his irascible fairy companion into one of the prison's shifting walls and been done with his guide altogether.

Instead, Snedeker hovered on the other side of the room. And Richard could not muster the might to yet again put the fairy in his place.

"Easy to say that when you aren't the one bleeding, Snedeker," Richard shot back.

"We fairies do *not* bleed," the other sniffed indignantly.

"Well," the Heliwr said, spitting red again. "Aren't *you* just the lucky one."

"Your sarcasm is not going to sav—"

"Shut the *hell up*, Snedeker."

The Oakwell fairy frowned bits of leaves and bark before returning his attention to their dangerous situation. Richard cursed inwardly. In the past they had broken into more fortified locations than the Parisian mansion. This time it had been different. Once inside, the home had become a living entity, a labyrinth of shifting walls and changing rooms, and occupied by a fey guard so intelligent and savage that the Heliwr had been outmatched from the outset.

Richard gripped the Dark Thorn close. He gathered what magic the staff afforded him. And waited for the walls to change yet again, to give them a new path.

And possibly a new chance at escape.

Long minutes slipped away.

"The creature must have a weakness," Richard said mostly to himself.

"Elychher are very hard to kill. You see, they grow stronger with pain. It drives them mad until they are unstoppable and kill the prey they have stalk—"

"I know, Snedeker," the knight growled.

"Well. Fine then."

"Where did it go though?" Richard asked.

"How the *Lady* should I know?" Snedeker retorted. "You drug us into this mess!"

"And I'll get us out," the knight said, even as the walls began grinding into a new configuration. "Now go. Something new must be better than this."

Snedeker flew into the next room, already seeking a way out. Using the Dark Thorn more as a crutch than a staff, Richard followed. Honestly he didn't know if they *would* get free. The home of the wizard was one large trap. Even the power of the Dark Thorn could not seek the way out, its ability to find what was lost compromised by the mutable nature of the home. The walls had been fortified, enhanced to withstand magic. And then there was the elychher. Richard had come to end the fey creature, the elychher controlled by Christophe Moreau and sent into the Paris portal for some time to acquire magical artifacts, gems, and weapons. Arnaud Lovel, the knight who warded the portal into Annwn, had not been strong enough to prevent the incursions. It was only when Merle, the ancient wizard known as Myrddin Emrys and architect of the portal knights, had decided enough was enough that he charged Richard with ending the threat.

After hours of research, both men had agreed it was time. Christophe Moreau had grown too dangerous. Power corrupted. Left unchecked, Moreau would acquire a magical arsenal larger than even what the Vatican housed.

And now, barely able to stand, Richard bled for it.

The Heliwr tried to remember everything Merle had taught him about the elychher. They were fey creatures, catlike and lethal, highly intelligent and feared by even their own Unseelie Court brethren. How Christophe Moreau had discovered, caged, and learned to control an elychher, Richard didn't know. It didn't matter at the moment. Even with his experience, the Heliwr had struck the creature just twice in the last hour, and both times the cat had fled, leaving behind only its high-pitched hyena laugh, the walls shifting into a new configuration before the unfettered knight could pursue it.

–How does it feel, McAllister, being the fly instead of the spider?–

The voice of Christophe Moreau echoed in the silence of the new room that held ancient chairs, older paintings, and no doorways of any kind.

"Why don't you show yourself and find out, wizard?"

—I am here. In these very walls. I am all around you. I have made you bleed. Do you not know that?—

"It will take more than my blood to kill me," Richard grated, sending his senses into the mansion to discover the wizard's whereabouts. He found nothing. "Others have done the same. I'm still here."

—And yet you weaken with every breath. I sense it. It is clear Myrddin Emrys chose his newest Heliwr poorly—

Rage strengthened Richard. "Come in here and find out how poorly, fucker."

—I will not be goaded, knight. You will see me when I wish it. I have not survived within the machinations of other European wizards and witches by being daft. You are nothing to me. Nothing to the world. You are an amusement, one I am slowly growing tired—

Richard gave voice to his fear. "You are toying with us."

—Very perceptive, Heliwr—

"But why?"

—Many reasons. The least of which, you dared break into my home. The most being Myrddin Emrys. He sent you here. Yet I will outmatch his arrogance. I want to send a message. I want you *broken*. I want your death on his conscience. I want the guilt to cripple him as I will cripple you. I will make an example of you and your fairy friend just as one day I will make an example of him—

This last trailed off in a hiss of seething anger.

"Do you know what I heard in all of that?" Richard asked, grinning darkly. "I heard a lot of 'I' this and 'I' that. Bring your worst, you pompous coward."

—And you are a fool for coming here at a fool's behest—

The walls shifted anew, moving at a rate that matched the wizard's ire.

—Heliwr, enough of this game. How do the powerful men in government put it? You are now collateral damage—

At that, part of the stone wall on Richard's right suddenly slid open and the cat leaped from its shadows, the elychher on the Heliwr so quickly he barely had time to ward it off. The Dark Thorn and his own instincts saved him. Fire erupted down its length like the sun, the flames exploding against the creature. It was not enough. Claws raked his left ribs to the bone, rending muscle, spinning him like a top. The elychher kept at him, an elusive target, slashing at him on one side, passing, and returning to strike the other. Snedeker tried to drop explosive dust but the catlike creature was always a step ahead. The smell of burnt cat hair sat thick in his nostrils, but his own magic could not land a strong blow either. The fey beast was getting faster in the attack even as he slowed.

He sensed this was the end. The wizard had finally come for the knight's death. Desperate anger was the only thing that kept Richard alive. He brought the entirety of his will and magic to bear, creating a wall of force that pushed the elychher back. It would not last long. But it would give him the time he needed.

When the invisible wall crumbled seconds later, Richard sidestepped the attack that leaped in a blur.

And sent the Dark Thorn's magic where the fey monster would land.

The fire slammed into the elychher's side, sending it flying through the air to crash into a small round table and its chairs. Body smoking, the creature attempted to flee from the brutal attack, to regroup as it had done several times before.

It was exactly what the Heliwr expected. Just as one of the walls opened to allow the elychher escape—closing as soon as it did so to keep the knight and fairy behind and trapped—Richard called the entirety of power he yet possessed.

"*Tynnu rhaff!*" he roared.

Even as he fought the blackness threatening him from the expenditure of magic, an invisible line wrapped about the elychher's hind leg, anchored to the room—just as the fey beast attempted to bound to safety. Taken by surprise, the elychher fought the magical lasso that had caught it, fighting to flee. It kicked out to no avail. Flipping over, looking back into the room, and mewling in fearful panic.

As the wall closed upon its body.

Bones snapped as the beast roared pain, blood bursting from its broken chest, shoulders. and back. The wall ground to a sudden halt, but it was too late. The elychher lay jammed between two rooms, dying, crushed.

"Is it dead?" Snedeker asked, hovering high in the ceiling.

Richard took a steadying breath. He approached the elychher, the Dark Thorn held protectively before him.

He would not need it. The beast died with every slowing gulp of air.

"Your watchdog is dead, wizard!" the Heliwr yelled, euphoria replacing the weakness that gripped his being. "What do you have to say about that?!"

No answer came. He gripped the magical tendril that still roped about the elychher and pulled, to remove the beast and leave the room through the opening. Eyes of alien shape stared at the knight. With rage. Malevolence. But first of all, fear. As its life faded, Richard realized he saw more—an all too human and terrible intelligence.

"What now, Rick?" the fairy asked, landing on his shoulder. "Find the wizard and end his sorrowful existence?"

Before Richard could reply, the elychher began to change following its final breath. Fur gave way to skin; paws melted into hands. Even the bones that jutted out of the fey beast shrank and transformed, no less splintered but eerily recognizable.

Where the elychher had been, a naked man lay.

"*Goatsack,*" Snedeker cursed. "A shapeshifter."

"You are as observant as ever," Richard snorted, barely able to comprehend what had just happened. "It is Moreau. We were wrong. He never caught an elychher. He merely took on its form." The knight looked around at the walls that slowly began to shift back to their natural state. "Damn wizards. And especially damn *this* wizard."

"We need to get you a healer," Snedeker observed, picking past the knight's shredded clothing to examine his wounds.

"No. Not yet." Richard looked down on the dead wizard even

as he fought to bring what magic remained his to the fore. "Time to find this wizard's vault before it falls into the wrong hands."

Richard sent the butt of the Dark Thorn into the stone. The staff born of Glastonbury Abbey's Holy Thorn entered the building easily, becoming one with it through his magic. Richard focused, drawing on reserves he did not know he had. He sent his senses outward, seeking the room containing the most power. His magic snaked into the building, twisting and turning, finding its way out of the now dead labyrinth.

Results returned immediately. Richard knew the location of the wizard's most treasured possessions, the path seen by the fairy as well.

"Do you know your way, Snedeker?"

"Already gone."

The room's true door now revealed, Snedeker flew beyond, guiding the Heliwr, both companions still wary despite the death of Moreau. Wizards were notorious for their traps remaining active long after they had left a place or passed on. They encountered no danger though. Still bleeding from several major wounds, Richard was thankful he didn't need to call on his depleted magic again. After twists, turns, and staircases, he came to a wall that was no wall.

"How will you get in?" Snedeker asked, hovering over the knight's shoulder.

Richard gathered his will. "I hope with Moreau's death his vault is no longer sealed with traps."

The knight placed his hands upon the cool stone. He first sought any wards that were placed to prevent this very sort of attempt. There were none. Christophe Moreau had been arrogant to his very last, believing his labyrinth protection enough. Richard called upon the earth beneath the building, the magic inherent in the world bolstering his ability to dissolve stone. A glow spread from his fingertips as he concentrated. Then without a sound, part of the wall vanished in a flash, revealing a circular door as tall as a man.

Richard gestured to Snedeker. The fairy flew inside, seeking danger.

Not sensing any, the Heliwr followed.

It was a large square room, as ornate as the mansion but unlike any of the rooms Richard had been in thus far, the crystal chandelier overhead beginning to glow with their entrance. Magic thrummed in the air, power so palpable that the knight could feel it in his very bones. That was not what staggered him though. Items of various intent and design lay upon hundreds of pedestals throughout the room, each bearing a unique artifact from centuries past. A sword here. A helmet there. A scroll encased in glass or a bone from an unknown creature. Pieces of jewelry, leather books, and clothing. Relics filled the room, Christophe Moreau building a collection that rivaled even the Pope's secret vault in St. Peter's. There was no way the Heliwr could take it all with him. Instead, he would have to request help from Merle to gather it.

"We have done our job," Richard said, still gazing about the room with its marvelous collection. "The elychher is dead. Moreau is no more. I will seal the room. No one will enter. And Merle can decide how to best handle this."

Snedeker nodded absently, ignoring him as he flew throughout the room as if casting what to steal.

Just as the Heliwr was about to seal the annoying fairy within the room to prove yet another point, Richard's gaze fell on a crystal object larger than a Faberge egg but shaped similarly.

"Holy shit," he murmured.

"What is it?" Snedeker asked, now suddenly interested.

Richard limped toward the center of the room. The egg-shaped item sat on a pedestal of granite, higher than the rest. The crystal was not clear but ash-colored like black topaz. The Heliwr gained the item and stared into its depths. Within, an orange and purplish light danced, alive. Snedeker hovered before the relic and a look of greed Richard had observed in the fairy multiple times overtook him.

None of that mattered though. Richard could not believe what he beheld.

"Well?" the fairy whispered. "What is it, Rick?"

The knight couldn't bring himself to touch it. "It is one of the rarest items this world or Annwn has ever seen."

Snedeker couldn't take his eyes off of it.

"*So?!* What is it?"

Richard touched it then, even though it felt blasphemous to do so. The crystal was alive, warm to the touch. A soft whisper entered his mind, one of rising rebirth and fire, of desire to live once more after many centuries of not.

The knight took a deep breath.

And wondered what the hell he had just gotten himself into.

"It, my dear Snedeker, is a phoenix egg."

"This is not only an unrisen phoenix, McAllister," Aengus Doughal said, the ancient Arch Druid running his hand over the crystal facets of the beautiful egg that now sat upon his desk. "It is the *last* known phoenix egg in *either* world."

Richard watched the tiny dancing flame within the egg, wondering at its history. He had taken it from Christophe Moreau's home, the only item removed because it demanded immediate answers. He now sat in the highest tower of Caer Dathal the New, the northern home to the Druid order, mostly recovered from his ordeal in Paris. The sounds of rebuilding were faint, construction on the damaged castle keep beginning once the Everwinter had thawed and spring become renewed. The vault the two men sat within had not fallen to the machinations of witch and wraith, its contents secured and saved, even as the majority of the castle had been severely broken. The Druid keep would be rebuilt as it had before in the order's history, and life would return to eventual educational and magical normalcy.

Richard marveled at the strength of people. Evil took no root in ground that was not fertile for it.

And if it did, it could be overcome.

"What do you know about this egg?" Richard asked, his mind returning to the subject at hand. Snedeker sat next to the egg, small in comparison, wood hands on mossy beard, unable to take his gaze from it. "Merle seems to think your expertise is more adept than all others. That is why I am here."

"Myrddin Emrys does not know everything, Heliwr. And neither do I," Aengus answered, tugging at his thick russet beard. "I know little concerning this particular past. The phoenix has long been extinct. Although some of the Druids who came before me marked that passing, and with written sadness."

Richard nodded. "We now know it *not* to be extinct."

"No. It is not," Aengus said, nodding. "Very interesting."

Richard leaned back in his chair, thinking. "How did this egg survive then?"

The Arch Druid went to the wall behind his desk and spoke a combination of words Richard could not hear. He watched as the wall vanished to reveal a hidden cache of preserved histories. Aengus grabbed a tome larger than the others, its metal bindings more ancient and its leather more aged, cradling it as a mother would an infant. He set it on his desk. Once the Arch Druid read a book it became a part of him; he was possessed of an ability to recall exactly where he had learned something new. Richard liked Aengus a great deal. He had an impeccably organized mind and a scholarly nature; he also had a stubbornness that rivaled Richard's own, a talent that had seen him through the hardest of lives.

"Here is the first passage I read about the phoenixes of old," Aengus said, flipping to a specific page and showing Richard. The knight stood over the desk to look.

It was a simple message, scrawled in a beautiful but older script:

Ash upon the Mountain bed, Fire birthed beneath,
What has Fallen shall Rise from whence it came.

"That sounds like prophecy," Richard mused.

"I have learned to not put much stock in prophecy. It is merely a plot device for poor fairy tales," Aengus said, giving Richard a dark gaze. "This book, however, is a history that recounts many of Annwn's magical elements. In this case, the phoenix belongs to neither the Seelie nor the Unseelie. It is a creature born of fire, earth, and wind. The passage I read *does* give insight into the life and death of the phoenix before its supposed extinction and a set of directions about its rebirth. We have no way of knowing if this was written before or after the last known phoenix perished."

"Ashes. But no mention of an egg," Richard said. "Although I suppose a bed means something must lie upon it."

"All too true. But which mountain?" The Druid read on, his eyes flitting over the page. Then he turned another. And another. Richard waited. The scholarly part of his past wished to help, but he knew the Arch Druid understood more about the craft of hunting information than the Heliwr ever would.

Without looking up, Aengus growled low and guttural.

"Call upon Druid Aderyn Hier, Paetyn and Kehndyl. I request her presence."

Before Richard could ask to whom Aengus was speaking, bits of shadow separated from the room's area of darkness, ink stains that coalesced into catlike forms possessing more spines and teeth than seemed physically possible for any fey creature.

"Unseelie. Vorrels, if I'm not mistaken," Richard observed, watching the shadows dart from the private tower room. "You keep strange company, Arch Druid."

"Present company included?" Aengus smiled. "They are friends. Like you."

The men waited, comfortable in silence. Snedeker contemplated the phoenix egg, the fairy hypnotized by it. Richard watched it as well, considering, while the Arch Druid continued to peruse the book. There were answers to be had with the use of scholarly work. Richard understood all too well, though, that ancient knowledge tended to be fragmented—and usually useless. He hoped that would not be the case here. But he couldn't shake the feeling he had missed something. And that something was important.

After fifteen minutes, the tower door opened and a woman like a switchblade entered. The two Vorrels were not in evidence, although Richard knew they were likely hiding in their shadows. Instead, he observed the Druid. She possessed sharp features and wrinkles. But while older than those in the room, she stood with a steely confidence and strength that belied her lean frame. Gray eyes met his, two people of power assessing the other, before she looked upon the egg.

Recognition and the surprise that followed became anger.

"Where did you *find* it, Aengus?" the old woman hissed, unmoving.

"Calm yourself, Aderyn," the Arch Druid said. "You are here to ascert–"

"No!" The woman growled, already moving toward the desk. Richard gripped his seat, watching, ready to intervene if needed. "You would see it destroy Caer Dathal, Arch Druid. We must take this egg fro–"

"Silence!" Aengus thundered, leaning over his desk to prevent her from touching the egg. The other Druid went quiet, but the fire in her eyes matched that of the Arch Druid. Richard doubted it was the first time the two had butted heads.

"What is wrong?" the Heliwr asked, trying to cut the tension in the room.

"Speak with care, Aderyn," Aengus ordered. "This is Heliwr Richard McAllister of the Yn Saith. And I will not suffer extreme emotion in this office, no matter how warranted, during his visit."

The old woman nodded to Richard, but it held little respect, her eyes back to the egg. All the while her hands wrenched at one another. "We must leave at once with it, Arch Druid," Aderyn Hier said more evenly now. The Druid moved to the desk but did not touch the crystal. "This egg brings great peril here. As you undoubtedly already know, it is a phoenix egg. A treasure. A curse. I thought them extinct." She paused, her fear now mingling with something else. Wonder? "You have brought it here, Heliwr? From the world of the Misty Isles?" Richard nodded. "But you did not realize the moment you entered Annwn, the Erlqueen of the Unseelie Court became aware of its entrance as well. In this history, my studies have been clear.

"The phoenix, the dragons, and the dark fey have ever been enemies," she continued. "The Erlqueen will hunt this egg now that it has returned to Annwn. And by doing so, you have endangered us all."

"She can sense it?" the Heliwr asked. "How can that be?"

"The Erlqueen can sense power that matches her own," Aderyn stated. "After all, the darkness senses the fire that can end it."

"I know the Erlqueen. She would not do this."

"The young woman you knew is largely gone, moved by the higher purposes of her new kin now," Aderyn disagreed. "She has already sent the ashterbach—a creature created for one purpose—and it is already heading toward Caer Dathal from Mrenin Rath even while we sit here and waste time."

Richard and Aengus exchanged worried glances. Because every shadow in the room had suddenly become an enemy.

"What would you have me do?" Richard questioned.

"Aderyn has studied this ancient history. It is in her past. It is why I asked her here," Aengus offered, closing the book he had been looking over. "She has a great deal of information. I am hoping she will know. If she's right, we will need to move quickly. If she is wrong about the Erlqueen, your quest will be simple."

"I'd prefer simple," Richard said.

"There is a small mountain range, to the north and east, within the Forest of Rhos," Aderyn began, choosing her words with care as if remembering them from a long-lost book. "The phoenixes of old lived there. Far removed from the rest of Annwn and those who hated them. The wood there is quite forbidding, a natural barrier. When they died, they were reborn there, with the aid of the Anfarwol, a small sect created by those who wanted to save the rare creature." She paused, recovered from her earlier anger. "I do not know if that sect remains. It has been several centuries since I left my home."

Richard nodded, thinking. "You grew up there?"

"I did," she said, looking back to the egg.

"Is this even advisable?" Richard asked Aengus. "If we bring this egg to the Forest of Rhos, what does that mean? Will it be even more endangered? Can it protect itself once reborn?"

"I believe some events are random, some events are meant. We have no control over that." The Arch Druid folded his hands before him. "If the dragons discover this egg, it will not survive. If the Unseelie Court discovers it, the line of the phoenix will end again, possibly forever. It could be taken back through the portal where it would be safe. But I believe it has resurfaced now because it is time for it to do so." He paused. "Make no mistake though, McAllister. Anyone and anything in its presence will be hunted. Perhaps killed. That means you and your fairy guide. It will be a difficult road for you."

Richard wanted to laugh darkly. "That road I have traveled many times."

"Then I wish you both safe travels," Aengus said.

"You will not join us?"

The Arch Druid gave a grave look. "I would see these creatures restored. Extinction from prejudice is not natural. Yet the egg's presence within Caer Dathal has likely already drawn unwanted attention, attention that is all too powerful. I must remain to protect my charge as Arch Druid."

"I don't envy your role," Richard admitted.

The two men shook upon their parting. Richard saw understanding and empathy in the other. Aderyn stood nearby as if carved from stone.

"I would join you, Heliwr," she said.

"I cannot ask that of you, Aderyn Hier," Richard said, shaking his head. "I have been in these situations before. It will be dangerous. Likely more than you know."

"I am not a waif, knight."

Richard deferred to the Arch Druid. "Aderyn will accompany you," Aengus said, looking into the egg's interior. The purple-orange glow illuminated his rugged features. Richard wondered what he saw within those depths. "She is tougher than the winter's hardest leather, and she knows the area and the history."

Richard nodded. "It is settled then." The Heliwr retrieved the egg from the desk and gently returned it to a large knapsack. Snedeker watched, the fairy wilting when the egg vanished from sight.

"Prepare for the journey, Aderyn Hier," Richard said, ignoring his guide's odd behavior. "We leave now."

Richard sat upon Lyrian and watched Aderyn Hier ride toward him.

The Heliwr, his mount, and his guide had been waiting outside the newly built walls of Caer Dathal for less than an hour, the air warm and buzzing with insects and the songs of numerous birds. Snedeker sat upon his shoulder, grumping about the phoenix egg being covered and kept from view. Richard did not care how his fairy guide felt. The egg had become a burden, one that could get them killed. Best that it was hidden, kept away from eyes that almost certainly watched from the shadows. Given the danger their charge would attract, they had remained too long in one place already, and the Heliwr was ready to be on the road. He would not feel comfortable until they were miles from Caer Dathal and well on their way toward the Forest of Rhos.

When she reined in her mount, the Druid dismounted and came up to the large leather bag that hung from Lyrian's heavy riding blanket. She ran her hands over the sturdy case that held the egg.

"We must keep safe what is inside this bag at all costs," she said.

"I know," he agreed. "Which is why we should already be gone."

"The road will be dangerous."

"My roads are always dangerous."

The Druid snorted and undid the top of the bag to view its contents. She ran her fingers over the crystal. There was something in the way she now acted toward the egg that bothered Richard. Before becoming a Knight of the Yn Saith, he had played poker weekly with several associate professors and grad students. He learned then that he had a knack for reading people. The Arch Druid had secrets—every Druid had them—but his secrets were held behind a stoic reserve. Aderyn did not possess that. She could be read. Or perhaps she wanted him to believe she cared. Either way, there were lies to guess at. Richard sensed she had not told him everything.

Snedeker did not have a poker face either. The fairy gave the Druid a continued dark look even after she had covered the egg again. Richard knew what it meant.

Jealousy.

It looked like he had more to worry about than just the ashterbach.

They rode east out from Caer Dathal the New, the day vibrant with late spring. The Everwinter had retreated, the long winter allowing Annwn to recover from its centuries of false summer, and nature had returned finally with renewed health. Snedeker scouted ahead as he had done a hundred times before on their journeys, ensuring their way was clear and free of danger. He found none. But every time he returned to report, he couldn't help but check in on the phoenix egg, reaching in through the leather bag's top flap to touch the warm crystal. They met few travelers on the road, who gave them strange but civil looks, eyeing aspects of the knight's odd, otherworldly garb.

Aderyn kept to herself despite Richard's best efforts to learn more about her. She had steel, he had to give her that. She kept her eyes on the surrounding forests and hills, watching for possible attack. The afternoon waned. As the sun began to set and night with its myriad star shine returned, the companions took refuge in a copse of fir trees well off the road. As the fire cooked their meal, Richard decided it was time to confront his fairy companion.

"What is your fascination with the egg, Snedeker?"

The small guide sat upon the unflapped leather bag containing the egg, staring down into its depths, mesmerized by the light that swirled within. The fey creature did not seem to hear the knight. Aderyn turned from watching the darkness, her sharp gaze on the fairy.

"Snedeker!" Richard shouted.

"What? *What?*" the fairy growled, finally looking up. His beady eyes flashed at the knight. "What is *wrong* with you, Rick?!"

"Me? What the hell is wrong with *you*?" the Heliwr shot back, nearly swatting the fairy into the night to return some common sense to him. "You've been fixated with that egg ever since we found it. Why? Does it have you under a spell or something?"

"No fairy can be spell-cast upon," Snedeker sniffed. "I just . . . like it. It's nice."

"It's nice?" Richard asked, surprised.

"Yes," Snedeker said, looking back down into the egg, its glow suffusing him. "Unlike *someone* I know."

"You speak to it?"

"I do."

Worry crept into Richard. His guide was going crazy.

"What does it say exactly?"

"Speak isn't the right word. It doesn't talk. Not exactly. I can sense its thoughts, its feelings. And it knows mine. It is alone. It is scared. And it has been waiting a long time. For me." He darted a look at Richard. "For us, I guess."

Richard snorted. "That's not possible. The phoenix within that egg knows nothing. How could it? It's not even born again. And if it is capable of sensing us, it's only done so during the time it has been in our care."

"It knows," the fairy said simply.

Richard shook his head, adding another thick branch to the fire.

"The fairy speaks truly, Heliwr," Aderyn interrupted his thoughts from the other side of the fire, her eyes glittering through the sparks that rose briefly toward the stars. "Your fairy guide can sense what the unborn phoenix is feeling. Even thinking."

"And now *you* finally decide to talk," Richard said, all the more annoyed.

"Do not attribute my silence to being a poor travel companion," the Druid said. "There is much to discuss. And it has taken me this long to find a way to begin it."

Richard poked at the fire with a stick, the heat hot on his hand. "I was hoping that Aengus had asked you to his office for a reason beyond being a mute."

"Probably several reasons, if truth be known. Ever since I met him several centuries ago, the Arch Druid has been a man possessed of great insight. It suits his role, knowing those of others," the woman said, ignoring his rebuke. "My role is largely as a historian, documenting the ancient fey of Annwn." She paused, looking toward the egg. "Even though the phoenix is not part of the fey technically, it had enough interactions with those of the Seelie and Unseelie Courts that their history is well documented—

at least for those who care to know about such things."

"And you do," Richard said.

"I do indeed," she said, her silver hair made orange-red by the fire. "You see, the phoenix has always been of particular interest to me. It shaped my youth and it continues to direct my life. It is the reason I came to Caer Dathal and took up the mantle of knowledge, although other reasons have taken up my many decades since then."

"And now you are going back home. Aengus thought it important that you do."

"He and he alone knows my past."

"Until you share it with me," the knight urged.

"No need to pry. I would have you both know the danger we face."

At least she sounded like she was willing to reveal that past. "I'm not real big on secrets," he admitted.

"We all have secrets, Heliwr," the Druid said softly.

"It has been my experience that secrets kept can kill," he said. "If it matters in our quest, tell me now. I've held long-standing grudges with friends for less."

Aderyn looked away, the wrinkles of her face pinched and deep. Richard waited. She would talk. Eventually. The fire snapped, shooting an ember away from their campsite. Minutes passed, the only other sounds the waking night creatures. She joined them finally. "I grew up in the Forest of Rhos, as I said," the Druid began. "I was born to Mother Ahlena Hier of the Anfarwol Order, a member of an ancient sect devoted to the phoenix. It was founded many centuries before my birth as a way to preserve the knowledge of a creature precious and unique, so that the phoenix may one day return. The phoenixes of old resided and were reborn in the Forest of Rhos, you see, and the founders of the Anfarwol Order gleaned if it was to rise again, it would do so there. I grew up amid a dozen families, each person devoted to learning everything there is to know about the phoenix.

"I left home—left the only life I had known, really—for several reasons, but highest among them was my mother. She became the head of the Order and, after several years, she had become quite extreme about it."

"How so?" Richard asked.

"She introduced strange rituals, ones not seen before," Aderyn said, shaking her head. "At the time, I did not know why. I went along with it, but I was too young, too naive, to know better. Now I know she did it to maintain her position. Her power. After several years, I left. I had grown into a woman who questioned everything and eventually that led to questioning my own mother."

"You certainly strike me as someone who knows what she wants." Richard said. He frowned. "What kinds of rituals though?"

"Deep within the Forest of Rhos, the phoenixes of old rebirthed upon a set of white granite cliffs that oversee the forest and the ocean to the north. There, my mother would hold gatherings. It began as dances. Then the dances became rites under the moon, a sharing of blood from the families so that the phoenix might rise again. Then men and women from different families began coupling upon the very stone beds that had once belonged to the creatures we promised to return. When I left—the reason why I had no choice but to leave—my mother began using the sacred ashes of the fallen phoenixes. In small ways, true, but ways never done by the Order's original founders." Aderyn could not hide the anger she still felt after so many years, eyes as hard as agates and lips made severe. "The families of the Anfarwol Order followed her, throughout all of it. Ardently. I could not do it."

"You were of the original, purer faith," Richard said. She nodded. "You kept quiet, knowing the wrong but unable to do anything about it."

"She would have killed me if I had. More than likely. In the name of the phoenix. I knew my danger," she said. "I fled in the night, oh so long ago. I do not regret it."

"You wonder what has become of them."

Aderyn nodded. "I do. Often."

"Worried what you will find there?" Richard asked.

"I am, although those I knew died long ago."

"The Anfarwol Order sounds like a cult, Rick," Snedeker

chimed in, his attention drawn away from the egg for a moment. "I hate cults."

"When you discovered this and left, you traveled to Caer Dathal," Richard said. "You needed to know. To learn. Not only about the world you had been withheld from but also the truth about the phoenix."

Aderyn nodded. "I can see why Aengus is fond of you, Heliwr. You have insight like he possesses. For three centuries, I have worked to learn as much as I could about the phoenix, not from the Anfarwol Order but from outside sources. Aengus Doughal knows this. It is why he called me to his office. No one knows the phoenix history like I do. And if someone can aid you, it would be me." She stoked the fire like Richard had been doing.

Richard said nothing. He let the information settle, feeling its gravity. He now knew why Aderyn had looked at the egg with reverence when they had left Caer Dathal. She understood its importance in a way that few could. It also opened up another set of problems. The fire snapped anew, pitch exploding like a mini grenade. How ironic they talked about the phoenix in front of a fire.

"When you saw the egg in the Arch Druid's chambers, you were afraid," the knight said finally, trying to get at the root of their danger. "What do you know about this creature that hunts it?"

"I know it had better not cross your fairy there. He seems quite protective," Aderyn said as she looked toward Snedeker and the phoenix egg, the first hint of a smile on her weathered lips. It vanished fast. "The creature hunting it—which will try to kill it before it has a chance of hatching—is called the ashterbach."

"The ashterbach," Richard repeated. "What is it?"

"A very old creature, one created by the Erlking of the Unseelie Court for one purpose. To kill the phoenix," Aderyn answered. "Phoenix fire has ever had the ability to rend shadows. The dark fey feared it, obviously. Whereas the dragons of Tal Ebolyon were challenged in the sky by the phoenix, the light of the phoenix could penetrate the deepest darkness, even of hearts." She paused, adding a log to the fire. "Many centuries ago, long before the Arch Druid and I came to Caer Dathal, there was a great war. I have never discovered how it began. But the devastation it wrought is documented. The Forest of Rhos and the Rhyd Wilvre were once one great forest, the Gwynedd Rhyd, spanning much of Annwn and north. The power expended in the war's battles destroyed much of it, blasting apart and burning great swaths of the ancient wood. You can probably guess the combatants in that war. The phoenix and the dragons of Tal Ebolyon. Two fire entities ruling the skies, and mortal enemies in nature.

"The Erlking of the Unseelie Court, in a fit of desperation, ventured into the darkest depths of the remaining great forest, the most resilient and powerful part of the wood," she continued. "In those depths, where not even sunlight ventured, he took the shadows—filled with absolute sorrow from the loss of their home—and melded them into a terrible new form, one capable of quenching the fire that had obliterated so much.

"When the Erlking named it, the creature gained its intelligence and power. The ashterbach is that name."

"The Erlking died. I saw it," Richard said. "He is unable to call upon it."

"And the Erlqueen gained all of his memories and abilities," the Druid said. "She will not endanger her new Unseelie family."

"Sounds worse than the elychher wizard in Paris, Rick," Snedeker interrupted.

"It is, fairy," Aderyn agreed. "It has no known weakness, no known crux. At least not from what I have learned." She looked deep into the coals. "I am not sure if we can even stop it if it finds us."

"Maybe it has no idea the phoenix has returned home," Richard offered.

"A creature like the ashterbach knows no maybes."

Richard felt the coolness of the night on his back even as the fire warmed his front. He shook his head at the irony. Nature had balancing mechanisms. It made sense that, after the fiery battles between the phoenix and dragons, nature would find a way to right the imbalance. The ashterbach was that mechanism. The problem came when there was an overcorrection. Now the Erlking's creation could eradicate a species.

It begged a question though. Which way would that pendulum swing back if Richard helped Aderyn return the phoenix to its rightful place in Anwnn's hierarchy? What could *he* accidentally unleash?

"I will take first watch," Aderyn said. "Rest. We travel far the next two days."

The Heliwr nodded, knowing she needed some time to wind down from the conversation. He opened up his bedroll and realized how relieved he was to lay down. The injuries done him in Paris still lingered, and while he had the ability to heal faster than most, he needed the call of sleep to prepare for what would probably come.

"Snedeker, do not stay up all night," Richard said at last.

The fairy sat hypnotized by the light emitted by the egg. Richard turned away and looked up at the night sky strewn with diamonds. Before the warmth of the fire lulled him to sleep, he heard his fairy guide's quiet murmuring to the phoenix.

It sounded like Snedeker was singing a lullaby.

It felt as if he had only just closed his eyes.

"Heliwr! It is here!" Aderyn shouted him awake.

Richard bolted out of his bedroll. The fire had dwindled but had not gone out, its light now barely pushing back the shadows at the fringe of their campsite. The Druid stood by his side, shirtsleeves pushed up to her elbows. She looked toward the south and its darkness. Richard did the same, scanning the wild woods there, gripping the Dark Thorn that had materialized the moment he had been called awake. Adrenaline replaced his aches and pains. The magic of his office bolstered him.

Snedeker had taken up defense of the egg as well. Just as Richard was about to order him into a shielding position above, the knight's vision dimmed, as if fainting but without the faded loss of consciousness.

Next to him, fire sprang down the length of the Druid's bare arms.

"The ashterbach!" she hissed.

A low moan entered the wood, the sound of an eerie wind at great distance. The shadows of the night coalesced; the darkness deepened about them. Having a hard time even comprehending what he saw at first, the ink slithered through the wood from many different directions, advancing upon their position, the light of the campfire being slowly drained as if a black hole approached. Unsure of what he saw, Richard focused on his own power, ensuring any number of spells were ready, the Dark Thorn anchoring him to the magic in the world as well as his innate own.

The feathery tendrils of what Aderyn had called the ashterbach paused as if gauging them, their fire, or both.

Then, like a whip, they lashed out.

The first attack struck Aderyn. The Druid brought her fire up, warding them all from the living smoke that sought the companions, her fire filling the night's air with bright orange and yellow. Richard added his while also shielding the Druid, letting her work. Heat seared the campsite, dry hotness that the knight breathed. He could feel Aderyn's power, magic from the Druid growing in intensity. Pressure in his ears built, muffled like he was underwater, until Richard realized it was the screaming pain of the shadows around the group as the fire fought them off.

The pressure withdrew, along with the tendrils. Aderyn pulled back her power, arms still ablaze. Richard maintained his shield, the Dark Thorn hot in his hands. Snedeker sat upon the egg, scanning the dark, ready to add his own fey magic if needed.

Just when Richard wondered if the ashterbach had fled, the fire along Aderyn's arms flared brighter.

"It's back," she hissed.

The ashterbach struck faster. Richard almost didn't respond in time. The shadows coalesced more urgently, more fiercely, fighting the powerful fiery light that the Druid threw at it. The Heliwr kept the Dark Thorn anchored to the ground, drawing on the magic of Annwn, helping Aderyn keep the powerful Unseelie creation at bay, all the while trying to discover its real origin. Looking deeper into the night's gloom and at the edge of his vision where the forest met their campsite, Richard could just make out more movement, a shimmering void like an oil slick blacker than the night, and within it a large birdlike thing with wings, a sharp eagle beak, and eyes that glimmered cold silver. The shadows attacking them twisted from its dark wings, an extension of its obsidian feathers, infiltrating the campsite.

Before Richard could turn his power to fight the hidden creature, another shadowy wisp whipped out at the Druid's legs, catching one of them and spinning Aderyn aside and into the air like a doll, her power dying. She landed hard and cried out, her robe blackening and falling away to dust where the ashterbach had touched her.

Richard rushed to stand over her, bringing the might of his magic to bear. The ashterbach hated light and fire—he'd give it both. One of the first spells he learned sprang to his lips, and with the Dark Thorn hot in his hands, he unleashed the hellish fury, a combination of fire bright like the sun and spreading from him in a ring. The ashterbach shrieked in response but it fought him, trying to find a way through his assault and into his defenses. It was all he could do to keep it at bay. He dropped to one knee, the magic Richard needed to keep the spell alive draining him. He knew he would not be able to keep them safe for much longer.

"Snedeker!" Richard roared, even as Aderyn added her magic to his own.

The fairy guide did not falter. He rose up into the air, wings ablur, sprinkling silver dust from his pack over the fallen Druid and the Heliwr, the magic forming a bright cocoon of light over their campsite. The ashterbach did not stop. Its darkness rammed the fairy's shield even as the Druid and Heliwr regained their feet. The light began to dim then, dark tendrils from the ashterbach already breaking through the skein of magic.

If his spells, her power, and fairy magic couldn't stop it, their death would come quicker than he ever imagined possible.

The fairy guide left him, flying back to the egg. Keeping the fount of his power battling the creature, Richard cursed that the fairy just wanted one more look at the egg before their end.

Surely the fairy sensed the knight's power waned and would fail soon.

Nothing would be able to stop the ashterbach then.

Out of the corner of his eye, Richard saw the fairy untie the leather strings that held the egg within its pouch. Smooth crystal shown out of the bag, its depths growing brighter and brighter until even Richard had to look away. A swirl of orange, red, and yellow fire spilled into the night, seeking the ashterbach's tendrils, bulldozing them aside and pushing them back toward the creature's hidden space. The power from the egg slammed into the body of the ashterbach then, lifting it off the ground, the light crawling all over the creature like electricity over a magnet. The ashterbach let out an inhuman howl of anguish, the screech of a giant eagle filling the night with pain. Flung hard into the trees around it, the Unseelie beast fought to untangle itself, the fire running over its feathers and back. It got free and fled deeper into the forest, flames going with it.

The only sound in Richard's ears was his own heavy, strained breathing. It caught in his chest when he saw the egg.

The crystal had gone dark.

"No, no, no," Snedeker screamed with a panic Richard had never heard from his fairy companion before, tiny hands upon its smooth surface.

A spark rekindled within the depths of the crystal then. The purple and orange light within it blossomed once more.

But it had become smaller, less bright.

The Heliwr went to Aderyn. "How hurt are you?" he asked.

"I will live," Aderyn grumbled

"That thing," the Heliwr said, shaking his head. "I've never seen anything like it. Felt like it was draining me."

"It is as I feared. The ashterbach," she said, looking over her robes. "It absorbs magic driven by energy, by heat, by light. Any magic not of the shadows. It would have killed you. And me. To get at the phoenix."

"Why has the egg dimmed?" Richard asked.

"The phoenix is a powerful creature, even within its protective egg. It knows what transpires around us; it likely knows the ashterbach was trying to kill it. It reacted in the only way it knows how. But its magic is not infinite. It expends energy, its lifeforce, and by expending it becomes lesser than it was before."

Richard didn't like the sound of that. "And if the ashterbach returns enough times and we can't stop it . . ."

"The phoenix will die. Withered. Within its egg," the Druid said. "Lost to the world forever."

The mountain rose above all, the forest below paying homage to it.

Richard pulled Lyrian to a halt, giving his great mount a respite from their arduous flight through the Forest of Rhos. Truth be told, the Heliwr needed it too. The night, the next day, and the previous night had been exhausting. No sleep, no rest. The ashterbach had attacked four more times, coming at them at different times, in various ways, and in broken patterns. Just on the other side of the Saith yn Col ruins, a barely perceptible shift of the sunlight had alerted them that the ashterbach tried to steal the egg's pouch. That night, the beast had attacked from the nighttime sky. The last two times had been direct assaults like the first one. Each time the Heliwr, Snedeker, and Aderyn Hier fought it. With every means that they possessed. Each time, the ashterbach almost reached the egg. And every time, the only magic that had any effect on the dark Unseelie creature was that of the phoenix.

The fire within the egg had now shrunk dramatically, its once robust purple-orange flame reduced to the size of a candle's flame. Snedeker fretted over the egg constantly.

Richard feared the worst.

They had last fought the ashterbach that morning, the egg fending it off, before Richard and Aderyn gained the Forest of Rhos. Draped in the shadows of the ancient wood where the ashterbach could easily hide and pull strength from, the final leg of their journey to the distant white cliffs promised to be the most dangerous.

But the ashterbach had not attacked again. And as the afternoon waned to lengthening shadows of evening, uneasiness grew within Richard as Aderyn guided them to the heights of the white granite cliffs.

"Who do you suspect is here?" Richard asked. "You would not be bringing us if you did not know the answer to my question. And you are on edge, I can feel it. You did not share everything the other night."

Aderyn gave him a withering look. "As I said, my mother once ruled here. It could be anyone from the former families, descendants of the Anfarwol Order."

"Maybe they are gone," Snedeker offered.

"If so, it would be the first good luck we've had," Richard said. "I have no desire to fight a cult, let alone a cult *and* the ashterbach."

"Let us hope for the best then," Aderyn shared.

They made their way up the path, the giant cliffs above a warning to Richard. The Heliwr kept the Dark Thorn close, its magic at his command more readily. He knew the need would arise. The ashterbach could kill them in any number of ways now—through the forest or from the air or higher up where even the forest dropped away from the path that clung to the side of the mountain and snaked upward. Richard had once found out the hard way how dangerous high mountain footpaths could be when Unseelie creatures had attacked him just below the dragon stronghold of Tal Ebolyon. The ashterbach could try to send them tumbling to their deaths below. The egg would be easy prey then, especially as weak as it had become.

Swaying upon Lyrian as they gained elevation, Richard pushed his senses into the natural world, seeking the ashterbach. He felt no presence of the deadly wraith.

The Heliwr wondered why it did not attack.

He looked back at Aderyn. She rode behind him, keeping her eyes locked on the reaches above where the trees had begun to thin, giving way to stubborn rock. This part of the world she knew well. Richard hated to admit it, but he was pleased the Arch Druid requested her for this journey. Especially if the Anfarwol Order still existed somewhere in these environs, a cult world that only she could navigate.

"Where did you live here, once upon a time?" Richard asked her.

The Druid pointed. "On the other side of the mountain. This path leads us to the top where the phoenix may birth, but there is another similar path on the other side that leads down into the village."

"Are you not curious to see if your home still stands?"

"I would be lying if I said no," Aderyn said, her steely confidence the only thing keeping her weariness at bay. "But we are not here for a social gathering, are we?"

"Not at all," the Heliwr agreed.

The two went quiet. Snedeker continued to scout and return at various times. He had nothing to report; they encountered no one. Birds sang and insects buzzed, nothing amiss. The exposed granite above glowed in the sunlight, drawing them on as if a beacon, the rest of the world falling away as they climbed. The wildness of the Forest of Rhos disappeared, its living sentience left behind, but ancient fir trees that had long ago found purchase on the mountain still offered shade and places where the ashterbach could hide. Richard remained vigilant. One never could tell where an attack would come from until it was too late. Better safe than dead.

The path began to level eventually. The forest grew wild again to either side of the trail, trees growing larger, their trunks wide and boughs thick into their heights. The air had become cooler, a reprieve from the heat below. Richard led upon Lyrian, heading directly toward a heart of shattered stone that rose above even the ancient trees like a throne for a giant sitting on top of the mountain.

"The home of Annwn's phoenix is ahead," Aderyn shared.

Richard appraised the situation as they grew closer. It was level ground leading up to the stone, much better to fend off the ashterbach than the steep trail they had just taken. The trees offered cover from the air once more. But the bed of upheaved granite stood before them, scarred by ash and exposed to the sky.

"The place looks recently used," he said. "You can tell by the soot."

"Agreed," Aderyn said, eyes scanning about.

"Snedeker, take a look around."

The fairy grumped about his lot in life while flying off, circling the top of the mountain. It did not take him long to return. "I found nothing," he said. "The only thing on the other side of this precipice is more white stone. Although there is artwork carved upon the rock here. Images in relief of the phoenix in various stages of life. And at its base the entire way around? Stacked wood as if ready for a bonfire."

"No ashes? Anywhere?" Richard asked.

"None."

"For the new phoenix to rise, we need the ashes of the old. The egg requires it, if history recounts fact," Aderyn said, dismounting and walking toward the stone edifice. She pointed to the place most blackened by ages of soot. "McAllister, place your ward there. Maybe the residual ash can split the crystal and free the phoenix."

Richard did just that, although he didn't think it would work. He had to try though, despite the hope in the other's voice. He took the egg from its leather bag—the sunlight of the day shimmering within the crystal and drowning out the weak flame within—and carried it toward a long smooth stone that almost looked like a bench. He glanced up at the frieze that had been carved into the mountain granite, able to make out images of a full-grown phoenix as it grew from egg to adult, its entire life cycle in one amazing and beautiful work of art.

He then placed the warm egg on the stone where soot seemed to be the most concentrated.

Nothing happened.

"This does not bode well," Richard said, glancing around. "I wonder wha—"

His eyes fell on the woman then.

She stood in the shadows, watching them, made a part of the wild wood about them by the dark green hooded cloak she wore. When she realized that she had been noticed, she strode forward then even as other shapes materialized out of the forest's gloom, a dozen men and women, all bearing weapons. And a lot of them.

The woman in front stopped about a dozen yards away and lowered her cowl. Sharp features. Long braided brunette hair.

And striking blue eyes that held eons of insight. At once, Aderyn breathed surprised acknowledgment.

"Mother?" she whispered. "This cannot be."

The woman approached the Druid, reaching out hands. Aderyn returned the gesture, gripping the other's gently. She laughed, a happy sound. "It cannot be because I should be long dead? You as well. Yet here you are."

"I am a Druid of Caer Dathal. We lead long lives."

The other nodded, eyes glimmering pleasure. "Out of all of my children, you always did have a powerful spirit. Intuitive. Smart. I am not surprised."

"But how is this possible?" Aderyn asked. "It's been centuries."

"You mean, why am I not buried?" the woman asked. "Let us just say that the power of this place is rooted in the permanence of fire."

Richard peered more intently at the two, trying to glean more about this new woman and what kind of family relationship she had with her daughter. There was a family resemblance, no doubt, although Aderyn's mother appeared far younger than her Druid daughter. He gave Snedeker a dark look. The fairy returned it. They had not expected this. But if there was one thing Richard had to constantly remind himself, magic had the ability to make the impossible possible. This was just one more instance. It was important to remain steady despite the surprise. The cult leader having magic at her disposal clearly opened up a box with even more questions than answers—would she be friend or foe in this endeavor that they had set out on? How would Richard handle it if the Anfarwol Order turned against his mission? And what magic did she possess?

Aderyn turned to him. "I am honored for you to meet Fianna Hier, Ard-Sagart of the Anfarwol Order. Mother, this is Richard McAllister, Heliwr of the Yn Saith, and his fairy companion, Snedeker of the Oakwell clan. Both friends to the Arch Druid of Caer Dathal the New and friends of my own as well."

The Druid had mentioned Aengus Doughal. She had done it with intent. Aderyn was trying to impress his importance upon her mother. An introduction but a warning too. Power had a way of only recognizing other power. Richard did not know how Fianna Hier had become Ard-Sagart—the High Priestess of the Anfarwol Order—but her daughter had made sure the mother would take him seriously.

"The Oakwell fairy there has a most prized object in his possession," Fianna Hier said, eyes narrowed upon the exposed egg. Her excitement was obvious. Whispers gathered at her back, the Anfarwol Order members taking note. "But we should not talk of it here. I sense shadows speaking. The ashterbach has been loosed once more." She paused, frowning at her daughter. "You should have known better, Aderyn, bringing a phoenix egg here without first sending word. We have protections and protocols for this event. You know this."

"I do, mother," Aderyn said. "I had no way of knowing if you were alive or the Order still even here. We have been adept at keeping the egg safe thus far. The Unseelie hunter has attacked several times. The egg is still here."

"All the more reason to go. We have much to discuss and prepare for."

"Ard-Sagart, I am pleased to be here and at service," Richard said, playing the role of politician that he always hated but which Merle forced upon him. "It is a dark visit though. I would rather finish this journey with a birth. Now." He pointed at the egg. "We need ashes from the previous phoenix. You have knowledge on this, I believe."

"That is what we must talk about," Fianna Hier said, averting her eyes. "Better to do so at our home from a position of strength. We have might at our disposal, Heliwr. Best we are protected by it."

Richard nodded, annoyed at being put off. He had no choice in the matter though, and he had to play by her rules until he could gauge more about the situation. Before he could acknowledge the request, a man from her group approached with measured steps. He was young, tall, and lean, handsome in the way that most bearded redhead men were in their twenties.

"Ard-Sagart, if I may," he said, unwilling to look her in the eye, deference in his every movement. "Do you believe that the Heliwr and the Druid could help with Laura?"

"My consort," Fianna Hier said in apology rather than introduction. She looked at Richard, measuring him. He knew distrust when he saw it. It unsettled him further. "One of my daughters is quite ill. A wasting sickness. I have done all that is within my own meager power. Her loss would be of a great pain to the Anfarwol Order."

"I am not a healer," Richard said. "But I know a few things. And Aderyn has likely learned a great deal during her time at Caer Dathal."

"Very well. I welcome your aid. You shall be our guests tonight," she said, glancing back at her consort and those behind him. "We will celebrate in this clearing tomorrow night as the moon rises. The phoenix has returned!"

Excited murmuring filled those behind her. Fianna Hier nodded to Richard, replaced her cowl, and headed back the direction they had come, into the forest and beyond. The Heliwr gathered the egg while Aderyn gained their mounts.

"Are you sure about this?" Snedeker said, watching the phoenix egg go back into its bag. "I don't trust her. And we should be trying to birth the phoenix tonight."

"What other recourse do we have?" the Heliwr said.

"Troll-fack, Rick. The phoenix doesn't trust her!"

"Oh?" Richard said. "It told you that, did he?"

"She," the fairy corrected. "And yes."

Richard slung the pack over his shoulder and walked after Aderyn. "Then I suggest you keep an eye out," he said. "And keep listening to her."

Snedeker flew ahead and upward as he had done so many times during their tenure as Heliwr and guide. Even though he adored the egg, he would keep watch from the trees as his duty required, the best way the Oakwell fairy could protect the unborn phoenix and the Heliwr as well. Aderyn led the on her steed with Richard mounted upon Lyrian, the congregation of Fianna Hier long since vanished back the way they had come.

"We must be cautious, Heliwr," Aderyn whispered from ahead,

turning in her seat. "These are people who have shut out the world."

"Feeling uneasy about this?"

The Druid nodded. "Something does not feel right."

"It doesn't," Richard agreed. "The ashterbach attacked us multiple times on our journey. Now here, nothing. Haven't seen even a hint of it. Why?"

"I don't know," Aderyn said. "But it is still out there. And it still wants to kill that phoenix, one way or another."

The Heliwr of the Yn Saith hiked the pack up higher on his shoulder, keeping it safe as they rode. None of it made any sense. Then again, events in Annwn rarely did. Preconceptions could kill in this land and survival meant being open to all possibilities—no matter how odd or inconceivable. Richard had survived a long time, longer than most in his position. He had done so by being cautious, by looking at all angles, and keeping focused on the problem at hand. Right now, he was entering a viper pit of cultists, even if their intentions may be in the right place. He would wait to discover that on his own.

It didn't take long to reach the village. It was clear that the Anfarwol Order had remained a small sect, the homes relegated to several dozen just down the hill from the mountain's stone summit. The massive trees above them had been limbed high, and many paths connected one home to another below. After the group had been shown comfortable accommodations, the Ard-Sagart escorted them to a larger home, one better constructed and filled with lavish items. Richard knew it to be her residence.

"Tomorrow night will see the Anfarwol Order's dedication come to fruition, a celebration. Tonight, though, I thought it would be a good time to see to the needs of my daughter, Laura Goodnight," Fianna Hier said, having made some tea and guiding them to a door that led to a side room. Her consort listened to her, then bowed his head and left. "And possibly become reacquainted with my first daughter after so long."

"You had a Goodnight as a consort, Mother?" Aderyn asked.

"I did. You remember that honorable line then," Fianna Hier said, nodding her approval. "He was a good man, like those you knew so long ago. Now dust ten years gone. He did give me Laura, and I thank the phoenix for that."

Richard couldn't imagine living so long that one could have multiple wives or husbands, multiple sets of children in different centuries. He found it unnerved him in some visceral way.

Fianna Hier opened the door. Beyond was a room lit by several candles that drove back the darkness of the coming night outside the window. On the bed lay a blanketed woman, lithe and fair, long dark hair framing a face serene and beautiful. Though dark circles swam under her eyes and her skin carried a waxy sheen. She did not awaken, eyes fitfully darting beneath their lids. She had been ill for some time.

"What is wrong with her?" Richard asked.

"We do not know. But there seems to be no cure."

The Heliwr went to her bedside. He sat beside her.

"May I?"

The girl's mother mulled it over, eyes taking in Richard's measure, before drinking a sip of her tea and shrugging, stepping aside. The Heliwr picked up the young woman's hands, warming them with his own, calling upon the magic of two worlds. The heat of magic responded, and he sent the abilities the Dark Thorn afforded him into her body, seeking what he knew would be there, hunting for the affliction. In a moment, he returned to himself.

"She is dying," Richard said. "Burning up. A malignancy unlike anything I've ever encountered before. But not of the flesh. In the blood. Dank gray spots traveling through her, clotting, a moving fever. I could not pin down its origin. Was she in contact with anything unusual before this?"

"Nothing that the rest of us haven't been," Fianna Hier said. She looked down on her daughter, concern etched in her features. "I had hoped that Aderyn would take on the mantle that I would pass along one day. When she left, I took it upon myself to find another who would do so. From the moment she was born, I knew it would be Laura. But now she is dying. And all my greatest fears are here."

"That you may lose another daughter," Aderyn said.

"That the Anfarwol Order would end without the wisdom I

can pass on to one of my children," Fianna Hier said. She took a sip of her tea and moved to sit on the bed next to her daughter. "A life's work wasted, knowledge lost."

"Losing a loved one is never easy," Richard said, thinking back to his long-dead wife. He decided to ask the hard question. "How is it that you've lived these many centuries? A Druid like Aderyn can live with quite an extended life. But you are not a Druid. And not one of the Seelie or Unseelie, as far as I can tell."

The woman darkened, eyes turned fiery. "There are many forms of longevity in this world. And there are some secrets that should not be shared."

"You can tell me," Richard pressed. "After all, I'm beholden to Myrddin Emrys, a man who has lived far longer than even you."

"It may help, Mother," Aderyn added.

"Knight of the Yn Saith," Fianna Hier said, her mouth twisting ugly. "I have encountered your kind twice before. You do not know everything, and nor should you. If you cannot help her, the fate of my daughter will be as the phoenix wills it." She paused, looking out the window. "On to happier things. We will have a joyous feast tonight. We will celebrate. And we will free the phoenix within its egg. We will dance and chant and call to those who came before and pray it will bless Laura back to health."

Richard did not want to fight with the Ard-Sagart. Too much was at stake with birthing the phoenix once more. Fianna Hier acted like cult leaders he had witnessed in the past—hiding information to create mystery that could be leveraged.

Fianna Hier tipped her tea cup to Laura's lips. Some of the liquid entered the other's mouth. Richard was not sure, but he thought he saw vitality color her cheeks and a reduction in darkness beneath her eyes.

The Heliwr gave Snedeker a look. The fairy returned it.

What had transpired had not been lost on his fairy guide.

"It has been a long trip," Richard said. "I would love some of that tea to help rid the road's dust from my tongue."

"The tea is for my family, and none other. But I shall find you refreshment that will be to your liking," Fianna Hier said, standing to leave, brushing aside the knight's wishes. "There is much to do. I will prepare the Order for the forthcoming joy."

"The fire . . . is . . . coming. And darkness," Laura said then, eyes fluttering but not fully opening. Her mother stopped and turned, shock on her face.

"What fire? What darkness?" Richard asked, leaning closer.

"They rise, together," Laura added. She turned her head then, weakly, eyes still closed but facing toward the backpack with the egg in it.

As if she sensed it.

"Laura, come back to us," her mother said. "Please."

The daughter said nothing further though, returned to whatever coma she had been in. Fire and darkness couldn't rise together. It made no sense. The words she had spoken infiltrated Richard, took root as worry. The phoenix. The ashterbach. The Anfarwol Order and its cult leader. The Druid. A fairy enchanted by the egg. It left Richard feeling cold inside, the Heliwr unable to unravel the puzzle before him.

And all the while, he could not ignore how the Ard-Sagart had reacted to his request for a cup of tea.

A tea that had lent a flush to her cheeks.

He stood as well then, aware that his own magic might not be up to the test.

What had he gotten himself into?

The knock at the door tore Richard from fitful sleep.

He swung his legs off the bed, awake in an instant. He had been tossing and turning, aware of every nighttime sound, discerning if it could be the ashterbach. He looked over at Aderyn. She sat in a chair across the room, having taken the first watch to keep the egg safe. Their eyes met. Snedeker had awoken too, the fairy fallen asleep upon the egg, in the best place to protect it. The Unseelie creature had not shown itself again—yet—leaving Richard with growing unease at why. And having observed the Anfarwol Order the previous evening, the Heliwr now believed they had fallen into a pit of vipers without knowing which snake would strike first.

Richard stood and called the Dark Thorn. The warm wood materialized. With a nod to Aderyn, he went to the door and opened it.

Fianna Hier stood in the doorway, cloaked and hooded. "We must go, Heliwr. Now."

Richard did not move. "Why?"

The Ard-Sagart pushed her way in and closed the door. "By design," she said, looking to her daughter. "The Anfarwol Order believes we will be releasing the phoenix tomorrow night. I wished that. A rebirth has never been done, not so long after its fiery death. I do not want outside influence impeding us."

"Like any group, there are factions?" Aderyn guessed.

"I do not fear my Order companions, daughter," she said. "I simply do not want a committee telling me how to do this. Even with centuries of study, I do not know how this will go, only the bits and pieces I've gleaned."

"Do you have the ashes?" Snedeker asked.

Fianna Hier brought forth a small rock-hewn urn with a flame chiseled into its side.

"The sooner the better," Richard said, already gathering the pack with the egg. "We have waited too long already."

The four of them left the little home. Richard walked with the Dark Thorn before him, sending tendrils of magic into the night, seeking any danger that could lie in wait. He discovered none. The moon had risen, casting a weak light for them to see by, and the shadows lay thick beneath the canopy of ancient trees they passed under. Snedeker flew from tree to tree, a blur of quicksilver above. Only the sounds of an awake night greeted them as they traveled upward along well-worn paths, diamonds within the star-strewn sky seen between thinning leaves. Upon reflection, the Heliwr was pleased Fianna Hier had decided this course of action. Fewer people present meant he could focus on protecting the egg if the ashterbach attacked—without worry of innocent people getting hurt.

When they gained the massive thrust of white granite at the mountain's top, Richard swept the area with his magic, as did Snedeker. They were alone. The Heliwr noticed the Anfarwol Order had been busy during the day, dry firewood logs added to the existing stacks along the rock edifice. It was the only change that he witnessed though; the carved life stages of the phoenix still bore the scars of past fire.

"Bring forth the egg, Heliwr of the Yn Saith Richard McAllister," Fianna Hier said with formality, standing upon the ash-smeared stone. She held the urn with its ashes.

Richard let the Dark Thorn fade and did as he was instructed, removing the egg from its pack. The crystal warmed his hands, pulsing with life. The orange-purple light of the phoenix within had lessened after so many attacks, but the Heliwr could feel its vibrant life still. He took a steadying breath as he placed the egg upon the ashes that Fianna Hier had scattered upon the rock at her feet.

"Step back," Fianna Hier instructed, eyes alight.

Richard and Aderyn did, but only a few steps. Snedeker sat upon the Heliwr's shoulder, hopeful eyes staring at the egg.

Fianna Hier began to chant then, arms raised as if calling power from the sky.

"What is she doing?" Richard whispered to Aderyn.

"I do not know," the Druid said, frowning. "I have been gone a long time, but this chant and language is not something I have discovered in my own pursuits. It is . . . dark."

As the words echoed off the granite, the light inside the egg began to twist this way and that, becoming more frantic with every word spoken.

"Rick!" Snedeker yelled. "The phoenix is afraid."

Recalling the Dark Thorn, the Heliwr strode forward, to put an end to whatever was going on and to demand answers, when he caught a vast darkness gathering in the night sky. It deepened until the ashterbach landed upon the rock face above, giant talons gripping the granite, baleful eyes glinting malevolence.

"Mother!" Aderyn yelled, bringing her fiery magic to bear.

The Ard-Sagart paid her no heed.

"Do not approach, daughter!"

Snedeker shot like a dart at the creature, unwavering, his silver dust thrown above and at the ashterbach. The Unseelie screeched rage and deflected it, the dust exploding fire along the birdlike monster's shielding wings, the fairy's magic not harming it. Roaring, Richard sent his fire at the beast as well, trying to keep the ashterbach from falling upon Fianna Hier and destroying the egg.

"Mother, no!" Aderyn screamed from his side. Richard glimpsed what the Druid had already seen.

A hammer in her hand—even as she brought it down as if to an anvil.

The crystal shrieked at the strike, as did the light within. It couldn't be the way to rebirth the phoenix. Confirming his fears, Aderyn was upon her mother like a wailing banshee, arms coated in angry flame, the Druid trying to wrestle the weapon away and keep it from hitting the egg again.

Richard had no time to help or even react. The ashterbach attacked, flying at the knight, a landslide of darkness falling. It was all he could do to stay on his feet, bringing the power of the Dark Thorn up as a shield like he had done so many times already. The Unseelie creature raged at the magic, trying to fight through its protection. It clawed and bit. It smothered him with its tendrils and wings. The Heliwr felt his limited strength waning, the man pressed into the ground, the air about him filled with the shadow of rotting, dead things.

One giant talon made its way through his magic—and picked him up effortlessly, flinging him like a pebble.

Encasing himself in a cocoon of magic, Richard still gritted his teeth as he slammed into the ground yards away from the carved stone edifice. Stunned, he regained his footing.

It was too late. The ashterbach already rushed toward the egg.

Richard yelled warning, running to help, but Snedeker had already seen the danger. The fairy had taken up a defensive posture over Aderyn, who now cradled her unmoving mother in her arms near the phoenix egg, the leader of the Anfarwol Order staring vacantly at nothing. When Snedeker saw the coming

Unseelie, he flew overhead, tiny pack with its dust held at the ready. The feathery tendrils of the ashterbach reached for him. The fairy threw his remaining silvery dust at the beast, a last-ditch effort to keep safe the phoenix.

It was not enough. The Unseelie creature swiped the dust away even as its beak snapped upon the body of the fairy, dark magic coursing into its prey.

Snedeker vaporized, spit out as ash on the air.

"No!" Richard yelled.

The Dark Thorn became hotter in his hands than it had ever been, the wood barely able to channel all the fury within him to the fore.

Wrapped in its darkness, the ashterbach reached for the egg.

Powered by the death of his longtime fairy guide and friend, Richard sent his magic at the nightmare creature. Fire became a hurricane within him. Driven by need. By vengeance. By sorrow. The Unseelie creature fought him, dark wings beating at the knight, but it would not relent. Magic coursed in his blood and heart, but it would not be enough. He didn't care though. He would burn it to cinders or be consumed himself.

"Heliwr! The fire to me!" Aderyn screamed.

Heat threatened to undo him, the flames he had called into existence hotter than any dragon's furnace. He saw what the Druid wanted then. He sent his power forward, not at the descending ashterbach but at Aderyn Hier. She sat now with the egg upon her dead mother's lap even as she cradled both, the Druid alive with fire that did not kill her somehow. When Richard's fire met her own, Aderyn absorbed the torrent of power, channeling it, becoming one with it. It twisted around her and upward in a tornado of yellows, reds, and oranges, fending off the ashterbach for a small time. Not immune to the fire, Fianna Hier blackened, hair disintegrating, then flesh, and after that even her bones. Red-hot ash of her mother coated Aderyn while the Druid held onto the egg, but the ashterbach did not stop.

A loud crack shattered the night—and the phoenix rose from the broken crystal of its egg, the orange-purple flame coming into contact with the air and erupting into a brilliance of fire forming the shape of a bird, not as a hatchling but as a rival to the ashterbach's size. The phoenix rose above them, growing, expanding, its fire-tipped wings reaching wide into the night sky. It seemed to encompass the world.

The ashterbach attacked, seemingly not concerned by the great bird's appearance, grappling with its fiery foe. The phoenix pulled power from Aderyn Hier, draining the fire that she and Richard had created. It latched onto the Unseelie creature with talons of its own and sent the fire coursing into an enemy that had killed so many of its kind.

The ashterbach howled once—fighting to get free—before the power flushed the darkness of its body and disintegrated it into melted nighttime shadows.

Peace filled the night.

The Unseelie hunter was no more.

—Heliwr of the Yn Saith Richard McAllister—

The voice entered his mind; it sounded like the crackling of a fire.

Richard looked up from where he knelt, where he had seen the ashes of his fairy guide fall, tears for the loss of his friend making his vision blurry. The phoenix hovered above him, brighter than the day, its form etched in flame, heat pouring off of it from its ethereal release. The heat should have burned him but it did him no harm, as if it had embraced him. He had rarely seen anything so beautiful or more alive.

"I am here," he said simply.

—I am what once was, from whence my long days had forgotten. You gave my memory remembrance. Your companion gave his life so that memory could become real again. It is a life that I owe you—

Richard looked around, dazed. Aderyn lay on the stone shelf, unmoving. No evidence of her mother existed. All that remained there were the crystal shards of the phoenix egg, crystal that had once been lovingly caressed by Snedeker—a fairy who only wanted to help another creature live.

Heavier tears came unbidden to the Heliwr, the weight in his chest pressing his sorrow out. His fairy. His guide. His friend.

Dead.

The tears increased, and the world swam within them.

—Snedeker—

The name of his longtime fairy friend.

Richard blinked the tears away as he felt magic. Ancient magic not in existence for centuries. He understood that much. The Heliwr saw the ashes of the fairy that had seemingly been lost rise into the air, could feel they did so at the bidding of the phoenix. Its power gently gathered all that was left of his friend, the remains spinning in the air, like a person deciding where pieces fit in a jigsaw puzzle. The gray grit swirled in a mini tornado, taking form once more, and slowly began to move toward Richard.

Unsure why he did so, he reached out, closing his eyes with hope of what could be happening.

When he opened his eyes, Snedeker lay upon his hands, little wings flexing.

His friend. Alive again.

—Keep safe in this most dangerous of worlds, Heliwr of the Yn Saith. It is the greatest gift I can give you. The gift of each other—

"Thank you," Richard whispered. It was all he could say.

The phoenix rose then, the fire of its form cooling. In a few minutes, the phoenix had become a regular bird in appearance if not in size, to vanish into the wild. Richard watched the space where it had gone, disbelieving the magic that had just happened. Still cradling the sleeping fairy, he then went to Aderyn. The Heliwr sat next to her and called upon the remaining magic he possessed of his office, its warmth spreading from him into her. He closed his eyes, concentrating. After a few minutes, her eyes fluttered open.

Confusion became worry.

"What happened?" she croaked, voice ragged.

"The phoenix happened," Richard said, still trying to believe it all. "How do you feel? It can't be good."

"My mother," the Druid said, shaking her head. She looked so frail. "I had to kill her. She would not stop and would have ended me if given the choice between me or more magic. More magic of the phoenix."

"With the ash she was taking in her tea," Richard said, thinking back on the previous day and meeting Laura Goodnight. Aderyn nodded. "Phoenix ash that kept her young somehow. The same ash that made her other daughter ill probably. Your mother wanted more of it. That's why she wanted to kill the creature in the egg."

"I told you," Aderyn said, sitting up with his help. "The phoenix is a powerful creature. Even its ashes are potent. For centuries, my mother used the remaining ash of the last phoenix to keep herself vital. That is clear to me now, the phoenix rising once placed upon her ashes—ashes mingled with those she had absorbed to stay so young. For decades I thought I had forsaken her. Now I understand I did the right thing without even knowing it. I took a different path, one I hoped would make a difference."

"It did make a difference. I suppose we'll never know how the phoenix was able to bring Snedeker back."

Aderyn looked down on the little fairy. "We know exactly what did that. Love."

"Love?"

"Snedeker cared for the phoenix. They were friends. He gave his life for his friend. Is that not what friends do, Heliwr?" the Druid asked.

Richard couldn't argue. He realized he would have given his life for Snedeker if need be. "What of you now? The Anfarwol Order will want to know what happened here? How their leader died? What became of the phoenix?"

"I will remain here," Aderyn said. "To recover as well as plan. My sister needs someone to care for her, someone who can help. Perhaps in time, if she recovers, I can teach her the power I've gained as a Druid. Maybe . . . maybe . . . she can take our mother's place as leader of the Anfarwol Order."

"They won't turn on you?" he asked. "Blame you for her death?"

She smiled wanly. "I am old but still quite formidable."

Richard nodded. "You are definitely that. You still think there is need for the Order though?"

"There is always a need for knowledge, especially for the wise who seek it."

Richard looked down on Snedeker, who had awoken, sat up, yawned, and stretched his wings as if testing them for the first time. "Are you okay?" Richard asked. "You were out for quite some time."

"Cramplepuss, I'm *fine*," the fairy snapped, clearly agitated. He then looked to Richard, frowning deeper. "Are those *tears* on your cheeks?"

Richard smiled. "Don't flatter yourself."

"What happened?" Snedeker asked, alarm on his face as he viewed the broken crystal remnants of the phoenix egg.

"You don't remember dying?"

The fairy's face screwed up in the fashion of a small child being lied to by an adult. "You really think I am foolish, don't you? Here I am, alive, you dolt!"

Richard couldn't hide his grin. Aderyn stood on shaky legs. The Heliwr helped her. As they slowly made their way back toward the village, he wondered at the night's events. He had witnessed one of the most powerful creatures in Annwn history—seen its rebirth, experienced its power. But he had seen more than that, hadn't he? Friendship. Love. Sacrifice. Caring for others ahead of oneself. As Heliwr, Richard had given of his time, his energy, his mind, and his body. But Snedeker had made the ultimate sacrifice.

It was testament that Richard still had a lot to learn about the nature of life.

And that of his friend.

Because perhaps the greatest magic this night had been of the giving kind.

ACKNOWLEDGMENTS

Unfettered III would not exist without some extraordinary people helping in various and different ways. I am indebted to one and all of them.

Richard and Kathy Speakman
Who encouraged in all the right ways

Kristin Speakman
Who dreams with me every day

Soren Speakman
Who is learning the magic he truly possesses

Darren and Sherry Lamb
Who give of their time and hearts

Jeff, Becky, Payton, and Kendall Lawson
Who journey with me into unknown territory

Rachelle Longé McGhee
Who wields editing lasers with pinpoint accuracy

Todd Lockwood
Who lends friendship and paint

Kaitlund Zupanic
Who joined late but finished early

My story contributors
Who answer my call ready with story

And finally, the readers
Who support these anthologies with love